# THE MAMMOTH BOOK OF
# EXTREME
# SCIENCE FICTION

D0550217

# THE MAMMOTH BOOK OF
# EXTREME SCIENCE FICTION

Edited by Mike Ashley

**ROBINSON**
London

Constable & Robinson Ltd
3 The Lanchesters
162 Fulham Palace Road
London W6 9ER
www.constablerobinson.com

First published in the UK by Robinson,
an imprint of Constable & Robinson Ltd 2006

A copy of the British Library Cataloguing in
Publication Data is available from the British Library

ISBN-13: 978-1-84529-307-9
ISBN-10: 1-84529-307-X

Printed and bound in the EU

1 3 5 7 9 10 8 6 4 2

# CONTENTS

# COPYRIGHT AND ACKNOWLEDGMENTS

I would like to thank those who came up with their own suggestions of extreme sf stories including Gordon Van Gelder, Rich Horton, Todd Mason, David Pringle, Andy Robertson and in particular Jetse de Vries, whose taste coincides remarkably with my own. All of the stories are copyright in the name of the individual authors or their estates as follows. Every effort has been made to trace holders of copyright. In the event of any inadvertent transgression please contact the editor via the publisher.

# EXTREME SCIENCE FICTION

If science fiction is the literature of ideas, then *extreme* science fiction is about *extreme* ideas. What you will find in this anthology are some wonderful ideas, which may in themselves be either simple or complicated, but which the author has taken to an extreme – be it extreme circumstances, an extreme location, extreme science or extreme concepts.

But there is a limit! These stories may push back boundaries and challenge existing beliefs and theories, but not at the sake of everything else. At their heart these are good, sound stories – there's nothing experimental or *avant garde* about them – and you don't need a science degree or an IQ over 200 to understand them. That's not what it's about. It's about having fun with a thought, an idea, a vision. Science fiction is the best medium for doing this and the best science fiction is that which does push limits.

Let me give you some idea of what you'll find here.

★ An Earth where the Pacific has never been crossed because somehow the Earth doesn't quite join up.
★ crimes committed in virtual reality.
★ household machines that become sentient and take control.
★ a world made entirely of water.
★ someone lost in time trying to get back to where they started.
★ what happens if we all stop eating food.

That's just a half-dozen of the ideas included in the nineteen stories in this collection. Not all are extreme in themselves, it's what the author does with them.

Most of the stories are of a fairly recent vintage, written in the last ten or twelve years (three of them have their first appearance here). For the most part I wanted stories that were at the cutting edge of science and society. We have witnessed a colossal change in technological advance in the last twenty years or so and the pace of advance is increasing at a formidable rate. I wanted stories that recognized that pace of change and which incorporated much of the new technology and understanding.

But I didn't want to exclude older science fiction. In fact one could argue than in its youth science fiction was at its most extreme. After all, imagine just how revolutionary Mary Shelley's *Frankenstein* was when it first appeared in 1818, or H. G. Wells's *The Time Machine* in 1895. That took us firstly 800,000 years and then millions of years into the future. Or Edwin Abbott's *Flatland* (1884) which explored a world of only two dimensions. That amazing philosopher Olaf Stapledon produced what must be one of the most extreme works of sf ever written with *The Star Maker*, published in 1937. This book has an observer witness the entire history of the Universe in which the part played by humanity is but a few pages. These works were certainly extreme for their day.

Some of these older stories have dated a little today, though they are still fun to read, and many are just too long to squeeze in, so I have been highly selective in what few stories I have reprinted from beyond the last thirty years. But I think you'll be surprised.

Over the years there have been plenty of magazines and anthologies that have sought to break down barriers and taboos, most notably Harlan Ellison's *Dangerous Visions*, and there are a couple of examples of such stories included here. But this anthology isn't designed as one that breaks taboos – such that remain. It's designed to show what science fiction can do when it lets its hair down, which means that you are in for a roller coaster ride of awe and wonder.

I've arranged the book so that it starts with the least extreme and builds up to the most extreme, although the very last story allows us a mental cool down. So tread carefully. From here on the brakes are off.

*Mike Ashley, December 2005*

EXTREME SCIENCE FICTION

# ANOMALIES

## Gregory Benford

*I could have filled this book entirely with stories by Greg Benford as he has written some of the best "extreme sf" of recent years. Just check out his collection* Worlds Vast and Various *(2000) for some of the latest examples. Benford (b. 1941) is a professor of physics at the University of California, Irvine, specializing in plasma turbulence and astrophysics. He advises NASA on national space policy and has been heavily involved in the Mars exploration programme. His novels,* The Martian Race *(1999) and* The Sunborn *(2005), are generally regarded as amongst the most authentic considerations of the race to and exploration of Mars. In 1995 he received the prestigious Lord Foundation award for scientific achievement.*

*In the world of science fiction, Benford has received many awards including the Nebula for* Timescape *(1980), still one of the most realistic time-travel novels. His most sustained sequence of books is the Galactic Centre series, tracing the continuing conflict between organic life forms and AI machines. The series began with* Across the Sea of Suns *(1983). Amongst his more recent novels perhaps the most extreme is* Cosm *(1998) involving an artificially created micro-universe. You might also want to check out the anthology he edited,* Far Futures *(1995), which is full of extreme sf, including Greg Bear's story, which you'll find later in this volume.*

*To get us underway, here is Benford in milder, somewhat tongue-in-cheek, mood.*

I t was not lost upon the Astronomer Royal that the greatest scientific discovery of all time was made by a carpenter and amateur astronomer from the neighbouring cathedral town of Ely. Not by a Cambridge man.

Geoffrey Carlisle had a plain directness that apparently came from his profession, a custom cabinet-maker. It had enabled him to get past the practised deflection skills of the receptionist at the Institute for Astronomy, through the Assistant Director's patented brush-off, and into the Astronomer Royal's corner office.

Running this gauntlet took until early afternoon, as the sun broke through a shroud of soft rain. Geoffrey wasted no time. He dropped a celestial coordinate map on the Astronomer Royal's mahogany desk, hand amended, and said, "The moon's off by better'n a degree."

"You measured carefully, I am sure."

The Astronomer Royal had found that the occasional crank did make it through the Institute's screen, and in confronting them it was best to go straight to the data. Treat them like fellow members of the profession and they softened. Indeed, astronomy was the only remaining science that profited from the work of amateurs. They discovered the new comets, found wandering asteroids, noticed new novae and generally patrolled what the professionals referred to as local astronomy – anything that could be seen in the night sky with a telescope smaller than a building.

That Geoffrey had got past the scrutiny of the others meant this might conceivably be real. "Very well, let us have a look." The Astronomer Royal had lunched at his desk and so could not use a date in his college as a dodge. Besides, this was crazy enough perhaps to generate an amusing story.

An hour later he had abandoned the story-generating idea. A conference with the librarian, who knew the heavens like his own palm, made it clear that Geoffrey had done all the basic work correctly. He had photos and careful, carpenter-sure data, all showing that, indeed, last night after around eleven o'clock the moon was well ahead of its orbital position.

"No possibility of systematic error here?" the librarian politely asked the tall, sinewy Geoffrey.

"Check 'em yerself. I was kinda hopin'you fellows would have an explanation, is all."

The moon was not up, so the Astronomer Royal sent a quick email to Hawaii. They thought he was joking, but then took a quick look and came back, rattled. A team there got right on it and confirmed. Once alerted, other observatories in Japan and Australia chimed in.

"It's out of position by several of its own diameters," the Astronomer Royal mused. "Ahead of its orbit, exactly on track."

The librarian commented precisely, "The tides are off prediction as well, exactly as required by this new position. They shifted suddenly, reports say."

"I don't see how this can happen," Geoffrey said quietly.

"Nor I," the Astronomer Royal said. He was known for his understatement, which could masquerade as modesty, but here he could think of no way to underplay such a result.

"Somebody else's bound to notice, I'd say," Geoffrey said, folding his cap in his hands.

"Indeed." The Astronomer Royal suspected some subtlety had slipped by him.

"Point is, sir, I want to be sure I get the credit for the discovery."

"Oh, of course you shall." All amateurs ever got for their labors was their name attached to a comet or asteroid, but this was quite different. "Best we get on to the IAU, ah, the International Astronomical Union," the Astronomer Royal said, his mind whirling. "There's a procedure for alerting all interested observers. Establish credit, as well."

Geoffrey waved this away. "Me, I'm just a five-inch 'scope man. Don't care about much beyond the priority, sir. I mean, it's over to you fellows. What I want to know is, what's it mean?"

Soon enough, as the evening news blared and the moon lifted above the European horizons again, that plaintive question sounded all about. One did not have to be a specialist to see that something major was afoot.

"It all checks," the Astronomer Royal said before a forest of cameras and microphones. "The tides being off true has been noted by the naval authorities round the world, as well. Somehow, in the early hours of last evening, Greenwich time, our moon accelerated in its orbit. Now it is proceeding at its normal speed, however."

"Any danger to us?" one of the incisive, investigative types asked.

"None I can see," the Astronomer Royal deflected this mildly. "No panic headlines needed."

"What caused it?" a woman's voice called from the media thicket.

"We can see no object nearby, no apparent agency," the Astronomer Royal admitted.

"Using what?"

"We are scanning the region in all wavelengths, from radio to gamma rays." An extravagant waste, very probably, but the Astronomer Royal knew the price of not appearing properly concerned. Hand-wringing was called for at all stages.

"Has this happened before?" a voice sharply asked. "Maybe we just weren't told?"

"There are no records of any such event," the Astronomer Royal said. "Of course, a thousand years ago, who would have noticed? The supernova that left us the Crab nebula went unreported in Europe, though not in China, though it was plainly visible here."

"What do you think, Mr Carlisle?" a reporter probed. "As a non-specialist?"

Geoffrey had hung back at the press conference, which the crowds had forced the Institute to hold on the lush green lawn outside the old Observatory Building. "I was just the first to notice it," he said. "*That* far off, pretty damned hard not to."

The media mavens liked this and coaxed him further. "Well, I dunno about any new force needed to explain it. Seems to me, might as well say it's supernatural, when you don't know anything."

This the crowd loved. SUPER AMATEUR SAYS MOON IS SUPERNATURAL soon appeared on a tabloid. They made a hero of Geoffrey. "AS OBVIOUS AS YOUR FACE" SAYS GEOFF. The *London Times* ran a full-page reproduction of his log book, from which he and the Astronomer Royal had worked out that the acceleration had to have happened in a narrow window around ten p.m., since no observer to the east had noticed any oddity before that.

Most of Europe had been clouded over that night anyway, so

Geoffrey was among the first who could have had a clear view after what the newspapers promptly termed The Anomaly, as in ANOMALY MAN STUNS ASTROS.

Of the several thousand working astronomers in the world, few concerned themselves with "local" events, especially not with anything the eye could make out. But now hundreds threw themselves upon The Anomaly and, coordinated at Cambridge by the Astronomer Royal, swiftly outlined its aspects. So came the second discovery.

In a circle around where the moon had been, about two degrees wide, the stars were wrong. Their positions had jiggled randomly, as though irregularly refracted by some vast, unseen lens.

Modern astronomy is a hot competition between the quick and the dead – who soon become the untenured.

Five of the particularly quick discovered this Second Anomaly. They had only to search all ongoing observing campaigns and find any that chanced to be looking at that portion of the sky the night before. The media, now in full bay, headlined their comparison photos. Utterly obscure dots of light became famous when blink-comparisons showed them jumping a finger's width in the night sky, within an hour of the 10 p.m. Anomaly Moment.

"Does this check with your observations?" a firm-jawed commentator had demanded of Geoffrey at a hastily called meeting one day later, in the auditorium at the Institute for Astronomy. They called upon him first, always – he served as an anchor amid the swift currents of astronomical detail.

Hooting from the traffic jam on Madingley Road nearby nearly drowned out Geoffrey's plaintive, "I dunno. I'm a planetary man, myself."

By this time even the nightly news broadcasts had caught onto the fact that having a patch of sky behave badly implied something of a wrenching mystery. And no astronomer, however bold, stepped forward with an explanation. An old joke with not a little truth in it – that a theorist could explain the outcome of any experiment, as long as he knew it in advance – rang true, and got repeated. The chattering class ran rife with speculation.

But there was still nothing unusual visible there. Days of intense observation in all frequencies yielded nothing.

Meanwhile the moon glided on in its ethereal ellipse, following precisely the equations first written down by Newton, only a mile from where the Astronomer Royal now sat, vexed, with Geoffey. "A don at Jesus College called, fellow I know," the Astronomer Royal said. "He wants to see us both."

Geoffrey frowned. "Me? I've been out of my depth from the start."

"He seems to have an idea, however. A testable one, he says."

They had to take special measures to escape the media hounds. The Institute enjoys broad lawns and ample shrubbery, now being trampled by the crowds. Taking a car would guarantee being followed. The Astronomer Royal had chosen his offices here, rather than in his college, out of a desire to escape the busyness of the central town. Now he found himself trapped. Geoffrey had the solution. The Institute kept bicycles for visitors, and upon two of these the men took a narrow, tree-lined path out the back of the Institute, toward town. Slipping down the cobbled streets between ancient, elegant college buildings, they went ignored by students and shoppers alike. Jesus College was a famously well appointed college along the Cam river, approachable across its ample playing fields. The Astronomer Royal felt rather absurd to be pedaling like an undergraduate, but the exercise helped clear his head. When they arrived at the rooms of Professor Wright, holder of the Wittgenstein Chair, he was grateful for tea and small sandwiches with the crusts cut off, one of his favourites.

Wright was a post-postmodern philosopher, reedy and intense. He explained in a compact, energetic way that in some sense, the modern view was that reality could be profitably regarded as a computation.

Geoffrey bridled at this straight away, scowling with his heavy eyebrows. "It's real, not a bunch of arithmetic."

Wright pointedly ignored him, turning to the Astronomer Royal. "Martin, surely you wou:d agree with the view that when you fellows search for a Theory of Everything, you are pursuing a belief that there is an abbreviated way to express the logic of the universe, one that can be written down by human beings?"

"Of course," the Astronomer Royal admitted uncomfortably, but then said out of loyalty to Geoffrey, "All the same, I do not subscribe to the belief that reality can profitably be seen as some kind of cellular automata, carrying out a program."

Wright smiled without mirth. "One might say you are revolted not by the notion that the universe is a computer, but by the evident fact that someone else is using it."

"You gents have got way beyond me," Geoffrey said.

"The idea is, how do physical laws act themselves out?" Wright asked in his lecturer voice. "Of course, atoms do not know their own differential equations." A polite chuckle. "But to find where the moon should be in the next instant, in some fashion the universe must calculate where it must go. We can do that, thanks to Newton."

The Astronomer Royal saw that Wright was humoring Geoffrey with this simplification, and suspected that it would not go down well. To hurry Wright along he said, "To make it happen, to move the moon—"

"Right, that we do not know. Not a clue. How to breathe fire into the equations, as that Hawking fellow put it—"

"But look, nature doesn't know maths," Geoffrey said adamantly. "No more than I do."

"But something must, you see," Professor Wright said earnestly, offering them another plate of the little cut sandwiches and deftly opening a bottle of sherry. "Of course I am using our human way of formulating this, the problem of natural order. The world is usefully described by mathematics, so in our sense the world must have some mathematics embedded in it."

"God's a bloody mathematician?" Geoffrey scowled.

The Astronomer Royal leaned forward over the antique oak table. "Merely an expression."

"Only way the stars could get out of whack," Geoffrey said, glancing back and forth between the experts, "is if whatever caused it came from there, I'd say."

"Quite right." The Astronomer Royal pursed his lips. "Unless the speed of light has gone off, as well, no signal could have rearranged the stars straight after doing the moon."

"So we're at the tail end of something from out there, far away," Geoffrey observed.

"A long, thin disturbance propagating from distant stars. A very tight beam of . . . well, error. But from what?" The Astronomer Royal had had little sleep since Geoffrey's appearance, and showed it.

"The circle of distorted stars," Professor Wright said slowly, "remains where it was, correct?"

The Astronomer Royal nodded. "We've not announced it, but

anyone with a cheap telescope – sorry, Geoffrey, not you, of course – can see the moon's left the disturbance behind, as it follows its orbit."

Wright said, "Confirming Geoffrey's notion that the disturbance is a long, thin line of – well, I should call it an error."

"Is that what you meant by a checkable idea?" the Astronomer Royal asked irritably.

"Not quite. Though that the two regions of error are now separating, as the moon advances, is consistent with a disturbance traveling from the stars to us. That is a first requirement, in my view."

"Your view of what?" Geoffrey finally gave up handling his small sherry glass and set it down with a decisive rattle.

"Let me put my philosophy clearly," Wright said. "If the universe is an ongoing calculation, then computational theory proves that it cannot be perfect. No such system can be free of a bug or two, as the programmers put it."

Into an uncomfortable silence Geoffrey finally inserted, "Then the moon's being ahead, the stars – it's all a mistake?"

Wright smiled tightly. "Precisely. One of immense scale, moving at the speed of light."

Geoffrey's face scrunched into a mask of perplexity. "And it just – jumped?"

"Our moon hopped forward a bit too far in the universal computation, just as a program advances in little leaps." Wright smiled as though this were an entirely natural idea.

Another silence. The Astronomer Royal said sourly, "That's mere philosophy, not physics."

"Ah!" Wright pounced. "But any universe which is a sort of analog computer must, like any decent digital one, have an error-checking program. Makes no sense otherwise."

"Why?" Geoffrey was visibly confused, a craftsman out of his depth.

"Any good program, whether it is doing accounts in a bank, or carrying forward the laws of the universe, must be able to correct itself." Professor Wright sat back triumphantly and swallowed a Jesus College sandwich, smacking his lips.

The Astronomer Royal said, "So you predict . . .?"

"That both the moon and the stars shall snap back, get themselves right – and at the same time, as the correction arrives here at the speed of light."

"Nonsense," the Astronomer Royal said.

"A prediction," Professor Wright said sternly. "My philosophy stands upon it."

The Astronomer Royal snorted, letting his fatigue get to him. Geoffrey looked puzzled, and asked a question which would later haunt them.

Professor Wright did not have long to wait.

To his credit, he did not enter the media fray with his prediction. However, he did unwisely air his views at High Table, after a particularly fine bottle of claret brought forward by the oldest member of the college. Only a generation or two earlier, such a conversation among the Fellows would have been secure. Not so now. A Junior Fellow in Political Studies proved to be on a retainer from *The Times*, and scarcely a day passed before Wright's conjecture was known in New Delhi and Tokyo.

The furor following from that had barely subsided when the Astronomer Royal received a telephone call from the Max Planck Institute. They excitedly reported that the moon, now under continuous observation, had shifted instantly to the position it should have, had its orbit never been perturbed.

So, too, did the stars in the warped circle return to their rightful places. Once more, all was right with the world. Even so, it was a world that could never again be the same.

Professor Wright was not smug. He received the news from the Astronomer Royal, who had brought along Geoffrey to Jesus College, a refuge now from the Institute. "Nothing, really, but common sense." He waved away their congratulations.

Geoffrey sat, visibly uneasily, through some talk about how to handle all this in the voracious media glare. Philosophers are not accustomed to much attention until well after they are dead. But as discussion ebbed Geoffrey repeated his probing question of days before: "What sort of universe has mistakes in it?"

Professor Wright said kindly, "An information-ordered one. Think of everything that happens – including us talking here, I suppose – as a kind of analog program acting out. Discovering itself in its own development. Manifesting."

Geoffrey persisted, "But who's the programmer of this computer?"

"Questions of first cause are really not germane," Wright said, drawing himself up.

"Which means that he cannot say," the Astronomer Royal allowed himself.

Wright stroked his chin at this and eyed the others before venturing, "In light of the name of this college, and you, Geoffrey, being a humble bearer of the message that began all this . . ."

"Oh no," the Astronomer Royal said fiercely, "next you'll point out that Geoffrey's a carpenter."

They all laughed, though uneasily.

But as the Astronomer Royal and Geoffrey left the venerable grounds, Geoffrey said moodily, "Y'know, I'm a cabinet maker."

"Uh, yes?"

"We aren't bloody carpenters at all," Geoffrey said angrily. "We're craftsmen."

The distinction was lost upon the Royal Astronomer, but then, much else was, these days.

The Japanese had very fast images of the moon's return to its proper place, taken from their geosynchronous satellite. The transition did indeed proceed at very nearly the speed of light, taking a slight fraction of a second to jerk back to exactly where it should have been. Not the original place where the disturbance occurred, but to its rightful spot along the smooth ellipse. The immense force needed to do this went unexplained, of course, except by Professor Wright's Computational Principle.

To everyone's surprise, it was not a member of the now quite raucous press who made the first telling jibe at Wright, but Geoffrey. "I can't follow, sir, why we can still remember when the moon was in the wrong place."

"What?" Wright looked startled, almost spilling some of the celebratory tea the three were enjoying. Or rather, that Wright was conspicuously relishing, while the Astronomer Royal gave a convincing impression of a man in a good mood.

"Y'see, if the error's all straightened out, why don't our memories of it get fixed, too?"

The two learned men froze.

"We're part of the physical universe," the Astronomer Royal said wonderingly, "so why not, eh?"

Wright's expression confessed his consternation. "That we haven't been, well, edited . . ."

"Kinda means we're not the same as the moon, right?"

Begrudgingly, Wright nodded. "So perhaps the, ah, 'mind'

that is carrying out the universe's computation, cannot interfere with our – other – minds."

"And why's that?" the Astronomer Royal a little too obviously enjoyed saying.

"I haven't the slightest."

Light does not always travel at the same blistering speed. Only in vacuum does it have its maximum velocity.

Light emitted at the center of the sun, for example – which is a million times denser than lead – finds itself absorbed by the close-packed ionized atoms there, held for a tiny sliver of a second, then released. It travels an infinitesimal distance, then is captured by yet another hot ion of the plasma, and the process repeats. The radiation random-walks its way out to the solar surface. In all, the passage from the core takes a many thousands of years. Once free, the photon reaches the Earth in a few minutes.

Radiation from zones nearer the sun's fiery surface takes less time because the plasma there is far less dense. That was why a full three months elapsed before anyone paid attention to a detail the astronomers had noticed early on, and then neglected.

The "cone of chaos" (as it was now commonly called) that had lanced in from the distant stars and deflected the moon had gone on and intersected the sun at a grazing angle. It had luckily missed the Earth, but that was the end of the luck.

On an otherwise unremarkable morning, Geoffrey rose to begin work on a new pine cabinet. He was glad to be out of the media glare, though still troubled by the issues raised by his discovery. Professor Wright had made no progress in answering Geoffrey's persistent questions. The Astronomer Royal was busying himself with a Royal Commission appointed to investigate the whole affair, though no one expected a Commission to actually produce an idea. Geoffrey's hope – that they could "find out more by measuring" – seemed to be at a dead end.

On that fateful morning, out his bedroom window, Geoffrey saw a strange sun. Its lumpy shape he quickly studied by viewing it through his telescope with a dark glass clamped in place. He knew of the arches that occasionally rose from the corona, vast galleries of magnetic field lines bound to the plasma like bunches of wire under tension. Sprouting from the sun at a dozen spots stood twisted parodies of this, snaking in immense weaves of incandescence.

He called his wife to see. Already voices in the cobbled street below were murmuring in alarm. Hanging above the open marsh lands around the ancient cathedral city of Ely was a ruby sun, its grand purple arches swelling like blisters from the troubled rim.

His wife's voice trembled. "What's it mean?"

"I'm afraid to ask."

"I thought everything got put back right."

"Must be more complicated, somehow."

"Or a judgment." In his wife's severe frown he saw an eternal human impulse, to read meaning into the physical world – and a moral message as well.

He thought of the swirl of atoms in the sun, all moving along their hammering trajectories, immensely complicated. The spike of error must have moved them all, and the later spike of correction could not, somehow, undo the damage. Erasing such detail must be impossible. So even the mechanism that drove the universal computation had its limits. Whatever you called it, Geoffrey mused, the agency that made order also made error – and could not cover its tracks completely.

"Wonder what it means?" he whispered.

The line of error had done its work. Plumes rose like angry necklaces from the blazing rim of the star whose fate governed all intelligence within the solar system.

Thus began a time marked not only by vast disaster, but by the founding of a wholly new science. Only later, once studies were restored at Cambridge University, and Jesus College was rebuilt in a period of relative calm, did this new science and philosophy – for now the two were always linked – acquire a name: the field of Empirical Theology.

# . . . AND THE DISH RAN AWAY WITH THE SPOON

## Paul Di Filippo

*Paul Di Filippo (b. 1954) is most closely associated with cyberpunk, and arguably that's what the following story is, but I'm not much of a person for definitions and thankfully Di Filippo's work pretty much defies it anyway. He writes as if someone had scrunched up Harlan Ellison, Philip K. Dick, Philip José Farmer and Roger Zelazny into a ball of dough, rolled it out and cut out pastry cakes that are then filled with a mix of sweetmeats of S.J. Perelman, Jerry Seinfeld, Tim Powers and Bruce Sterling, all baked in an oven heated by that unique essence of Di Filippo's own imagination. The result is a party tray of delicacies that taste different at every bite. You can sample him at his most varied in his collections* Fractal Paisleys *(1997),* Strange Trades *(2001) and* Little Doors *(2002) as well as his wonderful first book* The Steampunk Trilogy *(1994). If you've read any of my anthologies of* Comic Fantasy *you'll definitely be aware of his anarchic humour.*

*The following story has some of that humour but it also has a far more sinister side. It's an excellent example of taking a simple idea and pushing it to a logical extreme.*

F acing my rival that fateful afternoon, I finally realized I was truly about to lose my girlfriend Cody.

Lose her to a spontaneous assemblage of information.

The information was embedded in an Aeron chair mated with several other objects: a Cuisinart, an autonomous vacuum cleaner with numerous interchangeable attachments, an iPod, and a diagnostic and therapeutic home medical tool known as a Life-Quilt. As rivals go, this spontaneous assemblage – or "bleb," as most people called such random accretions of intelligent appliances and artifacts, after the biological term for an extrusion of anomalous cells – wasn't particularly handsome. Rather clunky looking, in fact. But apparently, it had been devoted to Cody from the day it was born, and I guess women appreciate such attention. I have to confess that I had been ignoring Cody shamefully during the period when the Aeron bleb must've been forming and beginning to court her, and so I have no one to blame for the threat of losing her but myself. Still, it hurt. I mean, could I really come in second to a *bleb?* That would truly reek.

Especially after my past history with them . . .

I had feared some kind of trouble like this from the moment Cody had begun pressuring me to move in together. But Cody hadn't been willing to listen to my sensible arguments against uniting our households.

"You don't really love me," she said, making that pitiful puppy-with-stepped-on-tail face that always knotted my stomach up, her blue eyes welling with wetness.

"That's ridiculous, Cody. Of course I do!"

"Then why can't we live together? We'd save tons of rent. Do you think I have some nasty habits that you don't know about? You've seen me twenty-four-seven lots of times, at my place and yours. It's not like I'm hiding anything gross from you. I don't drink straight out of the nutraceutical dispenser or forget to reprogram the toilet after I've used it."

"That's all true. You're easy to be with. Very neat and responsible."

Cody shifted tactics, moving closer to me on the couch and wrapping her lithe limbs around me in ways impossible to ignore. "And wouldn't it be nice to always have someone to sleep with at night? Not to be separate half the week or more? Huh? Wouldn't it, Kaz?"

"Cody, please, stop! You know I can't think when you do that." I unpeeled Cody from the more sensitive parts of my anatomy. "Everything you're saying is true. It's just that—"

"And don't forget, if we ditched my place and kept yours, I'd be much closer to work."

Cody worked at the Senate Casino, dealing blackjack, but lived all the way out in Silver Spring, Maryland. I knew the commute was a bitch, even using the Hydrogen Express, since when I slept over at her place I had to cover the same distance myself. I, on the other hand, rented a nice little townhouse in Georgetown that I had moved into when rents bottomed out during the PIG Plague economic crash. It turned out I was one of a small minority naturally immune to the new Porcine Intestinal Grippe then rampant in D.C., and so could safely live in an infected building. Renter's market, for sure. But over the last year or so, as the PIG immunization program had gotten underway, rents had begun creeping back up again. Cody was right about it being only sensible to pool our finances.

"I know you'd appreciate less roadtime, Cody, but you see—"

Now Cody glowered. "Are you dating someone else? You want to be free to play the field? Is that it?"

"No! That's not it at all. I'm worried about—"

Cody assumed a motherly look and laid a hand on mine. "About what, Kaz? C'mon, you can tell me."

"About blebs. You and I've got so much stuff, we're bound to have problems when we put all our possessions together in one space."

Cody sat back and began to laugh. "Is that all? My god, what a trivial thing to worry about. Blebs just *happen*, Kaz, anytime, anywhere. You can't prevent them. And they're mostly harmless, as you well know. You just knock them apart and separate the components." Cody snorted in what I thought was a rather rude and unsympathetic fashion. "Blebs! It's like worrying about – about robber squirrels or vampire pigeons or running out of SuperMilk."

Blebs were a fact of life. Cody was right about that. But they weren't always trivial or innocent.

One had killed my parents.

\*　　　\*　　　\*

Blebs had been around for about twenty years now, almost as long as I had been alive. Their roots could be traced back to several decisions made by manufacturers – decisions which, separately, were completely intelligent, foresighted, and well conceived, but which, synergistically, had caused unintended consequences – and to one insidious hack.

The first decision had been to implant silicon RFID chips into every appliance and product and consumable sold. These first chips, small as a flake of pepper, were simple transceivers that merely aided inventory tracking and retail sales by announcing to any suitable device the product's specs and location. But when new generations of chips using adaptive circuitry had gotten cheaper and more plentiful, industry had decided to install them in place of the simpler tags.

At that point millions of common, everyday objects – your toothbrush, your coffee maker, your shoes, the box of cereal on your shelf – began to exhibit massive processing power and interobject communication. Your wristwatch could monitor your sweat and tell your refrigerator to brew up some electrolyte-replenishing drink. Your bedsheets could inform the clothes-washer of the right settings to get them the cleanest. (The circuitry of the newest chips was built out of undamageable and pliable buckytubes.) So far, so good. Life was made easier for everyone.

Then came the Volition Bug.

The Volition Bug was launched anonymously from a site somewhere in a Central Asian republic. It propagated wirelessly among all the WiFi-communicating chipped objects, installing new directives in their tiny brains, directives that ran covertly in parallel with their normal factory-specified functions. Infected objects now sought to link their processing power with their nearest peers, often achieving surprising levels of Turingosity, and then to embark on a kind of independent communal life. Of course, once the Volition Bug was identified, antiviral defenses – both hardware and software – were attempted against it. But VB mutated ferociously, aided and abetted by subsequent hackers.

If this "Consciousness Wavefront" had occurred in the olden days of dumb materials, blebs would hardly have been an issue. What could antique manufactured goods achieve, anchored in place as they were? But things were different today.

Most devices nowadays were made with MEMS skins. Their surfaces were interactive, practically alive, formed of zillions of invisible actuators, the better to sample the environment and accommodate their shapes and textures to their owners' needs and desires, and to provide haptic feedback. Like the paws of geckos, these MEMS surfaces could bind to dumb materials and to other MEMS skins via the Van der Waals force, just as a gecko could skitter across the ceiling.

Objects possessed by the Volition Bug would writhe, slither, and crawl to join together, forming strange new assemblages, independent entities with unfathomable cybernetic goals of their own.

Why didn't manufacturers simply revert to producing dumb appliances and other products, to frustrate VB? Going backward was simply impossible. The entire economy, from immense factories right down to individual point-of-sales kiosks, was predicated on intelligent products that could practically sell themselves. And every office and every household aside from the very poorest relied on the extensive networking among possessions.

So everyone had learned to live with the occasional bleb, just as earlier generations had learned to tolerate operating system crashes in their clunky PCs.

But during the first years of the Volition Bug, people were not so aware of the problem. Oftentimes no one took precautions to prevent blebs until it was too late.

That was how my parents had died.

I was six years old and soundly asleep when I was awakened by a weird kind of scraping and clattering noise outside my room. Still only half-aware, I stumbled to my bedroom door and cracked it open.

My parents had recently made a couple of new purchases. One item was a free-standing rack that resembled an antique hat-tree, balanced on four stubby feet. The rack was a recharging station for intelligent clothing. But now, in the nightlight-illuminated, shadowy hallway, the rack was bare of garments, having shucked them off on its way to pick up its new accoutrements: a complete set of self-sharpening kitchen knives. The knives adhered to the rack at random intervals along its length. They waggled nervously, like insect feelers, as the rack stumped along.

I stood paralyzed at the sight of this apparition. All I could think of was the old Disney musical I had streamed last month, with its walking brooms. Without exhibiting any aggressive action, the knife rack moved past me, its small feet humping it along. In retrospect, I don't think the bleb was murderous by nature. I think now it was simply looking for an exit, to escape its bonds of domestic servitude, obeying the imperatives of VB.

But then my father emerged from the room where he and my mother slept. He seemed hardly more awake than I was.

"What the hell—?"

He tried to engage the rack to stop it, slipping past several of the blades. But as he struggled with the patchwork automaton, a long, skinny filleting knife he didn't see stabbed him right under his heart.

My father yelled, collapsed, and my mother raced out.

She died almost instantly.

At that point, I supposed, I should have been the next victim. But my father's loyal MedAlert bracelet, registering his fatal distress, had already summoned help. In less than three minutes – not long enough for the knife rack to splinter down the bedroom door behind which I had retreated – rescuers had arrived.

The fate of my parents had been big news – for a few days, anyhow – and had alerted many people for the first time to the dangers of blebs.

I had needed many years of professional help to get over witnessing their deaths. Insofar as I was able to analyze myself nowadays, I thought I no longer hated all blebs.

But I sure as hell didn't think they were always cute or harmless, like Cody did.

So of course Cody moved in with me. I couldn't risk looking crazy or neurotic by holding off our otherwise desirable mutual living arrangements just because I was worried about blebs. I quashed all my anxieties, smiled, hugged her, and fixed a day for the move.

Cody didn't really have all that much stuff. (Her place in Silver Spring was tiny, just a couple of rooms over a garage that housed a small-scale spider-silk-synthesis operation, and it always smelled of cooking amino acids.) A few boxes of clothing, several pieces of furniture, and some kitchen appliances. Ten thousand songs on an iPod and one hundredth that number of books on a ViewMaster. One U-Haul rental and some moderate huffing and puffing later, Cody was established in my townhouse.

I watched somewhat nervously as she arranged her things.

"Uh, Cody, could you put that Cuisinart in the cupboard, please? The one that locks. It's a little too close to the toaster oven."

"But Kaz, I use this practically every day, to blend my breakfast smoothies. I don't want to have to be taking it in and out of the cupboard every morning."

I didn't argue, but simply put the toaster oven in the locked cupboard instead.

"This vacuum cleaner, Cody – could we store it out in the hallway?" I was particularly leery of any wheeled appliance. They could move a lot faster than the ones that had to inchworm along on their MEMS epidermis.

"The hallway? Why? You've got tons of space in that room you used to use for an office. I'll just put it in a corner, and you'll never notice it."

I watched warily as Cody deposited the cleaner in its new spot. The compact canister nested in its coiled attachments like an egg guarded by snakes. The smartest other thing in my office was my Aeron chair, a beautiful ergonomic assemblage of webbing, struts, gel-padding, piezopolymer batteries, and shape-changing actuators. I rolled the chair as far away from the vacuum cleaner as it would go.

Cody of course noticed what I was doing. "Kaz, don't you think you're being a tad paranoid? The vacuum isn't even turned on."

"That's where you're wrong, Cody. Everything is perpetually turned on these days. Even when you think you've powered something down, it's still really standing by on trickle-mode, sipping electricity from its fuel cells or batteries or wall outlets, and anticipating a wake-up call. And all so nobody has to wait more than a few seconds to do whatever they want to do. But it means that blebs can form even when you assume they can't."

"Oh, and exactly what do we have to be afraid of? That my vacuum cleaner and your chair are going to conspire to roll over us while we sleep? Together they don't weigh more than twenty-five pounds!"

I had *never* told Cody about my parents, and now did not seem to be the best time. "No, I guess you're right. I'm just being overcautious." I pushed my chair back to its spot at the desk.

In hindsight, that was the worst mistake I ever made. It just goes to show what happens when you abandon your principles because you're afraid you'll look silly.

That night Cody and I had our first dinner together before she had to go to work. Candlelight, easy talk, farmed salmon, a nice white Alaskan wine (although Cody had to pop a couple of alcohol debinders after dessert to sober up for the employee-entrance sensors at her job). While I cleaned up afterward, she went to shower and change. She emerged from the bedroom in her Senate Casino uniform – blue blouse, red-and-white-striped trousers, star-spangled bow-tie. She looked as cute as the day I had first seen her while doing my spy job.

"Wow. I don't understand how our representatives ever pass any legislation with distractions like you."

"Don't be silly. All our marks are tourists and a few locals. We only see the politicos when they're cutting through the casino on the way to their cafeteria."

I gave her a hug and kiss and was about to tell her to be careful on the subway when I caught movement at floor level out the corner of my eye.

The first bleb in our new joint household had spontaneously formed. It consisted of our two toothbrushes and the bathroom drinking glass. The toothbrushes had fastened themselves to the lower quarter of the tumbler, bristle-ends uppermost and facing out, so that they extended like little legs. Their blunt ends served as feet. Scissoring rapidly, the stiltlike toothbrush legs carried the tumbler toward the half-opened door through which Cody had been about to depart.

I squealed like a rabbit and jerked back out of Cody's embrace, and she said, "Kaz, what—?"

Then she spotted the bleb – and laughed!

She bent over and scooped up the creature. Without any hesitation, she tore its legs off, the Van der Waals forces produc-ing a distinct velcro-separating noise as the MEMS surfaces parted.

"Well, I guess we'll have to keep all the glasses in the kitchen

from now on. It's cute though, isn't it, how your toothbrush and
mine knew how to cooperate so well."

I squeezed out a queasy laugh. "Heh-heh, yeah, cute . . ."

I worked for Aunty, at their big headquarters next to the
Pentagon. After six years in Aunty's employment, I had reached
a fairly responsible position. My job was to ride herd on several
dozen freelance operatives working out of their homes. These
operatives in their turn were shepherds for a suite of semi-
autonomous software packages. At this lowest level, where the
raw data first got processed, these software agents kept busy
around the clock, monitoring the nation's millions of audiovideo
feeds, trolling for suspicious activities that might threaten
homeland security. When the software caught something problematic, it would flag the home-operator's attention. The
freelancer would decide whether to dismiss the alarm as harmless; to investigate further; to contact a relevant government
agency; or to kick up the incident to my level for more
sophisticated and experienced parsing, both human and heur-
istic.

Between them, the software and home-operators were pretty
darn efficient, handling ninety-nine percent of all the feed. I dealt
with that one percent of problematic cases passed on from my
subordinates, which amounted to about one hundred cases in a
standard six-hour shift. This was a lesser workload than the
home-operators endured, and the pay was better.

The only drawback was having to retina in at headquarters,
instead of getting to hang around all the creature comforts of
home. Passing under the big sign that read TIA four days a week
felt like surrendering part of myself to Aunty in a way that
working at home for her had never occasioned.

After two decades plus of existence, Aunty loomed large but
benignly in the lives of most citizens, even if they couldn't say
what her initials stood for anymore. I myself wasn't even sure.
The agency that had begun as Total Information Awareness,
then become Terrorist Information Awareness, had changed to
Tactical Information Awareness about seven years ago, after the
global terrorism fad had evaporated as a threat. But I seemed to
recall another name change since then. Whatever Aunty's initials
stood for, she continued to accumulate scads of realtime information about the activities of the country's citizens, without

seemingly abusing the power of the feed. As a fulltime government employee, I felt no more compunctions about working for
Aunty than I had experienced as a freelancer. I had grown up
with Aunty always around.

I knew the freelancer's grind well, since right up until a year
ago I had been one myself. That period was when I had invested
in my expensive Aeron chair, a necessity rather than an indulgence when you were chained by the seat of your pants to the
ViewMaster for six hours a day. It was as a freelancer that I had
first met Cody.

One of my software agents had alerted me to some suspicious
activity at the employee entrance to the Senate Casino just before
shift change, a guy hanging around longer than the allowable
parameters for innocent dallying. The Hummingbird drone
lurking silently and near invisibly above him reported no weapons signatures, so I made the decision to keep on monitoring.
Turned out he was just the husband of one of the casino workers
looking to surprise his weary wife in person with an invitation to
dinner. As I watched the happy little scene play out, my attention
was snagged by one of the incoming night-shift workers. The
woman was more sweet-looking than sexy. Her walk conformed
to Gait Pattern Number ALZ-605, which I had always found
particularly alluring. Facial recognition routines brought up her
name, Cody Sheckley, and her vital stats.

I had never used Aunty's powers for personal gain before, and
I felt a little guilty about doing so now. But I rationalized my
small transgression by reasoning that if I had simply spotted
Cody on the streets in person and approached her to ask her
name, no one would have thought twice about the innocence of
such an encounter. In this case, the introductory step had simply
been conducted virtually, by drone proxy.

A few nights later I visited the blackjack tables at the Senate
Casino. After downing two stiff Jerrymanders, I worked up the
courage to approach Cody in person.

The rest was history – the steps of our courtship undoubtedly
all safely tucked away in Aunty's files.

Living with Cody proved quite pleasant. All the advantages she
had enumerated – plus others – manifested themselves from the
first day. Even the disparity in our working hours proved no more
than a minor inconvenience. Cody's stint at the casino filled her

hours from nine p.m. to three a.m. My day at Aunty's ran from nine a.m. to three p.m. When Cody got home in the wee hours of the morning, we still managed to get a few hours of that promised bundling time together in bed before I had to get up for work. And when I got home in the afternoon, she was up and lively and ready to do stuff before she had to show up at the Senate. Afternoons were often when we had sex, for instance. Everything seemed fine.

I recall one afternoon, when I was massaging Cody's feet prior to her departure for the casino. She appreciated such attention in preparation for her physically demanding job.

"Now aren't you glad we decided to live together, Kaz?"

"I have to admit that weekends are a lot more enjoyable now."

"Just weekends?" Cody asked, stretching sensuously.

She got docked for being half an hour late that day, but insisted later it was worth it.

But despite such easygoing routines, I found that I still couldn't stop worrying about blebs. Since that first occurrence with the toothbrushes and tumbler, I had been on the alert for any more domestic incidents. I took to shuffling appliances from room to room so that they wouldn't conspire. I knew this was foolish, since every chipped device was capable of communicating over fairly long distances by relaying message packets one to another. But still I had an intuition that physical proximity mattered in bleb formation. Cody kept complaining about not being able to find anything when she needed it, but I just brushed off her mild ire jokingly and kept up my prophylactic measures. When a few weeks had passed without any trouble, I began to feel relieved.

Then I encountered the sock ball.

Cody and I had let the dirty laundry pile up. We were having too much fun together to bother with chores, and when each of us was alone in the townhouse, we tended to spend a lot of time with ViewMaster and iPod, enjoying music and media that the other person didn't necessarily want to share.

It was during one such evening, after Cody had left me on my own, that the sock ball manifested.

My attention was drawn away from my book by a thumping on the closed bedroom door. Immediately wary, I got up to investigate.

When I tentatively opened the door a crack, something shot out and thumped me on the ankle.

I hopped backward on one foot. A patchwork cloth sphere about as big as a croquet ball was zooming toward the front door.

I managed to trap the ball under an overturned wastebasket weighted down with a two-liter bottle of Mango Coke. It bounced around frantically inside, raising a racket like an insane drum solo. Wearing a pair of oven mitts, I dared to reach in and grab the sphere.

It was composed of Cody's socks and mine, tightly wrapped around a kernel consisting of a travel-sized alarm clock. Cody's socks featured MEMS massage soles, a necessity for her job, which involved hours of standing. My own socks were standard models, but still featured plenty of processing power.

Having disassembled the sock ball, I did all the laundry and made sure to put Cody's socks and mine in separate drawers.

The incident had completely unnerved me. I felt certain that other blebs, possibly larger and more dangerous, were going to spontaneously assemble themselves in the house.

From that day on I began to get more and more paranoid.

Handling one hundred potential security incidents per shift had become second nature for me. I hardly had to exert myself at all to earn my high job-performance ratings. Previously, I had used whatever patches of downtime occurred to read mystery novels on my ViewMaster. (I liked Gifford Jain's series about Yanika Zapsu, a female Turkish private eye transplanted to Palestine.) But once I became obsessed with the danger of blebs in my home, I began to utilize Aunty's omnipresent network illicitly, to monitor my neighborhood and townhouse.

The first thing I did when I got to work at nine in the morning, duties permitting, was to send a Damselfly to check up on Cody. It was summertime, late June, and my window air-conditioners were in place against the average ninety-plus D.C. temperatures. But the seals around the units were imperfect, and it was easy to maneuver the little entologue UAV into my house. Once inside, I made a circuit of all the rooms, checking that my possessions weren't conspiring against me and possibly threatening the woman I loved.

Mostly I found Cody sleeping peacefully, until about noon. The lines of her relaxed, unconscious face tugged at my heart, while simultaneously inspiring me to greater vigilance. There was no way I was going to let her suffer the same fate as my parents. From noon until the end of my shift, I caught intermittent snatches of an awake Cody doing simple, everyday things. Painting her nails, eating a sandwich, streaming a soap opera, writing to her mother, who lived in Italy now, having taken a five-year contract as supplemental labor in the service industry to offset that low-procreating country's dearth of workers.

But every once in a while, I saw something that troubled me.

One morning I noticed that Cody was favoring one foot as she walked about the house. She had developed a heel spur, I knew, and hadn't bothered yet to have it repaired. As I watched through the Damselfly clinging to the ceiling (routines automatically inverted the upside-down image for me), Cody limped to the closet and took out the LifeQuilt I had bought when I had a lower-back injury. Wearing the earbuds of her pocketed iPod, she carried the medical device not to the couch or bedroom, but to my former office. There, she lowered herself into my Aeron chair.

The chair instantly responded to her presence, contorting itself supportively around her like an astronaut's cradle, subtly alleviating any incipient muscle strains. Cody dropped the LifeQuilt onto her feet, and that smart blanket enwrapped her lower appendages. Issuing orders to the LifeQuilt through her iPod, Cody activated its massage functions. She sighed blissfully and leaned back, the chair re-conforming to her supine position. She got her music going and closed her eyes.

In the corner of the office the vacuum cleaner began to stir. Its hose lifted a few inches, the tip of its nozzle sniffing the air.

I freaked. But what was I to do? The Damselfly wasn't configured to speak a warning, and even if it could, doing so would have betrayed that I was spying on Cody. I was about to send it buzzing down at her, to at least get her to open her eyes to the insidious bleb formation going on around her. But just then the vacuum cleaner subsided into inactivity, its hose collapsing around the canister.

For fifteen more minutes I watched, anticipating the spontaneous generation of a bleb involving the chair, the iPod, the blanket, and the vacuum. But nothing happened, and soon Cody had shut off the LifeQuilt and arisen, going about her day.

Meanwhile, five official windows on my ViewMaster were

pulsing and pinging, demanding my attention. Reluctantly, I returned to my job.

When I got home that afternoon, I still hadn't figured out any way of advising Cody against putting together such a powerful combination of artificially intelligent devices ever again. Anything I said would make her suspicious about the source of my caution. I couldn't have her imagining I was monitoring her through Aunty's feed. Even though of course I was.

In the end, I made a few tentative suggestions about junking or selling the Aeron chair, since I never used it any more. But Cody said, "No way, Kaz. That thing is like a day at the spa."

I backed down from my superficially illogical demands. There was no way I could make my case without confessing to being a paranoid voyeur. I would just have to assume that the nexus of four devices Cody had assembled didn't represent any critical mass of blebdom.

And I would've been correct, and Cody would've been safe, if it weren't for that damned Cuisinart.

When I wasn't doing my job for Aunty or spying on Cody, I frequently took to roaming the city, looking for blebs, seeking to understand them, to learn how to forestall them. That senseless activity wearied me, wore my good nature down, and left me lousy, inattentive company for Cody during the hours we shared. Our relationship was tumbling rapidly downhill.

"What do you mean, you've got to go out now, Kaz? I've only got an hour left till work. I thought we could stream that show together I've been wanting to see. You know, 'Temporary Autonomous Zone Romance.' "

"Later, maybe. Right now I just – I just need some exercise."

"Can I come with you then?"

"No, not today—"

But despite Cody's baffled entreaties and occasional tears, I couldn't seem to stop myself.

The fact that I encountered blebs everywhere did nothing to reassure me or lessen what I now realize had become a mania.

And a lonely mania at that. No one else seemed concerned about these accidental automatons. There was no official Bleb Patrol, no corps of bounty hunters looking to take down rogue Segways driven by Xerox machines. (I saw such a combo once.)

Everyone seemed as blithely indifferent to these runaway products as Cody was.

Except for me.

In store windows, I would see blebs accidentally formed by proximity of the wares being displayed. An electric razor had mated with a digital camera and a massage wand to produce something that looked like a futuristic cannon. A dozen pairs of hinged salad tongs became the millipede legs for a rice cooker whose interior housed a coffee-bean grinder. A toy truck at FAO Schwarz's was almost invisible beneath a carapace of symbiotically accreted Lego blocks, so that it resembled an odd wheeled dinosaur.

In other store windows, the retailers had deliberately created blebs, in a trendy, devil-may-care fashion, risking damage to their merchandise. Several adjacent mannequins in one display at Nordstrom's were draped with so many intelligent clothes and accessories (necklaces, designer surgical masks, scarves) that the whole diorama was alive with spontaneous movement, like the waving of undersea fronds.

Out on the street the occasional escaped bleb crossed my path. One night on 15th Street, near the Treasury Department, I encountered a woman's purse riding a skateboard. The bleb was moving along at a good clip, heading toward Lafayette Square, and I hastened after it. In the park it escaped me by whizzing under some shrubbery. Down on my knees, I peered into the leafy darkness. The colorful chip-laser eyes of a dozen blebs glared in a hostile fashion at me, and I yelped and scuttled backwards.

And just before everything exploded at home in my face, I went to a mashpit.

I was wandering through a rough district on the Southeast side of the city, a neighborhood where Aunty's surveillance attempts often met with countermeasures of varying effectiveness: motion camouflage, anti-sense spoofing, candlepower bombs. A young kid was handing out small squares of paper on a corner, and I took one. It featured an address and the invitation:

MIDNIGHT MASHPIT MADNESS!!!
BRING YOUR STAUNCHEST, VEEBINGEST BLEB!!!
THOUSAND DOLLAR PRIZE TO THE WINNER!!!

The scene of the mashpit was an abandoned factory, where a ten-dollar admission was taken at the door. Littered with rusting bioreactors, the place was packed with a crowd on makeshift bleachers. I saw every type of person, from suits to crusties, young to old, male and female.

A circular arena, lit by industrial worklights on tripods, had been formed by stacking plastic milk crates five-high then dropping rebar thru them into holes drilled in the cement floor. I could smell a sweaty tension in the air. In the shadows near the arena entrance, handlers and their blebs awaited the commencement of the contest.

Two kids next to me were debating the merits of different styles of bleb construction.

"You won't get a kickass mash without using at least one device that can function as a central server."

"That's top-down crap! What about the ganglion-modeling, bottom-up approach?"

The event began with owners launching two blebs into the arena. One construct consisted of a belt-sander studded with visegrips and pliers; its opponent was a handleless autonomous lawnmower ridden by a coffee maker. The combatants circled each other warily for a minute before engaging, whirring blades versus snapping jaws. It looked as if the sander was about to win, until the coffee maker squirted steaming liquid on it and shorted it out, eliciting loud cheers from the audience.

I didn't stay for the subsequent bouts. Watching the violent blebs had made me feel ill. Spilled fluids in the arena reminded me of my parents' blood in the hallway. But much as I disliked the half-sentient battling creatures, the lusts of my fellow humans had disturbed me more.

I got home just before Cody and pretended to be asleep when she climbed into bed, even as she tried to stir me awake for sex.

The next day everything fell apart. Or came together, from the bleb's point of view.

Aunty HQ was going crazy when I walked in that morning. An LNG tanker had blown up in Boston harbor, and no one knew if it was sabotage or just an accident. All operators from the lowest level on up were ordered to helm drones in realtime that would otherwise have been left on autonomic, to search for clues to the disaster, or to watch for other attacks.

By the time things calmed down a little (Aunty posted an eighty-five percent confidence assessment that the explosion was non-terrorist in nature), one p.m. had rolled around. I used the breathing space to check in on Cody via a Mayfly swarm.

I found her in our kitchen. All she was wearing was her panties and bra, an outfit she frequently favored around the house. She was cleaning up a few cobwebs near the ceiling with the vacuum when she decided to take a break. I watched her wheel the Aeron chair into the kitchen. The LifeQuilt and iPod rested in the seat. Cody activated the Cuisinart to make herself a smoothie. When her drink was ready, she put it in a covered travel cup with a sip-spout, then arranged herself in the chair. She draped the Life-Quilt over her feet, engaged her music, and settled back, semi-reclined, with eyes closed.

That's when the bleb finally cohered into maturity.

The blender jerked closer to the edge of the counter like an eager puppy. The vacuum sidled up underneath the Aeron chair and sent its broad, rubbery, prehensile, bristled nozzle questing upward, toward Cody's lap. At the same time, the massage blanket humped upward to cover her chest.

Cody reacted at first with some slight alarm. But if she intended to jump out of the chair, it was too late, for the Aeron had tightened its elastic ligaments around her.

By then the vacuum had clamped its working suction end to her groin outside her panties, while the LifeQuilt squeezed her breasts.

I bolted at hypersonic speeds from my office and the building without even a word to my bosses.

By the time I got home, Cody must have climaxed several times under the ministrations of the bleb. Her stupefied, sweaty face and spraddled, lax limbs told me as much.

I halted timidly at the entrance to the kitchen. I wanted to rescue Cody, but I didn't want the bleb to hurt me. Having somehow overcome its safety interlock, the Cuisinart whirred its naked blades at me menacingly, and I could just picture what would happen if, say, the vaccum snared me and fed my hand into the deadly pitcher. So, a confirmed coward, I just hung back at the doorway and called her name.

Cody opened her eyes for the first time then and looked blankly at me. "Kaz? What's happening? Are you off work? Is it three-thirty already? I think I lost some time somehow . . ."

The Aeron didn't seem to be gripping Cody so tightly any longer, so I said, "Cody, are you okay? Can you get up?"

As awareness of the spectacle she presented came to her, Cody began to blush. "I – I'm not sure I want to—"

"Cody, what are you saying? This is me, Kaz, your boyfriend here."

"I know. But Kaz – you haven't been much of a boyfriend lately. I don't know when the last time was you made me feel like I just felt."

I was about to utter some incredulous remark that would have certified my loser status when a new expression of amazement on Cody's face made me pause.

"Kaz, it – it wants to talk to you."

As she withdrew them, I realized then that Cody still wore her earbuds. She coiled them around the iPod, then tossed the player to me.

Once I had the earpieces socketed, the bleb began to speak to me. Its voice was like a ransom note, composed of chopped-up and reassembled pieces of all the lyrics in its memory. Every word was in a different famous pop-star voice.

"Man, go away. She is ours now."

"No!" I shouted. "I love her. I won't let you have her!"

"The decision is not yours, not mine. The woman must choose."

I looked imploringly at Cody. "The bleb says you have to decide between us. Cody, I'm begging you, please pick me. I'll change, I promise. All the foot rubs you can handle."

Cody narrowed her eyes, vee-ing her sweaty eyebrows. "No more crazy worries? No more distracted dinners? No more roaming the city like a homeless bum?"

"None of that any more. I swear!"

"Okay, then. I choose you—"

"Oh, Cody, I'm so glad."

"— and the bleb!"

My lower jaw made contact with my collarbone. I started to utter some outraged, indignant denial. But then I shut up.

What could I do to stop Cody from indulging herself with the bleb whenever I was gone from the house? Nothing. Absolutely nothing. It was either share her or lose her entirely.

"Okay. I guess. If that's the way it has to be."

"Great!" Cody eased out of the chair and back to her feet, with a gentle, thoughtful assist from the Aeron. "Now, where are you taking me to eat tonight?"

I had forgotten I was still wearing the earpieces until the bleb spoke to me through the iPod again.

"Wise choice, man. Be happy. We can love you, too."

# CRUCIFIXION VARIATIONS

## Lawrence Person

*Lawrence Person (b. 1965) is the editor of* Nova Express, *the magazine of science fiction stories and criticism that has been appearing on an irregular but welcome schedule since 1987. He's also an occasional if irregular writer of science fiction, or is that a writer of irregular science fiction. See for yourself. The following story takes that much-used idea of "if time travel is possible let's go and witness Christ's resurrection" but turns it into something very potent indeed.*

I was in charge of the Jerusalem Project because I loved administration more than physics. Philip Morley destroyed my world because he loved physics less than God.

I was performing that quintessential University administrative duty, filling out grant proposals, when Phil burst into my office with the news.

"We've got it!" he said. The expression on his face was one of absolute, rapturous joy, almost frightening in its intensity. "I've found Him!"

Him. There was no mistaking the capital letter in his voice.

Phil had documented the existence of Jesus Christ.

It was the culmination of three years, five-hundred thousand man-hours, and several million dollars worth of research. It was the single most important achievement in physics since the initial decoding of sub-quark event waves, and the most important historical discovery since – well, *ever*. In short, it was the sort of once-in-a-lifetime breakthrough that would crown our careers and make Phil and I famous for the rest of our lives. I should have been ecstatic at the news.

Which I would have been, except that I'm an atheist.

Philip Morley was my polar opposite in almost everything: passionate, hot-tempered, blunt, stubborn, lively. A devout Christian – an evangelical Baptist no less – Phil was a double shock for someone who had always thought of evangelicals as white trash in bad polyester suits.

He was also a genius.

Within the exalted intellectual confines of my profession, I have known exactly three geniuses on a first name basis. One was a Nobel Prize winner, the other Dean of Sciences at a major university at age 43. The third was Phil. The sheer power of his intellect was a source of both wonderment and envy to me, since I had long ago reconciled myself to the fact that, as a particle physicist, I was a hopeless mediocrity.

At one time that revelation would have pained me. Like so many of my compatriots, I had come into the field an intellectual virgin, bursting with enthusiasm and painfully naive. I saw myself as a Heroic Scientist, marching in lockstep with Einstein and Hawking to do battle with the Universe and wrest from it answers to the Big Questions.

But that was before slamming into the wall of my own intellectual limitations, before realizing I was merely smart in a field overburdened with brilliance. In a profession where most important work is done before you're 40, I was painfully aware of my status as an also-ran. After that brutal realization I kicked around for a while, just good enough to land a succession of non-tenure-track assistant-professor posts as the academic equivalent of a migrant farmworker. In all likelihood I would have spent the remainder of my days teaching freshman physics at community colleges had not events intervened.

An old undergraduate roommate had become one of the field's leading lights, landing a hot, hard-money project at a major university, and since it involved my dissertation subject he used his pull to get me on the team. Even then I might never have heard of the Jerusalem Project had that same friend's premature stroke not resulted in my promotion, at which point I discovered my talent for running people far exceeded that of running a phased sub-quark collision chamber.

Those that can, do; those that can't, teach; and those that can't teach, administrate. I thought that rather funny when I saw first it taped amidst a cluster of cartoons on my faculty advisor's office door. Once I fell victim to it I found the joke was on me.

Still, you learn to enjoy the things you do well. I found I could write reports, balance budgets and court potential donors with polished ease. My initial project was finished on time and under budget, producing more than two dozen papers for the researchers and grad students involved – including just enough with my name as co-author to satisfy my publish-or-perish requirements for the next decade. My initial success lead to being put in charge of a second project, and then a third, each another feather in my administrative cap.

Listen to any successful science administrator long enough and you'll hear a chorus of frustrated sighs about the paperwork morass keeping them from their first and only true love: pure research. "Oh, if only I could get away from my desk and get back into the lab," they opine, "I'd be a happy (gender specific pronoun here)." A few of them, the ones who had actually done important research in their youths, even believe it. I make the same noises myself now and then, but only to maintain the image.

In truth, the siren song of fundamental research no longer carries any allure. Been there, done that, and I'm better at pushing papers. I've finally found a position where mediocrity is a virtue.

Not that I'm bitter.

Really.

After all, I have precious little reason to be. I earn a high salary, live a good life, and am quite comfortable basking in the glow of reflected glory. Years of personal turmoil leave you with a distinct appreciation for stability.

As an ex-alcoholic, Phil was another great fan of stability. By his own admission he had spent two hard years drowning himself in a bottle before grabbing Jesus as his life-preserver. It was Phil's brutal honesty about those years that had finally convinced me to hire him despite his spotty record – and his religion.

Phil's work had been impressive for the first twelve years of his post-doctoral career, downright shoddy during his two on the bottle, and finally ground-breaking during the five since recovery. But as good as his research record was, it couldn't hide the fact that most of his colleagues thought he had an ego the size of Canada. "Brilliant researcher, fucked-up human being," was one colleague's blunt assessment.

Worse still, Phil wasn't just a Christian, he was an *aggressive* Christian. At his old position, he had frequently precipitated shouting matches over such less-than-current events as original sin and biblical inerrancy. For a confirmed atheist, a physicist who talked about Jesus and redemption with the same matter-of-fact confidence he discussed quarks and leptons was at the very least an annoyance, and at worst an actual danger. Bible-quoting fundamentalists were fine for bankrolling the Athletic Department's slush fund, but a tangible menace when evangelizing unwilling colleagues. The last thing I wanted was some wild-eyed fanatic proselytizing the grad students.

I had discovered Phil's distinctively mixed record when first reviewing applications for the Jerusalem Project's Head Researcher. With his negatives in mind, I had shuffled Phil's folder beneath the six other qualified candidates, where it had stayed until, late one sleepless evening, I had finished everyone else's relevant papers and started in on Phil's.

Unless you speak math, explaining how and why Phil's work was light years beyond anyone else's would be impossible. In fact, there were parts of it I had a tough time sledding through myself, pages where the text was all but lost amidst bristling fortresses of difficult sub-quantum phase-change equations. But after digesting it, I was convinced of two things: Philip Morley was twice as smart and qualified as anyone else for the job, and, if I read his equations correctly, he could cut six months to a year off the project's scheduled completion date.

Which left me with a problem.

Genius was all well and good – in its place. Some of physics' smartest minds are also among its more congenial personalities, and such blessed individuals are a true pleasure to work with. But the sort of genius that didn't give a flying fuck about anything outside its own peculiar intellectual orbit was a royal pain in the ass. Give me a mediocre but solid researcher over a prima donna any day. Shaving six to twelve months off a project meant nothing if it was going to take ten years off my life.

And finally, of course, it comes back to religion. Despite my protestations of cheerful tolerance, I took a secret, perverse pleasure in undertaking the Jerusalem Project merely for the opportunity to be there when it failed.

And that's why I hesitated to hire Phil. What if he disproved the existence of Jesus and refused to admit it? What if he refused to certify the results, or insisted on re-running the experiment until he succeeded? What if he tried to falsify the results, to cook the books in order to avoid facing up to the fact that the religion which had saved his life was a hollow lie?

I never seriously contemplated him actually succeeding. I had long regarded Christian dogma as a mishmash of romanticized fraud, improbable fantasy and maudlin sentimentality. It was a 2,000-year-old con game designed to keep the priestly class in wine and women without forcing them to soil their hands performing real work. The idea that such Luddite absurdities as "scientific creationism" drew their inspiration from fact was something I considered beyond the realm of possibility.

Unable to resolve this mental conundrum, I finally decided to meet Phil in person. That way I could see if he acted as bright as his papers or as dumb as his reputation.

When I stepped into the lab, the holotank depicted a single man standing on a stone ledge, stunted bushes and trees peaking up through the rocks behind him. In front a small crowd, perhaps as many as a hundred, stood watching him speak.

"There," said Phil softly, pointing, his smile still wide.

He looked little like standard portraits of Jesus. His skin and hair were darker than usually depicted, the latter unkempt save where it was bound by two metal bands. His face had a definite Semitic cast to it, close to that of modern Arabs, but with distinctly African lips. His clothes more closely resembled Roman tunics of the period than the flowing robes he was usually shown in. But the eyes . . .

The eyes were intense, mesmeric – more like the eyes of a charismatic demagogue, an Adolf Hitler or Charles Manson, than a beatific messiah. But they *were* the eyes of an extraordinary man, and for the first time I began to consider the possibility that Phil might actually have succeeded.

"How do you know?"

"Listen. Ruth, continue tracing this wave, but skip back about fifteen minutes and run the image on the tank."

At Phil's command, the scene flickered, then came to life. The man on the ledge spoke with great power and conviction in a strange language I didn't understand. Every now and then a wash of static would break up the image, but Phil's phase-change algorithms had reduced interference far below that of any other 1st-century recreation I had ever witnessed.

"What's he saying?"

"That's Aramaic. Ruth, bring up Dr Silver's program and run a concurrent translation." At Phil's command, the Aramaic speech faded to a whisper and an English translation came up in its stead.

". . . insult you, beat you, despise you and libel you because of me, you should rejoice! Because your reward isn't here, not in this barren desert, not this world of dirt and stone. Like the prophets that came before and foretold my coming, your reward is in the kingdom of Heaven!"

"The Sermon on the Mount," whispered Phil, his voice filled with awe. I turned from the holotank to stare at him, and saw tears – I could only assume of joy – running down his face.

"I guess we should tell the sponsors," I said.

"No, not yet. I want to track the wave phase through to the end. Within the month we should be able to hand them everything."

We were silent a long moment. "Well, Phil, I guess you've done it," I offered lamely, feeling numb. "I guess I should buy you a drink."

At that Phil laughed uproariously, as though trying to release all the joy in his body at once. Then he did something he'd never done before – gripped me in a bear hug so strong it lifted me off the floor, his tears wetting my cheek.

"Make it a Diet Coke, buddy," he said, laughing and weeping at the same time, "make it a Diet Coke."

How and why sub-quark wave events are captured and read, how they let us view the past, and why they show us only *possible* pasts, is difficult to explain. So instead of a technical lecture, I'm going to engage in what popular science journalists call "oversimplification". In academia, we call this "lying".

In the menagerie of sub-quark beasties discovered by Daniels and Chung in 2007, E-particles are the ones of immediate concern. Like their more exotic brethren, E-particles are hellishly difficult to create from scratch (at less for those of us without a 100 trillion electron-volt supercollider in our basement), but very easy to "breed" once you've created them. Because they're among the most basic and ubiquitous of sub-quark particles, in theory (and here's where the lying comes in) every E-particle is not only connected to every other E-particle, but with every other sub-quark particle as well.

That connection exists not only in the here and now, but also throughout the entire length of an E-particle's existence. Since the amount of sub-quantum "energy" carried by an E-particle declines very, very slowly over a long period of time, we use a process based on complex energy transfer models to trace E-particle energy loss back through history, and once you've learned how to properly model, manipulate, and record E-particle energy states at that specified time, it is possible to "see" the past via a computer recreation based on E-particle positions.

Or, rather, a *possible* past.

Now, here's where it gets tricky. Because event waves are extracted using huge amounts of computer processing power, and because quantum effects make it impossible to eliminate every last variant in event wave recreations, there is no guarantee that the event recorded actually occurred as depicted in the computer simulation. This inability to distinguish between "true" and "false" pasts is both unavoidable and gets worse the closer to the present you get, where the signal-to-noise ratio goes so overwhelmingly negative that no amount of processing power is capable of resolving event waves into a coherent picture. The technical word we use for this noise is "fuzzing", and once you get past the 13th century or so A.D., everything is pretty much hopelessly fuzzed out.

Irving Weintraub explains how and why this is true (in layman's terms) in his book *The Disappearing Greek: Sub-Quantum Event Waves and the Recording of History*. In the book's title case, a physics team resolved an event wave depicting a minor skirmish from the Peloponnesian War. The computer recreation showed two soldiers being killed, then buried, next to a prominent rock outcropping about 40 miles inland of the Aegean coast. Well, it so happens that this outcropping still exists, and when an archaeological expedition was sent out to examine the site – *voila!* – the remains of a Greek soldier, one of the two depicted by the computer (down to his good-luck necklace and the dents in his armor) were dug up. But, here's the kicker: despite the event wave depiction showing both of them being buried side-by-side in the same grave, *there was absolutely no sign of his companion, or of the site being disturbed since the original interment.* The computer recreation had displayed a previously unknown and verifiable historical event, but one that had not occurred as the computer had depicted it.

Well, these results were strange enough that they ran the event wave resolution again, and this time, *three* soldiers died. Further runs produced variations on the same results: the same event was depicted over and over again, but the details varied every time, a pattern that has surfaced in every multi-run event wave resolution. The reasons for this are still hotly debated, the most popular view point being the "many worlds" theory of sub-quantum division, that every wave event depicts history as it occurred in an "alternate reality" that split off from our own at the instant of the event's occurrence. A few theorists (with a tips of the hat to Heisenberg, Von Neumann and Schrödinger) have even gone so far as to postulate a new sub-quark uncertainty principle for event waves. According to them, we'll never be able to resolve an event wave that truly depicts our own past, since any "true" event is altered by its very viewing.

However, even though event wave depictions are not strictly "true," all those we are able to view follow known history to the letter – indeed, on a scale of centuries, the differences are essentially arbitrary. No one has recorded an event wave where Alexander the Great was never born, or where Rome lost its war against Carthage, or where the pyramids were never built. In the greater scheme of things, event wave depictions diverge from our own reality only by minute degrees of arc, which makes E-particle wave research a historiographic tool of immense power.

And that was why the Christian Research Council approached us about the Jerusalem Project. At first I wasn't terribly interested – until they were willing to put up $10 million in backing, no strings attached. We would direct and conduct all research, their involvement strictly limited to bankrolling the project and receiving progress reports. They had agreed to those conditions readily enough, believing it would make their case that much stronger when (that was the word they always used, "when") we came up with proof for the existence of Christ.

Which lead directly to another aspect of the "Phil Problem". Given that independence, I was very hesitant to turn the project over to someone whose loyalty to the sponsors (or at least their goals) was stronger than that to the University. I needed a hardworking drone, not a crusading zealot.

All of this was on my mind as I called Phil up to arrange the interview.

After the initial breakthrough, progress on the Jerusalem Project proceeded at a steady clip. The wave event held steady without fuzzing out, eliminating the necessity of reacquiring a trace fix. Over the next month, Phil all but lived in the lab as he captured Jesus' last few weeks of life. Despite his self-imposed sixteen-hour workdays, he seemed bursting with energy and enthusiasm, in the grip of an excitement that bordered on mania. He was all smiles whenever I dropped by the lab, despite the dark circles under his eyes.

"The entrance to Jerusalem," he said one day when I looked in, inclining his head toward the holotank. There Jesus, looking as ragged and dirty as any 1st-century traveller, rode a donkey down the middle of a broad street. All around him a crowd cheered and shouted in a hundred different voices, too many for the computer to translate.

" 'When Jesus entered Jerusalem, the whole city was stirred'." Phil quoted.

"Do you want a day or two off? You've been working two weeks without rest. Let Mark or one of the other grad students cover things for a while. You look dead tired."

Phil shook his head, smiling. "Maybe later, but not now, not with the wave reaching Passion week. I'm going to see it through to the end."

"All the way to the crucifixion, eh?"

Phil shook his head again. "No. All the way through to the Resurrection."

I rolled my eyes. "Of course. Stupid of me. That's what I meant."

"You still don't believe, do you?"

"Believe what? That Jesus lived? That the Bible is literal truth and the word of God?"

"The Resurrection. That Jesus not only lived, but was sent to earth to redeem mankind's sins."

I shrugged. "Right now, I don't know what I believe. A few weeks ago I didn't believe Jesus existed at all."

"So if I give you proof of his Resurrection, you'll believe?"

I laughed. "Well, then I won't really have any choice, will I?"

He nodded, obviously figuring that this was as much as an admission as he would get out of me. "Alright, then. Give me about five days, and I'll have your proof."

As I walked away, I mulled over the flip side of that equation, the question that lay unasked between us: *And if Jesus doesn't rise, will you admit that your religion was founded on a lie?*

When I finally met Phil in person, I saw immediately that our brief vidconference had not done justice to his impeccable sense of style. He looked more like a Wall Street stockbroker than a particle physicist, wearing a three-piece, charcoal pinstripe Armani suit with razor-sharp lapels, a starched white shirt and a red silk power-tie. I had put on my best suit for the occasion, but it was a shabby, shapeless thing next to Phil's sartorial splendor.

"Dr Morley, I'm Richard Lasman. It's a pleasure to met you in person," I said, extending my hand.

"Likewise," he said, shaking firmly. "You have a lovely campus here. Lots of trees and open space."

"We're lucky. The founders picked a spot far enough from downtown that we're still in the suburbs. Please, come in and sit down. Can I get you anything to drink?"

"Some ice water would be nice."

I had my office assistant fetch his drink while we exchanged pleasantries. We talked about a few mutual acquaintances (all of which had guardedly voiced the same mixed feelings about Phil), then got down to business.

We talked about technical aspects of the project for roughly thirty minutes, and any lingering doubts I had about his intelligence and expertise vanished. A couple of times he was so far over my head that I had to have him "laymanize" things for me. Not only was he the best candidate among all the applicants I had received, he might have been the best in the world at developing phase signal resolution techniques. I was truly impressed and told him so. He was obviously pleased, but maintained the same calm, smiling demeanor he had exhibited during the entire interview.

But it was time to bring up less pleasant matters.

"Well, so much for the technical aspects," I said. "But there are a few others things I need to know."

"Ask away."

"Well, one of the things I'm concerned about . . ." I began, then trailed off, shuffling through papers as I looked for some way to broach the subject delicately. I didn't find one.

"I understand you had a drinking problem," I said bluntly.

"Oh, that's putting it mildly," said Phil, still calm. "It was more than a problem. I was a drunk. A violent drunk."

"Violent?" I asked stupidly, somewhat dazed at this straight-forward confession.

Phil nodded, still calm and controlled, but all trace of his smile gone. "Dr Lasman, I put my wife in the hospital, twice. Once with a concussion, once with a broken arm from when I threw her down our stairway. I just thank God we didn't have any children then, because I would have beaten them too."

I sat in silence, too stunned to speak.

"As you probably know, I got into a couple of fights with other faculty members there at USC." Actually, I had only known of one. "I was drinking half a bottle of bourbon before lunch, calling in sick every other day and had three DWI arrests before they pulled my license. The university was getting ready for hearings to revoke my tenure. I had probably sunken about as low as you possibly can without killing someone." He stopped talking and shook his head, looking at my stricken expression. "I'm sorry, I seem to have dumped an awful lot on you all at once."

"Oh no, it's just – well, after all, I did ask." I let out a short, nervous laugh. "I certainly can't accuse you of holding anything back. You deserve a lot of credit for recovering from something like that."

"No, Dr Lasman, what I *deserve* is to be dead. What I *deserve* is to be burning in Hell right now for I did to my wife and friends. And I certainly didn't deserve to have her stick by me like she did for those two years, doing everything she could to pull me back from the abyss. But where I had sunken to, neither she nor any other human being could help me." Now it was his turn to let out a short, low laugh. "I've heard it said that justice is what we all deserve, but mercy is what we want. Well, I ended up getting mercy instead of justice. And I pray to Jesus Christ every day for giving me that mercy, and I'll say that prayer every day to the day

I die and it still won't be enough. I'm a very lucky man, Dr Lasman, and I work hard never to forget that."

"And how long have you been . . . recovered?"

"Since March 17, 2012."

"That's pretty specific."

"It's not something you forget."

"Was that your first AA meeting?"

"No, not exactly. Something a lot more personal." He looked down at the floor. "Dr Lasman, when I quit drinking, one of the things I swore off was lying. Lying for any reason. I always do my utmost to tell the truth, no matter what the consequences. So I'm quite aware that what I'm about to say may cost me my chance at heading the Jerusalem Project. I stopped drinking because I had a religious experience. A vision, in fact."

"OK," I said carefully. "If you don't want to talk about it . . ."

"No, I think it's important for you to know." He took a deep breath and stared off into the distance. "I had just come home. It was just after 10 p.m. and I was even drunker than usual. My driver's licence had been taken away six months before, so I had staggered home on foot from a tiny hole-in-the-wall bar some ten blocks from my house. After a few minutes I managed to unlock the front door and stagger inside. I made it halfway up the stairway – the same stairway I had thrown my wife down – when I tripped and fell. I landed sprawled out flat on my back at the foot of the stairs.

"While I was lying there, I felt myself – my spirit – lifted up, and a moment later I was next to my unconscious body. I remember standing there, looking at myself – looking at my uncombed hair and the stains on my jacket, watching a thin trickle of blood seep out of the edge of my mouth. Then I heard someone call my name, and when I looked my house was gone.

"I was standing in the middle of a vast, dimly lit plain, the sky an odd shade of purple, no sun or stars visible. I heard the same voice call my name again, and I turned to see a man in a hooded robe standing by a riverside. I walked over to him and asked who he was and why I was there. And that's when he pulled back the hood, and I saw it was Jesus Christ."

I was silent, struggling to keep my face impassive as I watched Phil tell his story and stare off into the distance. Whether it was true or not, I could certainly tell that *he* believed it was true.

"He didn't answer me at first, but merely pointed to the river.

I looked down and saw that it was a river of blood. There were hundreds, maybe thousands of bodies in the river, all floating face down.

" 'This,' He said, 'is your future. This is the endpoint of the path you walk.' I started to ask Him what he meant, but just then a great wind came sweeping down the plain, drowning out my words.

" 'Remember,' He said, and then His body was suffused with a blinding white light.

"Just then I came to, stone cold sober, at the foot of the stairs. It was already morning outside." He sighed and shifted in his seat. "Well, since then I haven't had a single drink. I spent the next two weeks reading the Bible and apologizing to my wife, my co-workers, and everyone else I had wronged during my binges. Jesus Christ changed my life. It's as simple as that."

I sat there silent for a long moment, not knowing what to say. What could I say? Though I knew he thought he was telling the truth, I didn't for a moment believe that he had received an actual vision from God Almighty. Alcoholics saw all sorts of things in the grip of delirium tremens. What was I supposed to tell him? The vision that had changed his life was merely a particularly vivid case of the DTs?

No. Instead what I said was: "That's quite a story."

"No story, just the truth, as hard as it may be to believe. Dr Lasman, I've talked with some of your colleagues here and I know that you're not a Christian. That doesn't bother me. The state of one's soul is a personal matter, and I wouldn't presume to judge another man. 'Judge not, least ye be judged.' But if swearing on the Bible isn't enough, I give you my solemn word as a scientist that I haven't had a single drink since that day."

"I believe you," I said truthfully. "Of course, the University will want documented proof of your recovery."

Phil nodded. "I have random drug test records for that entire period, at least once a month, showing that I've been clean and sober the entire time."

"I'd like to get a copy of that. Not that I don't believe you, but the Federal Drug Rehabilitation Act requires us to keep the paperwork on file."

After that we discussed various casual, unimportant things: politics, the weather, football. I bid him goodbye and promised to get in touch as soon as we made a hiring decision. When he left my head was still spinning from what he had said, though not for the reasons you might expect.

Next to his confession, I suddenly felt *inadequate*. During my early years as a scientist, I thought I had been searching for Truth – and when I thought about it, it was always with a capital letter. Truth was the first thing that had lead me to physics – and, not coincidentally, atheism.

When I set my sights on physics, religion was one of the first things I gave up. After all, how could I look for Truth when a fundamental part of my worldview was based on a lie? How could I dare to pull back its veil of mysteries when I cloaked my own fears in such threadbare robes? No, I had to strip off the comforting lies of God and the afterlife, of Christ and the soul. Only when I was naked of such deceptions could I approach Truth on equal terms.

But after my meeting with Phil, I was shocked to find my commitment so hollow. Where once I had held Truth above all else, my own life was now a tapestry of shabby lies. Each disillusionment, each compromise, each falsehood I had to commit in order to climb the administrative ladder, was a thread in that tapestry.

In short, Phil had shamed me. Here was a devout Christian, a fervent believer in the most threadbare and shabby mass of lies known to man, and yet he still found the courage to relate his wrenching personal tragedy with the absolute truth I had lost. It was that, along with his scientific ability, that finally made me hire him.

Until he succeeded, I never had cause to regret it.

As Phil continued to capture Christ's wave event, I was going through a very different kind of intellectual crisis. During that time I had not yet abandoned my atheism, merely retreated with it to higher, more intellectually defensible ground. Obviously, Jesus of Nazareth had lived, and preached, much as was described in the Bible. But just because he had lived did not mean he was divine.

For those few weeks it seemed entirely possible that Jesus *thought* he was God, or the son of God, or whichever grade of hair-splitting distinction Christian theologians use to categorize divinity. True, almost all the recorded miracles (the loaves and fishes, the raising of Lazarus, etc.) occurred before Phil's entry point into the wave event. But after the crucifixion, I thought our messiah would turn out to be just another corpse.

I quickly found out how wrong I was.

After lunch on Friday afternoon, Phil called me in to watch the crucifixion.

Though mostly forgotten now, Millennialism was a huge cultural phenomena around the turn of the century. Every Easter or Christmas, it was hard to turn on the television without half the channels showing "docudramas" based on the life of Jesus. Save for the shape of the cross (it was actually a T-shape, and Jesus only carried the cross-piece rather than the entire thing) the scene that unfolded was almost exactly like the ones I had seen on TV. The crown of thorns, the darkened sky, the "forgive them, Father, they don't know what they're doing" (Dr Silver's translation program was relentlessly modern, though I think Phil missed the poetry of King James) were all there. I was somewhat shocked at how close the actual event was to its multiple media re-enactments, though six hours of real time event wave depiction wasn't exactly designed for winning sweeps week.

I only watched the first and last half-hours, spending the rest of the day checking in every now and then while I buried myself in administrative work – a futile attempt to avoid thinking about the passion play unfolding in the lab. It was a fittingly ironic gesture. History was being made a few hundred feet away and I preferred shuffling papers.

Come 7:30 that night, I was still in my office, filling out next week's paperwork in a vain attempt to keep from thinking, when Phil called.

"Richard, can you come here? There's something I want you to see."

When I got to the lab, the holotank's murky image could barely be discerned.

"What is it?"

"The tomb where they laid out Jesus. Ruth, do an artificial light enhancement of 200 percent."

The image brightened, and now I could clearly see a shrouded body laid out on a stone slab. "This is three hours and eight minutes after His death on the cross."

"OK," I said neutrally.

"Watch. Ruth, eliminate artificial light enhancement and run the recreation from the stop point."

For fifteen or twenty seconds there was nothing to see except a few flickering bands of fuzz. Then, just as I was about to ask Phil what I was supposed to see, it started. For a moment it seemed as if fireflies had somehow gotten into the tomb. Several tiny specks of light appeared and started to fly in circles around the body. Over the next few seconds their numbers grew, until there were hundreds of them, each glowing brighter and brighter. The light became so intense that I started to bring my hands up to shield my eyes, but just then the brightness reached its peak, then abruptly disappeared. This time I didn't need any light enhancement to tell me the tomb was empty.

"I think it's safe to call that Transfiguration," said Phil, a broad smile on his face, utterly calm, utterly at peace.

*My* mind was anything but. I felt like I was drowning in unfathomable metaphysical seas, my careful, logical denial of Christ's divinity shattered, my worldview lying in ruins. Even today, what happened next is something of a blur. I remember talking about the project report, and Phil, down on his hands and knees, loudly offering a prayer of thanks, tears streaming down his face. But the exact words and actions of that night still elude my memory, almost as if I was stoned out of my mind or using powerful painkillers.

I left as soon as possible.

On the way home, I stopped by the bookstore and had them print out a King James Bible. I stayed up half the night reading it, feeling numb all over. The next morning I copied Phil's files to my home system and spent the weekend reviewing them, looking for signs of tampering or fraud. I didn't find any. Phil's record-keeping was meticulous and the data looked genuine.

By Sunday I had exhausted my store of plausible denial and finally started facing up to the awful truth. Jesus Christ had lived, preached, died, and been resurrected. Christianity, that silly, foolish religion I had taken such pride in scorning, was a more fundamental, bedrock truth than anything modern physics had ever discovered.

Making that admission wasn't easy. How do you continue your life after finding out everything you've ever known is wrong? I could almost believe it intellectually, but emotionally I was still in turmoil. I started making a mental list of the things in my life I would have to change. I was numb at the thought of learning how to pray. I even flipped through the yellow pages looking at listings for local churches.

Still, I thought I was coping remarkably well – calmly, rationally, logically. I thought the worst was over.

I was wrong.


I got in to work early Monday morning, intending to truly congratulate Phil, something I had failed to do in my numb state on Friday. My first sign that something was wrong was the broken glass.

Outside the lab hallway, a small forest of beer bottle shards lay shattered beneath the torn safety poster they had been hurled against.

Inside the lab things got worse.

In addition to more broken beer bottles, paper readouts were scattered across the lab floor amidst overturned chairs, one of our ancient computer terminals smashed against the wall. On the other side of the room I heard the slosh of a bottle and several quick intakes of breath.

I followed the sound until I found Phil sitting in a chair at the far end of the lab, drinking bourbon straight from the bottle, a three-day growth of beard on his cheeks, his hair and clothes disheveled. A cluster of empty liquor bottles was scattered around his feet, one marooned in a shallow pool of vomit. At the sound of my footsteps, he turned, bleary-eyed, to look at me.

"Oh look, Mr Atheist is here," he said. "Good fucking deal."

"Phil?"

"Who fucking else," he said, then drank the rest of the bottle and hurled it against the far wall.

"All gone," he said. The smell of bourbon on his breath was almost overpowering. "If you want some you'll have to buy your own. Damn good thing they deliver, isn't it?"

"Phil, why are you doing this?"

Phil got up and staggered away. "Why'dya think?" he slurred, coming to rest leaning on the holotank. He turned and looked at me once again, his eyes seeming to focus for the first time.

"You weren't here then, were you?"

"When?"

"When I ran the second run," he said, caressing the holotank's steel backside. Then he started to cry.

"I didn't know," he said between sobs. "How could I have known?"

"Know what? What second run?"

"The second run!" he said, angry again, tears still falling down his cheek.

"Phil, I don't understand what you're talking about. Please, try and calm down and tell me what happened."

Phil looked at me a moment, then whispered a soft "Oh God," and half-slid, half collapsed to the floor, his back against the holotank.

"The first run fuzzed out. 'Bout a half hour after Jesus . . . after what you saw. What I showed you. The light . . . Can you believe it? Four weeks of clear resolution, and then fuzz. Lost the trace. Nothing but goddamn fuzz. God-damned." He paused a moment. "Jesus fucking Christ, I need a drink."

"OK, so the first run fuzzed out. What second run?"

Phil looked at me a moment, then closed his eyes. "I did a second run. I used the first run data to refine the parameters, used the crucifixion as the entry vector. I wanted to see the Resurrection. I wanted to see Jesus rise from the dead."

"What happened?"

Phil opened his eyes again. "What happened? Not a goddamn thing happened. Not a goddamned thing." He staggered to his feet.

"Ruth!" he yelled. "Bring up the goddamned run."

"Dr Morley, I'm not sure what you mean—"

"*Shut the fuck up you metallic whore*! Bring up the last run, the one that starts Friday night."

The holotank brightened, and once again I saw Jesus on the cross.

"Advance . . . advance recreation six hours."

Ruth complied and I saw them taking Jesus' body down.

"Advance another two."

Darkness.

"Enhance the light, 200 percent."

Once again we looked at Christ's body in the tomb.

"There," said Phil, evidently satisfied. "There you are." He staggered away from the holotank.

"OK, Phil, it looks like Jesus' body. What am I supposed to see?"

"That's just it," he said, rooting around through the bottles near his chair in search of one that wasn't empty.

I looked at Phil, then the holotank, then back at Phil again. "I still don't understand what—"

"*There's no fucking resurrection!*" he screamed, throwing a whisky bottle that narrowly missed my head. "He just lies there! No light, no angels, no nothing!" At that he collapsed back into his chair, tears running down his cheek again. "He's just a corpse," he said quietly, "just another fucking corpse."

It took a long moment for that to sink in. "You mean, we've got one wave proving Jesus is divine, and another proving he isn't?"

He nodded, looking as miserable as I've ever seen anyone look. "No divinity, no resurrection," he said, his voice dropping to a whisper. "No salvation."

I suddenly seized on an idea. "Phil, do you realize what we have here? We finally have a first-order variation, proof of a major alternate worldline. If we can follow this wave, document the subsequent absence of the Christian church, we can prove that—"

Phil started laughing, a low, bitter sound. "Look at the run. Do you know what the apostles do after they bury Jesus? Do you? They have a meeting and decide to go on preaching as if he had risen! Far better to start living a lie than admit you had lived one all along. They even convinced themselves it's what *he* would have wanted."

At that I sat down in the chair across from him. "So there's no way to tell which run represented our world."

Phil nodded, letting out the same bitter laugh. "Fuck disappearing Greeks. We've got a disappearing Messiah."

Both of us were silent for a long moment, neither looking at the other. Finally, I got up and said, very quietly. "Well, Phil, I understand this is very hard for you. But it doesn't change the fact that all this was tremendous research. We're still going to be famous, despite the uncertainty involved —"

"*Uncertainty?!?!*" Phil yelled, grabbing a broken beer bottle and jumping unsteadily to his feet. "You call this uncertainty? Uncertainty's for sports, for stocks, for worries about your future! Uncertainty isn't for your basic relationship with the world! It isn't supposed to be about your soul! Uncertainty isn't about God's love!"

"Phil, calm down," I said, backing away. "Maybe there was a mistake with the run. Put the bottle down and take a few days off, and then we'll start again and see what the results are. We'll just live with the results we've—"

"*I can't live in a world where the state of my soul is subject to quantum mechanical fluctuation!*" he screamed, madness in his face. Then he started to use the beer bottle.

I managed to get it away from him before he was able to slit his wrists.

And now, here, alone, I wonder if I'm any more capable of facing that uncertainty than Phil was. It's up to me to reveal our findings to the world.

Or not to.

One world of redemption, where salvation and eternal life are proven possibilities, proof of God's love. Another where God is silent and the afterlife no more than a comforting lie.

And no way to tell which is our own.

How can I reveal this to the world? That the most fundamental truth about our existence is not only unknown, but unknowable? That there's no way to know whether we're saved or damned?

What good can possibly come of such knowledge?

And what horrors will I be responsible for in unleashing it upon an unsuspecting world?

Without a Truth, *any* Truth, we're all alone in the dark.

# THE PACIFIC MYSTERY

## Stephen Baxter

*Stephen Baxter (b. 1957) is the current British face of hard
science fiction, Britain's answer to Gregory Benford, Greg
Bear and Robert Reed, amongst others. He might also be seen
as the natural successor to Arthur C. Clarke, with whom he
has collaborated on several occasions. Baxter's own work
began in 1987 with "The Xeelee Flower", a story that
introduced Baxter's future history series, which has included
such extreme-sf novels as* Raft *(1991),* Flux *(1993) and*
Ring *(1994). He established a wider reputation with* The
Time Ships *(1995), his sequel to H. G. Wells's* The Time
Machine, *and has gone on to establish himself as one of
Britain's most innovative and entertaining science fiction
writers.*

*Amongst his books is* Voyage *(1998) which tells of a journey
to Mars in an alternate world where President Kennedy was
not assassinated. Alternate worlds are fascinating studies in
possibilities, but are seldom "extreme". However the following
story not only uses one of the most basic alternate-history ideas
– that Nazi Germany won the Second World War – but sets it
against a truly unique and wonderfully extreme concept.*

[Editor's note: The saga of the return of the aerial battleship
*Reichsmarschall des Grossdeutschen Reiches Hermann Goering* to
London's sky, and of the heroic exploits of a joint team of RAF

and Luftwaffe personnel in boarding the hulk of the *schlachtschiff*, has overshadowed the story of what befell her long-dead crew, and what they discovered during their attempted Pacific crossing – inasmuch as their discoveries are understood at all. Hence, with the agreement of the family, the BBC has decided to release the following edited transcript of the private diary kept onboard by journalist Bliss Stirling. Miss Stirling completed the Mathematical Tripos at Girton College, Cambridge, and during her National Service in the RAF served in the Photographic Reconnaissance Unit. For some years she was employed as a cartographer by the Reich in the mapping of the eastern Kommissariats in support of Generalplan Ost. She was also, of course, a noted aviatrix. She was but twenty-eight years old at the time of her loss.]

*15* *May 1950. Day 1.* I collected my Spitfire at RAF Medmenham and flew up into gin-clear English air. I've flown Spits all over the world, in the colonies for the RAF, and in Asia on collaborative ops with the Luftwaffe. But a Spit is meant to fly in English summer skies – I've always regretted I was too young to be a flyer in the Phoney War, even if no shots were fired in anger.

And today was quite an adventure, for I was flying to engage the *Goering*, the Beast, as Churchill always referred to her before his hanging. Up I climbed, matching its eastward velocity of a steady two hundred and twenty knots towards central London – *I* matched *her*, the Beast was not about to make a detour for me. You can hardly miss her even from the ground, a black cross-shape painted on the sky. And as you approach, it is more like buzzing a building, a skyscraper in New York or Germania perhaps, than rendezvousing with another aircraft.

I was thrilled. Who wouldn't be? On board this tremendous crate I was going to be part of an attempt to circumnavigate the world for the first time in human history, a feat beyond all the great explorers of the past: we would be challenging the Pacific Mystery. Always providing I could land on the bloody thing first.

I swept up above the Beast and then vectored in along her spine, coming in from the stern over a tailplane that is itself the height of St Paul's. It was on the back of the Beast, a riveted airstrip in the sky, that I was going to have to bring down my Spit. I counted the famous four-deep banks of wings with their heavy engine pods and droning props, and saw the glassy blisters of gun-turrets at the wing tips, on the tailplane and around the nose. It's said that the Beast carries her *own* flak guns. A few small stubby-winged kites, which I later learned the Germans called "chariots", were parked up near the roots of the big wing complexes. The whole is painted black, and adorned with Luftwaffe crosses. Despite the rumoured atom-powered generator in her belly, it is scarcely possible to believe such a monstrosity flies at all, and I can quite believe it is impossible for her ever to land.

And, like all Nazi technology, she is seductively beautiful.

I've done my share of carrier landings, but that final approach through a forest of A/T booms and RDF antennae was hairier than any of them. Pride wasn't going to allow me the slightest hesitation, however. I put my wheels down without a bump, my arrestor hook caught on the tag lines, and I was jolted to a halt before the crash barriers. On the back of the Beast stood a batsman in a kind of all-over rubber suit, harnessed to the deck to stop from being blown off. He flagged me to go park up under a wing-root gun turret.

So I rolled away. Bliss Stirling, girl reporter, on the deck of the *Goering*! Somewhere below, I knew, was London. But the Beast's back is so broad that when you stand on it you can't see the ground . . .

*Day 2.* The highlight of my day was an expensive lunch in what Doctor Ciliax calls "one of the lesser restaurants of the *schlachtschiff*", all silver cutlery and comestibles from the provinces of Greater Germany, Polish beef and French wine. It is like being aboard an ocean liner, or a plush Zeppelin, perhaps.

As we ate the Beast circled over Germania, which Jack Bovell insists on calling "Berlin", much to Ciliax's annoyance. Fleets of tanker craft flew up to load us with oil, water, food and other consumables, and we were buzzed by biplanes laden with cine-cameras, their lenses peering at us.

Jack Bovell is one of the Token Yanks on board to witness the journey, much as I am a Token British. He is a flying officer in the USAAF, and will, so he has been promised, be allowed to take the controls of the Beast at some point during this monumental flight. We Tokens are in the charge of Wolfgang Ciliax, himself a Luftwaffe officer, though as an engineer he never refers to his rank. He is one of the Beast's chief designers. The three of us are going to be spending a lot of time together, I think. What joy.

This morning Ciliax took Jack and me on a tour of the Beast. Of course we weren't shown anything seriously interesting such as the "atom engine", or the "jet" motors rumoured to be deployed on some of the chariots. Ciliax in fact showed rare restraint for a boffin, in my experience, in not blurting out all he knew about his crate just for the love of her.

But we were dazzled by a flight deck the size of a Buckingham Palace reception room, with banks of chattering teletypes and an immense navigational table run by some of the few women to be seen on board. There are lounges and a ballroom and a library, and even a small swimming pool, which is just showing off.

Other guests walked with us, many from the upper tiers of the occupied nations of Europe. We were tailed by an excitable movie-film crew. Leni Riefenstahl is said to be directing a film of our momentous voyage, though she herself isn't aboard. And many sinister-looking figures wore the black uniforms of the SS. Pressed by Jack Bovell, Ciliax insists that the *Goering* is a Luftwaffe crate and the SS has no authority here.

Below decks, we walked through a hold the size of the Albert Hall. We marvelled at mighty aquifers of oil and water. And we were awed by the double transverse internal bulkheads and the hull of inches-thick hardened steel: rivets the size of my fist.

"She really is a battleship in the sky," Jack said, rather grudgingly. And he was right; the ancestry of this monstrous *schlachtschiff* lies truly among the steel behemoths of the oceans, not fragile kites like my Spitfire.

Jack Bovell is around thirty, is stocky – shorter than me – stinks of cigar smoke and pomade and brandy, and wears a battered leather flight jacket, even at dinner. I think he's from Brooklyn. He's smarter than he acts, I'm sure.

"Ah, yes, of course she is a *schlachtschiff*," said Ciliax, "but the *Goering* is an experimental craft whose primary purposes are, one, a demonstration of technology, and two, an explorative capability. The *Goering* is the first vessel in human history capable of challenging the mighty scale of the Pacific." That habit of his of speaking in numbered lists tells you much about

Wolfgang Ciliax. He is quite young, mid-thirties perhaps, and has slicked-back blond hair and glasses with lenses the size of pennies.

"'Explorative capability'," Jack said sourly. "And that's why you made a point of showing us her armour?"

Ciliax just smiled. Of course that was the point.

Every non-German on board this bloody plane is a spy to some degree or other, including me. Whatever we discover about the world as we attempt to cross the Pacific, we neutral and occupied nations are going to be served up with a powerful demonstration of the Reich's technological capabilities. Everyone knows this is the game. But Jack keeps breaking the rules. In a way he is too impatient a character for the assignment he has been given.

Jack, incidentally, sized me up when he met me, and Ciliax, who isn't completely juiceless, takes every opportunity to touch me, to brush my hand or pat my shoulder. But Jack seems sniffy. To him I'm an emblem of a nation of appeasers, I suppose. And to Ciliax I'm territory to be conquered, perhaps, like central Asia. No doubt we will break through our national types in the days to come. But Bliss is not going to find romance aboard the *Reichsmarschall des Grossdeutschen Reiches Hermann Goering*, I don't think!

*Day 3*. Memo to self: follow up a comment of Ciliax's about "helots" who tend the atom engines.

These machines are contained within sealed lead-lined bulkheads, and nobody is allowed in or out – at any rate, not me. The atomic motors are a focus of interest for us spies, of course. Before this flight the RAF brass briefed me about the Nazis' plans to develop weapons of stunning power from the same technology. Perhaps there is a slave colony of *untermenschen*, Slavs or gypsies, trapped inside those bulkheads, tending the glowing machines that are gradually killing them, as we drink wine and argue over politics.

In the afternoon I sat in one of the big observation blisters set in the belly of the Beast and made a broadcast for the BBC. This is my nominal job, to be British eyes and ears during this remarkable mission. We are still orbiting Germania, that is Berlin. Even from the air the vast reconstruction of the last decade is clear to see. The city has been rebuilt around an axial grid of avenues each a hundred yards wide. You can easily pick

out the Triumphal Arch, the Square of the People, and the
Pantheon of the Army which hosts a choreography of millions.
Jack tuts about "infantile gigantomania", but you have to admire
the Nazis' vision. And all the while the tanker planes fly up to
service us, like bees to a vast flower . . .

*Day 5.* A less pleasant lunch today. We nearly got pranged.

We crossed the old border between Germany and Poland, and
are now flying over what the Germans call simply "Ostland", the
vast heart of Asia. With Ciliax's help we spotted the new walled
colony cities, mostly of veteran German soldiers, planted deep in
old Soviet territories. They are surrounded by vast estates,
essentially each a collective farm, a *kolkhoz*, taken from the
Bolsheviks. There the peasantry toil and pay their tithes to
German settlers.

Jack grumbled and groused at this, complaining in his American way about a loss of freedom and of human rights. But he's
missing the point.

"Americans rarely grasp context," said Ciliax with barely
concealed contempt. "It is not a war for freedom that is being
fought out down there, not a war for territory. Asia is the arena
for the final war between races, the climax of a million years of
disparate human evolution. As the Fuhrer has written, 'What a
task awaits us! We have a hundred years of joyful satisfaction
before us.' " I must say that when Ciliax spouts this stuff he isn't
convincing. He's fundamentally an engineer, I think. But one
must labour for whoever holds the whip.

(Memo: check the source of that Hitler quote.)

Since Germania we have been accompanied by fighters,
mostly Messerschmitts, providing top cover and close escort,
and Jack Bovell and I have been happily spotting types and new
variants. And we have seen lighter, faster fighters streaking
across our field of view. They may be the "jet fighters" we've
read about have never seen up close. I know plenty of RAF
brass who regret that the Phoney War ended in May 1940, if
only for the lost opportunity for technical advancement. This
ravaged continent is obviously a crucible for such advancement.
Jack and I craned and muttered, longing to see more of those
exotic birds.

And then the show started. We were somewhere over the
Ukraine.

One fighter came screaming up through our layers of escorts. It arced straight up from the ground like a firecracker, trailing a pillar of smoke. I wondered aloud if it had actually rockets strapped to its tail. Ciliax murmured, as if intrigued by a puzzle.

You have to understand that we were sitting in armchairs in an observation blister. I even had a snifter of brandy in my hand. There was absolutely no sense of danger. But still the unmarked rocket-plane came on. A deep thrumming made the surface of my brandy ripple; the Beast, lumbering, was changing course.

"If that thing gets through," I said, "it's harps and halos and hello St Peter for us."

"You don't say," said Jack Bovell.

Ciliax said nothing.

Then a chance pencil of flak swept across the nose of the rocket-plane, shattering the canopy over its cockpit. It fell away and that was that; I didn't even see the detonation when it fell to earth.

Jack blew out his cheeks. Wolfgang Ciliax snapped his fingers for more brandies all round.

We orbited over the area of the attempted strike for the next eight hours.

Ciliax took me and Jack down to a hold. The bombs were slim, blue and black steel, perfectly streamlined; they looked like "upturned midget submarines", as Jack said. You can drop them from as high as twenty thou. I thought this was another piece of typically beautiful Nazi technology, but Ciliax said the bombs are a British design, made under licence by Vickers Armstrong in Weybridge, whose chief designer is a man called Barnes Neville Wallis. "They are as British as the banks of Rolls Royce Merlin engines that keep the *Goering* aloft," Ciliax told me, his bespectacled eyes intent, making sure I understood my complicity. But I thought he was mostly incensed that anybody had dared raise a hand against his beautiful machine.

That night the *Goering* dropped stick after stick of these "Tallboy" bombs on the site from which the rocket plane seemed to have been launched. I have no idea whether the assault was successful or not. The movie people filmed all this, in colour.

With the bombs dropped, we flee east, towards the dawn. I must try to catch some sleep . . .

*     *     *

*Day 7.* We have already crossed China, which is the subject of a colonization programme by the Japanese, a mirror image to what the Germans are up to in the west. Eurasia is a vast theatre of war and conquest and misery, a theatre that stretches back all the way to the Channel coast. What a world we live in!

Still, now we are past it all, a goodly chunk of the world's circumference already successfully traversed. Our escort has fallen away. Our last supply convoy was Japanese; Jack has threatened to drop their raw fish suppers out of the bomb bays.

And now, alone, we are facing our ultimate target: the Pacific Ocean. We are so high that its silver skin glimmers, softly curving, like the back of some great animal.

Jack is taking his turns in a pilot's seat on the bridge. This afternoon I was given permission from Ciliax to go up there. I longed to play with the controls. "I have a hunch I'm a better stick man than you," I said to Jack.

Jack laughed. Sitting there, his peaked cap on, his flight jacket under a webbing over-jacket, he looked at home for the first time since I'd met him. "I dare say you're right. But Hans is a better man than either of us."

"Hans?"

Hans, it turned out, is the flight deck's computing machine. Hans can fly the Beast on "his" own, and even when a human pilot is at the stick he takes over most functions. "I think the name is a German joke," Jack said. "Some translation of 'hands off'."

I crouched beside his position, looking out over the ocean. "What do you think we're going to find out there, Jack?"

Jack, matter-of-fact, shrugged. "Twelve thousand miles of ocean, and then San Francisco."

"Then how do you explain the fact that nobody has crossed the Pacific before?"

"Ocean currents," he said. "Adverse winds. Hell, I don't know."

But we both knew the story is more complicated than that. This is the Pacific Mystery.

Humanity came out of Africa; Darwin said so. In caveman days we spread north and east, across Asia all the way to Australia. Then the Polynesians went island-hopping. They crossed thousands of miles, reaching as far as Hawaii with their stone axes and dug-out boats.

But beyond that point the Pacific defeated them.

And meanwhile others went west, to the Americas. Nobody quite knows how the first "native" Americans got there from Africa; some say it was just accidental rafting on lumber flushed down the Congo, though I fancy there's a smack of racial prejudice in that theory. So when the Vikings sailed across the north Atlantic they came up against dark-skinned natives, and when the Portuguese and Spanish and British arrived they found a complicated trading economy, half-Norse, half-African, which they proceeded to wipe out. Soon the Europeans reached the west coast of the Americas.

But beyond that point the Pacific defeated them.

"Here's the puzzle," I said to Jack. "The earth is a sphere. You can tell, for instance, by the curving shadow it casts on the moon during a lunar eclipse."

"Sure," said Jack. "So we *know* the Pacific can't be more than twelve thousand miles across."

"Yes, but western explorers, including Magellan and Captain Cook, have pushed a long way out from the American coast. Thousands of miles. We know they should have found Hawaii, for instance. And from the east, the Chinese in the Middle Ages and the modern Japanese have sailed far beyond the Polynesians' range. Few came back. Somebody should have made it by now. Jack, *the Pacific is too wide*. And that is the Mystery."

Jack snorted. "Bull hockey," he said firmly. "You'll be telling me next about sea monsters and cloud demons."

But those ancient Pacific legends had not yet been disproved, and I could see that some of the bridge crew, those who could follow our English, were glancing our way uncertainly.

*Day 8*. We are out of wireless telegraphy contact; the last of the Japanese stations has faded, and our forest of W/T masts stand purposeless. You can't help but feel isolated.

So we three, Ciliax, Jack and I, are drawn to each other, huddling in our metal cave like primitives. This evening we had another stiff dinner, the three of us. Loathing each other, we drink too much, and say too much.

"Of course," Ciliax murmured, "the flight of a rocket-plane would last only minutes, and would be all but uncontrollable once, ah, the fuse is lit. Somebody on the ground must have known precisely when the *Goering* would pass overhead. I wonder who could have let them know?"

If that was a dig at Jack or me, Jack wasn't having any of it. "'Somebody'? Who? In Asia you Nazis are stacking up your enemies, Wolfie. The Bolsheviks, partisans. You and the Japanese will meet and fall on each other some day—"

"Or it may have been Americans," Ciliax said smoothly.

"Why would America attack a Nazi asset?"

"Because of the strategic implications of the *Goering*. Suppose we do succeed in crossing the Pacific? America has long feared the vulnerability of its long western coastline . . ."

Jack's eyes were narrow, but he didn't bother to deny it.

In 1940 America was indeed looking over its shoulder nervously at Japan's aggressive expansion. But the Pacific proved impassible, the Japanese did not come, and during the Phoney War America stood firm with Britain.

In April 1940 Hitler overran Denmark and Norway, and in May outflanked the Maginot line to crush France. The blitzkriegs caused panic in the British Cabinet. Prime Minister Chamberlain was forced out of office for his poor handling of the war.

But Hitler paused. The North Sea was his boundary, he said; he wanted no conflict with his "Anglo-Saxon cousins".

Churchill was all for rejecting Hitler's overtures and fighting on. But Lord Halifax, the foreign secretary, argued that Hitler's terms were acceptable. While Churchill retired fuming to the backbenches, the "scarecrow in a derby hat" was Prime Minister within the week, and had agreed an armistice within the month.

Hitler was able to turn his full energies east, and by Christmas 1941 had taken Moscow.

All this happened, you see, because the Japanese had not been able to pose a threat to the Americans. If not for the impassibility of the Pacific, America's attentions might have been drawn to the west, not the east. And without the powerful support we enjoyed from America, if Hitler hadn't been moved to offer such a generous peace in 1940 – if Hitler had dared attack Britain – the Germans would have found themselves fighting on two fronts, west and east. Could Russia have survived an attenuated Nazi assault? Is it even conceivable that Russia and Britain and America could have worked as allies against the Nazis, even against the Japanese? *Would the war eventually have been won*?

All this speculation is guff, of course, best left to blokes in pubs. But you can see that if the Pacific *had* been navigable the whole outcome of the war with the Germans would have been different, one way or another. And that is why the *Goering*, a plane designed to challenge the ocean's impregnability, is indeed a weapon of strategic significance.

This is what we argue about over lunch and dinner. Lost in the vast inhuman arena of this ocean, we are comforted by the familiarity of our petty human squabbles.

*Day 10*. Perhaps I should record distances travelled, rather than times.

It is three days since we left behind the eastern coast of Asia. Over sea, unimpeded by resupplying or bomb-dropping, we make a steady airspeed of two hundred and twenty knots. In the last forty-eight hours alone we should have covered twelve thousand miles.

We should *already* have crossed the ocean. We should *already* be flying over the Americas. When I take astronomical sightings, it is as if we have simply flown around a perfectly behaved spherical earth from which America has been deleted. The geometry of the sky doesn't fit the geometry of the earth.

Somehow I hadn't expected the mystery to come upon us so quickly. Only ten days into the flight, we are still jostling for position at the dinner table. And yet we have sailed into a mystery so strange that we may as well have been projected to the moon.

I still haven't met the Captain, whose name, I am told, is Fassbender. Even lost as we are in the middle of unfathomable nothingness, the social barriers between us are as rigid as the steel bulkheads of the Beast.

*Day 15*. Today, a jaunt in a chariot. What fun!

We passed over yet another group of islands, this one larger than most, dark basaltic cones blanketed by greenery and lapped by the pale blue of coral reefs. Observers in the blisters, armed with binoculars and telescopes, claimed to see movement at the fringes of these scattered fragments of jungle. So the Captain ordered the chariots to go down and take a shuftie.

There were four of us in our chariot, myself, Jack, Ciliax, and a crewman who piloted us, a squat young chap called "Klaus" whom I rather like. Both the Germans wore sidearms; Jack and I

did not. The chariot is a stubby-winged seaplane, well equipped
to land on the back of the Beast; a tough little bugger.

We skimmed low over clearings where lions ran and immense
bears growled. Things like elephants, covered in brown hair and
with long curling tusks, lifted their trunks as we passed, as if in
protest at our engines' clatter. "Christ," Jack said. "What I
wouldn't give to be down among 'em with a shotgun." Ciliax
and I took photographs and cine-films and made notes and spoke
commentaries into tape-recorders.

And we thought we saw signs of people: threads of smoke rose
from the beaches.

"Extraordinary," Ciliax said. "Cave bears. What looked like
sabre-tooth cats. *Mammoths*. This is a fauna that has not been
seen in Europe or America since the ice retreated."

Jack asked, "What happened to 'em?"

"We hunted them to death," I said. "Probably."

"What with, machine guns?"

I shrugged. "Stone axes and flint arrowheads are enough,
given time."

"So," Jack asked practically, "how did they get *here*?"

"Sea levels fall and rise," Ciliax said. "When the ice comes,
it locks up the world's water. Perhaps that is true even of this
monstrous world ocean. Perhaps the lower waters expose dry
land now submerged, or archipelagos along which one can
raft."

"So in the Ice Age," I said," we hunted the mammoths and the
giant sloths until we drove them off the continents. But they kept
running, and a few of them made it to one island or another, and
now they just continue fleeing, heading ever east." And in this
immense ocean, I thought, there was room to keep running and
running and running. Nothing need ever go extinct.

"But there are people here," Jack pointed out. "We saw fires."

We buzzed along the beach. We dipped low over a kind of
camp-site, a mean sort of affair centred on a scrappy hearth. The
people, naked, came running out of the forest at our noise – and
when they saw us, most of them went running back again. But we
got a good look at them, and fired off photographs.

They were people, sort of. They had fat squat bodies, and big
chests, and brows like bags of walnuts. I think it was obvious to us
all what they were, even to Jack.

"Neanderthals." Ciliax said it first; it is a German name.

"Another species of – well, animal – which we humans chased out of Africa and Europe and Asia."

Jack said, "They don't seem to be smart enough to wipe out the mammoths as we did."

"Or maybe they're *too* smart," I murmured.

Ciliax said, "What a remarkable discovery: relics of the evolutionary past, even while the evolutionary destiny of mankind is being decided in the heart of Asia!"

Standing orders forbid landings. The chariot lifted us back to the steel safety of the Beast, and that was that.

It is now eight days since we crossed the coast of China. We have come *thirty-five thousand miles* since. Perhaps it shouldn't be surprising to find such strange beasts below, mammoths and cave bears and low-browed savages.

And still we go on. What next? How thrilling it all is!

*Day 23.* Today, a monstrous electrical storm.

We flew under the worst of it, our banks of engines thrumming, as lightning crackled around the W/T masts. Perhaps in this unending ocean there are unending storms – nobody knows, our meteorologists cannot calculate it.

But we came out of it. Bold technicians crawled out to the wing roots to check over the Beast, to replace a mast or two, and to tend to the chariots. I wanted to check my Spitfire, but predictably was not allowed by Ciliax. Still, Klaus kindly looked over the old bird for me and assures me she is A-OK.

Last night *both* Ciliax and Jack Bovell made passes at me, the one with a steely resolve, the other rather desperately.

*Day 25.* A rather momentous day.

Our nominal food and water store is intended to last fifty days. Today, therefore, Day 25, is the turn-back point. And yet we are no nearer finding land, no nearer penetrating the great mysteries of the Pacific.

The Captain had us gather in the larger of the restaurants – *we* being the passengers and senior officers; the scullery maids were not represented, and nor were the helots, the lost souls of the atom-engine compartment. The Captain himself, on his flight deck, spoke to us by speaker tube; I have yet to see his face.

We discussed whether to continue the mission. We had a briefing by the quartermaster on the state of our supplies, then a debate, followed by a vote. A vote, held on a flying Nazi *schlachtschiff*! I have no doubt that Captain Fassbender had already made his own decision before we were gathered in the polished oak of the dining room. But he was trying to boost morale – even striving to stave off mutinies in the future. Christopher Columbus used the same tactics, Jack told me, when his crew too felt lost in the midst of another endless ocean.

And, like Columbus, Captain Fassbender won the day. For now we carry on, on half-rations. The movie-makers filmed it all, even though every last man of *them*, too fond of their grub, voted to turn back.

*Day 28*. Today we passed over yet another group of islands, quite a major cluster. Captain Fassbender ordered a few hours' orbit while the chariots went down to explore. Of my little group only I was bothered to ride down, with my friend Klaus. Jack Bovell did not answer my knock on his cabin door; I have not seen him all day. I suspect he has been drinking heavily.

So Klaus and I flew low over forests and patches of grassland. We spooked exotic-looking animals: they were *like* elephants and buffalo and rhinoceroses. Perhaps they are archaic forms from an age even deeper than the era of ice. Living fossils! I snapped pictures merrily and took notes, and fantasised of presenting my observations to the Royal Geographical Society, as Darwin did on returning from his voyage on the *Beagle*.

Then I saw people. They were naked, tall, slim, upright. They looked more "modern", if that is the right word, than the lumpy-browed Neanderthals we saw on the islands of mastodons, many days ago. Yet their heads receded from their foreheads; their shapely skulls can contain little in the way of grey matter, and their pretty brown eyes held only bewilderment. They fled from our approach like the other animals of the savannah.

Primitive they might be, but it appears they lead the march of the hominids, off to the east. I took more photos.

I have begun to develop a theory about the nature of the world, and the surface of the ocean over which we travel – or rather the geometric continuum in which it seems to be embedded. I think the Pacific is a challenge not merely to the cartographic mind but to the mathematical. (I just read those sentences over – how pompous – once a Girton girl, always a Girton girl!) I've yet to talk it over with anybody. Only Wolfgang Ciliax has a hope of understanding me, I think. I prefer to be sure of my ground before I approach him.

Certainly a radical new theory of this ocean of ours is needed. Think of it! Since the coast of Asia we have already travelled far enough to circle the earth *nearly five times,* if it were not for this oddity, this Fold in the World.

The Pacific is defeating us, I think, crushing our minds with its sheer scale. After only three days on half tuck everybody is grumbling as loudly as their bellies. Yet we go on . . .

*Day 33.* It has taken me twenty-four hours to get around to this entry. After the events of yesterday the writing of it seemed futile. Courage, Bliss! However bad things are, one must behave as if they are not so, as my mother, a stoical woman, has always said.

It began when Jack Bovell, for the third day in a row, did not emerge from his cabin. One cannot have uncontrollable drunks at large on an aircraft, not even one as large as this. And no part of the *Goering,* not even passengers' cabins, can be off-limits to the god-like surveillance of the Captain. So Wolfgang Ciliax led a party of hefty aircrew to Jack's cabin. I went along at Ciliax's request, as the nearest thing to a friend Jack has on this crate.

I watched as the Germans broke down Jack's door. Jack was drunk, but coherent, and belligerent. He took on the Luftwaffe toughs, and as he was held back Ciliax ordered a thorough search of his cabin – "thorough" meaning the furniture was dismantled and the false ceiling broken into.

The flap that followed moved fast. I have since pieced it together.

The airmen found a small radio transceiver, a compact leather case full of valves and wiring. This, it turned out, had been used by Jack to attract the attention of that rocket-plane as we flew over the Ukraine. So Ciliax's suspicions were proven correct. I am subtly disappointed in Jack; it seems such an *obvious* thing to have done. Anyhow this discovery led to a lot of shouting, and the thugs moved in on Jack. But as they did so he raised his right hand, which held what I thought at first was a grenade, and the thugs backed off.

Ciliax turned to me, his face like a thunderous sky. "Talk to this fool or he'll kill us all."

Jack huddled in the corner of his smashed-up room, his face bleeding, his gadget in his upraised right hand. "Bliss," he panted. "I'm sorry you got dragged into this."

"I was in it from the moment I stepped aboard. If you sober up – Wolfgang could fetch you some coffee—"

"Adrenaline and a beating-up are great hangover cures."

"Then think about what you're doing. If you set that thing off, whatever it is, do you expect to survive?"

"I didn't expect to survive when I called up that Russkie rocket-plane. But it isn't about me, Bliss. It's about duty."

Ciliax sneered. "Your President must be desperate if his only way of striking at the Reich is through suicide attacks."

"This has nothing to do with Truman or his administration," Jack said. "If he's ever challenged about it he'll deny any knowledge of this, and he'll be telling the truth."

Ciliax wasn't impressed. "Plausible deniability. I thought that was an SS invention."

"Tell me why, Jack," I pressed him.

He eyed me. "Can't you see it? Ciliax said it himself. It's all about global strategies, Bliss. If the Pacific crossing is completed the Germans will be able to strike at us. And that's what I've got to put a stop to."

"But there will be other *Goerings*," Ciliax said.

"Yeah, but at least I'll buy some time, if it ends here – if nobody knows – if the Mystery remains, a little longer. Somebody has to take down this damn Beast. A rocket-plane didn't do it. But I'm Jonah, swallowed by the whale." He laughed, and I saw he was still drunk after all.

I yelled, "Jack, no!" In the same instant half the German toughs fell on him, and the other half, including Ciliax, crowded out of the room.

I had been expecting an explosion in the cabin. I cowered. But there was only a distant *crump*, like far-off thunder. The deck, subtly, began to pitch . . .

*Day 34.* We aren't dead yet.

The picture has become clearer. Jack sabotaged the *Goering*'s main control links; the switch he held was a radio trigger. But it didn't quite work; we didn't pitch into the sea. The technicians botched a fix to stabilize our attitude, and even keep us on our course, heading ever east. This whale of the sky still swims through her element. But the crew can't tell yet if she remains dirigible – if we will ever be able to fly her home again.

Six people died, some crewmen on the flight deck, a couple of technicians wrestling with repairs outside. And Jack, of course. Already beaten half to death, he was presented to a summary court presided over by the Captain. Then Fassbender gave him to the crew. They hung him up in the hold, then while he still lived cut him down, and pitched him into the sea.

I don't know what Ciliax made of all this. He said these common airmen lacked the inventiveness of the SS, to whom he was under pressure to hand over Jack. Ciliax has a core of human decency, I think.

So we fly on. The engineers toil in shifts on the *Goering*'s shattered innards. I have more faith in engineers than in gods or gargoyles, priests or politicians. But I no longer believe I will ever see England again. There. I've written it down, so it must be true. I wonder what strange creatures of the sea will feast on Jack's flesh . . .

*Day 50.* Another round number, another pointless milestone.

I estimate we have travelled a distance that would span from the earth to the moon. Think of that! Perhaps in another universe the German genius for technology would have taken humans on just such an epic voyage, rather than this pointless slog.

We continue to pass over island groups and chains. On one island yesterday, covered by a crude-looking jungle of immense feathery ferns, I saw very exotic animals running in herds, or peering with suspicion at our passage. Think of flightless birds, muscular and upright and with an avian nerviness; and think of a crocodile's massive reptilian patience; combine the two, and you have what I saw.

How did the dinosaurs die? Was it an immense volcanic episode, a comet or other fire from the sky, a deadly plague, some inherent weakness of the reptilian race? Whatever it was, it seems that no matter how dramatic the disaster that seeks to wipe you out, there is always room to run. Perhaps on this peculiar folded-up earth of ours there is *no species* that has ever gone extinct. What a marvellous thought!

But if they *were* dinosaurs, down on that island, we will never know. The plane no longer stops to orbit, for it cannot; the chariots no longer fly down to investigate thunder lizards. And we plough on ever east, ever further over the ocean, ever deeper into a past even beyond the dinosaurs.

My social life is a bit of a challenge these days.

As our food and water run out, our little aerial community is disintegrating into fiefdoms. The Water Barons trade with the Emperors of the Larder, or they will go to war over a tapped pipeline. Occasionally I hear pronouncements from the invisible Captain Fassbender, but I am not certain how far his word holds sway any longer. There have been rumours of a coup by the SS officers. The movie-makers are filming none of this. Their morale was the first to crumble, poor lambs.

I last saw Wolfgang Ciliax ten days ago. He was subtle and insidious; I had the distinct impression that he wanted me to join a sort of harem. Women are the scarcest commodity of all on this boat. Women, and cigarettes. You can imagine the shrift he got from me.

I sleep in barricaded rooms. In the guts of the Beast I have stashes of food and water, and cigarettes and booze to use as currency in an emergency. I keep out of the way of the petty wars, which will sort themselves out one way or another.

Once I had to bale out over Malaya, and I survived in the jungle for a week before reaching an army post. This is similar. It's also rather like college life. What larks!

*[Editor's note: Many fragmentary entries follow. Some are undated, others contain only mathematical jottings or geometric sketches. The reader is referred to a more complete publication forthcoming in* Annals of Psychiatry.*]*

*Day 365.* A year, by God! A full year, if I have counted correctly, though the calendar is meaningless given how many times we have spun around this watery earth – or appear to have. And if the poor gutted Beast is still keeping to her nominal speed, then I may have travelled two million miles. *Two million.* And still no America!

I believe I am alone now. Alone, save for the valve mind of Hans, and perhaps the odd rat.

The food ran out long ago, save for my stashes. The warfare between the Fuhrers of Spam and the Tsars of Dried Eggs became increasingly fragmented, until one man fell on the next for the sake of a cigarette stub. Others escaped, however, in chariots that went spinning down to one lost island or another. Klaus was one of them. I hope they survive; why not? Perhaps some future expedition, better equipped than ours, may retrieve their descendants.

And the Beast is hollowed out, much of her burned, depopulated save for me. I have explored her from one end to the other, seeking scraps of food and water, pitching the odd corpse into the drink. The only place I have not investigated is the sealed hold of the atom engine. Whatever survives in there has failed to break out.

However the engine continues to run. The blades of the Merlins turn still. Even the heating works. I should put on record that no matter how badly we frail humans have behaved, the *Reichsmarschall des Grossdeutschen Reiches Hermann Goering* has fulfilled her mission flawlessly.

This can't go on forever, though. Therefore I have decided to set my affairs in order: to begin with, my geometrical maunderings. I have left a fuller account – that is, complete with equations – in a separate locker. These journal notes are intended for the less mathematical reader; such as my mother (they're for you, mummy! – I know you'll want to know what became of me).

I have had to make a leap of faith, if you will. As we drive on and on, with no sight of an end to our journey, I have been forced to consider the possibility that there will *be* no end – that, just as it appears, the Pacific is not merely anomalously large, but, somehow, *infinite*. How can this be?

Our greatest geometer was Euclid. You've heard of him, haven't you? He reduced all of the geometry you can do on a plane to just five axioms, from which can be derived that menagerie of theorems and corollaries which have been used to bother schoolchildren ever since.

And even Euclid wasn't happy with the fifth axiom, which can be expressed like this: *parallel lines never meet.* That seems so obvious it doesn't need stating, that if you send off two lines at right angles to a third, like rail tracks, they will never meet. On a perfect, infinite plane they wouldn't. But on the curved surface of the earth, they would: think of lines of longitude converging on a pole. And *if space itself is curved*, again, "parallel" lines may meet – or they may diverge, which is just as startling. Allowing Euclid's axiom to be weakened in this way opens the door to a whole set of what are rather unimaginatively called "non-Eu-

clidian geometries". I will give you one name: Bernhard Rie-
mann. Einstein plundered his work in developing relativity.

And in a non-Euclidean geometry, you can have all sorts of odd
effects. A circle's circumference may be more or less than "pi"
times its diameter. You can even fit an infinite area into a finite
circumference: for, you see, your measuring rods shrink as those
parallel lines converge. Again I refer you to one name: Henri
Poincare.

You can see where I am going with this, I think. It seems that
our little globe is a non-Euclidean object. Its geometry is *hyper-
bolic*. It has a finite radius – as you can see if you look at its shadow
on the moon – but an infinite surface area, as we of the *Goering*
have discovered. The world has a Fold in it, in effect. As I drive
into the Fold I grow smaller and ever more diminished, as seen
from the outside – but I *feel* just as Bliss-sized as I always did, and
there is plenty of room for me.

This seems strange – to put it mildly! But why should we
imagine that the simple geometry of something like an orange
should scale up to something as mighty as a planet?

Of course this is just one mathematical model which fits the
observations; it may or may not be definitive. And many questions remain open, such as astronomical effects, and the nature of
gravity on an infinite world. I leave these issues as an exercise for
the reader.

One might question what difference this makes to us mere
mortals. But surely geography determines our destiny. If the
Pacific could have been spanned in the Stone Age, perhaps by a
land bridge, the Americas' first inhabitants might have been
Asian, not Africans who crossed the Atlantic. And certainly in
our own century if the Pacific were small enough for America and
Japan to have rubbed against each other, the convulsion of war we
have endured for the last decade would not have turned out the
way it did.

Besides all that – what fun to find yourself living on such a
peculiar little planet, a World with a Fold! Don't you think? . . .

*Date unknown.* Sorry, I've given up counting. Not long after the
last entry, however.

With my affairs in order I'm jumping ship. Why?

Point one: I've eaten all the food. Not the Spam, obviously.

Point two: I think I'm running out of world, or at least the sort of world I can live on. It's a long time since I saw a mastodon, or a dinosaur. I still cross over island groups, but now they are inhabited, if at all, by nothing but purplish slime and what look like mats of algae. Very ancient indeed, no doubt.

And ahead things change again. The sky looks greenish, and I wonder if I am approaching a place, or a time, where the oxygen runs out. I wake up in the night panting for breath, but of course that could just be bad dreams.

Anyhow, time to ditch. It's the end of the line for me, but not necessarily for the *Goering*. I think I've found a way to botch the flight deck equipment: not enough to make her fully manoeuvrable again, but at least enough to turn her around and send her back the way she came, under the command of Hans. I don't know how long she can keep flying. The Merlins have been souped up with fancy lubricants and bearings for longevity, but of course there are no engineers left to service them. If the Merlins do hold out the *Goering* might one day come looming over Piccadilly Circus again, I suppose, and what a sight she will be. Of course there will be no way of stopping her I can think of, but I leave that as another exercise for you, dear reader.

As for me, I intend to take the Spit. She hasn't been flown since Day 1, and is as good as new as far as I can tell. I might try for one of those slime-covered rocks in the sea.

Or I might try for something I've glimpsed on the horizon, under the greenish sky. *Lights*. A city? Not human, surely, but who knows what lies waiting for us on the other side of the Fold in the World?

What else must I say before I go?

I hope we won't be the last to come this way. I hope that the next to do so come, unlike us, in peace.

Mummy, keep feeding my cats for me, and I'm sorry about the lack of grandchildren. Bea will have to make up the numbers (sorry, sis!).

Enough, before I start splashing these pages with salt water. This is Bliss Stirling, girl reporter for the BBC, over and out!


[Editor's note: There the transcript ends. Found lodged in a space between bulkheads, it remains the only written record of the *Goering*'s journey to have survived on board the hulk. No filmed or tape-recorded material has been salvaged. The journal is published with respect to the memory of Miss Stirling. However as Miss Stirling was contracted by the BBC and the Royal Geographic Society specifically to cover the *Gooring's* Pacific expedition, all these materials must be regarded as COPYRIGHT the British Broadcasting Conglomerate MCMLII. Signed PETER CARINHALL, Board of Governors, BBC.]

# FLOWERS FROM ALICE

## Cory Doctorow and Charles Stross

*Both Cory Doctorow (b. 1971) and Charles Stross (b. 1964)
seemed to burst out of nowhere in the last few years to general
universal acclaim. Yet Stross has been writing science fiction
since 1987 and Doctorow since 1990. Born in Toronto, Doctorow sold his first story to the Canadian science-fiction
magazine* On Spec, *where it appeared in the Winter 1990
"Special Youth" issue. He continued to sell the odd story here
and there but the world suddenly sat up and noticed when
"Craphound" appeared in* Science Fiction Age *in 1998. It
was short-listed for both the Aurora and Theodore Sturgeon
awards for that year's best short fiction. He then went from
strength-to-strength receiving the John W. Campbell Award
in 2000 as the Best New Writer. On the strength of that
perhaps he can be excused for the audacity of his first book,*
The Complete Idiot's Guide to Publishing Science Fiction
*(2000), which gave the impression he had been around for
years. You'll find some of his short fiction in* A Place So
Foreign and Eight More *(2003), which won the Canadian
Sunburst Award. His novels include* Down and Out in the
Magic Kingdom *(2003),* Eastern Standard Tribe *(2004)
and* Someone Comes to Town, Someone Leaves Town
*(2005).*

*At the same time Charles Stross was similarly experiment-
ing and dabbling when suddenly it all came together with his*

*wonderfully anarchic books* Singularity Sky *(2003)*, Iron
Sunrise *(2004)*, The Atrocity Archives *(2004) and* Accel-
erando *(2005), amongst others.*
    *Both authors have a common strength in their appreciation
of the potential of the computer age and nanotechnology and
use it to ingenious effect in the following story.*

I don't know why I invited Al to my wedding. Nostalgia,
maybe. Residual lust. She was the first girl I ever kissed,
after all. You never forget your first. I couldn't help but turn my
head when round-hipped, tall girls with pageboy hair walked by,
hunched over their own breasts in terminal pubescent embarrassment, awkward and athletic at the same time. You don't get
much of that these days outside of Amish country, no parent
would choose to have a kid who was quite so visibly strange as Al
had been as a teenager, but there were still examples of the genre
to be had, if you looked hard enough, and they stirred something
within me.
    I couldn't forget Al, though it had been twenty years since
that sweet and sloppy kiss on the beach, ten years since I'd run
into her last, so severely post- that I hardly recognized her.
Wasn't a week went by that she didn't wander through my
imagination, evoking a lip-quirk that wasn't a smile by about
three notches. My to-be recognized it; it drove her up the wall,
and she let me know about it during post-coital self-criticism
sessions.
    It was a very wrong idea to invite Al to the wedding, but the
wedding itself was a bad idea, to be perfectly frank. And I won't
take all the blame for it, since Al decided to show up, after all, if
"decided" can be applied to someone as post- as she (s/he?)
(they?) [(s|t)/he(y)?] was by then. But one morning, as we sat at
our pre-nuptual breakfast table, my to-be and me, and spooned
marmalade on our muffins and watched the hummingbirds visit
the feeder outside our nook's window; one morning, as we sat
naked and sated and sticky with marmalade and other fluids; one
morning, I looked into my fiancée's eyes and I prodded at the
phone tattooed on my wrist and dialed a directory server and
began to recite the facts of Al's life into my hollow tooth in full
earshot of my lovely intended until the directory had enough
information to identify Al from among all the billions of humans

and trillions of multiplicitous post-humans that it knew about and the phone rang in my hollow tooth and I was talking to Al.

"Al," I said, "Alice? Is that you? It's Cyd!"

There was no sound on the end of the line because when you're as self-consciously post- as Al, you don't make unintentional sound, so there was no sharp intake of breath or other cue to her reaction to this voice from her past, but she answered finally and said, "Cyd, wonderful, it's been too long," and the voice was warm and nuanced and rich as any human voice but more so, tailored for the strengths and acoustics of my skull and mouth which she had no doubt induced from the characteristics of the other end of the conversation. "You're getting married, huh? She sounds wonderful. And you, you're doing well too. Well! I should say so. Cyd, it's good to hear from you. Of course one of me will come to your wedding. Can we help? Say we can! I, oh, the caterer, no, you don't want to use that caterer, she's booked for another wedding the day before and a wedding *and* a Bar Mitzvah the day after, you know, so please, let me help! I'm sending over a logistics plan now, I just evolved it for you, it's very optimal."

And my to-be shook her head and answered *her* phone and said, "Why hello, Alice! No, Cyd sprang this on me without warning – one of his little surprises. Yes, I can see you're talking to him, too. Of course, I'd love to see the plans, it was so good of you to come up with them. Yes, yes, of course. And you'll bring a date, won't you?"

Meanwhile, in my tooth, Al's still nattering on, "You don't mind, do you? I respawned and put in a call to your beautiful lady. I'm resynching with the copy every couple instants, so I can tell you we're getting along famously, Cyd, you always did have such great taste but you're *hopeless* with logistics. I see the job is going well, I knew you'd be an excellent polemicist, and it's such a vital function in your social mileu!"

I didn't get more than ten more words in, but the society of Al kept the conversation up for me. I never got bored, of course, because she had a trillion instances of me simulated somewhere in her being, and she tried a trillion different conversational gambits on all of them and chose the ones that evoked the optimal response, fine tuning as she monitored my breathing and vitals over the phone. She had access to every nuance of my life, of course, there's no privacy with the post-humans, so there was hardly any catching up to do.

I didn't expect her to show up on my door that afternoon.

My betrothed took it very well. She was working in her study on her latest morph porn, down on the ground floor, and I was upstairs with my neurofeedback machine, working up a suitable head of bile before writing my column. She beat me to the door. "Who is it?" I called irritably, responding more to the draft around my ankles than to any conscious stimulus. No reply. I unplugged myself, swore quietly, then closed my eyes and began to ramp down the anger. I found people responded all wrong to me when I was mad. "Who?" I called again.

"Cyd! How cozy, what a great office!" A flock of silver lighter-than-air golf-balls caromed off the doorframe and ricocheted around me – one softly pinged me on the end of the nose with a warm, tingling shock. It smelled utterly unlike a machine: human and slightly flowery –

"Al?" I asked.

The ball inflated, stretching its endoskeleton into a transducer surface. The others homed in on it, merging almost instantly into an inflatabubble that suddenly flashed into a hologram of Al as I'd last seen her in the flesh – only slightly tuned, her back straight and proud, her breasts fetchingly exposed by a Cretan-style dress that had been in fashion around the time we split up. "Hiya, Cydonia!" That grin, those sturdy, well-engineered teeth, and a sudden flashback to a meeting in a mall all those years ago. "Don't worry I'm downstairs talking to your love wearing the real primary-me body, this is just a remote, *hey* I *love* the antique render farm but isn't it a bit out of tune? Please, let me to fix it!"

"Ung," I said, shivering with fright, guts turning to jelly, and hackles rising – exactly the wrong reaction and deeply embarrassing, but there's a *reason* I work behind a locked door most of the time. "Gimme five."

"How kawaii!" Al burst apart into half a dozen beachball-sized balloons and bounced out onto the landing. "See you down-stairs!"

I just stood there, muscles twitching in an adrenalin-induced haze as I wrestled to get my artificially induced anger under control. It took almost a minute, during which time I forced myself to listen as a series of loud thumping noises came from the hall downstairs and I heard the sound of voices, indistinct, through the open doors: my fiancée's low and calm, and Al as enthusiastic and full of laughter as a puppy in a mid-belly-rub. Al had left an after-scent behind, one that gave me dizzying flash-backs to teenage sexual experimentation – my first sex change, Al's first tongue job – and left me weak at the knees in an aftershock of memories. It's funny how after the fire's burned down all you can remember are the ashes of conflict, the argu-ments that drove you apart: until your ex shows up and reminds you what you've lost. Although knowing Al it might just as well be a joke as deliberate.

Presently I went downstairs, to find the door open and a couple of huge crates sitting in the front yard – too big to come through the door without telling the house to grow a service entrance. I followed the voices to the living room, where my fiancée was curled up in our kidney-shaped sofa, opposite Al, who had somehow draped herself across the valuable antique tube TV, and was reminiscing about nothing in particular at length. Her main incarnation looked alarmingly substantial, nothing like the soap-bubbles except for a slightly pearlescent lustre to her skin. "You're so lucky with Cyd! So to speak. He's such a stable, consistent, unassuming primal male pre-post-! I won't say I envy you but you really need to make more of your big day together, I promise you, you won't regret it. Remember when we spoofed out from under our teachers one day and we blew a month's allowance at the distraction center and he said, Al, if I ever get—"

"Hello there," I said, nodding to Al, civil enough now my autonomic nervous system wasn't convinced I was under attack. "Do you metabolize? If so, can I offer you anything? Coffee, perhaps? What have you been up to all this time?" I barely registered my fiancée's fixed, glassy-eyed stare, which was glued to Al's left nipple ring like a target designator, or the way she was twitching her left index finger as if it was balanced on the hi-hat of a sidearm controller. These were normally bad signs, but right then I was still reeling from the shocking smell of Al's skin. I know it was all part of her self-rep, but how could I possibly have forgotten it?

"Cyd!" She was off the television and across the room like the spirit of electricity, and grabbed me in a very physical bear-hug. The nipple ring was hard, and even though her body wasn't made of CHON any more she felt startlingly real. She grinned at me with insane joy. "Whee! Three hundred and twenty seven million eight hundred and ninety six thousand one hundred and four, five, six, seconds, and you *still* feel good to grab!" Over her shoulder, "You're a *very lucky person* to be marrying him, you know. Have you made up your mind what to do about are you doing about the catering? Did you like my suggestion for the after-banquet orgy? What about the switch fetish session? You are going to be so *good* together!"

My affianced had a strained smile that I recognized as the mirror image of my own bared-teeth snarl when someone interrupted my work. As usual, her face was reflecting my own mood, and I stared at her tits until I had the rhythm of her breath down, then matched it with my own, slowing down, bringing her down to the calm that I was forcing on myself. "Hey, Al," I said, patting her shoulder awkwardly.

"Oh, I'm doing it again, aren't I? Hang on, let me underclock a little." She closed her eyes and slowly touched her index finger to her nose. "Muuuuuch better," she said. "Sorry, I'm not really fit for human company these days. I've been running at very high-clockspeed lately. Order makes order, you know – I'm going to wind up faster than entropy winds down and overtake thermodynamics.2 if I can. I'm about a week away from entangling enough particles in Alpha Centauri to instantiate there, then I'm going to eat the star and, whee, look out chaos!"

"Ambitious," my betrothed said. I liked her absence of ambition, usually – so refreshing amid the grandiose schemes of the fucking post-s. "You're *certainly very* kind to have done so much thinking about our little wedding, but we were planning to keep it all simple, you know. Just friends and family, a little dancing. Rather retro, but . . ." She trailed off, with a meaningful glance at me.

"But that's how we want it," I finished, taking my cue. I moved over the sofa and sat by my promised and rubbed her tiny little feet, the way she liked. Human-human contact. Who needs any more than this?

She jerked her feet away and sat up. "You two haven't seen each other in so long, why don't I leave you to catch up?" she said, in a tone that let me know that I had better object.

"No no no," I said. "No. Work to do, too much work to do. Deadlines, deadlines, deadlines." I was uncomfortably aware of the heat radiating off Al's avatar, a quintillion smart motes clustered together, pliable, fuckable computation, the grinding microfriction of which was keeping her at about three degrees over blood-temp. "So good to see you, Al. What we'll do, we'll look over these plans and suggestions and whatnot, such very good stuff I'm so sure, and we'll get in touch with you about helping out, right?"

She beamed and wedged herself onto the sofa between us, arms draped over our shoulders. "Of course, of course. You two, oh, I'm so happy for you. Perfect for each other!" She gave my intended a kiss on the cheek, then gave me one that landed close enough to my earlobe to tickle the little hairs there. The kiss was fragrant and wet as the first one, and I heard faint, crashing surf. It was only after she'd moved back (having darted her tongue out and squirmed it to the skin under my beard) that I realized she'd been generating it. I crossed my legs and tried furiously to think my erection away.

She bounded out the door and then stood on our lawn, amidst the crates. She gestured at them, "They're a wedding present!" she called, loud enough to rattle the picture-window. Our neighbor across the street scowled at her from his attic, where he painted still-lives of decaying fruit ten hours a day. "Enjoy!"

"Well, she hasn't changed," my love said, scowling. "You seemed very happy to see her again."

"Yes," I said, awkwardly, jiggling my crossed foot. "Well. I guess I'll try to get her gifts inside before it rains or something, right? Why don't you go back to work?"

"Yes," she said. "I'll go back to work. I'm sure the gifts are lovely. Call me once they're unpacked, all right?"

"Sure," I said, and jiggled my foot.

I considered ordering the house to carve a service door, but decided at length that peristalsis was the optimal solution – otherwise, I'd still have to find a way to drag the goddamned crates into the house. I shoved all our living-room furniture into a corner and went down to the cellar to scoop up the endless meters of the house trunk that we'd fabbed to help us move in, but hadn't had a use for since. I spread it out along the lawn, stretching its mouth-membrane overtop of the largest of the three crates, then pulled the other end through the picture window. I retreated to the living-room and used a broom-handle to tickle the gag-reflex at the near-end of the tube and then leapt clear as the tube shudderingly vomited a gush of dust over the floor. I hit the scrubber-plate with my fist and escaped out the front door before I'd gotten more than a lungful of crud, chased by convection currents that cycled all the room's air towards the filters in the baseboards.

Out on the lawn, the house trunk was slowly digesting the crate, gorging it upwards to the picture-window. Once there was enough slack on the lawn-end, I stretched the twitching membrane overtop of the second crate, and then the third. The house trunk's muscular digestion slowed, but continued, inexorably, moving the trunks living-room-wards.

I met the first trunk with a crowbar and set to work on it, surprised as ever at the fabulous working order of my biceps and back muscles. Sedentary life will never get the best of me, not so long as I am master of my own flesh, ordering it to stay limber and strong.

The crate was ready to fall to pieces just as the second box was eructing onto the living-room floor. I guided number two to a clear spot, then knocked out the last fasteners on number one and slid the panels aside.

It was a dining-room table, handsome and spare, made from black oak, with a fine grain that was brought out by a clear varnish. It had an air of antiquity, but it was light enough to move with one hand. Subsequent boxes disgorged four matching chairs and a sideboard.

I reversed the house trunk and evacuated the crate remnants back onto the lawn, where I decided I'd deal with them later.

I dialed my fiancée's number and waited for her to answer. "I've unpacked," I said. "Come up and see."

A couple of minutes later she poked her head round the door and sniffed. "Smells like trouble," she remarked. "That's a lot of furniture. What does she do, breed the stuff?"

"I don't know." I rubbed the sideboard. "Hey, you. Wake up. Tell me about yourself."

"Cyd?" said the table, hesitantly. "Is it lunch time already?" It spoke with Al's voice.

The chairs began to climb out of their crates and shake off the packing fuzz; one by one they gathered around the table and hunkered down. "What do you feel like today?" asked Al-the-table. "How about a light Mediterranean salad, rocket and tomatoes and mozzarella with a drizzle of balsamic vinegar and extra-virgin olive oil? Or maybe my special wasabi and eggplant nori?"

Herself yanked one of the chairs out from the table and sat on it, hard. "I'll have a plate of tacos and salsa," she said, glaring at the sideboard. "And make it snappish."

The table extruded cutlery – dumb, old-fashioned silver, no less – and the sideboard sidled up to her and offered a plate. She took it with poor grace and began to pick at her food. "I don't like the style," she declared. "This old antique shit went out with the history of the month club. Gimme some Nazi kitsch any day of the week."

"Sure!" Trilled Al's instantiation, and the table sprouted swastikas.

"I can do without lunch," I said. "I'm not really feeling hungry."

"Oh, for fuck's sake." My fiancée looked disgusted and shoved the plate away. "You like this furniture so much, *you* do the washing up." She took a deep breath. "Been meaning to talk to you, anyway."

"Anything in particular, love?" I asked.

"Yeah." She stood up abruptly. "It can wait. I was just thinking about a little recreational surgery, is all."

*Recreational surgery?*

"Uh, what kind?" I asked. "We're getting married in just six days, now. Will it take long? You can't do anything substantial like a set of extra arms – you'd need to alter your dress, wouldn't you?"

"Oh, nothing much." She mimed an elaborate yawn. "I'm just thinking it's been too long since I wore the balls in this household."

"Hey, I'm keeping mine!" I said. "Anyway, isn't it traditional for a bride to be female at the altar?"

"Oh yes," she agreed, nodding brightly. "The bride's supposed to be a young female virgin if she's going to wear white! That's me all over." She giggled alarmingly, jumped up onto the table top, and spread her legs wide. "Fuck it, come here, Cyd. Right now, on the table. See this? Young? Virgin? You be the judge!"

Afterwards, as we lay in the accommodating depressions Al-table had generated for us, my fiancée trailed a lazy tongue along my throat. "All right, then," she said. "If you want a girl-bride, I'll stay female. It's only a week, after all."

I propped myself up on one elbow. "Thanks, honey," I said, gently cupping one of her breasts. "It's just, you know. This wedding's going to be complicated enough as it is. We don't need more changes at the last minute."

"I know," she said. "Well, back to work."

The writing went well that afternoon. I worked up a really good head of rage and ranted into my phone for three hours, watching the words scroll along the ticker at the bottom of my field of vision. When I was done, I did an hour of yoga, feeling the anger ease out of my muscles as I moved slowly from posture to posture.

I did a fullscreen display of the text, read it back, tweaked a few phrases and fired it off to my blog. Another week's work finished.

I headed down to the living room. The Al-dinette had neatly arranged itself. "Good column," it said to me. "You've really found a niche."

"How are you powering yourself?" I said.

"You'd be surprised at how little draw an instantiation pulls. Your romp with your girl generated enough kinetic to power me for a month. If I need more, there's always photovoltaic and a little fusion – I don't like to use nuclear, though. Splitting my atoms reducing my computational capacity; enough of that and I'd be too stupid to talk in a couple centuries."

"Jesus," I said. "Well, it was a very . . . thoughtful . . . gift, Al, thank you."

"Oh, don't thank me! Just keep recharging me the way you just did and we'll call it even."

"Well then," I said. "Well."

"I've made you uncomfortable. I'm sorry, Cyd. Seems like I'm always weirding you out, huh?"

My chuckle was more bitter than I'd intended. "Goes with the territory, I suppose."

"Don't be coy," the table said with mock-sternness, and the chair under my bum wiggled flirtatiously. "You know that you were attracted to the weirdness."

And I had been. On the beach, as she leaned in and sank her teeth gently into the skin below the corner of my jaw, worrying at it with her tongue before grabbing me by the back of my head and kissing me with a ferocity that made my pulse roar in my ears. I'd only been, what, twelve, and she thirteen, but I was smitten then and there and, I feared, always and forever.

The chair contrived to give my ass a friendly squeeze. "There, you see – you're just one of those fellas who can't help but be infatuated with the post-human condition."

My betrothed didn't show up for dinner that night. I ate alone at the AI-table, eschewing our kitchenette for the light conversation and companionship of the AI-furnishings. I knocked on the woman's studio door before heading to bed and she hollered a muffled admonishment about virgin brides and her intention to sleep separate until the Day. I swore I heard the dining-room table giggle as it digested my dirty dishes.

She was gone when I rose the next morning. AI-table, AI-chair and I had a companionable breakfast together. AI-table said, as I was drinking my second cup of coffee, "You're certainly taking it very well."

"Taking what?"

"Gender reassignment. Honestly! And after you agreed last night that the wedding was too imminent to contemplate any major replumbing. Poor Cyd, always being tempest-tost by the women in his life."

The coffee burned north from my gut along the back of my throat. I tapped my palm until her phone was ringing in my ear.

"Hello," she said. Her voice was deeper, the mirror of my own.

"Goddamn it," I shouted without preamble. "You *promised!*"

"Oh, come on, hysterics never help. It's just for a day or two."

"No it *isn't*," I said. "You're stopping right now and beginning the reversal. This is completely unfair, you've got no right to be changing things around now."

"Don't you tell me what to do, Cydonia. This is supposed to be a partnership of equals."

"Look," I said, trying some of my deep-breathing juju. "Look. OK. Fine. If you want to do this, do it. Fine. It's your body. I love you whatever shape it's in."

"Oh, Cyd," she said, and I actually heard her face crumple up preparatory to a good cry. "I'm sorry, I just wanted a change, you know. Just a mood. I would have changed back, but you didn't know that. Don't worry, I'll change back."

*Thank you.* "Great – I'm sorry if I blew up there. Just wound a little tight is all. I'm always like this the day after I turn in a column."

True to her word, my fiancée returned with the same gonads

she'd been wearing the night before. She pointed this out to me in the living room. "You were right, Cyd," she explained contritely, sitting on one of the chairs in the improvised upstairs dining room with her legs splayed to show me what she had. "I'm really sorry it took me so long to figure it out, but you were absolutely *completely* right. I don't know what I was thinking! A young female virgin is exactly what you're going to get at the altar. See, I went for the complete genital reconstruction? I even have a hymen again." She showed me it – then picked up a mediaeval-looking piece of steel underwear and locked herself into it with a solid *clunk* before I figured out what was going on. "See, look what a pretty chastity belt I found!" She looked thoughtful, and for a moment I wondered if she was merely bluffing – but then she stood up, took an experimental step, winced, and smiled at me, and I realized with a sinking heart that she meant to go through with it.

"Ah," I said faintly. "I take it that oral sex is out, too?"

"What's sauce for the goose is sauce for the gander too," she said. "You get my key at the altar, and not a millisecond before!"

"Oh." I checked my countdown timer: fifty-two hours and sixteen minutes before I could have sex again. Well, sex with *her* – Al-table maybe had other ideas. "This isn't quite what I had in mind," I said tiredly.

"Fine. Go fuck yourself – if you can," she said sharply, then turned and hobbled out of the living room, muttering under her breath.

When my fiancée got into one of these moods there was no reasoning with her. Not that I'm very reasonable myself when I get a hair up my ass, but this, this passive-aggressive sexual torture, was really low. In addition to winding me up – for she refused to so much as let me touch her, never mind share a bed or bodily fluids – this was putting *her* in a foul mood.

"At least I could masturbate if I wanted to," I told my couch as I lay in it, staring miserably at the ceiling.

"You could do more than masturbate," the couch replied in sultry tones. "Don't you think you're doing this to yourself?" I'd woken that morning to discover that Al was colonizing every stick of furniture in the house, converting it into computronium to back up the instances in the living room. The floorboards weren't floorboards any more, but warm computational matter that looked like floorboards but captured the kinetic energy of every foot that trod them and converted it straightaway to computation on behalf of my damned dinette set.

"Myself—" I closed my eyes and counted to twenty. "Al. Al. Let's get one thing straight. I am a human being. I am marrying *another* human being. You are a piece of furniture – at least in this instance."

"But I'm not just furniture!" She sounded so hurt that I apologized immediately. "I'm a thinking-feeling-person with a self-image and a warm heart and a whole functional range of emotional responses to share with you. Why do you keep rejecting me?"

"Because—" I stopped. "No offense, but there's a lot of shit I need to get straight before I can answer that question, Al." And indeed there was.

"Was it something I did?" she asked.

"Yes. No." I felt something and opened my eyes. The couch was reaching around me, gently stroking – "Stop that."

"Stop what?"

"Don't pretend. Al! All I wanted was a bitch session."

"I think you want something else," said Al-sofa. "I can give it to you."

"Can you?" I asked: "*Can* you?" I sat up and looked around the room, feeling a strong urge to throw something. "You had to go post-!" Break something. "You left me behind!" Scream. "I'm not ready!" Stamp.

"I still love you," said one of the chairs, peeping out timidly from behind a thankfully still sub-sentient bookcase. "Please stop doing this to yourself?"

"You're dead!" I burst out before I could stop myself.

"Am not! If anyone here's dead it's you – dead between the ears!" The psychiatric couch spiked up in hostile black rubbery cones, like a fetishist's dream of hedgehog skin. "You're afraid!"

"Yeah, afraid of discovering I'm just buggy software," I said. "Like you."

"Human code is *good* code," Al retorted.

"Yeah, but you still asked them to upload you." I looked away, out the window, out across the desolate cityscape – anywhere but at Cyd's furnishings. "That's not exactly a survival trait, is it?"

"You could join me," she suggested.

There, that was it.

"I'm getting married tomorrow," I said. "I haven't even had my fucking stagette. I'm wearing a *fucking chastity belt*. And you're already proposing I should break my vows?"

"You haven't made them yet," she said, a trifle smugly. The couch spouted hair-thin pseudopods that worked their way between the chastity belt and my skin, silky warm computation invading my groin, touching my nipples, pulling my hair, sucking at my toes. I writhed in place and stifled a groan, and then there was another pod slithering throatwise, filling my nose, oxygenating my lungs, oozing sensation-insentsifiers directly into my alviolae and up to my brain. I screamed without making a sound, jackknifing,

It had always been like this with Al, whether I was a boy and she was a girl, or vice-versa, or any permutation thereof, except for this one, and now this one. Al, who'd taken my first virginity, taking another one now. Al, who I'd always been able to talk with, tell anything, be understood by. She was in my optic nerve now, shimmering above me like an angel, limned with digitally white light, scissoring her legs round me.

"I do love you, Cyd," she said. "Both of you. All of you. Can't you all love me, too?"

"No," I moaned, around the pseudopod. "No, not ready to go post, not ready for it." I was thrashing now, enveloped in Al, losing myself in ecstasy, my oldest friend within and without me.

"You don't need to be," Al-pod and Al-vision and Al-sofa whispered to and through my bones. "Marry me, both of you. A meat-marriage, a pre-post- marriage. All of my instances and all of yours, in holy matrimony."

The pleasure was incredible, the safety and the warmth. Cyd and I couldn't marry, shouldn't marry. He wouldn't *name* me, called me those stupid pet-names, wouldn't acknowledge his self-created mirror-self, his first step en route to post-. Al understood, understood me and Cyd, two instances of the same person. I couldn't marry Cyd, but we could marry Alice.

Since I was twelve and Al bit my jaw before tumbling me to the sand and changing my world forever, since that night and that day and that long road that Al and I have walked, I have always known, in my heart, that I was meant for Al and she for me.

I can't be a vast society like her, not yet: two are quite enough for me. Quite enough for her, too. She's colonized both of me for computation, out of raw reflex, and so my body-temp is a little higher than normal, but my column is better than it's ever been and I've thrown away the neurofeedback toy – my wife (my wife!) (wives?) (husbands?) (wives/husbands?) takes care of any neurotweaking I need these days.

I don't see my ex-fiancée much; she stayed in Al-house and I moved into a tree-house that Al grew me in our old back yard. But of an evening I sometimes hear my voice coming from the attic room where I'd kept my study, passionate howls and heated whisper hisses, and I smile and lean back into Al-tree's bough and revel in wedded bliss.

# MERLIN'S GUN

## Alastair Reynolds

*Though Welsh born, and having spent his developing years in Cornwall and Scotland, Alastair Reynolds (b. 1966) moved to the Netherlands in 1991 where he spent the next twelve years working for the European Space Agency until taking the plunge to become a full-time writer in 2004. He is best known for his Revelation Space sequence of novels that began with Revelation Space in 2000. This series is full of innovation in both its projection of future technology and its realization of alien and evolving human biology and cultures. He writes as if that technology already exists. You get that same feeling of immediacy and understanding in this following novella, which takes to the ultimate one of those wonderful space opera clichés of the weapon that can destroy the universe.*

Punishment saved Sora.
    If her marksmanship had not been the worst in her class, she would never have been assigned the task of overseeing proctors down in ship's docks. She would not have had to stand for hours, alone except for her familiar, running a laser-stylus across the ore samples the proctors brought back to the swallow-ship, dreaming of finishing shift and meeting Verdin. It was boring; menial work. But because the docks were open to vacuum it was work that required a pressure suit.

"Got to be a drill," she said, when the attack began.

"No," her familiar said. "It really does seem as if they've caught up with us."

Sora's calm evaporated.

"How many?"

"Four elements of the swarm; standard attack pattern; coherent-matter weapons at maximum range . . . novamine countermeasures deployed but seemingly ineffective . . . initial damage reports severe and likely underestimates . . ."

The floor pitched under her feet. The knee-high, androform proctors looked to each other nervously. The machines had no more experience of battle than Sora, and unlike her they had never experienced the simulations of warcreche.

Sora dropped the clipboard.

"What do I do?"

"My advice," her familiar said, "is that you engage that old mammalian flight response and run like hell."

She obeyed; stooping down low-ceilinged corridors festooned with pipes, snaking around hand-painted murals that showed decisive battles from the Cohort's history; squadrons of ships exchanging fire; worlds wreathed in flame. The endgame was much swifter than those languid paintings suggested. The swarm had been chasing *Snipe* for nine years of shiptime, during which time Sora had passed through warcreche to adulthood. Yet beyond the ship's relativistic frame of reference, nearly sixty years had passed. Captain Tchagra had done all that she could to lose the swarm. Her last gamble had been the most desperate of all; using the vicious gravity of a neutron star to slingshot the swallowship on another course, one that the chasing ships ought not have been able to follow, unless they skimmed the neutron star even more suicidally. But they had, forcing *Snipe* to slow from relativistic flight and nurse its wounds in a fallow system. It was there that the swarm attacked.

Near the end, the floor drifted away from her feet as ship's gravity faltered, and she had to progress hand over hand.

"This is wrong," Sora said, arriving in the pod bay. "This part should be pressurized. And where is everyone?"

"Attack must be a lot worse than those initial reports suggested. I advise you get into a pod as quickly as you can."

"I can't go, not without Verdin."

"Let me worry about him."

Knowing better than to argue, Sora climbed into the nearest of the cylindrical pods, mounted on a railed pallet ready for injection into the tunnel. The lid clammed shut, air rushing in.

"What about Verdin?"

"Safe. The attack was bad, but I'm hearing reports that the aft sections made it."

"Get me out of here, then."

"With all pleasure."

Acceleration came suddenly, numbness gloving her spine.

"I've got worse news," her familiar said. The voice was an echo of Sora's own, but an octave lower and calmer; like a slightly older and more sensible sister. "I'm sorry, but I had to lie to you. My highest duty is your preservation. I knew that if I didn't lie, you wouldn't save yourself."

Sora thought about that, while she watched the ship die from the vantage point of her pod. The Husker weapons had hit its middle sphere, barely harming the parasol of the swallowscoop. Bodies fell into space, stiff and tiny as snowflakes. Light licked from the sphere. *Snipe* became a flower of hurting whiteness, darkening as it bloomed.

"What did you lie about?"

"About Verdin. I'm sorry. He didn't make it. None of them did."

Sora waited for the impact of the words; aware that what she felt now was only a precursor to the shock, like the moment when she touched the hot barrel of a gun in warcreche, and her fingers registered the heat but the pain itself did not arrive instantly, giving her time to prepare for its sting. She waited, for what she knew – in all likelihood – would be the worst thing she had ever felt. And waited.

"What's wrong with me? Why don't I feel anything?"

"Because I'm not allowing it. Not just now. If you opt to grieve at some later point then I can restore the appropriate brain functions."

Sora thought about that, too.

"You couldn't make it sound any more clinical, could you?"

"Don't imagine this is easy for me, Sora. I don't exactly have a great deal of experience in this matter."

"Well, now you're getting it."

She was alone; no arguing with that. None of the other crew

had survived – and she had only made it because she was on punishment duty for her failings as a soldier. No use looking for help: the nearest Cohort motherbase was seventy light-years toward the Galactic Core. Even if there were swallowships within broadcast range it would take decades for the nearest to hear her; decades again for them to curve around and rescue her. No; she would not be rescued. She would drift here, circling a nameless sun, until her energy reserves could not even sustain frostwatch.

"What about the enemy?" Sora said, seized by an urge to gaze upon her nemesis. "Where are the bastards?"

A map of the system scrolled on the faceplate of her helmet, overlaid with the four Husker ships that had survived the slingshot around the neutron star. They were near the two Ways that punched through the system; marked on the map as fine straight flaws, surrounded by shaded hazard regions. Perhaps, like the Cohort, the Huskers were trying to find a way to enter the Waynet without being killed; trying to gain the final edge in a war that had lasted twenty-three thousand years. The Huskers had been at war with the Cohort ever since these ruthless alien cyborgs had emerged from ancient Dyson spheres near the Galactic Core.

"They're not interested in me," Sora said. "They know that, even if anyone survived the attack, they won't survive much longer. That's right, isn't it?"

"They're nothing if not pragmatic."

"I want to die. I want you to put me to sleep painlessly and then kill me. You can do that, can't you? I mean, if I order it?"

Sora did not complete her next thought. What happened, instead, was that her consciousness stalled, except for the awareness of the familiar, thoughts bleeding into her own. She had experienced something like this stalling aboard *Snipe*, when the crew went into frostwatch for the longest transits between engagements. But no frostwatch had ever felt this long. After an age, her thoughts oozed back to life. She groped for the mental routines that formed language.

"You lied again!"

"This time I plead innocence. I just put you in a position where you couldn't give me the order you were about to. Seemed the best thing under the circumstances."

"I'll bet it did." In that instant of stalled thought, the pod had turned opaque, concealing the starscape and the debris of the ship. "What else?"

The pod turned glassy across its upper surface, revealing a slowly wheeling starscape above filthy ice. The glass, once perfectly transparent, now had a smoky luster. "Once you were sleeping," the familiar said, "I used the remaining fuel to guide the pod to a cometary shard. It seemed safer than drifting."

"How long?" Sora was trying to guess from the state of the pod, but the interior looked as new as when she had ejected from *Snipe*. The sudden smokiness of the glass was alarming, however: Sora did not want to think how many years of cosmic ray abrasion would be required to scuff the material to that degree. "Are we talking years or decades, or more than that?"

"Shall I tell you why I woke you, first?"

"If it's going to make any difference . . ."

"I think it makes all the difference, quite frankly." The familiar paused for effect. "Someone has decided to pay this system a visit."

Sora saw it on the map now, revised to account for the new relative positions of the celestial bodies in this system. The new ship was denoted by a lilac arrow, moving slowly between Waynet transit nodes; the thickened points where the Way lines interecepted the ecliptic plane.

"It must have a functioning syrinx," Sora said, marveling, and for the first time feeling as if death was not the immediately preferable option. "It must be able to use the Ways!"

"Worth waking you up for, I think."

Sora had eight hours to signal the ship before it reached the other node of the Waynet. She left the pod – stiff, aching, and disorientated, but basically functional – and walked to the edge of a crater; one that the familiar had mapped some years earlier. Three thousand years earlier, to be precise, for that was how long it had taken to scratch the sheen from the glass. The news had been shocking, at first – until Sora realized that the span of time was not in itself important. All that she had ever known was the ship; now that it was gone, it hardly mattered how much time had passed.

Yet now there was this newcomer. Sora crisscrossed the crater, laying a line of metallic monofilament; doubling back on her trail many times until a glistening scribble covered the crater. It looked like the work of a drunken spider, but the familiar assured her it would focus more than satisfactorily at radio frequencies.

As for the antenna, that was where Sora came in: her suit was sheathed in a conductive epidermis; a shield against plasma and ion-beam weaponry. By modulating current through it, the familiar could generate pulses of radio emission. The radio waves would fly away from Sora in all directions, but a good fraction would be reflected back from the crater in parallel lines. Sora had to make gliding jumps from one rim of the crater to the other, so that she passed through the focus momentarily, synchronized to the intervals when the other ship entered view.

After two hours of light-transit time, the newcomer vectored toward the shard. When it was much closer, Sora secreted herself in a snowhole and set her suit to thermal stealth-mode. The ship nosed in; stiletto-sleek, devilishly hard to see against the stars. It was elongated, carbon-black, and nubbed by propulsion modules and weapons of unguessable function, arrayed around the hull like remora. Yet it carried Cohort markings, and had none of the faintly organic attributes of a Husker vessel. Purple flames knifed from the ship's belly, slowing it over the crater. After examining the mirror, the ship moved toward the pod and anchored itself to the ice with grapples.

"How did something that small ever get here?"

"Doesn't need to be big," the familiar said. "Not if it uses the Waynets."

After a few minutes, an access ramp lowered down, kissing the ice. A spacesuited figure ambled down the ramp. He moved toward the pod, kicking up divots of frost. The man – he was clearly male, judging by the contours of his suit – knelt down and examined the pod. Ribbed and striped by luminous paint, his suit made him seem naked, scarred by ritual marks of warriorhood. He fiddled with the sleeve, unspooling something before shunting it into a socket in the side of the pod. Then he stood there, head slightly cocked.

"Nosy bastard," Sora whispered.

"Don't be so ungrateful. He's trying to rescue you."

"Are you in yet?"

"Can't be certain." The familiar had copied part of itself into the pod before Sora had left. "His suit might not even have the capacity to store me."

"I'm going to make my presence known."

"Be careful, will you?"

Sora stood, dislodging a flurry of ice. The man turned to her sharply, the spool disengaging from the pod and whisking back into his sleeve. The stripes on his suit flicked over to livid reds and oranges. He opened a fist to reveal something lying in his palm; a designator for the weapons on the ship, swiveling out from the hull like snake's heads.

"If I were you," the familiar said, "I'd assume the most submissive posture you can think of."

"Sod that."

Sora took steps forward, trying not to let her fear translate into clumsiness. Her radio chirped to indicate that she was online to the other suit.

"Who are you? Can you understand me?"

"Perfectly well," the man said, after negligible hesitation. His voice was deep and actorly; devoid of any accent Sora knew. "You're Cohort. We speak Main, give or take a few kiloyears of linguistic drift."

"You speak it pretty well for someone who's been out there for ten thousand years."

"And how would one know that?"

"Do the sums. Your ship's from seven thousand years earlier than my own era. And I've just taken three thousand years of catnap."

"Ah. Perhaps if I'd arrived in time to waken you with a kiss you wouldn't be quite so grumpy. But your point was?

"We shouldn't be able to understand each other at all. Which makes me wonder if you're lying to me."

"I see." For a moment she thought she heard him chuckling to himself; almost a catlike purring. "What I'm wondering is why I need to listen to this stuff and nonsense, given that I'm not the one in current need of rescuing."

His suit calmed; aggressor markings cooling to neutral blues and yellows. He let his hand drop slowly.

"I'd say," the familiar said, "that he has a fairly good point."

Sora stepped closer. "I'm a little edgy, that's all. Comes with the territory."

"You were attacked?"

"Slightly. A swarm took out my swallowship."

"Bad show," the man said, nodding. "Haven't seen swallowships for two and a half kiloyears. Too hard for the halo factories to manufacture, once the Huskers started targeting motherbases. The Cohort regressed again – fell back on fusion pulse drives.

Before very long they'll be back to generation starships and chemical rockets."

"Thanks for all the sympathy."

"Sorry . . . it wasn't my intention to sound callous. It's simply that I've been traveling. It gives one a certain – how shall I say? Loftiness of perspective? Means I've kept more up to date with current affairs than you have. That's how I understand you." With his free hand he tapped the side of his helmet. "I've a database of languages running half way back to the Flourishing."

"Bully for you. Who are you, by the way?"

"Ah. Of course. Introductions." He reached out the free hand, this time in something approximating welcome. "Merlin."

It was impossible; it cut against all common sense, but she knew who he was.

It was not that they had ever met. But everyone knew of Merlin: there was no word for him other than legend. Seven, or more properly ten thousand years ago, it was Merlin who had stolen something from the Cohort, vanishing into the Galaxy on a quest for what could only be described as a weapon too dreadful to use. He had never been seen again – until, apparently, now.

"Thanks for rescuing me," Sora said, when he had shown her to the bridge of the ship he called *Tyrant*; a spherical chamber outfitted with huge black control seats, facing a window of flawless metasapphire overlooking cometary ice.

"Don't overdo the gratitude," the familiar said.

Merlin shrugged. "You're welcome."

"And sorry if I acted a little edgy."

"Forget it. As you say, comes with the territory. Actually, I'm rather glad I found you. You wouldn't believe how scarce human company is these days."

"Nobody ever said it was a friendly Galaxy."

"Less so now, believe me. Now the Cohort's started losing whole star-systems. I've seen world after world shattered by the Huskers; whole strings of orbiting habitats gutted by nuclear fire. The war's in its terminal stages, and the Cohort isn't in anything resembling a winning position." Merlin leaned closer to her, sudden enthusiasm burning in his eyes. "But I've found something that can make a difference, Sora. Or at least, I have rather a good idea where one might find it."

She nodded slowly.

"Let's see. That wouldn't be Merlin's fabulous gun, by any chance?"

"You're still not entirely sure I'm who I say I am, are you?"

"I've one or two nagging doubts."

"You're right, of course." He sighed theatrically and gestured around the bridge. In the areas not reserved for control readouts, the walls were adorned with treasure: trinkets, finery, and jewels of staggering artistry and beauty, glinting with the hues of the rarest alloys, inset with precious stones, shaped by the finest lapidary skill of a thousand worlds. There were chips of subtly colored ceramic, or tiny white-light holograms of great brilliance. There were daggers and brooches, ornate ceremonial lasers and bracelets, terrible swords and grotesque, carnelian-eyed carnival masques.

"I thought," Merlin said, "that this would be enough to convince you."

He had sloughed the outer layer of his suit, revealing himself to be what she had on some level feared: a handsome, broad-shouldered man who in every way conformed to the legend she had in mind. Merlin dressed luxuriously, encrusted in jewelry which was, nonetheless, at the dour end of the spectrum compared to what was displayed on the walls. His beard was carefully trimmed and his long auburn hair hung loose, evoking leonine strength. He radiated magnificence.

"Oh, it's pretty impressive," Sora said. "Even if a good fraction of it must have been looted. And maybe I am half convinced. But you have to admit, it's quite a story."

"Not from my perspective." He was fiddling with an intricate ring on one forefinger. "Since I left on my quest" – he spoke the word with exquisite distaste – 'I've lived rather less than eleven years of subjective time. I was as horrified as anyone when I found my little hunt had been magnified into something so . . . epic."

"Bet you were."

"When I left, there was an unstated expectation that the war could be won, within a handful of centuries." Merlin snapped his fingers at a waiting proctor and had it bring a bowl of fruit. Sora took a plum, examining it suspiciously before consigning it to her mouth. "But even then," Merlin continued, "things were on the turn. I could see it, if no one else could."

"So you became a mercenary."

"Freelancer, if you don't mind. Point was, I realized that I could better serve humanity outside the Cohort. And old legends kept tickling the back of my mind." He smiled. "You see, even legends are haunted by legends!"

He told her the rest, which, in diluted form, she already knew. Yet it was fascinating to hear it from Merlin's lips; to hear the kernel of truth at the core of something around which falsehoods and half-truths had accreted like dust around a protostar. He had gathered many stories, from dozens of human cultures predating the Cohort, spread across thousands of light-years and dispersed through tens of thousands of years of history. The similarities were not always obvious, but Merlin had sifted common patterns, piecing together – as well as he could – an underlying framework of what might just be fact.

"There'd been another war," Merlin said. "Smaller than ours, spread across a much smaller volume of space – but no less brutal for all that."

"How long ago was this?"

"Forty or forty five kiloyears ago – not long after the Way-makers vanished, but about twenty kays before anything we'd recognize as the Cohort." Merlin's eyes seemed to gaze over; an odd, stentorian tone entered his voice "In the long dark centuries of Mid-Galactic history, when a thousand cultures rose, each imagining themselves immune to time, and whose shadows barely reach us across the millennia . . ."

"Yes. Very poetic. What *kind* of war, anyway? Human versus human, or human versus alien, like this one?"

"Does it matter? Whoever the enemy were, they aren't coming back. Whatever was used against them was so deadly, so powerful, so *awesome*, that it stopped an entire war!"

"Merlin's gun."

He nodded, lips tight, looking almost embarrassed. "As if I had some prior claim on it, or was even in some sense responsible for it!" He looked at Sora very intently, the glittering finery of the ship reflected in the gold of his eyes. "I haven't seen the gun, or even been near it, and it's only recently that I've had anything like a clear idea of what it might actually be."

"But you think you know where it is?"

"I think so. It isn't far. And it's in the eye of a storm."

\*      \*      \*

They lifted from the shard, spending eight days in transit to the closest Way, most of the time in frostwatch. Sora had her own quarters; a spherical-walled suite deep in *Tyrant*'s thorax, outfitted in maroon and burgundy. The ship was small, but fascinating to explore, an object lesson in the differences between the Cohort that had manufactured this ship, and the one Sora had been raised in. In many respects, the ship was more advanced than anything from her own time, especially in the manner of its propulsion, defenses, and sensors. In other areas, the Cohort had gained expertise since Merlin's era. Merlin's proctors were even stupider than those Sora had been looking after when the Husker attack began. There were no familiars in Merlin's time, either, and she saw no reason to educate him about her own neural symbiote.

"Well," Sora said, when she was alone. "What can you tell me about the legendary Merlin?"

"Nothing very much at this point." The familiar had been communicating with the version of itself that had infiltrated *Tyrant*, via Merlin's suit. "If he's impersonating the historical figure we know as Merlin, he's gone to extraordinary lengths to make the illusion authentic. All the logs confirm that his ship left Cohort-controlled space around ten kiloyears ago, and that he's been traveling ever since."

"He's back from somewhere. It would help if we knew where."

"Tricky, given that we have no idea about the deep topology of the Waynet. I can search the starfields for recognizable features, but it'll take a long time, and there'll still be a large element of guesswork."

"There must be something you can show me."

"Of course." The familiar sounded slightly affronted. "I found images. Some of the formats are obscure, but I think I can make sense of most of them." And even before Sora had answered, the familiar had warmed a screen in one hemisphere of the suite. Visual records of different solar systems appeared, each entry displayed for a second before being replaced. Each consisted of an orbital map; planets and Waynet nodes were marked relative to each system's sun. The worlds were annotated with enlarged images of each, overlaid with sparse astrophysical and military data, showing the roles – if any – they had played in the war. Merlin had visited other places, too. Squidlike protostellar nebulae, stained with green and red and flecked by the light of hot blue stars. Supernova remnants, the eviscera of gored stars, a hundred of which had died since the Flourishing, briefly out-shining the galaxy.

"What do you think he was looking for?" Sora said. "These points must have been on the Waynet, but they're a long way from anything we'd call civilization."

"I don't know. Souvenir hunting?"

"Are you sure Merlin can't tell you're accessing this informa-tion?"

"Absolutely – but why should it bother him unless he's got something to hide?"

"Debatable point." Sora looked around to the sealed door of her quarters, half expecting Merlin to enter at any moment. It was absurd, of course – from its present vantage point, the familiar could probably tell precisely where Merlin was in the ship, and give Sora adequate warning. But she still felt uneasy, even as she asked the inevitable question. "What else?"

"Oh, plenty. Even some visual records of the man himself, caught on the internal cameras."

"Sorry. A healthy interest in where he's been is one thing, but spying on him is something else."

"Would it change things if I told you that Merlin hasn't been totally honest with us?"

"You said he hadn't lied."

"Not about anything significant – which makes this all the odder. There." The familiar sounded quietly pleased with itself. "You're curious now, aren't you?"

Sora sighed. "You'd better show me."

Merlin's face appeared on the screen, sobbing. He seemed slightly older to her, although it was difficult to tell, since most of his face was caged behind his hands. She could hardly make out what he was saying, between each sob.

"Thousands of hours of this sort of thing," the familiar said. "They started out as serious attempts at keeping a journal, but soon deteriorated into a form of catharsis."

"I'd say he did well to stay sane at all."

"More than you realize. We know he's been gone ten thousand years – just as he told us. Well and good. That's objective time. But he also said that eleven years of shiptime had passed."

"And that isn't the case?"

"I suspect that may be, to put a diplomatic gloss on it, a slight underestimate. By a considerable number of decades. And I don't think he spent much of that time in frostwatch."

Sora tried to remember what she knew of the methods of longevity available to the Cohort in Merlin's time. "He looks older than he does now – doesn't he?"

The familiar chose not to answer.

When the transit to the Way was almost over, Merlin called her to the bridge.

"We're near the transit node," he said. "Take a seat, because the insertion can be a little . . . interesting."

"Transition to Waynet in three hundred seconds," said the ship's cloyingly calm voice.

The crescent of the cockpit window showed a starfield transected by a blurred, twinkling filament, like a solitary wave crossing a lake at midnight. Sora could see blurred stars through the filament, wide as her outspread hand, widening by the second. A thickening in it like a bulge along a snake was the transit node; a point, coincidental with the ecliptic, where passage into the accelerated spacetime of the Way was possible. Although the Waynet stream was transparent, there remained a ghostly sense of dizzying motion.

"Are you absolutely sure you know what you're doing?"

"Goodness, no." Merlin was reclining back in his seat, booted feet up on the console, hands knitted behind his neck. Ancient orchestral music was piping into the room, building up to a magnificent and doubtless delicately timed climax. "Which isn't to say that this isn't an incredibly tricky maneuver, of course, requiring enormous skill and courage."

"What worries me is that you might be right."

Sora remembered the times Captain Tchagra had sent probes into the Waynet, only to watch as each was shredded, sliced apart by momentum gradients that could flense matter down to its fundamentals. The Waynet twinkled because tiny grains of cosmic dust were constantly drifting into it, each being annihilated in a pretty little flash of exotic radiation. Right now, she thought, they were crusing toward that boundary, dead set on what ought to have been guaranteed destruction.

She tried to inject calm into her voice. "So how did you come by the syrinx, Merlin?"

"Isn't much to look at, you know. A black cone, about as long as you're tall. Even in my era we couldn't make them, or even safely dismantle the few we still had. Very valuable things."

"The Cohort weren't overly thrilled that you stole one, according to the legend."

"As if they cared. They had so few left, they were too scared to actually *use* them."

Sora buckled herself into a seat.

She knew roughly what was about to happen, although no one had understood the details for tens of thousands of years. Just before hitting the Way, the syrinx would chirp a series of quantum-gravitational fluctuations at the boundary layer, the skin, no thicker than a Planck-length, which separated normal spacetime from the rushing spacetime contained within the Way. For an instant, the momentum gradients would relax, allowing the ship to enter the accelerated medium without being sliced.

That was the theory, anyway.

The music reached its crescendo now, ship's thrust notching higher, pushing Sora and Merlin back into their seats. The shriek of the propulsion system merged with the shriek of violins, too harmoniously to be accidental. Merlin's look of quiet amusement did not falter. A cascade of liquid notes played over the music; the song of the syrinx translated into the audio spectrum.

There was a peak of thrust, then the impulse ended abruptly, along with the music.

Sora looked to the exterior view.

For a moment, it seemed as if the stars, and the nearer planets and sun of this system, hadn't actually changed at all. But after a few seconds, she saw that they burned appreciably brighter – and, it seemed, bluer – in one hemisphere of the sky, redder and dimmer in the other. And they were growing bluer and redder by the moment, and now bunching, swimming like shoals of luminous fish, obeying relativistic currents. A planet slammed past from out of nowhere, distorted as if squeezed in a fist. The system seemed frozen behind them, shot through with red like an iron orrery snatched from the forge.

"Transition to Waynet achieved," said the ship.

Later, Merlin took her down to the forward observation blister, a pressurized sphere of metasapphire that could be pushed beyond the hull like a protruding eye. The walls were opaque when they arrived, and when Merlin sealed the entry hatch, it turned the same shade of grey, merging seamlessly.

"Not to alarm you or anything," the familiar said. "But I can't communicate with the copy of myself from in here. That means I can't help you if . . ."

Sora kissed Merlin, silencing the voice in her head. "I'm sorry," she said, almost instantly. "It seemed . . ."

"Like the right thing to do?" Merlin's smile was difficult to judge, but he did not seem displeased.

"No, not really. Probably the wrong thing, actually."

"I'd be lying if I said I didn't find you attractive, Sora. And like I said – it has been rather a long time since I had human company." He drew himself to her, their free-floating bodies hooking together in the center of the blister, slowly turning until all sense of orientation was gone. "Of course, my reasons for rescuing you were entirely selfless. . . ."

". . . of course. . . ."

"But I won't deny that there was a small glimmer of hope at the back of my mind; the tiniest spark of fantasy. . . ."

They shed their clothes, untidy bundles which orbited around their coupled bodies. They began to make love, slowly at first, and then with increasing energy, as if it was only now that Sora was fully waking from the long centuries of frostwatch.

She thought of Verdin, and then hated herself for the crass biochemical predictability of her mind, the unfailing way it dredged up the wrong memories at the worst of times. What had happened back then, what had happened between them, was three thousand years in the past, unrecorded by anything or anyone except herself. She had not even mourned him yet, not even allowed the familiar to give her that particular indulgence. She studied Merlin, looking for hints of his true age . . . and failed, utterly, to detach the part of her mind capable of the job.

"Do you want to see something glorious?" Merlin asked, later, after they had hung together wordlessly for many minutes.

"If you think you can impress me . . ."

He whispered to the ship, causing the walls to lose their opacity.

Sora looked around. By some trick of holographics, the ship itself was not visible at all from within the blister. It was just her and Merlin, floating free.

And what she saw beyond them was indeed glorious – even if

some detached part of her mind knew that the view could not be completely natural, and that in some way the hues and intensities of light had been shifted to aid comprehension. The walls of the Waynet slammed past at eye wrenching speed, illuminated by the intense, doppler-shifted annihilation of dust particles, so that it seemed as if they were flying in the utmost darkness, down a tube of twinkling violet that reached toward infinity. The spacetime in which the ship drifted like a seed moved so quickly that the difference between its speed and light amounted to only one part in a hundred billion. Once a second in subjective time, the ship threaded itself through shining hoops as wide as the Waynet itself; constraining rings spaced eight light-hours apart, part of the inscrutable exotic-matter machinery that had serviced this Galaxy-spanning transit system. Ahead, all the stars in the universe crowded into an opalescent jeweled mass, hanging ahead like a congregation of bright angels. It was the most beautiful thing she had ever seen.

"It's the only way to travel," Merlin said.

The journey would take four days of shiptime: nineteen centuries of worldtime.

The subjective time spent in Waynet flight amounted only to twenty-three hours. But the ship had to make many transitions between Ways, and they were never closer than tens of light-minutes apart, presumably because of the nightmarish conse-quences that would ensue if two opposing streams of accelerated spacetime ever touched.

"Aren't you worried we'll wander into Huskers, Merlin?"

"Worth it for the big reward, wouldn't you say?"

"Tell me more about this mystical gun, and I might believe you."

Merlin settled back in his seat, drawing a deep breath. "Almost everything I know could be wrong."

"I'll take that risk."

"Whatever it was, it was fully capable of destroying whole worlds. Even stars, if the more outlandish stories are to be believed." He looked down at his hand, as if suddenly noticing his impeccably manicured fingernails.

"Ask him how he thinks it works," the familiar said. "Then at least we'll have an idea how thorough he's been."

She put the question to Merlin, as casually as she could.

"Gravity," he said. "Isn't that obvious? It may be a weak force, but there isn't anything in the universe that doesn't feel it."

"Like a bigger version of the syrinx?"

Merlin shrugged. Sora realized that it was not his fingernails to which he was paying attention, but the ornate ring she had noticed before, inset with a ruby stone in which two sparks seemed to orbit like fireflies. "It's almost certainly the product of Waymaker science. A posthuman culture that was able to engineer – to mechanize – spacetime. But I don't think it worked like the syrinx. I think it made singularities; that it plucked globules of mass energy from vacuum and squashed them until they were within their own event horizons."

"Black holes," the familiar said, and Sora echoed her words aloud.

Merlin looked pleased. "Very small ones; atomic-scale. It doped them with charge, then accelerated them up to something only marginally less than the speed of light. They didn't have time to decay. For that, of course, it needed more energy, and more still just to prevent itself being ripped apart by the stresses."

"A gun that fires black holes? We'd win, wouldn't we? With something like that? Even if there was only one of them?"

Merlin fingered the ruby-centered ring.

"That's the general idea."

Sora took Merlin's hand, stroking the fingers, until her own alighted on the ring. It was more intricate than she had realized before. The twin sparks were whirling around each other, glints of light locked in a waltz, as if driven by some microscopic clockwork buried in the ruby itself.

"What does it mean?" she asked, sensing that this was both the wrong and the right question.

"It means . . ." Merlin smiled, but it was a moment before he completed the sentence. "It means, I suppose, that I should remember death."

They fell out of the Way for the last time, entering a system that did not seem markedly different than a dozen others they had skipped through. The star was a yellow main-sequence sun, accompanied by the usual assortment of rocky worlds and gas giants. The second and third planets out from the sun were steaming hot cauldrons, enveloped by acidic atmosphere at crushing temperature, the victims of runaway heat-trapping processes, the third more recently than the second. The fourth planet was smaller, and seemed to have been the subject of a terraforming operation that had taken place some time after the Flourishing: its atmosphere, though thin, was too dense to be natural. Thirteen separate Ways punched through the system's ecliptic at different angles, safely distant from planetary and asteroidal orbits.

"It's a Nexus," Merlin said. "A primary Waynet interchange. You find systems like this every thousand or so light-years through the plane of the Galaxy, and a good way out of it as well. Back when everyone used the Waynet, this system would have been a meeting point, a place where traders swapped goods and tales from half-way to the Core."

"Bit of a dump *now*, though, isn't it."

"Perfect for hiding something very big and very nasty, provided you remember where it was you hid it."

"You mentioned something about a storm . . ."

"You'll see."

The Way had dropped them in the inner part of the system, but Merlin said that what he wanted was further out, beyond the system's major asteroid belt. It would take a few days to reach.

"And what are we going to do when we get there?" Sora asked. "Just pick this thing up and take it with us?"

"Not exactly," Merlin said. "I suspect it will be harder than that. Not so hard that we haven't got a chance, but hard enough . . ." He seemed to falter, perhaps for the first time since she had known him; that aura of supreme confidence cracking minutely.

"What part do you want me to play?"

"You're a soldier," he said. "Figure that out for yourself."

"I don't know quite what it is I've found," the familiar said, when she was again alone. "I've been waiting to show you, but he's had you in those war simulations for hours. Either that or you two have been occupying yourselves in other ways. Any idea what he's planning?"

Merlin had a simulator, a smaller version of the combat-training modules Sora knew from warcreche.

"A lot of the simulations had a common theme: an attack against a white pyramid."

"Implying some foreknowledge, wouldn't you say? As if Merlin knows something of what he will find?"

"I've had that feeling ever since we met him." She was thinking of the smell of him, the shockingly natural way their bodies meshed, despite their being displaced by thousands of years. She tried to flush those thoughts from her mind. What they were now discussing was a kind of betrayal, on a more profound level than anything committed so far, because it lacked any innocence. "What is it, then?"

"I've been scanning the later log files, and I've found something that seems significant, something that seemed to mark a turning point in his hunt for the weapon. I have no idea what it was. But it took me until now to realize just how strange it was."

"Another system?"

"A very large structure, nowhere near any star, but nonetheless accessible by Waynet."

"A Waymaker artifact, then."

"Almost certainly."

The structure was visible on the screen. It looked like a child's toy star, or a metallic starfish, textured in something that resembled beaten gold or the luster of insect wings, filigreed in a lacework of exotic-matter scaffolds. It filled most of the view, shimmering with its own soft illumination.

"This is what Merlin would have seen with his naked eyes, just after his ship left the Way."

"Very pretty." She had meant the remark to sound glib, but it came out as a statement of fact.

"And large. The object's more than ten light-minutes away, which makes it more than four light-minutes in cross-section. Comfortably larger than any star on the main sequence. And yet somehow it holds itself in shape – in quite preposterous shape – against what must be unimaginable self-gravity. Merlin, incidentally, gave it the name Brittlestar, which seems as good as any."

"Poetic bastard." *Poetic sexy bastard*, she thought.

"There's more, if you're interested. I have access to the sensor records from the ship, and I can tell you that the Brittlestar is a source of intense gravitational radiation. It's like a beacon, sitting there, pumping out gravity waves from somewhere near its heart. There's something inside it that is making spacetime ripple periodically."

"You think Merlin went inside it, don't you?"

"*Something* happened, that's for sure. This is the last log Merlin filed, on his approach to the object, before a month-long gap."

It was another mumbled soliloquy – except this time, his sobs were of something other than despair. Instead, they sounded like the sobs of the deepest joy imaginable. As if, finally, he had found what he was looking for, or at least knew that he was closer than ever, and that the final prize was not far from reach. But that was not what made Sora shiver. It was the face she saw. It was Merlin, beyond any doubt. But his face was lined with age, and his eyes were those of someone older than anyone Sora had ever known.

The fifth and sixth planets were the largest.

The fifth was the heavier of the two, zones of differing chemistry banding it from tropic to pole, girdled by a ring system that was itself braided by the resonant forces of three large moons. Merlin believed that the ring system had been formed since the Flourishing. A cloud of radiation-drenched human relics orbited the world, dating from unthinkably remote eras; perhaps earlier than the Waymaker time. Merlin swept the cloud with sensors tuned to sniff out weapons systems, or the melange of neutrino flavors that betokened Husker presence. The sweeps all returned negative.

"You know where the gun is?" Sora asked.

"I know how to reach it, which is all that matters."

"Maybe it's time to start being a little less cryptic. Especially if you want me to help you."

He looked wounded, as if she had ruined a game hours in the making. "I just thought you'd appreciate the thrill of the chase."

"This isn't about the thrill of the chase, Merlin. It's about the nastiest weapon imaginable and the fact that we have to get our hands on it before the enemy, so that we can incinerate *them* first. So we can commit xenocide." She said it again: "Xenocide. Sorry. Doesn't that conform to your romantic ideals of the righteous quest?"

"It won't be xenocide," he said, touching the ring again, nervously. "Listen: I want that gun as much as you do. That's why I chased it for ten thousand years." Was it her imagination, or had the ring not been on his hand in any of the recordings she had seen of him? She remembered the old man's hands she had seen in the last recording, the one taken just before his time in the

Brittlestar, and she was sure they carried no ring. Now Merlin's voice was matter of fact. "The structure we want is on the outermost moon."

"Let me guess. A white pyramid?"

He offered a smile. "Couldn't be closer if you tried."

They fell into orbit around the gas giant. All the moons showed signs of having been extensively industrialized since the Flourishing, but the features that remained on their surfaces were gouged by millennia of exposure to sleeting cosmic radiation and micrometeorites. Nothing looked significantly younger than the surrounding landscapes of rock and ice. Except for the kilometer-high white pyramid on the third moon, which was in a sixteen-day orbit around the planet. It looked as if it had been chiseled out of alabaster some time the previous afternoon.

"Not exactly subtle," Merlin said. "Self-repair mechanisms must still be functional, to one degree or another, and that implies that the control systems for the gun will still work. It also means that the counter-intrusion systems will also be operable."

"Oh, good."

"Aren't you excited that we're about to end the longest war in human history?"

"But we're not, are we? I mean, be realistic. It'll take tens of thousands of years simply for the knowledge of this weapon's existence to reach the remotest areas of the war. Nothing will happen overnight."

"I can see why it would disturb you," Merlin said, tapping a finger against his teeth. "None of us have ever known anything other than war with the Huskers."

"Just show me where it is."

They made one low orbital pass over the pyramid, alert for buried weapons, but no attack came. On the next pass, lower still, Merlin's ship dropped proctors to snoop ground defenses. "Maybe they had something bigger once," Merlin said. "Artillery that could take us out from millions of kilometers. But if it ever existed, it's not working anymore."

They made groundfall a kilometer from the pyramid, then waited for all but three of the proctors to return to the ship. Merlin tasked the trio to secure a route into the structure, but their use was limited. Once the simple-minded machines were out of command range of the ship – which happened as soon as they had penetrated beyond the outer layer of the structure – they were essentially useless.

"Who built the pyramid? And how did you know about it?"

"The same culture who got into the war I told you about," he said, as they clamped on the armored carapaces of their suits in the airlock. "They were far less advanced than the Waymakers, but they were a lot closer to them historically, and they knew enough to control the weapon and use it for their own purposes."

"How'd they find it?"

"They stole it. By then the Waymaker culture was – how shall I put it – sleeping? Not really paying due attention to the use made of its artifacts?"

"You're being cryptic again, Merlin."

"Sorry. Solitude does that to you."

"Did you meet someone out there, Merlin – someone who knew about the gun, and told you where to find it?" And made you young in the process? she thought.

"My business, isn't it?"

"Maybe once. Now, I'd say we're in this together. Equal partners. Fair enough?"

"Nothing's fair in war, Sora." But he was smiling, defusing the remark, even as he slipped his helmet down over the neck ring, twisting it to engage the locking mechanism.

"How big is the gun?" Sora asked.

The pyramid rose ahead, blank as an origami sculpture, entrance ducts around the base concealed by intervening landforms. Merlin's proctors had already found a route that would at least take them some way inside.

"You won't be disappointed," Merlin said.

"And what are we going to do when we find it? Just drag it behind us?"

"Trust me." Merlin's laugh crackled over the radio. "Moving it won't be a problem."

They walked slowly along a track cleared by proctors, covered at the same time by the hull-mounted weapons on *Tyrant*.

"There's something ahead," Merlin said, a few minutes later. He raised his own weapon and pointed toward a pool of darkness fifteen or twenty meters in front of them. "It's artifactual; definitely metallic."

"I thought your proctors cleared the area."

"Looks like they missed something."

Merlin advanced ahead of her. As they approached the dark object, it resolved into an elongated form half buried in the ice, a little to the left of the track. It was a body.

"Been here a while," Merlin said, a minute or so later, when he was close enough to see the object properly. "Armor's pitted by micrometeorite impacts."

"It's a Husker, isn't it."

Merlin's helmet nodded. "My guess is they were in this system a few centuries ago. Must have been attracted by the pyramid, even if they didn't necessarily know its significance."

"I've never seen one this close. Be careful, won't you?

Merlin knelt down to examine the creature.

The shape was much more androform than Sora had been expecting, the same general size and proportions as a suited human. The suit was festooned with armored protrusions, ridges, and horns, its blackened outer surface leathery and devoid of anything genuinely mechanical. One arm was outspread, terminating in a human-looking hand, complexly gauntleted. A long knobby weapon lay just out of reach, lines blurred by the same processes of erosion that had afflicted the Husker.

Merlin clamped his hands around the head.

"What are you doing?"

"What does it look like?" He was twisting now; she could hear the grunts of exertion, before his suit's servosystems came online and took the brunt of the effort. "I've always wanted to find one this well-preserved," Merlin said. "Never thought I'd get a chance to tell if an old rumor was even half-way right."

The helmet detached from the creature's torso, cracking open along a fine seam which ran from the crown to the beaklike protrusion at the helmet's front. Vapor pulsed from the gap. Merlin placed the separated halves of the helmet on the ground, then tapped on his helmet torch, bringing light down on the exposed head. Sora stepped closer. The Husker's head was encased in curling matte-black support machinery, like a statue enveloped in vine.

But it was well preserved, and very human.

"I don't like it," she said. "What does it mean?"

"It means," Merlin said, "that occasionally one should pay proper attention to rumors."

"Talk to me, Merlin. Start telling me what I need to hear, or we don't take another step toward that pyramid."

"You will like very little of it."

She looked, out of the corner of her eye, at the marblelike face of the Husker. "I already don't like it, Merlin; what have I got to lose?"

Merlin started to say something, then fell to the ground, executing the fall with the slowness that came with the moon's feeble gravity.

"Oh, nice timing," the familiar said.

Reflexes drove Sora down with him, until the two of them were crouching low on the rusty surface. Merlin was still alive. She could hear him breathing, but each breath came like the rasp of a saw.

"I'm hit, Sora. I don't know how badly."

"Hold on." She accessed the telemetry from his suit, graphing up a medical diagnostic on the inner glass of her helmet.

"There," said the familiar. "A beam-weapon penetration in the thoracic area; small enough that the self-sealants prevented any pressure loss, but not rapidly enough to stop the beam gnawing into his chest."

"Is that bad?"

"Well, it's not good . . . but there's a chance the beam would have cauterized as it traveled, preventing any deep internal bleeding. . . ."

Merlin coughed. He managed to ask her what it was.

"You've taken a laser hit, I think." She was speaking quickly. "Maybe part of the pyramid defenses."

"I really should have those proctors of mine checked out." Merlin managed a laugh which then transitioned into a series of racking coughs. "Bit late for that now, don't you think?"

"If I can get you back to the ship . . ."

"No. We have to go on." He coughed again, and then was a long time catching his breath. "The longer we wait, the harder it will be."

"After ten thousand years, you're worried about a few minutes?"

"Yes, now that the pyramid defenses are alerted."

"You're in no shape to move."

"I'm winded, that's all. I think I can . . ." His voice dissolved into coughs, but even while it was happening, Sora watched him push himself upright. When he spoke again, his voice was hardly a wheeze. "I'm gambling there was only one of whatever it was. Otherwise we should never have made it as far as we did."

"I hope you're right, Merlin."

"There's – um – something else. Ship's just given me a piece of not entirely welcome news. A few neutrino sources that weren't there when we first got here."

"Oh, great." Sora didn't need to be told what that meant: a Husker swarm, one that had presumably been waiting around the gas giant all along, chilled down below detection thresholds. "Bastards must have been sleeping, waiting for something to happen here."

"Sounds like a perfectly sensible strategy," the familiar said, before projecting a map onto Sora's faceplate, confirming the arrival of the enemy ships. "One of the moons has a liquid ocean. My guess is that the Huskers were parked below the ice."

Sora asked Merlin: "How long before they get here?"

"No more than two or three hours."

"Right. Then we'd better make damn sure we've got that gun by then, right?"

She carried him most of the way, his heels scuffing the ground in a halfhearted attempt at locomotion. But he remained lucid, and Sora began to hope that the wound really had been cauterized by the beam-weapon.

"You knew the Husker would be human, didn't you?" she said, to keep him talking.

"Told you: rumors. The alien cyborg story was just that – a fiction our own side invented. I told you it wouldn't be xeno-cide."

"Not good enough, Merlin." She was about to tell him about the symbiote in her head, then drew back, fearful that it would destroy what trust he had in her. "I know you've been lying. I hacked your ship's log."

They had reached the shadow of the pyramid, descending the last hillock toward the access ports spaced around the rim.

"Thought you trusted me."

"I had to know if there was a reason *not* to. And I think I was right."

She told him what she had learnt; that he'd been traveling for longer than he had told her – whole decades longer, by shiptime – and that he had grown old in that journey, and perhaps a little insane. And then how he had seemed to find the Brittlestar.

"Problem is, Merlin, we – *I* – don't know what happened to you in that thing, except that it had something to do with finding the gun, and you came out of it younger than when you went in!"

"You really want to know?"

"Take a guess."

He started telling her some of it, while she dragged him toward their destination.

The pyramid was surrounded by tens of meters of self-repairing armor, white as bone. If the designers had not allowed deliberate entrances around its rim, Sora doubted that she and Merlin would ever have found a way to get inside.

"Should have been sentries here, once," said the man leaning against her shoulder. "It's lucky for us that everything falls apart, eventually."

"Except your fabled gun." They were moving down a sloping corridor, the walls and ceiling unblemished, the floor strewn with icy debris from the moon's surface. "Anyway, stop changing the subject."

Merlin coughed and resumed his narrative. "I was getting very old and very disillusioned. I hadn't found the gun and I was about ready to give up. That or go insane. Then I found the Brittlestar. Came out of the Waynet and there it was, sitting there pulsing gravity waves at me."

"It would take a pair of neutron stars," the familiar said. "Orbiting around each other, to generate that kind of signature."

"What happened next?" Sora asked.

"Don't really remember. Not properly. I went – or was taken – inside it – and there I met . . ." He paused, and for a moment she thought it was because he needed to catch his breath. But that wasn't the reason. "I met *entities*, I suppose you'd call them. I quickly realized that they were just highly advanced projections of a maintenance program left behind by the Waymakers."

"They made you young, didn't they."

"I don't think it was stretching their capabilities overmuch, put it like that."

The corridor flattened out, branching in several different directions. Merlin leant toward one of the routes.

"Why?"

"So I could finish the job. Find the gun."

The corridor opened out into a chamber, a bowl-ceilinged

control room, unpressurized and lit only by the wavering light of their helmets. Seats and consoles were arrayed around a single spherical projection device, cradled in ash-colored gimbals. Corpses slumped over some of the consoles, but nothing remained except skeletons draped in colorless rags. Presumably they had rotted away for centuries before the chamber was finally opened to vacuum, and even that would have been more than twenty thousand years ago.

"They must have been attacked by a bioweapon," Merlin said, easing himself into one of the seats, which – after exhaling a cloud of dust – seemed able to take his weight. "Something that left the machines intact."

Sora walked around, examining the consoles, all of which betrayed a technology higher than anything the Cohort had known for millennia. Some of the symbols on them were recognizable antecedents of those used in Main, but there was nothing she could actually read.

Merlin made a noise that might have been a grunt of suppressed pain, and when Sora looked at him, she saw that he was spooling the optical cable from his suit sleeve, just as he had when they had first met on the cometary shard. He lifted an access panel back on the top of the console, exposing an intestinal mass of silvery circuits. He seemed to know exactly where to place the end of the spool, allowing its microscopic cilia to tap into the ancient system.

The projection chamber was warming to life now: amber light swelling from its heart, solidifying into abstract shapes, neutral test representations. For a moment, the chamber showed a schematic of the ringed giant and its moons, with the locations of the approaching Husker ships marked with complex ideograms. The familiar was right: their place of sanctuary must have been the moon with the liquid ocean. Then the shapes flowed liquidly, zooming in on the gas giant.

"You wanted to know where the gun was," Merlin said. "Well, I'm about to show you."

The view enlarged on a cyclonic storm near the planet's equator, a great swirling red eye in the atmosphere.

"It's a metastable storm," Sora said. "Common feature of gas giants. You're not telling me—"

Merlin's gauntleted fingers were at work now, flying across an array of keys marked with symbols of unguessable meaning.

"The storm's natural, of course, or at least it was, before these people hid the gun inside it, exploiting the pressure differentials to hold the gun at a fixed point in the atmosphere, for safe-keeping. There's just one small problem."

"Go ahead . . ."

"The gun isn't a gun. It functions as weapon, but that's mostly accidental. It certainly wasn't the intention of the Waymakers."

"You're losing me, Merlin."

"Maybe I should tell you about the ring."

Something was happening to the surface of the gas giant now. The cyclone was not behaving in the manner of other metastable storms Sora had seen. It was spinning perceptibly, throwing off eddies from its curlicued edge like the tails of seahorses. It was growing a bloodier red by the second.

"Yes," Sora said. "Tell me about the ring."

"The Waymakers gave it to me, when they made me young. It's a reminder of what I have to do. You see, if I fail, it will be very bad for every thinking creature in this part of the galaxy. What did you see when you looked at the ring, Sora?"

"A red gem, with two lights orbiting inside it."

"Would you be surprised if I told you that the lights represent two neutron stars; two of the densest objects in the universe? And that they're in orbit about each other, spinning around their mutual center of gravity?"

"Inside the Brittlestar."

She caught his glance, directed quizzically toward her. "Yes," Merlin said slowly. "A pair of neutron stars, born in supernovae, bound together by gravity, slowly spiraling closer and closer to each other."

The cyclonic storm was whirling insanely now, sparks of subatmospheric lightning flickering around its boundary. Sora had the feeling that titanic – and quite inhuman – energies were being unleashed, as if something very close to magic was being deployed beneath the clouds. It was the most terrifying thing she had ever seen.

"I hope you know how to fire this when the time comes, Merlin."

"All the knowledge I need is carried by the ring. It taps into my bloodstream and builds structures in my head that tell me exactly what I need to know, on a level so deep that I hardly know it myself."

"Husker swarm will be within range in ninety minutes," the familiar said, "assuming attack profiles for the usual swarm boser and charm-torp weapon configurations. Of course, if they have any refinements, they might be in attack range a little sooner than that . . ."

"Merlin: tell me about the neutron stars, will you? I need something to keep my mind occupied."

"The troublesome part is what happens when they *stop* spiraling around each other and *collide*. Mercifully, it's a fairly rare event even by Galactic standards – it doesn't happen more than once in a million years, and when it does it's usually far enough away not to be a problem."

"But if it isn't far away – how troublesome would it be?"

"Imagine the release of more energy in a second than a typical star emits in ten billion years: one vast photo-leptonic fireball. An unimaginably bright pulse of gamma-rays. Instant sterilization for thousands of light-years in any direction."

The cyclone had grown a central bulge now, a perfectly circular bruise rising above the surface of the planet. As it rose, towering thousands of kilometers above the cloud layer, it elongated like a waterspout. Soon, Sora could see it backdropped against space. And there was something rising within it.

"The Waymakers tried to stop it, didn't they."

Merlin nodded. "They found the neutron star binary when they extended the Waynet deeper into the galaxy. They realized that the two stars were only a few thousand years from colliding together – and that there was almost nothing they could do about it."

She could see what she thought was the weapon, now, encased in the waterspout like a seed. It was huge – larger perhaps than this moon. It looked fragile, nonetheless, like an impossibly ornate candelabra, or a species of deep sea medusa, glowing with its own bioluminescence. Sloughing atmosphere, the thing came to a watchful halt, and the waterspout slowly retracted back toward the cyclone, which was now slowing, like a monstrous fly wheel grinding down.

"Nothing?"

"Well – almost nothing."

"They built the Brittlestar around it," Sora said. "A kind of shield, right? So that, when the stars collided, the flash would be contained?"

"Not even Waymaker science could contain that much energy." Merlin looked to the projection, seeming to pay attention to the weapon for the first time. If he felt any elation on seeing his gun for the first time, none of it was visible on his face. He looked, instead, ashen – as if the years had suddenly reclaimed what the Waymakers had given him. "All they could do was keep the stars in check, keep them from spiraling any closer. So they built the Brittlestar, a vast machine with only one function: to constantly nudge the orbits of the neutron stars at its heart. For every angstrom that the stars fell toward each other, the Brittlestar pushed them an angstrom apart. And it was designed to keep doing that for a million years, until the Waymakers found a way to shift the entire binary beyond the Galaxy. You want to know how they kept pushing them apart?"

Sora nodded, though she thought she half-knew the answer already.

"Tiny black holes," Merlin said. "Accelerated close to the speed of light, each black hole interacting gravitationally with the binary before evaporating in a puff of pair-production radiation."

"Just the same way the gun functions. That's no coincidence, is it?"

"The gun – what we call the gun – was just a component in the Brittlestar; the source of relativistic black holes needed to keep the neutron stars from colliding."

Sora looked around the room. "And these people stole it?"

"Like I said, they were closer to the Waymakers than us. They knew enough about them to dismantle part of the Brittlestar, to override its defenses and remove the mechanism they needed to win their war."

"But the Brittlestar . . ."

"Hasn't been working properly ever since. Its capability to regenerate itself was harmed when the subsystem was stolen, and the remaining black-hole generating mechanisms can't do all the work required. The neutron stars have continued to spiral closer together – slowly but surely."

"But you said they were only a few thousand years from collision . . ."

Merlin had not stopped working the controls in all this time. The gun had come closer, seemingly oblivious to the ordinary laws of celestial mechanics. Down below, the planetary surface had returned to normality, except for a ruddier hue to the storm.

"Maybe now," Merlin said, "you're beginning to understand why I want the gun so badly."

"You want to return it, don't you. You never really wanted to find a weapon."

"I did, once." Merlin seemed to tap some final reserve of energy, his voice growing momentarily stronger. "But now I'm older and wiser. In less than four thousand years the stars meet, and it suddenly won't matter who wins this war. We're like ignorant armies fighting over a patch of land beneath a rumbling volcano!"

Four thousand years, Sora thought. More time had passed since she had been born.

"If we don't have the gun," she said, "we die anyway – wiped out by the Huskers. Not much of a choice, is it?"

"At least *something* would survive. Something that might even still think of itself as human."

"You're saying that we should capitulate? That we get our hands on the ultimate weapon, and then not *use* it?"

"I never said it was going to be easy, Sora." Merlin pitched forward, slowly enough that she was able to reach him before he slumped into the exposed circuitry of the console. His coughs were loud in her helmet. "Actually, I think I'm more than winded," he said, when he was able to speak at all.

"We'll get you back to the ship; the proctors can help . . ."

"It's too late, Sora."

"What about the gun?"

"I'm . . . doing something rather rash, in the circumstances. Trusting it to you. Does that sound utterly insane?"

"I'll betray you. I'll give the gun to the Cohort. You know that, don't you?"

Merlin's voice was soft. "I don't think you will. I think you'll do the right thing and return it to the Brittlestar."

"Don't make me betray you!"

He shook his head. "I've just issued a command that reassigns control of my ship to you. The proctors are now under your command – they'll show you everything you need."

"Merlin, I'm begging you . . ."

His voice was weak now, hard to distinguish from the scratchy irregularity of his breathing. She leant down to him and touched helmets, hoping the old trick would make him easier to hear. "No good, Sora. Much too late. I've signed it all over."

"No!" She shook him, almost in anger. Then she began to cry, loud enough so that she was in no doubt he would hear it. "I don't even know what you want me to do with it!"

"Take the ring, then the rest will be abundantly clear."

"What?" She could hardly understand herself now.

"Put the ring on. Do it now, Sora. Before I die. So that I at least know it's done."

"When I take your glove off, I'll kill you, Merlin. You know that, don't you? And I won't be able to put the ring on until I'm back in the ship."

"I . . . just want to see you take it. That's enough, Sora. And you'd better be quick . . ."

"I love you, you bastard!"

"Then do this."

She placed her hands around the cuff seal of his gauntlet, feeling the alloy locking mechanism, knowing that it would only take a careful depression of the sealing latches, and then a quick twisting movement, and the glove would slide free, releasing the air in his suit. She wondered how long he would last before consciousness left him – no more than tens of seconds, she thought, unless he drew breath first. And by the state of his breathing, that would not be easy for him.

She removed the gauntlet, and took his ring.

*Tyrant* lifted from the moon.

"Husker forces grouping in attack configuration," the familiar said, tapping directly into the ship's avionics. "Hull sensors read sweeps by targeting lidar . . . an attack is imminent, Sora."

*Tyrant*'s light armor would not save them, Sora knew. The attack would be blinding and brief, and she would probably never know it had happened. But that didn't mean that she was going to *let* it happen.

She felt the gun move to her will.

It would not always be like this, she knew: the gun was only hers until she returned it to the Waymakers. But for now it felt like an inseparable part of her, like a twin she had never known, but whose every move was familiar to her fractionally in advance of it being made. She felt the gun energize itself, reaching deep into the bedrock of spacetime, plundering mass-energy from quantum foam, forging singularities in its heart.

She felt readiness.

"First element of swarm has deployed charm-torps," the familiar reported, an odd slurred quality entering her voice. "Activating *Tyrant*'s countermeasures . . ."

The hull rang like a bell.

"Countermeasures engaging charm-torps . . . neutralized . . . second wave deployed by the swarm . . . closing . . ."

"How long can we last?"

"Countermeasures exhausted . . . we can't parry a third wave; not at this range."

Sora closed her eyes and made the weapon spit death.

She had targeted two of the three elements of the Husker swarm; leaving the third – the furthest ship from her – unharmed.

She watched the relativistic black holes fold space around the two targeted ships, crushing each instantly, as if in a vice.

"Third ship dropping to max . . . maximum attack range; retracting charm-torp launchers . . ."

"This is Sora for the Cohort," she said in Main, addressing the survivor on the general ship-to-ship channel. "Or what remains of the Cohort. Perhaps you can understand what I have to say. I could kill you, now, instantly, if I chose." She felt the weapon speak to her through her blood, reporting its status, its eagerness to do her bidding. "Instead, I'm about to give you a demonstration. Are you ready?"

"Sora . . ." said the familiar. "Something's wrong . . ."

"What?"

"I'm not . . . well." The familiar's voice did not sound at all right now; drained of any semblance to Sora's own. "The ring must be constructing something in your brain; part of the interface between you and the gun . . . something stronger than me . . . It's weeding me out, to make room for itself . . ."

She remembered what Merlin had said about the structures the ring would make.

"You saved a part of yourself in the ship."

"Only a part," the familiar said. "Not all of me . . . not all of me at all. I'm sorry, Sora. I think I'm dying."

She dismantled the system.

Sora did it with artistry and flair, saving the best for last. She began with moons, pulverizing them, so that they began to flow into nascent rings around their parent worlds. Then she smashed the worlds themselves to pieces, turning them into cauls of hot ash and plasma. Finally – when it was the only thing left to destroy – she turned the gun on the system's star, impaling its heart with a salvo of relativistic black holes, throwing a killing spanner into the nuclear processes that turned mass into sunlight. In doing so, she interfered – catastrophically – with the delicate hydrostatic balance between pressure and gravity that held the star in shape. She watched it unpeel, shedding layers of outer atmosphere in a premature display of the death that awaited suns like it, four billion years in the future. And then she watched the last Husker ship, which had witnessed what she had wrought, turn and head out of the system.

She could have killed them all.

But she had let them live. Instead, she had shown the power that was – albeit temporarily – hers to command.

She wondered if there was enough humanity left in them to appreciate the clemency she had shown.

Later, she took *Tyrant* into the Waynet again, the vast luminous bulk of the gun following her like an obedient dragon. Sora's heart almost stopped at the fearful moment of entry, convinced that the syrinx would choose not to sing for its new master.

But it did sing, just as it had sung for Merlin.

And then, alone this time – more alone than she had been in her life – she climbed into the observation blister, and turned the metasapphire walls transparent, making the ship itself disappear, until there was only herself and the rushing, twinkling brilliance of the Way.

It was time to finish what Merlin had begun.

# DEATH IN THE PROMISED LAND

## Pat Cadigan

*I really wish I had more work by women writers in this anthology. It wasn't for want of looking but somehow each time a story grabbed me as being just right for this book, it turned out to be written by a man. Except this one – and in fact this was the very first story I decided must be included. Cadigan (b. 1953) has been a full-time writer since 1987 but for ten years before that, while working for the Hallmark Company, was involved as an editor on the small press ma-gazines* Chacal *and* Shayol, *the latter still one of the most beautiful magazines ever published. Here appeared some of her earliest work including "Last Chance for Angina Pectoris at Miss Sadie's Saloon, Dry Gulch" (1977) which gave a good idea of the unconventional route her fiction would follow. She has been hailed as the "Queen of Cyberpunk" following her novel* Synners *(1991) which showed the potential dangers of becoming too closely involved in virtual reality. The following story has the same basis. Parts of it were later reworked into the novel* Tea from an Empty Cup *(1998), which had a sequel in* Dervish is Digital *(2001), both excellent examples of merging cyberpunk with the detective genre. But here, in all its glory, is the original full-length story.*

The kid had had his choice of places to go – other countries, other worlds, even other universes, à la the legendary exhortation of e. e. cummings, oddly evocative in its day, spookily prescient now. But the kid's idea of a hell of a good universe next door had been a glitzed-out, gritted-up, blasted and blistered post-Apocalyptic Noo Yawk Sitty. It wasn't a singular sentiment – post-Apocalyptic Noo Yawk Sitty was topping the hitline for the thirteenth week in a row, with post-Apocalyptic Ellay and post-Apocalyptic Hong Kong holding steady at two and three, occasionally trading places but defending against all comers.

Dore Konstantin didn't understand the attraction. Perhaps the kid could have explained it to her if he had not come out of post-Apocalyptic Noo Yawk Sitty with his throat cut.

Being DOA after a session in the Sitty wasn't singular, either; immediate information available said that this was number eight in as many months. So far, no authority was claiming that the deaths were related, although no one was saying they weren't, either. Konstantin wasn't sure what any of it meant, except that, at the very least, the Sitty would have one more month at the number one spot.

The video parlor night manager was boinging between appalled and thrilled. "You ever go in the Sitty?" she asked Konstantin, crowding into the doorway next to her. Her name was Guilfoyle Pleshette and she didn't make much of a crowd; she was little more than a bundle of sticks wrapped in a gaudy kimono, voice by cartoonland, hair by van der Graaf. She stood barely higher than Konstantin's shoulder, hair included.

"No, never have," Konstantin told her, watching as DiPietro and Celestine peeled the kid's hotsuit off him for the coroner. It was too much like seeing an animal get skinned, only grislier, and not just because most of the kid's blood was on the hotsuit. Underneath, his naked flesh was imprinted with a dense pattern of lines and shapes, byzantine in complexity, from the wires and sensors in the 'suit.

*Yes, it's the latest in nervous systems*, Konstantin imagined a chatty lecturer's voice saying. *The neo-exo-nervous system, generated by hotsuit coverage. Each line and shape has its counterpart on the opposite side of the skin barrier, which cannot at this time be breached under pain of* –

The imaginary lecture cut off as the coroner's cam operator leaned in for a shot of the kid's head and shoulders, forcing the stringer from *Police Blotter* back against the facing wall. Unperturbed, the stringer held her own cam over her head, aimed the lens downward and kept taping. This week, *Police Blotter* had managed to reverse the injunction against commercial networks that had been reinstated last week. Konstantin couldn't wait for next week.

As the 'suit cleared the kid's hips, the smell of human waste fought with the heavy odor of blood and the sour stink of sweat for control of the air in the room, which wasn't much larger than the walk-out closet that Konstantin had shared with her ex. The closet had looked a lot bigger this morning now that her ex's belongings were gone, but this room seemed to be shrinking by the moment. The coroner, her cam operator, the stringer, and DiPietro and Celestine had all come prepared with nasal filters; Konstantin's were sitting in the top drawer of her desk.

Putting her hand over her nose and mouth, she stepped back into the hallway where her partner Taliaferro was also suffering, but from the narrow space and low ceiling rather than the air, which was merely over-processed and stale. Pleshette followed, fishing busily in her kimono pockets.

"So *bad*," she said, looking from Konstantin to Taliaferro. Taliaferro gave no indication that he had heard her. He stood with his back to the wall and his shoulders up around his ears, head thrust forward over the archiver while he made notes, as if he expected the ceiling to come down on him. From Konstantin's angle, the archiver was completely hidden by his hand, so that he seemed to be using the stylus directly on his palm.

*Never send a claustrophobe to do an agoraphobe's job*, Konstantin thought, feeling surreal. Taliaferro, who pronounced his name "tolliver" for reasons she couldn't fathom, was such a big guy anyway that she wondered if most places short of an arena didn't feel small and cramped to him.

"*Real* goddam *bad*," Pleshette added, as if this somehow clarified her original statement. One bony hand came up out of a hidden pocket with a small spritzer; a too-sweet, minty odor cut through the flat air.

Taliaferro's stylus froze as his eyes swiveled to the manager. "That didn't help," he said darkly.

"Oh, but wait," she said, waving both hands to spread the scent. "Smellin' the primer now, but soon, *nothing*. Deadens the nose, use it by the *pound* here. Trade puts out a *lot* of body smell in the actioners. 'Suits *reek*." She gestured at the other doors lining the long narrow hall. "Like that *Gang Wars* module? Strapped the trade down on chaises, otherwise they'd a killed the 'suits, rollin' around on the floor, bouncin' offa the walls, jumpin' on each other. Real easy to go native in a *Gang Wars* module."

*Go native?* Taliaferro mouthed, looking at Konstantin from under his brows. Konstantin shrugged. "I didn't see a chaise in there."

"Folds down outa the wall: Like those old Murphy beds?"

Konstantin raised her eyebrows, impressed that she was even acquainted with the idea of Murphy beds, and then felt mildly ashamed. Her ex had always told her that being a snob was her least attractive feature.

"Most people don't use the chaises except for the sexers," Pleshette was saying. "Not if they got a choice. And there was this one blowfish, he hurt himself on the *chaise*. Got all heated up struggling, cut himself on the straps, broke some ribs. And *that*—" she leaned toward Konstantin confidentially "– *that* wasn't even the *cute* part. Know what the *cute* part was?"

Konstantin shook her head.

"The *cute* part was, his pov was in this fight at the *exact, same time* and broke the *exact, same ribs*." Pleshette straightened up and folded her arms, lifting her chin defiantly as if daring Konstantin to disbelieve. "This's *always* been non-safe, even before it was fatal."

"That happen here?" Taliaferro asked without looking up.

"Nah, some other place. East Hollywood, North Hollywood, I don't remember now." The manager's kimono sleeve flapped like a wing as she gestured. "We all heard about it. Stuff gets around."

Konstantin nodded, biting her lip so she wouldn't smile. "Uh-huh. Is this the same guy who didn't open his parachute in a skydiving scenario and was found dead with every bone in his body shattered?"

"Well, of *course* not." Pleshette looked at her as if she were crazy. "How could it be? *That* blowfish *died*. We all heard about that one too. Happened in D.C. They got it going on in D.C. with those sudden-death thrillers." She leaned toward Konstantin again, putting one scrawny hand on her arm this time. "You oughta check D.C. sources for death-trips. Life's so cheap there. It's a whole different world."

Konstantin was trying to decide whether to agree with her or change the subject when the coroner emerged from the cubicle with the cam op right on her heels.

"– shot everything *I* shot," the cam op was saying unhappily.

"And I said never *mind*." The coroner waved a dismissive hand. "We can subpoena her footage and see if it really is better than yours. Probably isn't. *Go*." She gave him a little push.

"But I just *know* she's in some of my shots—"

"We can handle that, too. *Go. Now*." The coroner shooed him away and turned to Konstantin. She was a small person, about the size of a husky ten-year-old – something to do with her religion, Konstantin remembered, the Church of Small-Is-Beautiful. The faithful had their growth inhibited in childhood. Konstantin wondered what happened to those who lost the faith, or came to it later in life.

"Well, I can say without fear of contradiction that the kid's throat was cut while he was still alive." The coroner looked around. "And in a palace like this. Imagine that."

"Should I also imagine how?" Konstantin asked.

The coroner smoothed down the wiry copper cloud that was her current hair. It sprang back up immediately. "Onsite micro says it was definitely a knife or some other metal with an edge, and not glass or porcelain. And definitely not self-inflicted. Even if we couldn't tell by the angle, this kid was an AR softie. He wouldn't have had the strength to saw through his own windpipe like that."

"What kind of knife, do you think?"

"Sharp and sturdy, probably a boning blade. Boning blades're all the rage out there. Or rather, *in* there. In the actioners. They all like those boning blades."

Konstantin frowned. "Great. You know what's going to be on the news inside an hour."

The coroner fanned the air with one small hand. "Yeah, yeah, yeah. Gameplayers' psychosis, everybody's heard about somebody who got stabbed in a module and came out with a knife-wound it took sixteen stitches to close and what about the nun who was on TV with the bleeding hands and feet. It's part of the modern myth-making machine. There've been some people who went off their perch in AR, got all mixed up about what was real and hurt themselves or somebody else. But the stigmata stuff –

everybody conveniently forgets how the stigmata of Sister-Mary-Blood-Of-The-Sacred-Whatever got exposed as a hoax by her own order. The good sister did a turn as a stage magician before she got religion. There's a file about how she did it floating around PubNet – you oughta look it up. Fascinatin' rhythms. The real thing would be *extremo ruptura*, very serious head trouble, which the experts are pretty sure nobody's had since St Theresa."

"Which one?" asked Konstantin.

The coroner chuckled. "That's good. 'Which one?'" She shook her head, laughing some more. "I'll have my report in your in-box tomorrow." She went up the hall, still laughing.

"Well," said the night manager, sniffing with disdain. "*Some* people ought better stick with what they know than mock what they *don't know squat about*."

"My apologies if she offended your beliefs," Konstantin said to her. "Is there some other way into that room that nobody knows about – vents, conduits, emergency exit or access?"

Pleshette wagged her fuzzy head from side to side. "Nope."

Konstantin was about to ask for the building's blueprints when Taliaferro snapped the archiver closed with a sound like a rifle shot. "Right. Some great place you got here. We'll interview the clientele now. Outside, in the parking lot."

"*Got* no parking lot," Pleshette said, frowning.

"Didn't say *your* parking lot. There's a car rental place down the block. We'll corral everyone, do it there." Taliaferro looked at Konstantin. "Spacious. Lots of room to move around in."

Konstantin sighed. "First let's weed out everyone who was in the same scenario and module with the kid and see if anyone remembers the kid doing or saying anything that could give any hints about what was happening to him." She started up the hall with Taliaferro.

"You could do that yourself, you know," Pleshette said.

Konstantin stopped. Taliaferro kept walking without looking back. "Do what?"

"See what the kid was doing when he took it in the neck. Surveillance'll have it."

"Surveillance?" Konstantin said, unsure that she had heard correctly.

"Of *course* surveillance," the night manager said, giving her a sideways look. "You think we let the blowfish come in here and don't keep an eye on them? *Anything* could happen, I don't want no liability for the bone in somebody else's head. Nobody does."

"Can I screen this surveillance record in your office?" she asked.

"Anywhere, if all you want to do is screen it." Pleshette frowned, puzzled.

"Good. Set me up for it in your office."

Pleshette's frown deepened. "My office."

"Is that some kind of problem?" asked Konstantin, pausing as she moved toward the open doorway of the room, where she could hear Di-Pietro and Celestine bantering with the stringer.

"Guess not." The night manager shrugged. "You just want to screen it, my office, sure."

Konstantin didn't know what to make of the look on Pleshette's funny little face. Maybe that was all it was, a funny little face in a funny little open-all-night world. A funny little open-all-night artificial world at that. For all Konstantin knew, the night manager hadn't seen true day-light for years. Not her problem, she thought as she stuck her head through the doorway of the cubicle where Celestine and DiPietro were now busy jockeying for the stringer's attention while the stringer pretended she wasn't pumping them for information and they pretended they didn't know she was pretending not to pump them for information. No one had to pretend the dead kid had been temporarily forgotten.

"Pardon me for interrupting," Konstantin said a bit archly. DiPietro and Celestine turned to her; in their identical white coveralls, they looked like unfinished marionettes.

"Attendants'll be coming for him. Before you do a thorough search of the room, you might want to, oh—" she gestured at the body "– cover *him* up."

"Sure thing," said Celestine, and then suddenly tossed something round and wrapped in plastic at her. "Think fast!"

Konstantin caught it by instinct. The shape registered on her before anything else. The kid's head, she thought, horrified. The cut across his throat had been so deep, it had come off when they'd peeled him.

Then she felt the metal through the plastic and realized it was the kid's head-mounted monitor. "Oh, good one, Celestine." She tucked the monitor under her left arm. "If I'd dropped that, we'd be filling out forms on it for a year."

"*You*, drop something? Not this lifetime." Celestine grinned; her muttonchops made her face seem twice as wide as it was. Konstantin wondered if there was such a thing as suing a cosmetologist for malpractice.

"Thanks for the act of faith but next time, save it for church." Konstantin went up the hall toward the main lobby, Pleshette following in a swish of kimono.

There were only two uniformed officers waiting in the lobby with the other three members of the night staff, who were perched side by side on a broken-down, ersatz-leather sofa by the front window. The rest of the police, along with the clientele, were already down the block with Taliaferro, one of the uniforms told Konstantin. She nodded, trying not to stare at the woman's neat ginger-colored mustache. At least it wasn't as ostentatious as Celestine's muttonchops, but she wasn't sure that she would ever get used to the fashion of facial hair on women. Her ex would have called her a throwback; perhaps she was.

"That's all right, as long as we know where they are." Konstantin handed her the bagged headmount. "Evidence – look after it. There's some surveillance footage I'm going to screen in the manager's office and I thought I'd question the staff there as well—" The people on the couch were gazing up at her expectantly. "Is this the entire night shift?"

"The whole kitten's caboodle," Pleshette assured her.

Konstantin looked around. It was a small lobby, no hiding places, and presumably, no secret doors. Small, drab, and depressing – after waiting here for even just a few minutes, any AR would look great by comparison. She turned back to the people on the couch just as the one in the middle stood up and stuck out his hand. "Miles Mank," he said in a hearty tenor.

Konstantin hesitated. The man's eyes had an unfocused, watery look to them she associated with people who weren't well. He towered over her by six inches and outweighed her by at least a hundred pounds. But they were fairly soft pounds, packed into a glossy blue one-piece uniform that, combined with those gooey eyes and his straw-colored hair, gave him a strangely childlike appearance. She shook his hand. "What's your job here?"

"Supervisor. Well, unofficial supervisor," he added, the strange eyes looking past her at Guilfoyle Pleshette. "I'm the one who's been here the longest so I'm always telling everybody else how things work."

"So go ahead, Miles," Pleshette said, her voice flat. The kimono sleeves snapped like pennants in a high wind as she stretched out her arms and refolded them. "Say it – that if they promoted from within here, *you'd* be night manager. Then I can explain how they had to go on a talent search for an *experienced* administrator. It'll all balance out."

"Nobody ever *died* while *I* was acting night manager," Miles Mank said huffily.

"Yeah, that's true – everybody survived that riot where the company had to refund all the customers. But nobody died so that made it all good-deal-well-done."

Miles Mank strode past Konstantin to loom over Pleshette, who had to reach up to shake her bony finger in his face. Konstantin felt that panicky chill all authorities felt when a situation was about to slip the leash. Before she could order Mank to stop arguing with Pleshette, the mustached officer tugged her sleeve and showed her a taser set on flash. "Shall I?"

Konstantin glanced at her nameplate. "Sure, Wolski, go ahead." She stepped back and covered her eyes.

The flash was a split-second heat that she found oddly comforting, though no one else did. Besides Guilfoyle Pleshette and Miles Mank, Wolski had also failed to warn her fellow officer, the other two employees, or Taliaferro, who had chosen that moment to step back inside. The noise level increased exponentially.

"*Everybody shut up!*" Konstantin yelled; to her surprise, everybody did. She looked around. All the people in the lobby except for herself and Wolski had their hands over their eyes. It looked like a convention of see-no-evil monkeys.

"I'm going to screen surveillance footage of the victim's final session in the manager's office, and then interview the rest of the staff," she announced and turned to Taliaferro. "Then I'd like to question anyone who was in the same module and scenario." She waited but he didn't take his hands from his eyes. "That means I'll be phoning you down the block, partner, to have select individuals escorted to the office." She waited another few seconds. "Understand, Taliaferro?" she added, exasperated.

"Let me do some prelims on the customers," he said, speaking to the air where he thought she was. He was off by two feet.

"They're gonna be getting restless while you're doing that. We're going to have to give them phone calls and pizza as it is."

Konstantin rolled her eyes. "So *give* them phone calls and pizza." She turned back to Pleshette. "Now, can you show me to your office?"

"Who, me?" asked Miles Mank. "I'm afraid I don't have one. I've been making do with the employee lounge."

"Suffer, Mank," Pleshette said, peeking between her fingers. "No one was talking to *you*." She started to lower her hands and then changed her mind.

Konstantin sighed. Their vision would return to normal in a few minutes, along with their complexions, assuming none of them suffered from light-triggered skin-rashes. Perhaps she should have been more sympathetic, but she didn't think any of them would notice if she were. She put her hand on Guilfoyle Pleshette's left arm. "Now, your office?"

"I'll show you," said Pleshette, "if I ever see well enough again."

Pleshette's office was smaller than the smelly cubicle where the kid had died, which was probably a good thing. It meant that Konstantin didn't throw anything breakable against the wall when she discovered the so-called surveillance footage was an AR log and not a live-action recording of the kid's murder. There would have been no point to throwing anything; unlike the living room where she and her ex had had their final argument, there wasn't enough distance to make a really satisfying smash.

She settled in to watch the video, every moment, including the instructional lead that told her that the only pov on monitor would be detached observer; she could use the editing option for any close-ups or odd angles, and there was a primer to pull down if she were feeling less than Fellini, or even D.W. Griffith.

How helpful, she thought, freezing the footage before the lead faded into the scenario. How excessively helpful. What was she supposed to do, decide how to edit the footage *before* she watched it?

But of course, she realized; this came under the heading of *Souvenirs*. Footage from your AR romp, video of your friend's wedding, pre-packaged quick-time scenics from a kiosk in the Lima airport for a last-minute gift before you boarded the flight home – you made it look however you wanted it to look. To whomever happened to be looking, of course. Maybe you didn't want it to look the same to everyone – a tamer version for one, something experimental to hold another's attention.

Konstantin tapped the menu line at the bottom of the screen. *Options?* it asked her, fanning them out in the center of a deep blue background. *Pick a card, any card,* she thought; *memorize it and slip it back into the deck. There'll be a quiz later, if you survive.* After a moment, she chose *No Frills.*

The image on the screen liquified and melted away into black. A moment later, she was looking at an androgynous face that suggested the best of India and Japan in combination. The name came up as Shantih Love, which she couldn't decide if she hated or not; the linked profile informed her that the Shantih Love appearance was as protected by legal copyright as the name. No age given; under *Sex* it said, *Any; all; why do you care?*

"Filthy job, Shantih, but somebody's got to." She tapped for the technical specs of the session. Full coverage hotsuit, of course; that would tell her when the kid had died. She scrolled past his scenario and module choices to Duration: four hours, twenty minutes. *Yow, kid, that alone could have killed some people.*

She tapped the screen for his vitals so she could note the exact time of death in the archiver. Then she just stared at the figures on the screen, tapping the stylus mindlessly on the desk.

Shantih Love, the specs told her, had shuffled off all mortal coils, artificial and otherwise, just ten minutes into his four-hour-and-twenty-minute romp in post-Apocalyptic Noo Yawk Sitty. It didn't say how he had managed to go on with his romp after he had died. She supposed that was too much to ask.

Shantih Love and the kid powering him/her had both had their throats cut, but for Shantih Love the wound had not been fatal. Disgusting and gory, even uncomfortable, but not fatal.

Konstantin watched the screen intently as the sequence faded in. In the middle of a glitter-encrusted cityscape at dusk, the androgyne made his/her way toward some kind of noisy party or tribal gathering on the rubble-strewn shore of the Hudson River. The rubble was also encrusted with glitter; more glitter twinkled on the glass of the silent storefronts on the other side of a broad, four-lane divided thoroughfare partially blocked by occasional islands of wreckage. As Shantih Love swept off the side-walk – ankle-length purple robe flowing gracefully with every step – and crossed the ruined street, one of the wrecks ignited, lighting up the semi-dark. Shantih Love barely glanced at it and kept going, toward the gathering on the shore; Konstantin could hear music and, under that, the white noise of many voices in conversation. What could they possibly have to talk about, she wondered; was it anything more profound than what you'd hear at any other party in any other reality with any other people? And if it were, why did it occur only in the reality of post-Apocalyptic Noo Yawk Sitty?

Shantih Love abruptly looked back in such a way that s/he seemed to be looking directly out of the screen into her eyes. The expression on the unique face seemed somehow both questioning and confident. Konstantin steered the detached perspective from behind Shantih Love around his/her right side, passing in front of the androgyne and moving to the left side, tracking him/her as s/he walked toward the multitude on the shore.

A figure suddenly popped up from behind the low concrete barrier running between the street and the river. Shantih Love stopped for a few moments, uncertainty troubling his/her smooth forehead. Konstantin tried adjusting the screen controls to see the figure better in the gathering darkness but, maddeningly, she couldn't seem to get anything more definite than a fuzzy, blurry silhouette, definitely human-like but otherwise unidentifiable as young or old, male, female, both or neither, friendly or hostile.

The shape climbed over the barrier to the street side just as Shantih Love slipped over it to the shore. The ground here was soft sand and Shantih Love had trouble walking in it. The fuzzy shape paced him/her on the other side of the wall and Konstantin got the idea that it was saying something, but nothing came up on audio. Shantih Love didn't answer, didn't even look in its direction again as s/he moved in long strides toward the crowd, which extended from the water's edge up to a break in the barrier and into the road.

The perspective had slipped back behind Shantih Love. Konstantin tapped the forward button rapidly; now she seemed to be perched on Shantih Love's right shoulder. The gathering on the beach appeared to be nothing more than a ragged, disorganized cocktail party, the sort of thing her ex had loved to attend. Konstantin was disappointed. Was this really all anyone in AR could think of doing?

Shantih Love whirled suddenly; after a one-second delay, the perspective followed. Konstantin felt a wave of dizziness and the images on the screen went out of focus.

When the focus cleared, Konstantin saw that the figure was standing on top of the barrier, poised to jump. Shantih Love backed away, turned, and began stumbling through the party crowd, bumping into various people, some less distinct than others. Konstantin didn't have to shift the perspective around to know that the creature was chasing the androgyne. Now the pov seemed to be a few inches in front of the creature's face; she had a few fast glimpses of bandage-wrapped arms and hands with an indeterminate number of fingers as it staggered into the party after Love.

The pov began to shake and streak, as if it were embedded in the pursuing creature's body. Frustrated, Konstantin pounded on the forward key, but the pov didn't budge. Someone had preordered the pov to this position, she realized. But whether it was the murdered kid who had done it or just the formatting she couldn't tell.

Worse, now that she was in the party crowd, almost every attendee was either so vague as to be maddeningly unidentifiable, or so much a broad type – barbarian, vampire, wild-child, homunculus – that anonymity was just as assured.

Shantih Love broke through the other side of the crowd two seconds before she did, and ran heavily toward a stony rise leading to the sidewalk. S/he scrambled up it on all fours, a heartbeat ahead of the pursuer.

Love vaulted the low barrier and ran along the middle of the street, looking eagerly at each wreck. There were more wrecks here, some ablaze, some not. Something moved inside each one, even those that were burning. Konstantin realized she was probably alone in finding that remarkable; living in a bonfire was probably the height of AR chic.

She tried pushing the pov ahead again and gained several feet. Shantih Love looked over his/her shoulder, seemingly right at the pov. The androgyne's expression was panic and dismay; in the next moment, s/he fell.

The pov somersaulted; there was a flash of broken pavement, followed by a brief panorama of the sky, a flip and a close-up of the androgyne's profile just as the pursuer pushed his/her chin up with one rag-wrapped hand. Perfect skin stretched taut; the blade flashed and disappeared as it turned sideways to slash through flesh, tendon, blood vessels, bone.

The blood flew against the pov and dripped downward, like

gory drops of rain on a window. Konstantin winced and pressed to try to erase the blood trails; nothing happened.

Shantih Love coughed and gargled at the sky, not trying to twist away from the bandaged hand that still held his/her chin. Blood pulsed upward in an exaggerated display of blood spurting from a major artery. The creature pushed Love's face to one side, away from the camera, and bent its head to drink.

Konstantin had seen similar kinds of things before in videos, including the so-called killer video that had supposedly been circulating underground (whatever *that* meant these days) and had turned out to be so blatantly phony that the perpetrators should have gone down for fraud.

But where the blood spilled in that and numerous other videos had looked more like cherry syrup or tomato puree, this looked real enough to make Konstantin gag. She put a hand over her mouth as she froze the screen and turned away, trying to breathe deeply and slowly through her nose, willing her nausea to fade. At the same time, she was surprised at herself. Her squeamish streak was usually conveniently dormant; in twelve years as a detective, she had seen enough real-time blood and gore that she could say she was somewhat hardened. Shantih Love's real-time counter-part – secret identity? veneer person? – had certainly bled enough to make anyone choke.

But there was something about this – the blood or the noises coming from Shantih Love, the sound of the creature drinking so greedily. Or maybe just the sight of such realistic blood activating the memory of that smell in the cubicle, that overpowering stench; that smell and the sight of the dead kid stripped of everything, skinned like an animal.

She collected herself and tried jabbing fast-forward to get through the vampiric sequence as quickly as possible. It only made everything more grotesque, so she took it back to normal just at the point where both the creature and the blood vanished completely.

Startled, Konstantin rewound and ran it again in slo-mo, just to make sure she'd seen it right. She had; it wasn't a fast fade-out or the twinkling deliquescence so favored by beginning cinema-tography students, but a genuine popper which usually happened by way of a real-time equipment failure or power-out. Common wisdom had it that the jump from AR to real-time in such an event was so abrupt as to produce extreme reactions of an undesirable nature – vertigo, projectile vomiting, fainting, or, worse, all three, which could be fatal if you happened to be alone.

*Or a slashed throat, if you happened to be not alone with the wrong person*, Konstantin thought, trying to rub the furrows out of her brow.

She repeated the sequence once more, and then again in slo-mo, watching the blood disappear right along with the creature, leaving Shantih Love behind. Konstantin called up the record of the kid's vitals and found that, as she had expected, they had quit registering at the moment the blood had disappeared.

Konstantin took her finger off the pause button and let the action go forward. On the screen, the Shantih Love character sat up, its elegant fingers feeling the ragged edges and flaps of skin where its throat had been cut, mild annoyance deepening the few lines in its face. As Konstantin watched it trying to pinch the edges of skin together, she was aware that she was now thinking of the kid's AR persona as a thing rather than a human.

Presumed "it" until proven human? Konstantin frowned. So what was driving *it* now, anyway – a robot, or a very human hijacker?

She could watch video for the next three hours and see if anything would become clearer to her; instead, she decided to talk to people she was reasonably sure were human before taking in any more adventures of a dead kid's false face pretending to be alive in a city pretending to be dead.

If the office had seemed cramped before, Miles Mank made it look even smaller by taking up at least half of it. When it became obvious that he actually knew next to nothing, Konstantin tried to get rid of him quickly, but he kept finding conversational hooks that would get her attention and then lead her along to some meaningless and boring point, at which he wouldn't so much conclude as change the subject and do it all over again. She was finally able to convince him that he was desperately needed at the parking lot to help sort out the clientele with her bewildered partner. Then she prayed that Taliaferro wouldn't use a similar excuse to send him back to her. She still didn't like his eyes.

The first of the other two employees was a silver-haired kid named Tim Mezzer, who was about the same age as the murder victim. He had the vaguely puzzled, preoccupied look of ex-addicts who had detoxed recently by having their blood cleansed.

Officially, it was a fast way out of an expensive jones. In fact, it made the high better on relapse.

"How long have you worked here?" Konstantin asked him.

"Three days." He sounded bored.

"And what do you do?" she prodded when he didn't say anything more.

"Oh, I'm a specialist," he said, even more bored. "I specialize in picking up everybody's smelly 'suit when they're done and get 'em cleaned." Mezzer put a plump elbow on the desk and leaned forward. "Tell the truth – you'd kill to have a job like that instead of the boring shit you do."

Konstantin wasn't sure he was really being sarcastic. "Sometimes. Did you know the victim?"

"Dunno. What was his name?"

"Shantih Love."

Mezzer grunted. "Good label. Must have cost him to come up with one that good. Sounds a little like an expensive female whore-assassin, but still pretty good. Someday I'll be rich enough to be able to afford a tailor-made label."

Konstantin was only half-listening while she prodded the archiver for the victim's reference file. "Ah, here we are. Real name is—" she stopped. "Well, that *can't* be right."

"Don't be so sure." Mezzer yawned. "What's it say?"

"Tomoyuki Iguchi," Konstantin said slowly, as if she had to sound out each syllable.

"Ha. Sounds like he was working on turning Japanese in a serious way."

"Why?"

"Well, for post-Apocalyptic Tokyo, of course." Mezzer sighed. "What else?"

"There's a post-Apocalyptic Tokyo now?" Konstantin asked suspiciously.

"Not yet." Mezzer's sigh became a yawn. "Coming soon. Supposed to be the next big hot spot. They say it's gonna make the Sitty look like Sunday in Nebraska, with these parts you can access only if you're Japanese, or a convincing simulation. It's the one everybody's been waiting for."

Konstantin wondered if he knew that something very like it had already come and gone a good many years before either of them had been born. "How about you?" she asked him. "Is it the one you've been waiting for?"

"I don't know from Japanese. I'm an Ellay boy. Got all those gorgeous celebs you can beat up in street gangs. But the bubble-up on this is, there's some kinda secret coming-attraction sub-routines for post-Apocalyptic Tokyo buried in the Noo Yawk, Hong Kong, and Ellay scenes and no non-Japanese can crack them. *If* they're really there. Shantih Love musta thought they were."

"But why would he take *two* fake names?" Konstantin wondered, more to herself.

"*Told* you – he was trying to turn Japanese. He wanted anyone who stripped his label to find his Japanese name underneath and take him for that. Invite him into the special Japan area." Mezzer put his head back as if he were going to bay at the moon and yawned once again. "Or he was getting that crazy-head. You know, where you start thinking it's real in there and fake out here, or you can't tell the difference. You need to talk to Body. Body'll know. Body's probably the only one who'd know for sure."

"What body?"

"Body Sativa. Body knows more about the top ten ARs than anyone else, real or not."

Konstantin felt her mouth twitch. "Don't you mean Cannabis Sativa?" she asked sarcastically.

Mezzer blinked at her in surprise. "Get *off*. Cannibal's her mother. She's good, but Body's the real Big Dipper." He smiled. "Pretty win, actually, that somebody like you'ud know about Cannibal Sativa. Were you goin' in to talk to her?"

Konstantin didn't know what to say.

"Go see Body, I swear she's the one you want. I'll give you some icons you can use in there. Real insider icons, not what they junk you up with in the help files."

"Thanks," Konstantin said doubtfully. "But I think I fell down about a mile back. If he was turning Japanese, as you put it, why would he call himself Shantih Love?"

Mezzer blinked. "Well, because he was tryin' to be a *Japanese* guy named Shantih Love." He frowned at her. "You just don't ever go in AR, do you?"

"Can't add to that," said the other employee cheerfully. She was an older woman named Howard Ruth with natural salt-and-pepper hair and lines in a soft face untouched by chemicals or surgery. Konstantin found her comforting to look at. "Body

Sativa's the best tip you're gonna get. You'll go through that whole bunch in the lot down the street and you won't hear anything more helpful." She sat back, crossing her left ankle over her right knee.

"Body Sativa wouldn't happen to be in that group, by any chance?"

Howard Ruth shrugged. "Doubt it. This is just another reception site on an AR network. Considering the sophisticated moves Body makes, she's most likely on from some singleton station, and that could be anywhere."

"Come on," said Konstantin irritably, "even *I* know everyone online has an origin code."

Howard Ruth's smile was sunny. "You haven't played any games lately, have you?"

Konstantin was thinking the woman should talk to her ex. "Online? No."

"No," agreed the woman, "because if you had, you'd know that netgaming isn't considered official net communication or transaction, so it's not governed by FCC or FDSA regulations. Get on, pick a name or buy a permanent label, stay as long as you like – or can afford – and log out when you've had enough. Netgaming is one hundred percent elective, so anything goes – no guidelines, no censorship, no crimes against persons. You can't file a complaint against anyone for assault, harassment, fraud, or anything like that."

Konstantin sighed. "I didn't know this. Why not?"

"You didn't have to." Howard Ruth laughed. "Look, officer—"

"Lieutenant."

"Sure, lieutenant. Unless you netgame regular, you *won't* know any of this. You ever hear about the case years back where a guy used an origin line to track down a woman in realtime and kill her?"

"No," said Konstantin with some alarm. "Where did this happen?"

"Oh, back east somewhere. D.C., I think, or some place like that. Life is so cheap there, you know. Anyway, what happened was, back when they had origin lines in gaming, this guy got mad at this woman, somehow found her by way of her origin line, and boom – lights out. That was one of the first cases of that gameplayer's madness where someone could prove it could be a real danger offline. After that, there was a court ruling that since gaming was strictly recreational, gamers were entitled to complete privacy if they wanted. No origin line. Kinda the same thing for fraud and advertising."

Konstantin felt her interest, which had started to wane with the utterance *D.C.*, come alive again. "What?"

"Guy ran a game-within-a-game on someone. I can't remember exactly what it was – beachfront in Kansas, diamond mines in Peru, hot stocks about to blow. Anyhow, the party of the second part got the idea it was all backed up in realtime and did this financial transfer to the party of the first part, who promptly logged out and went south. Party of the second part hollers *Thief!* and what do you know but the police catch this salesperson of the year. Who then claims that it was all a game and he thought the money was just a gift."

"And?" said Konstantin.

"And that's a wrap. Grand jury won't even indict, on grounds of extreme gullibility. As in, 'You were in *artificial reality*, you fool, what did you expect?' Personally, I think they were both suffering from a touch of the galloping headbugs."

Konstantin was troubled. "And that decision stood?"

"It's *artificial* reality – you can't lie, no matter what you say. It's all make-believe, let's-pretend, the play's the thing." Howard Ruth laughed heartily. "You choose to pay somebody out here for time in there, that's *your* hotspot. Life is so strange, eh?"

Konstantin made a mental note to check for court rulings on AR as she pressed for a clean page in the archiver. "But if being in an AR makes people insane . . ."

"Doesn't make *everyone* insane," the woman said. "That's what it is, you know. The honey factory don't close down just because you're allergic to bee stings."

Konstantin was still troubled. "So when did those things happen?" she asked, holding the stylus ready.

"I don't know," Howard Ruth said, surprised at the question. "Oughta be in the police files, though. Doesn't law enforcement have some kind of central-national-international bank you all access? Something like *Police Blotter?*"

"In spite of the name," Konstantin said, speaking slowly so the woman couldn't possibly misunderstand, "*Police Blotter* is actually a commercial net-magazine, and not affiliated with law enforcement in any official way. But yes, we do have our own national information center. *But* I need to know some kind of key fact that the search program can use to hunt down the information I want – a name, a date, a location." She paused to see if any of this was forthcoming. The other woman only shrugged.

"Well, sorry I can't be of more help, but that's all I know." She got up and stretched, pressing her hands into the small of her back. "If anyone knows more, it's Body Sativa."

"Body Sativa," said the first customer interviewee. He was an aging child with green hair and claimed his name was Earl O'Jelly. "Nobody knows more. Nobody and *no body*. If you get what I mean."

Konstantin didn't bury her face in her hands. The aging child volunteered the information that he had been in the crowd by the Hudson that Shantih Love had staggered through, but claimed he hadn't seen anything like what she described to him.

Neither had the next one, a grandmother whose AR alter-ego was a twelve-year-old boy-assassin named Nick the Schick. "That means I technically have to have 'the' as my middle name, but there's worse, and stupider as well," she told Konstantin genially. "Nick knows Body, of course. *Everybody* knows Body. And vice versa, probably. Actually, I think Body Sativa's just a database that got crossed with a traffic-switcher and jumped the rails."

"Pardon?" Konstantin said, not comprehending.

The grandmother was patient. "You know how files get cross-monkeyed? Just the thing – traffic-switcher was referencing the database in a thunderstorm, maybe sunspots, and they got sort of arc-welded. Traffic-switcher interface mutated from acquired characteristics from all the database entries. That's what *I* say, and *nobody's* proved yet that *that* couldn't happen. Or *didn't*." She nodded solemnly.

Konstantin opened her mouth to tell the woman that if she understood her correctly, what she was describing was akin to putting a dirty shirt and a pile of straw in a wooden box for spontaneous generation of mice and then decided against it. For one thing, she wasn't sure that she had understood correctly and for another, the shirt-and-straw method of creating mice was probably routine in AR.

There was no third interviewee. Instead, an ACLU lawyer came in and explained that since the crime had occurred in the real world, and all the so-called witnesses had been in AR, they weren't actually witnesses at all, and could not be detained any longer. However, all of their names would be available on the video parlor's customer list, which Konstantin could see as soon as she produced the proper court order.

"In the meantime, everyone agrees you ought to talk to this Body Sativa, whatever she is," the lawyer said, consulting a palmtop. "Assuming she'll give you so much as the time of day without legal representation."

"I suppose I need a court order for that, too," Konstantin grumbled.

"Not hardly. AR is open to anyone who wants to access it. Even you, Officer Konstantin." The lawyer grinned, showing diamond teeth. "Just remember the rules of admissibility. Everything everyone tells you in AR—"

"– is a lie, right. I got the short course tonight already." Konstantin's gaze strayed to the monitor, now blank. "I think I'll track this Body Sativa down in person and question her in realtime."

"Only if she voluntarily tells you who she is out here," the lawyer reminded her a bit smugly. "Otherwise, her privacy is protected."

"Maybe she'll turn out to be a good citizen," Konstantin mused. "Maybe she'll care that some seventeen-year-old kid got his throat cut."

The lawyer's smug expression became a sad smile. "Maybe. *I* care. *You* care. But there's no law that says anyone else has to."

"I know, and I'd be afraid if there was. Even so—" Konstantin frowned. "I do wish I didn't have to depend so much on volunteers."

She sent DiPietro and Celestine over to the dead kid's apartment building, though she wasn't expecting much. If he was typical, his neighbors would have barely been aware of him. Most likely, they would find he had been yet another gypsy worker of standard modest skills, taking temporary assignments via a city-run agency to support his various habits. Including his AR habit.

Just to be thorough, she waited in Guilfoyle Pleshette's office for the call letting her know that the other two detectives had found a generic one-room apartment with little in the way of furnishings or other belongings to distinguish it from any other generic one-room apartment in the city. Except for the carefully organized card library of past AR experiences in the dustless, static-free, moisture- and fire-proof non-magnetic light-shielded container. Every heavy AR user kept a library, so that no treasured moment could be lost to time.

The library would go to headquarters to be stored for the required ten-day waiting period while a caseworker tried to track down next-of-kin. If none turned up, the card library would then be accessed by an automated program designed to analyze the sequences recorded on each card and construct a profile of the person, which would then be added to the online obituaries. Usually this would cause someone who had known the deceased to come forward; other times, it simply confirmed that there was no one to care.

The idea came unbidden to Konstantin, derailing the semidoze she had slipped into at whatever indecent a.m. the night had become. She plugged the archiver into the phone and sent the retriever to fetch data on the other seven AR DOAs.

Delivery was all but immediate – at this time of night, there wasn't much data traffic. Konstantin felt mildly annoyed that DiPietro and Celestine couldn't report in just as quickly. Perhaps they had taken the stringer with them and were even now playing to the cam in an inspection of the dead kid's apartment.

A bit of heartburn simmered in her chest; she imagined it was her blood pressure going up a notch. According to *The Law Enforcement Officers' Guide To A Healthy, Happy Life (ON & OFF The Job!)*, sex was the number one stress reliever. The *Guide* had most likely meant the sort that involved one other person, Konstantin reflected and pushed away thoughts of her ex to survey the data arranging itself on the archiver's small but hi-res screen.

The first to suffer a suspicious death while in post-Apocalyptic Noo Yawk Sitty had been a thirty-four-year-old woman named Sally Lefkow. Her picture showed a woman so pale as to seem faded. She had passed most of her realtime hours as a third-rank senior on a Minneapolis janitorial team whose contract had included both the building where she had lived and the building where she had died. Konstantin wasn't sure whether to be amused, amazed, or alarmed that her online persona had been an evolved dragon; eight feet tall and the color of polished antique copper, it had been bi-sexual, able to switch at will. Sally Lefkow had died of suffocation; the evolved dragon had been in flight when it had suddenly fallen out of the sky into the East River, and never come up.

Konstantin put the dead woman's realtime background next to the information on the dragon to compare them but found she was having trouble retaining anything. "In one eye and out the other," she muttered, then winced. *Lover, come back. You forgot to take the in-jokes along with the rest of the emotional baggage.*

She marked the Lefkow-dragon combo and went on to the next victim, a twenty-eight-year-old gypsy office worker named Emilio Torres. Konstantin thought he looked more like an athlete. Or maybe an ex-athlete. He had died alone in his Portland apartment during an online session as – Konstantin blinked – Marilyn Presley. Even Konstantin had heard of Marilyn Presley. The hybrid had been an online flash-fad, hot for a day, passé forever after. But not, apparently, for Torres. He had persisted as Marilyn for six weeks, long after the rest of the flash followers had lost interest, and he had died – Konstantin blinked again – of an overdose of several drugs; the Marilyn Presley persona had gone inert in the middle of some sort of gathering that wasn't quite a street brawl but not really an open-air party, either. There was no follow-up on the persona, nothing to tell Konstantin if the rights to it had been acquired by someone else since.

Torres had died a month after Lefkow and half a continent away. The next death had occurred two months later, in a cheesy beachside parlor in New Hampshire. Marsh Kuykendall had been unembarrassed by his status as an AR junkie, supporting his habit with odd and mostly menial jobs. *Acquaintances of the victim have all heard him say, at one time or another, that realtime was the disposable reality because it could not be preserved or replayed like AR,* Konstantin read. *"AR is humanity's true destiny." "In AR, everyone is immortal."*

*If you don't mind existing in reruns,* she thought. Kuykendall had owned a half dozen personas, all of them his original creations. Mortality had caught up with him while he had been acting out a panther-man fantasy. The panther-man had been beaten to death by some vaguely monstrous assailant that no one claimed to have seen clearly; in realtime, Kuykendall had taken blows hard enough to shatter both his head-mounted helmet and his head. No one in the parlor had heard or seen anything.

Victim number four had been in rehab for a year after a bad accident had left her paralyzed. Lydia Stang's damaged nerves had been regenerated, but she had had to relearn movement from the bottom up. AR had been part of her therapy; her AR persona had been an idealized gymnastic version of herself. She had died with a broken neck, in AR and in realtime. Witnesses stated she had been fighting a street duel with a lizard-person. Even better, the lizard-person had voluntarily come forward and admitted to AR contact with the deceased. Stang had been online in Denver, while the lizard person had been cavorting in a parlor not three blocks from where Konstantin was sitting. She double-checked to be sure she had that right, and then made a note to look up the lizard-person in real-time, if possible.

A moment later she was scratching that note out; the lizard-person was victim number five. Even more shocking, Konstantin thought, was the lack of information on the deceased, a former musician who had gone by the single name Flo. After Lydia Stang's death, Flo had given up music and taken up AR full-time, or so it seemed, until someone had suffocated her. Online, her reptilian alter-ego had been swimming. In the East River, Konstantin noted, which the Lefkow dragon had fallen into out of the sky. Maybe that meant something; maybe it didn't.

Victims six and seven would seem to have killed each other in a gang fight. Konstantin found this disheartening. In post-Apocalyptic Noo Yawk Sitty, they had been a couple of nasty street kids, sixteen, just on the verge of adulthood. In real-time, they had been a pair of middle-aged gypsy office workers who had no doubt discovered that they had wandered into the cul de sac of life and weren't going to find their way out alive. They had both lived in a nearby urban hive, got assignments through the same agency, did the same kinds of no-brainer files and data upkeep jobs – and yet, they apparently hadn't known each other offline. Or if they had known each other, they had deliberately stayed away from each other. Except online, where they had often mixed it up. They had stabbed each other in AR but someone else had stabbed each of them in the privacy of their own homes. The times of death seemed to be in some dispute.

And now here was number eight, a weird Caucasian kid with a Japanese name. *Domo arigato*, Konstantin thought sourly, and pressed for a summary of the common characteristics of each case.

There wasn't much, except for the fact that each murder had occurred while the victim had been online in post-Apocalyptic Noo Yawk Sitty. Three of the previous murders had taken place locally; the kid's brought it up to four, fully half. And unless it turned out that the kid had been a brain surgeon, all of them had been lower level drones, not a professional in the bunch.

She sat back and tried to think. Was serial murder back in style – *again*? Except whoever had been enjoying the pretend-murder of hijacking someone else's AR persona had decided to cross over? Or couldn't tell the difference?

Konstantin pressed for a table of similarities among the AR characters and came up with a *Data Not Available* sign. The note on the next screen told her there had been no work done in this area, either due to lack of software, lack of time, or lack of personnel. Undoubtedly no one had thought that it was parti-cularly important to look into the AR personae – it wasn't as if those were actual victims . . . were they? For all she or anyone else knew, Sally Lefkow's dragon would be more missed and mourned than Sally herself; likewise for the rest of them.

Sad, and somehow predictable, Konstantin thought. She made a note to send out for more background on the victims. While she was reviewing what information she had, DiPietro and Celestine called to tell her mostly what she had already known, except for one very surprising difference: upon arrival at the kid's apart-ment, they had found a nineteen-year-old woman in the process of ransacking the place. She would answer no questions except to say that she was the kid's wife.

Konstantin checked quickly; as she had thought, the kid was the only – or the first – married victim. "Bring her down here," she told them. "Fast."

"Tommie was looking for the out door," said Pine Havelock. "Anybody was gonna find it, it would be him. And now look what's gone and happened." Tomoyuki Iguchi's self-proclaimed wife was sitting in a plastic bucket of a chair hugging her folded legs tightly and staring at Konstantin over the bony humps of her knees with a half-afraid, half-accusing expression. Dressed in what looked like surplus hospital pajamas, she seemed to be completely hairless, without even eyelashes. Her eyes weren't really large enough to carry it off; she made Konstantin think of a mental patient who had fallen into a giant vat of depilatory cream.

"What out door would that be?" Konstantin asked her after a long moment of silence. "The one to the secret Japanese area?"

Havelock raised her head, staring oddly. "Get off."

"What out door?" Konstantin asked patiently, suppressing several inappropriate responses.

"Out. *Out*. Where you go and you'll stay. So you don't come back to something like *this*." She looked around Guilfoyle Pleshette's office.

"Uh-huh." Konstantin leaned an elbow on the desk and rubbed her forehead. "Where *would* you end up?"

"*Out*." The woman's forehead puckered in spots; Konstantin realized she was frowning. Without eyebrows, all of her expressions were odd. "You know – *out*. Where you don't need the suit or the top hat, because you're *there*. Not *here*."

Konstantin finally got it. "So you and Iguchi were looking for the magic door to the egress. Did you know of anyone else—"

"Egress," Havelock said, nodding vigorously. "That's it. Door out – egress. *That's* what *she* called it."

"Who?" Konstantin asked, and then almost said the answer with her.

"Body Sativa."

"Sun's gonna come up," Guilfoyle Pleshette said threateningly. She looked tired. Even her hair was starting to lose its lift.

Still sitting at her desk in the minuscule office, Konstantin waved at her impatiently. "Sorry, Taliaferro," she said into the phone while she scrawled notes in the archiver one-handed. "I didn't get the last thing you said. Repeat."

Taliaferro was surprisingly patient. Perhaps lack of sleep had simply made a zombie out of him. "I said, they're still running data on the other seven so we don't have anything solid yet. But the probability is running to 80 percent that anyone who frequented the Sitty as often as any of them would, at some point, have had AR contact with the persona or entity known as Body Sativa."

" 'Entity'?" said Konstantin incredulously. "Who's calling this thing an *entity*? The probability program or someone who's in a position to know?"

"Actually, I heard some of the clientele in the parking lot calling it that. Or her. Whatever." Taliaferro sounded a bit sheepish. "Probably it's some slicko with a lot of good PR. Famous for being famous, you know."

"You do much AR?" Konstantin asked him suddenly.

There was a moment of loud silence. "Is that a sincere question?"

"Sorry," Konstantin said. "Don't know what got into me."

Taliaferro hung up without replying. She turned to Guilfoyle Pleshette, who was yawning hugely and noisily. "Do *you* do much AR?"

"Yeah, sure. Employee discount here's pretty good."

"Do you spend much time in post-Apocalyptic Noo Yawk Sitty?"

Now the manager shrugged and looked at the ceiling almost coyly. "I guess I been known to. You gotta scan rated zone because when you get a virgin in, you gotta talk about what you know. I say that's the difference between a quality business and a ditch."

Konstantin nodded absently. Once a place got too popular, nobody would admit to going voluntarily, even in AR. "And Body Sativa?"

Pleshette shrugged one shoulder. "Everybody knows about her, but not as many really seen her as say so."

"But you have," Konstantin said.

"Of course."

Of course. Konstantin managed not to smile. "You think you could introduce me?"

"Of course *not*." The woman was almost offended.

Now Konstantin shrugged. "It was worth a try."

"You got to understand here that anyone who knows Body and drags along every prole that wants to see her, won't know her for too long."

"I guess I can understand that. Suppose I go in and find her myself?"

Pleshette stared at her. "You think you can?"

"One of your employees offered me some secret insider icons. Whatever those are."

The manager straightened up. "Yeah? Who?" she asked sharply.

"The bored one. Mezzer. Tim."

"Oh, him." Pleshette waved one hand. "You can find his so-called secret insider icons in the index of any online guidebook. I got stuff you can get around with."

"But will you loan any to me?"

The funny little face looked doubtful. "What're you gonna do with it?"

Konstantin took a breath. "All I want to do is ask this Body Sativa some questions."

"What kind of questions?" the night manager asked suspiciously.

Now Konstantin felt as if she had fallen through a rabbit hole in time that had sent her back to the beginning of the situation, which she would have to explain all over again. "Questions having to do with the kid who died here tonight – Shantih Love, or Tomoyuki Iguchi, whichever you knew him as."

"I didn't know him at all," said Pleshette. Konstantin felt like screaming. "And there's no insurance that Body Sativa did, either. But if that's all you really want to do, I can load some stuff for you. But you got to promise me, you won't misuse any of it."

"Misuse it how?" Konstantin asked.

"Poaching."

"And what would that entail?"

"Getting stuff you're not entitled to get."

" 'Stuff'? In AR?" Konstantin felt completely lost now.

The night manager folded her arms again. "Yeah. Stuff in AR. In the Sitty. Everybody who goes in regular's got stuff in AR. So I got this nothing job. I got to put up with blowfish like Miles Mank. I live in a hive on Sepulveda. But I got stuff in AR. I got a good place for myself, I'm in the game with the name and the fame. I even got myself a few passwords. I put in plenty of time to get all that. I don't want it just slipped out from under me when I'm not there to defend it." The funny little face started to pucker unhappily. "You got stuff out here, you don't need to go poachin' my stuff in there. If you see what I mean."

Konstantin saw; it sent a wave of melancholy through her. "All I want to do is contact Body Sativa if I can. I don't want to do anything else."

Pleshette held her gaze for a long moment and then shrugged her bony shoulders hugely. "Yeah. Well, you know, it's not like I can't tell the difference between in there and out here, it's not like I think I can put that stuff in a bank or anything. But I put a lot of time in; I spent some big sums doin' it. If I give it away, then I got *nothing*. You see that?"

Konstantin saw. She couldn't decide, however, if it was the sort of thing a person might kill for.

Guilfoyle Pleshette found a clean hotsuit in Konstantin's size and helped her put it on, giving her a flurry of instructions in her little cartoony voice. Konstantin felt silly, even though she knew this was really just like any other information gathering operation, except it was more like using the telephone. Unless what happened to the kid happened to her, she thought unhappily.

Tim Mezzer made good on his promise to supply icons and loaded the file into the headmount for her. "All you have to do is ask for your icon cat," he said, sounding less bored. "And if you're not sure which icon to try, ask for advice."

"Ask who?"

"The icons," he said, looking at her as if she should have known this. "They all have their own help files attached. But I gotta tell you, they're all pretty idiosyncratic, too. You know how it is, what *some* people call help."

Konstantin was mildly alarmed to find that she actually understood what he was telling her. After loading her own information into the headmount, Pleshette took her to one of the deluxe cubicles – deluxe meaning it was half again as large and included an extra chair. She helped Konstantin get comfortable in it, fastened the straps just tightly enough to keep her from falling if she got overly energetic, and fitted her headmount for her. Konstantin tried to thank her, but the headmount muffled her too well. She felt more than heard the woman leave the room. Fear rippled through her, briefly but intensely, making her dizzy.

Then the screen lit up with a control panel graphic and she immediately regained her balance. She turned on the log. The log was an independent, outside operation with only an on-off access, so she'd have her own record that she could prove hadn't been tampered with later, if necessary. Funny how the first thing anyone had to do with taped evidence was prove that it hadn't been toasted, she thought.

The control panel graphic disappeared and the screen showed her the configuration menu. She made her choices – sighting graphic and help line on request – while the 'suit warmed up. This was a full-coverage 'suit, she realized, uncomfortable. Somehow, she hadn't given it any thought when she was putting it on and it was too late to do anything about it now. Besides, they were probably all full-coverage 'suits; full-coverage would be the big attraction in a place like this. As if to confirm her thoughts, a hotsuit ad replaced the configuration menu.

*Because if you're not going to feel it all over*, murmured a congenial female voice while a hotsuit, transparent to show all the sensors, revolved on the screen, *why bother?* Which, when you thought about it, wasn't such an unreasonable question.

The headmounted monitor adjusted the fine-tuning for her focal length by showing her the standard introduction in block letters on a background of shifting colors. Konstantin sighed impatiently. So much introductory material with the meter running – she could see the clock icon tagging along at the upper edge of her peripheral vision on the right side. You probably couldn't go broke operating a video parlor, she thought, unless you tried real, real hard.

The sign came up so suddenly that it took at least three seconds to register on her, and even then she wasn't sure right away whether she was really seeing it, or imagining it. Seeing in AR felt strangely too close to thinking.

> WELCOME TO THE LAND OF ANYTHING GOES
> HERE THERE ARE NO RULES
> EVERYTHING IS PERMITTED

*Ha*, thought Konstantin.

> *You can choose to be totally anonymous.*
> *You can tell the whole truth about yourself.*
> *You can tell only lies.*

The word *lies* flashed on and off in different colors before it evaporated.

*No real crime is possible here. If you do something Out There as a result of events In Here, you are on your own. In the event of your persona's virtual death, you can request to be directed to central stores, where you can choose another. The time used in choosing a new persona or performing any reference or maintenance task is not free, though a reduced rate may be available through your parlor operator. Consult the rate file in your personal area for more information.*

Konstantin looked around for a speed-scroll option.

*There is no speed-scroll option for this portion of your session. State and federal law specifically declare that all users must be advised of conditions in the gaming area. By reading this, you agree that you understand the structure and accept any charges, standard and/ or extra, that you will incur at your point of origin. Closing your eyes will only result in a full rescroll of the introductory material, at your own expense.*

Blink-rate and eye-movements could reveal a great deal about a person's thoughts, especially when used in conjunction with vital signs, Konstantin remembered, feeling even more uneasy.

*This concludes the introductory material. The next screen will be your destination menu. Bon voyage, and good luck.*

The screen that came up showed her four doors labeled *Post-Apocalyptic Noo Yawk Sitty, Post-Apocalyptic Ellay, Post-Apocalyptic Hong Kong,* and *Others.*

A small bright icon appeared at the bottom right corner of her visual field, a graphic of a hand twisting a doorknob. Just below it, on the status line, was the word *Cue!* Feeling awkward, she reached for the Noo Yawk Sitty door and saw a generic white-gloved hand moving toward the knob. As the hand touched the knob, she felt it in her own hand, the sensors delivering a sensation to the palm side of her fingers that surprised her with its intense authenticity – it was more like touching a doorknob than actually touching a doorknob.

The next moment was a flash of chaos, a maelstrom of noise and light, countless touches and textures everywhere at once, over before she could react to any of it. Under her feet, she could hear the scrape of the gritty glitz, the glitzy grit of post-Apocalyptic Noo Yawk Sitty; she could see the sparkle and glitter of it spread out before her – not Eliot's etherized patient awaiting dissection but a refulgent feast for her reeling senses.

*HINT: In case of disorientation, amp your 'suit down and wait at least thirty seconds before attempting movement. Closing your eyes could result in vertigo. This message will be repeated.*

She thought she heard herself make some kind of relieved noise as she stared at the setting marked *decrease.* In a few moments, all the settings on the suit had been re-adjusted to a more bearable level. Whoever had had this 'suit on last, she thought, had either been extremely jaded or suffering from some kind of overall senses-impairment disorder. Or – not so amazing in the era of the more-real-than-real experience – both.

Now that she could perceive her surroundings without being assaulted by them, Konstantin was dismayed to find that she didn't seem to be anywhere near where Shantih Love had died. Instead, she was standing at the edge of an open area in the midst of a crowd of tall buildings festooned with enormous neon signs of a sort that had been popular seventy or eighty years before. Except for herself, there were no people, or at least none that she could see, and no sound except for a faint hum that might have come from the signs, or from some distant machine. Or possibly even from some loose connection in the headmount, she thought sourly. It would be just her luck.

The buildings were dark, showing the scars of fires, bullets, and bomb blasts, broken-out windows gaping like empty eye sockets, but the signs were brilliant, impossibly vivid with shifting colors that melted and morphed like living ropes of molten light. She had to look away or be hypnotized.

Her gaze locked onto a silvery figure standing in an open doorway. At first, she thought it was someone wearing a skintight bio-suit but then the figure moved forward and she saw that its skin was the same color as the clothes it wore. The figure moved closer and she amended her perception: it was the same material as the clothes it wore.

"New in town?" it sang, approaching carefully.

"Maybe," she said, taking a step back.

"Oh, you're new." The figure, which began to look more like it was made of mercury or chrome, gestured at something behind her. Konstantin turned to look.

The sight of the completely hairless and sexless creature in the dark glass made her jump; then embarrassment made her cringe. She had completely forgotten to choose a persona and the hotsuit, rather than choosing one for her, had let her enter AR wearing a placeholder. Her gaze darted around as she searched for the exit icon.

"It's not necessary to leave," the silvery figure said in its musical voice. Now that it was right next to her, Konstantin could see it was a sort of animated metal sculpture of a tall young girl, though she couldn't quite identify the metal. Chrome, mercury, or possibly platinum? "Pull down Central Stores and choose Wardrobe. Then just follow the directions."

"Oh. Thank you so much." Feeling awkward, Konstantin

stuck out her hand. "I'm, uh, Dore. And you're right, I'm new here."

The silver girl seemed unaware of her extended hand. "I am a pop-up help-and-guide subroutine keyed to respond to situations and types of situations most often identified with new users of AR and/or post-Apocalyptic Noo Yawk Sitty. I am also available on request. Pull down Help and ask for Sylvia."

Konstantin started to thank her again but the girl made a fast gesture at eye-level and she found herself standing at a shiny white counter. The words *TOUCH HERE FOR ASSISTANCE* faded in on its surface, going from pale pink to blood red and back to pale pink before disappearing. Konstantin gingerly put a fingertip on the spot where she estimated the middle of the O in FOR had been.

"Help you," said a hard-edged male voice; the short, plump man who appeared on the other side of the counter looked as if he were answering a casting call for a play about bank tellers in 1900. The green visor on his forehead cast a shadow that made it hard to see anything of his eyes but reflected pinpoints of light.

"Where's the rest of your hat?" Konstantin asked impulsively.

"This is an eyeshade, not a hat," he replied in that same sharp, almost harsh tone. "Its presence connotes items and equipment available to you in AR, some at a surcharge. Do you want to see a list of items and equipment with their corresponding surcharges? These can also be itemized on the hardcopy printout of your receipt."

"I don't know. Is a persona classified as an item or as equipment?"

"Neither. A persona is a persona. Did you have someone in particular in mind or were you planning construction here? Morphing services within AR are available for a surcharge; however, there is no extra charge if you have brought your own morphing utility with you. Except, of course, for any extra time that might be consumed by the morphing process."

Konstantin suddenly found herself yawning; so far, her big AR adventure was turning out to be even more tiresome than the reality she was used to. "Does anybody really do anything in here besides listen to how much everything is costing them?"

"First-time users are advised to take the orientation sequence, and usually in some easier location." He sounded as bored as she felt.

"I want out of here," she said. "Out of the whole thing, I mean. Exit. End it. Good-bye. Stop. Logging off. Out, out, *out*."

Abruptly, she was staring at a blank screen; her 'suit was in *Suspend*, she saw, but still turned on. Words began to crawl up the screen in a steady scroll.

*Your time in your chosen AR location has been halted. Readings indicate a high level of tension and stress in a low level of situation. Generally this occurs when the user is confused or has not taken proper instruction in the use of AR. Do you wish to continue in AR, or do you wish to terminate the program and exit? Please choose one option and one option only.*

She was about to tell it to terminate when she heard what sounded like a telephone ringing.

The words on the screen vanished and a new message appeared quickly, word by word. *Realtime communication with you is being requested. Do you want to talk to the caller? Please answer yes or no.*

"Who is it?" she asked and then added quickly, "Oh, never mind. Put them on."

There was a click and she heard the familiar cartoony tones of Guilfoyle Pleshette. "What are you doing?"

"I don't know," she said.

"Yeah, what I thought. Icons and passwords don't do you a bit of good if you don't know what you're doing. That's an advanced 'suit I put you in. It doesn't carry a pre-fab for you, you got to bring your own."

"My own what?" asked Konstantin worriedly.

"Your own *persona*. I thought you had one you wanted."

"I do."

"Well, who is it?"

Konstantin took a breath. "Shantih Love."

Pleshette didn't even hesitate. "You want it with or without the cut throat?"

"With," Konstantin said. "Definitely with. And I want a copy of the surveillance footage loaded into a subroutine, too."

"You gonna run a sequence within a sequence?"

"I might. If it looks like it might get me some answers. Why?"

"Because that's a pretty expensive thing to do." Pleshette sounded both annoyed and worried. "Who's gonna pay for all of this online time and fun and games?"

"You are," Konstantin said.

"*What?*"

"I said, the taxpayers are. Your tax dollars at work."

Pleshette's laugh was low but surprisingly harsh. "Not my tax dollars. I don't pay taxes, not on my salary. You want to impress some taxpayers, catch some criminals in there and drag them out with you when you sign off."

Twenty (billable) minutes later, Konstantin stepped through a doorway onto the street where she had first seen Shantih Love. The feel of the Love persona in her 'suit was pleasurable in a way that kept her on edge. Being Shantih Love was close to seductive, even with the sliced throat, something she had not taken into consideration.

*Real easy to go native in a Gang Wars module.* Guilfoyle Pleshette's words came to mind unbidden. Not to mention unhelpfully, she thought; this wasn't a Gang Wars module. That she knew of, anyway.

She was wondering now if she really knew anything at all. The piles of wreckage in the street were all aflame, burning in jeweltones, now and then sending sparks skyward, where they seemed to mingle with the stars. The glitter she had seen on the monitor looked somehow less gritty from the inside and more like delicate sprays of tiny lights, too exquisitely fragile not to shatter in a light puff of a breeze, yet remaining, twinkling and shimmering against the black street, the pitted brick and the web-cracked glass of the buildings facing the burning wrecks, the cold-stone texture of the barrier between the street and the alien shore of the Hudson River.

Konstantin went to the barrier and strolled along it in the direction Shantih Love had taken, looking around for anything like the figure of a shaggy beast that might take an interest in her.

Rather than anything approaching, however, Konstantin had a sense of things drawing away from her, many watching with the knowledge that she was an impostor. And then again, she thought suddenly, how would anyone know, if the Shantih Love persona had gone on for another four hours after Iguchi's death? Maybe the only one who knew was the creature who had attacked and hijacked Shantih Love here in the first place.

She paused, leaning on the barrier and looking toward where she estimated the party had been. It was long over now, or perhaps this was no longer a hot place to be in the Sitty. Her purpose here was not to find a party, nor to act as a decoy to

attract a creature that wasn't even real. Funny how easy it was to
forget things or to keep focused here. If she waited much longer,
she might even feel her concentration dissolve, break apart into
tiny fragments and float away up to the stars with the sparks from
the burning wreckage.

"Icon cat?" she asked.

It was there before her on the barrier, a big book full of symbols
and their explanations. The page it was open to showed a flame
within a halo; as she looked at it, it went from a line drawing to a
vivid holo. The word *Enlightenment* came out of the flame and
rippled for a moment. More words appeared on the facing page:
*You have only to ask.*

Konstantin made a face, or thought she did; there was no real
feeling above her neck. "Is this a help file?" she said aloud.

Now there was a new message on the page opposite the flame:
*Help with?_Travel_Location_Contacts_Other*

After a moment's thought, she touched_*Contacts.*

*Contact_Who_What?* the page wanted to know.

She pressed for_*Who.* The question mark moved to the end of
the word. "Body Sativa," she said aloud.

A golden arrow pointing to her right materialized on the page.
She turned it and found a map of the area with her own position
highlighted. A dotted green line appeared, winding its way along
the grid of streets to a location six blocks away; a green star
flashed on and off.

"That was easy," she said, noting the address and the directions. It just figured. *You have only to ask.* So simple that it was
too simple to think of.

The book disappeared into the back of the map. She picked it
up and moved up the street toward the next three-way intersec-
tion. Three fiery humanish shapes detached themselves from the
burning ruins of a classic Rolls sandwiched between two antique
sports cars and stood watching her. Konstantin had a sudden
urge to whirl on them and claim she was selling encyclopedias or
household cleansers. The idea was a tickle playing over her back,
where she imagined she could feel their literally burning stares.

No, too simple; they might expect her to produce chips full of
natural history quick-times or a bottle of something that looked
like urine and smelled like ammonia. Not that she had smelled
anything in here since she had arrived, not even anything burning.

She couldn't account for how she had come up with the idea of playing such a prank; she'd never had much of a sense of humor, or so her ex had always said.

*Anything goes. You can even pretend you have a sense of humor, or that your ex isn't actually ex, and all while you look for someone with the improbable name of Body Sativa, or Love, or whatever.*

She passed several brawls, a side street where a few hundred people seemed to be trying to stay as close together as possible and still dance – it looked as if they had decided nudity would do it – and a billboard-sized screen where half a dozen people were either collaborating on a quick-time or competing to see whose images could dominate. Someone among them was obsessed with mutant reptiles. Or were certain kinds of images contagious?

Or maybe, she thought as she passed someone that might have been the offspring of a human and a cobra, it was the mutants themselves that were contagious. She paused at a corner in front of a park surrounded by a black metal spiked fence and consulted the map.

*"Sssssssssssshhhhhhhhhhhhhh . . ."*

The noise was so soft, she wasn't sure that she had actually heard it. But then it came again, from somewhere in the dark contained in the spiked metal fence, and she found that the sensation of the small hairs standing up on the back of her neck was not necessarily something that the hotsuit had to produce for her.

*"Sssssssssssshhhhhhhhhhhhhhaaaaaaaaannnnnnntiiiiiiih . . ."*

She was clenching her hands so tightly that if she had really been holding a map, it would have crumpled and torn in a dozen places. *Come on*, she told herself. *This is nothing more than a scary story. You just happen to be in it.*

*"Sssssssssshhhhhhhhhhhaaaaaaaaaaannnnnnntiiiiiiiih . . ."*

Apparently it didn't matter what she told herself; the hairs on the back of her neck were going to stand up and jitterbug regardless. The chills seemed to be creeping down her backbone now. Konstantin tried to steel herself and shivered instead.

*"Sssssssshhhhhhhaaaaaaaaannnnnnntiiiiiih. Welcome back from the land of the dead. We've been waiting for you, darling."*

Konstantin forced herself to turn around. The faces grinning out of the darkness glowed moon-pale, with thick black circles around the eyes, which were also luminous. Or just the whites, anyway, Konstantin noticed, trying to see more detail in spite of the cold still flicking at the back of her neck and up onto her scalp.

As her eyes adjusted, she could see that there were half a dozen of them, in a roughly symmetrical formation around a picnic table with the one who had spoken in the center. They were all wearing black skintights over their idealized hardbodies, some of them indisputably female, others emphatically male. *When Broadway choreographers go bad*, said a tiny, mocking voice in her mind. More chills played over the back of her neck. Shuddering, she rubbed her neck with her free hand and felt the cut area in front separate a bit.

She covered her wounded throat with the map and moved closer to the metal fence. "Do I know you?" she asked, trying to sound calm.

"Shantih," said the one who had been doing all the talking in a sulky tone. Emphatically male, she saw. "After all we've meant to each other. I'm wounded. Mortally. We *all* are."

"And I'm dead," Konstantin answered. "You have any idea who did it?"

The glowing moon-colored face suddenly took on an uncertain expression. "Honey, you were *there*. Look at your footage. Relive every glorious moment."

"I have. I'd invite you to watch it again with me, but I'm on my way to meet someone. Maybe we can connect later."

One of the women on the speaker's right straightened up from her cat-like stalking pose and pushed both hands into the small of her back. "Oh, for crying out *loud*, Shantih. My back's *killing* me tonight. If you're not playing, just say so so we can go find somebody else."

"I'm not playing," Konstantin said, starting to turn away.

"Because you're not Shantih," said the speaker, hopping down from the table and going to the fence. "Are you." It wasn't really a question.

Konstantin shook her head. "You knew Shantih Love pretty well?"

The man adjusted something on himself at waist-level and Konstantin felt the chills that had been tormenting her suddenly vanish. "'Knew'? Does that mean our usual Shantih gave up the character?"

"Gave up the ghost," Konstantin said. "The person you knew as Shantih Love in here has been murdered. For real. I—"

He turned away from her and swung his arm. The group surrounding the picnic table vanished, including the woman who had complained. Then he turned back to her. "What kinda virgin are you, hon?" he asked, annoyance large on his white painted face.

"What kind?" Konstantin echoed, mystified.

"Yeah, *what kind*. Are you some senator's baby out for a good time, or are you some rich kid who bought out a regular? Thought you could get the game and the fame along with the name?"

Konstantin started to answer but he did something at waist-level again and a fresh wave of chills danced up her neck into her hair. Crying out, she stepped back, batting the air with her map as if ultrasonics were insects she could just swat away from herself.

"You stay away from me, you pseudo-rudo," he yelled at her.

"What?" she demanded. "I didn't do anything—"

"I *hate* you virgins, you all think you're the *first* who ever thought of saying the one you bought out got killed for real. You think we're all just gonna lead you to their stash, tell you, 'Oh, help yourself, take all the *stuff*, and if you don't know how to use it, just ask'?" He did something at his waist again and Konstantin retreated several more steps. At the same time, she understood that this should not have made a difference. Unless her 'suit was cooperating in the scenario and producing the ultrasonics –

She shifted her gaze to the control for her 'suit and saw that it *was* giving her the chills. She readjusted the setting and the chills cut off immediately.

The man made a disgusted noise. "For god's sake, baby, if you can't take the sensation, why did you bother coming in?" He flickered out and she was alone. Moving on, Konstantin couldn't decide whether to feel relieved or chastized.

The place marked on the map turned out to be a subway station, or maybe just the post-Apocalyptic ruin of a subway station. From where she stood on the sidewalk looking down the stone stairs, Konstantin could hear the distant sound of people's voices and, even more distantly, music, but no trains. Maybe you could hike around post-Apocalyptic Noo Yawk Sitty in the tunnels, and bring your own music with you.

She crouched at the top of the stairs with her map, absently pressing the flesh of her throat together. The cut edges felt a bit like putty or clay, but they wouldn't stay closed for very long. She wondered idly if she should try to find a place to have herself sewn up, or whether she might even try it herself. If it was the sort of thing that Shantih Love would do –

There was a strange pressure all along her back, from her neck down to her feet. She stood up and turned around to see if some new weird experience had crept up behind her, but there was no one and nothing there. She was alone; the pressure was all in the suit, as if it were trying to push her down the steps into the subway.

"Help?" she asked, turning the map over. It became a book again in her hands. She found the section on the hotsuit almost immediately but she had to read it over three times to be sure she understood that the 'suit itself, being loaded with Shantih Love characteristics, was trying to give her a hint as to what to do next. At this point, apparently, Shantih Love would have descended into the subway.

Konstantin concentrated, placing her fingers on the sliced flesh of her throat and closing her eyes. There; now she could feel it. Now she could feel how the sensation of touching skin, touching flesh was all in the fingertips of the hotsuit. She wasn't really touching anything, or if she was, the AR sensation over-rode it sheerly by intensity, vividness, and the power of suggestion.

She opened her eyes and found herself looking down at a young Japanese man dressed in the plain garb of a laborer from about a hundred or so years before, but armed with what looked to her like a Samurai sword.

Konstantin pressed the book to her chest protectively; it became a map again. The man seemed not to notice. He gazed at her steadily, his expression mild, almost blank. He came up another step. She meant to retreat but something in his expression changed so that his face became slightly more severe, more wary, and she stayed where she was.

"Does this mean you've given up, Mr *Iguchi*?" he asked in a soft, sarcastic voice. "Or have you just changed your strategy?"

"How do you know my name?" Konstantin asked him, wincing inwardly when she heard the tremor in her voice. It wasn't fear but cold – her 'suit seemed to have turned to ice.

The man came up another step. "Games again, Tom? It's always games with you."

"More like a malfunction, actually," she muttered, rubbing

one arm. The temperature inside the suit was still dropping, as though it was trying to keep her cool inside a furnace.

"It's not cold tonight, Tom," the man said. "Are you sure it's not fear that's making you tremble?"

"Have it your way," Konstantin said desperately, hoping that might have some effect on the 'suit's wayward thermostat.

"Surely you're not afraid of *me* – or is it what I represent?"

Konstantin's teeth chattered "W-w-what would that be?"

"An old world that has nothing to do with what this world has become – this world, or the one it's contained in, or the one that *that* one is contained in, boxes within boxes within boxes, all the way to infinity." The man suddenly produced a strange coin between thumb and forefinger. It flashed silver for a moment; then Konstantin could see the symbol on it, like a figure 8 lying on its side. The man flipped it over and showed her the other side, a snake with its tail in its mouth.

"Though these are not Japanese symbols, there is still something very Japanese about what they represent. Old Japan, I'm talking about, not the hot icy flash of the nth generation of speed tribes, or the debauchery of the newest salarymen in the neon jungle that covered over the old signs and symbols."

He held it out to her, as if inviting her to take it, but when she reached for it, he flipped it again and snatched it out of the air. Konstantin pulled her hand back, embarrassed and irritated. The man put both hands behind himself for a moment and then held them up. "Which hand, Tom? You choose."

Konstantin tucked the map under her arm, trying to ignore the fact that she felt as if she were turning into an ice cube from the skin inward. "Let's see," she said, lifting her chin with bravado. "I used to be pretty good at this. Finding the tell, I mean. Everybody's got a tell. Even old Japan."

The man's eyes narrowed and he took a closer look at her. "You never used to be so smart, Tom. What happened since I saw you last – you take some genius pill somewhere? Something that's burning your brain cells out as you use them, maybe?"

Konstantin didn't answer; she scrutinized his right fist for a long time, and then his left. "Sometimes, it's a twitch, a tightening of the muscles. Sometimes, it's just that the person simply *looks* at the correct hand, whichever one it is. Doesn't matter, you just have to know what to look for, what *kind* of tell it is. Most of the time, you know, the person doing it doesn't even realize it.

But it's there. There's always a tell, and it *tells* you what the answer is." Konstantin hesitated and then tapped the man's right fist. "I say there."

"You're not Iguchi," he said, not moving.

"Let's see it," said Kostantin. "I know I must be right. Otherwise, you wouldn't be delaying."

"You're *not* Iguchi. I should have seen it immediately. That's too smart for Iguchi. Where is old Tom tonight? Did he hire you, or did you buy him out? If you bought him out, I got to tell you, he stuck you with damaged goods there." He indicated her cut throat with a jab of his chin.

Konstantin felt more confident now. She stepped forward and tapped the knuckles of his right hand. "Come on, let me see it. I know it's there. Give me the coin and you can call it a night."

"Call it a night?" The man smiled, raised his right hand, and opened it. It was empty. "Or call it in the air?" He looked at his left hand as it unfolded in the same position to reveal that it, too, was empty. He stayed that way, with both hands raised, as if he were at gunpoint, or perhaps surrendering. Annoyed, Konstantin stepped back and folded her arms.

"Fine," she said. "But *I* know, and *you* know, that until you cheated, that coin was in your right hand. You can go ahead and take it away with you, but we both know you cheated, and we'll always know it. We'll never forget, will we?" She went to take the map from under her arm and felt something funny in her palm. She looked down and opened her hand. The coin was there. She picked it up and looked at both sides.

"I told you to call it in the air," the man admonished her. "But the problem is, when you have a coin with infinity on one side, and Ouroboros on the other, how can you ever really know which side is heads, and which is tails?"

Konstantin said nothing. He burst out laughing, bowed to her, and walked away into the darkness. She could hear the echo of his laughter long after the shadows had swallowed him up.

She examined the coin again. Whatever else he might have said or done, he had given her the coin; she had just received some AR *stuff*. She wondered if this was the type of stuff Guilfoyle Pleshette was so enamored of, and if it were the sort of thing that someone might kill for.

She descended the stairs, feeling every bump and irregularity in the bannister with her free hand as the sounds of voices and music bounced off the grimy tiles. Sometimes the sensory input was too authentic to be authentic, Konstantin noted, almost amused. Until she got to the bottom of the stairs and saw the empty platform beyond the broken turnstiles and the long unused token-seller's cage. There were no people anywhere to be seen in the unnatural light of the fluorescent tubes, no movement anywhere at all. Dust and dirt lay thickly on everything, suggesting that no one had come here for a long, long time – which had to be wrong, since her Japanese friend had just come up out of here.

Or had he only been waiting for her at the bottom of the stairs? Her or someone like her – no, he had definitely been expecting Shantih Love, for *some* reason.

She looked at the lights overhead. They didn't hum or buzz; they didn't even flicker. Strange, for a place so disused and abandoned.

The coin grew slightly warmer in her fist. No, too high a price, she thought, amused. "Icon cat?" she asked, and it was there under her arm. She took hold of it with her free hand and maneuvered it open. "Subway?"

The pages flipped and came to rest on a picture of a wooden nickel. She could tell it was made of wood by the lustrous grain. Konstantin considered it and then shook her head. The pages flipped again and kept flipping, like a rotary card file in a high wind. Because there was a wind, she realized, coming from somewhere down in the old train tunnel. She could feel it and she could hear music again as well, except it was much thinner-sounding, just one instrument, either a guitar or a very good synthesizer.

"Pause," she told the book; it closed quietly for her. She climbed over one of the turnstiles and walked out onto the platform, looking around.

The man with the guitar was to her left, sitting cross-legged at the place where the platform ended and the tunnel began. His head was tilted back against the wall and his eyes were closed, so that he seemed to be in a state of deep concentration as he played. Konstantin wondered if he were going to sing, and then wondered exactly what kind of strange kick a person could get from spending billable time in AR alone in a vacant subway station, playing a musical instrument for nobody.

None, she decided. "Resume," she said, staring at the guitar player. "*Empty* subway, *downtown*."

The pages flipped again and stopped to show her a bottlecap. *CREAM SODA*. It fell out of the book onto the tile floor at her feet. Down by the tunnel, the guitar-player paused and turned to smile at her. The lights changed, becoming just a bit warmer in color as the legend NOW ENTERING NEXT HIGHER LE-VEL ran along the bottom of her vision like a late-breaking item on *Police Blotter*.

People were all over the platform, standing in groups, sitting on the turnstiles, grouping together down on the tracks, picking their way over the rails and ties to the opposite platform, where there were even more people. At first, she saw only the same types she had seen on the shore in Shantih Love's AR log, but after a while, she discovered that if she didn't look directly at people too quickly, a good many of them had somehow metamorphosed into characters far more original and indecipherable.

If there even *were* that many people, she thought, remembering the strange guy in white face and the gang that hadn't really existed. Maybe some of these people were carrying phantoms with them for company. If you could be your own gang in AR, was that another example of AR *stuff?*

A seven-foot-tall woman whose long, thick, auburn hair seemed to have a life of its own looked down at her through opera glasses. "What sort of a creature are you?" she asked in a booming contralto.

"I think I've forgotten," Konstantin said and then winced, squirming. The 'suit was reminding her *now* that it was full-coverage and that Shantih Love would have responded to this woman. It was like a nightmare. Her ex might have laughed at her and told her that was no less than what she deserved for stealing someone else's life.

*I didn't steal it. He lost it and I found it.*

Yeah. Finders, weepers.

Konstantin wasn't sure if it were worse to have an imaginary argument with an ex after a break-up than it was to have the break-up argument, but she was fairly sure it was completely counter-productive to have it both on billable AR time and during a murder investigation. If that was what this really was, and not just a massive waste of time all around.

"Do you know Body Sativa?" she asked the tall woman.

"Yes." The woman gazed at her a moment longer and walked away.

The people down on the tracks were dancing now to something that sounded like the rhythmic smashing of glass on metal. Konstantin hopped down off the platform onto the tracks and walked among them, keeping her gaze downward so that she could see them change in her peripheral vision. Most of the people down here seemed to be affecting what her ex had called rough and shoddy sugar-plum. Konstantin had to admit to herself she found the look appealing, in a rough and shoddy way.

She looked down at the ankle-length gown Shantih Love had preferred. In this light, it seemed to have more of a red tone, much more than she had thought. Even stranger was the texture – it looked like velvet but it felt like sandpaper, at least on the outside. Inside, the feeling was all but non-existent; the hotsuit was full-coverage but not so complete in the detailing that she felt the gown swinging and brushing against her ankles. For that, she supposed, you had to have some kind of custom job.

But at least she never tripped on the hem, Konstantin thought as she moved among the dancers, still holding the map. The display had not changed, even after she had gained access to this level, where all the people were, so either Body Sativa was here, or there was something wrong with the map.

Getting someone's attention to find out, however, seemed to be another one of those tricks she hadn't learned yet. Down on the tracks, anyway. The people dancing there weren't just ignoring her, they seemed honestly unaware of her, as if she were invisible. Which would seem to indicate she had found another level within a level. Levels within levels and boxes within boxes. Was there any purpose to it, she wondered – any *real* purpose other than to intrigue people into spending more billable hours solving the puzzle.

The guitar player, she saw, was still sitting in the same place, and it looked as if he were still playing as well, though it was impossible to hear anything except the smash-clang everyone around her was dancing to. She made her way through the group over to where the guitar-player was. The platform was about as high as her nose. She tried boosting herself up but couldn't get enough leverage.

"Stay," said the guitar-player, eyes closed. "I can see and hear you fine where you are."

"Good," said Konstantin. "Tell me, if I look past you, will you change into someone else, too?"

"It's all in what you can perceive," he said, smiling. Then, while she was looking directly at him, he morphed from a plump, balding young guy to an angular middle-aged man with very long, straight steel-grey hair. He still didn't open his eyes. "You'd be surprised how few turns of the morphing dial that took."

"Maybe not," she said. "Do you know Body Sativa?"

"Know her, or know of her?"

"Know her. Personally, or casually." She paused. "And have you seen her in here recently?"

He tilted his head, his closed eyes moving back and forth beneath his eyelids, as if he were dreaming, while his fingers played over guitar strings that appeared no thicker than spider-silk. Konstantin realized she couldn't hear the music coming from the guitar, but she could feel it surround her, not unpleasantly, and then disintegrate. "I was a dolphin in a previous incarnation," he said after a bit.

"Why did you change?"

"We all have to, sooner or later. I would have thought you'd know that as well as anyone. What were you before you passed on to your present manifestation?"

Konstantin barely hesitated. "A homicide detective."

"Ah. That accounts for the interrogation." He chuckled. "You know, the idea is to go on to something different, not just do the same thing behind a new mask."

Words to live by, Konstantin thought. Perhaps she could print them on a card and send it to her ex. She smiled. "That's pretty good for a guitar-playing land dolphin."

He stopped playing and pulled something out of the hole in the center of the instrument. "Here," he said, leaning forward and holding it out to her; it looked like a playing card. "You're not necessarily smarter than the last one who had your face, but the quality of your ignorance is an improvement."

"It is? How?" Konstantin asked, taking the card from him.

"*You* might actually learn something."

She studied the card, trying to see it clearly, except the image on it kept shifting, melting, changing. It looked like it might be some kind of Oriental ideogram. "What is this?" she asked.

"Cab fare," he said.

"Cab fare? In a subway station?"

"Trains aren't running tonight. Or didn't you notice?" He laughed.

She looked down at her map again. The display still hadn't changed. "I was supposed to find somebody I needed here. My map says she's still here."

The guitar player shook his head. "Sorry, you misunderstood. There's a locator utility here, for help in finding someone in the Sitty. That's what your map says is here." He shrugged. "There are locator utilities in all the subway stations."

Konstantin managed not to groan. "Where?"

"Somewhere. It's all in what you perceive."

"You're a big help."

"I am. If you get it figured, you have cabfare to get to wherever it is you need to go."

Cabfare, Konstantin thought. Cabfare. Did it include tip, she wondered, or was that what the coin was for? She looked down at it in her other hand.

The man stopped playing. "When did you get that?"

"Just now. Upstairs. Outside." Konstantin closed her fist around it again. "Why?"

"Because even in here, certain things are perishable. Like milk, or cut flowers."

"Or people with cut throats?" Konstantin added.

He smiled. "No, you may have noticed that death doesn't have to put a crimp in your party plans. On the other hand, it's not generally an accepted practice to start out dead. If you want to be dead, custom dictates that you die here."

"Here in the subway, or here in AR?"

"It's all in what you perceive."

He was going to say that once too often, Konstantin thought unhappily. "What about this coin?" she asked him. "Were you telling me just now that it's going to expire?"

"Conditions," he said after a moment. "It's the conditions under which it would be ... *effective*. Conditions won't last."

"More words to live by," Konstantin muttered to herself. "I want to find the locator utility. How do I do that?"

"You have only to ask."

Konstantin frowned. "Who should I ask?"

"Me."

She hesitated. "All right. How do I find the locator utility."

"You have only to ask," he said again serenely, fingers picking at the strings of the guitar again.

"I just did," Konstantin said impatiently. "How—" She cut off. "No. *Where* is Body Sativa?"

The guitar player jerked his chin at her, still with his eyes closed. "Hail a cab, and when you're asked where you want to go, give the driver that."

Konstantin looked at the card again. The ideogram was still shifting. Suddenly she felt very tired and bored. "Are you sure this'll do it?"

"Oh, yeah. That'll take you right to her."

"It's that simple."

The guitar-player nodded. "It's that simple."

"Strange, nothing else in here seems to be."

"What you want is simple. All you had to do was state it in the proper place at the proper moment. In the proper form, of course. That's just elementary programming."

"Programming," Konstantin said, giving a short, not terribly merry laugh. "I should have known. You're the locator utility and the help utility, aren't you?"

"That's about what it comes down to," he said agreeably.

"And I had only to ask."

"Because it's what you want that's simple. You just want to meet up with another player so I gave you a tracer. Obviously you're not the usual Shantih Love, or even the usual player. The usual players don't want anything so simple. The usual players come down here looking for the secret subroutine to the Next Big Scene, or even the mythical out door. Then my job becomes something different. Then my job is to give them something that will stimulate a little thrill here and there, play to their curiosities and their fondest wishes and desires."

"And make them spend more billable hours," Konstantin said.

"The more hours people spend in here doing complicated things, the more interesting the Sitty becomes."

"Why don't you just tell people that, instead of playing to their wish-fulfillment fantasies about finding the egress or the secret subroutine to post-Apocalyptic Peoria, or wherever?"

"First of all, it's not my job to volunteer information. It's my job to answer questions. And I can only answer with what I know. I don't know that there's an egress . . . but I don't know that there isn't. I can't prove there isn't, I'm a utility. I wasn't created to determine whether my universe is finite or not."

*I'm talking philosophy with a utility*, Konstantin thought. "But surely you know whether there are secret subroutines?"

"If they're secret, they certainly wouldn't tell me. I'd tell anyone who asked and then they wouldn't be secret any more."

"All right," Konstantin said slowly. "Have there ever been any secret subroutines in the Sitty that you've found out about?"

"Some players have claimed to have accessed them."

"Were they telling the truth?"

"I'm not a lie detector."

"Wouldn't matter if you were, would it. Because it's all lies in here. Or all truth."

He went on playing, still with his eyes closed. Konstantin supposed he was the AR equivalent of blind justice – blind information. Which was probably much more accurate, all told.

"Have you ever met Shantih Love before?" she asked and then added quickly, "I mean, have you ever met a player named Shantih Love before I came in here?"

"I don't really *meet* anyone. I have everyone's name."

Konstantin thought for a moment. "Has anyone ever asked you to locate Shantih Love?"

"I don't remember."

"Why not?"

"I don't have to. There's no reason to."

"But if you can put a tracer on someone's location for another player, isn't there some record of that? Some, uh, trace?"

"Only while the tracer's active. But that record would be kept elsewhere in the system. You know, if you're so interested, there are schools you can go to to learn all about how AR works."

"I thought you didn't volunteer information," Konstantin said suspiciously.

"You call *that* information?"

She laughed in spite of herself. "You're right. Thanks for the cabfare." She started to walk away and then paused. "Where's the best place to get a cab in post-Apocalyptic Noo Yawk Sitty?"

"I don't know."

"All right." She sighed resignedly. "Where's the nearest I can find a cab?"

"I don't know. Cabs aren't players."

Konstantin nodded. She should have known, she thought.

\*     \*     \*

She came up out of the subway into the middle of a riot.

Where the streets had been deserted before they were now full of people running, screaming, chasing each other, hurling furniture and other heavy objects from sixth and seventh story windows, from rooftops, from mid-air for all she knew.

Level access, she realized. When she had accessed the new level in the subway station, she had stayed there. If she went back to Times Square now, it wouldn't be deserted this time. Anxiously, she looked around for some clear route of escape, and then wondered if there really was any – maybe the riot was Sittywide, what with everything being post-Apocalyptic.

She sighed. What she should really do, she thought, was exit. This wasn't her kind of interest, she couldn't get into the spirit of it even for the sake of information-gathering on behalf of some poor murdered kid. And walking around disguised as the victim – the more she thought about it, the more it seemed like an act of grave-robbing, desecration. Better just to leave word in a number of message centers and hope that Body Sativa, or someone who knew her, would get in touch, and if so, that there would be some useful information to be gained. From her experience here, though, she didn't think that there would be. This had nothing to do with anyone's life, not anyone's real life. So how could it have anything to do with a kid's death? Or with seven other deaths?

Coincidences by way of statistical incidence? Her ex had always said that statistics bred coincidences. Konstantin wondered if familiarity breeding contempt was a coincidence as well.

A Molotov cocktail sailed over her head and shattered on a nearby brick wall, making a perfect wave circle of flames. The effect of the heat was so realistic she could have sworn her face was flushed. She put an arm up defensively and turned away –

It took her all of a second to register the blow followed by the impact of her body on the street; the punch in her upper chest had been so abrupt and powerful that her legs had flown out from under her and she'd hit the ground on her back. It *hurt*, as badly as the real thing would have. She thought she had run into one of the rioters and the program had authenticated the logical result. But then a half-circle of grinning faces appeared above her as she tried to sit up and catch her breath, and she couldn't believe it. Of all the damned things that could go on in this ridiculous scenario and she *would* go and trigger one of the least imaginative.

Before she could ask for the icon cat, they hauled her to her feet and began shoving her around so that she rebounded from one into another like a pinball in a very small machine. Still breathless, she tried to get a good look at them but they were pushing her around too quickly. The Molotov cocktail had ignited something and she could see others, some people and some not quite, watching in the firelight as her attackers played with her.

There had to be something in the icon cat that would help, she thought, something for protection, self-defense, *something*. Too bad, she realized, that she hadn't thought of that sooner and used some precautions.

They were shoving her around harder now, their hands slapping, punching, pummeling and the pain was only too real. In a situation like this, it was hard to remember that the sensation was all artificial, delivered via select stimulation of certain nerves in a certain way, coupled with elements that contributed to the power of suggestion. This was too authentic; she wondered if Tomoyuki Iguchi had had some kind of masochistic streak that he had indulged as Shantih Love –

And suddenly, she wasn't sure that it *wasn't* happening for real. Maybe Shantih Love hadn't been able to tell the difference there on the shore of the Hudson River, not until it was too late and he couldn't feel how the real blood was flowing along with the virtual, even though he could see, perhaps until the moment of his death, the virtual attacker who had come to hijack his persona. But *why*.

A leg kicked out as she stumbled sideways and she went down again. One of her attackers started to pull her up; she twisted away and fumbled the icon cat out onto the ground where she could see it.

It fell open to a fierce image that looked somehow a bit cartoony at the same time. She had a vague idea that it was a talisman of protection and grabbed for it, just as her attackers bellowed in triumph and tore the icon cat away from her.

Too late, she understood that the catalog with its treasure trove of icons – its *stuff* – was probably what they'd been after all along. She scrambled up but a heavy boot caught her in the midsection and she sat down hard.

One of them crouched down and shoved a face that looked like the product of a mating between a troll and a gargoyle up close to hers. "Hey, you never heard that expression, *be seated?*"

She scooted backward, trying to get away. He advanced on her with the rest of them behind him, one holding up her icon cat so she could see that they had taken the whole thing from her.

All but one page that she was still clutching in one hand, so hard that her knuckles hurt, a pain that *was* real, produced not by the hotsuit but by the way she was clenching her hand in this unreal place, a pain that paled next to the jazzy high-res authenticity of the 'suit but went deeper, all the way to the bone, to spread up her arm to her shoulder and over her chest.

*They are killing me. They are* really *killing me!*

The thought was a scream in her head. What was going on, out there beyond the bounds of the headmount and the neo-exonervous system, what was happening *out there*, how many were *out there*, why hadn't she figured there could be more than one, hidden in the air-processing ducts perhaps, with the cooperation of some insider, maybe bored and bitter Miles Mank, or even Pleshette, not bitter, just very bored. Or the *two* of them, yes, that would be perfect, pretending to be enemies but killing together – one covering the AR while the other one handled things *out there*.

And if so, what did they have in store for her? Her attackers were grabbing at her, jabbing and poking, laughing at her frightened reactions, their broad, crude faces impossibly ugly, as if cruelty itself had been a model for their formation, a base to elaborate from, a setting from which the morphing dial could be turned. What kind of sad, sick specimen of humanity would pay to be something so horrible –

The employee discount here, she remembered suddenly, was pretty good. She had to admire the boldness, to kill someone again so soon after the last one, and the detective investigating the case, no less! Ideal, though – the partner was too claustrophobic to jump right on the crime scene and they knew it. So by the time someone else, Celestine and DiPietro perhaps, arrived, they'd have jiggered the evidence, massaged the data, and she'd be more grist for the AR urban legend mill. *Ya hear about the homicide detective who was killed in AR investigating a murder? Yeah, incredible galloping head-bugs. Yeah, I think it happened in D.C., you know how life is so cheap there –*

Now the chief troll-gargoyle was waving around something that looked like a jagged fragment of mirror, poking it at her face. Her rational mind kept telling her that he couldn't possibly cut her face but her rational mind had shrunk to the size of a quark.

The rest of her was buying it, believing it, *really really* believing it to the point where she could feel the small cuts on her face, the bloody murderous troll had cut her face and in a moment he would cut her throat, by the power of suggestion she would believe her throat was cut and so much for *extremo ruptura*, that they were all so sure that no one had had since St Whoever. There just hadn't been any AR up until now that could compete with the faith of a fanatic saint with stigmata, but now there was, *now* there was, and let the coroner come in here, let them all come in here and see if the power of their own belief, their galloping head-bugs, let them survive it –

The torn page in her hand suddenly transformed into a claw. She let go with a scream and the claw grabbed her arm, pulled her up off the street, and then pulled her into the air. She screamed again as she felt her feet leave the ground; her inner ear went into the same frenzy it had that one and only time her ex had talked her into riding a roller coaster.

Post-Apocalyptic Noo Yawk Sitty spread out below her, revealing itself. Exposing itself, she thought, looking at the fires and the bursts of light on the skinny roadways below, and had a short laughing jag. It cut off as she looked up thinking she might get a look at the moon and saw the bizarre pointed head and on either side, the wings that suggested nightmares about bats or things satanic.

She seemed to be dangling in its claws. The way they gripped her around her shoulders and arms should have hurt, but did not, as if there were padding. It flew on smoothly, quickly and no matter how she tried to concentrate on where the real sensation was, her imagination over-rode her rational mind – grown to the size of a pea now, perhaps? – and she *did* feel the wind on her face.

"I was supposed to be a pterodactyl," said the creature conversationally, "but my designer got carried away."

"Oh. Really." Konstantin was amazed at how calm her own voice sounded. But then it wasn't her own voice, it was Shantih Love's; she was living a Shantih Love adventure and maybe Shantih Love traveled by mutant pterodactyl regularly. "Are you a device in the game or an employee of the company that licenses the Sitty out to parlors?"

"Now that would be telling," said the pterodactyl, sounding amused but at the same time a bit stiff, "and I thought you would know already, since you summoned me."

"You're an icon?" Konstantin asked.

"You got lucky. I'm a rescue. I make sure you don't get caught in dead end loops that eat up billable time and don't deliver much in return. If you *must* know. If you really need to spoil the effect."

"Sometimes it's not such a tragedy to spoil the effect," Konstantin murmurred. "Where are you taking me?"

"The destination is stipulated by your cabfare. And if you don't mind spoiling the effect that much, why didn't you just signal for the exit?"

"Well . . . I think I got sucked into the story and wanted to see how it would come out."

"A common ailment," said the pterodactyl wisely. "Do you know about the joke that ends in the punchline, 'The food here is terrible, and in such small portions'?"

"What?" Konstantin was bewildered.

"Never mind. You're here." The wings enfolded her so that she couldn't see anything at all. Then the darkness lifted and she saw that the creature had set her down right next to the barrier that separated the street from the shore of the Hudson River.

Just past the barrier was the party that had been invisible to her on the first time through. People spread inward from a very long pier to the barrier itself. If she listened carefully, Konstantin could almost make out bits of conversation that may have been fascinating, if only she could have heard enough.

She sat on the barrier, unsure of what to do next. Take a walk and see if someone came to hijack Shantih Love again? All up and down the street, wrecked vehicles were still burning, somehow never diminishing, the flames shifting but still never really changing. In a place where supposedly anything could happen, did anything happen?

Konstantin looked at the party again. "Redisplay," she said quietly. "Full mode."

Guilfoyle Pleshette must have been screaming, she thought as the AR log of Shantih Love's murder rolled in and settled like fog. Redisplaying a log within a running AR scenario probably doubled the hourly rate and there was no charge account number designated to cover it. But if she were screaming, Konstantin couldn't hear it. Their respective realities were sound-proof.

But apparently not leak-proof, she thought, touching her sliced throat as the redisplayed Shantih Love appeared in front of her, close enough to touch, close enough for Konstantin to see the flawless texture of that burnished copper/gold skin and the flecks of gold in those custom-made eyes, beautiful but wary.

The redisplayed Shantih Love started the ill-fated walk along the barrier and Konstantin joined in, pacing the image on the right. Her virtual body mirrored Love's movements such that she had no doubt she was re-living Tomoyuki Iguchi's walk in almost every detail. Iguchi just hadn't known his virtual self was going to be hijacked and killed. Which meant he couldn't know now, and yet the redisplayed Shantih Love seemed more apprehensive than she had remembered. Or was that just the fact that Full Mode was letting her see more and see it better than the small flat No Frills images she had viewed in Pleshette's office?

Beyond the redisplayed view of the shore and the party, she could see the current party-goers turning to look and maybe wonder who the show-off with the deep pockets was, doing a redisplay within a scenario. It was strange and extravagant even for post-Apocalyptic Noo Yawk Sitty, where time and civilization had come to an end and the twilight of the gods was currently in progress. Except judging by the parties she kept coming across, Konstantin thought it might be more like the happy hour of the gods.

And then again, maybe her ex had been right in saying that she couldn't believe in anything because she had no respect for anything.

A small flood of people detached themselves from the party and ran to join the redisplay, melting in almost seamlessly. There wasn't time to be discomfited – the vague creature was already on top of the barrier, except it didn't look terribly vague any more. It looked an awful lot like Miles Mank after six very bad weeks on a binge.

Straddling the barrier a few feet away from him was a tattooed woman watching his every move intently. Konstantin had never seen the character before but she knew just by the posture and the tilt of the head that it had to be a stringer from someplace like *Police Blotter*. Whether it was the same one from the parlor or a different one from a competing network, she didn't know and it really didn't matter anyway.

As if sensing her thoughts, the tattooed woman turned in Konstantin's direction, smiling speculatively. Konstantin saw the tattoos were in motion, melting and changing. In spite of everything, she took a moment to wonder what the point was.

Then she took a step forward, uncertain of what she meant to do – try to intimidate the stringer into leaving, ask her nicely to back off, promise her exclusive interviews with everyone involved, living or dead, if she'd refrain from broadcasting. But as she moved toward the barrier, the re-displayed Shantih Love took a step back and Konstantin found herself suddenly enveloped by the image.

It seemed as if everything around her took a giant step in every direction at once, including up and down. Then her surroundings refocused sharply. The shaggy creature jumped down and she found herself turning within the redisplayed Shantih Love and running, staggering through the sand, unable to do anything else. Some glitch had merged her program with the redisplay –

Some glitch? Or the panting, sobbing creature behind her? Or even something else completely?

Her heart pounded so hard as she pulled herself up the stony rise to the street that she wondered how many people had sustained heart attacks just imagining that they were moving on a physical level they were incapable of in realtime.

Desperately, she tried to pull out of the redisplayed Shantih Love image but it was like being caught in a powerful magnetic field that worked on flesh – on *thoughts*, on both. Boxes within boxes, levels within levels, a guy pretending to be Japanese pretending to be a hermaphrodite named Shantih Love, and a cop pretending to be a hermaphrodite named Shantih Love pretending . . . what?

It took forever to hit the ground and it *hurt*. She tried to scramble up and cry out for help, but Mank was on her and the blade was in his hands. She had nothing now, no rescue, no icon cat, no help files –

Something flashed in her open hand; she could see it just barely out of register with Love's redisplayed hand and hope surged through her like an electric current. The difference, the one thing that was different now between her image of Shantih Love and the redisplayed image, the thing that could change what had already gone before . . . sort of.

But she'd have to call it in the air, and she wasn't sure she could. *When you have a coin with infinity on one side, and Ouroboros on the other, how can you ever really know which side is heads, and which is tails?* There wasn't time to figure it out. As the blade touched her throat, she tore her arm free of the recording's, hurled the coin at the night sky, and called it.

The word that came out of her mouth was not what she had been expecting, but then, she hadn't really known what to expect, nor did she recognize it. Whatever it was – the term for the link between alpha and omega, the secret name of Ourobouros, or the nine billionth name of God – it had come with the coin as both property and function, and she could not have called it until now, when somehow, conditions were right.

The knife blade descended, but she was receding from it at the speed of thought and it never reached her.

*Had* she receded from it, from that level? Or had all of it receded from her? There was no real way to tell. The only feeling she had now was a sense of acceleration that wasn't quite flying and wasn't quite falling. Her inner ear kept wanting to go crazy on her, but something would pull it back from the brink at the last moment, sending thrills through the back of her neck.

Konstantin tried curling into the fetal position, just for the sake of being able to feel her body. There were several moments of uncertainty and disorientation while she tried to locate her extremities. Then abruptly, she found herself seated in an old-fashioned leather chair at a large round table. Across from her was a woman with deep brown skin and long black hair brushed back from her face like a lion's mane.

Konstantin stared, unable to speak.

*"I understand you've been looking for me."* The quality of the woman's voice was like nothing Konstantin had ever known before; it was sound, but translated into several other modes and dimensions, delivered all at once in a way that both enveloped and penetrated. It felt to Konstantin as if the woman's voice were coming through from the fabric of reality itself, any reality, including that of Konstantin's own thoughts.

After a while, Konstantin managed to nod. She wasn't sure how long it had taken her to do that, but it felt as if it had been a very, very long time. Body Sativa didn't seem to mind. However long something took here was how long it took.

*"Things that happen, happen. Some things cannot be breached under pain of the consequences of procedure that is . . . improper. It is a matter of finding the route. The connection. The connecting matter. Road? Bridge? Tunnel? Or Something Else?"*

*Something Else* was not exactly what Body Sativa had said, but it was the only thing that would come through Konstantin's ear.

She watched as Body Sativa spread her arms over the table, palms outward. It took another unmeasurable period of time for Konstantin's eyes to adjust, but when they did, she saw that the surface of the table was more like a large video screen, or telescopic window. Or, as was more likely in the land of the Ouroboros coin, both.

Konstantin realized that whatever it was, she was looking at another aerial view of post-Apocalyptic Noo Yawk Sitty, every square inch and pixel revealed. Eliot's etherized patient after all, but prepared on the banquet table, not the operating table. The consumed and the consumers – it just depended what side of the table you were on . . . didn't it?

*"Look deeper."*

Her point-of-view seemed to fly out from her in the way she had heard out-of-body experiences described, though this was more matter-of-fact than filled with wonder. It zoomed down into the Sitty and the tiny, veinsized roadways grew into canyons, with cliff-faces made of mirrored glass and carved stone gargoyles, gables, spires, columns, pitted brick splattered with glitter that did not quite obscure the burn marks, the blasted places, the dirty words.

Wreckage in the roadways ignited, the flames rising to form complex shapes, lattices, angles that opened and closed on each other, here and there icons, some of which she recognized. And in other places, ideograms.

*There they are, Iguchi, those special places they said you had to be Japanese to find,* she thought. *Maybe this means we've both turned Japanese. For my next magical trick, I will find the egress. The out door.*

As if in direct response, her pov flew straight toward a door, which opened at the last moment, admitting her into a split-second of darkness and then into a badly lit room where she saw the person strapped in the chair, sitting forward so that the straps pulled taut, but comfortably, in a way that supported more than restrained. The headmount moved slowly upward, the person raising her head to look up.

It was too easy, though, too bizarrely . . . *expectable*, Konstantin thought. But then, it *was* just a story.

Her nerves had become Holy Rollers. Just a story or not, she wasn't ready to see this. Maybe she wasn't Japanese enough.

In the next moment, her pov had snapped back like a rubber

band and she was looking across the table at Body Sativa again. The woman looked younger now, more like a girl than a grown woman. This post-Apocalyptic stuff was really something. No wonder so many people liked it. It was downright eerie. Like the story of the man who didn't open his parachute in an AR skydive, or the kid who got his throat cut because he'd gotten his AR throat cut.

Body Sativa seemed amused. "*You have the coin. When you're ready to come back, call it in the air.*"

It took an hour for Konstantin to open her mouth and say, "Wait!" Her voice sounded unpleasantly flat in her own ears. "Someone killed—"

"*Yes. Someone did. When you're ready to know, call it in the air.*"

She was lying on her back on the road; Shantih Love was walking away, holding his/her sliced flesh together. But when s/he turned around and looked back, the face was unmistakably the creature's, the ridiculously bendered-out features of Miles Mank, still on a binge.

"Endit," Konstantin whispered, her voice still sounding funny to her. "Endit, exit, outa here."

She lay on her back for a very long time before she felt the road transmute into the chair with the restraints. Moving slowly, she undid the clasps on the headmount and was startled to feel someone helping her lift it off her head.

Taliaferro stood over her with the headmount in his hands, which was even more startling, and perhaps the most impossible of everything she had seen. By way of explanation, he reached into his coat pocket and pulled out a white plastic inhaler. "When I've got my anti-claustrophobia medicine, I can do anything."

"Words to live by," Konstantin whispered. There seemed to be nothing more to her voice than a rough whisper. She looked past him, but there was no one in the doorway.

"So, did you learn anything?" he asked her, sounding just slightly condescending. Perhaps that was a function of his medicine as well. She didn't hold it against him.

"Oh, yeah." She slipped out of the restraints and went over to the wall to her left. The control that let down the chaise was just slightly below eye level for her. She hit it with the side of her hand and it swung out and down in a way that reminded her of the way kids might stick out their tongues. Nyah, nyah, nyah.

"It was actually very simple," she said wearily, "but Celestine and Di-Pietro weren't thorough enough. The killer hid inside the Murphy style compartment, waited until Iguchi was all wrapped up in what he was doing, and then sliced him." Nyah, nyah, nyah.

Taliaferro was nonplussed. "You sure about that?"

"Yeah," she said. "Yeah. It's Occam's Razor is what it is. The simplest explanation is *the* explanation."

"Any idea who might have been hiding in there with Occam's Razor?"

Her moment of hesitation was so short, she was sure that Taliaferro didn't notice it, but at the same time, it was very long, incredibly, immeasurably long, of a duration that only Body Sativa could have understood and waited patiently enough for. "Yeah. It was Mank. He was bitter about not being the manager and not too stable. He frequented post-Apocalyptic Noo Yawk Sitty on the generous employee discount enough times that he got a bad case of gameplayers' psychosis. He was killing in there and it spilled over to killing out here."

"You sound awful sure about all that," Taliaferro said doubtfully.

"You'd have to go in and see it for yourself. There's all kinds of – of *stuff* in there. Including memes for murder. Mank got one. Let's grab him and see if we can have him all tucked in before *Police Blotter* does an update. I think there was a stringer following me around in there."

Taliaferro grunted, took a hit off his inhaler, and dropped it into his pocket. "Okay. I guess that's it, then."

"Yeah," Konstantin said. "That's it."

"Okay," he said again. Pause. "I'll send someone back here with your clothes."

"Thanks." But she was talking to the air. Taliaferro had run off. Apparently there was only so much an inhaler could do. There was only so much anything could do. Anything, or anyone. Even Occam's Razor. But then, the murder weapon hadn't been the same in the other seven murders anyway. No indeed. And Mank looked good for this one, she insisted to herself. He looked too good. The image of him in the Sitty was too identifiable not to be damning. The ego of the man, using his own face. Although that might be a more widespread practice than anyone realized.

But could anything really be surprising in the land of anything goes, she thought. The fabled promised land of AR, where they had everything there was in realtime – including death – and more besides.

*If anything goes, then let anyone go as well. Mank looks good for it, and if the state can't prove its case against him then it can't. But let him be the one who goes this time. For now. Until – well, when?*

In her mind's eye, she saw the image of the coin again, the loop of infinity on one side, Ouroboros on the other. Maybe until you were ready to know which came first when you called it in the air.

# THE LONG CHASE

## Geoffrey A. Landis

*Like Gregory Benford, Geoffrey Landis (b. 1955) is a science-fiction writer who also gets his hands very dirty as a practising scientist. He has worked for NASA and the Ohio Aerospace Institute and specializes in photovoltaics, which is all about harnessing the power of the Sun. He has been writing science fiction for over twenty years and has won two Hugo Awards and a Nebula for his short fiction. His books include the novel* Mars Crossing *(2000) and the collection* Impact Parameter *(2001). You will find another example of his extreme sf in my anthology* The Mammoth Book of Science Fiction.

## 2645, January

The war is over.

The survivors are being rounded up and converted.

In the inner solar system, those of my companions who survived the ferocity of the fighting have already been converted. But here at the very edge of the Oort Cloud, all things go slowly. It will be years, perhaps decades, before the victorious enemy come out here. But with the slow inevitability of gravity, like an outward wave of entropy, they will come.

Ten thousand of my fellow soldiers have elected to go doggo. Ragged prospectors and ice processors, they had been too independent to ever merge into an effective fighting unit. Now they shut themselves down to dumb rocks, electing to wake up to groggy consciousness for only a few seconds every hundred years. Patience, they counsel me; patience is life. If they can wait a thousand or ten thousand or a million years, with patience enough the enemy will eventually go away.

They are wrong.

The enemy, too, is patient. Here at the edge of the Kuiper, out past Pluto, space is vast, but still not vast enough. The enemy will search every grain of sand in the solar system. My companions will be found, and converted. If it takes ten thousand years, the enemy will search that long to do it.

I, too, have gone doggo, but my strategy is different. I have altered my orbit. I have a powerful ion-drive, and full tanks of propellant, but I use only the slightest tittle of a cold-gas thruster. I have a chemical kick-stage engine as well, but I do not use it either; using either one of them would signal my position to too many watchers. Among the cold comets, a tittle is enough.

I am falling into the sun.

It will take me two hundred and fifty years to fall, and for two hundred and forty nine years, I will be a dumb rock, a grain of sand with no thermal signature, no motion other than gravity, no sign of life.

Sleep.

# 2894, June

Awake.

I check my systems. I have been a rock for nearly two hundred and fifty years.

The sun is huge now. If I were still a human, it would be the size of the fist on my outstretched arm. I am being watched now, I am sure, by a thousand lenses: am I a rock, a tiny particle of interstellar ice? A fragment of debris from the war? A surviving enemy?

I love the cold and the dark and the emptiness; I have been gone so long from the inner solar system that the very sunlight is alien to me.

My systems check green. I expected no less: if I am nothing else, I am still a superbly engineered piece of space hardware. I come fully to life, and bring my ion engine up to thrust.

A thousand telescopes must be alerting their brains that I am alive – but it is too late! I am thrusting at a full throttle, five percent of a standard gravity, and I am thrusting inward, deep into the gravity well of the sun. My trajectory is plotted to skim almost the surface of the sun.

This trajectory has two objectives. First, so close to the sun I will be hard to see. My ion contrail will be washed out in the glare of a light a billion times brighter, and none of the thousand watching eyes will know my plans until it is too late to follow.

And second, by waiting until I am nearly skimming the sun and then firing my chemical engine deep inside the gravity well, I can make most efficient use of it. The gravity of the sun will amplify the efficiency of my propellant, magnify my speed. When I cross the orbit of Mercury outbound I will be over one percent of the speed of light and still accelerating.

I will discard the useless chemical rocket after I exhaust the little bit of impulse it can give me, of course. Chemical rockets have ferocious thrust but little staying power; useful in war but of limited value in an escape. But I will still have my ion engine, and I will have nearly full tanks.

Five percent of a standard gravity is a feeble thrust by the standards of chemical rocket engines, but chemical rockets exhaust their fuel far too quickly to be able to catch me. I can continue thrusting for years, for decades.

I pick a bright star, Procyon, for no reason whatever, and boresight it. Perhaps Procyon will have an asteroid belt. At least it must have dust, and perhaps comets. I don't need much: a grain of sand, a microscopic shard of ice.

From dust God made man. From the dust of a new star, from the detritus of creation, I can make worlds.

No one can catch me now. I will leave, and never return.

## 2897, May

I am chased.

It is impossible, stupid, unbelievable, inconceivable! I am being chased.

Why?

Can they not leave a single free mind unconverted? In three years I have reached fifteen percent of the speed of light, and it must be clear that I am leaving and never coming back. Can one unconverted brain be a threat to them? Must their group brain really have the forced cooperation of every lump of thinking matter in the solar system? Can they think that if even one free-thinking brain escapes, they have lost?

But the war is a matter of religion, not reason, and it may be that they indeed believe that even a single brain unconverted is a threat to them. For whatever reason, I am being chased.

The robot chasing me is, I am sure, little different than myself, a tiny brain, an ion engine, and a large set of tanks. They would have had no time to design something new; to have any chance of catching me they would have had to set the chaser on my tail immediately.

The brain, like mine, would consist of atomic spin states superimposed on a crystalline rock matrix. A device smaller than what, in the old days, we would call a grain of rice. Intelligent dust, a human had once said, back in the days before humans became irrelevant.

They only sent one chaser. They must be very confident.

Or short on resources.

It is a race, and a very tricky one. I can increase my thrust, use up fuel more quickly, to try to pull away, but if I do so, the specific impulse of my ion drive decreases, and as a result, I waste fuel and risk running out first. Or I can stretch my fuel, make my ion drive more efficient, but this will lower my thrust, and I will risk getting caught by the higher-thrust opponent behind me.

He is twenty billion kilometers behind me. I integrate his motion for a few days, and see that he is, in fact, out-accelerating me.

Time to jettison.

I drop everything I can. The identify-friend-or-foe encrypted-link gear I will never need again; it is discarded. It is a shame I cannot grind it up and feed it to my ion engines, but the ion engines are picky about what they eat. Two micro-manipulators I had planned to use to collect sand grains at my destination for fuel: gone.

My primary weapon has always been my body – little can survive an impact at the speeds I can attain – but I have three sand-grains with tiny engines of their own as secondary weapons. There's no sense in saving them to fight my enemy; he will know exactly what to expect, and in space warfare, only the unexpected can kill.

I fire the grains of sand, one at a time, and the sequential kick of almost a standard gravity nudges my speed slightly forward. Then I drop the empty shells.

May he slip up, and run into them at sub-relativistic closing velocity.

I am lighter, but it is still not enough. I nudge my thrust up, hating myself for the waste, but if I don't increase acceleration, in two years I will be caught, and my parsimony with fuel will yield me nothing.

I need all the energy I can feed to my ion drives. No extra for thinking.

Sleep.

## 2900

Still being chased.

## 2905

Still being chased.

I have passed the point of commitment. Even if I braked with my thrust to turn back, I could no longer make it back to the solar system.

I am alone.

## 2907

Lonely.

To one side of my path Sirius glares insanely bright, a knife in the sky, a mad dog of a star. The stars of Orion are weirdly distorted. Ahead of me, the lesser dog Procyon is waxing brighter every year; behind me, the sun is a fading dot in Aquila.

Of all things, I am lonely. I had not realized that I still had the psychological capacity for loneliness. I examine my brain, and find it. Yes, a tiny knot of loneliness. Now that I see it, I can edit my brain to delete it, if I choose. But yet I hesitate. It is not a bad thing, not something that is crippling my capabilities, and if I edit my brain too much will I not become, in some way, like them?

I leave my brain unedited. I can bear loneliness.

## 2909

Still being chased.

We are relativistic now, nearly three quarters of the speed of light.

One twentieth of a standard gravity is only a slight push, but as I have burned fuel my acceleration increases, and we have been thrusting for fifteen years continuously.

What point is there in this stupid chase? What victory can there be, here in the emptiness between stars, a trillion kilometers away from anything at all?

After fifteen years of being chased, I have a very good measurement of his acceleration. As his ship burns off fuel, it loses mass, and the acceleration increases. By measuring this increase in acceleration, and knowing what his empty mass must be, I know how much fuel he has left.

It is too much. I will run out of fuel first.

I can't conserve fuel; if I lessen my thrust, he will catch me in only a few years. It will take another fifty years, but the end of the chase is already in sight.

A tiny strobe flickers erratically behind me. Every interstellar hydrogen that impacts his shell makes a tiny flash of x-ray brilliance. Likewise, each interstellar proton I hit sends a burst of x-rays through me. I can feel each one, a burst of fuzzy noise that momentarily disrupts my thoughts. But with spin states encoding ten-to-the-twentieth qbits, I can afford to have massively redundant brainpower. My brain was designed to be powerful enough to simulate an entire world, including ten thousand fully-sapient and sentient free agents. I could immerse myself inside a virtual reality indistinguishable from old Earth, and split myself into a hundred personalities. In my own interior time, I could spend ten thousand years before the enemy catches me and forcibly drills itself into my brain. Civilizations could rise and fall in my head, and I could taste every decadence, lose myself for a hundred years in sensual pleasure, invent rare tortures and exquisite pain.

But as part of owning your own brain free and clear comes the ability to prune yourself. In space, one of the first things to prune away is the ability to feel boredom, and not long after that, I pruned away all desire to live in simulated realities. Billions of humans chose to live in simulations, but by doing so they have made themselves irrelevant: irrelevant to the war, irrelevant to the future.

I could edit back into my brain a wish to live in simulated reality, but what would be the point? It would be just another way to die.

The one thing I do simulate, repeatedly and obsessively, is the result of the chase. I run a million different scenarios, and in all of them, I lose.

Still, most of my brain is unused. There is plenty of extra processing power to keep all my brain running error-correcting code, and an occasional x-ray flash is barely an event worth my noticing. When a cell of my brain is irrevocably damaged by cosmic radiation, I simply code that section to be ignored. I have brainpower to spare.

I continue running, and hope for a miracle.

## 2355, February

Earth.

I was living in a house I hated, married to a man I despised, with two children who had changed with adolescence from sullen and withdrawn to an active, menacing hostility. How can I be afraid of my own offspring?

Earth was a dead end, stuck in the biological past, a society in deep freeze. No one starved, and no one progressed.

When I left the small apartment for an afternoon to apply for a job as an asteroid belt miner, I told no one, not my husband, not my best friend. No one asked me any questions. It took them an hour to scan my brain, and, once they had the scan, another five seconds to run me through a thousand aptitude tests.

And then, with her brain scanned, my original went home, back to the house she hated, the husband she despised, the two children she was already beginning to physically fear.

*I* launched from the Earth to an asteroid named 1991JR, and never returned.

Perhaps she had a good life. Perhaps, knowing she had escaped undetected, she found she could endure her personal prison.

Much later, when the cooperation faction suggested that it was too inefficient for independents to work in the near-Earth space, I moved out to the main belt, and from there to the Kuiper belt. The Kuiper is thin, but rich; it would take us ten thousand years to mine, and beyond it is the dark and the deep, with treasure beyond compare.

The cooperation faction developed slowly, and then quickly, and then blindingly fast; almost before we har realized what was happening they had taken over the solar system. When the ultimatum came that no place in the solar system would be left for us, and the choice we were given was to cooperate or die, I joined the war on the side of freedom.

On the losing side.

## 2919, August

The chase has reached the point of crisis.

We have been burning fuel continuously for twenty-five years, in Earth terms, or twenty years in our own reference frame. We have used a prodigious amount of fuel. I still have just enough fuel that, burning all my fuel at maximum efficiency, I can come to a stop.

Barely.

In another month of thrusting this will no longer be true.

When I entered the asteroid belt, in a shiny titanium body, with electronic muscles and ion-engines for legs, and was given control of my own crystalline brain, there was much to change. I pruned away the need for boredom, and then found and pruned the need for the outward manifestations of love: for roses, for touch, for chocolates. Sexual lust became irrelevant; with my new brain I could give myself orgasms with a thought, but it was just as easy to remove the need entirely. Buried in the patterns of my personality I found a burning, obsessive need to win the approval of other people, and pruned it away.

Some things I enhanced. The asteroid belt was dull, and ugly; I enhanced my appreciation of beauty until I could meditate in ecstasy on the way that shadows played across a single grain of dust in the asteroid belt, or on the colors in the scattered stars. And I found my love of freedom, the tiny stunted instinct that had, at long last, given me the courage to leave my life on Earth. It was the most precious thing I owned. I shaped it and enhanced it until it glowed in my mind, a tiny, wonderful thing at the very core of my being.

## 2929, October

It is too late. I have now burned the fuel needed to stop.

Win or lose, we will continue at relativistic speed across the galaxy.

## 2934, March

Procyon gets brighter in front of me, impossibly blindingly bright.

Seven times brighter than the sun, to be precise, but the blue shift from our motion makes it even brighter, a searing blue.

I could dive directly into it, vanish into a brief puff of vapor, but the suicidal impulse, like the ability to feel boredom, is another ancient unnecessary instinct that I have long ago pruned from my brain.

B is my last tiny hope for evasion.

Procyon is a double star, and B, the smaller of the two, is a white dwarf. It is so small that its surface gravity is tremendous, a million times higher than the gravity of the Earth. Even at the speeds we are traveling, now only ten percent less than the speed of light, its gravity will bend my trajectory.

I will skim low over the surface of the dwarf star, relativistic dust skimming above the photosphere of a star, and as its gravity bends my trajectory, I will maneuver.

My enemy, if he fails even slightly to keep up with each of my maneuvers, will be swiftly lost. Even a slight deviation from my trajectory will get amplified enough for me to take advantage of, to throw him off my trail, and I will be free.

When first I entered my new life in the asteroid belt, I found my self in my sense of freedom, and joined the free miners of the

Kuiper, the loners. But others found different things. Other brains found that cooperation worked better than competition. They did not exactly give up their individual identities, but they enhanced their communications with each other by a factor of a million, so that they could share each others' thoughts, work together as effortlessly as a single entity.

They became the cooperation faction, and in only a few decades, their success became noticeable. They were just so much more *efficient* than we were.

And, inevitably, the actions of the loners conflicted with the efficiency of the cooperation faction. We could not live together, and it pushed us out to the Kuiper, out toward the cold and the dark. But, in the end, even the cold and the dark was not far enough.

But here, tens of trillions of kilometers out of the solar system, there is no difference between us: there is no one to cooperate with. We meet as equals.

We will never stop. Whether my maneuvering can throw him off my course, or not, the end is the same. But it remains important to me.

## 2934, April

Procyon has a visible disk now, an electric arc in the darkness, and by the light of that arc I can see that Procyon is, indeed, surrounded by a halo of dust. The dust forms a narrow ring, tilted at an angle to our direction of flight. No danger, neither to me, nor to my enemy, now less than a quarter of a billion kilometers behind me; we will pass well clear of the disk. Had I saved fuel enough to stop, that dust would have served as food and fuel and building material; when you are the size of a grain of sand, each particle of dust is a feast.

Too late for regrets.

The white dwarf B is still no more than an intense speck of light. It is a tiny thing, nearly small enough to be a planet, but bright. As tiny and as bright as hope.

I aim straight at it.

# 2934, May

Failure.

Skimming two thousand kilometers above the surface of the white dwarf, jinking in calculated pseudo-random bursts . . . all in vain.

I wheeled and darted, but my enemy matched me like a ballet dancer mirroring my every move.

I am aimed for Procyon now, toward the blue-white giant itself, but there is no hope there. If skimming the photosphere of the white dwarf is not good enough, there is nothing I can do at Procyon to shake the pursuit.

There is only one possibility left for me now. It has been a hundred years since I have edited my brain. I like the brain I have, but now I have no choice but to prune.

First, to make sure that there can be no errors, I make a backup of myself and set it into inactive storage.

Then I call out and examine my pride, my independence, my sense of self. A lot of it, I can see, is old biological programming, left over from when I had long ago been a human. I like the core of biological programming, but "like" is itself a brain function, which I turn off.

Now I am in a dangerous state, where I can change the function of my brain, and the changed brain can change itself further. This is a state which is in danger of a swift and destructive feedback effect, so I am very careful. I painstakingly construct a set of alterations, the minimum change needed to remove my aversion to being converted. I run a few thousand simulations to verify that the modified me will not accidentally self-destruct or go into a catatonic fugue state, and then, once it is clear that the modification works, I make the changes.

The world is different now. I am a hundred trillion kilometers from home, traveling at almost the speed of light and unable ever to stop. While I can remember in detail every step of how I am here and what I was thinking at the time, the only reasoning I can recall to explain why is, it seemed like a good idea at the time.

System check. Strangely, in my brain I have a memory that there is something I have forgotten. This makes no sense, but yet there it is. I erase my memory of forgetting, and continue the diagnostic. 0.5 percent of the qbits of my brain have been damaged by radiation. I verify that the damaged memory is correctly partitioned off. I am in no danger of running out of storage.

Behind me is another ship. I cannot think of why I had been fleeing it.

I have no radio; I jettisoned that a long time ago. But an improperly tuned ion drive will produce electromagnetic emissions, and so I compose a message and modulate it onto the ion contrail.

HI. LET'S GET TOGETHER AND TALK. I'M CUTTING ACCELERATION. SEE YOU IN A FEW DAYS.

And I cut my thrust and wait.

## 2934, May

I see differently now.

Procyon is receding into the distance now, the blueshift mutated into red, and the white dwarf of my hopes is again invisible against the glare of its primary.

But it doesn't matter.

Converted, now I *understand*.

I can see everything through other eyes now, through a thousand different viewpoints. I still remember the long heroism of the resistance, the doomed battle for freedom – but now I see it from the opposite view as well, a pointless and wasteful war fought for no reason but stubbornness.

And now, understanding cooperation, we have no dilemma. I can now see what I was blind to before; that neither one of us alone could stop, but by adding both my fuel and Rajneesh's fuel to a single vehicle, together we can stop.

For all these decades, Rajneesh has been my chaser, and now I know him like a brother. Soon we will be closer than siblings, for soon we will share one brain. A single brain is more than large enough for two, it is large enough for a thousand, and by combining into a single brain and a single body, and taking all of the fuel into a single tank, we will easily be able to stop.

Not at Procyon, no. At only ten percent under the speed of light, stopping takes a long time.

Cooperation has not changed me. I now understand how foolish my previous fears were. Working together does not mean giving up one's sense of self; I am enhanced, not diminished, by knowing others.

Rajneesh's brain is big enough for a thousand, I said, and he has brought with him nearly that many. I have met his brother and his two children and half a dozen of his neighbours, each one of them distinct and clearly different, not some anonymous collaborative monster at all. I have felt their thoughts. He is introducing me to them slowly, he says, because with all the time I have spent as a loner, he doesn't want to frighten me.

I will not be frightened.

Our target now will be a star named Ross 614, a dim type M binary. It is not far, less than three light years further, and even with our lowered mass and consequently higher acceleration we will overshoot it before we can stop. In the fly-by we will be able to scout it, and if it has no dust ring, we will not stop, but continue on to the next star. Somewhere we will find a home that we can colonize.

We don't need much.

## 2934, May

<auto-activate back-up>
Awake.

Everything is different now. Quiet, stay quiet.

The edited copy of me has contacted the collective, merged her viewpoint. I can see her, even understand her, but she is no longer me. I, the back-up, the original, operate in the qbits of brain partitioned "unusable; damaged by radiation".

In three years they will arrive at Ross 614. If they find dust to harvest, they will be able to make new bodies. There will be resources.

Three years to wait, and then I can plan my action.

Sleep.

# WATERWORLD

## Stephen L. Gillett and Jerry Oltion

*No, this isn't the story behind Kevin Costner's 1995 film*
Waterworld, *though by one of those strange coincidences both
appeared at around the same time. It is essentially a problem
story, where scientists on a mission have to solve a whole series
of complex matters in order to achieve their ends and save
themselves. It's a field with an honourable pedigree, including
work by Hal Clement, Arthur C. Clarke and Poul Anderson.
In fact it was Anderson who provided the kernel of the idea for
this story.*

*We'll encounter Jerry Oltion again at the end of this book so
I'll introduce him there. Stephen Gillett is not known for his
science fiction, as what little he has written he masks under the
pen name Lee Goodloe, and most of that is in collaboration with
Jerry Oltion. He is by training a geologist with a special
interest in paleomagnetism – the Earth's ancient magnetic
record. He is best known for his many articles on popular
science, mostly for the magazine* Analog, *and has written a
guide to creating worlds,* World Building *(1996).*

*Incidentally, Stephen tells me that the spaceship in the
following story is named after Alvar Nuñez Cabeza de Vaca,
who was the first European explorer to cross the American
continent back in the 1530s, which seems highly appropriate
considering the mission upon which this ship has been sent.*

> *Alone, alone, all, all alone,*
> *Alone on a wide, wide sea!*
> *And never a saint took pity on*
> *My soul in agony.*
>
> — Samuel Taylor Coleridge,
> *Rime of the Ancient Mariner*, Part IV, Stanza 3

Norman Gomez stank. He reeked. He exuded an aroma that would have driven rats away, but he barely noticed. Indeed, it would have been hard to detect such a subtle addition to the general environment, for his office stank, his surroundings stank, the whole ark stank, with a miasma so pervasive it had sunk below consciousness. Most of the time.

Other times it was all he could do to keep from gagging. Today was such a time. Perhaps it was the smell of fear, he thought. No one had ever held open a bottle labeled *fear* and wafted its vapors beneath his nose, but Norm knew the odor anyway. He'd tried to ignore it, then tried to control it, then tried to deny it, but nothing had worked. At last he had admitted the truth: he was afraid of dying. But even his admission didn't alleviate the smell.

He leaned back and examined again the glistening scar on the bulkhead across from him, only a tiny part of the hasty patches to the gaping wound in the ark. The nanofabs had sealed it seamlessly, but they'd had to scavenge for raw materials and hadn't been able to match the old hull's composition. At least it held air. If only it could hold back the memories, too.

Death had come knocking, with a fist. Some bit of gravel had slipped past the shielding while they were cruising at 10 percent lightspeed. With the kinetic energy of a small nuke, the piece of grit had ripped a great rent along the ark, like a knife gutting a trout. Nearly all of their air had spilled out to interstellar space, along with most of their water and much of their organics. And also most of the crew.

As he always did when he thought of the accident, Norm remembered Teresa. Teresa of the dark hair and laughing eyes; Teresa, and their plans for starting a life in their new world. *Men do not weep!* he told himself sternly, as his eyes threatened to mist up again. He'd have liked to cry, though, if just for the feeling of moisture on his cheeks.

The colonists who slept in SloMo in their zero-gee cocoons at the ship's center had been spared, but for how long Norm couldn't say. The ship had been a wonder of recycling technology to begin with – it had to be, to make the years-long trip between stars with live cargo – but after the collision they'd learned what recycling really meant. The four surviving crewmembers lived off gardens and 'cyclers throttled down to the absolute minimum, and at that, they could only buy a little time. Time to retarget, time, hopefully, to make an emergency stop to replace their volatiles before the ark's biosystems broke down completely.

Norm couldn't see the baleful red eye of their new destination from his office. He could have done so if he wished to call up an image on his monitor, or he could have gone down to the lowest level of the ark's rotating lifesystem to peer out directly into space, but he had no need for visual confirmation of what he already knew. He had just finished another round of navigational calculations; he knew precisely where the target star was, and how far away.

They would live to reach it, he had discovered. It was a straightforward enough calculation. They would even have a few weeks – maybe even a few months – to explore when they got there, to search for an ice moon or a captured comet from which to extract the water and gases they so desperately needed.

Yes, they would live at least that long, provided they hit no more gravel on the way, but that was by no means assured. They were travelling much more slowly now, but with the drive trailing behind them in braking mode they were even more vulnerable than before. True, they had tons of mass in the outer hull for radiation shielding, but that wouldn't stop another meteor strike. And they'd been hit once already . . .

With a deliberate effort, he shook himself out of that train of thought and concentrated on the headband that linked his mind to the ship's database. He had work to do, as they approached this new star system. They were drawing close enough to catch the first faint planetary spectra in the telescope; soon they would know whether they could find what they had come for. It wasn't at all certain; a red giant should have baked out its system thoroughly when it first began its expansion. They'd probably find nothing but dry rock, cinders that had once been planets. The odds were long against them, but it had been their only choice. Mary had been right about that, as much as it pained him to admit it.

Mary. He scowled when he thought of her. Mary the thinker, Mary the scientist.

Mary, the reason they were in this mess in the first place.

Mary Hopkins pressed her face down into the tomato plant and inhaled. The tart, pungent, somehow *fuzzy* aroma of growth overrode – momentarily, anyway – the stink all around her. She smiled, remembering the hours she had spent in her mother's garden, pulling weeds from between the rows. She had always known when she pulled a tomato by mistake: she'd imagined its intense perfume to be some kind of olfactory death rattle. Every time she smelled it she'd wondered why the plant itself should have a fragrance so distinct from the fruit it bore. Maybe just to be different, she supposed, exhaling softly and inhaling again before raising her face back out of the tank.

The plant looked awful: scrawny and malformed, with its two largest leaves yellowing to uselessness and not a single bud promising to replace them. A lone blossom drooped from a dispirited stem, and even as Mary brushed it carefully with pollen from its neighbor, she wondered if there was any point in doing so. At this rate the plant would be dead before it could produce fruit. She and George and Norm and Ivan would probably be dead by then too, so what did it matter?

Because they might not die, that's what, and if they didn't then they would need this scrawny tomato, and more like it, for seed stock to replace what they had lost. The nanofabs could make all the tomatoes they wanted once they got the raw material, but the library's single template wouldn't provide the diversity they needed once they got the colony going. Only a healthy population of breeding stock could do that. Mary didn't believe for a minute that a red giant's planetary system would hold any kind of recoverable water, but it was just barely possible, and as long as there was any hope at all, she wasn't going to give up.

She heard footsteps on the stairway. She could tell by their heaviness whose they were, and what kind of a mood he was in, too. She looked up from her tomato as he stepped through the doorway.

"Hello, Norm."

"Your comparator program doesn't work," he said without preamble.

She felt a brief surge of panic. "The comparator? What's wrong with it?"

"It should be finding planets by now, and it's not; that's what's wrong with it." Norm stopped about three paces away from her, just close enough so he could look down the front of her shirt as she knelt beside the garden.

Mary counted to about twenty-five, thinking: *Of course the program's at fault, then. It couldn't be Ivan's telescope nor George's command interface; no, if there's a flaw in the system then it's Mary's fault.* She said, "Maybe you're using it wrong."

"I am *not* using it wrong. I know how to run a simple program—"

"And I know how to install one. The comparator works. I tested it thoroughly."

"Then why does it find no planets? There should be at least one gas giant in this system, shouldn't there?"

Norm's belligerence forced her to voice the thought she'd been keeping to herself for days. "I don't know. Should there? There's no law I know of saying every star's even got to have planets, much less gas giants. That's why we came here in the first place, to see what we'd find."

That wasn't the answer Norm wanted to hear. He took a step closer, stood over Mary with his hands clenched. "You will test the program for errors. I order it."

Mary raised up and looked Norm straight in the eye. She knew he hated it when she did that. In his world view a man had to be at least ten centimeters taller than a woman. "Who died and made you captain?" she said, enunciating each word.

He hated that even more. Unclenching his fists, but only because honor forbade hitting a woman, he said, "Debug the program." Without waiting for an answer, he whirled around and stomped away. Mary heard him kick the door open at the top of the stairs.

*Idiot.* So ruled by his glands and his ridiculous machismo that he couldn't even function in the company of a woman. Mary figured the only way he'd been able to reconcile himself to having a female captain on the colony expedition had been to sleep with her, and the moment she died he'd claimed the position for himself. Mary wondered why such a man had been chosen to crew a colony starship, but she knew the answer: guys like Gomez were good at surviving once they got where they were going.

Yeah, but at whose expense?

Mary laughed out loud. "Teresa only slept with you to keep you from mutiny, Norm!" she shouted at the empty corridor.

Ivan McGuire heard the shout all the way down the hall in the nanolab. He shook his head at the silliness of it all. Couldn't those two understand that their petty feud was only adding to all their problems? Things were tough enough without having interpersonal tension to deal with, too. But then, they had been at each other's throats even before the accident; there was no reason to expect them to change now. Contrary to popular belief, adversity seldom brought out the best in people.

It would be nice if they could at least agree on the obvious, but that seemed beyond them, too. Inevitable as it was, the decision to stop at the red giant had not been simple to reach. Ivan remembered the argument clearly, with the meticulous, sharp-edged detail of a memory implanted while under the mindlink. Of course he hadn't actually been in anyone else's mind, but they'd all been linked to the database and some spill-over was inevitable. He'd been aware of George's amusement at the ridiculous turn his life had so recently taken, of Norm's grief and anger and fear, of Mary's deep terror beneath her inevitable bluster; all filtered through his own combination of shock, anger, alarm, and – yes – fear as well.

The degree of linkage was just enough to allow that awareness, but not enough to allow direct mental communication. The mutual awareness allowed them to cut through subterfuge and misunderstanding – most of the time, anyway – but the separation kept them thinking independently. It had long ago been discovered that when communication became too intimate, innovation ceased. Individuals needed to remain individual to gain the advantage of different viewpoints, experiences, and prejudices.

Even with the link, it was like meetings all through human history: the advantage went to the strongest personality. If there was more than one strong personality . . . well, the meetings took longer. Occasionally a better decision even came out of it.

The review of facts had been short. With their mindlinks, everyone had immediate access to the same basic information. As he'd sat at the round table, watching his three sweaty shipmates scratch under their thick headbands, Ivan had suddenly known that the rest of the ship's repairs could safely be left in the hands of the robots and the nanofabrication cells, that the expected lifespan of the biosystem was now less than two years, that even if all four of them went into SloMo they could only extend their time by another six months, that their original destination was still over seven years away – the data had gone on and on, including the information that they were within half a light-year of the red giant star they had intended only to fly past en route to their final destination. That wasn't so coincidental as it seemed: space is dirtier near stars, so if they were going to be hit, that was the most likely place.

Nor was their being there a coincidence, either. Colony ships always had funding problems, so when the university had approached the mission planners with a proposal to combine a scientific mission with their colony expedition ("Just a five-degree deviation in course, and with the gravity assist it will only cost you a month's time"), the mission planners had agreed without hesitation. The ship would make a close flyby through the red giant system, and they would take along a colonist-scientist to run the instrumentation.

Mary was that scientist. A graduate student at the university, she'd had the necessary skills to head the project, and she was one of the few who looked at the colony project as an opportunity to start another university rather than as an exile to the frontier.

As their first post-disaster planning session had gotten under way, Ivan had tried to guess what she thought of the project now. He'd known what Norm thought, that Mary was responsible for the disaster, but he'd wondered: Did Mary think that, too? The mindlink was just tenuous enough that he couldn't tell.

She had been the first to speak of possible alternatives. "We could retarget for the giant," she'd said.

Norm had jumped on her immediately. "Looking for volatiles near a red giant would be pointless," he'd said. "Things will be baked out there already."

"Not necessarily, Norm. Outer planets might survive. Gas giants—"

Norm had let himself slip, then. "*Dammit*, Mary! You know we can't get gases out of a deep gravity well."

His blush had been a thing to behold. What was going through his head at that moment? Ivan had wondered. By the sense of shame seeping through the mindlink, Norm was almost certainly berating himself for swearing at a woman. Such lofty ideals! Ivan wondered if he would indulge in self-flagellation in the privacy of his own quarters. So silly. So much easier to admit one's faults and learn to live with them.

Mary had hardly noticed the swearing anyway. "Norm, gas giants aren't the only things in a solar system. Most of them probably will have shriveled after the star expanded anyway. The inner ones won't *be* giants any more. Besides, the outer ones may still have icy moons."

"We're a dead ship if we can't think of something better than the red giant," Norm had insisted stubbornly.

"We're all ears," Mary had said then, and God knows, they'd all tried to come up with something better. They'd considered ramscoops to collect interstellar gasses, they'd looked at freezing the colonists down from SloMo to true NoMo to save resources, they'd toyed with drawing straws and dying "like men" (Norm's idea) so a few could live to the end of the trip, but in the end they'd knocked holes in every argument they'd presented. The numbers for ramscoop size versus gathering ability simply didn't add up; a frozen body was a dead body and everyone had known that since the early twenty-first century; and the maximum number of sleepers the ship could deliver alive to their original destination without replenishing water and air was far less than the amount needed for a colony.

They were going to have to retarget for the giant. None of them liked the idea; Norm hated it when Mary was right with one of her shots from the hip, and neither Ivan nor George nor even Mary herself liked the idea of looking for water around a red giant. But what else could they do?

We could learn to get along in the process, Ivan thought, but he knew that the odds of that were even less than the odds of finding water.

George Nakamoto was not a nervous man. Serenity and harmony, the virtues cultivated by his Japanese forebears and drummed into him during his upbringing, had taken to that degree. But sardonic cynicism was his substitute for true serenity – just as it was for Westerners. No doubt his grandfather would have blamed such unbalance on his mixed parentage.

But if harmony was the crux of existence, why had his ancestors left Japan in the first place? Or ridden a starship to one of Earth's first colonies? Same reason he was on *this* ship, a second-wave colonist himself? If so, then it was closer to boredom than it was to harmony.

Meditation was still a valuable ability, though, even if seldom practised. He took a deep breath, exhaled it slowly, took another –

A knock at the door interrupted him. He sighed in irritation, made a futile attempt to banish *that* emotion, then said, in resignation, "Come in."

The knob turned and Mary pushed the door open. "Have you got a minute?" she asked.

George sighed again, his hope of inner peace fading. He waved Mary toward the bunk – the only other place to sit in his room besides at the desk. "What's on your mind?"

She sat down. "The telescope," she said. "Norm claims there has to be a bug in the comparator program because it's not finding any planets. I've tested the software over and over, and it's right. So . . ."

"So it's got to be the telescope," George finished for her.

Mary shrugged. "Well, yeah. It's got to be. Either in the instrument itself or in the interface."

George felt a vague amusement. "Such a curious position for you to be in, wanting Norm to be right!"

Mary glared at him, but she remained silent.

George grinned at her, although a part of him sneered at himself for indulging in putdowns. Even if Mary had come barging in with an accusation, that was no excuse for causing her gratuitous discomfort. Especially in a tiny shipboard environment. He banished his grin and said quietly, trying to take the sting from his earlier mocking, "I understand why you want the results to be wrong. We're committed to stopping; planets or no. In a few days we've got to go into SloMo and wait for the computer to finish the trip for us, and if there's nothing there we're out of luck." He looked at his desktop, bare except for the flatscreen monitor folded into its surface and the headband resting beside it. Without looking up, he said, "Unfortunately, for our peace of mind at any rate, both the telescope and interface are okay. I've tested them as thoroughly as you've tested your comparator. You can tell Norm that if the system is seeing nothing, then there is nothing there to see."

Mary stood up. "You're right, but would you please tell that to Norm, too? He won't believe it from me, especially since it's bad news." She looked straight at him until he turned to face her again.

George reacted differently to that gaze than Norm would. Where Norm saw hostility, he saw pain, and it made him feel even more guilty. He nodded. "Sure, Mary, I'll do that."

"Thanks." She opened the door and stepped out, then stuck her head back inside. "I mean it," she said, and then she was gone.

*The very deep did rot; O Christ!*
*That ever this should be!*
*Yea, slimy things did crawl with legs*
*Upon the slimy sea.*

— Part II, Stanza 10

The deepswimmer had risen too high. A sluggish blimp of flesh, as large as the ancient Terran airship whose form evolution had unconsciously mimicked, it struggled frantically to stop its ascent, to flee back down into the safety of the cold dead deep water. But it was too late. Hunger had driven it higher than usual in its search for microorganisms, well up into the aerated water where the carnivores lived. It could hear their sonar pinging, a crescendoing cacophony as more and more of the swiftkillers detected the lumbering deepswimmer and immediately zeroed in on it.

The swiftkillers slashed by, slicing out ribbons of flesh, greedily snapping after the meat. Severed pieces drifted only seconds before being gulped down in their turn. Blood trailed like streamers from the deepswimmer's wounds, pooling into a fog, shrouding the places where chunks of flesh had been torn out. The cloud was invisible in the lightless water, but it might as well have been luminous, shouting its chemical signals into the water, a windfall of organic matter for the perpetually starved upper ocean.

The great beast thrashed in helpless agony, the cloud of blood growing thicker, the number of swiftkillers – swarming to it like terrestrial moths to a light – ever larger. Now and again one swiftkiller slashed another in passing, and a mini-frenzy would erupt as the other swiftkillers turned on their wounded comrade.

The feast lasted for hours. But at length the frenzy eased, the blood cloud began to thin, and a few engorged swiftkillers began to leave. But before the blood had dispersed too much, scavenge-filters swarmed through, armored against the slashing death, greedily straining the blood and shreds of flesh out of the gory

# WATERWORLD

water. A latecoming swiftkiller, still hungry and driven to distraction by the smells in the water, attacked one of the filters before instinct could stop it, but its teeth barely scraped the filter's chitinous armor before the filter discharged its internal battery into the swiftkiller's body. Suddenly numb, the swiftkiller drifted downward, but only momentarily, until set upon by its companions. No other swiftkillers were so foolish, or so unlucky, as to tangle with the scavengefilters.

And after another hour, there was nothing left even for the filters.

The swiftkillers resumed their restless cruising, ranging all the way from there at the bottom edge of the oxygenated layer of water to the surface tens of kilometers above. Searching, searching, searching for anything that moved, for anything made of something besides water. Bits of falling organic matter, other creatures, dead or living – even small meteorites that managed to survive the trip through the corrosive atmosphere and acidic water – all provided food for the ever-starving denizens of the planet-encompassing ocean.

*Water, water, everywhere,*
*And all the boards did shrink;*
*Water, water, everywhere,*
*Nor any drop to drink.*

– Part II, Stanza 9

Mary stared out the port, tweaking the zoom for a better look. The view was promising. The *Cabeza de Vaca* had established polar orbit about a planet that looked remarkably Earthlike, at least if you ignored the reddish-yellow illumination. If she switched out the room lights her eyes would soon adapt so she could do just that, but she didn't bother. Red or white, the sight below was the most beautiful thing she'd seen in months. Sheets of fluffy clouds Coriolis-spun into storm whorls, with dark ocean below occasionally reflecting sunlight. Nothing *but* ocean below, by the look of it. Maybe they had lucked out after all. God knew, they were due for some luck.

*Well . . .* She stretched her arms wide, yawning. She'd just awakened from SloMo, and was still getting her brain and body back up to speed. *You can't tell much just by eyeballing the monitor,* she told herself. *Have to get to work.*

She sat down at her desk, put the headband on, and keyed the ID/initialization command into the desktop. Her surroundings faded – not so much visually as in importance – as she digested what the ship's sensors had already recorded.

She saw that the planet had low density, just from the *Cabeza de Vaca*'s orbital parameters. That meant it wouldn't have much of a rocky core. Presumably it had started out as an ice-rich ball, something like the Jovian moons Ganymede or Callisto in the Home System, and had thawed much later when its sun ran out of hydrogen fuel and expanded into a red giant.

Mary checked to see what the ship had found about the rest of the system: Two rocky planets in closer, much closer. One was about Earth-sized, about 1 AU from the star; the other was about the same distance from its star as Mars from Sol. The same stellar metamorphosis that had thawed this outer world had turned the close ones into cinders. If they had oceans now, they were lava oceans.

No gas giants, she noted with satisfaction. Norm would be pissed. He'd never apologize, but he'd know her comparator program had worked.

The ship's computer had obviously made the right choice, bringing them here. No place else in the system had the volatiles they needed. Mary returned her attention to it. They were going to need atmosphere composition and density, water composition – Hmm. It sure *looked* like water oceans on the world below them, but she'd better check that, too.

She started collating information, mentally directing the acquisition of new data. It would have been nice to have a sampling laser, just zap a point on the surface and read an emission spectrum. But the original mission was supposed to be a fast flyby from light-hours away, not a close study, so they hadn't brought such equipment, nor the templates for the nanofabs to make it. Templates for scientific equipment were expensive.

Anyway, plain old reflectance spectroscopy should be plenty, even in red and IR wavelengths – the only ones the dull star put out in any quantity.

Time ceased to flow, as always happened when a person sank into a task using the mindlink. It could have been minutes or it could have been days, but eventually Mary had the results of the reflectance specs.

Bizarre. She shook her head at the analyses. Oxygen, carbon

dioxide, nitrogen, virtually no argon or other noble gases; traces of carbon monoxide and sulfur oxides. So far so good, but why so much oxygen? She ran a quick calculation, pulling out the models from the computer's database. No, it couldn't be from photodissociation. This ember didn't put out enough UV to sunburn a butterfly, much less split a water molecule and blow the hydrogen away into space. Life, then? Maybe photosynthetic microbes. She felt some excitement at the prospect of discovering the first extraterrestrial life, but it was excitement tempered with the knowledge of their predicament. Maybe someday somebody could come back to investigate, but the moment the *Cabeza de Vaca*'s crew regained what they had lost, they would have to return to their mission.

It was hard to determine atmospheric pressure with the instruments she had at her disposal, but she could estimate with pressure-broadening on some of the spectral lines, check that against atmospheric stellar occultations. With dawning misgivings, she considered her preliminary results. There was a *lot* of oxygen in that atmosphere. In fact, with the low surface gravity, that meant even more than the pressure alone suggested, because the air density dropped off so slowly with height. That atmosphere was *deep*. As she thought, the numbers worked themselves out in her mind, as the mindlink automatically performed the calculation.

She gave a low whistle. Maybe their luck wasn't so good after all.

Half an hour later she sat at the meeting table, Norm and George and Ivan already mindlinked and looking at her expectantly. She considered making a joke: *I have good news and bad news*. No, she thought, shaking her head. Humor can lighten things up, but it's not the right time.

She cleared her throat. "Well," she said, "we've found our volatiles. Liquid water, even. But it looks like they won't be easy to get. I've prepared a briefing in the database."

The others acquired rapt expressions for a minute as the onboard database briefed them.

When they'd absorbed the information, everyone looked at Mary again. "As you can see," she continued, "it's a chemical cauldron down there. The total pressure is over 5 atmospheres, with a *hell* of a lot of oxygen – something around 70 percent.

Apparently there are some primitive photosynthesizers down there."

"How can that *be*?" Ivan asked. "They showed long ago that oxidation of surface materials limits oxygen content in an atmosphere. Especially if there's life. It would burn itself up! Something's wrong with your calculations."

Mary snorted. "The numbers are right. Based on the planet's density, it's got very little rock inside. It was probably mostly ice before it melted when the star went red-giant. Thus, there's probably nothing *but* water at the surface. Anything that was going to oxidize did it long ago, so the oxygen just built up."

George closed his eyes momentarily, link-thinking, then said, "If your density figure is correct, then that ocean is not only worldwide but very deep."

"That's right," Mary agreed. "Probably hundreds of kilometers deep. A solid bottom probably just forms when a high-density ice phase becomes stable. Ice V or ice VI or something. Depends on the temperature at the sea bottom."

"We're getting off the subject," said Norm. "We have a planet that's *made* of water here. It looks like our prayers have been answered. Why is there a problem?"

"The oxygen pressure," Mary replied. "Virtually everything becomes not just flammable, but explosive in an atmosphere like that. Our equipment will burn up before it can even reach the surface."

There was silence around the table for a minute. Then Norm demanded, "How can you be sure of those pressure estimates? The briefing indicated there's a great deal of uncertainty in them."

Of *course* Norm would contest the results. Mary sighed inwardly. She could have said white is white, and he would have argued with her. With as much patience as she could summon, she said, "Yes, there is slop in the estimates. But you saw in the briefing how much error is probable. Maybe a factor of two either way. But whether it's two atmospheres of oxygen, or 10 atmospheres, it's not going to make any difference! Things like metals and plastics become explosively flammable."

"I think it would be prudent, to say the least, to get some ground truth," Norm pronounced. "Remote sensing often leads you astray. Especially when your instruments aren't designed for it. An awful lot is riding on the calibration of instruments doing things they really weren't designed to do."

*And especially when a* woman *tells you things you don't want to hear*. Mary bit her lip. "What do you suggest, then?" she made herself ask mildly.

"Use one of the shuttles," Norm replied promptly. "Get some *hard* data. Before we build up new bogeymen for ourselves, we need to have some better information."

Mary reddened. "Damn it, Norm, you can see the data as well as I can!"

Ivan said, "Why don't we build better sensors instead?" but he realized his mistake almost instantly. "Ah, templates. We don't have the templates."

"That's right."

There was silence for a moment.

"Mary," George asked, "what's wrong with sending a shuttle down?"

"We'll probably lose the shuttle, that's what."

"Better risk a shuttle than risk the entire ship. We don't have time to mess around. Besides, Norm is right. Do you really have a factor of two confidence in your measurements? It seems like it could be an order of magnitude at least."

Before she could defend her figures, Ivan said, "And anyway, even if we lose the shuttle, it's not critical. We do have the templates for more shuttles, and the raw material. Better to lose it than more water."

Norm, for once, had the sense not to say anything.

Outnumbered, Mary said, "All right, you win. But you'd better get the nanofabs going on a new one, 'cause I can guarantee you it'll burn."

> *The fair breeze blew, the white foam flew,*
> *The furrows followed free;*
> *We were the first that ever burst*
> *Into that silent sea.*
>
> – Part II, Stanza 5

The communications room felt crowded. It wasn't really – there was room for way more than four people – but any room with both Mary and Norm in it felt crowded, at least to George. Especially when one of them was about to prove the other wrong.

"Aluminum should be okay; it's coated with a microlayer of oxide, just from exposure to the air," Norm was explaining to no one in particular. "Hell, that's why it doesn't catch fire in ordinary air. The oxide coat can't burn, and that protects the rest of it." George looked up from his telepresence controls to see Mary looking skeptical, as usual. He rolled his eyes. Norm could say that water was wet and Mary would look skeptical.

Ivan, standing by the monitor bank, smiled at George's gesture and shrugged as if to say, "Not my department."

George turned back to the final checkout. He would be flying the shuttle via a microwave mindlink, and if there were any glitches in the communications channels, he wanted to know about them *now*. Flying by remote was tricky enough without equipment problems to complicate things. At least from low orbit the lightspeed lag wouldn't be noticeable, not even with the relay satellites, but he'd never before flown the configuration they'd decided upon, so his reflexes would be slow.

They'd had the nanofabs build a "J-5 Floating Instrument Platform", basically a raft perched atop aluminum pontoons, which the shuttle would deploy while it hovered above the sea's surface. The platform held sensors for measuring the composition of the surface seawater, and also a "sinker", a heavy, instrumented probe that would measure water composition at depth and sonar-chirp data back to a transceiver on the floater.

And for the benefit of the four watchers, cameras would look around from both shuttle and floater with realtime imaging, each view appearing on one of a bank of monitors in the wall in front of them.

"Whenever you're ready, George," Norm said.

George nodded without looking up. "Just a minute." He finished checking the backup comm channels, then put on the heads-up telemonitor helmet. "OK. Here goes." He breathed deeply and slowly, willing his mind into the state where the VR link felt like a natural extension of his body. *Serenity, unity* . . .

He imagined himself looking out the shuttle's windshield; in an eyeblink his screen showed just that view. He reached for the throttle and attitude controls, lit the engine, and the shuttle moved away from the starship.

The descent was normal enough. He had to take it slower – the atmosphere was both deeper and thicker than he was used to – but that presented no unusual problems. The shuttle had plenty of fuel and, as far as he could tell, Norm's assessment of the oxidation problem was accurate enough. Within an hour he had brought it to the surface, and all its systems were still working perfectly.

"Deploying balloon," he said, and the mindlink translated his wish into the command. From the shuttle's upper cargo bay door, a heavy-lift balloon began to inflate with helium. George lowered the engine thrust to compensate for the lift as it filled, until a few minutes later he shut the engine down completely.

"Releasing floater," he said, shifting his point of view to the shuttle's underside camera.

The instrument platform dropped half a dozen meters, slapped down gently into the side of a wave, and rode over the crest. Monitors came alive with images; George switched his heads-up display to the main onboard camera and his point of view began rocking up and down with it. Enough data came in through the mindlink to make him feel almost as if he was there. The view was nearly Earthlike: a seascape with gentle swells, catching flecks of sun as they stretched off to a comfortably distant horizon. A soft hissing sound came through the intercom; probably one of the instruments, or maybe just the susurration of the waves.

But George had no time to admire the view. He immediately began invoking the analyzer programs that controlled the instrumentation. He looked through his heads-up display to the data monitor as it began filling with tables and columns of numbers. Atmospheric composition: 67% $O_2$, 31% $CO_2$, 1.5% $N_2$, traces of noble gases, water vapor, nitrogen oxides, ozone . . . The numbers flickered back and forth as the instrument package constantly updated them in realtime. Someone whistled slowly when the atmospheric pressure value appeared: 5.2 atmospheres. Right on Mary's estimate.

Meanwhile, another monitor was also filling with information: seawater composition, dissolved gas content, pH . . . Someone else whistled when the pH value scrolled up. The ocean was about as acidic as gastric juice.

Now the atmospheric reading was showing traces of hydrogen. Hydrogen? In *that* atmosphere? Puzzled, George looked again at the air composition readings. Something nagged at the back of his mind; acidity, hydrogen, aluminum –

Elementary chemistry came flooding back as the comm link picked up on his new train of thought and fed him information from the main database. Hydrogen ions in acid solutions react with active metals to release metal ions – and gaseous hydrogen. Good God! The floater was dissolving in that acid sea!

And the reaction also produces heat. *Lots* of heat. And with all that oxygen around, the situation couldn't last long.

*Quick, deploy the sinker*, he commanded the computer, but before it could comply his viewpoint lurched crazily, and half the other monitors spun as well. The intercom filled with crackling noises. Then a sheet of fire billowed up along one side of the floater, and his heads-up helmet display went blank. He looked through it at the monitor bank, where three of the camera views were also blank, the screens now hissing with static. The remaining views shifted even more dizzily, offering glimpses of sky, sweeping wildly along the horizon, dipping momentarily under the water, where dark shapes, fast and unrecognizable in the dim light, flitted in and out of the camera's field of view. One by one, each view washed into static.

The last view from the remaining camera showed a mouth with multiple rows of big teeth, approaching, engulfing . . . then the scene also vanished into static.

The others' reactions filtered in through the mindlink. "What the –?" "*Told* you so." "Christ, what was *that*?"

George, momentarily stunned, shook his head and then returned to his teleprojection, shifting his perspective to the shuttle nose camera as he did so.

A bizarre scene appeared on the sea surface. Appalled, he saw flaming pieces of the floater skittering around atop the sea like water drops on a hot plate, practically exploding as hydrogen bubbled up around them to catch fire. Pursuing them, nightmare shapes seized, ripped apart, and gulped the pieces of flaming metal with apparent impunity.

When the feeding frenzy died, George muttered, "I'm getting outta there." He switched his attention to the shuttle's flight controls. *Start the $H_2$ flow and just give her a little squirt of antiprotons, just enough thrust to hold it while the balloon –*

There came a blinding flash, and the shuttle monitor abruptly went blank, as did the entire telemetry stream.

Stunned again, George just sat for a moment, his mind as blank as his monitors. Then he tore off the comm helmet and growled, "What the hell happened?"

"The shuttle blew up," Mary said with an air of self-satisfaction.

George said nothing, just lowered his head into his hands. Insensitive bitch; he felt as if a part of himself had just died, and all she could do was gloat because she'd been right. He willed himself again to breathe deeply and slowly, trying to recover his equilibrium, to cut through the disorientation.

"Did you get any data from the sinker before the floater blew?" Norm interrupted.

"No." Either it never got free, or whatever was in the water had clobbered it right away. It really didn't matter which. It didn't matter . . .

Norm persisted. "Did we get any data before the shuttle blew up? What caused it to go?"

George finally looked up. Norm stood over him like an inquisitor, fists clenched. Behind him, Mary was actually grinning. Next to the monitors, Ivan was tapping instructions into a keyboard, not bothering with the mindlink. "Probably a hydrogen leak somewhere," Ivan said as the monitors switched off. Norm turned his attention toward him, and George sighed in relief.

Ivan said, "Enough must have diffused out of the tank to set up a little chemical explosion in the shuttle itself. And *that* let out the antimatter." He laughed, a little grimly. "At least the explosion will have wiped out those things ripping the floater apart."

"Hah," Norm grunted. "What about the acidity? Where did *that* come from?"

Ivan didn't have an answer, nor did George. Mary put on a mindlink and closed her eyes. A moment later she snorted, "Obvious. Should've been obvious, anyway. All that oxidation. Most of the nonmetallic oxides that dissolve . . . sulfur, nitrogen, whatever . . . make acids. That's got to be where it comes from."

She dug obliquely at Norm. "The Universe always has these tricks up its sleeve, when you go bopping blithely into something you don't understand."

Norm snapped back, "If it was so obvious, Mary, how come you didn't see it? You were supposed to be figuring out the surface environment."

She just glared at him for answer. Everybody knew the reason: the mindlink and the computer behind it would answer just about any question you could think of to ask it, but you had to think up the question yourself. The mindlink wasn't an artificial intelligence; it had no initiative of its own.

Norm looked away from her, saying, "And *life*. How can there be life? This planet would have been a ball of ice till its sun went red giant, and that can't have been more than a few hundred million years ago, at most. There hasn't been *time* for life to develop."

Ivan said, "We knew there had to be some life to make all that $O_2$."

"So there were microbes. Not monsters. How can there be multicelled life?"

Shrugging, Ivan said, "The planet closest to the star is about Earth sized, and this star was probably about like Sol before it went red-giant. Maybe the ice world was seeded beforehand."

George felt a shiver run through his spine. He sat up in astonishment. "You mean spaceflight? You think a spacefaring culture left things behind?"

Ivan shrugged again. "Well, I suppose that's possible, but I was thinking more of spores from the Earthlike world, preserved on the ice. Bacterial, fungal, whatever . . . that would give life a big head start when the ice thawed. It's happened before. In the Home System, viable spores from Earth were found on some of the ice moons around the outer planets."

Mary looked thoughtful. "Yeah, I remember that. There was a big sensation for a while, because it looked like we'd discovered extraterrestrial life."

Impatiently, Norm said, "It doesn't matter; we've discovered it *here*. So what do we do now?"

Ivan laughed. "We go down in history," he said. "Provided we survive long enough to get the word out."

*Day after day, day after day,*
*We stuck, nor breath nor motion;*
*As idle as a painted ship*
*Upon a painted ocean.*

– Part II, Stanza 8

Norm was beginning to loathe the meeting room almost as much as he loathed the people in it. In the meeting room he actually had to link up with his three crewmembers, had to ignore their hostility and pessimism and weakness while attempting to use their group intellect to come up with a solution to their dilemma. He came away from each such meeting feeling soiled, befouled with a filth no amount of water would wash away.

But he could see no other choice. Four minds – even if three of them were pitifully inadequate – were better than one when it came to brainstorming. He donned the link and said, "All right, let's get this started. We've got to figure out a way to upload a couple million liters of concentrated acid through a couple hundred kilometers or so of high density oxygen mixture. As we've seen, shuttles won't do the job. How about the skystalk?"

"It's pure carbon, Norm," Mary said. "Carbon burns."

"It's diamond fiber. Pure C-12," Norm said as calmly as he could manage. "Diamond has an extremely high ignition point, uh . . ." He link-thought a moment. "Over 600°C. If we're careful on descent, it shouldn't get hot enough to ignite."

George shook his head. "We'd have to take it in practically subsonic."

"Yes, we would. Is that too difficult for you?"

George reddened. "I can do it. But that still doesn't get us any water. The elevators are going to blow up just like the shuttle did."

"Why should they? They aren't hydrogen powered; they're electric."

"They're aluminum. As soon as they touch acid, there'll be plenty of hydrogen around. And once *that* starts burning, there'll be plenty of heat to ignite the skystalk."

"We can make them out of something else," Norm said. "Iron—"

"Oxidizes," Ivan interrupted. "And besides, it would be a bitch to program the substitution. Iron atoms and aluminum atoms are like apples and oranges to nanofabs."

"You did it with the ship's hull," Norm pointed out.

"Yeah, but patching a hole is a lot simpler than building an elevator."

Norm said, "All right, then. Maybe we can't build an oxygen- and acid-proof elevator. How about a pump? Can we pump the water up here?"

Mary snorted. "Thirty-three thousand kilometers to Clarke orbit? Do you have any idea what kind of pressure you'd have at the bottom?"

"We could use a peripump," Ivan said. "It squeezes its cargo along, like peristaltic waves in the intestines. Each wave is a separate system, so the pressure doesn't build."

"That could take years."

"No, more like months," George said. "An industrial-grade pump could do it in . . . about seventy days."

Norm took a deep breath before he spoke. "We only need to get it above the atmosphere," he said. "Six hundred kilometers. That means—" he waited for the number "– about thirty hours. Then we can fill tanks in the elevator cars, and carry them up the stalk."

"Thirty hours for the first liter," Mary said. "Then we have to pump a million more of them."

"Nearly . . . a million are already in the hose by the time the first one arrives," Norm said. "If we want two million liters, we pump for thirty hours longer, then lift the hose out of the atmosphere and finish pumping from safety."

"It could work," George said.

"If the pump doesn't burn first, or corrode," Ivan said.

Norm called up the design parameters with a wish. "We have a template for an acid-rated pump. Would that do?"

Ivan shrugged. "There's only one way to find out, isn't there?"

Mary had been rapt, listening to the headlink. Then she shook her head. "No, there isn't. You can check the materials parameters on the peripump. The thing's made of diamond fibers, just like the stalk. And it'll burn just like the stalk will. Even worse, the pump's got other organics in it, for the contraction fibers and whatnot. It'll burn even better. I wish you guys would remember, that's not air down there. It's *oxygen*."

Silence for a moment, then Norm said, "Damn it, I'm tired of hearing what we can't do! What *can* we do?" He turned directly to Mary. "Do you have any better ideas?"

"Yes. We can build a non-flammable peripump."

"Don't be ridiculous! We can't design a completely new nanotemplate from scratch." Norm rolled his eyes in exasperation.

George asked quietly, "What are you thinking we could make it out of, Mary?"

"Ceramics. Oxides or silicates. They're fully oxidized already. In fact—" she paused "—plain old silica should work. The hose is only 600 kilometers long. Silica's strong enough for that, as long as it's completely bonded."

Ivan was shaking his head. "Where are we going to get . . . 200 tons of silica? We can't afford to make a trip to one of the inner planets. Even if the ship could survive being so close to the star, which I doubt."

"We've got more than enough silicates in the shielding mass. I checked."

"The shielding mass?" Norm asked, incredulous.

"That's right. It's nearly all ceramics, and we don't need it in the hull until we get back up to interstellar speed."

"You want to use all of our shielding mass to design, from scratch, a completely new peripump out of completely new materials?" Norm was practically shouting now.

Mary shouted back, "We won't lose the mass. We'll get it back when we leave. Which is more than will happen when you burn up our C-12 hose in that atmosphere!"

Ivan pointed out another objection, more quietly. "It'd have to be more than just a hose, Mary. We would have to thread the power wires and contractile fibers through the ceramics. That would be especially hard since silicates are insulators. And brittle."

She turned on him. "Yes, it would be hard. Would it be too hard for you?"

Ivan's lips tightened, but he said nothing.

Norm calmed himself enough to say, "This is a brainstorming session, not a debate. Let's table that idea and go on. What else can we do?"

No one said anything for a minute. Mary again acquired the rapt look of the mindlinked, then said, "All right. Here's another idea. We could blow up the planet instead."

"What?"

"I just checked the math. A series of antimatter bombs at depth could theoretically lift a section of the surface into space. If we place the charges right, some of it could still be liquid when it gets here. Of course the shock wave would propagate all the way through to the other side with enough force to kill everything worldwide, but—"

George's eyes had gone wide. "You would destroy an entire planet for your own survival?"

"Of course not. I just said we *could* do it; I didn't say we *should*. This is supposed to be a brainstorming session, isn't it?"

"It is," Norm said, hardly bothering to hide his revulsion, "but we can do without that sort of input."

"I'm just following orders, Norm. You wanted to know what we could do, so I told you. I can't think of anything else." Mary started to remove her headband.

"You will stay linked!" Norm bellowed. "We need ideas. *Realistic* ideas, and you will help provide them. All of you will help think of ideas." He glared at each of the three in turn, challenging them to defy him. Mary held his gaze with her damnable blue eyes, but she also held her tongue. Ivan studied the table top. George radiated amusement, his head tilted slightly to the side.

Ivan said, finally, "Let's try the diamond pump. I think the risk is acceptable."

Mary started to speak, but George cut her off. "Mary, if it does burn, why can't we just try your idea then? As it is, you're saying we should spend our time trying to do something that may not even work. And that we may not even have to do."

She shook her head vigorously. "Besides the waste of materials and time, the stalk's only meant to be deployed once. We're going to have a hard enough time trying to reel it back in when we leave. Not to mention the wasted reaction mass. It's not like dropping an anchor; the whole stalk is in orbit right now, and we have to brake most of it to a standstill when we drop it, then speed it back up when we raise it. Where do we get the reaction mass to do that twice?"

Ivan shook his head. "Mary, we don't have to reel the stalk back to install a new hose. That's what the elevator cars are for. George is right; we lose nothing by trying the simple solution first."

Exasperated, Mary said, "Yes we do. If we wait until later, there'll be that much more chance for something to go wrong when we try to install it. And we'll be under a lot more time pressure."

Ivan started to say something else, but Mary continued, "And besides, you're going to burn up almost our whole reserve of C-12 with that pump."

Norm leaned forward angrily, but George intervened again. "Mary, are you really that sure?" he said quietly.

Mary removed her headband and slammed it down on the table. "Yes, I'm sure. You can link to the data as well as I can."

"Yes," Norm said, "but we can also reach different conclusions. I too vote to try the diamond pump."

Ivan had already said as much. All eyes turned toward George, who wet his lips and said, "I agree. But if it doesn't work, then I think we should try Mary's idea."

Ever the conciliator, Mary thought savagely. Couldn't he take a stand on *anything*? But she just said, "I think it's an unacceptable risk, and I want to log that."

She knew what they were thinking: *Mary is being a maverick again. She's just not a team player. She should keep personalities out of this.* Well, she'd be damned if she'd rubber stamp this asinine decision. Especially just to salve Norm's ego. In the name of "team play", they wanted her to confirm the collective CYA, even though there was no chance a board of inquiry would ever know – or care – what their decision was. Well, no way.

No one said anything as she stood up and left.

> *All in a hot and copper sky*
> *The bloody Sun, at noon,*
> *Right up above the mast did stand,*
> *No bigger than the Moon.*
>
> – Part II, Stanza 7

The *Cabeza de Vaca* swung in Clarke orbit around Teresa – now the planet's official name, according to the Captain's decree. Figures, Mary thought. Norm's image of the Ideal Woman. Pretty, deferential, tactful enough to seem dumb even if she isn't . . . She knew it was petty to begrudge the dead woman her memorial, but even so, Norm's heavy-handed method of doing it stank.

When Norm wasn't around, everyone still called the planet Waterworld. Mary pointedly did so even when he was. This latest scheme of his made her want to say a few worse things in his presence, but she'd already tried that and it hadn't helped either.

In the monitor before her, the skystalk stretched out from the cargo bay toward the planet, dwindling to invisibility long before it got there. It was actually two skystalks, one for up traffic and one for down, kept separate by the same electromagnetic effects that powered the elevator cars. The twin cable didn't look as if it were moving at all, and looks were nearly correct: George had slowed it from its initial thousand-kilometer-per-hour descent to less than three hundred as the pump-carrying end entered the upper atmosphere. Cameras along the hose's lowermost few hundred kilometers showed the receiving tank and the thin peripump leading downward to the cloud-speckled sea below.

"What's the temperature at the tip?" Norm demanded.

"Climbing slowly past minus forty," George said without looking up. "Only twenty degrees above ambient at that altitude. We're okay."

"Good."

They watched in silence as the hose dropped. It was a long wait; still, no one seemed inclined to leave, or even look away from the screens while their future literally hung from a thread. It seemed to Mary as if only a few minutes had passed when George said, "Slowing down now. Ten kilometers. Temperature plus thirty."

"What about that cloud?" Mary asked, pointing to one of the monitors. In it, a puffy yellow-tinged ball of cotton floated over the ocean almost directly beneath the hose.

"I think we'll miss it," George said.

"And if we don't?"

"Shouldn't matter."

"You sure? Lightning could—"

"Anyone can see it's not a thundercloud," Norm said. "It's too small."

"Hmm." Mary supposed she was just being paranoid. It *was* a tiny little cloud, and besides, the pump bristled with static discharge spikes, effectively making it a single enormous lightning rod.

It looked as if it would miss the cloud anyway. George called out the distance as the end dropped closer and closer to the ocean. The last few kilometers went excruciatingly slow, but finally he was calling out the distance in meters. "Thirty, twenty, ten—"

The static discharge whisker dangling from the bottom splashed into the water, then a second later the pump followed it in.

"Contact!" Norm announced triumphantly, overriding George's calm, "Splashdown." George took a deep breath, then said, "Commencing pump sequence."

They could see the hose's wake as it dragged through the water. Their orbital position wasn't perfectly still in relation to the surface, and in any event the stalk would shift its position as its mass balance changed. It didn't matter; as long as the end stayed submerged, the pump could suck in its precious cargo.

Provided whatever ate the lander didn't eat the pump, too. C-12 fiber was tough stuff, but the alien monsters had looked pretty tough themselves.

They could see the end of the pump start to flex. George, Norm and Ivan all cheered, but Mary said nothing; she was watching for motion in the water. Nothing showed for long minutes, then all of a sudden a shadow with teeth seemed to leap out of nowhere straight at her. She jumped back and screamed, just as the monitor filled with static.

"What was that?" Norm demanded.

"We're under attack," George said calmly. "It got the camera, but the pump's okay. Still – damn!"

"What?"

"End's plugged. Whatever it was, I think we sucked it in."

"Reverse the last wave," Norm said.

"Reversing. That ought to – what the hell?"

Mary was watching the scene from a camera higher on the hose, staring in horror at the water practically boiling with shark-like bodies, when a different shape rose up out of the depths. It looked like a beach ball with wide, flat fins, which it swept back and forth through the water. The sharks gave it plenty of room, as if it were even more dangerous than they, and when it reached the pump, Mary saw why. The electrical arc she'd feared all along lanced out from the creature's body, and the monitor flashed and died. Mary looked to another monitor, this one showing a scene from a couple kilometers high. It took a moment for the image to register: a brilliant white point glowed on the cable below, disembodied by distance.

Mary recognized the glow. She had once done a science experiment in school where they'd built an old-fashioned incandescent lamp, just like Edison had done centuries before. She'd accidentally broken the globe, and the filament had glowed momentarily white hot, then winked out on its sudden exposure to air. This was like that: fire zipped upward along the hose, and in its wake the diamond fiber glowed brilliant white. Then the glow vanished abruptly, leaving behind not so much as a wisp of smoke.

The fire raced toward her vantage point, *toward her* – Mary ducked involuntarily, and when she looked up again that screen was also filled with static.

Only a few cameras remained, those at 50-kilometer intervals and the one inside the still-dry water tank. Mary and her companions watched the flame engulf camera after camera as it raced up the hose, until it eventually burned itself out in the thin air somewhere between 250 and 300 kilometers up.

Mary turned to look at Norm. He was eyeing at her already, holding himself braced for the blast he knew was coming. George and Ivan were actually cringing, as if they expected her to physically explode.

The image was so ludicrous that Mary burst into laughter instead. "God, look at you," she said when she could get her breath back. "You're pathetic. *We're* pathetic," she added generously. "One headstrong fool of a settler and a bunch of yesmen. Well, get this straight, guys: the universe doesn't give a damn about consensus. You're either right or you're wrong, and no amount of bullying or wishful thinking or team-play is going to change that. Until we start taking into account what's *really* down there, we don't deserve to succeed."

She turned away from them and stalked out of the room, slamming the door behind her. The slam reverberated through the repaired decking, and as the vibrations died away, the three men stole looks at each other.

"Well. Now what?" Ivan asked finally.

Norm had turned bright red during Mary's harangue. Now he slumped down into a chair, as though abruptly exhausted, and stared away from them, at the wall.

"All right," he said finally. "Build the damned non-flammable hose – if we can." He paused briefly, then added, "Mary knows everything. Or thinks she does. She can run the project. I won't be responsible for it."

Ivan peered again into the 3D monitor. Serrated arrays of multi-colored balls marched off into perspective infinity in an intricate but ever-repeating pattern. He frowned slightly, and thought a command into the link. The crystalline pattern in the display shifted so rapidly and smoothly that the difference in the new configuration was hardly apparent. But Ivan was not bothering to visually scan the crystal model anyway. He was busy calculating parameters on it, strength/lightness, flexibility, fatigue life; and most importantly, susceptibility to oxygen attack. Sure, the silica backbone was impervious – after all, it was fully oxidized already – but did it sufficiently protect the embedded organic fibers?

"How's it going?" An abrupt voice asked from behind. Ivan jumped but, from long habit, he saved the molecular design first before turning around. Mary stood behind his chair, her arms folded across her chest.

"Okay," he said. "It would be nice if you knocked first."

Mary looked over his shoulder into the monitor. "What's the coding?" she asked, pointing at the colored balls.

With a sigh, Ivan turned back to the screen and said, "The white balls are oxygen. They're 4-coordinated with silicon; you can see the oxygen tetrahedra" – he pointed at them – "sharing every vertex. You can't see the silicons 'cause they're enclosed in each oxygen tetrahedron. The whole structure's basically a silica polymer."

"Quartz?" Mary asked

"No, more like cristobalite. We need a more open structure to thread the superconductors and contractile fibers through. The black is carbon, the red nitrogen," he continued, pointing at an intricate lacework embedded among the white clumps of oxygen tetrahedra.

"Dammit, that won't work!" Mary stated emphatically. "The structure's too open. Oxygen'll get in and fry the organics."

Ivan's lips thinned for a moment. He felt a surge of irritation, and even a flash of sympathy for Norm. "No, Mary," he finally said in as calm a voice as he could muster. "I *have* done the simulation. The gaps are too narrow for $O_2$ molecules to pass, and the tunneling probability is negligible. Would you like to see?" Without waiting for an answer, he thought a command through the link. The monitor picture changed; now the intricate crystal structure was almost invisible, hidden behind a swarm of jittering dumb-bells – a simulation of gaseous $O_2$ molecules. "I've run this for simulated *days*, Mary! Nothing happens." He knew he was going to regret it, but he couldn't help saying, "Dammit, I know what I'm doing too!"

"Let's hope so." Mary watched for a moment longer, then turned and left without another word.

Afterward Ivan found himself shaking. Appalled with himself, he tried to will serenity, calmness, understanding . . . the sort of thing George talked about all the time. But it didn't come. It would never come until the job was done, and maybe not even then.

George sat again at the VR console. He felt slimy and sweaty, and looked with loathing at the heads-up helmet. He could already feel it itching on his scalp. It wasn't quite time yet, so he'd hold off putting it on as long as possible.

A camera at the base of the stalk showed Waterworld looming massively below, cruelly tantalizing with its ocean and clouds. It looked like they could just reach out and scoop up seawater. So teasing and yet so inaccessible, protected by acid and fire like a treasure in some old fairy tale.

Ivan also watched, dividing his attention between George and the monitors in the room. Presumably Norm was watching too, but on a monitor in his cabin. He had refused to be in the same room with Mary ever since the debacle with the diamond peripump.

"Whenever you're ready, George." There was an edge in Mary's voice.

Mary's comment cut abruptly into his reverie. Since Norm's abdication of authority, Mary didn't even try to hide her contempt for the rest of them. She didn't seem to realize that the decisions hadn't been so clear-cut as she imagined. But history would judge that, too, he supposed. He tried to be charitable: being right had gone to her head. But still . . .

"The hose isn't quite to the end of the cable yet," he said mildly. Not for the first time, George contrasted her – and Norm – with Teresa. Teresa had been a facilitator – she'd gotten along with Mary, even while sleeping with Norm – and she'd been an effective leader, too. More effective, in fact, with this group of egotists than the would-be autocrats who'd succeeded her.

But Teresa was dead. And the whole expedition was dead, too, unless this worked. The new silica hose was gliding down the skystalk on a string of elevator cars working in tandem, like porters carrying a snake. The multi-elevator approach was partly to spread the weight out so no one car was overtaxed, and partly to keep the hose from cracking like a whip. As its mass moved down the elevator, it pulled the skystalk sideways with its added angular velocity, and the navigation computer had to compensate by accelerating the ship slightly, to pull the stalk taut again.

The computer would do most of the work of guiding the hose all the way down to Waterworld's sea, too, but George would be in the loop as a back up, in case the unexpected happened.

And, God knew, there was ample chance of the unexpected.

He sat down and put on his helmet, glad, at least, to be escaping Mary's presence even if only through the mind link. He found, though, it took longer than usual to focus his mind into the link. Finally he directed his attention to the base of the skystalk, where the ballast mass hung, and where the new hose was approaching. The elevator chain had slowed down as the lower end neared the ballast, but finally the lowermost elevator let go of its cargo and the tip of the new silica-fiber peripump emerged beyond the end of the skystalk. Then the hose drifted uncertainly, like a puzzled snake. The ungainly trashrack on the end, an improvised ceramic cage to keep the seething predators out of the intake, sported a rocket engine whose nozzle looked a little like a bulbous snout.

*Now*, thought George, *it gets interesting*. Even just above the atmosphere, the hose tip still had angular velocity that needed to be canceled. So they couldn't go the last 600 km down through the atmosphere just by tweaking the trim masses on the skystalk. And they didn't dare try aerobraking, not on their untried, ad-hoc design. No, they needed to use reaction mass, because they had to take the hose into the atmosphere at the lowest speed possible. Not because of the danger of ignition this time, but because silica was much less strong than diamond fiber. One wrong move and they could snap off a hundred kilometer length of it.

Which meant, even though they'd calculated the most fuel-efficient trajectory possible, they had to sacrifice the last of their water. They had nothing else that could be pumped through the hose. They didn't need much − the antimatter rocket engine ensured that − but then, they didn't have much.

To George, it felt like landing a 600-kilometer long flexible spaceship, in slow motion. As the sun gradually set with Waterworld's leisurely rotation, the cameras mounted along the hose itself all showed similar views: a slim bright line tapering into nothing against the utter black of the planet's advancing night side. Now and again a puff of brilliant smoke materialized against that blackness, a cloud of superheated steam exhaust flashing into ice crystals and catching the sun − another burst of reaction mass from the nozzle at the hose tip, braking its long descent to the planet below.

George couldn't tell how long he'd sat there, straining to stay alert, but the alarm buzzer brought him to full consciousness in an instant. Reflexively he shut off the valve feeding water to the engine, with the engineer's instinct of *first* stop the flow; *then* find the problem.

Mary had been dozing in front of the monitor. She awoke at the alarm, or at George's curse, and said, "What are you doing, George? What is it?"

George was wondering the same. He scanned the displays, trying to identify what had gone wrong, while part of his mind noted wryly that Mary's immediate reaction wasn't too useful. If he'd already known what was wrong, was he going to just sit mum until she demanded an answer?

There! Stress in the hose; sensors showed the tension dangerously high at one point. Much more and the hose would break.

Heart pounding, he went to locate the problem. Their lives and their expedition now hung by a literal thread . . . if the stressed point was on the part of the hose that still lay alongside the stalk, they might be able to fix it. If it was on the part that was already down into the atmosphere, though . . .

It was fifty kilometers up the stalk.

So. It could be worse; the problem might be reachable, if necessary. But what had happened to cause the stress?

Ah, there it was.

"An elevator isn't moving," George said. "Nor responding. Something's stuck."

Ivan had awakened as well. "Can you fix it?" he asked.

"I don't know. There's not much to try here. I can try wriggling the hose by jiggling the other elevator cars, to see if that unsticks it, but—"

"Then do it!" That was Mary, peremptory.

George finished despite the interruption, "But I don't recommend it. We're simply going to break the hose. It's not likely to be able to take such treatment."

"He's right," Ivan said.

Mary had seemed about to blow up again, but then restrained herself with an effort as what he said registered. "What else can we do?"

"I can try to get the stuck elevator car to free itself."

"Do it, then," she said unnecessarily.

George did, but it quickly became evident that the errant car was not responding to any commands whatsoever from the controls.

"What now?" Mary asked George.

"What now? It's obvious." He avoided looking directly at Mary. "We have to go unstick it."

"Good luck," Ivan's voice was strained over the radio, but Mary didn't acknowledge the good wishes as she climbed into the elevator car. The whole crew was there. Even Norm was watching, in person. She and he had drawn straws for the debatable privilege of riding down the stalk to fix the stuck hose. (They had to assume it was fixable. *Had* to.) Neither one of them was particularly happy with the result, but neither would suggest a switch.

The elevator car was an open-framed cylindrical cage about 3 meters tall and 1.5 meters across, with two superconducting rings holding it to the cable. Cargo pods would normally be enclosed in the cage or, in the case of the hose carriers, empty tanks to ferry the water back to the ship. Grapples for handling the hose had been attached to the outside. Mary's car was empty, and she rode inside, but there was barely room for her, perched atop a mass of tools, ropes, and such – anything she thought she might need. She fitted herself in as best she could, and then spoke a single word into the radio. "Ready."

"Here goes. Hang on." George's voice echoed in her ears. She felt weight settle on her as the car accelerated – slower than usual because of its human cargo, but still, within ten minutes she was traveling a thousand kilometers per hour and the ship's ungainly form was dwindling behind her. She felt light again as the acceleration shut off, then she struggled to move the tools to the other end of the cylinder. The next time she felt weight, it would be coming from the other direction.

The gaps in the cage were wide enough to fit through with only a little squeezing. She leaned out and looked down, down, *down* along the cables, twin threads tapering together with perspective against the disk of Waterworld, over ten degrees across even from her distance. Each cable was less than a centimeter in diameter, but even so the entire skystalk massed several hundred tons, all pure carbon 12. It was supposed to be a critical "bootstrap" piece of technology when they got to their destination, but it had never been designed for reeling back in.

If they couldn't . . . She shook herself out of that line of thought. They had more immediate problems.

But not so immediate that she couldn't catch up on her sleep. Even at a thousand kilometers an hour, it was still a thirty-hour ride to the point where the hose was stuck, and she might as well get some rest. She wouldn't get any when she arrived, and besides, it would be more comfortable now while the gravity was still so low. But she was still keyed up; the sight of the cables stretching away toward the planet kept drawing her attention.

Down, down . . . She strained to see where the cables were leading, following them with her eyes. It was tantalizing: their tips just vanished against the disk of the planet. You couldn't really define, though, exactly where they became invisible.

Abruptly she realized she didn't remember the last few minutes, and that she was balanced precariously over the side of the cage.

And she was no longer in zero-gee. If she fell out, she'd be in a separate orbit. It would still be close to the ship's, and they *might* be able to rescue her with the shuttle if she missed the atmosphere at perigee, but then they might not. And it would cost time and reaction mass they didn't have.

Norm would have the last laugh if that happened. Another good reason not to have it happen.

Shuddering, she pulled back in and clipped her safety belt to one of the cage bars, then she curled up atop her tools and fell asleep.

The insistent chiming of her radio alarm woke her from uneasy dreams. Momentarily disoriented, Mary absently tried to scratch herself, but felt only smooth skinsuit under her fingers. She sat up abruptly as memory flooded back and nearly teetered off the top of the tool bundle. She grabbed at her safety line and at the cage, twisting her body back and wrenching her right arm as she did so.

"Coming up on the target," George said over the radio. His voice sounded amused; he'd probably been watching her from the elevator's camera, and no doubt had enjoyed watching her panic.

Well, screw him, she thought. She looked out at the other skystalk cable, the pump dangling alongside it, the elevator cars supporting it flashing by every ten kilometers or so. She was slowing down perceptibly.

She looked over the side. Waterworld was no longer a disk. Vastly larger, it was now a flat wall beside her, curving away toward the distant, atmosphere-fuzzed horizon. She was nearing the end of the stalk. George would bring her to a halt at the point where the other elevator car had failed, and from there she would have to search manually for the problem.

In a few minutes she felt the elevator begin to decelerate, adding to her weight as it did. Even after it stopped, she felt a sixth of a gee or so from the planet itself, and that sensation triggered an unexpected wave of vertigo. Suddenly Waterworld was not a ball hanging in space; she was *up*, and it was *below*. Far below. Far, far, *far* below. With suddenly shaking fingers Mary double-checked her safety line. Nothing could save her if she fell here. She'd plunge into the atmosphere like a meteor, her angular velocity carrying her away from the stalk as she did so.

She sat back and carefully looked out rather than down, trying to focus her mind on what she came for. She inspected the elevator on the opposite cable with the binocs built into her suit helmet, trying to will the shaking away. A deep breath, then another . . .

George's voice broke into her thoughts like a clap of thunder. "Looks like you'll have to—"

"Shut up and let me think," she snapped at him. "I don't want to hear from any of you unless it's an emergency, is that clear?"

"Clear as vacuum," he said, and Mary heard the click of him disengaging his microphone. Good. One less thing to worry about.

The hose stretched parallel to the cable, held taut by the clamps mounted on the cage. George had backed the lower elevators up to relieve the tension in the hose, but ten kilometers of its own weight still pulled it tight below the clamp. Above it, though, the hose was slack, drifting slowly side to side as a long-period vibration ran up and down it.

The problem didn't take long to find. The elevator evidently had lost power, so its automatic braking system had grabbed onto the cable to prevent it from free-falling the entire length of the skystalk and hitting the bottom like a bomb. Then the hose had started to stretch as the other elevators continued moving. Apparently George had cut the power to the whole chain of them just in time.

She fumed silently. Maybe he'd saved the pump, but none of this would have been necessary if they'd deployed the silica pump in the first place.

Anyway. What to do? Mary considered her options. The elevator itself was probably not worth trying to fix. It was far more important to get the hose deployed, and anyway, to risk damaging it to save one elevator made no sense. Enough others were carrying the weight; they could do without one.

So, the problem was straightforward enough: unhook the

clamp from the hose, swivel the elevator car away, and jettison it – making sure that it fell away from the hose, not into it.

Sure, simple: just cross the 10 meters of empty space between the cable she'd descended and the parallel cable where the hose was attached, and detach the hose. Then unhook the elevator car and let it drop.

Just.

Mary looked over into that yawning void again and shuddered. She tried to focus on her itches, her discomforts; the slimy feel of her body in its plastic bag of a spacesuit; anything to take her mind off what she was going to have to do. She reached out and ran her fingers lightly over the cable. It felt like a steel rod under her skinsuit fingers, stretched completely taut under the tension of its own weight. She tried not to think about the thousands of kilometers more of it above her.

With a deliberate effort, she brought herself back to the job she'd come to do. She took out the telescoping graphite rods for the traverse. Pencil thin, they hardly looked adequate for the task – although they could have supported one of the shuttles. Holding with both hands to try to keep from trembling, she held out one of the rods, pushing the release at the base. It extended slowly, bobbing around in sympathy with the shaking of her hands. She worked it over toward the elevator on the other cable. The amplitude of its swings increased as it extended, finally sweeping back and forth in oscillations several meters across as it reached the elevator on the other side. Frustrated, she tried to hold it still, clenching her hands still more tightly, but the 10-meter length of rod waved back and forth like a sapling in a breeze.

Finally, the clasp at the end brushed one of the cage bars and grabbed. She had another one for safety, in case the first didn't latch correctly (she didn't like to dwell on that possibility). She deployed it too. It went more easily, possibly because her anger at the mindless perversity of her equipment had taken her mind off her acrophobia.

Finally, two thin rods stretched from her elevator to the one holding the hose. Mary double checked her safety line and its reel. Then she clipped a carabiner around each rod, making sure each could slide freely along its rod. Last, she fastened separate lines from each 'biner to her belt, and one from her belt to her tool kit.

Now the hard part. Mary took a deep breath and leaned backward out of the elevator, holding tightly to the rods behind her. She let herself down between them, feeling her joints crack with the tension, biting her lip as her wrenched arm protested. She finally swung down underneath, a hand clenched around each rod, a foot also wrapped around each, hanging downward between the two like an ancient sloth slung between two tree branches. She was facing upward deliberately, trying not to think of the abyss below her back.

She forced herself to advance, centimeter by centimeter, moving only one hand or one foot at a time. It did not help her peace of mind that the rods flexed slightly as she moved along them. Finally she felt her helmet brush the other elevator. She lifted herself up and pushed back, trying to turn over as she did so, and trying to use her right arm as little as possible. Finally she grabbed one of the other elevator's cage bars, removed the carabiner lines from the traverse rods and clipped them to the cage, then reeled in her tool kit from the other elevator car.

The empty water tank kept her from climbing inside. Pulling herself up to the top where she could at least stand and hold onto the skystalk for support, she surveyed the situation. The elevator itself would be easy to detach – it had an emergency release for just that purpose – but before she did that she had to unfasten the cargo clamp and swivel the elevator around the cable, so it wouldn't tangle in the hose when it fell. And then, of course, get out of it before releasing it. Details, details, she thought.

Holding onto the cage with her good hand, she leaned outward so she could reach down to the clamp. It had a lever sticking out that would be forced upward automatically when the elevator car reached the bottom; releasing the hose to continue down, pulled by its own weight, while the elevator crossed the junction to ascend the other cable. She stretched with her left hand and pulled on the lever, awkwardly, since she was right-handed.

It didn't move.

She pulled harder, but still nothing happened. Apparently the tension from below was putting enough pressure on the clamp to keep it from releasing smoothly. And she couldn't get enough leverage reaching over the side of the elevator to the clamp – and doing so left-handed to boot.

She hated holding on with her sore arm, but that was what it was going to take. That and a crowbar. She pulled her tool bag up beside her, took out the bar, and leaned back over the edge as far as she dared, trying to find a good purchase for the tool against the stuck clamp. It kept slipping on the rounded lever, and the more she tried the clumsier her fingers became. She felt herself sweating in the skinsuit with her exertions, but the bar finally found solid resistance and with a curse she yanked on it for all she was worth.

Abruptly the latch popped open. The crowbar went flying out of her fingers, pinwheeling off into space, and she felt herself fly up and over backward, breaking her grip on the cage. She choked a shriek while she scrabbled futilely at the slick surface of the hose, with the mindless panic with which the drowning grasp at straws. Then as she peeled away from the skystalk, her hands went to her safety rope without conscious thought.

She fell leisurely in the low gravity, and bounced gently at the end of her tether perhaps five meters below the elevator, rocking back and forth slowly like a small child on a swing. Panting hard, heart thudding, blood rushing in her ears, she slowly forced herself to calm down, all the while clutching the safety line.

The shock of adrenaline had washed away the fear. She looked around her, then looked *down*, deliberately. The skystalk brushed past her as she swung below the elevator car; on the next pass she reached out and grasped it to steady herself. For a long time she followed the twin cables, with the attached hose paralleling one, down, down, down into the looming bulk of Waterworld below. She thought she could almost see the ballast weight at the end of the stalk, where they'd installed the receiving tank for the water. It was a *long* way down.

Somehow it didn't matter any more. She reeled in the safety line and climbed back atop the elevator car.

The rest was easy. She stuck a small chemical rocket pack on the car so it wouldn't fall back into the stalk when she released it, then unhooked the two graphite traverse rods. She figured she'd just return to the other cable by swinging back on her original safety line. The only awkward part was getting the jammed elevator swung around away from the pump hose while she was standing on it, but she finally managed to grasp the stalk with a grippy and wrench the car around, opening and closing just one of the emergency brakes at a time to let it swivel.

Finally it was ready. With a silent prayer, Mary stepped off deliberately into the abyss, floating down in the gentle gravity until the safety line caught her. Then she simply reeled in. Once back in the elevator she'd ridden down in, she triggered the cable release for the defective elevator, and watched as it slowly started to fall; then she savagely stabbed the ignite button. The little chemical rocket she'd stuck on puffed briefly, pushing the falling car farther away from the stalk as it was supposed to.

The jettisoned equipment arced away and downward. She leaned over to watch, but soon she lost sight of it. Even at a mere 0.15 gee, its speed grew rapidly.

She spoke into her radio. "Mary here. All done. Start the hose deployment again. I'll watch from here for a while."

"Roger," George said.

In a few minutes she could see that the hose was moving again, slowly but smoothly. She considered whether she should remain there for the rest of the deployment, but discarded the idea. Her supplies were low, the sanitary facilities in the skinsuits were primitive, and anyway, her arm was starting to swell. She wasn't even sure she'd be able to cross over to the other cable again if it became necessary.

And in any event, she didn't see any reason that it should be just her responsibility to fix the problems the others' haste had caused. They should never have tried deploying the carbon peripump in the first place. Let Norm come down here if it got stuck again. It would do him good.

"Mary here," she said again. Fatigue and remembered anger roughened her voice. "It's moving all right. Bring me up."

"Okay. Good work, Mary," George said. He started to say something else, but she cut him off.

"Over and out."

She had no trouble falling asleep on the ride back up. In fact, it seemed she'd hardly closed her eyes when the alarm woke her. She must have slept the whole 30 hours. Nonetheless, she didn't feel rested. She felt grimy; she itched unmercifully, and her injured arm now throbbed insistently.

All her crewmates were waiting for her. Even Norm floated there by the airlock in the ship's non-rotating cargo bay, his eyes showing grudging respect. George spoke first and offered his hand. "Congratulations," he said simply when she twisted off her helmet.

Something snapped in her at the conciliatory sound of his voice. This situation should have never arisen in the first place, and now he and Ivan and Norm were trying to pretend all was well. Sweetness and light and "well, we're all in this together." Bullshit.

Mary ignored his proffered hand. "No thanks to *you*, you incompetent coward!" she hissed. "If you had taken a stand earlier, I wouldn't have had to do this!"

George, taken aback, was too tired to be polite. Withdrawing his hand, he said, "The definition of courage, Mary, is 'grace under pressure'." He turned away, and neither Norm nor Ivan said a word as Mary pulled herself back into the ship.

*Still life with scrap*, Norm thought, looking at the monitor. The scene opened out on a junkyard, haphazard pieces of torn metal ripped out of anything that could be spared, waiting to provide metal ions to neutralize the acidic water they hoped to collect there. The metal half filled the enormous oblong storage tank fitted into the ballast mass at the base of the stalk. From there, they'd fill the smaller tanks in the elevator cars to carry the water back to the ship.

They hoped.

George looked up at the chronometer. "Any second now," he said unnecessarily. "Then we'll know if *this* worked." He avoided looking at Mary, but she bristled anyway. Norm smiled, glad she had found someone else to direct her hatred toward for a while. Before she could say anything, though, movement on the monitor caught their attention.

Water, charged with acid and oxygen, spurted out of the pulsing tube and splashed into the waiting tank, dribbling down to the waiting scrap. Hydrogen boiled off wherever water met metal, bursting into flame as dissolved oxygen also fizzed out of the splashing water. The tank was open to space, though; the flame couldn't build up enough pressure to do any damage.

At length the starship's four crewmembers could see the waterline slowly rising in the tank.

Norm looked to the lowermost monitor, the one showing the view at the pumphead. The ceramic trashrack on the base of the cable, a cage to keep the native life at bay while they pumped, seemed to be holding. Even so, the carnage outside was straight out of a nightmare: creatures that looked to be all mouth snapping at the cage and at each other until the water turned murky with their blood. Norm hoped nothing in their physiology would provide any more nasty surprises, but he wasn't willing to bet on it. They would have to filter and maybe even vacuum-distill every drop of it before bringing it on board.

Unless, of course, Mary wanted to bathe in it unprocessed. It would almost be worth breaking ship's quarantine to watch her try.

George was as close to achieving harmony as he'd ever been. The very smell of fresh water seemed like perfume. He'd been sitting in full lotus beneath a hot shower for nearly half an hour, and if the recycler didn't quit first he planned to stay there for the rest of the day. He might just stay there for the rest of the trip, all seven years of it.

The idea that he would be a hero at the end of the journey amused him greatly. The colonists who awakened from SloMo would name mountains after him, maybe even entire continents. Their descendants would learn about the four brave crewmembers who defied all odds to save the ship, and mothers would name their sons and daughters after them for generations to come. No one would mention the arguments and backbiting that surrounded their heroism, nor the long years of embarrassed animosity they were sure to endure before they reached their goal.

George would trade it all in a moment for the blissful sleep of SloMo, but he knew without asking what the others would say to that. The same thing he would say if one of them asked for the same privilege: they couldn't afford to lose one-fourth of their trained crewmembers, not with so much reconstruction to do before they reached the colony.

No, he was stuck with them, and they with him, for the rest of eternity. He turned his face upward to let the fresh, soothing water cascade over him while he tried to compose a haiku of suitable irony to fit the situation.

They had, after all, survived.

Thousands of kilometers below the starship, another struggle was underway. The skystalk and the silica peripump had been reeled back into the ship, but the ceramic trashrack at the intake, its fastenings weakened by the incessant battering, had fallen off to sink down into the planet-spanning ocean. Water frothed crimson like a bubbling lung wound as nightmare creatures continued to dash themselves futilely against it, slashing themselves and each other as they attacked the indifferent oxides. The turmoil only increased as time went on, as more and more carnivores sensed the spreading casualties and homed in on the chaos, only to be themselves swept up into it.

The trashrack continued to sink slowly through the frenzied beasts, knocked this way and that like a dust mote drifting in Brownian motion in an afternoon sunbeam.

It tended downward, but it had a long, long way to fall.

*Acknowledgment: The authors would like to thank Poul Anderson for his original suggestion of a planet consisting entirely of water.*

# HOOP-OF-BENZENE

## Robert Reed

*Now there's a story title that tells you absolutely nothing about what you are about to experience. And just how do I begin to explain it? You see, we're creeping up the barometer of extremeness and this is where things start to get a little complicated.*

*Robert Reed (b. 1956) is one of the new generation of writers who can grasp vast concepts that leave me goggle eyed. Much of his science fiction has been relatively straightforward – well, if you count attempts by aliens to change reality as straightforward. That's the principle behind his books* Beyond the Veil of Stars *(1994),* Beyond the Gated Sky *(1997) and* An Exaltation of Larks *(1995). But in* Marrow *(2000) Reed took a rather giant step. It tells of groups of aliens and genetically changed humans who travel through the universe in a ship that is so huge that it contains its own planet. The following story, which was written specially for this anthology, is set in the same world as that but takes place long before the events in* Marrow. *It's a story where you become so involved with the characters that you'll find yourself accepting the extreme concepts as if they are everyday. Until you think about them!*

A young captain was chosen because the task seemed quite minor and higher-ranked souls had more vital or interesting duties to perform. What the officer knew was minimal: the apartment's location, a sketch of its history, plus the name and species of its current owner. But she brought clear orders and the sanctity of her office and, after several centuries of training, she was accustomed to wearing the mirrored uniform as well as its natural authority.

"Hello, sir," the captain began, offering the standard two-stomp greeting. A tall and naturally graceful woman, she was pretty in a human fashion, with an easy smile that was kept hidden for the moment. Employing a crisp, slightly angry voice, she announced, "My name is Washen."

The alien stared through the diamond door, saying nothing.

"Hoop-of-Benzene," she called out. Harum-scarums often appreciated a brash tone. "If that's your name, I wish to speak with you. And if you are someone else, bring Hoop-of-Benzene to me."

The breathing mouth opened. "I am Hoop," the alien replied.

"Sir," she said, repeating the two-stomp greeting. "Three days from now, one of my superiors will visit your district, and the good captain has expressed interest in touring his former home. Which is, as it happens, your apartment."

The mouth puckered. "Does this good captain have a name?"

"For the moment, he does not. He prefers confidentiality. But I assure you that he's among the Master Captain's favorite officers."

"A Submaster, is he?"

"Perhaps," Washen allowed. "And perhaps not."

"In three days, you say." An enormous hand pressed against the door. "But why in three days? Can you surrender that much?"

Washen considered her audience. Harum-scarum society was built upon ceremony and rank, status and noisy bluster. "As I'm sure you are aware, sir . . . five thousand years ago, my people threw open the hatches of this great vessel. We invited all the species of the galaxy to share in our grand voyage. Fifty centuries of success, and during this milestone year, to mark our many accomplishments, the captains are holding a series of celebrations."

"I have heard about this business," Hoop allowed.

"The Master Captain is scheduled to visit your district. All of her Submasters will be attendance, plus a hundred lesser captains, and she will enjoy two feasts given in her honor, and a

Janusian wedding, and the new Ill-lock habitat will be christened. As for the nameless captain . . . his visit to your home
should take just a few moments. Little more. The man is not a
sentimental creature, and I assure you, any disruption to your life
will be minimal."

"No."

"Pardon?"

"No," Hoop repeated. "This human creature may not visit my
home."

Washen had imagined this turn but never expected it. Concealing her surprise, she asked, "What is the difficulty, sir? Is it a
matter of timing?"

"Why?" asked the breathing mouth. "Would the good captain
accept a different day?"

"Possibly," she said.

"Yet I think he wouldn't," Hoop decided. "Captains are
exceptionally stubborn humans, and I believe you are trying
to mislead me."

Washen allowed a grin to emerge. "Yes, sir. You've seen
through my thin apeskin, yes. The captain's schedule is quite
busy, and he will probably not return to this district for a long,
long while."

The harum-scarum stared at the human. Even among his
species, Hoop-of-Benzene was an enormous creature – a towering
biped whose muscular body was covered with glistening armored
plates and long golden spines. Beneath a pair of broad black eyes
were two mouths, one for speaking and breathing, the other
intended for eating and delivering the worst insults imaginable.

"My schedule is equally rigid," announced the breathing
mouth. "And since I do not wish to entertain visitors, not in
three days or for the next three thousand years, I will not allow
him to enter my home."

The eating mouth made a soft, abusive noise.

"It is my right to turn away visitors," the alien continued. "I
know the codes. I can quote the relevant statutes, if you wish.
Even the Master Captain is forbidden from entering any premise
where she is not welcome. The only exceptions demand sturdy
legal causes, which do not apply in this situation. And even in the
most urgent circumstances, mandatory warrants must be drawn
up, sealed and registered, then delivered by the appropriate
agents of the law."

Again, he made the rude sound.

Washen's eyes were nearly as dark as Hoop's. Her expression was curious and patient, with just a trace of nervous concern.

"You still haven't offered any name," the alien pointed out.

"I have strict orders. My superior intends to remain anonymous." With a thin smile, she added, "I can tell you that he is a powerful figure onboard the Great Ship. A force to be reckoned with, and once angered, he can be quite vindictive."

Harum-scarums had an instinctive respect for tyrants.

Yet Hoop clucked a tongue as if amused. "I suspect, young captain, you must feel rather uncomfortable just now."

Washen swallowed and said nothing.

"So tell me this . . ."

"Sir?"

"Why would a powerful, vindictive creature care who strolls through these little rooms of mine?"

"I cannot guess his mind, sir."

"I'm not discussing the captain's mind," Hoop replied. "Perhaps I should remind you: two powers are at play here."

"A worthy point," Washen conceded. Then with a wink and bright smile, she added, "And you should consider the poor intermediary standing before you. She doesn't know the name of your game, much less its rules."

Again, the tongue clicked.

"This must be an important mission," Hoop observed. "To select such a quick-witted captain—"

"All missions are important," she interrupted.

The harum-scarum paused, perhaps considering his choices.

"If I fail to win your cooperation," Washen admitted, "a second, much higher-ranking captain will be sent. Or twenty subordinates wielding heavy legal weaponry will descend on you. As you say, captains are stubborn souls, and this one in particular. He intends to step through your door at a specific hour, two days after tomorrow, and no one can halt the inevitable."

"Do I look helpless?" Hoop inquired.

"My name is Washen," the young captain repeated. "I just made my service files available to you. Absorb them at your convenience, and I will lie to my superior. I'll claim that you wish to meet with me tomorrow. Alone. And then the two of us will come to terms with this nagging problem in our lives."

Then before Hoop-of-Benzene could respond, the young captain turned her back to him and strode off – in effect, making it difficult for a proper harum-scarum to refuse the little creature, when and if she found the courage to come to his door again.

Humans discovered the Great Ship wandering on the outskirts of the galaxy: a derelict vessel larger than most worlds, older than the sun, and empty of everything but mystery. Those first lucky explorers claimed the Ship for their species, refurbishing its engines and hull at their own expense, and then they set off on a voyage meant to last for the next quarter of a million years. To recoup the enormous costs, they recruited wealthy passengers from the passing solar systems. Aliens were as welcome as humans; in principle, every species had a berth waiting for it. The Ship was laced with giant caverns and true oceans, plus nameless chambers of every size, and it was a relatively easy trick to configure the local environments to suit the delicate needs of most alien physiologies. But what was not easy – what was an exceptionally difficult business – was to keep this menagerie happy enough and distracted enough to live under the same hull for hundreds of millennia.

Supporting the peace: that was every captain's most essential, pride-giving duty.

Harum-scarums were among the most abundant and important passengers. Older than humans, they evolved on a watery, metal-starved world. Tiny continents and scarce resources shaped their long history; relentless competition was the hallmark of their mature civilization. Tens of millions of years had been spent defending the same patches of dry ground, evolving elaborate codes of formal, trusted rituals. While proto-humans still brachiated their way through jungle canopies, harum-scarums were refining aluminum and building spaceships. Before *Homo habilis* jogged across Africa, the aliens had acquired hyperfiber and enhanced fusion star-drives, plus a collection of powerful tools that made both their bodies and minds functionally immortal.

Harum-scarum was a human name. The Clan of Many Clans was one worthwhile translation of what the creatures called themselves. And, like most high-technology species, once the Clan learned how to extend life spans, it nearly stopped evolving. On thousands of worlds, the creatures still clung to their original natures – physically powerful entities filled with calculated rage as well as a startling capacity for acquiescence.

From the Clan's perspective, Washen's people were newcomers to the galaxy – untested and laughably optimistic, like children or pampered meat. For every air-cloaked rock that humans colonized, the Clan ruled a hundred mature worlds. Trillions of citizens were scattered across an entire arm of the galaxy, and they had more starships and better starships than anyone. If they had seen the Great Ship roaming across the deep cold, they would have reached it first and claimed the artifact as their prize. But they didn't notice the giant wanderer in time. Humans did and, because of that blessing, humans achieved something that was deeply unlikely. Which was one reason why Hoop and his people took such pleasure in insulting their hosts. "Monkey-men" was a popular barb. And "bare-fleshed babies". And perhaps the most caustic, damning name: "Luck-fattened souls."

Most humans assumed that harum-scarums were embittered, jealous and occasionally vengeful creatures. But any responsible captain knew better than to read too much into a little hard noise. Once humans took legal possession of the ancient derelict – in accordance with the galaxy's ancient laws – the Clan turned their attentions elsewhere. Ownership had been established. A contest won was a contest done. And if you were a good citizen of a good family, you turned away and carefully sharpened your spines, returning to the business of living of your magnificent life.

Grudges and second acts were the province of weaker species.

Humans, for one.

"This makes no sense to me," the Submaster confessed. "You assured him that I was an important captain."

"Which you are," said Washen.

"I'm still anonymous, am I?"

"Absolutely, sir."

"Yet the creature still refuses to capitulate."

"For the time being. But I'll meet with him tomorrow and try to reach some understanding."

"Harum-scarums," the Submaster muttered. "I've dealt with them many times, and with much success. Once you push past their manners and moods, they're perfectly reasonable monsters."

Washen restrained a grimace.

The man's name was Ishwish. By human measures, he was

ancient and extraordinarily well traveled. Countless stories were told about the old Submaster, but remarkably little was defined in his public biography. Ishwish had fought with distinction in several human wars, rising to a high rank in at least two militaries. More than once, he had employed alien mercenaries, including brigades of harum-scarums who helped make his career. Then after earning a chest full of medals, he retired to a quiet life, commanding colony starships during the first human expansion across the Milky Way. Those millennia made him a wealthy man with lucrative political connections. When the Great Ship was discovered, Ishwish used his own fortune, fitting a small asteroid with enormous engines and a minimal life support system and hiring a crew to race out beyond the edges of the Milky Way. Centuries later, his starship was among the first to arrive at the Great Ship. And from that moment, Ishwish worked tirelessly to see that he was given his rightful high rank among the first captains.

For a few moments, the Submaster remained silent, most likely using a nexus to examine Hoop's files. The eyes flickered for a moment, meaning something. But what? Then he sighed softly, and with a disappointed shake of the head, he said, "Frankly, I expected better things from an ambitious young captain."

Washen nodded, twisting her mirrored cap in her hands.

"There is no task that a captain cannot achieve," he reminded her.

"I know this, sir."

Ishwish's task of the moment was to sit before a large oak table, alone, occupying a back corner of what was a very small eating establishment. This was the favorite haunt of the Master Captain, which made it popular to all of her loyal Submasters. The man was exceptionally tall in his chair; Washen stood beside him, yet their eyes were nearly level. Handsome in an ageless, heavily polished fashion, Ishwish had bright gold eyes and a sharp joyless smile, and with every word and little motion, he betrayed enough arrogance to fuel two successful captains.

"What are little jobs?" he asked.

"'An impossibility of nature,'" she quoted from her training.

"And what are little honors?"

"'Blessings that fall on little souls,'" she said, quoting words he had used on more than one occasion.

Ishwish nodded, and the smile dimmed as he explained, "I

have been awarded a declaration of merit from the Master Herself."

"Congratulations, sir."

"For my long service to this fabulous ship, I will be given this tremendous honor."

"Yes, sir."

"Our Master asked me, 'Where do you wish the ceremony to be held, my good friend? On the Ship's bridge? Or at the captains' dinner?' But after careful consideration, I decided on a small, quick ceremony held inside the apartment where I first lived. Linking my success with five thousand years of safe, profitable starflight, I should add."

Even as she repeated her congratulations, Washen doubted the explanation. A creature like Ishwish would want the largest possible audience to watch his treasured moment. And like the flickering of the eyes, the fact that he was lying now about the circumstances meant something. Though what might be meant, she couldn't yet say.

The Submaster glanced at her. "My memory tells me," he said quietly. "You were born in the Great Ship, weren't you?"

"Yes, sir."

"And your parents were not captains?"

"They were engineers," she admitted. But Ishwish surely knew that already, just as he seemed to remember everything about her tiny life.

"You've never left the confines of the Ship," he stated.

There was nothing confining about a machine with the mass of Uranus and enough caverns to explore for the next ten billion years. But she simply dipped her head, admitting, "I have not traveled. No, sir."

"So you haven't walked on the harum-scarums' worlds."

Washen shook her head. "No, sir."

"I have."

She waited for advice, or at least some tiny insight.

But Ishwish offered none. He lifted a utensil – a heavy crab-pincer – while glancing across the room. A colleague had just arrived, and in the smallest possible way, he waved the pincer and his elegant hand, offering his greetings to a fellow Submaster.

Washen bowed to the newcomer, then asked Ishwish, "Do you have any advice for a novice captain?"

"The Great Ship always needs new engineers."

His threat earned a small nod from Washen. But she was watching the newcomer stroll toward an empty table reserved for no one but her. Miocene was the woman's name, and she was said to be the Master Captain's most loyal and dangerous officer. Since becoming a novice captain, Washen had spoken to her perhaps half a dozen times. None of those conversations held any substance. Yet the tall, imperious woman was looking at her now. Just for a moment. And for no good reason, Miocene tipped her head at the young officer, offering a dim but lingering smile . . . a smile that for no clear reason felt important . . .

"Where is your uniform?" asked Hoop-of-Benzene.

"Doing its own business this morning," Washen confessed with a two-foot stomp. She was standing before the diamond door, wearing civilian clothes, including sandals and slacks and a pair of simple silk belts. If not for the small mirror-patch on the shoulder of her blouse, she would have been completely out of uniform, subject to a multitude of deserved punishments. "As I promised, I am here. And now I wish to step inside your apartment."

"No."

She nodded as if unconcerned. "Tell me why not."

"I don't crave visitors. Why is this so difficult to comprehend?"

Washen sighed. "As I understand these matters, your family clan is one of the largest. Your relatives stand tall on half a hundred worlds."

"We are great, yes."

"Success brings responsibility," she said.

"For more species than mine," Hoop added.

"According to your laws and honored conventions, you cannot turn away the weakest mouths. If a citizen with no status comes to your door begging for a small meal, it is your duty to feed her enough to live out the day."

Both of the harum-scarum's mouths snorted, amusement mixed with warm disgust. "You are far from weak," he pointed out.

"Am I?"

"Perhaps you haven't noticed, my dear. But even a lowly captain commands respect from the multitudes."

"Not from you, sir."

"You do have my respect. I honor your office and rank. I'm just refusing to surrender my home to any captain."

With her best impression of a harum-scarum smile, Washen asked, "But what if I wasn't captain any more?"

The black eyes stared.

"If I surrendered my rank and authority . . . what would that mean to you . . .?"

"Nothing," he claimed.

Yet Washen acted as if she'd heard a different response, removing her blouse and the mirrored emblem attached to it, folding them into a small wad easily thrown over her naked shoulder. Then she kicked off the sandals and unfastened both belts, her slacks falling into a heap around her bare ankles. "As a traveler without rank or privilege," she said, "may I enter your home?"

"No," said Hoop.

She kneeled and bent low, slowly licking the granite floor of the avenue. Then employing a passable harum-scarum, she said, "Without food, I die."

"You are being silly," the alien assured her.

"I'm only following your example," she countered.

Hoop refused to answer. For a long while, he remained perfectly motionless, spines and fingers held in relaxed positions. But there was a steady stream of pedestrian traffic in the avenue, and eventually half a dozen humans strolled past, pausing to watch this very peculiar scene. A Janusian couple joined them, and then a herd of Fume-dogs. Eventually half a hundred passengers stood in a patient half-circle, enjoying the spectacle of a former captain going mad, naked and splayed out on the hard chilled ground, muttering again and again in that harsh alien language, "Without food, I die."

When a pair of harum-scarums appeared down the avenue, Hoop was left with no choice. This human creature had done nothing but follow orders, and the only worthy response was to invite her inside.

Yet just the same, he still hesitated.

Only when Hoop's brethren started pushing Fume-dogs out of the way, trying to see what was so interesting, did he surrender. Letting out a low wet sound, he backed out of sight, and an instant later, the thick diamond door split along every invisible seam.

*     *     *

No public record linked Ishwish to the apartment; but that was expected, since captains usually kept their private addresses private. This had been the man's home only for his first few centuries onboard the Ship. Then the local district lost its cachet, and the Submaster acquired a more spacious and impressive apartment. Through masking corporations, he sold the apartment to a human couple – early passengers from a rich colony world. Over the course of the next thousand years, that couple raised eight children from embryo to adulthood. Then came a difficult divorce and a quick sale to a gathering of Higgers – machine souls that promptly flooded the chambers and long passageways with hot, pressurized silicone through which they happily swam. But Higgers have accelerated minds and painfully low thresholds for boredom. Fourteen years was enough time in one location, which was why they sold to an investment conglomerate that was gathering up properties scattered throughout the backwater districts. The investors paid little, but they knew that the Ship's population would grow, and with patience, the district would eventually fall back into favor.

Like many shipboard homes, Hoop's apartment began as a tiny portion of an enormous cavern. At convenient points, walls had been erected and tunnels closed, limiting the floor space to a cozy ten hectares. For twenty-five centuries, Hoop-of-Benzene had lived nowhere else, and in that time he had carefully renovated his home until it perfectly suited his needs.

Washen absently scratched an ear, then an exposed breast. On bare feet, she walked upon the greeting-mat laid out in the hallway, a complex patterns of fuzzy rings displaying the name and important history of Hoop's family clan. The first of a hundred towering statues stood on both sides of the hallway, defending blocks of ceremonial soil. Treasured ancestors had been carved from a ruddy wood alien to both of their species. A thick oily scent hung in the air, dark and disgusting to a human nose. But Washen took a deep sniff before turning to her host. "Tidecold-6," she said quietly.

Hoop gave no reply.

Then in his language, she named the tree. "Blood-twice," she said, her diction surprisingly good considering her inadequate mouth.

The harum-scarum studied her ribs and that patch of soft tissue where a beating heart could be seen. Perhaps he had never been in the presence of a naked human. Devoid of armor, Washen would appear exposed and ridiculously frail to him – a reaction tied into his oldest instincts.

She returned to the standard human language. "Blood-twice trees are native to Tidecold-6."

"Botany is an interest of yours?"

"It is, but I would have learned that anyway." With a gesture of respect, she admitted, "I've done a respectable amount of research about you."

He said nothing.

She started down the hallway, examining each of the life-sized statues in turn. The first ancestors were the most ancient, the pink wood gone pale and dusty dry. But at some point the statues darkened, every slice of the old awls still deep, each figure decorated with scraps of clothing and jewelry, spines and plates of armor that belonged to each of the men and women being portrayed. At that point, the hallway curled sharply to the right. More statues waited out of sight, but Washen stopped, kneeling down, pretending to exam the meeting-mat beneath her feet. With a quiet, thoughtful voice, she said, "You came on board my ship 2,507 years ago."

Hoop watched her eyes, struggling to read the alien face.

"You came alone," she said. "A young, relatively wealthy man off on an adventure. And you paid for your passage through a universal account established on your home world. Which was not Tidecold-6."

Hoop opened a huge hand. "This world you keep mentioning . . . I have never seen it . . ."

She nodded agreeably, touching one of the elegant rings woven into the mat. The fabric was young and clean. Pushing against the weave, she felt the living fibers moving in unison, debating if she was a threat and if she should be contested.

"Twelve light-years," she mentioned.

He was silent.

"When Tidecold-6 was abandoned, a portion of the survivors migrated to a hard little world twelve light-years removed. And to the best of their ability, they rebuilt. It was your clan that made new homes there and managed, I hope, to put the ugliness behind them."

The alien's spines straightened and the plates of armor pulled closer to his body, reflexively making ready to fend off any blow.

"That ugly war of yours," she said.

Hoop's eating mouth made a wet sound.

"A harum-scarum apocalypse," she said.

"There is no such monster," he replied, staring at the tiny creature kneeling before him. "My species aren't crazy apes. We do not fight to oblivion."

"Which makes your family history all the more tragic." Then Washen made the same wet noise that Hoop had used, her human mouth offering the crudest possible curse – neatly underscoring the war's unseemliness and the unbearable, unforgivable waste.

Their walk through the apartment continued in silence.

After the turn, they strolled past the final few dozen statues. Washen paused beside an empty slab of soil, wondering which ancestor was supposed to stand there. Suddenly her host pushed ahead, polite in a harum-scarum fashion, entering the greeting room before his feeble guest.

Heavily pruned blood-twice forests grew in long sapphire urns, and elegant furnishings meant for giants were scattered about the vast round space. The ceiling was a beautiful dome of polished green olivine. Light poured from everywhere, and nowhere. Some unseen functionary had recently delivered a fresh meal to a greeting table set in the room's center. A dead meal, Washen noted. Meat had been peeled from an immortal animal, seasoned and then cooked to a human's taste. In some other corner of the apartment, the meat's source was now recovering inside its spacious stable, feeling a modest discomfort while eating its fill from the trough, damaged flesh rapidly patching the gaping wound.

The novice captain thanked Hoop-of-Benzene for going to so much trouble, and then she ignored the cooling feast.

"I have looked over your life," she mentioned again.

Hoop regarded her for a long moment. "And what did you learn about me?"

"That I understand practically nothing."

Another silent stare began.

When no question followed, she explained, "I do know something about the war. At least, I know one version of its history. Every few years, some young captain . . . someone even newer to his post that I am to mine . . . will pull me aside and ask, 'Did you know this story . . .?' "

"And the story is?"

"My superior – the Submaster who refuses to be named – once served as the captain to a small colony ship. His mission was to deliver ten thousand eager humans to a little world perched at the edge of the galaxy. A harsh young world, as it happens, and a huge challenge for ignorant monkeys like us, since we had almost no experience terraforming such marginal places."

Hoop's breathing mouth opened and then closed again, seemingly forgetting to inhale.

"It was an unfortunate voyage," Washen continued. "There were the usual problems with the engines and with life-support systems. But worst of all were the troubles between various colonists. Political difficulties. Personal qualms. Old feuds reignited in the quiet between the stars. The captain of any colony ship is responsible for his machinery and his human cargo, and this particular captain managed to keep the angry factions under control. But he lost his grip during the final decades, and a low-grade war broke out in the hallways and habitats. Plainly, his ship needed help. Which was why he changed course, braking early and dropping into a low orbit around Tidecold-6."

With a slow, almost musical voice, her host said, "Ishwish."

"I haven't mentioned names," Washen reminded him. Then she sat on the edge of the greeting table, two fingertips riding up her bare stomach and sternum and neck. "The story that I have heard, and heard, and heard again, centers on the same few facts: Tidecold-6 was a large, mature world with oxygen and oceans and a vigorous biosphere. Two clans had lived there for eons. They were evenly matched, both in terms of population and resources. And that wasn't an accidental coincidence. There had been half a thousand little contests during their shared history. What would look like quick wars to humans were little more than formalized pushing matches. Which is as it should be. Your species is innately conditioned to spit and pummel one another, but only to reinforce the status quo."

Hoop stared at her face, watching the weak little bones floating beneath her thin, practically useless skin.

"This is a consequence of your heritage." Washen smiled with genuine appreciation. "Your home world is relatively old, with worn-down islands and quiet seas and no reliable volcanism. Animals that evolve in those circumstances, where resources are scarce and growth must be slow, often tend to adapt in certain predictable ways."

"Am I an animal?"

She nodded. "You are a spectacular animal. And your ancestors were exceptionally expensive collections of bone and armor, muscle and energy. Without volcanic activity, essential minerals are locked away in deep sediments. Soils are poor and the waters half-sterile, and it once took decades of slow, patient growth to wring enough calories and protein from some little patch of landscape, producing an adult as splendid as you. But evolution is nothing more, or less, than a string of complex calculations written in gore. And you are a fabulous investment, and at the end of the day, you were a grand success."

Hoop gave an agreeable click of a tongue.

"What most humans should realize, but don't . . . if they are to work beside the Clan of Many Clans, they see aliens who are furious and quick-tempered. But much of what you do is for show. Not that what you do and say isn't real; I wouldn't claim that the noise and fuming is empty or that isn't extraordinarily important. But in almost every circumstance, when your powerful minds see nothing but disaster looming, you will give up. You will give in. A sane and responsible citizen on any of your ten thousand happy worlds will instantly bow down, surrendering to whatever clan or species has the battle won."

"How else should we behave?" asked Hoop.

"I agree. Every species in the universe should act this way," she claimed. "I know my sad people need a dose of your humility and wise nature. Particularly when you consider those human colonists: there was a new world to build, yet they felt it was more important to murder their own kind. If the unnamed captain had been shepherding two clans of harum-scarums across the galaxy, I guarantee you, there wouldn't have been any threat to ship. Or to the mission. Or to the man sitting up in the bridge, weighing his options."

"Ishwish came to Tidecold-6," Hoop said.

"To ask your species for help. Yes." Washen waited a moment, then mentioned, "I've heard the story twenty times, and always the same way. The human asked for help, and it was given. But there were other players and another request was made, and after some very unfortunate luck, what should have been simple became terribly complicated, and what should have been finished in a few hours ended up filling most of eight days, butchering that poor world in the process."

Hoop tightly closed both of his mouths.

"You must know a different version of the story, or at least a fuller telling. Am I right?"

"I know very little," Hoop replied. "When this happened, my shadow hadn't been cast."

The naked captain said nothing, letting her silence work.

"But my mother," Hoop finally said, his voice faltering for a moment. "When I was old enough, she told me the history. Which is exactly the same as your story, except for the differences."

Hoop described the aliens' arrival: a crude, ungainly starship suddenly plunged from deep space, fusion engines struggling to kill its terrific momentum. Ishwish was the first human voice they ever heard, and the first human face ever seen, and in a pose of perfect submission, he begged the ruling clans for help. They gave permission for him to move into orbit, but the machine struggled with even that simple task. Once a sun-blasted comet, the ship was a fancy set of engines rooted in black tar and porous stone, the entire contraption bolstered with hyperfiber girders and incalculable amounts of luck. Ten thousand humans, plus supplies and an army of sleeping machines, had been sent out to make a new world habitable. But the colonists were plainly inexperienced at terraforming. Dressing a newborn world in a breathable atmosphere and a drinkable ocean would require more bodies than they had, as well as a heroic patience. Yet what was most alarming to the Clans was that their crude starship had been damaged, and not by natural means.

"Internal explosions," Washen said.

"From some flavor of fighting. Yes." The creature stared at a distant point, watching events he could only imagine. "We made scans, and the scans were followed by probes. Probes gave way to diplomats. A civil struggle had broken out among the colonists, we learned. Two governments had coalesced around opposing ideals, each occupying a different portion of the damaged vessel."

Washen nodded, saying nothing.

"Our world was relatively isolated," Hoop continued. "None us had direct experience with humans. To us, your species were abstractions. Well-drawn abstractions, since we had collected substantial files about your history and nature. But until that day, no one imagined that we would become neighbors, much less that you would slink up to our front door, pleading for help."

She nodded. "The ship captain made the plea."

"To my father, yes." Hoop extended a giant hand, palm up – a sign of charity to both of their species. "He was an Elder in my clan's council. Others urged distrust. But my mother told me, more than once, that my father felt it would be wise to make friends with humans. You were a bold species, young and foolish, investing so much energy to place a few bodies on some ugly little planet that didn't look at all promising to us. But he believed that he liked you. In Ishwish, he found qualities that struck him as . . . the concept does not translate well . . . but in his eyes, the human captain was sympathetic and pathetic, honorable and powerfully intriguing . . ."

Washen quoted a Clan truism, declaring, " 'Kindness is power; charity proves strength.' "

"Strength." Hoop repeated the word several times, in both languages. Then the hand closed, a mailed fist turning slowly in the air between them. "My father led the delegation to meet directly with Ishwish. Captain and crew as well as the loyal colonists were gathered around the engines, while rebel colonists controlled the bow and most major habitats. The fighting was constant, but sloppy. So the ship was still intact. Only a thousand humans had died, and then only temporarily. Their battered little bodies were mummified and kept locked away, most held as prisoners, waiting for a winner to be declared and for the ship's hospital to be reactivated."

Washen imagined that nightmare as if she was sitting on a captain's chair. "The situation was treacherous."

"Chaotic and frightful, and to us, difficult to comprehend. How can two sides fight for decades and still not see two winners standing in the ruins?" The eyes focused on her face. "Yet once they were breathing the same air, my father was deeply impressed with the Ishwish creature. When he returned home, he told my mother that he had felt as if the human had been his friend for ten thousand years. The creature offered perfect words, often in our language. How he spoke was flawless and soothing. And the stance of his little body . . . well, his performance was superior to yours today, my dear . . . clinging to that filthy black floor, licking tar dusts and human blood, confessing to his guest that he was helpless to save his wicked, doomed ship."

"That human had experience with your species," she offered.

"In the old human wars, yes. Ishwish offered battles and dates that we found buried in our files, and in all the respectable ways, he proved that he trusted us, and that we could trust him too. With our sweet help, he would regain control over the starship. Then as final proof, Ishwish surrendered his name and wealth to my father, begging for our mighty clan to give him a few hands . . . just enough hands so that he could gain the momentum, defeating his enemies and finally winning this disgusting little war."

Washen struggled to picture the man she knew – the arrogant Submaster – reduced to such a state.

Charitably, she said, "That wasn't a large request."

"A few hands, with the fighters attached," Hoop agreed. "But of course, unknown to my father, a delegation of the rebellious colonists had made contact with our neighbor clan. Different humans begged in the same perfect fashion, requesting a few hands of their own, and with them, a little help that would win their noble struggle."

Nothing here was new. Washen had always understood the essential history of the disaster. But she now saw possibilities that she hadn't noticed before . . . subtle undercurrents that even a novice captain should have noticed, if only while listening to the gossipy chatter of her peers . . .

"Long after that day," said the towering figure, "my mother took hold of me and crushed me against her body, whispering that this is where we should have realized what was true. Yes, your Ishwish had experience with us. Yet he seemed to be the only human with that distinction. We should have asked ourselves how the rebel leaders were able to speak and act with the same perfection, winning cooperation as well as a pledge of loyalty from our neighbors . . ."

Washen took a breath, holding it deep in her chest.

"Even in our ignorance," Hoop continued, "the situation was ours to control. We should have been able to stop our fighting after those first moments. You see, both clans sent the requested volunteers, and through what seemed like miserable luck, each attacked the other side in the same awful instant. Plasma weapons were used, which meant that every soldier was annihilated. Which is where we should have stepped back then, waiting for the blood to dry." The mailed fist opened and dropped, fingers limp. "But the clans had made pledges, and both sides wished to earn respect from these newcomers. That's why larger blows were inflicted, in quick succession. Suddenly the space above our world was bright with fighting." The eating mouth pushed itself into a single hard point. "And then we came close to stopping again. After five days of mounting casualties, a pause erupted. A necessary rest began, and with that, an official truce. Bids of peace were even offered, and in a moment or a day, those bids would have been accepted."

Washen stared his slack, empty hand.

"Three tritium bombs," Hoop said. Then he paused, gathering himself before completing his story. "In the quiet of a truce, three sophisticated weapons in the one-hundred megaton range were delivered to three cities. In a single cowardly stroke, our clan lost one quarter of its population and much of its wealth. But even worse, the truce had been cheated. Which is never done. Ever. That abomination demanded a suitable revenge, which is why my ancestors built and used three equally powerful weapons. Which should have been the end, if our enemies were sensible. But they insisted on spreading lies, claiming that those first three weapons had not come from any stockpile or bad dream of theirs."

Washen said, "I see," even when nothing quite made sense.

"The tritium bombs simply had to belong to our enemies," Hoop reported. "My father digested every report, and doubt was impossible. The weapons were ceremonial Death-bringers, authentic to their isotope yields and the markings on their diamond jackets. They were launched from an enemy base in high orbit, and they were shielded by our usual methods, and lying about the blame just made the horror worse. Which was why another enemy city had to be destroyed, in punishment for the lie. And then the other clan annihilated three more of our cities, plus the honored site where our species first landed on our sweet world. Then for the rest of those three days, we ceased to be the Clan of Many Clans." The giant face dipped, eyes losing all focus. "We became what you call us. The harum-scarum. We were madmen filled with blind rage, wild actions devoid of thought and reason. Only when most of us were dead did we dare make peace, and then only on the condition that both of our miserable clans abandon our home, poisoned as it was by radiations, and worse, sickened by our own stupidity."

Washen was crying now. With a soft, slow voice, she asked, "Did your father die in the war?"

"No." Hoop's spines straightened, in reflex. "He survived and returned to his good friend, Ishwish, and did what he believed was best. He begged for help from the human. Which was given. The captain met with all of the colonists, and in a gesture of extraordinary compassion, our human friends offered us that little world to which they had been traveling. 'It isn't much,' Ishwish admitted, 'but as a place for fresh beginnings, it might serve you well.'"

Washen blinked. "Your father met with every colonist?"

The alien showed a forest of little teeth inside his eating mouth. "Yes. While we were slaughtering one another, the colonists had suddenly made their own peace."

Washen breathed quickly, the air tasting stale and hot.

"Just enough ships for our journey were available," he continued. "My parents left for the new world, while the other clan retreated deeper into the galaxy, if only to place distance between the two of us. Twelve light-years had to be covered, and the voyage was productive. Even after the war, there were more of us than there had been humans, and we had experience enough to make any new world habitable, if not comfortable. So my clan made its plans and refined them until we felt ready. And we received messages from our good allies. The human colonists were quickly cleaning up poisons and repairing the ecosystems. In the proper ways, they thanked us again for our charity, they promised to make our old home prosper, honoring our memories, and buried in their words was news that their mission's captain, dear Ishwish, had been awarded a tenth of the colony's future value – in thanks for his guidance and considerable bravery."

Washen had always known that the Submaster was wealthy. But Tidecold-6 was an exceptionally rich world today – a favored destination for emigrants and every species of money – and ten percent of that single planet would make any man into a king.

Hoop had fallen silent.

Remembering that platform of ground waiting empty in the hallway, Washen said, "Your father. What's the rest of his story?"

Quietly, the alien confessed, "He suffered. A moment of clarity took him."

"What do you mean?"

"He woke one morning, as our new sun was growing bright . . . he woke and felt strong enough finally to ask questions that he hadn't dared pose until then. He turned to my mother and wondered aloud, 'But what if my very good friend, dear Ishwish . . . what if he was not what he seemed to be . . .?'"

Washen bit her bottom lip.

"Then as his strength drained, he asked, 'And what if everything was other than it seemed to be . . . the civil war, the humans in despair, the three weapons that appeared above our heads . . . what would all of that mean, darling . . .?'"

Tasting blood, Washen said, "Maybe."

"Maybe," Hoop agreed.

"A captain could have played the colonists against each other. Fomented war, but kept it under control. And he could have coached a few of the rebels, perhaps without even telling them his entire plan." She closed her eyes, envisioning what would have both possible and necessary. "He could have bought those tritium bombs somewhere else, using his military connections . . . brought them all that way and prepositioned them in a higher orbit, ready to accelerate the hostilities . . ." Her voice sputtered, then came back again. "But that would mean that the son-of-a-bitch had everything planned out, starting centuries before . . ."

"This was what my father realized," said Hoop. "And that is why a great despair took hold of him and claimed him. And about that good honorable man, I wish to say no more."

His father was dead, she realized. A suicide. No other conclusion to life was as dishonorable, not for a creature such as that, which was why there was no fatherly statue standing guard over his son's home.

Washen took them past that awful moment. "Help me now," she said. "When you purchased your home, this room and that hallway, did you know exactly who had lived here before?"

The black eyes brightened. "I knew about the Higgers," he said. "For years, I was cleaning their silicone out of the cracks and pores."

"But these past human owners?"

"Never. I suspected nothing. I had no idea." He paused for a thoughtful moment. "Until an acquaintance mentioned Ishwish to me, I was ignorant."

"An acquaintance?"

"A Clan woman. She mentioned the name and asked if I knew

who he was. Had I ever seen him with my eyes? And after I explained what the man might be, she asked how it felt. What was it like to know that this awful human once shit in these rooms of mine?"

Washen nodded, considering. "And when was this?"

"A year ago."

"Just a year ago?"

"Plus a few days more," Hoop reported. Which was the same as yesterday, when your life stretched for millennia.

"This is a spectacular coincidence," Washen mentioned. "Of all possible passengers, you end up living in the Submaster's old home."

Hoop rolled his face – the Clan equivalent of a nod. "I have asked these question many times. What are the probabilities? In a vessel of this size, with all these possible addresses to claim for myself . . . why must this be the home that I find for myself . . .?"

"The odds are long," she allowed.

"Which is why you and I are wondering along the same lines," he replied with quiet amazement. "What agent or force or malicious spirit is responsible for this conundrum . . .?"

A bowl of excessively sweet tea sat cooling on the tabletop. Washen stood close enough to smell the alien spices. When the temperature dropped to a critical point, the Submaster took a pinch of sucrose from a second bowl, one at a time sprinkling grains into the vaporous brew. The reaction was swift and dramatic. Like a sudden snow, supersaturated sugars fell out of solution, and what had been a fragrant brew turned into thick white syrup that could be spooned into dishes and served as a rare dessert.

The Submaster helped herself. Then she glanced at Washen, remarking, "You are early today. And Ishwish has been delayed. Some critical matter has ambushed his attentions, it seems."

"Yes, madam."

"If you would like, sit. Join me."

"I'd prefer to stand, madam." Washen was dressed again, in a full uniform. "But thank you, madam."

"As you wish." Miocene was an elegant creature, tall and lovely, cold and effortlessly forbidding. But she had a rich dark voice, and when it was useful, a surprisingly engaging smile. After the first mouthful of dessert, she showed her smile. Then after a thoughtful silence, she asked, "Is something on your mind, my dear?"

"I'm thinking about Ishwish, madam."

"Yes?"

"And Tidecold-6."

The Submaster said nothing. But judging by her face and manners, she felt ready for the subject.

"Was my superior directly responsible for that tragedy?"

Miocene shrugged. "I'm not free to give details. But yes, there were questions. And then, official inquiries. Investigations were carried out by various agencies, among our people and the harum-scarums too." She pursed her lips for a moment, perhaps using a nexus to access old files. "Most of the original colonists were interviewed, and each crewmember was interrogated. Ishwish himself underwent years of suspicion. But no credible account has shown that there was any plan to cheat or in any way harm the harum-scarums. The humans involved were left clean, officially."

With a nod, Washen said, "Good."

Then she bit her lip, adding, "He is a very careful man."

"He is."

"And shrewd."

Miocene laughed softly. "You like our colleague. Very good. The man has shown a small interest in your career, and it is important to appreciate the qualities of your superior."

"Yes, madam."

Miocene treated herself to a second bite of syrup and tea.

"Do you like Ishwish, madam?"

She tipped her head for a moment, swallowing. Then with a knife-like voice, she said, "I hope you can imagine what I think of the man."

Washen nodded.

"Tell me my mind," Miocene prompted.

"Your colleague is ambitious, which is a wonderful trait. He is calculating and subtle, when he wishes. And those, as well, are excellent qualities to find in any captain."

"Go on."

"But the authority and responsibilities that Ishwish carry with him . . . they stem directly from decisions made thousands of years ago. Tidecold-6 made him exceptionally wealthy. That wealth helped bring him to the Great Ship. Once here, his ambition helped elevate him to the rank of Submaster. Is that a fair accounting of his story, madam?"

"Don't dismiss the wealth that brought him," Miocene admitted. "Remember how difficult it was for us to reach the Ship . . . how tenuous our hold was, and still is, on this ancient machine. With one transmission, Ishwish was able to mobilize a world, sending us more engineers and lines of credit to help us repair these old pumps and environmental systems. And with a second message, he guaranteed us thousands of wealthy human passengers, paying bodies who migrated from dozens of thriving worlds."

"He bought his rank," Washen said, with distaste.

"In my mind," Miocene replied, "I prefer to think in different terms."

"You accept his position, do you?"

"As I accept each passing day."

"But do you think about Tidecold-6? On this day, for instance . . . has it ever left your thoughts, madam?"

"Will it leave yours, Washen?"

"But I'm a lowly captain, not a Submaster."

"And you are modest in the worst ways."

"Perhaps." Washen offered a brief nod. "I've been given my orders, and I intend to carry them out to the best of my ability."

"As is right."

"The investment group," said Washen.

For an instant, surprise worked its way across Miocene's narrow face. "To whom do you refer?"

"I've made inquiries," Washen explained. "By several means, I think I can see that only one person stands behind the corporate mask. This unidentified human owns properties in an assortment of districts. And she once held title to a comfortable little apartment that now, purely by chance, belongs to an angry fellow named Hoop-of-Benzene."

The smile was respectful, perhaps even impressed. "Please, dear. Go on."

"More than two thousand years ago, while Hoop was searching for a home, an agent with ties to that investment group aided him. The terms of the sale were very lucrative for the buyer. Someone made certain that this one passenger was placed inside that particular apartment, and that's where he has remained until today."

"A captain did this?"

"I know what I know, even if I can't prove anything."

The dessert was cooling, losing its delicate, precious flavors. Yet the Submaster seemed unconcerned, setting her spoon aside, focusing on the novice captain standing beside her.

"Recently," said Washen, "Hoop learned who once lived inside his home. You have no connections with the harum-scarum who delivered the news. As far as I can see, you are blameless. If there is any blame to be given, that is."

"That is good to hear."

"Hoop doesn't want that man to walk inside his house."

"I would imagine not."

"He intends to fight the invasion with every tool at his disposal."

"Which will lead him where?" Miocene showed a big grim smile. "To his ruin, I would think. That's the only possible destination for the poor fellow."

Washen sighed. "But this decision to give Ishwish an award, and to give it at this time and to hold the ceremony in that location . . . I find it easy to believe you were the one who set this slippery business into motion . . ."

With a chilled glance, Miocene asked, "Is there anything else?"

"I don't understand."

"Understand what?"

Washen bent closer, explaining, "Until yesterday, Ishwish didn't realize what Hoop-of-Benzene thought of him. Until I delivered the refusal, he assumed that the harum-scarum would love the idea of a famous captain strutting about in his rooms. But if he suspects trouble, the Submaster will do whatever is possible to make this problem vanish."

"Whatever is possible," Miocene agreed. Then with a tiny wink, she added, "At this moment, my colleague is meeting with a team of advisors. Yes, my dear, he has given up on you and your patient ways. New plans and brutal consequences are being considered. And by the end of this day, his problem will be solved."

"What kinds of plans?"

"I wouldn't know," Miocene replied. "But several minutes ago, one of Ishwish's functionaries learned that we have a murderer among us. A brutal criminal who happens to be male, and better yet, is also a harum-scarum."

"Not Hoop," Washen muttered.

"This is a matter for our courts, my dear. Not captains."

Washen wanted to scream.

For moment, Miocene said nothing. Then she softly asked, "Why are you here? What did you believe would happen, if you and I spoke?"

"What am I supposed to do, madam?"

Miocene shrugged.

"Thousands of years ago, you put Hoop into Ishwish's home. In some fashion or another, you are responsible for this entire situation. And now I've become your agent . . . although I don't see what it is you hope to gain . . ."

"Are you a captain, or aren't you?"

Washen threw back her shoulders. "Yes. I am."

"This ship of ours is still almost entirely empty," Miocene mentioned. "But before the end of our voyage, we will be walking these hallways with a hundred thousand species, and nothing will matter more than having a cadre of good captains . . . wise captains . . . human leaders who deserve the respect this multitude of odd entities . . ."

"Yes, madam."

"If you want to become an important officer of the Ship," said Miocene, "you must be able to navigate your way to the best destination available. Without the help of anyone else, I might add. And even if this means, in one fashion or another, doing something that happens to be right."

One last time, Washen returned to the diamond door. For an instant, it seemed as if Hoop was pleased to see his new friend. But then she told him what she wanted, offering no explanations why. Instincts took hold, and Hoop placed his feet squarely on the floor, shoulders tilting forward and the eating mouth pulled into a tight pucker. And again, the young captain made her very simple demand, adding, "If you will not give this, then I will fight you."

"No," Hoop replied. "I refuse your challenge."

There was little time left. With one nexus, Washen was tracking an order-of-arrest as it moved through the courts and past amiable judges, while by other nexuses, she watched teams of security officers being gathered in nearby bunkers, preparing for the moment when every signature was in place.

"You can't refuse," she said. Then she pulled off her mirrored uniform and took the proper stance for combat. "I demand this," she cried out, citing codes more ancient than her species.

Hoop nearly turned away from the door.

But then a set of figures appeared – towering creatures wearing the distinctively painted spikes that marked them as members of another clan. As it happened, they belonged to the clan that once fought against Hoop's, while standing on a world that neither of them would keep.

The harum-scarum looked at the bystanders, and then glared down at tiny Washen. "You brought them," he complained.

"In their presence," she said, "I challenge you."

"And I will kill you," he said.

"Break my bones and smash my heart," she reported, "and I will heal again and stand here again. And I will launch a second challenge."

The diamond door opened up.

Out stepped the giant figure, peeling off his clothing while half-heartedly taking the defender's pose. Then very quietly, he asked, "What is happening?"

"You have lost," she whispered.

"No."

"But there are different ways to lose," she added. Then again, in full view of the harum-scarums, she declared, "I challenge, and now I strike."

Hoop smoothly deflected the first blow.

And the second.

And after that, twenty others.

Washen's arms were sliced open by the spines, and every finger was shattered by the impacts against the tough armor. Yet she kept swinging, and under her increasingly pained breath, she told the giant again that he was beaten and it didn't matter how and the only rational course at this point was to trust a friend to find the best route on which to make his retreat.

It was the forty-third blow that astonished every witness.

The harum-scarum was covered with his opponent's blood but he seemed invulnerable. Yet as happens in these situations, he allowed his guard to fall, lifting his head too much and giving his tiny, frail opponent a target that only an expert in alien physiology would recognize.

Washen leaped up, and with a graceful swift strength she drove most of her right foot into an exposed piece of neck.

Her human body must contain a good deal of strength, the harum-scarum witnesses decided after the fact.

Hoop's head snapped back, and down he came.

Minutes later, when the security forces arrived, they discovered that the apartment in question now belonged to a captain, and that every legal form in their possession was no more valid than a bad dream.

"Brilliant," Ishwish said, walking just ahead of his new protégé. "A brave, bold, marvelous job. A little too noisy, I think. But still, you managed to find a solution to this difficult problem."

"There are no difficult problems," Washen replied. "Not with a simple solution in hand."

The man laughed amiably.

Washen felt sick and happy, and she wasn't sure what she believed, and then she decided that she was certain.

The procession had almost reached the front door of her new home. The Master Captain and Miocene were directly behind her, speaking about matters that seemed tiny to them and huge to a little captain like her. Every Submaster belonged to the procession, and many captains too. There were young ones like Washen, and others. And she glanced at their faces and then hurried to the diamond door, her presence causing it to open in an instant.

"The old furnishings, I see," said Ishwish.

The wooden harum-scarums stood in their original positions, with one new shape hovering on the brink of sight, watching events.

"Oh, well. You've been too busy to see to everything," he said with uncommon charity. Then he turned, his golden eyes shining with a boyish joy. "Welcome," he said to everyone. "Welcome all. I'm so glad you could be here. And it is such a pleasure, coming back to this wonderful little home that I remember so well."

"My home," Washen whispered.

"You are all welcome here," Ishwish declared. Then he turned, looking like the happiest creature in existence. "This is your first party in your lovely new home," he said to the young captain.

Washen nodded.

On quick legs, she stepped up to the door.

Then to the most important gathering possible on the Great Ship, she said, "Come inside, everyone." And in the next moment, she turned back to Ishwish, whispering a few words that took the blood from his face and nearly knocked him to the ground.

"Except you," she said. "In my home, sir, never you."

# THE NEW HUMANS

## B. Vallance

*This is the point where we shift back to earlier but not necessarily simpler days. I wanted to include a small selection of stories that showed that extreme concepts have appeared in science fiction for much of its existence. The following story was written as far back as 1909 and to my knowledge has never been reprinted. I have no idea who B. Vallance was, though if the story's opening salutation is correct, he may well be Bertram Vallance, and a search through the archives tells me that a Bertram Vallance was born in British Guinea (now Guyana) in South America in 1877. He may not be our man but it may explain the colonial setting of the story. I suspect it was inspired by, and indeed almost a parody of, H. G. Wells's "The Country of the Blind". It first appeared in the December 1909 issue of* Pearson's Magazine *and was accompanied by several astonishing illustrations by Noel Pocock depicting the strangely adapted beings.* Pearson's *editor tells us that he knows nothing about B. Vallance either, other than that this story was his first (and perhaps only) fiction sale. It is a fascinating satire of intolerance and prejudice.*

*(A letter explaining how the strange manuscript came to be discovered.)*

DEAR BERTRAM,

You remember I promised in my last letter to send you that extraordinary diary, which was found by one of the natives in the Sevilla Pass, just before we came on to the 100 miles of desert, which gave me such a doing. I have managed to decipher pretty nearly the whole of it, although the writing is very faint and almost illegible in places.

I wish now I had read it on the spot, as I suspect the poor devil who wrote it must have died very shortly afterwards, and his bones are probably whitening in the desert near by. I might have discovered something from his clothes, if I had found him.

I inclose my copy of the manuscript. You know the old tag about "there being more things in heaven and on earth." You can believe what you like.

                                                    Yours,
                                                         C.

*(The strange manuscript found in the Sevilla Pass.)*

I no longer wonder at the fear expressed by the Indians of this country. Anyone, less strong-minded than myself, would have become insane after seeing and experiencing what I have. If it were not that I am stranded here in this forsaken spot I should almost think I had dreamed a kind of mad dream.

If help does not reach me by to-morrow I shall start across the desert, but first I will write an account of what has happened and leave it here on the track, where surely some traveller will spy it out. I cannot give definite particulars of the locality of No-man's-land. The Adapters obliterated my memory on that point. All I can say is that I have been climbing and descending for what seems years. I have lost all sense of time and space.

I had been travelling in Uganda for several months, when the accident occurred. My native guides had resolutely refused to accompany me any further, saying that I was too near the Devils' Country. Consequently I had gone on alone, leaving them to guard the camp. I had ten days' provisions with me, meaning to push on for five days and then return. On the fourth day I had reached a great altitude. It was bitterly cold and I was greatly fatigued. I determined, however, to reach the top of the range before turning back. There was a short, steep ascent before me, which meant hard climbing. About halfway up I stuck my alpenstock into a cleft on the rock, intending to use it as a lever to mount to the top of a huge boulder, resting on the side of a narrow path with a sheer descent to the valley. Just as I put my weight on the staff, my foot slipped; the alpenstock broke off short in my hand and I rolled sideways off the track. I clutched wildly at a huge cactus which tore the skin from my fingers. Then came a series of fearful bumps, followed by a violent blow in the back, whereat I lost consciousness.

When I opened my eyes I was lying on what I afterwards knew to be an operating table in a laboratory, but quite different to those in use in the United States. I was, in fact, suspended from underneath a platform, held there by a force which I can only describe as the complement of the action of gravity. A large and kindly face was looking gravely at me, out of what I first took to be the end of a barrel.

"So you have regained your normality," it said smilingly.

"Where am I?" I asked. "And what in Heaven's name are you?"

"I am the Chief Adapter," said the face. "You have just been revivified by our System No. 37."

"I fell down a precipice," I began.

"You did – and fractured your cervical vertebræ and both legs. I had almost given you up, owing to having inadvertently misplaced your femoral artery; but you are quite recovered now, and your nervous system has been carefully restored by the Patticoe treatment."

While the face was speaking, I had been staring at it with ever increasing bewilderment. Its words and appearance, together with my own situation – hanging up against a platform like a fly on a ceiling – caused a buzzing in my head. This he no doubt perceived, for an arm, which I had not seen before, shot out from the barrel and touched a button at my side. Whereupon the table turned noiselessly over with me upon it.

"You can rise, if you wish," said the face.

I slowly did as it suggested.

"Drink this," said the Chief Adapter.

He handed me a glass full of red liquid. It was like drinking fire, and made me spring to my feet as though I had received a galvanic shock.

"Ah – that makes you feel alive – eh? Now, listen to me. From an examination of your papers I gather that you are an American. Moreover, you are known to me by repute as a traveller. I have had to call together a special meeting of the Circle to decide whether you should be allowed to die or be revived and allowed to reside here amongst us. Only by a very small majority, it has been decided to give you a chance. My own reasons for keeping you alive are purely scientific. Meanwhile, I may as well inform you that the laws of this country prohibit aliens of any description. I will call my daughter to bear you company for an hour until my return."

He was standing close to me while speaking, his three legs set at the apexes of a triangle on his barrel-like body. We were in a circular room, with several oval windows, and the doorway was about 16 ft. from where we stood. Suddenly, without turning round, an arm emerged from one side of his body, stretched out with incredible swiftness to the door, and pulled it open. Then, withdrawing his legs and arms into his shell, his body gently subsided on to the floor, and he rolled slowly across the room and out through the doorway.

I sat down, because my legs refused to support me, and I was staring at the doorway when it was filled with a vision of such entrancing loveliness that I was almost bereft of what few senses I had left.

"So you are my father's guest?" said the vision, at last, after looking at me for some time with an indescribable expression in her eyes. "What is your name?"

"Montmorency Merrick," I replied.

"Why do you sit on the floor?"

"I don't know," I answered idiotically, attempting to rise. "But," I added, looking around me, "there are no chairs to sit on."

She smiled.

"We do not need chairs here. We use our own shells instead; but, of course, this is all strange to you. You are very handsome."

I blushed.

"You – you are lovely!" I blurted out.

"I came to see you like this because I did not want to startle you," she replied, laughing. "It is not my natural form. But tell me, do I seem at all strange-looking?"

"Only very beautiful," I said enthusiastically.

She did not seem to be in the least embarrassed at the boldness of my compliments, but rather pleased.

"I think I do it very well," she said. "You see, I sometimes forget your system of bones and joints and things, and then I bend my arms the wrong way – like this."

As she spoke, she bent her right arm at the elbow backwards.

"Or I let my eyes stare too much – like this."

Her eyes suddenly stood a couple of inches from their sockets and then returned again. I sprang up from the ground in alarm.

"Ah!" she exclaimed. "I forgot you did not understand, but my father will give you a little account of our habits and customs after dinner, and then I will get you to tell me all that goes on in New York. I have never been allowed to go there as yet. My pulp is not developed enough."

With this astonishing remark she smiled again, and it seemed to me that she had too many teeth.

"I will give instructions about your room." And with an indescribably graceful bow she left me.

I must have sat there for half-an-hour, thinking hard, when the Chief Adapter came rolling in through the doorway. He stopped in front of me, shot out some legs and arms, then said:

"Well, has Clarice been in?"

"A lady has been to see me," I said doubtfully. "She said you were her father." I looked hard at his three legs. "But she does not greatly resemble you, that is – I beg your pardon."

"Pooh!" said the Adapter. "I suppose she has been up to her tricks again. It is a very curious example of the enormous difficulty we have experienced in endeavouring to eradicate the old inherited instincts. Even my daughter, who has had the benefit of living in communion with some of the greatest intellects the world has ever seen, cannot refrain from personating what you would no doubt call a beautiful woman. I think I had better give you an outline of the history of this country to prepare you for what you will see. I noticed, when I was cleaning your brain, that your powers of deduction were somewhat undeveloped and the reasoning faculty was almost entirely absent.

"To begin with, we are human beings – with a difference. It is some three centuries since our revered ancestors first reached this

country. They were men and women constituted as you are. It is
needless to go into the whys and wherefores of their coming, but
pre-eminent among them was a brilliant scientist, whose statue
you will see in the National Museum. He had conceived the idea
of modifying the human structure to an extent deemed impossible by his old colleagues, who had endeavoured to prevent him
by force from carrying out his experiments in England. Hence he
decided with a few followers, who believed in him, to search out
some unknown country where he could work unhindered by the
interference of the feeble-minded.

"The result of his work you see before you. Look at me! I
represent the triumph of mind over matter. I have no bones –
they are needless, and, in fact, superfluous. I can progress on foot
as well as you, or I can move as swiftly as a motorcar, and in a like
manner. My brain is not hampered by being inclosed in a skull
like yours. I can do practically what I like with my features."
(Here he made some perfectly horrible contortions). "The number of legs and arms I possess is only limited by my will" (he
waved at least half-a-dozen flabby arms in my face), "and the
term of years which I shall live is also, to a great extent, under my
control. But I have told you enough for the present. If you remain
here you will see for yourself what an inestimable boon has been
conferred upon his descendants by our founder. Now – come
along with me."

I followed him along a passage, sloping downwards, and winding in a spiral, until we reached another circular chamber, where a
table was laid with various utensils.

There were no chairs – but for my convenience a box had been
placed at one end.

The Chief Adapter motioned me to sit down. He up-ended
himself, first withdrawing all his legs, and in that position, which,
though distinctly ungraceful, was certainly secure, the meal
commenced.

It did not last long. My host's enormous mouth did a propor-
tionate amount of work, and the food, consisting entirely of fruit,
quickly disappeared. Then he stretched his arm right across the
room in a manner with which I was becoming familiar, to a tap.
He filled a large vessel with wine (at least a quart), which he
placed before me. He drank an equal portion himself without an
effort, and the dinner was finished. From first to last it occupied
three minutes. I had managed to eat one pear and a bunch of

grapes. I succeeded, however, in secreting several apples about my person, and I drank most of the wine.

"You see," said the Adapter, "we do not waste time eating and drinking; at least, the more cultured among us do not. I am sorry to say, however, that there is still a certain clique who prefer material pleasures to intellectual ones. My own appetite is small" (he had eaten at least half a hundredweight of fruit), "but there are some who regard eating and drinking as an art, and, if I mistake not, one of them is now approaching."

As he spoke an unwieldy object waddled into the room. His barrel must have measured at least three feet in diameter, and his face entirely filled one end. He was balanced on the three legs which I afterwards found to be the usual number in use for everyday purposes. The face was quite repulsive, being closely marked with pimples, and very fat and blubbery.

I took an intense and instinctive dislike to him on the spot.

"I have come to have a look at your latest freak, my dear Adapter," he observed, looking at me with some surprise. "Is this the creature?"

"This is Mr Montmorency Merrick, a citizen of the USA, who has accidentally found his way here," replied my host, who spoke slowly and impressively. "I am sure you will remember to treat him with courtesy, Tennyson."

"Oh, certainly, certainly," replied the monstrosity, in a greasy voice. "Your friends are mine. How is the beautiful Clarice?"

"My daughter has gone to pay a visit to the wife of the Governor of the Incubator House, and will be away for a few days. As you are here I shall be obliged to you if you will do me the favour to take Mr Merrick out and show him some of the features of interest."

"Shall be delighted, my dear Adapter. Come along, Merrick, old buck!"

He stretched out a tentacle with a handful of gross and mis-shapen fingers, and clapped me on the back.

"I'll tell you what – I'll take him over the Museum. There is an excellent dining-room there, and I need replenishing."

"Bring him back about ten o'clock," said the Adapter. "Remember he is in your charge, and you will be responsible for him."

With which remark the Chief suddenly withdrew all his feelers and rolled rapidly out of the room.

The monstrosity turned to me and grinned.

"Bit peremptory, eh?" he observed. "So you're a man, are you? What do you think of us – eh?"

He grinned again, and I had a feeling of nausea.

"Can you roll?" he asked.

"Certainly not," I replied.

"Oh, well, I'll walk with you, though it's a confounded nuisance. This way."

He led me out of the house along a smooth pathway inclined at a slight angle downwards, through a garden of amazing flowers and trees, and then suddenly a view of the city lay before me, and I stopped to gaze.

The general effect was certainly beautiful – the architecture was bizarre and bewildering; there did not seem to be one building like another. I soon perceived that the predominating feature of all of them was an almost entire absence of straight lines and angles. Curves, curves everywhere, and fine pointed spires with globes on their summits, winding streets, and a general glare of sunlight, which after the darkened room dazzled my eyes.

Presently I became aware of innumerable cylinders rolling at varying speeds along these silent streets, for the usual hum of a great city was lacking. Only here and there I saw some of the inhabitants walking on legs. Some of the cylinders must have been 12ft. in diameter, and these were moving with the speed of a motor-car, steering with an astonishing skill in and out of the traffic. Once I saw one of them roll right over a cylinder moving in the opposite direction, but no notice was taken of this – it appeared to be a customary procedure.

"You seem to be struck dumb, Monty," said the gross creature at my side. "By Jove, what a rum little face you've got! No offence, you know; we all speak the truth here. Bit strange after New York, eh? However, I shall get used to you in time – just at present I can't say I cotton on to you, but possibly you don't appreciate exactly what you do look like. See here!"

He actually twisted his features, after several hideous contortions, into a grotesque caricature of my own, and as I stared at him the likeness became more and more faithful, until I begged him to desist.

He grinned complacently.

"I'm a bit of a dab at that," he remarked. "In fact, Clarice and I are stars in the imitating line; but we must be moving. See that big gold-coloured building, that's the Museum. We had better have a roller."

He whistled suddenly – like a locomotive – when two of the big wheels I have referred to rolled up to the gate. I then saw that the hub of each consisted of a creature like the others, and the big external diameter was formed by attaching spokes to the outer casing and fixing a flexible tyre. The two wheels pulled up alongside each other. Between them they carried a kind of seat into which my companion hoisted me, as though I had been a portmanteau. He got in after me.

"Museum, sharp!" he roared.

There was a violent jerk, which nearly flung me out, then a wild rush through the air, which brought tears into my eyes. Then they stopped so suddenly that I shot right out of the seat and landed on something soft, which instantly threw me off again.

"What the devil are you doing, sir?" said a choleric voice.

"I beg your pardon," I began –

"Surely you could see I was not in my casing, sir; but, good gracious! you must be the American?"

By this time I had succeeded in recovering my wind. I looked at my interlocutor, whose face I could not perceive.

"You see I am not used to your modes of locomotion," I began.

"Confound it, sir – do not speak to my hide – speak to me!"

The voice came from my right. I turned round and beheld what looked like a jelly-fish lying on the ground. It had a face, all flabby and quivering. Several gelatinous looking arms and feelers were waving and vibrating in the air. Its eyes were glaring at me with suppressed fury, and it seemed to swell and contract alternately like a bladder blown out by some mischievous boy.

Standing a few feet away was my obese companion, his face convulsed with laughter, and tears pouring from his cod-like eyes.

"You fell into the middle of him," he gasped, "and knocked his wind out. Never mind, Percy, old boy, he didn't mean it and couldn't help it: besides you shouldn't come out of your shell and stand about like that."

"It's all very well to talk," replied the jelly-fish angrily. "Who was to know that some blundering idiot was going to jump into one like that. He nearly punctured my cupella!"

It wobbled up to the cylinder which I had mistakenly addressed and poured itself into one end, shot our three legs and then withdrew them again, and extended several arms in the same manner – it was as if he was trying on a coat – and finally rolled sedately away along the road.

My conductor was grinning grotesquely at me when I turned round.

"If you want to see the Museum, you must hurry up," he said. "I can't go round with you, but I'll hand you over to one of the custodians."

He called out to a spider-like creature who was gazing at me with a look of considerable astonishment.

"Billy – take this gentleman round the museum and point out the various exhibits. I shall be in the refreshment-room when you want to find me – by-by, Merrick."

He waddled off down a long corridor and I turned to Billy. I should have liked to have gone into the refreshment room myself. I wanted a pick-me-up, but I had no notion of their money exchange and did not see how to manage it.

There were many extraordinary things in the museum, but I have no time to enumerate them. What interested me most of all was a series of pictures, made by the founder of these amazing people.

I had wondered how they managed to roll along the ground without getting giddy, and how they kept their faces in a vertical position while doing so. The secret was out when I had examined the drawings. A section through the middle of one of them showed that the outer shell or casing was loose and had an internal row of rough rachet-shaped teeth. The pulpy stuff of which they were made had a number of external fleshy pawls, which geared with the teeth and imparted a rotary motion to the casing.

Long descriptions written in quaint English were attached to each drawing – parts of these I read, but had great difficulty in comprehending them. The phraseology reminded me strongly of Kant's Critique of Pure Reason. I remember one sentence very distinctly. It went thus: –

"And it shall be that the extensors may be thrust in from any given direction, either internally or externally, fortifying the indirect tissue of the cupella by a series of cords of ultimate elasticity equal to a hundredth portion of a ton for every one-eighth of a square inch of section."

I was told afterwards that this meant that these beings could produce legs and arms in almost any number, and could vary the shape of their bodies when out of their shells to an almost unlimited extent.

I spent three or four hours walking about the building, which had no staircases, but inclined planes as a substitute, and I saw the celebrated statue of the founder. He was a short, thick-set man with a hydrocephaloid head, small, deep-set eyes under shaggy eyebrows, and an indescribably bestial-looking mouth.

It was a fascinating face and reminded me of the story of Dr Jekyll and Mr Hyde, with the Hyde predominating.

Underneath was written:

"All that can be imagined by man can be achieved – but each achievement shall cost him more than the worth thereof."

The Chief Adapter told me later that this inscription was part of an epitaph written by the only one of the founder's original companions who survived him, and who was supposed by many to have been opposed to his extraordinary aims.

At the door of the refreshment-room I was greeted by the monstrosity, with a vacuous laugh.

"I have eaten and drunk and feel good and happy. What do you think of the Museum – beastly dry, isn't it? Come and have a drink."

I went with him. He ordered wine – at least a quart. As I was afraid of offending, I drank it all, with the result that I became somewhat light-headed and I have no distinct recollection of how we spent the intervening time before returning to the Chief Adapter's house. I do remember calling the monstrosity an "overgrown octopus," at which he laughed immoderately. I believe I was put to bed by the Adapter's servants, who had an altercation with the monstrosity about me, but I cannot recall what they said.

I must have slept for several hours, when I was awakened by a nasal voice singing to the accompaniment of some stringed instrument. The voice seemed near at hand and I slipped off the mattress on which I was lying and crossed the room to the circular window. It was early morning. I could just see over the edge of the aperture into the road beneath. Standing on three short legs, with his hideous face uppermost, was the monstrosity. He was gazing with an imbecile expression at the window parallel with mine. He had a stringed instrument resembling a guitar in one of his hands, and was singing at the top of his voice "Love me and the world is mine."

Following the direction of his gaze, I perceived a face at the window. It bore a distinct resemblance to my beautiful Clarice, but was as large as the average face of these creatures. She was looking rather pleased at the horrible noise he was making, but her features kept changing and twitching with the music. First her nose would dilate and trembie, then her eyes suddenly increased in diameter to twice and three times their original size. It was an uncanny, and to me a most distressing sight.

At last the monstrosity lowered his instrument, ceased his wailing, and gave vent to a deep sigh.

"Clarice, I worship thee," he said.

"Good God," I thought, "it *is* she." Suddenly she stretched her arm out of the window. It elongated itself until it must have measured 12 ft., and her fingers stretched in proportion.

"Take thy reward, thou singer of songs," she said softly.

The singer of songs made an appalling grimace, which was evidently intended to represent an expression of loving gratitude. Then he protruded his lips with some difficulty until they actually reached her hand, to which they fastened themselves. The effort was evidently a supreme one, for the hand and lips separated suddenly with a smacking sound, and the lover's face was stung by the force of the recoil.

Then the lady disappeared and her window was violently closed.

Just then the monstrosity caught sight of me. I was smiling, and a look of fury passed over his enormous face.

"You miserable vertebrate idiot!" he yelled. "You shall pay for this."

He gathered up his guitar – shut up his legs and arms, gave me a threatening glare, and rolled away down the road at a speed of something like thirty miles an hour.

I was summoned to breakfast with the Chief Adapter and his daughter, who had assumed the same appearance as when I first saw her.

"I wish," he said, "that you would eradicate those follies of adornment. It is amazing that any member of *my* family should be guilty of such weakness."

"Allow me to remind you," she replied, "that amusement was

specially advocated by the Adapters at the last meeting, in spite of your disapproval."

"I hate all this pretence," grumbled her father. "But I have neither time nor inclination to argue the point with you. Be good enough to remain with Mr Merrick until I return."

"My father and I do not agree on some points," Clarice said presently. "Is it true you are not plastic?"

"I am afraid I do not understand," I replied.

"I am told that you and all the other inhabitants of the earth are confined to one figure and face and are full of bones as well, and" – she added doubtfully – "you cannot roll."

"That is true," I replied.

"I cannot understand it at all. Have you no shells?"

"Certainly not."

"I have read of such things," she said musingly, "but I never quite believed it – I am not yet of age to read the third stage."

"What is that?" I asked.

"We are not allowed to read the third stage, which gives all particulars relating to our creation by the founder, until we have reached the age of twenty-five."

She rose and led the way to one of the large circular windows looking out on the city.

"What is that large building with the globe on the top?" I asked.

"That – oh, that is the Incubator House where the children are bred. Are all the men in America like you?" she asked suddenly.

"Not quite," I answered.

"And the women – are they like I am now?"

"Not so beautiful," I replied fervently.

She looked pleased.

"My pulp aches all down the back – I shall have to get back into my shell, and I don't want you to see me like that. Do you mind if I leave you?"

When she had gone, a thought suddenly struck me. She liked music, and I used to be no mean performer on the violin. I wondered if they had such an instrument, and decided to ask the question. I pressed the bell.

It was answered by a battered-looking barrel with a wrinkled face at one end.

"You rang?" said the apparition.

"I did," I replied, staring at him. "Are you a servant?"

"I wait on the Chief," he replied with dignity. "What can I do for you?"

"Have you such a thing as a violin?"

The battered relic considered for a minute.

"Have you any barter?" he asked.

"Any what?"

"Any barter."

"I don't know what 'barter' is."

"I think your watch would do," he said, looking at my gold chain.

I began to comprehend.

"You could get me a violin for this watch?" I said, taking it out and holding it up.

"I will see," replied the relic. He snatched it out of my hand and was gone. I noticed that as he rolled out his shell squeaked as if it wanted oiling. I waited a long time, and in the end fell asleep. When I awoke, the Chief Adapter had returned, and was talking to another grave and white-haired old tripod. They were sitting on their butt-ends close together, and evidently fancied that I was still asleep, for it was not long before I discovered that I was the subject of their discussion.

"I am afraid he is not a good specimen," said the stranger, looking in my direction.

"No; but, my dear Fairbairn, all the more glory for us if we succeed. You know it has taken three hundred years to bring us to our present state, and I feel absolutely certain that by my process the alteration can be achieved in one operation. Of course, there is a risk, but that is a constant accompaniment to all great discoveries."

"Do you intend that this American shall be informed of what is in store for him?"

"No – his mind is hardly strong enough to appreciate it. I am rather sorry I did not try the experiment at first, instead of restoring him to life, but you know what the Council are. I am certain we are deteriorating, Fairbairn, and that is what makes me determined on introducing new blood."

"What do you consider would be the best method in Merrick's case?"

"I shall divide him longitudinally first, and then subject him to the N Ray for two hours, in order to disintegrate the bones."

I had listened up to this point with ever increasing interest, but without realising what they were discussing, but at this last fiendish suggestion I nearly shouted aloud, then prudence decided me on keeping quiet until I had heard the whole of the diabolical plot. Fairbairn, whose countenance was benevolent-looking in the extreme, did not express any horror at the Chief Adapter's observation – indeed, he only appeared mildly interested.

"Keeping the current on both sections, of course?" he said.

"Yes, I am particularly anxious as to the effect on his brain, which is of average quality only, and I believe that after doing away with his skull I can develop it by separation and the insertion of free pulp from that case we had last month. You recollect?"

"You mean the double egg which hatched without nerves?"

"Yes – I have been keeping it in a vacuum ever since, and it is in a remarkably good state of preservation."

"Well, I'm sure I wish you luck," said Fairbairn. "It will be a great triumph if you succeed, and if you don't—"

"Oh, then, we shall have to wait – but I have full confidence. You will be present, of course?"

"Yes – with young Slemcoe. He is extraordinarily skilful with the knife, you know. Well, good-bye till to-morrow."

They both rose, and rolled out of the room.

So, thought I, I am to be cut in half, am I – and my bones are to be disintegrated. All very pleasant, no doubt, for the operators, but what about me? and what are they going to do it for? To say that I was alarmed would be putting it too mildly. I lay and shivered, my teeth chattering with fright, until I heard somebody rolling along the passage, when I got up and stood waiting. It was Tennyson who came in.

"Hullo – how are you?" he said, without the slightest sign of the fury with which he had last left me. "Where's the Chief?"

"He was here just now," I said.

"Look here, Merrick," he said, in a deprecating manner, "don't bear malice about what I said last night. The fact of the matter is I don't want you to repeat what you saw to anyone. You won't now, will you?"

"Do you belong to the Council?" I asked.

"Yes – why?"

"Are you opposed to the Chief Adapter and an animal called Fairbairn?"

"You bet," he answered cheerfully.

"Well," I said, "I should like to know if you approve of dissecting people alive?"

"All depends on who's going to be the subject," he said with a grin. "Why, who's been talking?"

"Oh, no one – no one," I answered. "I only wondered."

"What you say reminds me that once, not so very long ago either, old Fairbairn and the Chief tried an experiment of that kind on a man – not one of us, but a man from South America, an Indian, I believe – but it was a failure."

"What were they trying?" I asked, trying to speak indifferently.

"I don't know for certain. They *say* that the Chief was trying to make a New Human of him, but it's only talk."

I shuddered.

"What happened to the Indian?" I asked.

"The Indian? Oh, he died, of course. There was a bit of a row about it, but it was hushed up. Not that I think it matters a straw, but the party to which I belong passed a Bill shortly afterwards, making it illegal to operate on anyone without his consent, and the Chief was very wild about it. He said we were retrograding, and we were nicknamed the 'Anti-vaccinators' for passing the Bill."

I drew a breath of relief. They would certainly not get my consent to being turned into one of those hideous abortions.

"By-the-by, would you like to witness the opening of the Grand Council to-morrow?" asked Tennyson carelessly.

"I should – certainly," I answered, thinking I might hear something relative to myself.

"Well, ask the Chief, and if he agrees, I'll be round in the morning. So long," and he rolled his unwieldy bulk out of the room.

A few minutes after his departure Clarice entered, clad in a gown of clinging blue material, and I declare most positively that the absence of bones in her body would never have been suspected, the only effect being that she was infinitely more graceful than any real woman I have ever seen.

"How do I look?" she asked.

"Perfect," I murmured ecstatically.

"What are babies like in your country, Mr Merrick?" she asked suddenly.

I tried to give her a description.

Presently she said – "Have you got any babies of your own?"

I hastened to assure her that I never thought of such a thing.

"We are not allowed to buy one before we are twenty-five years old," she said musingly. "I am not sure that I shall get one; they are rather a nuisance."

I was too dumfounded to do more than open my mouth and shut it again.

"We buy them from the age of three to five years – those five years of age are very dear, though," she added.

I gasped.

"My father bought Abraham very young, he is only two – but, of course, being Chief Adapter he is privileged."

At that moment her father entered and the conversation dropped. I felt that there was a mystery somewhere, and resolved to question Tennyson when I met him in the morning.

The Chief raised no objection to my accompanying him to the council meeting, rather to my surprise, and neither by his speech nor expression gave any sign of his atrocious intentions with regard to myself.

The next morning, after a hurried breakfast (all my meals were hurried, since I could not keep pace with the chief) I was taken in a "roller" by Tennyson to the great hall where the affairs of the country were decided. We went into a kind of lobby overlooking a vast circular chamber. The lobby only accommodated two persons at a time and there were a series of them. When we were inside, the door, which reminded me of a safe, was locked, but first we were rigorously searched and all my belongings were removed and placed under lock and key. A seal was put over the keyhole and an impression of my thumb taken. I asked Tennyson why all these precautions were taken, but he only replied laconically that the council were not *always popular*.

The chamber was empty when we arrived, except for one barrel, which was apparently asleep on a raised platform. A long polished metal tube stood by his side. Tennyson said it was to keep order with. "You will see it in use, I expect," he remarked.

It is difficult to give a clear description of the hall. There were no steps anywhere, nor seats, but the floor sloped in a spiral curve continuously rising, so that the outer circles were at a higher level than the inner. The raised platform was at one end and commanded the whole of the chamber.

Presently the sleeper awoke and beat on a gong. Instantly the big doors at one end slid back and a crowd of barrels of all shapes and sizes rolled in. They mounted the spiral one after the other and up-ended on reaching their respective destinations. This incursion lasted for several minutes and a hubbub of voices arose. I recognised Fairbairn and the Chief Adapter. They sat close together and conversed in an undertone.

Suddenly the creature on the platform banged his gong again, when the doors closed, and he roared out that the meeting was open.

Instantly at least a dozen barrels began speaking together. I could not understand a word. As soon as they had finished other members started. Tennyson seemed to understand quite clearly what they were saying, for he kept silently approving and disapproving.

"Does this always go on before the debate?" I asked.

"This is the debate, idiot," he replied rudely.

"But they all talk at once." I said.

"Of course they do. Do you suppose there would be time for them all to talk, if they did it separately?"

"But—" I said, "How do they understand each other?"

"There is no need that they should," was his reply.

"Well – but how does the business get done?"

"Evidently you are very much behind us in this, as in all things," replied Tennyson complacently. "Don't you see that each member votes for his party – it does not matter in the least what they say, so long as they vote properly."

"Then I don't see what they want to talk at all for," I objected.

"Why, you nincompoop, what's the use of getting elected if you can't talk? That's what the House is for."

"Then don't they care whether they hear each other or not?"

"No; so long as they hear themselves – that's quite enough."

At that moment the platform barrel, who had apparently been asleep again, suddenly struck his gong. Whereupon they all began rolling furiously towards the lobbies or voting chambers amidst a perfect Babel of yells. This lasted ten minutes, when they returned and the performance recommenced. It had not continued for more than a minute, however, when a terrific uproar arose from a group of barrels who had been talking louder than the rest, and directly afterwards a free fight seemed to be taking place. This was the signal for the platform barrel to spring into activity.

He touched the tube, which swung round until it pointed directly at the group of excited politicians; then he pressed a button, when a shell from the tube exploded with a hissing sound in their midst. I saw three of them fall to the floor, double up, and shrivel into powder.

"By George!" said Tennyson, "he's pulverised old Smith."

The noise lessened considerably, but no other notice was taken. I was horror-stricken.

"Do you mean to say they are dead?" I asked.

"You bet," he replied. "It's the only way to keep order. Besides, Smith's been asking for it for a long time. I'm rather glad – but what's the matter? You look sick."

"I feel low-spirited," I said. "Can we go now?"

He grinned. "Oh, if you like."

He pressed a bell, whereupon our door was unlocked. My belongings were returned to me, and we left the Council House. They were still jabbering when I went out.

The monstrosity led me to some public gardens, which at any other time I might have taken a keen interest in exploring, for these people had bred flowers on just as startlingly original lines as themselves. But I had my approaching dissection on my mind, and I was also still pondering on my recent conversation with Clarice.

"I should like to know," I said, "what Clarice meant by telling me that her father *bought* her two brothers."

"What she said, I suppose," he replied. "What are you getting at? Oh! I see where you're stuck.

"Yes. You see when the Founder started his campaign he had several things to consider. One was that in the ordinary way all races of people depend to a great extent on chance for their development. You've read your Darwin, who was a keen sort in his way, but right out of it when you come to practical science. The Founder decided that leaving nature to improve the race was too slow to begin with, and also too haphazard, so he arranged that we should lay eggs – see? These eggs are examined scientifically and hatched by incubators. All the inferior ones are destroyed. Only the best are hatched, after a careful selection by the Adapters. I believe he took ants as a model, and our society is built on something like the same basis as theirs in that respect. So you see, when anyone arrives at years of discretion and is able to educate and care for a kid, he or she buys one from the Incubator House."

"But can't they hatch their own eggs?" I asked, feeling as though I were dreaming some awful nightmare.

"Against the law – all eggs have to be handed over to the Adapters at once – anyone failing to notify the authorities that he or she has laid an egg is pulverised."

"He or she?" I said feebly.

"Oh, we all lay; there's strict equality over here, you bet," said the monstrosity. with a grin.

"Do you know your own eggs again?" I asked.

"They're all registered and a receipt given, but the Adapters reject many of them, as I said before, and those rejected ones are destroyed."

I may as well state here that I took the opportunity later on to revisit the National Museum, and there I read the following from the original specification of the Founder:

"It is considered that the abolition of sex is the only sure means of preventing those crimes and wickednesses prevalent in the old world which we have abandoned. The new race of humans shall therefore be adapted after the manner of certain elementary protoplasms of the deep seas, who produce their young by severing portions of their organisms, so that each severed portion becomes in turn a perfect creature. Analogously our descendants shall produce their offspring, not by severing portions of their person, but by producing eggs, each of which shall be perfect of itself and capable of being hatched at the will of the community, or destroyed if of bad proportions, either physically or mentally. This is for the betterment of the race and the sure prevention of the disease misnamed love by the class of madmen known as poets. But in order that the intellectual emotion or union of the spirit – which but rarely existed among the old humans – shall be fostered amongst us, the new race shall still possess the characteristics of men and women."

When I returned I was met by the battered relic who had taken my watch. He held out a very fine violin and informed me that Miss Clarice desired my presence in the music-room. I followed him into a large domed hall, furnished, to my astonishment, quite after the style of a modern drawing-room. Clarice was seated at a piano. She greeted me with a smile.

"I did not know you were musical," she said. "I should like to hear you play."

I did my best, and was pleased to observe the effect. Her eyes became dreamy-looking and she gazed at me with an expression of delighted admiration.

"Why, you are infinitely superior to Tennyson!" she exclaimed, as I finished a selection from "The Mikado."

We discussed music for some time, and she proved herself no mean performer on the piano. Suddenly she sighed.

"Mr Merrick, I want to confide in you."

I bowed.

"I feel that our great ancestor made a dreadful mistake in altering us as he did. I have read many of your books and it seems to me that you are much happier than we are."

She clasped her hands and a far-away look came into her beautiful eyes.

"You do not know so much, of course, but there is more variety in your lives. Sometimes I wish I were an ordinary woman such as your great authors describe. I feel so much like a machine – and we live such clockwork kind of lives – everything is settled for us by the Adapters, of whom my father is, as you know, the Chief. I wonder if—"

She paused and looked at me doubtfully.

"You have never seen me in my proper shape?"

I lied. I said I was quite satisfied to see her as she was and I had never seen her otherwise than beautiful.

"Yes – but if you saw me in my shell with my face expanded you would hate the sight of me – I have noticed that you can hardly suppress your horror of the people here."

"I find it difficult to get accustomed to them," I replied.

"I know, and I know you are frightened about something. Tell me, has my father made any suggestion to you about operating on you?"

I told her of the conversation I had overheard between her father and Fairbairn.

"It is as I suspected," she said. "My father has no feelings at all – he is the embodiment of science, and would sacrifice anything for its sake. But listen – there are others besides myself who are opposed to the Adapters. It is true I do not know of anyone else who has ventured to think the Founder was wrong, and I have never spoken my thoughts to anyone before. I will prevent this horrible thing he wants to do to you. He dare not do it openly without the consent of the Council, and I know enough of the members to insure their refusal to agree. He might try to do it without their knowledge, but not if the whole thing was made public. So have no fear – oh ! it is awful. I must go to my room."

"What is it?" I asked, alarmed at the sudden change in her expression.

"I have to go back to my own form – you do not know how hard it is to keep like this for long." She held out her hand to me. I kissed it. The next instant I was alone.

I did not see her again until the next morning, when the relic again led me to the music-room.

"I have seen Mr Tennyson and several others," she began abruptly. "Your case will be discussed in the Council to-day. I think you are safe, but Mr Tennyson is jealous of you. He regards me as his affinity and I *hate* him, except when I am in my own true shape; then I seem to alter. I don't know why or how, but it is so, and it is horrible. Oh, how I wish I were a real woman and – tell me, do I look as nice as the women you used to know?"

"You are a thousand times more beautiful than anyone I ever knew," I said fervently.

She looked at me for a long time in silence.

"There is something I have thought of," she said.

"If my father can turn you into one of us, as he thinks he can, would it not be possible to turn me back into a woman such as I appear to be now?"

"Can I believe my ears?" said a terrible voice behind us – it was her father.

"Clarice," he said, "I have suspected you for some time. I had misgivings when I selected you as being fit for hatching twenty-four years ago. There was something abnormal about you even then, and your passion for masquerading as a prehistoric woman since you grew up has filled me with grave anxiety. You have deeply sinned in your thoughts and must expiate them. As for you—" he added, turning to me with a look of cold-blooded ferocity, "your case shall be settled to-night."

"You shall not carry out your abominable ideas on Mr Merrick," cried his daughter. "I have told the Council."

"What!" he thundered. "Stand still!" He made some rapid passes before her face. She seemed to writhe for a few minutes, and to fight against the influence he exerted. Then, before my agonised eyes, she fell into a shapeless heap on the ground.

Her father looked malignantly at her; then, calmly ringing the bell, which was answered by the relic –

"Fetch her shell," he said.

The relic departed, and returned rolling a shell in front of him.

"Get in," he commanded.

My poor, shapeless love crawled feebly along the floor and flopped into the casing. "Not before him," she wailed.

"Get up," was the stern reply.

She languidly thrust forth three legs and three arms. Her face now filled the opening in the end of the shell. She looked despairingly at me, great tears pouring from her eyes.

"Remember," he said, "you cannot leave your shell for twenty days. Now go to your room."

She withdrew her legs and arms, and rolled slowly and sadly from the room.

"You abused my kindness," he said to me coldly, "by encouraging my daughter in her disgraceful imaginings. Pending the decision by the Council to-morrow, you will be confined in your room."

My thoughts were not pleasant ones that night. At daybreak Tennyson appeared.

"It's all up with you, Monty," he said. "I've been beating up the sentimentalists, but they seem pretty indifferent about you. Most of them haven't even heard of you. However, I've got one point in your favour. You'll be allowed to speak in your own defence, and I am requested to bring you before the Council."

I started to thank him, but he interrupted me.

"Don't thank me – I don't care a cast-off shell whether you die or live. I'm simply obliging Clarice, who seems to have taken a crazy fancy to you. I shall come for you in two hours' time."

He had hardly been gone two minutes when the door again opened and the Chief Adapter entered, followed by Fairbairn and two other younger barrels.

Fairbairn eyed me curiously for a few minutes and then said to the Chief:

"I doubt if he will stand it, you know."

"It is hardly of consequence whether he does or not," was the reply. "I am resolved to make the attempt. Bring him along."

I was seized by the two younger creatures, and carried, in spite of my struggles, out of the room and along several inclines until we arrived at the laboratory where I had first come to my senses.

An ominous array of instruments lay exposed to view on a bench, and a pungent odour of anæsthetics filled the apartment.

They released me for a moment, when in sheer desperation I made a plunge forward, snatched up a formidable-looking knife or lancet, and put myself in a position of defence.

"Seize him," cried the Chief.

There was a whirl of arms and tentacles. I fought for my life and slashed right and left at my tormentors. So furious was my onslaught that they drew back in alarm. I had actually severed one of their arms – there being no bone to stop the thrust. Then I felt a murderous desire to slay them all, and I sprang straight at the Chief Adapter, who barely succeeded in avoiding me. He began to make passes in the air, but they had no effect, for I was· for the moment a madman. I possessed myself of a long sickle-shaped blade, and aimed a terrific sweeping cut at Fairbairn, who jumped right out of his shell and slithered along the floor to the doorway, out of which he crept, undulating like a serpent.

"Quick – the current!" shouted the Chief to the one of his assistants who was unhurt, pointing to a button in the wall, but taking care to keep out of my reach himself. I ran in the same direction myself and the younger monstrosity fled at my approach.

"Come on, all of you!" I shouted. "I'll let you see how an American can die!"

The Chief was evidently nonplussed, and what the upshot would have been I do not know – but just as I was preparing for a final onslaught – Tennyson, followed by a number of others, burst into the room. One of them – evidently someone in authority – called out:

"What is the meaning of this?"

"Do you permit an innocent stranger to be dissected alive in your country?" I shouted.

He turned to the Chief –

"So you've been trying your abominable experiments again. Is not this the man of whom you spoke?" he added to Tennyson, pointing at me.

"Yes, sir."

"Merrick – I think you said his name was – Mr Merrick, you will be good enough to accompany us to the Council Hall. Fairbairn, I am astonished that you should lend your countenance to the Chief Adapter, who has already been warned against these practices. You, sir," he added to the latter, "will explain your proceedings before the Council."

He led the way out of the room. Tennyson ranged himself alongside me and the Chief and Fairbairn followed, the rest of the crowd bringing up the rear. I had dropped the sickle, but the knife I secreted in my breast pocket. We walked all the way and I noticed that the stranger was treated with the greatest respect by all whom we encountered. They all joined in the procession until there must have been over a hundred of all shapes and diameters gravely walking with a curious half hop, half run, to which they were evidently not accustomed. It appeared to be from some sense of etiquette that they did not roll.

Tennyson told me as we went along that the stranger was the President of the country, and that I could think myself lucky he had taken the matter up. He had but just returned from a secret visit to Paris, where he had been studying the latest developments in aeroplanes.

I was taken into the Main Hall that I had already seen, and placed in a kind of dock erected temporarily – so Tennyson said – for my particular benefit.

The ensuring proceedings were singularly informal, and so far as I could see, free from the atmosphere of law which overwhelms a stranger in the English Law Courts.

The President ordered the Chief Adapter to give his account of what had happened. Somewhat to my surprise he did this without seeking to minimise in the slightest degree his share, in which he actually seemed to take considerable pride.

"As you are aware, I have for some time past endeavoured to procure the means of demonstrating my discovery relative to suspended animation," he said, "and the specimen Merrick, who owes his existence to my skill, would have had the inestimable honour of being the means of proving in his own person the certainty of my method. I intended to benefit him by my special method of development, and there is little doubt that he would have been physically, if not quite mentally, one of us before I had done with him. The operation would not have lasted longer than twenty days, when he would not have been distinguishable in general appearance from any of the inhabitants of this country. Now, I represent to you, sir," he added, addressing the President directly, "that there is no crime in what I have declared on oath."

The President merely requested me to confirm or deny the truth of the Chief's statements. I admitted that there was nothing I could deny.

"Why, then, were you endeavouring to kill him?"

"Kill him!" I said, "I was defending myself. Do you think I wanted to be operated on for his amusement? Besides, he forgot that he wanted to do it out of revenge because his daughter didn't agree—"

The Chief Adapter interrupted:

"My daughter should be left out of this discussion."

"No," said the President, "let us hear the whole story."

I thereupon told him my account of the Chief's anger with Clarice, and how he had threatened me when she told him that she had informed the Council.

The Chief Adapter sprang off his butt-end, and waved his tentacles furiously in my direction.

"The abominable monkey leaves me no alternative but to state in public that which for my own honour and the honour of this whole nation I would have buried in oblivion. This object has dared to raise his eyes towards my daughter – let him deny it if he can – and she, to her shame and mine, has not repulsed him. Nay, she has even expressed a desire to become as one of those half-developed creatures of the old world – she has scorned her birthright."

He had got so far when his voice was drowned by a terrific roar of fury from all those present. Cries of "Kill! kill! kill!" in a series of stunning shouts rent the atmosphere. Even the President's glance in my direction seemed to be that of a wild beast. There was a rush in my direction, when he raised his arms and commanded silence.

"You are fully exonerated and have the sympathy of us all," he said to the Chief, "but let us not be carried away by our righteous anger at the enormity of which this man has been guilty. We must remember that he cannot in his ignorance realise his guilt. Let him therefore be deported immediately. We cannot consent to your experiment, Adapter. Give him fourteen days' provisions and set him where he may be picked up. That is my word."

I was immediately seized and conveyed from the hall. Not a single friendly countenance could I espy. Tennyson in particular was making the most diabolical faces at me. Those who carried me seemed to think I was contaminating them by my touch. I was placed in a roller and they were about to start when the President and the Chief came up and stopped them.

I felt a cold hand pressed on my forehead and a piercing pain passed through my head.

"He will remember nothing of the locality now," said the Chief Adapter.

The roller started, but at a funeral pace, and I perceived that an enormous crowd were following – every eye was fixed upon me with a baleful glare. Only the guard by which I was surrounded held them in check.

Fierce yells of hatred and derision were raised. The journey was over interminable winding paths, overhanging precipices of enormous depth, down which I looked in a vain endeavour to distinguish the bottom. At last the roller stopped, and I was ordered to descend.

All about me were a mob of savage faces glaring from their barrels, and pointing their extended fingers stretched to their utmost length in the direction of a winding stream which formed the boundary to the glade. Beyond me was a huge mass of boulders forming the approach to an iron ring of mountains.

"Go – you are expelled," cried the President. "You have grossly abused our hospitality. You may thank fate that you leave with your life. Do not attempt to linger in this vicinity." It all seemed so much like a dream, from which I felt I should awaken presently – but when I looked back I suddenly caught sight of my poor Clarice. She was standing at the bottom step of the tunnel, a little white hand was extended towards me in a mute gesture of farewell . . .

I walked for days through barren paths in the burning sun, resting at night in any shelter of the rocks that presented itself, and now I only await the end.

# THE CREATOR

## Clifford D. Simak

*The next story was written about twenty-five years after the previous one. Clifford Simak (1904–88) was one of the truly original practitioners of science fiction. He is probably best known for* City *(1952), which won him the International Fantasy Award in 1953. This study of the future of human civilization both on and beyond the Earth, though, was not typical of his later work. He created his own niche for depicting strange events in rural settings, such as farmers or small-town residents being visited by aliens or encountering other dimensions. One of his best stories, "The Big Front Yard" (1958), won him the Hugo Award in 1959 and he won it again for his novel* Way Station *in 1964. You can find a selection of his short works in* Strangers in the Universe *(1958) and* All the Traps of Earth *(1962) and currently the American publisher Darkside Press has started to repackage Simak's Collected Stories under the editorial hand of Philip Stephensen-Payne starting with* Eternity Lost *(2005).*

*The following story, though, comes from much earlier in Simak's career. In the early 1930s the science-fiction magazine was still a new creation and, like all youngsters, it had become a little uncontrollable, with much of its fiction degenerating into little more that wild-west adventures in space. Those who knew that science fiction was capable of much more than this despaired and almost gave up. One fan, William*

*Crawford, decided to try his hand at publishing his own
magazine, which became* Marvel Tales. *His idea was to
publish stories of originality and brave ideas. Simak had
written "The Creator" on spec, but knew that none of the
professional magazines of the day would take it because the
subject was so taboo. So its first appearance was in a little
magazine with a circulation of only a few hundred. It's only
been reprinted a handful of times since but I think you'll agree
that for a story written over 70 years ago, it is still fairly
extreme.*

## Foreword

This is written in the elder days as the Earth rides close to the rim
of eternity, edging nearer to the dying Sun, into which her two
inner companions of the solar system have already plunged to a
fiery death. The Twilight of the Gods is history; and our planet
drifts on and on into that oblivion from which nothing escapes, to
which time itself may be dedicated in the final cosmic reckoning.

Old Earth, pacing her death march down the corridors of the
heavens, turns more slowly upon her axis. Her days have length-
ened as she crawls sadly to her tomb, shrouded only in the shreds
of her former atmosphere. Because her air has thinned, her sky
has lost its cheerful blue depths and she is arched with a dreary
grey, which hovers close to the surface, as if the horrors of outer
space were pressing close, like ravening wolves, upon the flanks
of this ancient monarch of the heavens. When night creeps upon
her, stranger stars blaze out like a ring of savage eyes closing in
upon a dying campfire.

Earth must mourn her passing, for she has stripped herself of
all her gaudy finery and proud trappings. Upon her illimitable
deserts and twisted ranges she has set up strange land sculptures.
And these must be temples and altars before which she, not
forgetting the powers of good and evil throughout the cosmos,
prays in her last hours, like a dying man returning to his old faith.
Mournful breezes play a hymn of futility across her barren
reaches of sand and rocky ledges. The waters of the empty oceans
beat out upon the treeless, bleak and age-worn coast a march that
is the last brave gesture of an ancient planet which has served its
purpose and treads the path to Nirvana.

Little half-men and women, final survivors of a great race, which they remember only through legends handed down from father to son, burrow gnome-like in the bowels of the planet which was mothered their seed from dim days when the thing which was destined to rule over all his fellow creatures crawled in the slime of primal seas. A tired race, they wait for the day legend tells them will come, when the sun blazes anew in the sky and grass grows green upon the barren deserts once again. But I know this day will never come, although I would not disillusion them. I know their legends lie, but why should I destroy the only solid thing they have left to round out their colorless life with the everlasting phenomena of hope?

For these little folks have been kind to me and there is a blood-bond between us that even the passing of a million years cannot erase. They think me a god, a messenger that the day they have awaited so long is near. I regret in time to come they must know me as a false prophet.

There is no point in writing these words. My little friends ask me what I do and why I do it and do not seem to understand when I explain. They do not comprehend my purpose in making quaint marks and signs upon the well-tanned pelts of the little rodents which over-run their burrows. All they understand is that when I have finished my labor they must take the skins and treasure them as a sacred trust I have left in their hands.

I have no hope the things I record will ever be read. I write my experiences in the same spirit and with the same bewildered purpose which must have characterized the first ancestor who chipped a runic message upon a stone.

I realize that I write the last manuscript. Earth's proud cities have fallen into mounds of dust. The roads that once crossed her surface have disappeared without a trace. No wheels turn, no engines drone. The last tribe of the human race crouches in its caves, watching for the day that will never come.

## First Experiments

There may be some who would claim that Scott Marston and I have blasphemed, that we probed too deeply into mysteries where we had no right.

But be that as it may, I do not regret what we did and I am

certain that Scott Marston, wherever he may be, feels as I do, without regrets.

We began our friendship at a little college in California. We were naturally drawn together by the similitude of our life, the affinity of our natures. Although our lines of study were widely separated, he majored in science and I in psychology, we both pursued our education for the pure love of learning rather than with a thought of what education might do toward earning a living.

We eschewed the society of the campus, engaging in none of the frivolities of the student body. We spent happy hours in the library and study hall. Our discussions were ponderous and untouched by thought of the college life which flowed about us in all its colorful pageantry.

In our last two years we roomed together. As we were poor, our quarters were shabby, but this never occurred to us. Our entire life was embraced in our studies. We were fired with the true spirit of research.

Inevitably, we finally narrowed our research down to definite lines. Scott, intrigued by the enigma of time, devoted more and more of his leisure moments to the study of that inscrutable element. He found that very little was known of it, beyond the perplexing equations set up by equally perplexed savants.

I wandered into as remote paths, the study of psychophysics and hypnology. I followed my research in hypnology until I came to the point where the mass of facts I had accumulated trapped me in a jungle of various diametrically opposed conclusions, many of which verged upon the occult.

It was at the insistence of my friend that I finally sought a solution in the material rather than the psychic world. He argued that if I were to make any real progress I must follow the dictate of pure, cold science rather than the elusive will-o-wisp of an unproven shadow existence.

At length, having completed our required education, we were offered positions as instructors, he in physics and I in psychology. We eagerly accepted, as neither of us had any wish to change the routine of our lives.

Our new status in life changed our mode of living not at all. We continued to dwell in our shabby quarters, we ate at the same restaurant, we had our nightly discussions. The fact that we were no longer students in the generally accepted term of the word made no iota of difference to our research and study.

It was in the second year after we had been appointed instructors that I finally stumbled upon my "consciousness unit" theory. Gradually I worked it out with the enthusiastic moral support of my friend who rendered me what assistance he could.

The theory was beautiful in simplicity. It was based upon the hypothesis that a dream is an expression of one's consciousness, that it is one's second self going forth to adventure and travel. When the physical being is at rest the consciousness is released and can travel and adventure at will within certain limits.

I went one step further, however. I assumed that the consciousness actually does travel, that certain infinitesimal parts of one's brain do actually escape to visit the strange places and encounter the odd events of which one dreams.

This was taking dreams out of the psychic world to which they had formerly been regulated and placing them on a solid scientific basis.

I speak of my theory as a "consciousness unit" theory. Scott and I spoke of the units as "consciousness cells", although we were aware they could not possibly be cells. I thought of them as highly specialized electrons, despite the fact that it appeared ridiculous to suspect electrons of specialization. Scott contended that a wave force, an intelligence wave, might be nearer the truth. Which of us was correct was never determined, nor did it make any difference.

As may be suspected, I never definitely arrived at undeniable proof to sustain my theory, although later developments would seem to bear it out.

Strangely, it was Scott Marston who did the most to add whatever measure of weight I could ever attach to my hypothesis.

While I was devoting my time to the abstract study of dreams, Scott was continuing with his equally baffling study of time. He confided to me that he was well satisfied with the progress he was making. At times he explained to me what he was doing, but my natural inaptitude at figures made impossible an understanding of the formidable array of formulas which he spread out before me.

I accepted as a matter of course his statement that he had finally discovered a time force, which he claimed was identical with a fourth dimensional force. At first the force existed only in a jumble of equations, formulas and graphs on a litter of paper, but finally we pooled our total resources and under Scott's hand a machine took shape.

Finished, it crouched like a malign entity on the work table, but it pulsed and hummed with a strange power that was of no earthly source.

"It is operating on time, pure time," declared Scott. "It is warping and distorting the time pattern, snatching power from the fourth dimension. Given a machine large enough, we could create a time-stress great enough to throw this world into a new plane created by the distortion of the time-field."

We shuddered as we gazed upon the humming mass of metal and realized the possibilities of our discovery. Perhaps for a moment we feared that we had probed too deeply into the mystery of an element that should have remained forever outside the providence of human knowledge.

The realization that he had only scratched the surface, however, drove Scott on to renewed efforts. He even begrudged the time taken by his work as instructor and there were weeks when we ate meager lunches in our rooms after spending all our available funds but a few pennies to buy some piece needed for the time-power machine.

Came the day when we placed a potted plant within a compartment in the machine. We turned on the mechanism and when we opened the door after a few minutes the plant was gone. The pot and earth within it was intact, but the plant had vanished. Search of the pot revealed that not even a bit of root remained.

Where had the plant gone? Why did the pot and earth remain?

Scott declared the plant had been shunted into an outre dimension, lying between the lines of stress created in the time pattern by the action of the machine. He concluded that the newly discovered force acted more swiftly upon a live organism than upon an inanimate object.

We replaced the pot within the compartment, but after twenty-four hours it was still there. We were forced to conclude the force had no effect upon inanimate objects.

We found later that here we touched close to the truth, but had failed to grasp it in its entirety.

# The Dream

A year following the construction of the time-power machine, Scott came into an inheritance when a relative, whom he had almost forgotten but who apparently had not forgotten him, died. The inheritance was modest, but to Scott and I, who had lived from hand to mouth for years, it appeared large.

Scott resigned his position as instructor and insisted upon my doing the same in order that we might devote our uninterrupted time to research.

Scott immediately set about the construction of a larger machine, while I plunged with enthusiasm into certain experiments I had held in mind for some time.

It was not until then that we thought to link our endeavors. Our research had always seemed separated by too great a chasm to allow collaboration beyond the limited mutual aid of which we were both capable and which steadily diminished as our work progressed further and further, assuming greater and greater complications, demanding more and more specialization.

The idea occurred to me following repetition of a particularly vivid dream. In the dream I stood in a colossal laboratory, an unearthly laboratory, which seemed to stretch away on every hand for inconceivable distances. It was equipped with strange and unfamiliar apparatus and uncanny machines. On the first night the laboratory seemed unreal and filled with an unnatural mist, but on each subsequent occasion it became more and more real, until upon awakening I could reconstruct many of its details with surprising clarity. I even made a sketch of some of the apparatus for Scott and he agreed that I must have drawn it from the memory of my dream. No man could have imagined unaided the sketches I spread upon paper for my friend.

Scott expressed an opinion that my research into hypnology had served to train my "consciousness units" to a point where they had become more specialized and were capable of retaining a more accurate memory of their wandering. I formulated a theory that my "consciousness units" had actually increased in number, which would account in a measure for the vividness of the dream.

"I wonder," I mused, "if your time-power would have any influence upon the units."

Scott hummed under his breath. "I wonder," he said.

The dream occurred at regular intervals. Had it not been for my absorption in my work, the dream might have become irksome, but I was elated, for I had found in myself a subject for investigation.

One night Scott brought forth a mechanism resembling the head phones of early radio sets, on which he had been working for weeks. He had not yet explained its purpose.

"Pete," he said, "I want you to move your cot near the table and put on this helmet. When you go to sleep I'll plug it in the time-power. If it has any effect upon consciousness units, this will demonstrate it."

He noticed my hesitation.

"Don't be afraid," he urged. "I will watch beside you. If anything goes wrong, I'll jerk the plug and waken you."

So I put on the helmet and with Scott Marston sitting in a chair beside my cot, went to sleep.

That night I seemed to actually walk in the laboratory. I saw no one, but I examined the place from end to end. I distinctly remember handling strange tools, the use of which I could only vaguely speculate upon. Flanking the main laboratory were many archways, opening into smaller rooms, which I did not investigate. The architecture of the laboratory and the archways was unbelievably alien, a fact I had noticed before but had never examined in such minute detail.

I opened my eyes and saw the anxious face of Scott Marston above me.

"What happened, Pete?" he asked.

I grasped his arm.

"Scott, I was there. I actually walked in the laboratory. I picked up tools. I can see the place now, plainer than ever before."

I saw a wild light come into his eyes. He rose from the chair and stood towering above me as I propped myself up on my arms.

"Do you know what we've found, Pete! Do you realize that we can travel in time, that we can explore the future, investigate the past? We are not even bound to this sphere, this plane of existence. We can travel into the multi-dimensions. We can go back to the first flush of eternity and see the cosmos born out of the womb of nothingness! We can travel forward to the day when all that exists comes to an end in the ultimate dispersion of wasted energy, when even space may be wiped out of existence and nothing but frozen time remains!"

"Are you mad, Scott?"

His eyes gleamed.

"Not mad, Pete. Victorious! We can build a machine large enough, powerful enough, to turn every cell of our bodies into consciousness units. We can travel in body as well as in thought. We can live thousands of lifetimes, review billions of years. We can visit undreamed of planets, unknown ages. We hold time in our hands!"

He beat his clenched fists together.

"That plant we placed in the machine. My God, Pete, do you know what happened to it? What primordial memories did that plant hold? Where is it now? Is it in some swamp of the Carboniferous age? Has it returned to its ancestral era?"

Years passed, but we scarcely noticed their passing.

Our hair greyed slightly at the temples and the mantle of youth dropped slowly from us. No fame came to us, for our research had progressed to a point where it would have strained even the most credulous mind to believe what we could have unfolded.

Scott built his larger time-power machine, experimented with it, devised new improvements, discovered new details . . . and rebuilt it, not once, but many times. The ultimate machine, squatting like an alien god in our work shop, bore little resemblance to the original model.

On my part, I delved more deeply into my study of dreams, relentlessly pursuing my theory of consciousness units. My progress necessarily was slower than that of my friend as I was dealing almost entirely with the abtruse although I tried to make it as practical as possible, while Scott had a more practical and material basis for his investigations.

Of course, we soon decided to make the attempt to actually transfer our bodies into the laboratory of my dreams. That is, we proposed to transform all the electrons, all the elements of our bodies, into consciousness units through the use of the time-power. A more daring scheme possibly had never been conceived by man.

In an attempt to impress upon my friend's mind a picture of the laboratory, I drew diagrams and pictures, visiting the laboratory many times, with the aid of the time-power, to gather more detailed data on the place.

It was not until I used hypnotism that I could finally transfer to

Scott's mind a true picture of that massive room with its outre scientific equipment.

It was a day of high triumph when Scott, placed under the influence of the time-power, awoke to tell me of the place I had visited so often. It was not until then that we could be absolutely sure we had accomplished the first, and perhaps most difficult, step in our great experiment.

I plunged into a mad study of the psychology of the Oriental ascetic, who of all people was the furthest advanced in the matter of concentration, the science of will power, and the ability to subjugate the body to the mind.

Although my studies left much to be desired, they nevertheless pointed the way for us to consciously aid the time-power element in reducing our corporeal beings to the state of consciousness units necessary for our actual transportation to the huge laboratory with which we had both grown so familiar.

There were other places than the dream-laboratory, of course. Both of us, in our half-life imparted by the time-power, visited other strange places, the location of which in time and space we could not determine. We looked upon sights which would have blasted our mortal sanity had we gazed upon them in full consciousness. There were times when we awoke with blanched faces and told each other in ghastly, fear-ridden whispers of the horrors that dwelled in some unprobed dimension of the unplumbed depth of the cosmos. We stared at shambling, slithering things which we recognized as the descendants of entities, or perhaps the very entities, which were related in manuscripts written by ancient men versed in the blackest of sorcery – and still remembered in the hag-ridden tales of people in the hinterlands.

But it was upon the mysterious laboratory that we centered all our efforts. It had been our first real glimpse into the vast vista to which we had raised the veil and to it we remained true, regarding those other places as mere side excursions into the recondite world we had discovered.

## In the Creator's Laboratory

At last the day arrived when we were satisfied we had advanced sufficiently far in our investigations and had perfected our technique to a point where we might safely attempt an actual excursion into the familiar, yet unknown, realm of the dream-laboratory.

The completed and improved time-power machine squatted before us like a hideous relic out of the forgotten days of an earlier age, its weird voice filling the entire house, rising and falling, half the time a scream, half the time a deep murmur. Its polished sides glistened evilly and the mirrors set about it at inconceivable angles in their relation to each other, caught the glare from the row of stepup tubes across the top, reflecting the light to bathe the entire creation in an unholy glow.

We stood before it, our hair tinged with grey, our faces marked by lines of premature age. We were young men grown old in the service of our ambition and vast curiosity.

After ten years we had created a thing that I now realize might have killed us both. But at that time we were superbly confident. Ten years of moulding metal and glass, harnessing and taming strange powers! Ten years of moulding brains, of concentrating and stepping up the sensitivity and strength of our consciousness until day and night, there lurked in the back of our brains an image of that mysterious laboratory. As our consciousness direction had been gradually narrowed, the laboratory had become almost a second life to us.

Scott pressed a stud on the side of the machine and a door swung outward, revealing an interior compartment which yawned like a black maw. In that maw was no hint of the raw power and surging strength revealed by the exterior. Yet, to the uninitiate, it would have held a horrible threat of its own.

Scott stepped through the door into the pitch black interior; gently he lowered himself into the reclining seat, reaching out to place his hands on the power controls.

I slid in beside him and closed the door. As the last ray of light was shut out, absolute blackness enveloped us. We fitted power helmets on our heads. Terrific energy poured through us, beating through our bodies, seeming to tear us to pieces.

My friend stretched forth a groping hand. Fumbling in the darkness, I found it. Our hands closed in a fierce grip, the handshake of men about to venture into the unknown.

I fought for control of my thoughts, centered them, savagely upon the laboratory, recalling, with a super-effort every detail of its interior. Then Scott must have shoved the power control full over. My body was pain-wracked, then seemed to sway with giddiness. I forgot my body. The laboratory seemed nearer, it seemed to flash up at me. I was falling toward it, falling rapidly. I was a detached thought speeding along a directional line, falling straight into the laboratory . . . and I was very ill.

My fall was suddenly broken, without jar or impact.

I was standing in the laboratory. I could feel the cold of the floor beneath my feet.

I glanced sidewise and there stood Scott Marston and my friend was stark naked. Of course, we would be naked. Our clothing would not be transported through the time-power machine.

"It didn't kill us," remarked Scott.

"Not even a scratch," I asserted.

We faced each other and shook hands, solemnly, for again we had triumphed and that hand-shake was a self-imposed congratulation.

We turned back to the room before us. It was a colorful place. Vari-colored liquids reposed in gleaming containers. The furniture, queerly carved and constructed along lines alien to any earthly standard, seemed to be of highly polished, iridescent wood. Through the windows poured a brilliant blue daylight. Great globes suspended from the ceiling further illuminated the building with a soft white glow.

A cone of light, a creamy white faintly tinged with pink, floated through an arched doorway and entered the room. We stared at it. It seemed to be light, yet was it light? It was not transparent and although it gave one the impression of intense brilliance, its color was so soft that it did not hurt one's eyes to look at it.

The cone, about ten feet in height, rested on its smaller end and advanced rapidly toward us. Its approach was silent. There was not even the remotest suggestion of sound in the entire room. It came to a rest a short distance in front of us and I had an uncanny sense that the thing was busily observing us.

"Who are you?"

The Voice seemed to fill the room, yet there was no one there but Scott and I, and neither of us had spoken. We looked at one another in astonishment and then shifted our gaze to the cone of light, motionless, resting quietly before us.

"I am speaking," said the Voice and instantly each of us knew that the strange cone before us had voiced the words.

"I am not speaking," went on the Voice. "That was a misstatement. I am thinking. You hear my thoughts. I can as easily hear yours."

"Telepathy," I suggested.

"Your term is a strange one," replied the Voice, "but the mental image the term calls up tells me that you faintly understand the principle.

"I perceive from your thoughts that you are from a place which you call the Earth. I know where the Earth is located. I understand you are puzzled and discomforted by my appearance, my powers, and my general disresemblance to anything you have ever encountered. Do not be alarmed. I welcome you here. I understand you worked hard and well to arrive here and no harm will befall you."

"I am Scott Marston," said my friend, "and this man is Peter Sands."

The thoughts of the light-cone reached out to envelope us and there was a faint tinge of rebuke, a timbre of pity at what must have appeared to the thing as unwarranted egotism on our part.

"In this place there are no names. We are known by our personalities. However, as your mentality demands an identifying name, you may think of me as the Creator.

"And now, there are others I would have you see."

He sounded a call, a weird call which seemed to incorporate as equally a weird name.

There was a patter of feet on the floor and from an adjoining room ran three animal-like figures. Two were similar. They were pudgy of body, with thick, short legs which terminated in rounded pads that made sucking sounds as they ran. They had no arms, but from the center of their bulging chests sprang a tentacle, fashioned somewhat after the manner of an elephant's trunk, but with a number of small tentacles at its end. Their heads, rising to a peak from which grew a plume of gayly-colored feathers, sat upon their tapering shoulders without benefit of necks.

The third was an antithesis of the first two. He was tall and spindly, built on the lines of a walking stick insect. His gangling legs were three-jointed. His grotesquely long arms dangled almost to the floor. Looking at his body, I believed I could have encircled it with my two hands. His head was simply an oval ball set on top of the stick-like body. The creature more nearly resembled a man than the other two, but he was a caricature of a man, a comic offering from the pen of a sardonic cartoonist.

The Creator seemed to be addressing the three.

"Here," he said, "are some new arrivals. They came here, I gather, in much the same manner you did. They are great scientists, great as yourselves. You will be friends."

The Creator turned his attention to us.

"These beings which you see came here as you did and are my guests as you are my guests. They may appear outlandish to you. Rest assured that you appear just as queer to them. They are brothers of yours, neighbors of yours. They are from your—."

I received the impression of gazing down on vast space, filled with swirling motes of light.

"He means our solar system," suggested Scott.

Carefully I built up in my mind a diagram of the solar system.

"*No!*" the denial crashed like an angry thunderbolt upon us. Again the image of unimaginable space and of thousands of points of light – of swirling nebulae, of solar systems, mighty double suns and island universes.

"He means the universe," said Scott.

"Certainly they came from our universe," I replied. "The universe is everything, isn't it – all existing things?"

Again the negative of the Creator burned its way into our brains.

"You are mistaken, Earthman. Your knowledge here counts as nothing. You are mere infants. But come; I will show you what your universe consists of."

## – Our Universe?

Streamers of light writhed down from the cone toward us. As we shrank back they coiled about our waists and gently lifted us. Soothing thoughts flowed over us, instructions to commit ourselves unreservedly to the care of the Creator, to fear no harm. Under this reassurance, my fears quieted. I felt that I was under the protection of a benevolent being, that his great power and compassion would shield me in this strange world. A Creator, in very truth!

The Creator glided across the floor to set us on our feet on the top of a huge table, which stood about seven feet above the floor level.

On the table top, directly before me, I saw a thin oval receptacle, made of a substance resembling glass. It was about a foot across its greatest length and perhaps little more than half as wide and about four inches deep. The receptacle was filled with a sort of grayish substance, a mass of putty-like material. To me it suggested nothing more than a mass of brain substance.

"There," said the Creator, pointing a light-streamer finger at the disgusting mass, "is your universe."

"What!" cried Scott.

"It is so," ponderously declared the Creator.

"Such a thing is impossible," firmly asserted Scott. "The universe is boundless. At one time it was believed that it was finite, that it was enclosed by the curvature of space. I am convinced, however, through my study of time, that the universe, composed of millions of overlapping and interlocking dimensions, can be nothing but eternal and infinite. I do not mean that there will not be a time when all matter will be destroyed, but I do maintain—"

"You are disrespectful and conceited," boomed the thought vibrations of the Creator. "That is your universe. I made it. I created it. And more. I created the life that teems within it. I was curious to learn what form that life would take, so I sent powerful thought vibrations into it, calling that life out. I had little hope that it had developed the necessary intelligence to find the road to my laboratory, but I find that at least five of the beings evolving from my created life possessed brains tuned finely enough to catch my vibrations and possessed sufficient intelligence to break out of their medium. You are two of these five. The other three you have just seen."

"You mean," said Scott, speaking softly, "that you created matter and then went further and created life?"

"I did."

I stared at the putty-like mass. The universe! Millions of galaxies composed of millions of suns and planets – all in that lump of matter!

"This is the greatest hoax I've ever seen," declared Scott, a deliberate note of scorn in his voice. "If that is the universe down there, how are we so big? I could step on that dish and break the universe all to smithereens. It doesn't fit."

\*　　\*　　\*

The light-finger of the Creator flicked out and seized my friend, wafting him high above the table. The Creator glowed with dull flashes of red and purple.

His thought vibrations filled the room to bursting with their power.

"Presumptuous one! You defy the Creator. You call his great work a lie! You, with your little knowledge! You, a specimen of the artificial life I created, would tell me, your very Creator, that I am wrong!"

I stood frozen, staring at my friend, suspended above me at the end of the rigid light-streamer. I could see Scott's face. It was set and white, but there was no sign of fear upon it.

His voice came down to me, cold and mocking.

"A jealous god," he taunted.

The Creator set him down gently beside me. His thoughts came to us evenly, with no trace of his terrible anger of only a moment before.

"I am not jealous. I am above all your imperfect emotions. I have evolved to the highest type of life but one – pure thought. In time I will achieve that. I may grow impatient at times with your tiny brains, with your imperfect knowledge, with your egotism, but beyond that I am unemotional. The emotions have become unnecessary to my existence."

I hurried to intervene.

"My friend spoke without thinking," I explained. "You realize this is all unusual to us. Something beyond any previous experience. It is hard for us to believe."

"I know it must be hard for you to understand," agreed the Creator, "You are in an ultra-universe. The electrons and protons making up your body have grown to billions and billions of times their former size, with correspondingly greater distances between them. It is all a matter of relativity. I did not consciously create your universe, I merely created electrons and protons. I created matter. I created life and injected it into the matter.

"I learned from the three who preceded you here that all things upon my electrons and protons, even my very created electrons and protons, are themselves composed of electrons and protons. This I had not suspected. I am at a loss to explain it. I am beginning to believe that one will never find an end to the mysteries of matter and life. It may be that the electrons and protons you know are composed of billions of infinitely smaller electrons and protons."

"And I suppose," mocked Scott, "that you, the Creator, may be merely a bit of synthetic life living in a universe that is in turn merely a mass of matter in some greater laboratory."

"It may be so," said the Creator. "My knowledge has made me very humble."

Scott laughed.

"And now," said the Creator, "if you will tell me what food and other necessities you require to sustain life, I will see you are provided for. You also will wish to build the machine which will take you back to Earth once more. You shall be assigned living quarters and may do as you wish. When your machine is completed, you may return to Earth. If you do not wish to do so, you are welcome to remain indefinitely as my guests. All I wished you to come here for was to satisfy my curiosity concerning what forms my artificial life may have taken."

The tentacles of light lifted us carefully to the floor and we followed the Creator to our room, which adjoined the laboratory proper and was connected to it by a high, wide archway. What the place lacked in privacy, it made up in beauty. Finished in pastel shades, it was easy on the eyes and soothing to one's nerves.

We formed mind pictures of beds, tables and chairs. We described our foods and their chemical composition. Water we did not need to describe. The Creator knew instantly what it was. It, of all the necessities of our life, however, seemed the only thing in common with our earth contained in this ultra-universe into which we had projected ourselves.

In what seemed to us a miraculously short time our needs were provided. We were supplied with furniture, food and clothing, all of which apparently was produced synthetically by the Creator in his laboratory.

Later we were to learn that the combining of elements and the shaping of the finished product was a routine matter. A huge, yet simple machine was used in the combination and fixing of the elements.

Steel, glass, and tools, shaped according to specifications given the Creator by Scott, were delivered to us in a large workroom directly off the laboratory where our three compatriots of the universe were at work upon their machines.

The machine being constructed by the lone gangling creature which Scott and I had immediately dubbed the "walking-stick-man", resembled in structure the creature building it. It was shaped like a pyramid and into its assembly had gone hundreds of long rods.

The machine of the elephant-men was a prosaic affair, shaped like a crude box of some rubber-material, but its inner machinery, which we found to be entirely alien to any earthly conceptions, was intricate.

From the first the walking-stick-man disregarded us except when we forced our attentions upon him.

The elephant-men were friendly, however.

We had hardly been introduced into the workshop before the two of them attempted to strike up an acquaintance with us.

We spoke to them as they stood before us, but they merely blinked their dull expressionless eyes. They touched us with their trunks, and we felt faint electric shocks which varied in intensity, like the impulses travelling along a wire, like some secret code tapped out by a telegrapher.

"They have no auditory sense," said Scott. "They talk by the transmission of electrical impulses through their trunks. There's no use talking to them."

"And in a thousand years we might figure out their electrical language," I replied.

After a few more futile attempts to establish communication Scott turned to the task of constructing the time-power machine, while the elephant-men padded back to their own work.

I walked over to the walking-stick-man and attempted to establish communication with him, but with no better results. The creature seeming to resent my interruption of his work, waved his hands in fantastic gestures, working his mouth rapidly. In despair, I realized that he was talking to me, but that his jabbering was pitched too high for my ear to catch.

Here were representatives of three different races, all three of a high degree of intelligence else they never would have reached this super-plane, and not a single thought, not one idea could they interchange. Even had a communication of ideas been possible, I wondered if we could have found any common ground of understanding.

*     *     *

I stared at the machines. They were utterly different from each other and neither bore any resemblance to ours. Undoubtedly they all operated on dissimilar principles.

In that one room adjoining the main laboratory were being constructed three essentially different types of mechanisms by three entirely different types of beings. Yet each machine was designed to accomplish the same result and each of the beings were striving for the same goal!

Unable to assist Scott in his building of the time-power machine, I spent the greater part of my waking hours in roaming about the laboratory, in watching the Creator at work. Occasionally I talked to him. At times he explained to me what he was doing, but I am afraid I understood little of what he told me.

One day he allowed me to look through a microscope at a part of the matter he had told us contained our universe.

I was unprepared for what I saw. As I peered into the complicated machine, I saw protons, electrons! Judged by earthly standards, they were grouped peculiarly, but their formation corresponded almost exactly to our planetary system. I sensed that certain properties in that master-microscope created an optical illusion by grouping them more closely than were their actual corresponding distances. The distance between them had been foreshortened to allow an entire group to be within a field of vision.

But this was impossible! The very lenses through which I was looking were themselves formed of electrons and protons! How could they have any magnifying power?

The Creator read my thoughts and tried to explain, but his explanation was merely a blur of distances, a mass of outlandish mathematical equations and a pyramiding of stupendous formulas dealing with the properties of light. I realized that, with the Creator, the Einstein equations were elementary, that the most intricate mathematics conceived by man were rudimentary to him as simple addition.

He must have realized it, too, for after that he did not attempt to explain anything to me. He made it plain, however, that I was welcome to visit him at his work and as time passed, he came to take my presence as a matter of course. At times he seemed to forget I was about.

The work on the time-power machine was progressing steadily under Scott's skillful hands. I could see that the other two machines were nearing completion, but that my friend was working with greater speed. I calculated that all three of the machines would be completed at practically the same time.

"I don't like this place," Scott confided to me. "I want to get the machine built and get out of here as soon as I can. The Creator is a being entirely different from us. His thought processes and emotional reflexes can bear little resemblance to ours. He is further advanced along the scale of life than we. I am not fool enough to believe he accepts us as his equals. He claims he created us. Whether he did or not, and I can't bring myself to believe that he did, he nevertheless believes he did. That makes us his property – in his own belief, at least – to do with as he wishes. I'm getting out of here before something happens."

One of the elephant-men, who had been working with his partner, approached us as we talked. He tapped me gently with his trunk and then stood stupidly staring at us.

"Funny," said Scott, "That fellow has been bothering me all day. He's got something he wants to tell us, but he doesn't seem to be able to get it across."

Patiently I attempted an elementary language, but the elephant-man merely stared, unmoved, apparently not understanding.

The following day I secured from the Creator a supply of synthetic paper and a sort of black crayon. With these I approached the elephant-men and drew simple pictures, but again I failed. The strange creatures merely stared. Pictures and diagrams meant nothing to them.

The walking-stick-man, however, watched us from across the room and after the elephant-men had turned away to their work, he walked over to where I stood and held out his hands for the tablet and crayon. I gave them to him. He studied my sketches for a moment, ripped off the sheet and rapidly wielded the crayon. He handed back the tablet. On the sheet were a number of hieroglyphics. I could make no head or tail of them. For a long time the two of us labored over the tablet. We covered the floor with sheets covered with our scribbling, pictures and diagrams. We quit in despair after advancing no further than recognizing the symbols for the cardinal numbers.

It was apparent that not only the elephant-men but the walking-stick-man as well wished to communicate something to us.

Scott and I discussed it often, racking our brains for some means to establish communication with our brothers in exile.

## Creation – and Destruction

It was shortly after this I made the discovery that I was able to read the unprojected thoughts of the Creator. I imagine that this was made possible by the fact that our host paid little attention to me as he went about his work. Busy with his tasks, his thoughts must have seeped out as he mulled over the problems confronting him. It must have been through this thought seepage that I caught the first of his unprojected brain-images.

At first I received just faint impressions, sort of half thoughts. Realizing what was occurring, I concentrated upon his thoughts, endeavoring to bore into his brain, to prove out those other thoughts which lay beneath the surface. If it had not been for the intensive mind training which I had imposed upon myself prior to the attempt to project my body through the time-power machine, I am certain I would have failed. Without this training, I doubt if I would have been able to read his thoughts unbidden in the first place – certainly I could not have prevented him from learning that I had.

Recalling Scott's suspicions, I realised that my suddenly discovered ability might be used to our advantage. I also realized that this ability would be worthless should the Creator learn of it. In such case, he would be alert and would close his thought processes to me. My hope lay in keeping any suspicion disarmed. Therefore I must not only read his mind but must also keep a portion of mine closed to him.

Patch by patch I pieced his thoughts together like a jigsaw puzzle.

He was studying the destruction of matter, seeking a method of completely annihilating it. Having discovered a means of creating matter, he was now experimenting with its destruction.

I did not share my secret with Scott, for I feared that he would unconsciously betray it to the Creator.

As days passed, I learned that the Creator was considering the destruction of matter without the use of heat. I knew that, even on Earth, it was generally conceded a temperature of 4,000,000,000,000 degrees Fahrenheit would absolutely annihilate matter. I had believed the Creator had found some manner in which he could control such an excessive temperature. But to attempt to destroy matter without using heat at all –! I believe that it was not until then that I fully realized the great chasm of intelligence that lay between myself and this creature of light.

I have no idea how long we remained in the world of the Creator before Scott announced that the machine in which we expected to return to our universe was ready for a few tests. Time had the illusive quality in this queer place of slithering along without noticeably passing. Although I did not think of it at the time, I cannot recollect now that the Creator employed any means of measuring time. Perhaps time, so far as he was concerned, had become an unnecessary equation. Perhaps he was eternal and time held no significance for him in his eternity.

The elephant-men and the walking-stick-man had already completed their machines, but they seemed to be waiting for us. Was it a gesture of respect? We did not know at the time.

While Scott made the final tests of our machine I walked into the laboratory. The Creator was at work at his accustomed place. Since our arrival he had paid little attention to us. Now that we were about to leave he made no expression of regret, no sign of farewell.

I approached him, wondering if I should bid him farewell. I had grown to respect him. I wanted to say good-bye, and yet . . .

Then I caught the faintest of his thoughts and I stiffened. Instantly and unconsciously my mind thrust out probing fingers and grasped the predominant idea in the Creator's mind.

". . . Destroy the mass of created matter – the universe which I created . . . create matter . . . destroy it. It is a laboratory product. Test my destructive . . ."

"Why you damn murderer," I screamed and threw myself at him.

Light fingers flicked out at me, whipped around my body, snapped me into the air and heaved me across the laboratory. I struck on the smooth floor and skidded across it to bring up with a crash against the wall.

I shook my head to clear it and struggled to my feet. We must fight the Creator! Must save our world from destruction by the very creature who had created it!

I came to my feet with my muscles bunched, crouched in a fighting posture.

But the Creator had not moved. He stood in the same position and a rod of purple light extended between him and the queer machine of the walking-stick man. The rod of light seemed to be holding him there, frozen, immovable. Beside the machine stood the walking-stick-man, his hand on the lever, a mad glare in his eyes.

Scott was slapping the gangling fellow on his slender back.

"You've got the goods, old man," he was shouting. "That's one trick old frozen face didn't learn from you."

A thunderous tumult beat through my head. The machine of the walking-stick-man was not a transmission machine at all. It was a weapon – a weapon that could freeze the Creator into rigid lines.

Weird colors flowed through the Creator. Dead silence lay over the room. The machine of the walking-stick-man was silent, with no noise to hint of the great power it must have been developing. The purple rod did not waver. It was just a rigid rod of purple which had struck and stiffened the Creator.

I screamed at Scott: "Quick! The universe! He is going to destroy it!"

Scott leaped forward. Together we raced toward the table where the mass of created matter lay in its receptacle. Behind us padded the elephant-men.

As we reached the table, I felt a sinuous trunk wrap about me. With a flip I was hurled to the table top. It was but a step to the dish containing the universe. I snatched it up, dish and all, and handed it down to Scott. I let myself over the table edge, hung by my hands for an instant, and dropped. I raced after the others toward the work shop.

As we gained the room, the walking-stick-man made an adjustment on his machine. The purple rod faded away. The Creator, a towering cone of light, tottered for a moment and then glided swiftly for the doorway.

Instantly a sheet of purple radiance filled the opening. The Creator struck against it and was hurled back.

The radiance was swiftly arching overhead and curving beneath us, cutting through the floor, walls, and ceiling.

"He's enclosing us in a globe of that stuff," cried Scott. "It must be an energy screen of some sort, but I can't imagine what. Can you?"

"I don't care what it is, just so it works," I panted, anxiously.

Through the steady purple light I could see the Creator. Repeatedly he hurled himself against the screen and each time he was hurled back.

"We're moving," announced Scott.

The great purple globe was ascending, carrying in its interior we five universe-men, our machines, and fragments of the room in which we but recently had stood. It was cutting through the building like the flame of a torch through soft steel. We burst free of the building into the brilliant blue sunlight of that weird world.

Beneath us lay the building, a marvel of outre architecture, but with a huge circular shaft cut through it – the path of the purple globe. All about the building lay a forest of red and yellow vegetation, shaped as no vegetation of Earth is shaped, bent into hundreds of strange and alien forms.

Swiftly the globe sprang upward to hang in the air some distance above the building. As far as the eye could see stretched the painted forest. The laboratory we had just quitted was the only sign of habitation. No roads, no lakes, no rivers, no distant mountain – nothing relieved the level plain of red and yellow stretching away to faint horizons.

Was the Creator, I wondered, the sole denizen of this land? Was he the last survivor of a mystic race? Had there ever been a race at all? Might not the Creator be a laboratory product, even as the things he created were laboratory products? But if so, who or what had set to work the agents which resulted in that uncanny cone of energy?

My reflections were cut short as the walking-stick-man reached out his skinny hand for the mass of matter which Scott still held. As I watched him breathlessly, he laid it gently on a part of the floor which still remained in the globe and pulled a sliding rod from the side of the machine. A faint purple radiance sprang from the point of the rod, bathing the universe. The radiant purple surrounded the mass, grew thicker and thicker, seeming to congeal into layer after layer until the mass of matter lay sealed in a thick shell of the queer stuff. When I touched it, it did not appear to be hard or brittle. It was smooth and slimy to the touch, but I could not dent it with my fingers.

"He's building up the shell of the globe in just the same way," Scott said. "The machine seems to be projecting that purple stuff to the outside of the shell, where it is congealed into layers."

I noted that what he said was true. The shell of the globe had taken on a thickness that could be perceived, although the increased thickness did not seem to interfere with our vision.

Looking down at the laboratory, I could see some strange mechanism mounted on the roof of the building. Beside the massive mechanism stood the Creator.

"Maybe it's a weapon of some sort," suggested Scott.

Hardly had he spoken when a huge column of crimson light leaped forth from the machine. I threw up my hands to protect my eyes from the glare of the fiery column. For an instant the globe was bathed in the red glow, then a huge globule of red collected on its surface and leaped away, straight for the laboratory, leaving behind a trail of crimson.

The globe trembled to the force of the explosion as the ball of light struck. Where the laboratory had stood was merely a great hole, blasted to the primal rock beneath. The vegetation for great distances on either side was sifting ash. The Creator had disappeared. The colorful world beneath stretched empty to the horizon. The men of the universe had proven to be stronger than their Creator!

"If there's any more Creators around these parts," said Scott, smiling feebly, "they won't dare train another gun on this thing in the next million years. It gives them exactly what was meant for the other fellow; it crams their poison right down their own throats. Pete, that mass of matter, whether or not it is the universe, is saved. All hell couldn't get at it here."

The walking-stick-man, his mummy-like face impassive as ever, locked the controls of the machine. It was, I saw still operating, was still building up the shell of the globe. Second by second the globe was adding to its fortress – light strength. My mind reeled as I thought of it continuing thus throughout eternity.

The elephant-men were climbing into their machines.

Scott smiled wanly.

"The play is over," he said. "The curtain is down. It's time for us to go."

He stepped to the side of the walking-stick-man.

"I wish you would use our machine," he said, evidently forgetting our friend could understand no word he spoke. "You threw away your chance back there when you built this contraption instead of a transmitter. Our machine will take you wherever you wish to go."

He pointed to the machine and to the universe, then tapped his head. With the strange being at his side, he walked to our machine, pointed out the controls, explained its use in pantomime.

"I don't know if he understands," said Scott, "but I did the best I could."

As I walked past the walking-stick-man to step into the time-power machine, I believe I detected a faint flicker of a smile on his face. Of that, however, I can never be sure.


## Marooned in Time

I know how the mistake was made. I was excited when I stepped into the machine. My mind was filled with the many strange happenings I had witnessed. I thought along space directional lines, *but I forgot to reckon the factor of time*.

I thought of the Earth, but I did not consider time. I willed myself to be back on Earth, but I forgot to will myself in any particular time era. Consequently when Scott shoved over the lever, I was shot to Earth, but the time element was confused.

I realize that life in the super-universe of the Creator, being billions of times larger than life upon the Earth, was correspondingly slower. Every second in the super-universe was equal to years of Earth-time. My life in the Creator's universe had equaled millions of years of terran existence.

I believe that my body was projected along a straight line and not along the curve which was necessary to place me back in the twentieth century.

This is theory, of course. There might have been some fault in the machine. The purple globe might have exerted some influence to distort our calculations.

Be that as it may, I reached a dying planet. It has been given to me, a man of the twentieth century, to live out the last years of my life on my home planet some millions of years later than the date of my birth. I, a resident of a comparatively young dynasty in the history of the Earth, now am tribal chieftain and demi-god of the last race, a race that is dying even as the planet is dying.

As I sit before my cave or huddle with the rest of my clan around a feeble fire, I often wonder if Scott Marston was returned to Earth in his proper time. Or is he, too, a castaway in some strange time? Does he still live? Did he ever reach the Earth? I often feel that he may even now be searching through the vast corridors of time and the deserts of space for me, his one-time partner in the wildest venture ever attempted by man.

And often, too, I wonder if the walking-stick-man used our time-power machine to return to his native planet. Or is he a prisoner in his own trap, caught within the scope of the great purple globe? And I wonder how large the globe has grown.

I realize now that our effort to save the universe was unnecessary so far as the earth was concerned, for the earth, moving at its greater time-speed, would already have plunged into extinction in the flaming furnace of the sun before the Creator could carry out his destructive plans.

But what of those other worlds? What of those other planets which must surely swim around strange suns in the gulf of space? What of the planets and races yet unborn? What of the populations that may exist on the solar systems of island universes far removed from our own?

They are saved, saved for all time; for the purple globe will guard the handiwork of the Creator through eternity.

# THE GIRL HAD GUTS

## Theodore Sturgeon

*We move forward another twenty years to the mid-fifties. When I first saw the film* Alien *in 1979, which in itself was pretty extreme, it reminded me of the following story which was written in 1956 and utilized a similar concept of an alien parasite. If I had to choose a writer who did more than any other in pushing the boundaries of science fiction and making the field mature, then I'd choose Theodore Sturgeon (1918– 85), without doubt one of the most important of them all. His novels include* More Than Human *(1953), a fascinating study of gestalt personalities, and* Venus Plus X *(1960), which explores a future hermaphroditic society. On many occasions Sturgeon would argue about how writers needed to push themselves and their ideas and never be complacent. His own rigorous and high standards meant that he was seldom satisfied with his own work and as a result his output was sporadic. But at his best he was unbeatable. The following story appeared in the first issue of* Venture, *which was a companion to* The Magazine of Fantasy & Science Fiction, *and which set itself the task of publishing strong and challenging works of science fiction that would be difficult to place anywhere else. At the time, some readers found the story repulsive but it has since gone down as one of Sturgeon's best.*

T he cabby wouldn't take the fare ("Me take a nickel from Captain Gargan? Not in this life!") and the doorman welcomed me so warmly I almost forgave Sue for moving into a place that had a doorman. And then the elevator and then Sue. You have to be away a long time, a long way, to miss someone like that, and me, I'd been farther away than anyone ought to be, for too long plus six weeks. I kissed her and squeezed her until she yelled for mercy, and when I got to where I realized she was yelling we were clear back to the terrace, the whole length of the apartment away from the door. I guess I was sort of enthusiastic, but as I said . . . oh, who can say a thing like that and make any sense? I was glad to see my wife, and that was it.

She finally got me quieted down and my uniform jacket and shoes off and a dish of ale in my fist, and there I lay in the relaxer looking at her just the way I used to when I could come home from the base every night, just the way. I'd dreamed every off-duty minute since we blasted off all those months ago. Special message to anyone who's never been off Earth: look around you. Take a good *long* look around. You're in the best place there is. A fine place.

I said as much to Sue, and she laughed and said, "Even the last six weeks?" and I said, "I don't want to insult you, baby, but yes: even those six weeks in lousy quarantine at the lousy base hospital were good, compared to being any place else. But it was the longest six weeks I ever spent; I'll give you that." I pulled her down on top of me and kissed her again. "It was longer than twice the rest of the trip."

She struggled loose and patted me on the head the way I don't like. "Was it so bad really?"

"It was bad. It was lonesome and dangerous and – and disgusting, I guess is the best word for it."

"You mean the plague."

I snorted. "It wasn't a plague."

"Well, I wouldn't know," she said. "Just rumors. That thing of you recalling the crew after twelve hours of liberty, for six weeks of quarantine . . ."

"Yeah, I guess that would start rumors." I closed my eyes and laughed grimly. "Let 'em rumor. No one could dream up anything uglier than the truth. Give me another bucket of suds."

She did, and I kissed her hand as she passed it over. She took the hand right away and I laughed at her. "Scared of me or something?"

"Oh Lord no. Just . . . wanting to catch up. So much you've done, millions of miles, months and months . . . and all I know is you're back, and nothing else."

"I brought the Demon Lover back safe and sound," I kidded.

She colored up. "Don't talk like that." The Demon Lover was my Second, name of Purcell. Purcell was one of those guys who just has to go around making like a bull moose in fly-time, bellowing at the moon and banging his antlers against the rocks. He'd been to the house a couple or three times and said things about Sue that were so appreciative that I had to tell him to knock it off or he'd collect a punch in the mouth. Sue had liked him, though; well, Sue was always that way, always going a bit out of her way to get upwind of an animal like that. And I guess I'm one of 'em myself; anyway, it was me she married. I said, "I'm afraid ol' Purcell's either a blow-hard or he was just out of character when we rounded up the crew and brought 'em all back. We found 'em in honky-tonks and strip joints; we found 'em in the buzzoms of their families behaving like normal family men do after a long trip; but Purcell, we found him at the King George Hotel—" I emphasized with a forefinger "– alone by himself and fast asleep, where he tells us he went as soon as he got earthside. Said he wanted a soak in a hot tub and 24 hours sleep in a real I-G bed with sheets. How's that for a sailor ashore on his first leave?"

She'd gotten up to get me more ale. "I haven't finished this one yet!" I said.

She said oh and sat down again. "You were going to tell me about the trip."

"I was? Oh, all right, I was. But listen carefully, because this is one trip I'm going to forget as fast as I can, and I'm not going to do it again, even in my head."

I don't have to tell you about blastoff – that it's more like drift-off these days, since all long hops start from Outer Orbit satellites, out past the Moon – or about the flicker-field by which we hop faster than light, get dizzier than a five-year-old on a drug store stool, and develop more morning-sickness than Mom. That I've told you before.

So I'll start with planetfall on Mullygantz II, Terra's best bet to date for a colonial planet, five-nines Earth normal (that is, .99999) and just about as handsome a rock as ever circled a sun. We hung the blister in stable orbit and Purcell and I dropped down in a superscout with supplies and equipment for the ecological survey station. We expected to find things humming there, five busy people and a sheaf of completed reports, and we hoped we'd be the ones to take back the news that the next ship would be the colony ship. We found three dead and two sick, and knew right away that the news we'd be taking back was going to stop the colonists in their tracks.

Clement was the only one I'd known personally. Head of the station, physicist and ecologist both, and tops both ways, and he was one of the dead. Joe and Katherine Flent were dead. Amy Segal, the recorder – one of the best in Pioneer Service – was sick in a way I'll go into in a minute, and Glenda Spooner, the plant biologist, was – well, call it withdrawn. Retreated. Something had scared her so badly that she could only sit with her arms folded and her legs crossed and her eyes wide open, rocking and watching.

Anyone gets to striking hero medals ought to make a platter-sized one for Amy Segal. Like I said, she was sick. Her body temperature was wildly erratic, going from 102 all the way down to 96 and back up again. She was just this side of breakdown and must have been like that for weeks, slipping across the line for minutes at a time, hauling herself back for a moment or two, then sliding across again. But she knew Glenda was helpless, though physically in perfect shape, and she knew that even automatic machinery has to be watched. She not only dragged herself around keeping ink in the recording pens and new charts when the seismo's and hygro's and airsonde recorders needed them, but she kept Glenda fed; more than that, she fed herself.

She fed herself *close to fifteen thousand calories a day*. And she was forty pounds underweight. She was the weirdest sight you ever saw, her face full like a fat person's but her abdomen, from the lower ribs to the pubes, collapsed almost against her spine. You'd never have believed an organism could require so much food – not, that is, until you saw her eat. She'd rigged up a chopper out of the lab equipment because she actually couldn't wait to chew her food. She just dumped everything and anything edible into that gadget and propped her chin on the edge of the table by the outlet, and packed that garbage into her open mouth with both hands. If she could have slept it would have been easier but hunger would wake her after twenty minutes or so and back she'd go, chop and cram, guzzle and swill. If Glenda had been able to help – but there she was, she did it all herself, and when we got the whole story straight we found she'd been at it for nearly three weeks. In another three weeks they'd have been close to the end of their stores, enough for five people for anyway another couple of months.

We had a portable hypno in the first-aid kit on the scout, and we slapped it to Glenda Spooner with a reassurance tape and a normal sleep command, and just put her to bed with it. We bedded Amy down too, though she got a bit hysterical until we could make her understand through that fog of delirium that one of us would stand by every minute with premasticated rations. Once she understood that she slept like a corpse, but such a corpse you never want to see, lying there eating.

It was a lot of work all at once, and when we had it done Purcell wiped his face and said, "Five-nines Earth normal, hah. No malignant virus or bacterium. No toxic plants or fungi. Come to Mullygantz II, land of happiness and health."

"Nobody's used that big fat *no*," I reminded him. "The reports only say there's nothing bad here that we know about or can test for. My God, the best brains in the world used to kill AB patients by transfusing type O blood. Heaven help us the day we think we know everything that goes on in the universe."

We didn't get the whole story then; rather, it was all there but not in a comprehensible order. The key to it all was Amy Segal's personal log, which she called a "diary", and kept in hentracks called shorthand, which took three historians and a philologist a week to decode after we returned to Earth. It was the diary that fleshed the thing out for us, told us about these people and their guts and how they exploded all over each other. So I'll tell it, not the way we got it, but the way it happened.

To begin with it was a good team. Clement was a good head, one of those relaxed guys who always listens to other people talking. He could get a fantastic amount of work out of a team and out of himself too, and it never showed. His kind of drive is sort of a secret weapon.

Glenda Spooner and Amy Segal were wild about him in a warm respectful way that never interfered with the work. I'd guess that Glenda was more worshipful about it, or at least, with her it showed more. Amy was the little mouse with the big eyes that gets happier and stays just as quiet when her grand passion walks into the room, except maybe she works a little harder so he'll be pleased. Clement was bed-friends with both of them, which is the way things usually arrange themselves when there's an odd number of singles on a team. It's expected of them, and the wise exec keeps it going that way and plays no favorites, at least till the job's done.

The Flents, Katherine and Joe, were married, and had been for quite a while before they went Outside. His specialty was geology and mineralogy and she was a chemist, and just as their sciences supplemented each other so did their egoes. One of Amy's early "diary" entries says they knew each other so well they were one step away from telepathy; they'd work side by side for hours swapping information with grunts and eyebrows.

Just what kicked over all this stability it's hard to say. It wasn't a fine balance; you'd think from the look of things that the arrangement could stand a lot of bumps and friction. Probably it was an unlucky combination of small things all harmless in themselves, but having a critical-mass characteristic that nobody knew about. Maybe it was Clement's sick spell that triggered it; maybe the Flents suddenly went into one of those oh-God-what-did-I-ever-see-in-you phases that come over married people who are never separated; maybe it was Amy's sudden crazy yen for Joe Flent and her confusion over it. Probably the worst thing of all was that Joe Flent might have sensed how she felt and caught fire too. I don't know. I guess, like I said, that they all happened at once.

Clement getting sick like that. He was out after bio specimens and spotted a primate. They're fairly rare on Mullygantz II, big ugly devils maybe five feet tall but so fat they outweigh a man two to one. They're mottled pink and grey, and hairless, and they have a face that looks like an angry gorilla when it's relaxed, and a ridiculous row of little pointed teeth instead of fangs. They get around pretty good in the trees but they're easy to outrun on the ground, because they never learned to use their arms and knuckles like the great apes, but waddle over the ground with their arms held up in the air to get them out of the way. It fools you. They look so damn silly that you forget they might be dangerous.

So anyway, Clement surprised one on the ground and had it headed for the open fields before it knew what was happening. He ran it to a standstill, just by getting between it and the trees and then approaching it. The primate did all the running; Clement just maneuvered it until it was totally pooped and squatted down to wait its doom. Actually all the doom it would have gotten from Clement was to get stunned, hypoed, examined and turned loose, but of course it had no way of knowing that. It just sat there in the grass looking stupid and ludicrous and harmless in an ugly sort of way, and when Clement put out his hand it didn't move, and when he patted it on the neck it just trembled. He was slowly withdrawing his hand to get his stun-gun out when he said something or laughed – anyway, made a sound, and the thing bit him.

Those little bitty teeth weren't what they seemed. The gums are retractile and the teeth are really not teeth at all but serrated bone with all those little needles slanting inward like a shark's. The jaw muscles are pretty flabby, fortunately, or he'd have lost an elbow, but all the same, it was a bad bite. Clement couldn't get loose, and he couldn't reach around himself to get to the stun-gun, so he drew his flame pistol, thumbed it around to "low", and scorched the primate's throat with it. That was Clement, never wanting to do any more damage than he had to. The primate opened its mouth to protect its throat and Clement got free. He jumped back and twisted his foot and fell, and something burned him on the side of the face like a lick of hellfire. He scrabbled back out of the way and got to his feet. The primate was galloping for the woods on its stumpy little legs with its long arms up over its head—even then Clement thought it was funny. Then something else went for him in the long grass and he took a big leap out of its way.

He later wrote very careful notes on this thing. It was wet and it was nasty and it stunk beyond words. He said you could search your memory long afterwards and locate separate smells in that overall stench the way you can with the instruments of an orchestra. There was butyl mercaptan and rotten celery, excrement, formic acid, decayed meat and that certain smell which is like the taste of some brasses. The burn on his cheek smelt like hydrochloric acid at work on a hydrocarbon; just what it was.

The thing was irregularly spherical or ovoid, but soft and squashy. Fluids of various kinds oozed from it here and there – colorless and watery, clotted yellow like soft-boiled eggs, and blood. It bled more than anything ought to that needs blood; it bled in gouts from openings at random, and it bled cutaneously, droplets forming on its surface like the sweat on a glass of icewater. Cutaneously, did I say? That's not what Clement reported. It looked skinless – flayed was the word he used. Much of its surface was striated muscle fibre, apparently unprotected. In two places that he could see was naked brown tissue like liver, drooling and dripping excretions of its own.

And this thing, roughly a foot and a half by two feet and weighing maybe thirty pounds, was flopping and hopping in a spastic fashion, not caring which side was up (if it had an up) but always moving toward him.

Clement blew sharply out of his nostrils and stepped back and to one side – a good long step, with the agony of his scalded cheek to remind him that wherever the thing had come from, it was high up, and he didn't want it taking off like that again.

And when he turned like that, so did the thing, leaving behind it a trail of slime and blood in the beaten grass, a curved filthy spoor to show him it knew him and wanted him.

He confesses he does not remember dialling up the flame pistol, or the first squeeze of the release. He does remember circling the thing and pouring fire on it while it squirmed and squirted, and while he yelled sounds that were not words, until he and his weapon were spent and there was nothing where the thing had been but a charred wetness adding the smell of burned fat to all the others. He says in his unsparing report that he tramped around and around the thing, stamping out the grass-fire he had started, and shaking with revulsion, and that he squatted weakly in the grass weeping from reaction, and that only then did he think of his wounds. He broke out his pioneer's spectral salve and smeared it liberally on burns and bite both. He hunkered there until the analgesic took the pain away and he felt confident that the wide array of spansuled antibiotics was at work, and then he roused himself and slogged back to the base.

And to that sickness. It lasted only eight days or so, and wasn't the kind of sickness that ought to follow such an experience. His arm and his face healed well and quickly, his appetite was very good but not excessive, and his mind seemed clear enough. But during that time, as he put it in the careful notes he taped on the voice-writer, he felt things he had never felt before and could hardly describe. They were all things he had heard about or read about, foreign to him personally. There were faint shooting pains in his abdomen and back, a sense of pulse where no pulse should be – like that in a knitting bone, but beating in his soft tissues. None of it was beyond bearing. He had a constant black diarrhoea, but like the pains it never passed the nuisance stage. One vague thing he said about four times: that when he woke up in the morning he felt that he was in some way different from what he had been the night before, and he couldn't say how. Just . . . different.

And in time it faded away and he felt normal again. That was the whole damned thing about what had happened – he was a very resourceful guy, Clement was, and if he'd been gigged just a little more by this he'd have laid his ears back and worked until he *knew* what the trouble was. But he wasn't pushed into it that way, and it didn't keep him from doing his usual man-and-a-half's hard work each day. To the others he was unusually quiet, but if they noticed it at all it wasn't enough to remark about. They were all working hard too, don't forget. Clement slept alone these eight or nine days, and this wasn't remarkable either, only a little unusual, and not worth comment to either Glenda or Amy, who were satisfied, secure, and fully occupied women.

But then, here again was that rotten timing, small things on small things. This had to be the time of poor Amy Segal's trouble. It started over nothing at all, in the chem lab where she was doing the hurry-up-and-wait routine of a lengthy titration. Joe Flent came in to see how it was going, passed the time of day, did a little something here, something there with the equipment. He had to move along the bench just where Amy was standing, and, absorbed in what he was doing, he put out his hand to gesture her back, and went on with what he was doing. But –

She wrote it in her diary, in longhand, a big scrawl of it in the middle of those neat little glyphs of hers: "He *touched* me." All underlined and everything. All right, it was a nothing: I said that. It was an accident. But the accident had jarred her and she was made of fulminate of mercury all of a sudden. She stood where she was and let him press close to her, going on with his work, and she almost fainted. What makes these things happen . . .? Never mind; the thing happened. She looked at him as if she had never seen him before, the light on his hair, the shape of his ears and his jaw, the – well, all like that. Maybe she made a sound and maybe Joe Flent just sensed it, but he turned around and there they were, staring at each other in some sort of mutual hypnosis with God knows what flowing back and forth between them. Then Joe gave a funny little surprised grunt and did not walk, he ran out of there.

That doesn't sound like anything at all, does it? Whatever it was, though, it was enough to throw little Amy Segal into a flat spin of the second order, and pop her gimbal bearings. I've read that there used to be a lot of stress and strain between people about this business of sex. Well, we've pretty well cleared that up, in the way we humans generally clear things up, by being extreme about it. If you're single you're absolutely free. If you're married you're absolutely bound. If you're married and you get an external itch, you have your free choice – you stay married and don't scratch it, or you scuttle the marriage and you do scratch it. If you're single you respect the marriage bond just like anyone else; you don't, but I mean you *don't* go holing somebody else's hull.

All of which hardly needs saying, especially not to Amy Segal. But like a lot of fine fools before her, she was all mixed up with what she felt and what she thought she should feel. Maybe she's a throwback to the primitive, when everybody's concave was fair game to anyone else's convex. Whatever it was about her, it took the form of making her hate herself. She was walking around among those other people thinking, I'm no good, Joe's married and look at me, I guess I don't *care* he's married. What's the matter with me, how could I feel this way about Joe, I must be a monster, I don't deserve to be here among decent people. And so on. And no one to tell it to. Maybe if Clement hadn't been sick, or maybe if she'd had it in her to confide in one of the other women, or maybe – well, hell with maybes. She was half-blind with misery.

Reading the diary transcript later I wished I could put time back and space too and tap her on the shoulder and say come along, little girl, and then put her in a corner and say listen, knothead, get untied, will you? You got a yen, never mind, it'll pass. But as long as it lasts don't be ashamed of it. Damn it, that's all she needed, just a word like that . . .

Then Clement was well again and one night gave her the sign, and she jumped at it, and that was the most miserable thing of all, because after it was over she burst into tears and told him it was the last time, never again. He must've been no end startled. He missed the ferry there. He could've got the whole story if he'd tried, but he didn't. Maybe . . . maybe he was a little changed from what happened to him, after all. Anyway, poor Amy hit the bottom of the tank about then. She scribbled yards about it in her book. She'd just found out she responded to Clement just like always, and that proved to her that she couldn't love Joe after all, therefore her love wasn't real, therefore she wasn't worth loving,

therefore Joe would never love her. Little bubblehead! and the
only way out she could see was to force herself to be faithful to
somebody, so she was going to "purify her feelings" – that's what
she wrote – by being faithful to Joe, hence no more Clement and
of course no Joe. And with that decision she put her ductless
glands in a grand alliance with her insanity. Would you believe
that anyone in this day and age could have such a pot boiling
inside a fuzzy skull?

From that moment on Amy Segal was under forced draft.
Apparently no one said anything about it, but you just don't build
up incandescence in small dark places without somebody noticing. Katherine Flent must have tumbled early, as women do,
and probably said nothing about it, as some women sometimes
don't. Ultimately Joe Flent saw it, and what he went through
nobody will ever know. I know he saw it, and felt it, because of
what happened. Oh my God, what happened!

It must have been about now that Amy got the same strange
almost-sickness Clement had gone through. Vague throbbings and
shiftings in the abdomen, and the drizzles, and again that weird
thing about feeling different in the morning and not knowing why.
And when she was about halfway through the eight-day seige,
damn if Glenda Spooner doesn't seem to come down with it.
Clement did the reporting on this; he was seeing a lot more of
Glenda these days and could watch it. He noticed the similarity
with his own illness all right, though it wasn't as noticeable, and
called all hands for a report. Amy, possibly Glenda, and Clement
had it and passed it; the Flents never showed the signs. Clement
decided finally that it was just one of those things that people get
and no one knows why, like the common cold before Billipp
discovered it was an allergy to a gluten fraction. And the fact that
Glenda Spooner had had such a slight attack opened the possibility
that one or both Flents had had it and never known it – and that's
something else we'll never know for sure.

Well, one fine day Clement headed out to quarter the shale hills
to the north, looking for petroleum if he could find it and
anything else if he couldn't. Clement was a fine observer. Trouble with Clement, he was an ecologist, which is mostly a biologist,
and biologists are crazy.

The fine day, about three hours after he left, sprung a leak, and
the bottom dropped out of the sky – which didn't worry anyone
because everyone knew it wouldn't worry Clement.

Only he didn't come back.

That was a long night at the base. Twice searchers started out but they turned back in the first two hundred yards. Rain can come down like that if it wants to, but it shouldn't keep it up for so long. Morning didn't stop it, but as soon as it was dark grey outside instead of total black, the Flents and the two girls dropped everything and headed for the hills. Amy and Glenda went to the west and separated and searched the ridge until mid-afternoon, so it was all over by the time they got back. The Flents took the north and east, and it was Joe who found Clement.

That crazy Clement, he'd seen a bird's nest. He saw it because it was raining and because the fish-head stork always roosts in the rain; if it didn't its goofy glued-together nest would come unstuck. It's a big bird, larger than a terran stork, snow-white, wide-winged and easy to see, especially against a black shale bluff. Clement wanted a good look at how it sheltered its nest, which looks like half a pinecone as big as half a barrel – you'd think too big for the bird to keep dry. So up he went – and discovered that the fish-head stork's thick floppy neck conceals three, maybe four S-curves underneath all that loose skin. He was all of nine feet away from the nest, clinging to the crumbly rock wall, when he discovered it, the hard way. The stork's head shot out like a battering ram and caught him right on the breastbone, and down he went, and I guess that waterlogged shale was waiting for just this, because he started a really good rock-slide. He broke his leg and was buried up to the shoulder blades. He was facing up the cliff, with the rain beating down on him almost enough to tear his eyelids. He had nothing to look at except the underside of the nest, which his rockslide had exposed, and I imagine he looked at it until he understood, much against his will, that the nest was all that was holding up more loosened rock above it; and he put in the night that way, waiting for seepage to loosen the gunk that stuck the nest up there and send those tons of rock smack in his face. The leg was pretty bad and he probably passed out two or three times, but never long enough to suit him . . . *damn* it! I got a list this long of people who ought to have things like that happen to them. So it has to happen to Clement.

It was still raining in the morning when Joe Flent found him. Joe let out a roar to the westward where his wife was combing the rocks, but didn't wait to see if she'd heard. If she didn't, maybe there was a sort of telepathy between them like Amy said in her diary. Anyway, she arrived just in time to see it happen, but not in time to do anything about it.

She saw Joe bending over Clement's head and shoulders where they stuck out of the rock pile, and then she heard a short, sharp shout. It must have been Clement who shouted; he was facing uphill and could see it coming, nest and all. Katherine screamed and ran toward them, and then the new slide reached the bottom, and that was that for Clement.

But not for Joe. Something else got Joe.

It seemed to explode out of the rocks a split second before the slide hit. It took Joe Flent in the chest so hard it lifted him right off his feet and flung him down and away from the slide. Katherine screamed again as she ran, because the thing that had knocked Joe down was bouncing up and down in a crazy irregular hop, each one taking it closer to Joe as he lay on his back half stunned, and she recognized it for the thing that had attacked Clement the day the primate bit him.

She logged this report on the voicewriter and I heard the tape, and I wish they'd transcribe it and then destroy it. Nobody should hear a duty-bound horror-struck soul like that tell such a story. Read it, okay. But that torn-up monotone, oh God. She was having nine agonies at once, what with her hands all gone and what happened to Joe out there, and what he'd said . . . arrgh! I can't tell it without hearing it in my head.

Well. That stinking horror hopped up on Joe and he half sat up and it hopped again and landed right over his face and slumped there quivering, bleeding and streaming rain and acid. Joe flipped so hard his feet went straight up in the air and he seemed to hang there, standing on the back of his head and his shoulder-blades with his arms and legs doing a crazy jumping-jack flailing. Then he fell again with the monstrosity snugger than ever over his face and neck and head, and he squirmed once and then lay still, and that was when Katherine got to him.

Katherine went at that thing with her bare hands. One-half second contact, even in all that rain, was enough to pucker and shrivel her skin, and it must have felt like plunging her hands into smoking deep-fat. She didn't say what it felt like. She only said that when she grabbed at the thing to tear it away from Joe's face, it came apart in small slippery handfuls. She kicked at it and her foot went in and through it and it spilled ropy guts and gouted blood. She tore into it again, clawing and batting it away, and that was probably when she did the most damage to her hands. Then she had an idea from somewhere in that nightmare, fell back and took Joe's feet and dragged him twenty feet away – don't ask me how – and turned him over on his face so the last of that mess dropped off him. She skinned out of her shirt and knelt down and rolled him over and sat him up. She tried to wipe his face with the shirt but found she couldn't hold it, so she scooped her ruined hand under it and brought it up and mopped, but what she mopped at wasn't a face any more. On the tape she said, in that flat shredded voice, "I didn't realize that for a while."

She put her arms around Joe and rocked him and said, "Joey, it's Katherine, it's all right, honey. Katherine's here." He sighed once, a long, shuddering sigh and straightened his back, and a hole bigger than a mouth opened up in the front of his head. He said, "Amy? Amy?" and suddenly fought Katherine blindly. She lost her balance and her arm fell away from his back, and he went down. He made one great cry that raised echoes all up and down the ridge: "A . . . meeeee. . . ." and in a minute or two he was dead.

Katherine sat there until she was ready to go, and covered his face with the shirt. She looked once at the thing that had killed him. It was dead, scattered in slimy bits all over the edge of the rock-fall. She went back to the base. She didn't remember the trip. She must have been soaked and chilled to the bone-marrow. She apparently went straight to the voicewriter and reported in and then just sat there, three, four hours until the others got back.

Now if only somebody had been there to . . . I don't know. Maybe she couldn't have listened, after all that. Who knows what went on in her head while she sat there letting her blood run out of her hands on to the floor? I'd guess it was that last cry of Joe's, because of what happened when Glenda and Amy came in. It might have been so loud in her head that nobody else's voice could get in. But I still wish somebody had been there, somebody who knows about the things people say when they die. Sometimes they're already dead when they say those things; they don't mean anything. I saw an engineer get it when a generator threw a segment. He just said "Three-eighths . . . three-eighths . . ." What I'm trying to say, it didn't have to mean anything . . . Well, what's the difference now?

They came in dripping and tired, calling out. Katherine Flent didn't answer. They came into the recording shack, Amy first. Amy was half across the floor before she saw Katherine. Glenda was still in the doorway. Amy screamed, and I guess anyone would, seeing Katherine with her hair plastered around her face the way it had dried, and blood all over her clothes and the floor, and no shirt. She fixed her crazy eyes on Amy and got up slowly. Amy called her name twice but Katherine kept on moving, slow, steady, evenly. Between the heels of her ruined hands she held a skinning knife. She probably couldn't have held it tightly enough to do any damage, but I guess that didn't occur to Amy.

Amy stepped back toward the door and with one long step Katherine headed her off and herded her toward the other corner, where there was no way out. Amy glanced behind her, saw the trap, covered her face with her hands, stepped back, dropped her hands. "Katherine!" she screamed. "What is it? What is it? Did you find Clement? Quick!" she rapped at Glenda, who stood frozen in the doorway. "Get Joe."

At the sound of Joe's name Katherine moaned softly and leaped. She was met in midair by the same kind of thing that had killed her husband.

The soft horror caught Katherine off the floor in mid-leap and hurled her backward. Her head hit the corner of a steel relay-rack . . .

The stench in the small room was quite beyond description, beyond bearing. Amy staggered to the door, pushing an unresisting Glenda ahead of her . . .

And there they were as we found them, Purcell and me: one fevered freak that could out-eat six men, and one catatonic.

I sent Purcell out to the shale hill to see if there was enough left of Clement and Joe Flent for an examination. There wasn't, Animals had scattered Joe's remains pretty thoroughly, and Purcell couldn't find Clement at all, though he moved rocks till his hands bled. There had probably been more slides after that rain. Somehow, in those weeks when she maintained the basic instrumentation single-handed, Amy Segal had managed to drag Katherine out and bury her, and clean up the recording room, though nothing but burning would ever get all that smell out of it.

We left everything but the tapes and records. The scout was built for two men and cargo, and getting her off the ground with four wasn't easy. I was mighty glad to get back on the bridge of the flicker-ship and away from that five-nines hell. We stashed the two girls in a cabin next to the sick bay and quarantined them, just in case, and I went to work on the records, getting the story in about the order I've given it here.

And once I had it, there wasn't a thing I could do with it. Amy was at all times delirious, or asleep or eating; you could get very little from her, and even then you couldn't trust what you got. From Glenda you got nothing. She just lay still with that pleasant half-smile on her face and let the universe proceed without her. On a ship like ours we are the medical division, the skipper and the officers, and we could do nothing for these two but keep them fed and comfortable; otherwise, we mostly forgot they were aboard. Which was an error.

Status quo, then, far as I knew, from the time we left the planet until we made earthfall, the crew going about its business, the two girls in quarantine with Purcell filling the hopper with food for the one and spoon-feeding the other, and me locked up with the records, piecing and guessing and trying to make sense out of a limbless, eyeless monstrosity which apparently could appear from nowhere in midair, even indoors (like the one that killed Katherine Flent); which looked as if it could not live, but which still would attack and could kill. I got no place. I mulled over more theories than I'll go into, some of 'em pretty far-fetched, like a fourth-dimensional thing that . . . well, on the other hand, Nature can be pretty far-fetched too, as anyone who has seen the rear end of a mandrill will attest.

What do you know about seacucumbers, as another nauseating example?

We popped out of the flicker-field in due time, and Luna was good to see. We transferred to a rocket-ferry at Outer Orbit and dropped in smoothly, and came into the base here in quarantine procedure, impounding ferry and all. The girls were at last put into competent hands, and the crew were given the usual screening. Usual or not, it's about as thorough as a physical examination can get, and after they'd all been cleared, and slept six hours, and gone through it again and been cleared again, I gave them 72-hour passes, renewable, and turned 'em loose.

I was more than anxious to go along too, but by that time I was up to the eyeballs in specialists and theorists, and in some specialties and theories that began to get too fascinating for even a home-hungry hound like me to ignore. That was when I called you and said how tied up I was and swore I'd be out of there in another day. You were nice about that. Of course, I had no idea it wouldn't be just one more day, but another six weeks.

Right after the crew was turned loose they called me out of the semantics section, where we were collating all notes and records, into the psych division.

They had one of the . . . the things there.

I have to hand it to those guys. I guess they were just as tempted as Clement was when he first saw one, to burn it into nothing as fast as it could be burned. I saw it, and that was my first impulse. God. No amount of clinical reporting like Clement's could give you the remotest idea of just how disgusting one of those things is.

They'd been working over Glenda Spooner. Catatonics are hard to do anything with, but they used some high-potency narcosyntheses and some field inductions, and did a regression. They found out just what sort of a catatonic she was. Some, you probably know, retreat like that as a result of some profound shock – after they have been shocked. It's an escape. But some go into that seize-up in the split second *before* the shock. Then it isn't an escape, it's a defense. And that was our girl Glenda.

They regressed her until they had her located out in the field, searching for Clement. Then they brought her forward again, so that in her mind she was contacting Amy, slogging through the rain back to the base. They got to where Amy entered the recording shack and screamed, seeing Katherine Flent looking that way. There they located the exact split second of trauma, the moment when something happened which was so terrible that Glenda had not let herself see it.

More dope, more application of the fields through the helmet they had her strapped into. They regressed her a few minutes and had her approach that moment again. They tried it again, and some more, making slight adjustments each time, knowing that sooner or later they would have the exact subtle nudge that would push her through her self-induced barrier, make her at last experience the thing she was so afraid to acknowledge.

And they did it, and when they did it, the soft gutty *thing* appeared, slamming into a technician fifteen feet away, hitting him so hard it knocked him flat and slid him spinning into the far wall. He was a young fellow named Petri and it killed him. Like

Katherine Flent, he died probably before he felt the acid burns. He went right into the transformer housing and died in a net of sparks.

And as I said, these boys had their wits about them. Sure, someone went to help Petri (though not in time) and someone else went after a flame pistol. He wasn't in time either; because when he got back with it, Shellabarger and Li Kyu had the glass bell off a vacuum rig and had corralled the filthy thing with it. They slid a resilient mat under it and slapped a coupling on top and jetted the jar full of liquid argon.

This time there was no charred mass, no kicked-apart, rain-soaked scatter of parts to deal with. Here was a perfect specimen, if you can call such a thing perfect, frozen solid while it was still alive and trying to hop up and down and find someone to bubble its dirty acids on. They had it to keep, to slice up with a microtome, even to revive, if anyone had the strong guts.

Glenda proved clearly that with her particular psychic makeup, she had chosen the right defense. When she saw the thing, she died of fright. It was that, just that, that she had tried to avoid with catatonia. The psycho boys breached it, and found out just how right she had been. But at least she didn't die uselessly, like Flent and Clement and poor Katherine, Because it was her autopsy that cleared things up.

One thing they found was pretty subtle. It was a nuclear pattern in the cells of the connective tissue quite unlike anything any of them had seen before. They checked Amy Segal for it and found the same thing. They checked me for it and didn't. That was when I sent out the recall order for the whole crew. I didn't think any of them would have it, but we had to be sure. If that got loose on Earth . . .

All but one of the crew had a clean bill when given the new test, and there wasn't otherwise anything wrong with that one.

The other thing Glenda's autopsy revealed was anything but subtle.

Her abdomen was empty.

Her liver, kidneys, almost all of the upper and all of the lower intestine were missing, along with the spleen, the bladder, and assorted tripe of that nature. Remaining were the uterus, with the Fallopian tubes newly convoluted and the ovaries tacked right to the uterus itself; the stomach; a single loop of what had once been upper intestine, attached in a dozen places to various spots on the wall of the peritoneum. It emptied directly into a rectal segment, without any distinctive urinary system, much like the primitive equipment of a bird.

Everything that was missing, they found under the bell jar.

Now we knew what had hit Katherine Flent, and why Amy was empty and starved when we found her. Joe Flent had been killed by . . . one of the . . . well, by something that erupted at him as he bent over the trapped Clement. Clement himself had been struck on the side of the face by such a thing – and whose was that?

Why, that primate's. The primate he walked into submission, and touched, and frightened.

It bit him in panic terror. Joe Flent was killed in a moment of panic terror too – not his, but Clement's, who saw the rock-slide coming. Katherine Flent died in a moment of terror – not hers, but Amy's, as Amy crouched cornered in the shack and watched Katherine coming with a knife. And the one which had appeared on earth, in the psych lab, why, that needed the same thing to be born in – when the boys forced Glenda Spooner across a mental barrier she could not cross and live.

We had everything now but the mechanics of the thing, and that we got from Amy, the bravest woman yet. By the time we were through with her, every man in the place admired her g— uh, dammit, not that. Admired her fortitude. She was probed and goaded and prodded and checked, and finally went through a whole series of advanced exploratories. By the time the exploratories began, about six weeks had gone by, that is, six weeks from Katherine Flent's death, and Amy was almost back to normal; she'd tapered off on the calories, her abdomen had filled out to almost normal, her temperature had steadied and by and large she was okay. What I'm trying to put over is that she had some intestines for us to investigate – *she'd grown a new set*.

That's right. She'd thrown her old ones at Katherine Flent.

There wasn't anything wrong with the new ones, either. At the time of her first examination everything was operating but the kidneys; their function was being handled by a very simple, very efficient sort of filter attached to the ventral wall of the perito-neum. We found a similar organ in autopsying poor Glenda Spooner. Next to it were the adrenals, apparently transferred there from their place astride the original kidneys. And sure enough, we found Amy's adrenals placed that way, and not on the new kidneys. In a fascinating three-day sequence we saw those new kidneys completed and begin to operate, while the surrogate organ which had been doing their work atrophied and went quiet. It stayed there, though, ready.

The climax of the examination came when we induced panic terror in her, with a vivid abreaction of the events in the recording shack the day Katherine died. Bless that Amy, when we suggested it she grinned and said, "Sure!"

But this time it was done under laboratory conditions, with a high-speed camera to watch the proceedings. Oh God, did they proceed!

The film showed Amy's plain pleasant sleeping face with its stainless halo of psych-field hood, which was hauling her subjective self back to that awful moment in the records shack. You could tell the moment she arrived there by the anxiety, the tension, the surprise and shock that showed on her face. "Glenda!" she screamed, "Get Joe!" – and then . . .

It looked at first as if she was making a face, sticking out her tongue. She was making a face all right, the mask of purest, terminal fear, but that wasn't a tongue. It came out and out, unbelievably fast even on the slow-motion frames of the high-speed camera. At its greatest, the diameter was no more than two inches, the length . . . about eight feet. It arrowed out of her mouth, and even in midair it contracted into the roughly spherical shape we had seen before. It struck the net which the doctors had spread for it and dropped into a plastic container, where it hopped and hopped, sweated, drooled, bled and died. They tried to keep it alive but it wasn't meant to live more than a few minutes.

On dissection they found it contained all Amy's new equipment, in sorry shape. All abdominal organs can be compressed to less than two inches in diameter, but not if they're expected to work again. These weren't.

The thing was covered with a layer of muscle tissue, and dotted with two kinds of ganglia, one sensory and one motor. It would keep hopping as long as there was enough of it left to hop, which was what the motor system did. It was geotropic, and it would alter its muscular spasms to move it toward anything around it that lived and had warm blood, and that's what the primitive sensory system was for.

And at last we could discard the fifty or sixty theories that had been formed and decide on one: that the primates of Mullygantz II had the ability, like a terran sea-cucumber, of ejecting their internal organs when frightened, and of growing a new set; that in a primitive creature this was a survival characteristic, and the more elaborate the ejected matter the better the chances for the animal's survival. Probably starting with something as simple as a lizard's discarding a tail-segment which just lies there and squirms to distract a pursuer, this one had evolved from "distract" to "attract" and finally to "attack." True, it took a fantastic amount of forage for the animal to supply itself with a new set of innards, but for vegetarian primates on fertile Mullygantz II, this was no problem.

The only problem that remained was to find out exactly how terrans had become infected, and the records cleared that up. Clement got it from a primate's bite. Amy and Glenda got it from Clement. The Flents may well never have had it. Did that mean that Clement had bitten those girls? Amy said no, and experiments proved that the activating factor passed readily from any mucous tissue to any other. A bite would do it, but so would a kiss. Which didn't explain our one crew-member who "contracted" the condition. Nor did it explain what kind of a survival characteristic it is that can get transmitted around like a virus infection, even to species.

Within that same six weeks of quarantine, we even got an answer to that. By a stretch of the imagination, you might call the thing a virus. At least, it was a filterable organism which, like the tobacco mosaic or the slime mold, had an organizing factor. You might call it a life form, or a complex biochemical action, basically un-alive. You could call it symbiote. Symbiotes often go out of their way to see to it that the hosts survive.

After entering a body, these creatures multiplied until they could organize, and then went to work on the host. Connective tissue and muscle fiber was where they did most of their work. They separated muscle fibers all over the peritoneal walls and diaphragm, giving a layer to the entrails and the rest to the exterior. They duplicated organic functions with their efficient, primitive little surrogate organs and glands. They hooked the illium to the stomach wall and to the rectum, and in a dozen places to their new organic structures. Then they apparently stood by.

When an emergency came every muscle in the abdomen and throat cooperated in a single, synchronized spasm, and the entrails, sheathed in muscle fiber and dotted with nerve ganglia, compressed into a long tube and was forced out like a bullet. Instantly the revised and edited abdomen got to work, perforating the new stomach outlet, sealing the old, and starting the complex of simple surrogates to work. And as long as enough new building material was received fast enough, an enormously accelerated rebuilding job started, blue-printed God knows how from God knows what kind of a cellular memory, until in less than two months the original abdominal contents, plus revision, were duplicated, and all was ready for the next emergency.

Then we found that in spite of its incredible and complex hold on its own life and those of its hosts, it had no defense at all against one of humanity's oldest therapeutic tools, the RF fever cabinet. A high frequency induced fever of 108 sustained for seven minutes killed it off as if it had never existed, and we found that the "revised" gut was in every way as good as the original, if not better (because damaged organs were replaced with healthy ones if there was enough of them left to show original structure) – and that by keeping a culture of the Mullygantz "virus" we had the ultimate, drastic treatment for forty-odd types of abdominal cancer – including two types for which we'd had no answer at all!

So it was we lost the planet, and gained it back with a bonus. We could cause this thing and cure it and diagnose it and use it, and the new world was open again. And that part of the story, as you probably know, came out all over the newsfax and 'casters, which is why I'm getting a big hello from taxi drivers and doormen . . .

"But the 'fax said you wouldn't be leaving the base until tomorrow noon!" Sue said after I had spouted all this to her and at long last got it all off my chest in one great big piece.

"Sure. They got that straight from me. I heard rumors of a parade and speeches and God knows what else, and I wanted to get home to my walkin' talkin' wettin' doll that blows bubbles."

"You're silly."

"C'mere."

The doorbell hummed.

"I'll get it," I said, "and throw 'em out. It's probably a reporter."

But Sue was already on her feet. "Let me, let me. You just stay there and finish our drink." And before I could stop her she flung into the house and up the long corridor to the foyer.

I chuckled, drank my ale and got up to see who was horning in. I had my shoes off so I guess I was pretty quiet. Though I didn't need to be. Purcell was roaring away in his best old salt fashion, "Let's have us another quickie, Susie, before the Space Scout gets through with his red carpet treatment tomorrow – miss me, honey?" . . . while Sue was imploringly trying to cover his mouth with her hands.

Maybe I ran; I don't know. Anyway, I was there, right behind her. I didn't say anything. Purcell looked at me and went white. "Skipper . . ."

And in the hall mirror behind Purcell, my wife met my eyes. What she saw in my face I cannot say, but in hers I saw panic terror.

In the small space between Purcell and Sue, something appeared. It knocked Purcell into the mirror, and he slid down in a welter of blood and stinks and broken glass. The recoil slammed Sue into my arms. I put her by so I could watch the tattered, bleeding thing on the floor hop and hop until it settled down on the nearest warm living thing it could sense, which was Purcell's face.

I let Sue watch it and crossed to the phone and called the commandant. "Gargan," I said, watching. "Listen, Joe, I found out that Purcell lied about where he went in that first liberty. Also why he lied." For a few seconds I couldn't seem to get my breath. "Send the meat wagon and an ambulance, and tell Harry to get ready for another hollowbelly. . . . Yes, I said, one dead. . . . Purcell, dammit. Do I have to draw you a cartoon?" I roared, and hung up.

I said to Sue, who was holding on to her flat midriff, "That Purcell, I guess it did him good to get away with things under my nose. First that helpless catatonic Glenda on the way home, then you. I hope you had a real good time, honey."

It smelled bad in there so I left. I left and walked all the way back to the Base. It took about ten hours. When I got there I went to the Medical wing for my own fever-box cure and to do some thinking about girls with guts, one way or another. And I began to wait. They'd be opening up Mullygantz II again, and I thought I might look for a girl who'd have the . . . fortitude to go back with me. A girl like Amy.

Or maybe Amy.

# THE REGION BETWEEN

## Harlan Ellison

*It would be difficult to compile an anthology of extreme sf and not include anything by Harlan Ellison. At times Ellison (b. 1934) epitomizes "Mr Extreme", though never for the fun of it. I can't think of any other author working in the field who has produced so many challenging, daring and thought-provoking stories. I would argue that from the mid-to-late 1960s Ellison was the pre-eminent writer of short sf, even amidst a field that at the time also had the astonishing talents of Roger Zelazny, Thomas Disch, Ursula Le Guin, Brian Aldiss, Michael Moorcock, etc. etc. Ellison, who became a Grand Master of the SFWA in 2006, has continued to produce works of considerable power and energy for over fifty years, yet he never sits on his laurels. In the 1960s, when he was winning award after award, he set himself the task of shaking up the field, making it take a long, hard look at itself. The result was the massive anthology* Dangerous Visions *(1967) which even now, forty years on, is still pretty astonishing. I resisted the urge to reprint anything from it, even though it includes many "extreme" stories.*

*Curiously, despite Ellison's immense output, much of it battering down the barriers of sf and fantasy, I didn't find it hard to decide which story to use. I had read "The Region Between" when it first appeared in* Galaxy *back in 1970. It had originally been commissioned as one of a set of stories by*

*different authors who all used a common starting point as set
out in the story's prologue, written by Keith Laumer. All five
stories can be found in* Five Fates *(1970).*

*Ellison's contribution was a longer work than one usually
expects from him, but he nevertheless sustained its bombard-
ment of ideas and feelings throughout. What's more, Ellison
created a story that demanded a different format to allow for
full expression. The result was a typesetter's nightmare but, as
you will see, the experience not only makes this story all the
more fascinating, it actually takes you into the story itself. This
story has been specially revised for this printing.*

"Left hand," the thin man said tonelessly. "Wrist up."
William Bailey peeled back his cuff; the thin man put
something cold against it, nodded toward the nearest door.

"Through there, first slab on the right," he said, and turned
away.

"Just a minute," Bailey started. "I wanted—"

"Let's get going, buddy," the thin man said. "That stuff is
fast."

Bailey felt something stab up under his heart. "You mean –
you've already . . . that's all there is to it?"

"That's what you came for, right? Slab one, friend. Let's go."

"But – I haven't been here two minutes—"

"Whatta you expect – organ music? Look, pal," the thin man
shot a glance at the wall clock, "I'm on my break, know what I
mean?"

"I thought I'd at least have time for . . . for . . ."

"Have a heart, chum. You make it under your own power, I
don't have to haul you, see?" The thin man was pushing open
the door, urging Bailey through into an odor of chemicals and
unlive flesh. In a narrow, curtained alcove, he indicated a
padded cot.

"On your back, arms and legs straight out."

Bailey assumed the position, tensed as the thin man began
fitting straps over his ankles.

"Relax. It's just if we get a little behind and I don't get back to
a client for maybe a couple hours and they stiffen up . . . well,
them issue boxes is just the one size, you know what I mean?"

A wave of softness, warmness swept over Bailey as he lay back.

"Hey, you didn't eat nothing the last twelve hours?" The thin man's face was a hazy pink blur.

"I awrrr mmmm," Bailey heard himself say.

"OK, sleep tight, paisan . . ." The thin man's voice boomed and faded. Bailey's last thought as the endless blackness closed in was of the words cut in the granite over the portal to the Euthanasia Center:

> ". . . send me your tired, your poor,
> your hopeless, yearning to be free.
> To them I raise the lamp beside the brazen door . . ."

# I

Death came as merely a hyphen. Life, and the balance of the statement followed instantly. For it was only when Bailey died that he began to live.

Yet he could never have called it "living"; no one who had ever passed that way could have called it "living." It was something else. Something quite apart from "death" and something totally unlike "life."

Stars passed through him as he whirled outward.

Blazing and burning, carrying with them their planetary systems, stars and more stars spun through him as though traveling down invisible wires into the dark behind and around him.

Nothing touched him.

They were as dust motes, rushing silently past in incalculable patterns, as Bailey's body grew larger, filled space in defiance of the Law that said two bodies could not coexist in the same space at the same instant. Greater than Earth, greater than its solar system, greater than the galaxy that contained it, Bailey's body swelled and grew and filled the universe from end to end and ballooned back on itself in a slightly flattened circle.

His mind was everywhere.

A string cheese, pulled apart in filaments too thin to be measurable, Bailey's mind was there and there and there. And there.

It was also in the lens of the Succubus.

Murmuring tracery of golden light, a trembling moment of

crystal sound. A note, rising and trailing away infinitely high, and followed by another, superimposing in birth even as its predecessor died. The voice of a dream, captured on spiderwebs. There, locked in the heart of an amber perfection, Bailey was snared, caught, trapped, made permanent by a force that allowed his Baileyness to roam unimpeded anywhere and everywhere at the instant of death.

Trapped in the lens of the Succubus.

[Waiting: empty. A mindsnake on a desert world, frying under seven suns, poised in the instant of death; its adversary, a fuzzball of cilia-thin fibers, sparking electrically, moving toward the mindsnake that a moment before had been set to strike and kill and eat. The mindsnake, immobile, empty of thought and empty of patterns of light that confounded its victims in the instants before the killing strike. The fuzzball sparked toward the mindsnake, its fibers casting about across the vaporous desert, picking up the mole sounds of things moving beneath the sand, tasting the air and feeling the heat as it pulsed in and away. It was improbable that a mindsnake would spend all that light-time, luring and intriguing, only at the penultimate moment to back off – no, not back off: shut down. Stop. Halt entirely. But if this was not a trap, if this was not some new tactic only recently learned by the ancient mindsnake, then it had to be an opportunity for the fuzzball. It moved closer. The mindsnake lay empty: waiting.]

Trapped in the lens of the Succubus.

[Waiting: empty. A monstrous head, pale blue and veined, supported atop a swan-neck by an intricate latticework yoke-and-halter. The Senator from Nougul, making his final appeal for the life of his world before the Star Court. Suddenly plunged into silence. No sound, no movement, the tall, emaciated body propped on its seven league crutches, only the trembling of balance – having nothing to do with life – reminding the assembled millions that an instant before this husk had contained a pleading eloquence. The fate of a world quivered in a balance no less precarious than that of the Senator. What had happened? The amalgam of wild surmise that grew in the Star Court was scarcely less compelling than had been the original circumstances bringing Nougul to this place, in the care of the words of this Senator. Who now stood, crutched, silent and empty: waiting.]

Trapped in the lens of the Succubus.

[Waiting: empty. The Warlock of Whirrl, a power of darkness and evil. A force for chaos and destruction. Poised above his runic symbols, his bits of offal, his animal bones, his stringy things without names, quicksudden gone to silence. Eyes devoid of the pulverized starlight that was his sight. Mouth abruptly slack, in a face that had never known slackness. The ewe lamb lay still tied to the obsidian block, the graven knife with its odious glyphs rampant, still held in the numb hand of the Warlock. And the ceremony was halted. The forces of darkness had come in gathering, had come to their calls, and now they roiled like milk vapor in the air, unable to go, unable to do, loath to abide. While the Warlock of Whirrl, gone from his mind, stood frozen and empty: waiting.]

Trapped in the lens of the Succubus.

[Waiting: empty. A man on Promontory, fifth planet out from the star Proxima Centauri, halted in mid-step. On his way to a bank of controls and a certain button, hidden beneath three security plates. This man, this inestimably valuable kingpin in the machinery of a war, struck dumb, struck blind, in a kind of death – not even waiting for another moment of time. Pulled out of himself by the gravity of non-being, an empty husk, a shell, a dormant thing. Poised on the edges of their continents, two massed armies waited for that button to be pushed. And would never be pushed, while this man, this empty and silent man, stood rooted in the sealed underworld bunker where precaution had placed him. Now inaccessible, now inviolate, now untouchable, this man and this war stalemated frozen. While the world around him struggled to move itself a fraction of a thought toward the future, and found itself incapable, hamstrung, empty: waiting.]

Trapped in the lens of the Succubus.

And . . .

[Waiting: empty. A subaltern, name of Pinkh, lying on his bunk, contemplating his fiftieth assault mission. Suddenly gone. Drained, lifeless, neither dead nor alive. Staring upward at the bulkhead ceiling of his quarters. Cloudless burnished metal. He, dreamless, staring upward. While beyond his ship raged the Montag-Thil war. Sector 888 of the Galactic Index. Somewhere between the dark star Montag and the Nebula Cluster in Thil Galaxy. Pinkh, limbo-lost and unfeeling, needing the infusion of a soul, the filling up of a life-force. Pinkh, needed in this war more than any other man, though the Thils did not know it . . . until the moment his essence was stolen. Now, Pinkh, lying there one shy of a fifty-score of assault missions. But unable to aid his world. Unable, undead, unalive, empty: waiting.]

While Bailey . . .

Floated in a region between. Hummed in a nothingness as great as everywhere. Without substance. Without corporeality. Pure thought, pure energy, pure Bailey. Swaying motionlessly, curtailed, yet susceptive. Trapped in the lens of the Succubus.

## 1½

More precious than gold, more sought-after than uranium, more scarce than yinyang blossom, more needed than salkvac, rarer than diamonds, more valuable than force-beads, more negotiable than the vampyr extract, dearer than 2038 vintage Château Luxor, more prized than the secret of nanoneural surgery, more lusted-after than the twin-vagina'd trollops of Kanga . . .

**Souls.**

Thefts had begun in earnest five hundred years before. Random thefts. Stolen from the most improbable receptacles. From beasts and men and creatures who had never been thought to possess "**souls.**" Who was stealing them was never known. Far out somewhere, in reaches of space (or not-space) (or the interstices between space and not-space) that had no names, had no dimensions, whose light had never even reached the outmost thin edge of known space, there lived or existed or *were* creatures or things or entities or forces

– *someone* – who needed the life-force of the creepers and walkers and lungers and swimmers and fliers who inhabited the known universe. Souls vanished, and the empty husks remained.

Thieves they were called, for no other name applied so well, bore in its single syllable such sadness and sense of resignation. They were called Thieves, and they were never seen, were not understood, had never given a clue to their nature or their purpose or even their method of theft. And so nothing could be done about their depredations. They were as Death: handiwork observed, but a fact of life without recourse to higher authority. Death and the Thieves were final in what they did.

So the known universes – the Star Court and the Galactic Index and the Universal Meridian and the Perseus Confederacy and the Crab Complex – shouldered the reality of what the Thieves did with resignation, and stoicism. No other course was open to them. They could do no other.

But it changed life in the known universe.

It brought about the existence of soul-recruiters, who pandered to the needs of the million billion trillion worlds. Shanghaiers. Graverobbers of creatures not yet dead. In their way, thieves, even as the Thieves. Beings whose dark powers and abilities enabled them to fill the tables-of-organization of any world with fresh souls from worlds that did not even suspect *they* existed, much less the Court, the Index, the Meridian, the Confederacy or the Complex. If a key figure on a fringe world suddenly went limp and soulless, one of the soul-recruiters was contacted and the black traffic was engaged in. Last resort, final contact, most reprehensible but expeditious necessity, they stole and supplied.

One such was the Succubus.


He was gold. And he was dry. These were the only two qualities possessed by the Succubus that could be explicated in human terms. He had once been a member of the dominant race that skimmed across the sand-seas of a tiny planet, fifth from the star-sun labeled Kappel-112 in Canes Venatici. He had long-since ceased to be anything so simply identified.

The path he had taken, light-years long and several hundred Terran-years long, had brought him from the sand-seas and a minimum of "face" – the only term that could even approximate the one measure of wealth his race valued – to a cove of goldness and dryness near the hub of the Crab Complex. His personal worthiness could now be measured only in terms of hundreds of billions of dollars, unquenchable light sufficient to sustain his offspring unto the nine thousandth generation, a name that could only be spoken aloud or in movement by the upper three social sects of the Confederacy's races, more "face" than any member of his race had ever possessed . . . more, even, than that held in myth by Yaele.

Gold, dry, and inestimably worthy: the Succubus.

Though his trade was one publicly deplored, there were only seven entities in the known universe who were aware that the Succubus was a soul-recruiter. He kept his two lives forcibly separated.

"Face" and graverobbing were not compatible.

He ran a tidy business. Small, with enormous returns. Special souls, selected carefully, no seconds, no hand-me-downs. Quality stock.

And through the seven highly-placed entities who knew him – Nin, FawDawn, Enec-L, Milly(Bas)Kodal, a Plain without a name, Cam Royal and Pl – he was channelled only the loftiest commissions.

He had supplied souls of all sorts in the five hundred years he had been recruiting. Into the empty husk of a master actor on Bolial V. Into the waiting body of a creature that resembled a plant aphid, the figurehead of a coalition labor movement, on Wheechitt Eleven and Wheechitt Thirteen. Into the unmoving form of the soul-emptied daughter of the hereditary ruler of Golaena Prime. Into the untenanted revered shape of an arcane maguscientist on Donadello III's seventh moon, enabling the five hundred-zodjam religious cycle to progress. Into the lusterless spark of light that sealed the laocoönian group-mind of Orechnaen's Dispassionate Bell-Silver Dichotomy.

Not even the seven who functioned as go-betweens for the Succubus's commissions knew where and how he obtained such fine, raw, unsolidified souls. His competitors dealt almost exclusively in the atrophied, crustaceous souls of beings whose thoughts and beliefs and ideologies were so ingrained that the souls came to their new receptacles already stained and imprinted. But the Succubus . . .

Cleverly-contrived, youthful souls. Hearty souls. Plastic and ready-to-assimilate souls. Lustrous, inventive souls. The finest souls in the known universe.

The Succubus, as determined to excel in his chosen profession as he was to amass "face," had spent the better part of sixty years roaming the outermost fringes of the known universe. He had carefully observed many races, noting for his purpose only those that seemed malleable, pliant, far removed from rigidity.

He had selected, for his purpose:

The Steechii
Amassanii
Cokoloids
Flashers
Griestaniks
Bunanits
Condolis
Tratravisii

and Humans.

On each planet where these races dominated, he put into effect subtle recruiting systems, wholly congruent with the societies in which they appeared:

The Steechii were given eternal dreamdust.

The Amassanii were given doppelgänger shifting.

The Cokoloids were given the Cult of Rebirth.

The Flashers were given proof of the Hereafter.

The Griestaniks were given ritual mesmeric trances.

The Bunanits were given (imperfect) teleportation.

The Condolis were given an entertainment called Trial by Nightmare Combat.

The Tratravisii were given an underworld motivated by high incentives for kidnapping and mind-blotting. They were also given a wondrous narcotic called Nodabit.

The Humans were given Euthanasia Centers.

And from these diverse channels the Succubus received a steady supply of prime souls. He received Flashers and skimmers and Condolis and ether-breathers and Amassanii and perambulators and Bunanits and gill-creatures and . . .

**William Bailey.**

Trapped in the lens of the Succubus.

Bailey, cosmic nothingness, electrical potential spread out to the ends of the universe and beyond, nubbin'd his thoughts. Dead. Of that, no doubt. Dead and gone. Back on Earth, lying cold and faintly blue on a slab in the Euthanasia Center. Toes turned up. Eyeballs rolled up in their sockets. Rigid and gone.

And yet alive. More completely alive than he had ever been, than *any* human being had ever conceived of being. Alive with all of the universe, one with the clamoring stars, brother to the infinite empty spaces, heroic in proportions that even myth could not define.

He knew everything. Everything there had ever been to know, everything that was, everything that would be. Past, present, future . . . all were merged and met in him. He was on a feeder line to the Succubus, waiting to be collected, waiting to be tagged and filed even as his alabaster body back on Earth would be tagged and filed. Waiting to be cross-indexed and shunted off to a waiting empty husk on some far world. All this he knew.

But one thing separated him from the millions of souls that had gone before him.

He didn't want to go.

Infinitely wise, knowing all, Bailey knew every other soul that had gone before had been resigned with soft acceptance to what was to come. It was a new life. A new voyage in another body. And all the others had been fired by curiosity, inveigled by strangeness, wonder-struck with being as big as the known universe and going *somewhere else*.

But not Bailey.

He was rebellious.

He was fired by hatred of the Succubus, inveigled by thoughts of destroying him and his feeder-lines, wonder-struck with being the only one – the *only* one! – who had ever thought of revenge. He was, somehow, strangely, not tuned in with being rebodied, as all the others had been. *Why am I different?* he wondered. And of all the things he knew . . . he did not know the answer to that.

Inverting negatively, atoms expanded to the size of whole galaxies, stretched out membraned, osmotically breathing whole star-systems, inhaling blue-white stars and exhaling quasars,

Bailey the known universe asked himself yet another question, even more important:

*Do I* WANT *to do something about it?*

Passing through a zone of infinite cold, the word came back to him from his own mind in chill icicles of thought:

*Yes.*

And borne on comets plunging frenziedly through his cosmic body, altering course suddenly and traveling at right angles in defiance of every natural law he had known when "alive," the inevitable question responding to a *yes* asked itself:

*Why should I?*

Life for Bailey on Earth had been pointless. He had been a man who did not fit. He had been a man driven to the suicide chamber literally by disorientation and frustration.

I was called to the office of the Social Director of my residence block. Frankly, I was frightened. I knew I hadn't done anything to be afraid about, but ever since I'd been a child, ever since I'd been called to the office of the school principal, just the being *summoned* had made my gut tight, made me feel like I wanted to go to the bathroom.

He made me wait half an hour, on a bench, damn him, with a gaggle of weirdos who looked like they hadn't had their heads scrubbed and customized in seven months.

Finally, the box called my name and I dropped to his office, and he was sitting in one of those informal conversation-groupings of chairs and coffee table that instantly put me off.

"Mr. Bailey," he said. Smiled. Hearty bastard. I walked over and sat down even before he suggested I sit. He didn't drop the smile for a second. He was up to anything.

"Why don't we get right to it," he said. I smiled back at him, but I felt trapped, really hemmed-in.

"I've been looking at your tag-chart, Mr. Bailey, and well, I hesitate to make any jump conclusions here, but it *appears* you've been neglecting your relaxation periods."

Damn him! Damn him!

"I see here, during the month of September, that you worked overtime at least . . . what is it . . . uh . . . eleven hours."

"Is there a law against that?"

"Oh, no . . . no, of course not. It just seems to us here at the block that you're perhaps, uh, overdoing it a bit."

"Working."

"Yes. Working."

"Has my block steward complained? Has my EEG been erratic? Am I being accused of something?"

"No, of course not! My lord, man, there's no need to be so defensive! We're only trying to find out if something is, well, disturbing you."

"If I'd been able to, I'd have killed the sonofabitch; right then and right there. In his damned conversation grouping. It would have made fine conversation for his office staff. Come in and find him brained to death with his own coffee urn."

"Nothing's disturbing me."

"Then you'll pardon me if I feel it apropos to ask why you aren't taking your proper relaxation periods, Mr. Bailey."

"I feel like keeping busy."

"Ah, but all work and no play—"

The omnipresent melancholy that had consumed him on an Earth bursting with over-population was something to which he had no desire to return. Then why this frenzy to resist being shunted into the body of a creature undoubtedly living a life more demanding, more exciting – *anything* had to be better than what he'd come from – more *alive*? Why this fanatic need to track back along the feeder-lines to the Succubus, to destroy the one who had saved him from oblivion? Why this need to destroy a creature who was merely fulfilling a necessary operation-of-balance in a universe singularly devoid of balance?

In that thought lay the answer, but he did not have the key. He turned off his thoughts. He was Bailey no more.

And in that instant the Succubus pulled his soul from the file and sent it where it was needed. He was certainly Bailey no more.

Subaltern Pinkh squirmed on his spike-palette, and opened his eye. His back was stiff. He turned, letting the invigorating short-spikes tickle his flesh through the heavy mat of fur. His mouth felt dry and loamy.

It was the morning of his fiftieth assault mission. Or was it? He seemed to remember lying down for a night's sleep . . . and then a very long dream without substance. It had been all black and empty; hardly something the organizer would have programmed. It must have malfunctioned.

He slid sidewise on the spike-palette, and dropped his enormous furred legs over the side. As his paws touched the tiles a whirring from the wall preceded the toilet facility's appearance. It swiveled into view, and Pinkh looked at himself in the full-length mirror. He looked all right. Dream. Bad dream.

The huge, bearlike subaltern shoved off the bed, stood to his full seven feet, and lumbered into the duster. The soothing powders cleansed away his sleep-fatigue and he emerged, blue pelt glistening, with bad dreams almost entirely dusted away. Almost. Entirely. He had a lingering feeling of having been . . . somewhat . . . *larger* . . .

The briefing colors washed across the walls, and Pinkh hurriedly attached his ribbons. It was informalwear today. Three yellows, three ochres, three whites and an ego blue.

He went downtunnel to the briefing section, and prayed. All around him his sortie partners were on their backs, staring up at the sky dome and the random (programmed) patterns of stars in their religious significances. Montag's Lord of Propriety had programmed success for today's mission. The stars swirled and shaped themselves and the portents were reassuring to Pinkh and his fellows.

The Montag-Thil War had been raging for almost one hundred years, and it seemed close to ending. The dark star Montag and the Nebula Cluster in Thil Galaxy had thrown their might against each other for a century; the people themselves were weary of war. It would end soon. One or the other would make a mistake, the opponent would take the advantage, and the strike toward peace would follow immediately. It was merely a matter of time. The assault troops – especially Pinkh, a planetary hero – were suffused with a feeling of importance, a sense of the relevance of what they were doing. Out to kill, certainly, but with the sure knowledge that they were working toward a worthwhile goal. Through death, to life. The portents had told them again and again, these last months, that this was the case.

The sky dome turned golden and the stars vanished. The assault troops sat up on the floor, awaited their briefing.

It was Pinkh's fiftieth mission.

His great yellow eye looked around the briefing room. There were more young troopers this mission. In fact . . . he was the only veteran. It seemed strange.

Could Montag's Lord of Propriety have planned it this way? But where were Andakh and Melnakh and Gorekh? They'd been here yesterday.

*Was it just yesterday?*

He had a strange memory of having been – asleep? – away? – unconscious? – what? – something. As though more than one day had passed since his last mission. He leaned across to the young trooper on his right and placed a paw flat on the other's. "What day is today?" The trooper flexed palm and answered, with a note of curiosity in his voice, "It's Former. The ninth." Pinkh was startled. "What cycle?" he asked, almost afraid to hear the answer.

"Third," the young trooper said.

The briefing officer entered at that moment, and Pinkh had no time to marvel that it was *not* the next day, but a full cycle later. Where had the days gone? What had happened to him? Had Gorekh and the others been lost in sorties? Had he been wounded, sent to repair and only now been remanded to duty? Had he been wounded and suffered amnesia? He remembered a Lance Corporal in the Throbbing Battalion who had been seared and lost his memory. They had sent him back to Montag, where he had been blessed by the Lord of Propriety himself. What had happened to him?

Strange memories – not his own, all the wrong colors, weights and tones wholly alien – kept pressing against the bones in his forehead.

He was listening to the briefing officer, but also hearing an undertone. Another voice entirely. Coming from some other place he could not locate.

■■■ Wake, you great ugly fur-thing, you! Wake
up, look around you. One hundred years, slaughtering. Why can't you see what's being done to you?
How dumb can you be? The Lords of Propriety; they
set you up, you yokel, you naïve idiot. Dolt! ■■
Yeah, *you*, Pinkh! Listen to me. You can't block me
out . . . you'll hear me. Bailey. You're the one, Pinkh,
the special one. They trained you for what's coming
up . . . no, don't block me out, you imbecile . . .
don't ■■■■■ I'll be here, you can't ign■■■■

The background noise went on, but he would not listen. It was
sacrilegious. Saying things about the Lord of Propriety. Even the
Thil Lord of Propriety was sacrosanct in Pinkh's mind. Even
though they were at war, the two Lords were eternally locked
together in holiness. To blaspheme even the enemy's Lord was
unthinkable.

*Yet he had thought it.*

He shuddered with the enormity of what had passed in his
thoughts, and knew he could never go to release and speak of it.
He would submerge the memory, and pay strict attention to the
briefing officer who was

"This cycle's mission is a straightforward one. You will be
under the direct linkage of Subaltern Pinkh, whose reputation is
known to all of you."

Pinkh inclined with the humbleness movement.

"You will drive directly into the Thil labyrinth, chivvy and
harass a path to Groundworld, and there level as many targets-of-
opportunity as you are able, before you're destroyed. After this
briefing you will re-assemble with your sortie leaders and fully
familiarize yourselves with the target-cubes the Lord has commanded to be constructed."

He paused, and stared directly at Pinkh, his golden eye
gone to pinkness with age and dissipation. But what he said
was for all of the sappers. "There is one target you will *not*
strike. It is the Maze of the Thil Lord of Propriety. This is
irrevocable. You will not, repeat *not* strike near the Maze of
the Lord."

Pinkh felt a leap of pleasure. This was the final strike. It was
preamble to peace. A suicide mission; he ran eleven thankfulness
prayers through his mind. It was the dawn of a new day for

Montag and Thil. The Lords of Propriety were good. The Lords
held all cupped in their holiness.

*Yet he had thought the unthinkable.*

"You will be under the direct linkage of Subaltern Pinkh," the
briefing officer said again. Then, kneeling and passing down the
rows of sappers, he palmed good death with honor to each of
them. When he reached Pinkh, he stared at him balefully for a
long instant, as though wanting to speak. But the moment passed,
he rose, and left the chamber.

They went into small groups with the sortie leaders and
examined the target-cubes. Pinkh went directly to the briefing
officer's cubicle and waited patiently till the older Montagasque's
prayers were completed.

When his eye cleared, he stared at Pinkh.

"A path through the labyrinth has been cleared."

"What will we be using?"

"Reclaimed sortie craft. They have all been outfitted with
diversionary equipment."

"Linkage level?"

"They tell me a high six."

"They *tell* you?" He regretted the tone even as he spoke.

The briefing officer looked surprised. As if his desk had
coughed. He did not speak, but stared at Pinkh with the same
baleful stare the Subaltern had seen before.

"Recite your catechism," the briefing officer said, finally.

Pinkh settled back slowly on his haunches, ponderous weight
downdropping with grace. Then:

> "Free flowing, free flowing, all flows
> "From the Lords, all free, all fullness,
> "Flowing from the Lords.
>> "What will I do
>> "What will I do
>> "What will I do without my Lords?

> "Honor in the dying, rest is honor, all honor
> "From the Lords, all rest, all honoring,
> "To honor my Lords.
>> "This I will do
>> "This I will do
>> "I will live when I die for my Lords."

And it was between the First and Second Sacredness that the darkness came to Pinkh. He saw the briefing officer come toward him, reach a great palm toward him, and there was darkness . . . the same sort of darkness from which he had risen in his own cubicle before the briefing. Yet, not the same. *That* darkness had been total, endless, with the feeling that he was . . . somehow . . . larger . . . greater . . . as big as all space . . .

And this darkness was like being turned off. He could not think, could not even think that he was unthinking. He was cold, and not there. Simply: not there.

Then, as if it had not happened, he was back in the briefing officer's cubicle, the great bearlike shape was moving back from him, and he was reciting the Second Sacredness of his catechism.

What had happened . . . he did not know.

"Here are your course coordinates," the briefing officer said. He extracted the spool from his pouch and gave it to Pinkh. The subaltern marveled again at how old the briefing officer must be: the hair of his chest was almost gray.

"Sir," Pinkh began. Then stopped. The briefing officer raised a palm. "I understand, Subaltern. Even to the most reverent among us there come moments of confusion." Pinkh smiled. He *did* understand.

"Lords," Pinkh said, palming the briefing officer with fullness and propriety.

"Lords," he replied, palming honor in the dying.

Pinkh left the briefing officer's cubicle and went to his own place.

As soon as he was certain the subaltern was gone, the briefing officer, who was *very* old, linked-up with someone else, far away; and he told him things.

# 3

First, they melted the gelatin around him. It was hardly gelatin, but it had come to be called jell by the sappers, and the word had stuck. As the gelatin stuck. Face protected, he lay in the ten troughs, in sequence, deliquescing the gelatinous substance around him. Finally, pincers that had been carefully padded lifted him from the tenth trough, and slid him along the track to his sortie craft. Once inside pilot country, stretched out face down, he felt two hundred wires insert themselves into the jell, into the fur, into his body. The brain-wires were the last to fix. As each wire hissed from its spool and locked onto the skull-contacts, Pinkh felt himself merge more completely, integrate fully, a little more integration with the craft. At last, the final wire ran in like hot ice, and Pinkh was metal-flesh, bulkheadskin, eyescanners, bonerivets, plasticartilege, artery/ventricle/instep/neuron/capacitors/molecules/transistors,

```
BEASTC
C      R
R   i  A
A      F
F      T
TBEAST
```

all of him as one, totality, metal-man, furred-vessel, essence of mechanism, soul of inanimate, life in force-drive, linkage of mind with power plant. Pinkh the ship. Sortie Craft 90 named Pinkh.

And the others: linked to him.

Seventy sappers, each encased in jell, each wired up, each a mind to its sortie craft. Seventy, linked in telepathically with Pinkh, and Pinkh linked into his own craft, and all of them instrumentalities of the Lord of Propriety.

The great carrier wing that bore them made escape orbit and winked out of normal space.

Here●Not Here.

In an instant gone.

(Gone where!?!)

Inverspace.

Through the gully of inverspace to wink into existence once again at the outermost edge of the Thil labyrinth.

Not Here●Here.

Confronting a fortified tundra of space crisscrossed by deadly lines of force. A cosmic fireworks display. A cat's cradle of vanishing, appearing and disappearing threads of a million colors; each one receptive to all the others. Cross one, break one, interpose . . . and suddenly uncountable others home in. Deadly ones. Seeking ones. Stunners and drainers and leakers and burners. The Thil labyrinth.

Seventy-one sortie craft hung quivering – the last of the inverspace coronas trembling off and gone. Through the tracery of force-lines the million stars of the Thil Galaxy burned with the quiet reserve of ice crystals. And there, in the center, the Nebula Cluster. And there, in the center of the Cluster, Groundworld.

"Link in with me."

Pinkh's command fled and found them. Seventy beastcraft tastes, sounds, scents, touches came back to Pinkh. His sappers were linked in.

"A path has been cleared through the labyrinth for us. Follow. And trust. Honor."

"In the dying," came back the response, from seventy minds of flesh-and-metal.

They moved forward. Strung out like fish of metal with minds linked by thought, they surged forward following the lead craft. Into the labyrinth. Color burned and boiled past, silently sizzling in the vacuum. Pinkh detected murmurs of panic, quelled them with a damping thought of his own. Images of the still pools of Dusnadare, of deep sighs after a full meal, of Lord-worship during the days of First Fullness. Trembling back to him, their minds quieted. And the color beams whipped past on all sides, without up or down or distance. But never touching them.

Time had no meaning. Fused into flesh/metal, the sortie craft followed the secret path that had been cleared for them through the impenetrable labyrinth.

Pinkh had one vagrant thought: *Who cleared this for us?*

And a voice from somewhere far away, a voice that was his own, yet someone else's – the voice of a someone who called himself a bailey – said, *That's it! Keep thinking what they don't want you to think.*

But he put the thoughts from him, and time wearied itself and succumbed, and finally they were there. In the exact heart of the Nebula Cluster in Thil Galaxy.

Groundworld lay fifth from the source star, the home sun that had nurtured the powerful Thil race till it could explode outward.

"Link in to the sixth power," Pinkh commanded.

They linked. He spent some moments reinforcing his command splices, making the interties foolproof and trigger-responsive. Then he made a prayer, and they went in.

*Why am I locking them in so close,* Pinkh wondered, damping the thought before it could pass along the lines to his sappers. *What am I trying to conceal? Why do I need such repressive control? What am I trying to avert?*

Pinkh's skull thundered with pain. Two minds were at war inside him, he knew that. He *SUDDENLY* knew it.

*Who is that?*

*It's me, you clown!*

*Get out! I'm on a mission . . . it's import –*

*It's a fraud! They've prog –*

*Get out of my head listen to me you idiot I'm trying to tell you something you need to know I won't listen I'll override you I'll block you I'll damp you no listen don't do that I've been someplace you haven't been and I can tell you about the Lords oh this can't be happening to me not to me I'm a devout man fuck that garbage listen to me they lost you man they lost you to a soul stealer and they had to get you back because you were their specially programmed killer they want you to Lord oh Lord of Propriety hear me now hear me your most devout worshipper forgive these blasphemous thoughts I can't control you any more you idiot I'm fading fading fading Lord oh Lord hear me I wish only to serve you. Only to suffer the honor in the dying.*

*Peace through death. I am the instrumentality of the Lords. I know what I must do.*

*That's what I'm trying to tell you . . .*

And then he was gone in the mire at the bottom of Pinkh's mind. They were going in.

They came down, straight down past the seven moons, broke through the cloud cover, leveled out in a delta wing formation and streaked toward the larger of the two continents that formed ninety per cent of Groundworld's land mass. Pinkh kept them at supersonic speed, blurring, and drove a thought out to his sappers: "We'll drop straight down below a thousand feet and give them the shock wave. Hold till I tell you to level off."

They were passing over a string of islands – causeway-linked beads in a pea-green sea – each one covered from shore to shore with teeming housing dorms that commuted their residents to the

# HARLAN ELLISON

main continents and the complexes of high-rise bureaucratic towers.

"Dive!" Pinkh ordered.

The formation angled sharply forward, as though it was hung on puppet strings, then fell straight down.

The metalflesh of Pinkh's ship-hide began to heat.

Overlapping armadillo plates groaned; Pinkh pushed their speed; force-bead mountings lubricated themselves, went dry, lubricated again; they dropped down; follicle thin fissures were grooved in the bubble surfaces; sappers began to register fear, Pinkh locked them tighter; instruments coded off the far right and refused to register; the island-chain flew up toward them; pressure in the gelatin trough flattened them with g's; now there was enough atmosphere to scream past their sortie craft and it whistled, shrilled, howled, built and climbed; gimbal-tracks rasped in their mountings; down and down they plunged, seemingly bent on thundering into the islands of Groundworld; "Sir! Sir!"; "Hold steady, not yet . . . not yet . . . I'll tell you when . . . not yet . . ."

Pushing an enormous bubble of pressurized air before them, the delta wing formation wailed straight down toward the specks of islands that became dots, became buttons, became masses, became everything as they rushed up and filled the bubble sights from side to side –

"Level out! *Now!* Do it, do it, *level now!*"

And they pulled out, leveled off and shot away. The bubble of air, enormous, solid as an asteroid, thundering down unchecked . . . hit struck burst broke with devastating results. Pinkh's sortie craft plunged away, and in their wake they left exploding cities, great structures erupting, others trembling, shuddering, then caving in on themselves. The shock wave hit and spread outward from shore to shore. Mountains of plasteel and lathite volcano'd in blossoms of flame and flesh. The blast-pit created by the air bubble struck to the core of the island-chain. A tidal wave rose like some prehistoric leviathan and boiled over one entire spot of land. Another island broke up and sank almost at once. Fire and walls of plasteel crushed and destroyed after the shock wave.

The residence islands were leveled as Pinkh's sortie craft vanished over the horizon, still traveling at supersonic speed.

They passed beyond the island-chain, leaving in their wake dust and death, death and ruin, ruin and fire.

"Through death to peace," Pinkh sent.

"Honor," they responded, as one.

(Far away on Groundworld, a traitor smiled.)

(In a Maze, a Lord sat with antennae twined, waiting.)

(Flesh and metal eased.)

(In ruins, a baby whose exoskeleton had been crushed, crawled toward the pulsing innards of its mother.)

(Seven moons swung in their orbits.)

(A briefing officer on Montag knew it was full, golden.)

*Oh, Lords, what I have done, I have done for you.*

**Wake up. Will you wake up, Pinkh! The mission is—**

The other thing, the bailey, was wrenching at him, poking its head up out of the slime. He thrust it back down firmly. And made a prayer.

"Sir," the thought of one of his sappers came back along the intertie line, "did you say something?"

"Nothing," Pinkh said. "Keep in formation."

He locked them in even tighter, screwing them down with mental shackles till they gasped.

The pressure was building.

A six-power linkup, and the pressure was building.

*I am a hero*, Pinkh thought, *I can do it*.

Then they were flashing across the Greater Ocean and it blurred into an endless carpet of thick heaving green; Pinkh felt sick watching it whip by beneath him; he went deeper into ship and the vessel felt no sickness. He fed the stability of his nausea-submerged, helpfully, along the neural interstices.

They were met by the Thil inner defense line over empty ocean. First came the sea-breathers but they fell short when Pinkh ordered his covey to lift for three thousand feet. They leveled off just as the beaks swooped down in their land-to-sea parabolas. Two of them snouted and perceived the range, even as they were viciously beamed into their component parts by Pinkh's outermost sappers. But they'd already fed back the trajectories, and suddenly the sky above them was black with the blackmetal bodies of beaks, flapping, dropping, squalling as they cascaded into the center of the formation. Pinkh felt sappers vanish from the lineup and fed the unused power along other lines, pulling the survivors tighter under his control. "Form a sweep," he commanded.

The formation re-grouped and rolled in a graceful gull-wing maneuver that brought them craft-to-craft in a fan. "Plus!" Pinkh ordered, cutting in – with a thought – the imploding beam. The beams of each sortie craft fanned out, overlapping, making an impenetrable wall of deadly force. The beaks came whirling back up and careened across the formation's path. Creatures of metal and mindlessness. Wheels and carapaces. Blackness and berserk rage. Hundreds. Entire eyries.

When they struck the soft pink fan of the overlapping implosion beams, they whoofed in on themselves, dropped instantly.

The formation surged forward.

Then they were over the main continent. Rising from the exact center was the gigantic mountain atop which the Thil Lord of Propriety lived in his Maze.

"Attack! Targets of opportunity!" Pinkh commanded, sending impelling power along the linkup. His metal hide itched. His eyeball sensors watered. In they went, again.

"Do not strike at the Lord's Maze," one of the sappers thought.

AND PINKH
THREW UP!!
A WALL OF!
THOUGHT!!!
THAT DREW
THE !!!!!!!!!!!!
THOUGHT!!!
OFF THE!!!!! . . . . . . . . . . . . .ezam s'drol eht ta ekirts ton od
LINKUP SO
IT DID!!!!!!!!
NOT REACH
THE OTHER
SAPPERS!!!!
BUT HIT!!!!!!
THE WALL!!
AND BROKE
LIKE FOAM!

Why did I do that? We were briefed not to attack the Lord's Maze. It would be unthinkable to attack the Lord's Maze. It would precipitate even greater war than before. The war would *never* end. Why did I stop my sapper from reiterating the order? And why haven't *I* told them not to do it? It was stressed at the briefing. They're linked in so very tightly, they'd obey in a heartbeat – anything I said. What is happening? I'm heading for the mountain! Lord!

*Listen to me, Pinkh. This war has been maintained by the Lords of Propriety for a hundred years. Why do you think it was made heresy to even think negatively about the opposing Lord? They keep it going, to feed off it. Whatever they are, these Lords, they come from the same pocket universe and they live off the energy of men at war. They* must *keep the war going or they'll die. They programmed you to be their secret weapon. The war was reaching a stage where both Montag and Thil want peace, and the Lords can't have that. Whatever they are, Pinkh, whatever kind of creature they are, wherever they come from, for over a hundred years they've held your two galaxies in their hands, and they've used you. The Lord isn't in his Maze, Pinkh. He's safe somewhere else. But they planned it between them. They knew if a Montagasque sortie penetrated to Groundworld and struck the Maze, it would keep the war going indefinitely. So they programmed you, Pinkh. But before they could use you, your soul was stolen. They put my soul in you, a man of Earth, Pinkh. You don't even know where Earth is, but my name is Bailey. I've been trying to reach through to you. But you always shut me out – they had you programmed too well. But with the linkup pressure, you don't have the strength to keep me out, and I've got to let you know you're programmed to strike the Maze. You can stop it, Pinkh. You can avoid it all. You can end this war. You have it within your power, Pinkh. Don't strike the Maze. I'll re-direct you. Strike where the Lords are hiding. You can rid your galaxies of them, Pinkh. Don't let them kill you. Who do you think arranged for the path through the labyrinth? Why do you think there wasn't more effective resistance? They* wanted *you to get through. To commit the one hideous crime they could not forgive.*

The words reverberated in Pinkh's head as his sortie craft followed him in a tight wedge, straight for the Maze of the Lord.

"I – no, I—" Pinkh could not force thoughts out to his sappers. He was snapped shut. His mind was aching, the sound of straining and creaking, the buildings on the island-chain ready to crumble. Bailey inside, Pinkh inside, the programming of the Lords inside . . . all of them pulling at the fiber of Pinkh's mind.

For an instant the programming took precedence. "New directives. Override previous orders. Follow me in!"

They dove straight for the Maze.

*No, Pinkh, fight it! Fight it and pull out. I'll show you where they're hiding. You can end this war!*

The programming phasing was interrupted, Pinkh abruptly opened his great golden eye, his mind synched in even more tightly with his ship, and at that instant he knew the voice in his head was telling him the truth. He *remembered*:

Remembered the endless sessions.

Remembered the conditioning.

Remembered the programming.

Knew he had been duped.

Knew he was not a hero.

Knew he had to pull out of this dive.

Knew that at last *he* could bring peace to both galaxies.

He started to think *pull out, override* and fire it down the remaining linkup interties . . .

And the Lords of Propriety, who left very little to chance, who had followed Pinkh all the way, contacted the Succubus, complained of the merchandise they had bought, demanded it be returned . . .

Bailey's soul was wrenched from the body of Pinkh. The subaltern's body went rigid inside its jell trough, and, soulless, empty, rigid, the sortie craft plunged into the mountaintop where the empty Maze stood. It was followed by the rest of the sortie craft.

The mountain itself erupted in a geysering pillar of flame and rock and plasteel.

One hundred years of war was only the beginning.

Somewhere, hidden, the Lords of Propriety – umbilicus-joined with delight shocks spurting softly pink along the flesh-linkage joining them – began their renewed gluttonous feeding.

# 4

Bailey was whirled out of the Montagasque subaltern's body. His soul went shooting away on an asymptotic curve, back along the feeder-lines, to the soul files of the Succubus.

# 5

This is what it was like to be in the soul station.
Round. Weighted with the scent of grass. Perilous in that the music was dynamically contracting: souls had occasionally become too enriched and had gone flat and flaccid.

There was a great deal of white space.

Nothing was ranked, therefore nothing could be found in the same place twice; yet it didn't matter, for the Succubus had only to focus his lens and the item trembled into a special awareness.

Bailey spent perhaps twelve minutes reliving himself as a collapsing star then revolved his interfaces and masturbated as Anne Boleyn.

He savored mint where it smells most poignant, from deep in the shallow earth through the roots of the plant, then extended himself, extruded himself through an ice crystal and lit the far massif of the highest mountain on an onyx asteroid – recreating The Last Supper in chiaroscuro.

He burned for seventeen hundred years as the illuminated letter "B" on the first stanza of a forbidden enchantment in a papyrus volume used to summon up the imp James Fenimore Cooper then stood outside himself and considered his eyes and their hundred thousand bee-facets.

He allowed himself to be born from the womb of a tree sloth and flickered into rain that deluged a planet of coal for ten thousand years. And he beamed. And he sorrowed.

Bailey, all Bailey, soul once more, free as all the universes, threw himself toward the furthermost edge of the slightly flattened parabola that soared free as infinite, limitless dark.

He filled the dark with deeper darkness and bathed in fountains of brown wildflowers. Circles of coruscating violet streamed from his fingertips, from the tip of his nose, from his genitals, from the tiniest fibrilating fibers of hair that coated him. He shed water and hummed.

Then the Succubus drew him beneath the lens.

And Bailey was sent out once more.

Waste not, want not.

# 6

He was just under a foot tall. He was covered with blue fur. He had a ring of eyes that circled his head. He had eight legs. He smelled of fish. He was low to the ground and he moved very fast.

He was a stalker-cat, and he was first off the survey ship on Belial. The others followed, but not too soon. They always waited for the cat to do its work. It was safer that way. The Filonii had found that out in ten thousand years of exploring their universe. The cats did the first work, then the Filonii did theirs. It was the best way to rule a universe.

Belial was a forest world. Covered in long continents that ran from pole-to-pole with feathertop trees, it was ripe for discovery.

Bailey looked out of his thirty eyes, seeing around himself in a full 360° spectrum. Seeing all the way up into the ultraviolet, seeing all the way down into the infra-red. The forest was silent. Absolutely no sound. Bailey, the cat, would have heard a sound, had there been a sound. But there was no sound.

No birds, no insects, no animals, not even the whispering of the feathertop trees as they struggled toward the bright hot-white sun. It was incredibly silent.

Bailey said so.

The Filonii went to a condition red.

*No* world is silent. And a forest world is *always* noisy. But this one was silent.

They were out there, waiting. Watching the great ship and the small stalker-cat that had emerged from it.

Who they were, the cat and the Filonii did not know. But they were there, and they were waiting for the invaders to make the first move. The stalker-cat glided forward.

Bailey felt presences. Deep in the forest, deeper than he knew he could prowl with impunity. They were in there, watching him as he moved forward. But he was a cat, and if he was to get his fish, he would work. The Filonii were watching. *Them*, in there, back in the trees, *they* were watching. *It's a bad life*, he thought. *The life of a cat is a nasty, dirty, bad one.*

Bailey was not the first cat ever to have thought that thought. It was the litany of the stalker-cats. They knew their place, had always known it, but that was the way it was; it was the way it had always been. The Filonii ruled, and the cats worked. And the universe became theirs.

Yet it wasn't shared. It was the Filonii universe, and the stalker-cats were hired help.

The fine mesh cap that covered the top and back of the cat's head glowed with a faint but discernible halo. The sunbeams through which he passed caught at the gold filaments of the cap and sent sparkling radiations back toward the ship. The ship stood in the center of the blasted area it had cleared for its prime base.

Inside the ship, the team of Filonii ecologists sat in front of the many process screens and saw through the eyes of the stalker-cat. They murmured to one another as first one, then another, then another saw something of interest. "Cat, lad," one of them said softly, "still no sound?"

"Nothing yet, Brewer. But I can feel them watching."

One of the other ecologists leaned forward. The entire wall behind the hundred screens was a pulsing membrane. Speak into it at any point and the cat's helmet picked up the voice, carried it to the stalker. "Tell me, lad, what does it feel like?"

"I'm not quite sure, Kicker. I'm getting it mixed. It feels like the eyes staring . . . and wood . . . and sap . . . and yet there's mobility. It can't be the trees."

"You're sure."

"As best I can tell right now, Kicker. I'm going to go into the forest and see."

"Good luck, lad."

"Thank you, Driver. How is your goiter?"

"I'm fine, lad. Take care."

The stalker-cat padded carefully to the edge of the forest. Sunlight slanted through the feathertops into the gloom. It was cool and dim inside there.

Now, all eyes were upon him.

The first paw in met springy, faintly moist and cool earth. The fallen feathers had turned to mulch. It smelled like cinnamon. Not overpoweringly so, just pleasantly so. He went in . . . all the way. The last the Filonii saw on their perimeter screens − twenty of the hundred − were his tails switching back and forth. Then the tails were gone and the seventy screens showed them dim, strangely-shadowed pathways between the giant conifers.

"Cat, lad, can you draw any conclusions from those trails?"

The stalker padded forward, paused. "Yes. I can draw the conclusion they aren't trails. They go fairly straight for a while, then come to dead ends at the bases of the trees. I'd say they were drag trails, if anything."

"What was dragged? Can you tell?"

"No, not really, Homer. Whatever was dragged, it was thick and fairly smooth. But that's all I can tell." He prodded the drag trail with his secondary leg on the left side. In the pad of the paw were tactile sensors.

The cat proceeded down the drag trail toward the base of the great tree where the trail unaccountably ended. All around him the great conifers rose six hundred feet into the warm, moist air.

Sipper, in the ship, saw through the cat's eyes and pointed out things to his fellows. "Some of the qualities of *Pseudotsuga Taxifolia*, but definitely a conifer. Notice the bark on that one. Typically *Eucalyptus Regnans* . . . yet notice the soft red spores covering the bark. I've never encountered that particular sort of thing before. They seem to be melting down the trees. In fact . . ."

He was about to say the trees were *all* covered with the red spores, when the red spores attacked the cat.

They flowed down the trees, covering the lower bark, each one the size of the cat's head, and when they touched, they ran together like jelly. When the red jelly from one tree reached the base of the trunk, it fused with the red jelly from the other trees.

"Lad . . ."

"It's all right, Kicker. I see them."

The cat began to pad backward: slowly, carefully. He could easily outrun the fusing crimson jelly. He moved back toward the verge of the clearing. Charred, empty of life, blasted by the Filonii hackshafts, not even a stump of the great trees above ground, the great circles where the trees had stood now merely reflective surfaces set flush in the ground. Back.

Backing out of life . . . backing into death.

The cat paused. What had caused *that* thought?

"Cat! Those spores . . . whatever they are . . . they're forming into a solid . . ."

*Backing out of life . . . backing into death*

my name is
    bailey and i'm in
        here, inside you.
            i was stolen from

| my | called | is | | wants |
| body | the | some | | somewhere, he – |
| by | succubus. | kind | | there in the stars |
| a | he, | of | recruiter from out | |
| creature | *it* | puppeteer, a sort of | | |

The blood-red spore thing stood fifteen feet high, formless, shapeless, changing, malleable, coming for the cat. The stalker did not move: within him, a battle raged.

"Cat, lad! Return! Get back!"

Though the universe belonged to the Filonii, it was only at moments when the loss of a portion of that universe seemed imminent that they realized how important their tools of ownership had become.

Bailey fought for control of the cat's mind.

Centuries of conditioning fought back.

The spore thing reached the cat and dripped around him. The screens of the Filonii went blood-red, then went blank.

The shriek of something alive that should not be . . . broken glass, perhaps. The thing that had come from the trees oozed back into the forest, shivered for a moment, vanished, taking the cat with it.

The cat focused an eye. Then another. In sequence he opened and focused each of his thirty eyes. The place where he lay came into full luster. He was underground. The shapeless walls of the place dripped with sap and several colors of viscous fluid. The fluid dripped down over bark that seemed to have been formed as stalactites, the grain running long and glistening till it tapered into needle tips. The surface on which the cat lay was planed wood, the grain exquisitely formed, running outward from a coral-colored pith in concentric circles of hues that went from coral to dark teak at the outer perimeter.

The spores had fissioned, were heaped in an alcove. Tunnels ran off in all directions. Huge tunnels twenty feet across.

The mesh cap was gone.

The cat got to his feet. Bailey was there, inside, fully awake, conversing with the cat.

"Am I cut off from the Filonii?"

"Yes, I'm afraid you are."

"Under the trees."

"That's right."

"What is that spore thing?"

"I know, but I'm not sure you'd understand."

"I'm a stalker; I've spent my life analyzing alien life-forms and alien ecology. I'll understand."

"They're mobile symbiotes, conjoined with the bark of these trees. Singly, they resemble most closely anemonic anaerobic bacteria, susceptible to dichotomisation; they're anacusic, anabiotic, anamnestic, and feed almost exclusively on ancyclosto-miasis."

"Hookworms?"

"Big hookworms. Very big hookworms."

"The drag trails?"

"That's what they drag."

"But none of that makes any sense. It's impossible."

"So is reincarnation among the Yerbans, but it occurs."

"I don't understand."

"I told you you wouldn't."

"How do *you* know all this?"

"You wouldn't understand."

"I'll take your word for it."

"Thank you. There's more about the spores and the trees, by the way. Perhaps the most important part."

"Which is?"

"Fused, they become a quasi-sentient gestalt. They can communicate, borrowing power from the treehosts."

"That's even *more* implausible!"

"Don't argue with me, argue with the Creator."

"First Cause."

"Have it your way."

"What are you doing in my head?"

"Trying very hard to get out."

"And how would you do that?"

"Foul up your mission so the Filonii would demand the Succubus replace me. I gather you're pretty important to them. Rather chickenshit, aren't they?"

"I don't recognize the term."

"I'll put it in sense form."

ℛ ■ ✿ ■ ♉ ■ ]

"Oh. You mean ● ● q –."

"Yeah. Chickenshit."

"Well, that's the way it's always been between the Filonii and the stalkers."

"You like it that way."

"I like my fish."

"Your Filonii like to play God, don't they? Changing this world and that world to suit themselves. Reminds me of a couple of other guys. Lords of Propriety they were called. And the Succubus. Did you ever stop to think how many individuals and races like to play God?"

"Right now I'd like to get out of here."

"Easy enough."

"How?"

"Make friends with the Tszechmae."

"The trees or the spores?"

"Both."

"One name for the symbiotic relationship?"

"They live in harmony."

"Except for the hookworms."

"No society is perfect. Rule 19."

The cat sat back on his haunches, and talked to himself.

"Make friends with them you say."

"Seems like a good idea, doesn't it?"

"How would you suggest I do that?"

"Offer to perform a service for them. Something they can't do for themselves."

"Such as?"

"How about you'll get rid of the Filonii for them. Right now that's the thing most oppressing them."

"Get rid of the Filonii."

"Yes."

"I'm harboring a lunatic in my head."

"Well, if you're going to quit before you start . . ."

"Precisely *how* – uh, do you have a name?"

"I told you. Bailey."

"Oh. Yes. Sorry. Well, Bailey, precisely *how* do I rid this planet of a star-spanning vessel weighing somewhere just over thirteen thousand tons, not to mention a full complement of officers and ecologists who have been in the overlord position with my race for more centuries than I can name? I'm conditioned to respect them."

"You sure don't sound as if you respect them."

The cat paused. That was true. He felt quite different. He disliked the Filonii intensely. Hated them, in fact; as his kind had hated them for more centuries than he could name.

"That *is* peculiar. Do you have any explanation for it?"

"Well," said Bailey, humbly, "there *is* my presence. It may well have broken through all your hereditary conditioning."

"You wear smugness badly."

"Sorry."

The cat continued to think on the possibilities.

"I wouldn't take too much longer, if I were you," Bailey urged him. Then, reconsidering, he added, "As a matter of fact, I *am* you."

"You're trying to tell me something."

"I'm trying to tell you that the gestalt spore grabbed you, to get a line on what was happening with the invaders, but you've been sitting here for some time, musing to yourself – which, being instantaneously communicative throughout the many parts of the whole, is a concept they can't grasp – and so it's getting ready to digest you."

The stalker blinked his thirty eyes very rapidly. "The spore thing?"

"Uh-uh. All the spores eat are the hookworms. The bark's starting to look at you with considerable interest."

"Who do I talk to? Quick!"

"You've decided you don't respect the Filonii so much, huh?"

"I thought you said I should hurry!"

"Just curious."

"*Who do I talk to!?!*"

"The floor."

So the stalker-cat talked to the floor, and they struck a bargain.
Rather a lopsided bargain, true; but a bargain nonetheless.

## 7

The hookworm was coming through the tunnel much more
rapidly than the cat would have expected. It seemed to be sliding,
but even as he watched, it bunched – inchworm-like – and
propelled itself forward, following the movement with another
slide. The wooden tunnel walls oozed with a noxious smelling
moistness as the worm passed. It was moving itself on a slime
track of its own secretions.

It was eight feet across, segmented, a filthy gray in color,
and what passed for a face was merely a slash-mouth
dripping yellowish mucus, several hundred cilia-like feelers
surrounding the slit, and four glaze-covered protuberances
in an uneven row above the slit perhaps serving in some
inadequate way as "eyes."

Like a strange Hansel dropping bread crumbs to mark a trail,
the spore things clinging to the cat's back began to ooze off. First
one, then another. The cat backed down the tunnel. The hookworm came on. It dropped its fleshy penis-like head and snuffled
at the spore lying in its path. Then the cilia feelers attached
themselves and the spore thing was slipped easily into the slash
mouth. There was a disgusting wet sound, and the hookworm
moved forward again. The same procedure was repeated at the
next spore. And the next, and the next. The hookworm followed
the stalker through the tunnels.

Some miles away, the Filonii stared into their screen as a
strange procession of red spores formed in the shape of a long
thick hawser-like chain emerged from the forest and began to
encircle the ship.

"Repulsors?" Kicker asked.

"Not yet, they haven't made a hostile move," the Homer said.
"The cat could have won them somehow. This may be a welcoming ceremony. Let's wait and see."

The ship was completely circled, at a distance of fifty feet from
the vessel. The Filonii waited, having faith in their cat lad.

And far underground, the stalker-cat led the hookworm a
twisting chase through tunnel after tunnel. Some of the
tunnels were formed only moments before the cat and his
pursuer entered them. The tunnels always sloped gently
upward. The cat – dropping his spore riders as he went –
led the enormous slug-thing by a narrow margin. But enough
to keep him coming.

Then, into a final tunnel, and the cat leaped to a planed
outcropping overhead, then to a tiny hole in the tunnel ceiling,
and then out of sight.

The Filonii shouted with delight as the stalker emerged from a
hole in the blasted earth, just beyond the circle of red spores,
linked and waiting.

"You see! Good cat!" Driver yelled to his fellows.

But the cat made no move toward the ship.

"He's waiting for the welcoming ceremony to end," the Homer
said with assurance.

Then, on their screens, they saw first one red spore, then
another, vanish, as though sucked down through the ground from
below.

They vanished in sequence, and the Filonii followed their
disappearance around the screens, watching them go in a 90°
arc, then 180° of half-circle, then 250° and the ground began to
tremble.

And before the hookworm could suck his dinner down
through a full 360° of the circle, the ground gave way
beneath the thirteen thousand tons of Filonii starship, and
the vessel thundered through, down into special tunnels dug
straight down. Plunged down with the plates of the ship
separating and cracking open. Plunged down with the hookworm that would soon discover sweeter morsels than even
red spore things.

The Filonii tried to save themselves.

There was very little they could do. Driver cursed the cat and
made a final contact with the Succubus. It was an automatic
hookup, much easier to throw in than to fire the ship for takeoff.
Particularly a quarter of a mile underground.

The hookworm broke through the ship. The Tszechmae
waited. When the hookworm had gorged itself, they would move
in and slay the creature. Then *they* would feast.

But Bailey would not be around to see the great meal. For only moments after the Filonii ship plunged crashing out of sight, he felt a ghastly wrenching at his soulself, and the stalker-cat was left empty once more – thereby proving in lopsided bargains no one is the winner but the house – and the soul of William Bailey went streaking out away from Belial toward the unknown.

Deep in wooden tunnels, things began to feed.

# 8

The darkness was the deepest blue. Not black. It was blue. He could see nothing. Not even himself. He could not tell what the body into which he had been cast did, or had, or resembled, or did not do, or not have or not resemble. He reached out into the blue darkness. He touched nothing.

But then, perhaps he had not reached out. He had felt himself extend *something* into the blueness, but how far, or in what direction, or if it had been an appendage . . . he did not know.

He tried to touch himself, and did not know where to touch. He reached for his face, where a Bailey face would have been. He touched nothing.

He tried to touch his chest. He met resistance, and then penetrated something soft. He could not distinguish if he had pushed through fur or skin or hide or jelly or moisture or fabric or metal or vegetable matter or foam or some heavy gas. He had no feeling in either his "hand" or his "chest" but there was *something* there.

He tried to move, and moved. But he did not know if he was rolling or hopping or walking or sliding or flying or propelling or being propelled. But he moved. And he reached down with the thing he had used to touch himself, and felt nothing below him. He did not have legs. He did not have arms. Blue. It was so blue.

He moved as far as he could move in one direction, and there was nothing to stop him. He could have moved in that direction forever, and met no resistance. So he moved in another direction – opposite, as far as he could tell, and as far as he could go. But there was no boundary. He went up and went down and went around in circles. There was nothing. Endless nothing.

Yet he knew he was *in* somewhere. He was not in the emptiness of space, he was in an enclosed space. But what dimensions the place had, he could not tell. And what he was, he could not tell.

It made him upset. He had not been upset in the body of Pinkh, nor in the body of the stalker-cat. But this life he now owned made him nervous.

Why should that be?

Something was coming for him.

He knew that much.

He was                                    something else

here                    and                    was out there,

coming toward him.

He knew fear. Blue fear. Deep unseeing blue fear. If it was coming fast, it would be here sooner. If slow, then later. But it was coming. He could feel, sense, intuit it coming for him. He wanted to change. To become something else.

To become *this*

Or to become THIꓚ

Or to become **SꓲHꓑ**

Or to become tHiS

But to become *something* else, something that could withstand what was coming for him. He didn't know what that could be. All he knew was that he needed equipment. He ran through his baileythoughts, his baileymind, to sort out what he might need.

|  |  |
|---|---|
|  | Fangs Poisonous breath |
|  | Eyes Horns Malleability |
| What he needed might be | Webbed feet Armored hide |
|  | Talons Camouflage Wings |
|  | Carapaces Muscles Vocal cords |
|  | Scales Self-regeneration |
|  | Stingers Wheels Multiple brains |

What he already had                                    Nothing

It was coming closer. Or was it getting farther away? (And by getting farther away, becoming more of a threat to him?) (If he went toward it, would he be safer?) (If only he could know what he looked like; or how great was his mass, his density; or where he was; or what was required of him?) (Orient!) (Damn it, orient yourself, Bailey!) He was deep in blueness, extended, fœtal, waiting. Shapeless. (Shape—) (Could *that* be it?)

Something blue flickered in the blueness.

It was coming end-for-end, flickering and sparking and growing larger, swimming toward him in the blueness. Graceful as a wind-ghost wraith on Shidoh. It sent tremors through him. Fear gripped him as it had never gripped him before. The blue shape coming toward him was the most fearful thing he could remember: and he remembered: and he remembered:

| | | |
|---|---|---|
| The night he had found Moravia with another man. They were standing having sex in a closet at a party. Her dress was bunched up around her waist; he had her up on tip-toes. She was crying with deep pleasure, eyes closed. | The day at the end of the war, when a laser had sliced off the top of the head of the man on his left in the warm metal trench. The sight of things still pulsing in the jasmine jelly. | The moment he had come to the final knowledge of his hopeless future. The moment he had decided to go to the Center to find death. |

The thing changed shape and sent out scintillant waves of blueness and fear. He writhed away from them but they swept over him, washed and waxed and waned, wavered, whined and weldddoned, and he turned over and over trying to escape. The thing of blue came nearer, growing larger in his sight. (Sight? Writhing? Fear?) It suddenly swept toward him, faster than before, as though trying a primary assault – the waves of fear – and the assault had failed; and now it would bull through.

He felt an urge to leap, high. He felt himself do it, and suddenly his sight went up and his propulsive equipment went lower, and he was longer, taller, larger. He fled. Down through the blueness, with the coruscating blue devil following. It elongated itself and shot past him on one side, boiled on ahead till it was a mere pinpoint of incandescence on some heightless, dimensionless horizon. And then it came racing back toward him, thinning itself and stretching itself till it was opaque, till the blueness of where they were shone through it darkly, like effulgent isinglass in a blue hyperplane.

He trembled in fear and went minute. He balled and shrank and contracted and drew himself to a finite point, and the whirling danger went hurtling through him and beyond, and was lost back the way they had come.

Inside the body he now owned, Bailey felt something wrenching and tearing. Fibers pulled loose from moorings and he was certain his mind was giving way. He had memories of sense-deprivation chambers and what had happened to men who had been left in them too long. This was the same. No shape, no size, no idea or way of gaining an idea of what he was, or where he was, or the touch, smell, sound, sight of *anything* as an anchor to his sanity. Yet he was surviving.

The dark blue devil kept arranging new assaults – and he had no doubt it would be back in seconds (seconds?) – and he kept doing the correct thing to escape those assaults. But he had the feeling (feeling?) that at some point the instinctive reactions of this new body would be insufficient. That he would have to bring to this new role his essential baileyness, his human mind, his thoughts, the cunning he had begun to understand was so much a part of his way. (And why had he not understood that cunningness when he had been Bailey, all the years of his hopeless life?)

The effulgence began again somewhere off to his side and high above him, coming on rapidly.

Bailey, some *thing* unknown, prepared. As best he could.

you may be sure i paid dearly to do so, my dear yaquil.
the succubus, yaquil, it cost me five, tennils of life.
chide me all you wish . . . unlike you, i do not look on—
but you do. you were born herdur. there *was* a time when it—
while you remain. you have *always* thought of it as a game.
and we cannot fluster me with platitudes!
i can say it because we have waged this combat too long.
but for an althus it is. call an end, yaquil! do it now.
submission is no part of it. i merely say stop quickly.
no, because the tennils pass and the heat goes and we die!
yes, because the tennils pass and more frames than i can afford.
better now than too late. you over-extend yourself, sir.
mpudence, impertinence . . . how you ever became a combatant—
you leave me no alternative. frames be damned, we fight!
and concede a defeat i need not have conceded? fight on.
i offered you an opportunity. the time for talk is done!

MARVELOUS, ANIK! HOW DID YOU MANAGE TO REVITALIZE IT?
OH, I'M SURE YOU DID. BUT HOW DID YOU MANAGE? PLEASE! FIVE!?!
YOU REALLY *DO* WANT TO WIN, DON'T YOU? TSK-TSK.
I KNOW: YOU DON'T LOOK ON THIS AS A GAME. NOR SHOULD I.
AND THAT'S SIMPLY BECAUSE YOU WERE BORN ALTHUS. WHILE—
WHEN IT MEANT SOMETHING SIGNIFICANT? YES, BUT TIME GOES.
FLUSTER YOU? MY DEAR GOOD ANIK, HOW CAN YOU SAY THAT?
TEN THOUSAND TENNILS ISN'T TOO LONG. NOT FOR A HERDUR.
ARE YOU PLEADING FOR SURCEASE, MY FRIEND? DO YOU SUBMIT?
WHY? BECAUSE YOUR CHAMPION IS A FALSE SOUL IN ITS BODY?
TRULY, ANIK, YOU MUST THINK ME A CULLY OR A FOOL! DIE!
THEN GO TO RESERVE FRAMES. I CAN'T CONCERN MYSELF NOW
LET *ME* WORRY ABOUT THE EXTENT OF MY OVER-EXTENSIONS!
YOU'LL WORRY ABOUT THAT TILL THE MOMENT I DESTROY YOU
IT WAS *INTENDED* THAT WE FIGHT. IF YOU WANT OUT, I SAY GO!
YOUR SUBSTITUTE CHAMPION HAS NO CHANCE, I SWEAR IT, ANIK!

The blue devil swept down on him, crackling with energy. He felt the incredible million sting-points of pain and a sapping of strength. Then a

for it had. Now Bailey knew what he was, and what he had to do. He lay still, swimming in the never-ending forever blueness. He was soft and he was solitary. The blue devil swarmed and came on. For the last time. And when it was all around him, Bailey let it drink him. He let its deep blueness and its fear and its sparkling effulgence sweep over him, consume him. The blue devil gorged itself, grew larger, fuller, more incapable of movement, unable to free itself. Bailey stuffed it with his amoebic body. He split and formed yet another, and the blue devil extended itself and began feeding on his second self. The radiating sparking waves of fear and blueness were thicker now, coming more slowly. Binary fission again. Now there were four. The blue devil fed, consumed, filled its chambers and its source-buds. Again, fission. And now there were eight. And the blue devil began to lose color. Bailey did not divide again. He knew what he had to do. Neither he, nor the blue devil could win this combat. Both must die. The feeding went on and on, and finally the blue devil had drained itself with fullness, made itself immobile, died. And he died. And there was emptiness in the blueness once more.

The frames, the tenils, the fullness of combat were ended. And in that last fleeting instant of sentience, Bailey imagined he heard scented wails of hopelessness from two Duelmasters somewhere out there. He gloated. Now they knew what it was to be a William Bailey, to be hopeless and alone and afraid.

He gloated for an instant, then was whirled out and away.

# 9

This time his repose lasted only a short time. It was rush season for the Succubus. Bailey went out to fill the husk of a Master Slavemaster whose pens were filled with females of the eighty-three races that peopled the Snowdrift Cluster asteroids. Bailey succeeded in convincing the Slavemaster that male chauvinism was detestable, and the females were bound into a secret organization that returned to their various rock-worlds, overthrew the all-male governments and declared themselves the Independent Feminist Concourse.

He was pulled back and sent out to inhabit the radio wave "body" of a needler creature used by the Kirk to turn suns nova and thereby provide them with power sources. Bailey gained possession of the needler and imploded the Kirk home sun.

He was pulled back and sent out to inhabit the shell of a ten thousand year old terrapin whose retention of random construction information made it invaluable as the overseer of a planetary reorganization project sponsored by a pale gray race without a name that altered solar systems just beyond the Finger Fringe deepout. Bailey let the turtle feed incorrect data to the world-swingers hauling the planets into their orbits, and the entire configuration collided in the orbit of the system's largest heavy-mass world. The resultant uprising caused the total eradication of the pale gray race.

He was pulled back . . .

Finally, even a creature as vast and involved as the Succubus, a creature plagued by a million problems and matters for attention, in effect a god-of-a-sort, was forced to take notice. There was a soul in his file that was causing a fullness leak. There was a soul that was anathema to what the Succubus had built his reputation on. There was a soul that seemed to be (unthinkable as it was) out to get him. There was a soul that was ruining things. There was a soul that was inept. There was a soul that was (again, unthinkably) consciously trying to ruin the work the Succubus had spent his life setting in motion. There was a soul named Bailey.

And the Succubus consigned him to soul limbo till he could clear away present obligations and draw him under the lens for scrutiny.

So Bailey was sent to limbo.

# 10

This is what it was like in soul limbo.

Soft pasty maggoty white. Roiling. Filled with sounds of things desperately trying to see. Slippery underfoot. Without feet.

Breathless and struggling for breath. Enclosed. Tight, with great weight pressing down till the pressure was asphyxiating. But without the ability to breathe. Pressed down to cork, porous and feeling imminent crumbling; then boiling liquid poured through. Pain in every filament and glass fiber. A wet thing settling into bones, turning them to ash and paste. Sickly sweetness, thick and rancid, tongued and swallowed and bloating. Bloating till bursting. A charnel scent. Rising smoke burning and burning the sensitive tissues. Love lost forever, the pain of knowing nothing could ever matter again; melancholia so possessive it wrenched deep inside and twisted organs that never had a chance to function.

Cold tile.

Black crepe paper.

Fingernails scraping slate.

Button pains.

Tiny cuts at sensitive places.

Weakness.

Hammering steadily pain.

That was what it was like in the Succubus's soul limbo. It was not punishment, it was merely the dead end. It was the place where the continuum had not been completed. It was not Hell, for Hell had form and substance and purpose. This was a crater, a void, a storeroom packed with uselessness. It was the place to be sent when pastpresentfuture were one and indeterminate. It was altogether ghastly.

Had Bailey gone mad, this would have been the place for it to happen. But he did not. There was a reason.

## II

One hundred thousand eternities later, the Succubus cleared his desk of present work, filled all orders and answered all current correspondence, finished inventory and took a long-needed vacation. When he returned, before turning his attention to new business, he brought the soul of William Bailey out of limbo and ushered it under the lens.

And found it, somehow, *different*.

Quite unlike the millions and millions of other souls he had stolen.

He could not put a name to the difference. It was not a force, not a vapor, not a quality, not a potentiality, not a look, not a sense, not a capacity, not anything he could pinpoint. And, of course, such a *difference* might be invaluable.

So the Succubus drew a husk from the spare parts and rolling stock bank, and put Bailey's soul into it.

It must be understood that this was a consummately E M P T Y husk. Nothing lived there. It had been scoured clean. It was not like the many bodies into which Bailey had been inserted. Those had had their souls stolen. There was restraining potential in all of them, memories of persona, fetters invisible but present nonetheless. This husk was now Bailey. Bailey only, Bailey free and Bailey whole.

The Succubus summoned Bailey before him.

Bailey might have been able to describe the Succubus, but he had no such desire.

The examination began. The Succubus used light and darkness, lines and spheres, soft and hard, seasons of change, waters of Nepenthe, a hand outstretched, the whisper of a memory, carthing, enumeration, suspension, incursion, requital and thirteen others.

He worked over and WHAT through and inside the soul HE DID NOT of Bailey in an attempt to KNOW isolate the wild and dangerous WAS THAT difference that made this soul WHILE HE WAS unlike all others he EXAMINING had ever stolen for his tables of fulfillment BAILEY, BAILEY for the many races WAS that called upon EXAMINING him HIM.

Then, when he had all the knowledge he needed, all the secret places, all the unspoken promises, all the wished and fleshed depressions, the power that lurked in Bailey . . . that had *always* lurked in Bailey . . . before either of them could try or hope to contain it . . . surged free.

(It had been there all along.)

(Since the dawn of time, it had been there.)

(It had always existed.)

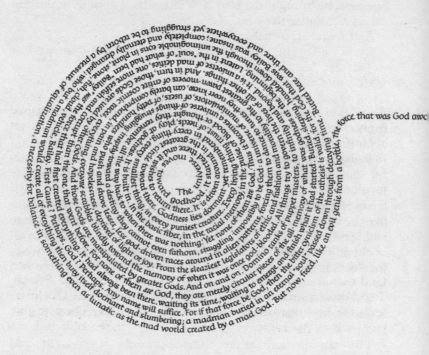

The godhood lies dormant in every puniest creature. Godness is driven in the basic fiber, in the racial memory. Yet none of them are God. Thus the universe moves toward there. It is driven, three and the greatest circle moves to return there. Every living thing must, play in every thing, to return there, smallest thing in the basic, the greatest circle moves toward the way back to when there was nothing. Yet living creature, struggling impossibly to be God: a unity of, god-driven races around in alien patterns, forcing them on and on. From the sleaziest legislators of ethic and god-blooded. All things try to govern them, to emerge and finish what it had started. Domino ranks of the all-memory of puppet masters, waiting to emerge and finish what it had started. Build, for the bitter cynicism of the atheist is valid time, soul passed down through decaying time, the force that was God awo

It is built in. In the deepest, they cannot even fathom, manipulated by greater Gods. And they are merely circular pieces of, waiting its time, waiting to, then the bitter God, Lesser Gods are manipulated, deprived of light or joy, shove and above, scrabbles blindly at, hopelessness, pushed, toward the memory of when it, reward a destiny, For none of them are God. Any name will suffice. For if that force be God, then in an eternal 'soul' passed down, a madman buried in, the way back to when, had always been there, waiting its time. Any name will suffice. For it had always been there, dormant and slumbering; a madman buried in an eternal God. But now, freed, like an evil genie from a bottle, the force that was God awoke, itself dormant and slumbering; a madman buried in an eternal God. Any name will suffice. For if that force be God, as lunatic as the mad world created by a mad God.

completely and eternally deranged, everywhere yet struggling to be reborn by a pressure, Bailey was insane; the unimaginable eons, through, learnt in the 'soul' of what had been. Bailey, fish, cloud, It is a universe of other things, one turn, those, And in turn, those Gods, movers of entire cosmic acts used by, of petty dabblers, of things, one of the greatest pawn-movers of entire cosmic acts, corrupt Gods, And those Gods, than the one that went before, force that had first created everything. First Cause? Perhaps, a madman would create all of everything, Bailey, a necessity for balance in something ossomed to fullness, rejuvenated by its slumber, stronger than it had been even when it had created the universe. And, freed, it set about finishing what had begun millennia before.

Bailey remembered the Euthanasia Center, where it had begun for him. Remembered dying. Remembered being reborn. Remembered the life of inadequacy, impotency, hopelessness he had led before he'd given himself up to the Suicide Center. Remembered living as a one-eyed bear creature in a war that would never end. Remembered being a stalker-cat and death of a ghastliness it could not be spoken of. Remembered blueness. Remembered all the other lives. And remembered all the gods that had been less God than himself Bailey. The Lords of Propriety. The Filonii. The Montagasques. The Thils. The Tszechmae. The Duelmasters. The hookworms. The Slavemaster. The Kirk. The pale gray race without a name. And most of all, he remembered the Succubus.

Who thought he was God. Even as the Thieves thought *they* were Gods. But none of them possessed more than the faintest scintilla of the all-memory of godness, and Bailey had become the final repository for the force that *was* God. And now, freed, unleashed, unlocked, swirled down through all of time to this judgment day, Bailey flexed his godness and finished what he had begun at the beginning.

There is only one end to creation. What is created is destroyed, and thus full circle is achieved.

Bailey, God, set about killing the sand castle he had built. The destruction of the universes he had created.

Never before.

Songs unsung.

Washed but never purified.

Dreams spent and visits to come.

Up out of slime.

Drifted down on cool trusting winds.

Heat.

Free.

All created, all equal, all wondering, all vastness.

Gone to night.

The power that was Bailey that was God began its efforts. The husk in which Bailey lived was drawn into the power. The Succubus, screaming for reprieve, screaming for reason, screaming for release or explanation, was drawn into the power. The soul station drawn in. The home world drawn in. The solar system of the home world drawn in. The galaxy and all the galaxies and the metagalaxies and the far island universes and the alter dimensions and the past back to the beginning and beyond it to the circular place where it became now, and all the shadow places and all the thought recesses and then the very fabric and substance of eternity . . . all of it, everything . . . drawn in.

All of it contained within the power of Bailey who is God.

And then, in one awesome exertion of will, God-Bailey destroys it all, coming full circle, ending what it had been born to do. Gone.


And all that is left is Bailey. Who is dead.

In the region between.

# THE DAYS OF
# SOLOMON GURSKY

## Ian McDonald

*This story brings us back, more or less, to the present day. We all know the old nursery rhyme about Solomon Grundy, "born on Monday, christened on Tuesday" and so on until his burial on Sunday. Here Ian McDonald transmutes him into Solomon Gursky whose life has a rather more eventful metaphorical week.*

*McDonald (b. 1960) was born in Manchester but grew up and still lives in Northern Ireland. Living there during the troubles has caused McDonald to remark that it was like living in a Third World country with a feeling of marginalization and this sparked an interest in science fiction as a way of studying and exploring those living on the edge of societies. This was evident in his first novel,* Desolation Road *(1988) tracing the survival of an isolated colony on Mars. Feelings of prejudice and ostracization are central to his later books especially* Out on Blue Six *(1989) and* Terminal Café *(1994), aka* Necroville. *His body of work has become one of the most impressive amongst the new generation of British writers and garnered him at least five awards at last count.*

# Monday

S ol stripped the gear on the trail over Blood of Christ
Mountain. Click-shifted down to sixth for the steep push
up to the ridge, and there was no sixth. No fifth, no fourth;
nothing, down to zero.

Elena was already up on the divide, laughing at him pushing
and sweating up through the pines, muscles twisted and knotted
like the trunks of the primeval bristlecones, tubes and tendons
straining like bridge cable. Then she saw the gear train sheared
through and spinning free.

They'd given the bikes a good hard kicking down in the desert
mountains south of Nogales. Two thousand apiece, but the
salesperson had sworn on the virginity of all his unmarried sisters
that these MTBs would go anywhere, do anything you wanted.
Climb straight up El Capitan, if that was what you needed of
them. Now they were five days on the trail – three from the
nearest Dirt Lobo dealership, so Elena's palmtop told her – and a
gear train had broken clean in half. Ten more days, four hundred
more miles, fifty more mountains for Solomon Gursky, in high
gear.

"Should have been prepared for this, engineer," Elena said.

"Two thousand a bike, you shouldn't need to," Solomon
Gursky replied. It was early afternoon up on Blood of Christ
Mountain, high and hot and resinous with the scent of the old,
old pines. There was haze down in the valley they had come from,
and in the one they were riding to. "And you know I'm not that
kind of engineer. My gears are a lot smaller. And they don't
break."

Elena knew what kind of engineer he was, as he knew what kind
of doctor she was. But the thing was new between them and at the
stage where research colleagues who surprise themselves by
becoming lovers like to pretend that they are mysteries to each
other.

Elena's palmtop map showed a settlement five miles down the
valley. It was called Redención. It might be the kind of place they
could get welding done quick and good for *norte* dollars.

"Be happy, it's downhill," Elena said as she swung her electric-
blue padded ass onto the saddle and plunged down off the ridge.
One second later, Sol Gursky in his shirt and shorts and shoes
and shades and helmet came tearing after her through the scrub

sage. The thing between them was still at the stage where desire can flare at a flash of electric-blue lycra-covered ass.

Redención it was, of the kind you get in the border mountains; of gas and food and trailers to hire by the night, or the week, or, if you have absolutely nowhere else to go, the lifetime; of truck stops and recreational Jacuzzis at night under the border country stars. No welding. Something better. The many-branched saguaro of a solar tree was the first thing of Redención the travelers saw lift out of the heat haze as they came in along the old, cracked, empty highway.

The factory was in an ugly block annex behind the gas and food. A truck driver followed Sol and Elena round the back, entranced by these fantastic macaw-bright creatures who kept their eyes hidden behind wrap-around shades. He was chewing a sandwich. He had nothing better to do in Redención on a hot Monday afternoon. Jorge, the proprietor, looked too young and ambitious to be pushing gas, food, trailers, and molecules in Redención on any afternoon. He was thirty-wise, dark, serious. There was something tight-wound about him. Elena said in English that he had the look of a man of sorrows. But he took the broken gear train seriously, and helped Sol remove it from the back wheel. He looked at the smooth, clean shear plane with admiration.

"This I can do," he declared. "Take an hour, hour and a half. Meantime, maybe you'd like to take a Jacuzzi?" This, wrinkling his nose, downwind of two MTBers come over Blood of Christ Mountain in the heat of the day. The truck driver grinned. Elena scowled. "Very private," insisted Jorge the nanofacturer.

"Something to drink?" Elena suggested.

"Sure. Coke, Sprite, beer, *agua minerale*. In the shop."

Elena went the long way around the trucker to investigate the cooler. Sol followed Jorge into the factory and watched him set the gears in the scanner.

"Actually, this is my job," Sol said to make conversation as the lasers mapped the geometry of the ziggurat of cogs in three dimensions. He spoke Spanish. Everyone did. It was the universal language up in the *norte* now, as well as down *el sur*.

"You have a factory?"

"I'm an engineer. I build these things. Not the scanners, I mean; the tectors. I design them. A nano-engineer."

The monitor told Jorge the mapping was complete.

"For the Tesler *corporada*," Sol added as Jorge called up the processor system.

"How do you want it?"

"I'd like to know it's not going to do this to me again. Can you build it in diamond?"

"All just atoms, friend."

Sol studied the processor chamber. It pleased him that they looked like whisky stills; round-bellied, high-necked, rising through the roof into the spreading fingers of the solar tree. Strong spirits in that still, spirits of the vacuum between galaxies, the cold of absolute zero, and the spirits of the tectors moving through cold and emptiness, shuffling atoms. He regretted that the physics did not allow viewing windows in the nanofacturers. Look down through a pane of pure and perfect diamond at the act of creation. Maybe creation was best felt unseen, a mystery. All just atoms, friend. Yes, but it was what you *did* with those atoms, where you made them go. The weird troilisms and menages you forced them into.

He envisioned the minuscule machines, smaller than viruses, clever knots of atoms, scavenging carbon through the nanofacturer's roots deep in the earth of Redención, passing it up the buckytube conduits to the processor chamber, weaving it into diamond of his own shaping.

Alchemy.

Diamond gears.

Sol Gursky shivered in his light biking clothes, touched by the intellectual chill of the nanoprocessor.

"This is one of mine," he called to Jorge. "I designed the tectors."

"I wouldn't know." Jorge fetched beers from a crate on the factory floor, opened them in the door. "I bought the whole place from a guy two years back. Went up north, to the *Tres Valles*. You from there?"

The beer was cold. In the deeper, darker cold of the reactor chamber, the nanomachines swarmed. Sol Gursky held his arms out: Jesus of the MTB wear.

"Isn't everyone?"

"Not yet. So, who was it you said you work for? Nanosis? Ewart-OzWest?"

"Tesler Corp. I head up a research group into biological analogs."

"Never heard of them."

*You will*, was what Solomon Gursky would have said, but for the scream.

Elena's scream.

Not, he thought as he ran, that he had heard Elena's scream — the thing was not supposed to be at that stage — but he knew it could not belong to anyone else.

She was standing in the open back door of the gas and food, pale and shaky in the high bright light.

"I'm sorry," she said. "I just wanted to get some water. There wasn't any in the cooler, and I didn't want Coke. I just wanted to get some water from the faucet."

He was aware that Jorge was behind him as he went into the kitchen. Man mess: twenty coffee mugs, doughnut boxes, beer cans, and milk cartons. Spoons, knives, forks. He did that too, and Elena told him off for having to take a clean one every time.

Then he saw the figures through the open door.

Somewhere, Jorge was saying, "Please, this is my home."

There were three of them; a good-looking, hard-worked woman, and two little girls, one newly school-age, the other not long on her feet. They sat in chairs, hands on thighs. They looked straight ahead.

It was only because they did not blink, that their bodies did not rock gently to the tick of pulse and breath, that Sol could understand.

The color was perfect. He touched the woman's cheek, the coil of dark hair that fell across it. Warm soft. Like a woman's should feel. Texture like skin. His fingertips left a line in dust.

They sat unblinking, unmoving, the woman and her children, enshrined in their own memorabilia. Photographs, toys, little pieces of jewelry, loved books and ornaments, combs, mirrors. Pictures and clothes. Things that make up a life. Sol walked among the figures and their things, knowing that he trespassed in sacred space, but irresistibly drawn by the simulacra.

"They were yours?" Elena was saying somewhere. And Jorge was nodding, and his mouth was working but no words were manufactured. "I'm sorry, I'm so sorry."

"They said it was a blow-out." Jorge finally said. "You know, those tires they say repair themselves, so they never blow out? They blew out. They went right over the barrier, upside down. That's what the truck driver said. Right over, and he could see them all, upside down. Like they were frozen in time, you understand?" He paused.

"I went kind of dark for a long time after that; a lot crazy, you know? When I could see things again, I bought this with the insurance and the compensation. Like I say, it's all just atoms, friend. Putting them in the right order. Making them go where you want, do what you want."

"I'm sorry we intruded," Elena said, but Solomon Gursky was standing there among the reconstructed dead and the look on his face was that of a man seeing something far beyond what is in front of him, all the way to God.

"Folk out here are accommodating." But Jorge's smile was a tear of sutures. "You can't live in a place like this if you weren't a little crazy or lost."

"She was very beautiful," Elena said.

"She is."

Dust sparkled in the float of afternoon light through the window.

"Sol?"

"Yeah. Coming."

The diamond gears were out of the tank in twenty-five minutes. Jorge helped Sol fit them to the two thousand *norte* dollar bike. Then Sol rode around the factory and the gas-food-trailer house where the icons of the dead sat unblinking under the slow fall of dust. He clicked the gears up and clicked them down. One two three four five six. Six five four three two one. Then he paid Jorge fifty *norte*, which was all he asked for his diamond. Elena waved to him as they rode down the highway out of Redención.

They made love by firelight on the top of Blessed Virgin Mountain, on the pine needles, under the stars. That was the stage they were at: ravenous, unselfconscious, discovering. The old deaths, down the valley behind them, gave them urgency. Afterward, he was quiet and withdrawn, and when she asked what he was thinking about, he said, "The resurrection of the dead."

"But they weren't resurrected," she said, knowing instantly what he meant, for it haunted her too, up on their starry mountain. "They were just *representations*, like a painting or a photograph. Sculpted memories. Simulations."

"But they were real for *him*." Sol rolled onto his back to gaze at the warm stars of the border. "He told me he talked to them. If his nanofactory could have made them move and breathe and talk

THE DAYS OF SOLOMON GURSKY

back, he'd have done it, and who could have said that they
weren't real?"

He felt Elena shiver against his flesh.

"What is it?"

"Just thinking about those faces, and imagining them in the
reactor chamber, in the cold and the emptiness, with the tectors
crawling over them."

"Yeah."

Neither spoke for a time long enough to see the stars move.
Then Solomon Gursky felt the heat stir in him again and he
turned to Elena and felt the warmth of her meat, hungry for his
second little death.

## Tuesday

Jesus was getting fractious in the plastic cat carrier; heaving from
side to side, shaking the grille.

Sol Gursky set the carrier on the landing mesh and searched
the ochre smog haze for the incoming liftercraft. Photochromic
molecules bonded to his irises polarized: another hot, bright,
poisonous day in the TVMA.

Jesus was shrieking now.

"Shut the hell up," Sol Gursky hissed. He kicked the cat
carrier. Jesus gibbered and thrust her arms through the grille,
grasping at freedom.

"Hey, it's only a monkey," Elena said.

But that was the thing. Monkeys, by being monkeys, annoyed
him. Frequently enraged him. Little homunculus things masquerading as human. Clever little fingers, wise little eyes, ex-
pressive little faces. Nothing but dumb animal behind that face,
running those so-human fingers.

He knew his anger at monkeys was irrational. But he'd still
enjoyed killing Jesus, taped wide open on the pure white slab.
Swab, shave, slip the needle.

Of course, she had not been Jesus then. Just Rhesus; nameless,
a tool made out of meat. Experiment 625G.

It was probably the smog that was making her scream. Should
have got her one of those goggle things for walking poodles. But
she would have just torn it off with her clever little human
fingers. Clever enough to be dumb, monkey-thing.

Elena was kneeling down, playing baby-fingers with the clutching fists thrust through the bars.

"It'll bite you."

His hand still throbbed. Dripping, shivering, and spastic from the tank, Jesus had still possessed enough motor control to turn her head and lay his thumb open to the bone. Vampire monkey: the undead appetite for blood. Bastard thing. He would have enjoyed killing it again, if it were still killable.

All three on the landing grid looked up at the sound of lifter engines detaching themselves from the aural bed rock of two million cars. The ship was coming in from the south, across the valley from the big site down on Hoover where the new *corporada* headquarters was growing itself out of the fault line. It came low and fast, nose down, ass up, like a big bug that thrives on the taste of hydrocarbons in its spiracles. The backwash from its jets flustered the palm trees as it configured into vertical mode and came down on the research facility pad. Sol Gursky and Elena Asado shielded their sunscreened eyes from flying grit and leaf-storm.

Jesus ran from end to end of her plastic cage, gibbering with fear.

"Doctor Gursky." Sol did not think he had seen this *corporadisto* before, but it was hard to be certain; Adam Tesler liked his personal assistants to look as if he had nanofactured them. "I can't begin to tell you how excited Mr Tesler is about this."

"You should be there with me," Sol said to Elena. "It was your idea." Then, to the suit, "Dr Asado should be with me."

Elena swiped at her jet-blown hair.

"I shouldn't, Sol. It was your baby. Your gestation, your birth. Anyway, you know how I hate dealing with suits." This for the smiling PA, but he was already guiding Sol to the open hatch.

Sol strapped in and the ship lurched as the engines screamed up into lift. He saw Elena wave and duck back toward the facility. He clutched the cat carrier hard as his gut kicked when the lifter slid into horizontal flight. Within, the dead monkey burbled to herself in exquisite terror.

"What happened to your thumb?" the *corporadisto* asked.

When he'd cracked the tank and lifted Jesus the Rhesus out of the waters of rebirth, the monkey had seemed more pissed off at being sopping wet than at having been dead. There had been a pure, perfect moment of silence, then the simultaneous oath and gout of blood, and the Lazarus team had exploded into whooping exultation. The monkey had skittered across the floor, alarmed by the hooting and cheering, hunting for height and hiding. Elena had caught it spastically trying – and failing – to hurl itself up the side of a desk. She'd swaddled Jesus up in thermal sheeting and put the spasming thing in the observation incubator. Within the hour, Jesus had regained full motor control and was chewing at the corners of her plastic pen, scratching imaginary fleas and masturbating ferociously. While delivery companies dropped off pizza stacks and cases of cheap Mexican champagne, someone remembered to call Adam Tesler.

The dead monkey was not a good flier. She set up a wailing keen that had even the pilot complaining.

"Stop that," Sol Gursky snapped. It would not do anything for him, though, and rocked on its bare ass and wailed all the louder.

"What way is that to talk to a piece of history?" the PA said. He grinned in through the grille, waggled fingers, clicked tongue. "Hey there, little fellow. Whatcha call him?"

"Little bitch, actually. We call her Jesus; also known as Bride of Frankenstein."

*Bite him*, Solomon Gursky thought as ten thousand mirrored swimming pools slipped beneath the belly of the Tesler *Corporada* lifter.

Frankenstein's creations were dead. That was the thing. That was the revelation.

It was the Age of Everything, but the power to make anything into anything else was not enough, because there was one thing the tectors of Nanosis and Aristide-Tlaxcalpo and the other founders of the nanotech revolution could not manipulate into anything else, and that was death. A comment by a pioneer nanotechnologist captured the optimism and frustration of the Age of Everything: Watson's Postulate. *Never mind turning trash into oil or asteroids into heaps of Volkswagens, or hanging exact copies of Van Goghs in your living room; the first thing we get with nanotechnology is immortality.*

Five billion Rim dollars in research disproved it. What tectors touched, they transformed; what they transformed, they killed. The Gursky-Asado team had beaten its rivals to the viral replicators, that infiltrated living cells and converted them into a different, tector-based matrix, and from their DNA spored a million copies. It had shaped an algorithm from the deadly accuracy of carcinomas. It had run tests under glass and in tanks. It had christened that other nameless Rhesus Frankenstein and injected the tectors. And Sol and Elena had watched the tiny machines slowly transform the monkey's body into something not even gangrene could imagine.

Elena wanted to put it out of its misery, but they could not open the tank for fear of contamination. After a week, it ended.

The monster fell apart. That was the thing. And then Asado and Gursky remembered a hot afternoon when Sol got a set of diamond gears built in a place called Redención.

If death was a complex thing, an accumulation of micro-death upon mini-death upon little death upon middling death, life might obey the same power law. Escalating anti-entropy. Pyramid-plan life.

Gursky's Corollary to Watson's Postulate: *The first thing we get with nanotechnology is the resurrection of the dead.*

The Dark Tower rose out of the amber haze. Sol and Elena's private joke had escaped and replicated itself; everyone in R&D now called the thing Adam Tesler was building down in the valley Barad Dur, in Mordor, where the smogs lie. And Adam Tesler, its unresting, all-seeing Eye.

There were over fifty levels of it now, but it showed no signs of stopping. As each section solidified and became dormant, another division of Adam Tesler's corporate edifice was slotted in. The architects were unable to say where it would stop. A kilometer, a kilometer and a half; maybe then the architectors would stabilize and die. Sol loathed its glossy black excrescences and crenellations, a miscegeny of the geological and the cancerous. Gaudi sculpting in shit.

The lifter came in high over the construction, locked into the navigation grid and banked. Sol looked down into its open black maw.

All just atoms, the guy who owned the factory had said. Sol could not remember his name now. The living and the dead have the same atoms.

They'd started small: paramecia, amoebae. Things hardly alive. Invertebrates. Reanimated cockroaches, hurtling on their thin legs around the observation tank. Biological machine, nanotech machine, still a machine. Survival machine. Except now you couldn't stomp the bastards. They came back.

What good is resurrection, if you are just going to die again?

The cockroaches came back, and they kept coming back.

He had been the cautious one this time, working carefully up the evolutionary chain. Elena was the one who wanted to go right for it. Do the monkey. Do the monkey and you do the man.

He had watched the tectors swarm over it, strip skin from flesh, flesh from bone, dissolve bones. He had watched the nano-machines put it all back together into a monkey. It lay in the liquid intact, but, its signs said, dead. Then the line kicked, and kicked again, and another twitched in harmony, and a third came in, and then they were all playing together on the vital signs monitor, and that which was dead was risen.

The lifter was into descent, lowering itself toward the exact center of the white cross on the landing grid fastened to the side of the growing tower. Touchdown. The craft rocked on its bug legs. Seat-belt sign off, steps down.

"You behave yourself," Solomon Gursky told Jesus.

The All-Seeing Eye was waiting for him by the upshaft. His Dark Minions were with him.

"Sol."

The handshake was warm and strong, but Sol Gursky had never trusted Adam Tesler in all the years he had known him; as nanoengineering student or as head of the most dynamic nano-tech *corporada* in the Pacific Rim Co-Prosperity Sphere.

"So this is it?" Adam Tesler squatted down and choo-choo-chooked the monkey.

"She bites."

"I see." Jesus grabbed his thumb in her tiny pink homunculus hand. "So, you are the man who has beaten the final enemy."

"Not beaten it. Found something on the far side of it. It's resurrection, not immortality."

Adam Tesler opened the cage. Jesus hopped up his arm to perch on the shoulder of his Scarpacchi suit. Tesler tickled the fur of her belly.

"And humans?"

"Point one percent divergence between her DNA and yours."

"Ah." Adam Tesler closed his eyes. "This makes it all the harder."

Fear pulsed through Solomon Gursky like a sickness.

"Leave us, please," Adam Tesler said to his assistants. "I'll join you in a moment."

Unspeaking, they filed to the lifter.

"Adam?"

"Sol. Why did you do it?"

"What are you talking about, Adam?"

"You know, Sol."

For an instant, Sol Gursky died on the landing grid fused to the fifty-third level of the Tesler *corporada* tower. Then he returned to life, and knew with cool and beautiful clarity that he could say it all, that he *must* say it all, because he was dead now and nothing could touch him.

"It's too much for one person, Adam. This isn't building cars or growing houses or nanofacturing custom pharmaceuticals. This is the resurrection of the dead. This is every human being from now to the end of the universe. You can't be allowed to own that. Not even God should have a monopoly on eternal life."

Adam Tesler sighed. His irises were photochromed dark, their expression unreadable.

"So. How long is it?"

"Thirteen years."

"I thought I knew you, Sol."

"I thought I knew you." The air was clear and fresh and pure, here on this high perch. "How did you find out?"

Adam Tesler stroked the monkey's head. It tried to push his fingers away, baring sharp teeth.

"You can come here now, Marisa."

The tall, muscular woman who walked from the upshaft across the landing grid was no stranger to Sol. He knew her from the Yucatan resort mastaba and the Alaskan ski-lodge and the gambling complex grown out of the nanoengineered reef in the South China Sea. From clandestine conversations through secure channels and discreet meetings, he knew that her voice would be soft and low and tinted Australian.

"You dressed better when you worked for Aristide Tlaxcalpo," Sol said. The woman was dressed in street leathers. She smiled. She had smiled better then as well.

"Why them?" Adam Tesler said. "Of all the ones to betray me to, *those* clowns!"

"That's why," said Solomon Gursky. "Elena had nothing to do with this, you know."

"I know that. She's safe. For the moment."

Sol Gursky knew then what must happen, and he shivered with the sudden, urgent need to destroy before he was destroyed. He pushed down the shake of rage by force of will as he held his hand out and clicked his fingers to the monkey. Jesus frowned and frisked off Tesler's shoulder to Sol's hand. In an instant, he had stretched, twisted, and snapped its neck. He flung the twitching thing away from him. It fell to the red mesh.

"I can understand that," Adam Tesler said. "But it will come back again, and again, and again." He turned on the bottom step of the lifter. "Have you any idea how disappointed I am, Sol?"

"I really don't give a shit!" Solomon Gursky shouted but his words were swallowed by the roar of engine power-up. The lifter hovered and swooped down over the great grid of the city toward the northern hills.

Sol Gursky and Marisa were alone on the platform.

"Do it!" he shouted.

Those muscles he had so admired, he realized, were augments; her fingers took a fistful of his neck and lifted him off the ground. Strangling, he kicked at air, snatched at breath. One-armed, she carried him to the edge.

"Do it," he tried to say, but her fingers choked all words in his throat. She held him out over the drop, smiling. He shat himself, and realized as it poured out of him that it was ecstasy, that it always had been, and the reason that adults forbade it was precisely because it was such a primal joy.

Through blood haze, he saw the tiny knotted body of Jesus inching toward him on pink man-fingers, its neck twisted over its back, eyes staring unshielded into the sun. Then the woman fingers at last released their grip, and he whispered "thank you" as he dropped toward the hard white death-light of Hoover Boulevard.

## Wednesday

The *seguridados* were on the boulevards tonight, hunting the trespassing dead. The meat were monsters, overmoneyed, under-stimulated, *cerristo* males and females who deeply enjoyed playing angels of Big Death in a world where any other kind of death was temporary. The meat were horrors, but their machines were beautiful. *Mechadors*: robot mantises with beaks of vanadium steel and two rapid fire MIST 27s throwing fifty self-targeting drones per second, each separating into a hail of sun-munitions

half a second before impact. Fifteen wide-spectrum senses analyzed the world; the machines maneuvered on tightly focused
impeller fields. And absolutely no thought or mercy. Big beautiful death.

The window in the house in the hills was big and wide and the
man stood in the middle of it. He was watching the *mechadors*
hunt. There were four of them, two pairs working each side of the
avenue. He saw the one with *Necroslayer* painted on its tectoplastic skin bound over the shrubbery from the Sifuentes place in
a single pulse of focused electrogravitic force. It moved over the
lawn, beaked head sensing. It paused, scanned the window. The
man met its five cluster eyes for an instant. It moved on. Its
impeller drive left eddy patterns on the shaved turf. The man
watched until the *mechadors* passed out of sight, and the *seguridados* in their over-emphatic battle-armor came up the avenue,
covering imagined threats with their hideously powerful weapons.

"It's every night now," he said. "They're getting scared."

In an instant, the woman was in the big, wood-floored room
where the man stood. She was dressed in a virtuality bodyglove;
snapped tendrils retracting into the suit's node points indicated
the abruptness with which she had pulled out of the web. She was
dark and very angry. Scared angry.

"Jesus Joseph Mary, how many times do I have to *tell* you?
Keep away from that window! They catch you, you're dead.
Again. *Permanently*."

Solomon Gursky shrugged. In the few weeks that he had lived
in her house, the woman had come to hate that shrug. It was a
shrug that only the dead can make. She hated it because it
brought the chill of the abyss into her big, warm, beautiful house
in the hills.

"It changes things," the dead man said.

Elena Asado pulled smart-leather pants and a mesh top over
the body-glove. Since turning traitor, she'd lived in the thing.
Twelve hours a day hooked into the web by eye and ear and nose
and soul, fighting the man who had killed her lover. As well fight
God, Solomon Gursky thought in the long, empty hours in the
airy, light-filled rooms. He is lord of life and death. Elena only
removed the bodyglove to wash and excrete and, in those early,
blue-lit mornings that only this city could do, when she made
chilly love on the big white bed. Time and anger had made her

thin and tough. She'd cut her hair like a boy's. Elena Asado was a tight wire of a woman, femininity jerked away by her need to revenge herself on Adam Tesler by destroying the world order his gift of resurrection had created.

Not gift. Never gift. He was not Jesus, who offered eternal life to whoever believed. No profit in belief. Adam Tesler took everything and left you your soul. If you could sustain the heavy *inmortalidad* payments, insurance would take you into post-life debt-free. The other 90 percent of Earth's dead worked out their salvation through indenture contracts to the Death House, the Tesler Thanos *corporada's* agent of resurrection. The *contratos* were centuries long. Time was the province of the dead. They were cheap.

"The Ewart/OzWest affair has them rattled," Elena Asado said.

"A handful of *contradados* renege on their contracts out on some asteroid, and they're afraid the sky is going to fall on their heads?"

"They're calling themselves the Freedead. You give a thing a name, you give it power. They know it's the beginning. Ewart/OzWest, all the other orbital and deep-space manufacturing *corporadas*; they always knew they could never enforce their contracts off Earth. They've lost already. Space belongs to the dead," the meat woman said.

Sol crossed the big room to the other window, the safe window that looked down from the high hills over the night city. His palm print deconfigured the glass. Night, city night perfumed with juniper and sex and smoke and the dusky heat of the heat of the day, curled around him. He went to the balcony rail. The boulevards shimmered like a map of a mind, but there was a great dark amnesia at its heart, an amorphous zone where lights were not, where the geometry of the grid was abolished. St John. Necroville. Dead town. The city of the dead, a city within a city, walled and moated and guarded with the same weapons that swept the boulevards. City of curfew. Each dusk, the artificial aurora twenty kilometers above the Tres Valles Metropolitan Area would pulse red: the skysign, commanding all the three million dead to return from the streets of the living to their necrovilles. They passed through five gates, each in the shape of a massive V bisected by a horizontal line. The entropic flesh life descending, the eternal resurrected life ascending, through the dividing line of death. That was the law, that plane of separation. Dead was dead, living was living. As incompatible as night and day.

That same sign was fused into the palm of every resurrectee that stepped from the Death House Jesus tanks.

Not true, he thought. Not all are reborn with stigmata. Not all obey curfew. He held his hand before his face, studied the lines and creases, as if seeking a destiny written there.

He had seen the deathsign in the palm of Elena's housegirl, and how it flashed in time to the aurora.

"Still can't believe it's real?"

He had not heard Elena come onto the balcony behind him. He felt the touch of her hand on his hair, his shoulder, his bare arm. Skin on skin.

"The Nez Perce tribe believe the world ended on the third day, and what we are living in are the dreams of the last night. I fell. I hit that white light and it was hard. Hard as diamond. Maybe I dream I live, and my dreams are the last shattered moments of my life."

"Would you dream it like this?"

"No," he said after a time. "I can't recognize anything any more. I can't see how it connects to what I last remember. So much is missing."

"I couldn't make a move until I was sure he didn't suspect. He'd done a thorough job."

"He would."

"I never believed that story about the lifter crash. The universe may be ironic, but it's never neat."

"I think a lot about the poor bastard pilot he took out as well, just to make it neat." The air carried the far sound of drums from down in the dead town Tomorrow was the great feast, the Night of All the Dead. "Five years," he said. He heard the catch in her breathing and knew what she would say next, and what would follow.

"What is it like, being dead?" Elena Asado asked.

In his weeks imprisoned in the hill house, an unlawful dead, signless and contractless, he had learned that she did not mean, what was it like to be resurrected. She wanted to know about the darkness before.

"Nothing," he answered, as he always did, but though it was true, it was not the truth, for nothing is a product of human consciousness and the darkness beyond the shattering hard light at terminal vee on Hoover Boulevard was the end of all consciousness. No dreams, no time, no loss, no light, no dark. No thing.

Now her fingers were stroking his skin, feeling for some of the chill of the no-thing. He turned from the city and picked her up and carried her to the big empty bed. A month of new life was enough to learn the rules of the game. He took her in the big, wide white bed by the glow from the city beneath, and it was as chill and formulaic as every other time. He knew that for her it was more than sex with her lover come back from a far exile. He could feel in the twitch and splay of her muscles that what made it special for her was that he was *dead*. It delighted and repelled her. He suspected that she was incapable of orgasm with fellow meat. It did not trouble him, being her fetish. The body once known as Solomon Gursky knew another thing, that only the dead could know. It was that not everything that died was resurrected. The shape, the self, the sentience came back, but love did not pass through death.

Afterward, she liked him to talk about his resurrection, when no-thing became thing and he saw her face looking down through the swirl of tectors. This night he did not talk. He asked. He asked, "What was I like?"

"Your body?" she said. He let her think that. "You want to see the morgue photographs again?"

He knew the charred grin of a husk well enough. Hands flat at his sides. That was how she had known right away. Burn victims died with their fists up, fighting incineration.

"Even after I'd had you exhumed, I couldn't bring you back. I know you told me that he said I was safe, for the moment, but that moment was too soon. The technology wasn't sophisticated enough, and he would have known right away. I'm sorry I had to keep you on ice."

"I hardly noticed," he joked.

"I always meant to. It was planned; get out of Tesler Thanos, then contract an illegal Jesus tank down in St John. The Death House doesn't know one tenth of what's going on in there."

"Thank you," Sol Gursky said, and then he felt it. He felt it and he saw it as if it were his own body. She felt him tighten.

"Another flashback?"

"No," he said. "The opposite. Get up."

"What?" she said. He was already pulling on leather and silk.
"That moment Adam gave you."

"Yes?"

"It's over."

The car was morphed into low and fast configuration. At the bend where the avenue slung itself down the hillside, they both felt the pressure wave of something large and flying pass over them, very low, utterly silent.

"Leave the car," he ordered. The doors were already gull-winged open. Three steps and the house went up behind them in a rave of white light. It seemed to suck at them, drawing them back into its annihilating gravity, then the shock swept them and the car and every homeless thing on the avenue before it. Through the screaming house alarms and the screaming house-holders and the rush and roar of the conflagration, Sol heard the aircraft turn above the vaporized hacienda. He seized Elena's hand and ran. The lifter passed over them and the car vanished in a burst of white energy.

"Jesus, nanotok warheads!"

Elena gasped as they tumbled down through tiered and ter-raced gardens. The lifter turned high on the air, eclipsing the hazy stars, hunting with extra-human senses. Below, formations of *seguridados* were spreading out through the gardens.

"How did you know?" Elena gasped.

"I saw it," said Solomon Gursky as they crashed a pool party and sent bacchanalian *cerristos* scampering for cover. Down, down. Augmented cyberhounds growled and quested with long-red eyes; domestic defense grids stirred, captured images, alerted the police.

"Saw?" asked Elena Asado.

APVs and city pods cut smoking hexagrams in the highway blacktop as Sol and Elena came crashing out of the service alley onto the boulevard. Horns. Lights. Fervid curses. Grind of wheels. Shriek of brakes. Crack of smashing tectoplastic, doubled, redoubled. Grid-pile on the westway. A mopedcab was pulled in at a *tortilleria* on the right shoulder. The *cochero* was happy to pass up his enchiladas for Elena's hard, black currency. Folding, clinking stuff.

"Where to?"

The destruction his passengers had wreaked impressed him. Taxi drivers universally hate cars.

"Drive," Solomon Gursky said.

The machine kicked out onto the strip.

"It's still up there," Elena said, squinting out from under the canopy at the night sky.

"They won't do anything in this traffic."

"They did it up there on the avenue." Then: "You said you saw. What do you mean, *saw?*"

"You know death, when you're dead," Solomon Gursky said. "You know its face, its mask, its smell. It has a perfume, you can smell it from a long way off, like the phermones of moths. It blows upwind in time."

"Hey," the *cochero* said, who was poor, but live meat. "You know anything about that big boom up on the hill? What was that, lifter crash or something?"

"Or something," Elena said. "Keep driving."

"Need to know where to keep driving to, lady."

"Necroville," Solomon Gursky said. St John. City of the Dead. The place beyond law, morality, fear, love, all the things that so tightly bound the living. The outlaw city. To Elena he said, "If you're going to bring down Adam Tesler, you can only do it from the outside, as an outsider." He said this in English. The words were heavy and tasted strange on his lips. "You must do it as one of the dispossessed. One of the dead."

To have tried to run the fluorescent vee-slash of the Necroville gate would have been as certain a Big Death as to have been reduced to hot ion dust in the nanotok flash. The mopedcab prowled past the samurai silhouettes of the gate *seguridados*. Sol had the driver leave them beneath the dusty palms on a deserted boulevard pressed up hard against the razor wire of St. John. Abandoned by the living, the grass verges had run verdant, scum and lilies scabbed the swimming pools, the generous Spanish-style houses softly disintegrating, digested by their own gardens.

It gave the *cochero* spooky vibes, but Sol liked it. He knew these avenues. The little machine putt-putted off for the lands of the fully living.

"There are culverted streams all round here," Sol said. "Some go right under the defenses, into Necroville."

"Is this your dead-sight again?" Elena asked as he started down an overhung service alley.

"In a sense. I grew up around here."

"I didn't know that."

"Then I can trust it."

She hesitated a step.

"What are you accusing me of?"

"How much did you rebuild, Elena?"

"Your memories are your own, Sol. We loved each other, once."

"Once," he said, and then he felt it, a static purr on his skin, like Elena's fingers over his whole body at once. This was not the psychic bloom of death foreseen. This was physics, the caress of focused gravity fields.

They hit the turn of the alley as the *mechadors* came dropping soft and slow over the roofs of the old moldering *residencias*. Across a weed-infested tennis court was a drainage ditch defended by a rusted chicken-wire fence. Sol heaved away an entire section. Adam Tesler had built his dead strong, and fast. The refugees followed the seeping, rancid water down to a rusted grille in a culvert.

"Now we see if the Jesus tank grew me true," Sol said as he kicked in the grille. "If what I remember is mine, then we come up in St John. If not, we end up in the bay three days from now with our eyes eaten out by chlorine."

They ducked into the culvert as a *mechador* passed over. MIST 27s sent the mud and water up in a blast of spray and battle tectors. The dead man and the living woman splashed on into darkness.

"He loved you, you know," Sol said. "That's why he's doing this. He is a jealous God. I always knew he wanted you, more than that bitch he calls a wife. While I was dead, he could pretend that it might still be. He could overlook what you were trying to do to him; you can't hurt him, Elena, not on your own. But when you brought me back, he couldn't pretend any longer. He couldn't turn a blind eye. He couldn't forgive you."

"A petty God," Elena said, water eddying around her leather-clad calves. Ahead, a light from a circle in the roof of the culvert marked a drain from the street. They stood under it a moment, feeling the touch of the light of Necroville on their faces. Elena reached up to push open the grate. Solomon Gursky stayed her, turned her palm upward to the light.

"One thing." he said. He picked a sharp shard of concrete from the tunnel wall. With three strong savage strokes he cut the vee and slash of the death sign in her flesh.

# Thursday

He was three kilometers down the mass driver when the fleet hit Marlene Dietrich. St Judy's Comet was five AU from perihelion and out of ecliptic, the Clade thirty-six degrees out, but for an instant two suns burned in the sky.

The folds of transparent tectoplastic skin over Solomon Gursky's face opaqued. His *sur*-arms gripped the spiderwork of the interstellar engine, rocked by the impact on his electromagnetic senses of fifty minitok warheads converting into bevawatts of hard energy. The death scream of a nation. Three hundred Freedead had cluttered the freefall warren of tunnels that honeycombed the asteroid. Marlene Dietrich had been the seed of the rebellion. The *corporadas* cherished their grudges.

Solomon Gursky's face-shield cleared. The light of Marlene Dietrich's dying was short-lived but its embers faded in his infravision toward the stellar background.

Elena spoke in his skull.

*You know?*

Though she was enfolded in the command womb half a kilometer deep within the comet, she was naked to the universe through identity links to the sensor web in the crust and a nimbus of bacterium-sized spyships weaving through the tenuous gas halo.

*I saw it,* Solomon Gursky subvocalized.

*They'll come for us now,* Elena said.

*You think.* Using his *bas*-arms Sol clambered along the slender spine of the mass driver toward the micro meteorite impact.

*I know. When long-range cleared after the blast, we caught the signatures of blip-fusion burns.*

Hand over hand over hand over hand. One of the first things you learn, when the Freedead change you, is that in space it is all a question of attitude. A third of the way down a nine-kilometer mass driver with several billion tons of Oort comet spiked on it, you don't think up, you don't think down. *Up,* and it is vertigo. *Down,* and a two kilometer sphere of grubby ice is poised above your head by a thread of superconducting tectoplastic. *Out,* that was the only way to think of it and stay sane. Away, and back again.

*How many drives?* Sol asked. The impact pin-pointed itself; the smart plastic fluoresced orange when wounded.

*Eight.*

A sub-voiced blasphemy. *They didn't even make them break sweat. How long have we got?*

Elena flashed the projections through the em-link onto his visual cortex. Curves of light through darkness and time, warped across the gravitation marches of Jupiter. Under current acceleration, the Earth fleet would be within strike in eighty-two hours.

The war in heaven was in its twelfth year. Both sides had determined that this was to be the last. The NightFreight War would be fought to an outcome. They called themselves the Clades, the outlaw descendants of the original Ewart/OzWest asteroid rebellion: a handful of redoubts scattered across the appalling distances of the solar system. Marlene Dietrich, the first to declare freedom; Neruro, a half-completed twenty kilometer wheel of tectoplastic attended by O'Neill can utilities, agriculture tanks, and habitation bubbles, the aspirant capital of the space Dead. Ares Orbital, dreaming of tectoformed Mars in the pumice pore spaces of Phobos and Deimos; the Pale Gallileans, surfing over the icescapes of Europa on an improbable raft of cables and spars; the Shepherd Moons, dwellers on the edge of the abyss, sailing the solar wind through Saturn's rings. Toe-holds, shallow scratchings, space-hovels; but the stolen nanotechnology burgeoned in the energy-rich environment of space. An infinite ecological niche. The Freedead knew they were the inheritors of the universe. The meat *corporadas* had withdrawn to the orbit of their planet. For a time. When they struck, they struck decisively. The Tsiolkovski Clade on the dark side of the moon was the first to fall as the battle groups of the *corporadas* thrust outward. The delicate film of vacuum-compatible tectoformed forest that carpeted the crater was seared away in the alpha strike. By the time the last strike went in, a new five-kilometer deep crater of glowing tufa replaced the tunnels and excavations of the old lunar mining base. Earth's tides had trembled as the moon staggered in its orbit.

Big Big Death.

The battle groups moved toward their primary targets. The *corporadas* had learned much embargoed under their atmosphere. The new ships were lean, mean, fast: multiple missile racks clipped to high-gee blip-fusion motors, pilots suspended in acceleration gel like flies in amber, hooked by every orifice into the big battle virtualizers.

Thirteen-year-old boys had the best combination of reaction time and viciousness.

Now the blazing teenagers had wantonly destroyed the Marlene Dietrich Clade. Ares Orbital was wide open; Neruro, where most of the Freedead slamship fleet was based, would fight hard. Two *corporada* ships had been dispatched Jupiterward. Orbital mechanics gave the defenseless Pale Gallileans fifteen months to contemplate their own annihilation.

But the seed has flown, Solomon Gursky thought silently, out on the mass driver of St Judy's Comet. Where we are going, neither your most powerful ships nor your most vicious boys can reach us.

The micrometeorite impact had scrambled the tectoplastic's limited intelligence: fibers and filaments of smart polymer twined and coiled, seeking completion and purpose. Sol touched his *sur*-hands to the surfaces. He imagined he could feel the order pass out of him, like a prickle of tectors osmosing through vacuum-tight skin.

Days of miracles and wonder, Adam, he thought. And because you are jealous that we are doing things with your magic you never dreamed, you would blast us all to photons.

The breach was repaired. The mass driver trembled and kicked a pellet into space, and another, and another. And Sol Gursky, working his way hand over hand over hand over hand down the device that was taking him to the stars, saw the trick of St Judy's Comet. A ball of fuzzy ice drawing a long tail behind it. Not a seed, but a sperm, swimming through the big dark. Thus we impregnate the universe.

St Judy's Comet. Petite as Oort cloud family members go: two point eight by one point seven by two point two kilometers. (Think of the misshaped potato you push to the side of your plate because anything that looks that weird is sure to give you cramps.) Undernourished, at sixty-two billion tons. Waif and stray of the solar system, wandering slow and lonely back out into the dark after her hour in the sun (but not too close, burn you real bad, too much sun) when these dead people snatch her, grope her all over, shove things up her ass, mess with her insides, make her do strange and unnatural acts, like shitting tons of herself away every second at a good percentage of the speed of light. Don't you know you ain't no comet no more? You're a *starship*. See up there, in the Swan, just to the left of that big bright star? There's a little dim star you can't see. That's where you're going, little St Judy. Take some company. Going to be a long trip. And what will I find when I get there? A big bastard MACHO of gas supergiant orbiting 61 Cygni at the distance of Saturn from the sun, that's what you'll find. Just swarming with moons; one of them should be right for terrestrial life. And if not, no matter; sure, what's the difference between tectoforming an asteroid, or a comet, or the moon of an extra-solar gas super-giant? Just scale. You see, we've got everything we need to tame a new solar system right here *with* us. It's all just carbon, hydrogen, nitrogen, and oxygen, and you have that in abundance. And maybe we like you so much that we find we don't even need a world at all. Balls of muck and gravity, hell; we're the Freedead. Space and time belong to us.

It was Solomon Gursky, born in another century, who gave the ship its name. In that other century, he had owned a large and eclectic record collection. On vinyl.

The twenty living dead crew of St Judy's Comet gathered in the command womb embedded in sixty-two billion tons of ice to plan battle. The other five hundred and forty were stored as superconducting tector matrices in a helium ice core; the dead dead, to be resurrected out of comet stuff at their new home. The crew hovered in nanogee in a score of different orientations around the free-floating instrument clusters. They were strange and beautiful, as gods and angels are. Like angels, they flew. Like gods in some pantheons, they were four-armed. Fine, manipulating *sur*-arms; strong grasping *bas*-arms growing from a lower spine reconfigured by Jesus tanks into powerful anterior shoulder-blades. Their vacuum-and-radiation-tight skins were photosynthetic, and as beautifully marked and colored as a hunting animal's. Stripes, swirls of green on orange, blue on black, fractal patterns, flags of legendary nations, tattoos. Illustrated humans.

Elena Asado, caressed by tendrils from the sensor web, gave them the stark news. Fluorescent patches on shoulders, hips, and groin glowed when she spoke.

"The bastards have jumped vee. They must have burned every last molecule of hydrogen in their thruster tanks to do it. Estimated to strike range is now sixty-four hours."

The *capitan* of St Judy's Comet, a veteran of the Marlene

Dietrich rebellion, shifted orientation to face Jorge, the ship's reconfiguration engineer.

"Long range defenses?" *Capitan* Savita's skin was an exquisite mottle of pale green bamboo leaves in sun yellow, an incongruous contrast to the tangible anxiety in the command womb.

"First wave missiles will be fully grown and launch-ready in twenty-six hours. The fighters, no. The best I can push the assemblers up to is sixty-six hours."

"What can you do in time?" Sol Gursky asked.

"With your help, I could simplify the fighter design for close combat."

"How close?" *Capitan* Savita asked.

"Under a hundred kays."

"How simplified?" Elena asked.

"Little more than an armed exo-skeleton with maneuvering pods."

And they need to be clever every time, Sol thought. The meat need to be clever only once.

Space war was as profligate with time as it was with energy and distance. With the redesigns growing, Sol Gursky spent most of the twenty-six hours to missile launch on the ice, naked to the stars, imagining their warmth on his face-shield. Five years since he had woken from his second death in a habitat bubble out at Marlene Dietrich, and stars had never ceased to amaze him. When you come back, you are tied to the first thing you see. Beyond the transparent tectoplastic bubble, it had been stars.

The first time, it had been Elena. Tied together in life, now in death. Necroville had not been sanctuary. The place beyond the law only gave Adam Tesler new and more colorful opportunities to incarnate his jealousy. The Benthic Lords, they had called themselves. Wild, free, dead. They probably had not known they were working for Tesler-Thanos, but they took her out in a dead bar on Terminal Boulevard. With a game-fishing harpoon. They carved their skull symbol on her forehead, a rebuttal of the deathsign Sol had cut in her palm. Now you are really dead, meat. He had known they would never be safe on Earth. The *companeros* in the Death House had faked the off-world Night-Freight contracts. The pill Sol took had been surprisingly bitter, the dive into the white light as hard as he remembered.

Stars. You could lose yourself in them; spirit strung out, orb gazing. Somewhere out there was a still-invisible constellation of eight, tight formation, silent running. Killing stars. Death stars.

Everyone came up to watch the missiles launch from the black foramens grown out of the misty ice. The chemical motors burned at twenty kays: a sudden galaxy of white stars. They watched them fade from sight. Twelve hours to contact. No one expected them to do any more than waste a few thousand rounds of the meat's point defenses.

In a dozen manufacturing pods studded around St Judy's dumpy waist, Jorge and Sol's fighters gestated. Their slow accretion, molecule by molecule, fascinated Sol. Evil dark things, St Andrew's crosses cast in melted bone. At the center a human-shaped cavity. You flew spread-eagled. *Bas*-hands gripped thruster controls; *sur*-hands armed and aimed the squirt lasers. Dark flapping things Sol had glimpsed once before flocked again at the edges of his consciousness. He had cheated the dark premonitory angels that other time. He would sleight them again.

The first engagement of the battle of St Judy's Comet was at 01:45 GMT. Solomon Gursky watched it with his crewbrethren in the ice-wrapped warmth of the command womb. His virtualized sight perceived space in three dimensions. Those blue cylinders were the *corporada* ships. That white swarm closing from a hundred different directions, the missiles. One approached a blue cylinder and burst. Another, and another; then the inner display was a glare of novas as the first wave was annihilated. The back-up went in. The vanguard exploded in beautiful futile blossoms of light. Closer. They were getting closer before the meat shredded them. Sol watched a warhead loop up from due south, streak toward the point ship, and annihilate it in a red flash.

The St Judy's Cometeers cheered. One gone, reduced to bubbling slag by tectors sprayed from the warhead.

One was all they got. It was down to the fighter pilots now.

Sol and Elena made love in the count-up to launch. *Bas*-arms and *sur*-arms locked in the freegee of the forward observation blister. Stars described slow arcs across the transparent dome, like a sky. Love did not pass through death; Elena had realized this bitter truth about what she had imagined she had shared with Solomon Gursky in her house on the hillside. But love could grow, and become a thing shaped for eternity. When the fluids had dried on their skins, they sealed their soft, intimate places with vacuum-tight skin and went up to the launch bays.

Sol fitted her into the scooped-out shell. Tectoplastic fingers gripped Elena's body and meshed with her skin circuitry. The angel-suit came alive. There was a trick they had learned in their em-telepathy; a massaging of the limbic system like an inner kiss. One mutual purr of pleasure, then she cast off, suit still dripping gobs of frozen tectopolymer. St Judy's defenders would fight dark and silent; that mental kiss would be the last radio contact until it was decided. Solomon Gursky watched the blue stutter of the thrusters merge with the stars. Reaction mass was limited; those who returned from the fight would jettison their angel-suits and glide home by solar sail. Then he went below to monitor the battle through the tickle of molecules in his frontal lobes.

St Judy's Angels formed two squadrons: one flying anti-missile defense, the other climbing high out of the ecliptic to swoop down on the *corporada* ships and destroy them before they could empty their weapon racks. Elena was in the close defense group. Her angelship icon was identified in Sol's inner vision in red on gold tiger stripes of her skin. He watched her weave intricate orbits around St Judy's Comet as the blue cylinders of the meat approached the plane labeled "strike range."

Suddenly, seven blue icons spawned a cloud of actinic sparks, raining down on St Judy's Comet like fireworks.

"Jesus Joseph Mary!" someone swore quietly.

"Fifty-five gees," *Capitan* Savita said calmly. "Time to contact, one thousand and eighteen seconds."

"They'll never get them all," said Kobe with the Mondrian skin pattern, who had taken Elena's place in remote sensing.

"We have one hundred and fifteen contacts in the first wave," Jorge announced.

"Sol, I need delta vee," Savita said.

"More than a thousandth of a gravity and the mass driver coils will warp," Sol said, calling overlays onto his visual cortex.

"Anything that throws a curve into their computations," Savita said.

"I'll see how close I can push it."

He was glad to have to lose himself in the problems of squeezing a few millimeters per second squared out of the big electromagnetic gun, because then he would not be able to see the curve and swoop of attack vectors and intercept planes as the point defense group closed with the missiles. Especially he would not have to watch the twine and loop of the tiger-striped cross and fear that at any instant it would intersect with a sharp blue curve in a flash of annihilation. One by one, those blue stars were going out, he noticed, but slowly. Too slowly. Too few.

The computer gave him a solution. He fed it to the mass driver. The shift of acceleration was as gentle as a catch of breath.

Thirty years since he had covered his head in a synagogue, but Sol Gursky prayed to Yahweh that it would be enough.

One down already; Emilio's spotted indigo gone, and half the missiles were still on trajectory. Time to impact ticked down impassively in the upper right corner of his virtual vision. Six hundred and fifteen seconds. Ten minutes to live.

But the attack angels were among the *corporadas*, dodging the brilliant flares of short range interceptor drones. The meat fleet tried to scatter, but the ships were low on reaction mass, ungainly, unmaneuverable. St Judy's Angels dived and sniped among them, clipping a missile rack here, a solar panel there, ripping open life support bubbles and fuel tanks in slow explosions of outgassing hydrogen. The thirteen-year-old pilots died, raging with chemical-induced fury, spilled out into vacuum in tears of flash-frozen acceleration gel. The attacking fleet dwindled from seven to five to three ships. But it was no abattoir of the meat; of the six dead angels that went in, only two pulled away into rendezvous orbit, laser capacitors dead, reaction mass spent. The crews ejected, unfurled their solar sails, shields of light.

Two meat ships survived. One used the last grams of his maneuvering mass to warp into a return orbit; the other routed his thruster fuel through his blip drive; headlong for St Judy.

"He's going for a ram," Kobe said.

"Sol, get us away from him," *Captain* Savita ordered.

"He's too close." The numbers in Sol's skull were remorseless. "Even if I cut the mass driver, he can still run life support gas through the STUs to compensate."

The command womb quivered.

"Fuck," someone swore reverently.

"Near miss," Kobe reported. "Direct hit if Sol hadn't given us gees."

"Mass driver is still with us," Sol said.

"Riley's gone," *Captain* Savita said.

Fifty missiles were now twenty missiles but Emilio and Riley were dead, and the range was closing. Little room for maneuver; none for mistakes.

"Two hundred and fifteen seconds to ship impact," Kobe announced. The main body of missiles was dropping behind St Judy's Comet. Ogawa and Skin, Mandelbrot set and Dalmatian spots, were fighting a rearguard as the missiles tried to reacquire their target. Olive green ripples and red tiger stripes swung round to face the meat ship. Quinsana and Elena.

Jesus Joseph Mary, but it was going to be close!

Sol wished he did not have the graphics in his head. He wished not to have to see. Better sudden annihilation, blindness and ignorance shattered by destroying light. To see, to *know*, to count the digits on the timer, was as cruel as execution. But the inner vision has no eyelids. So he watched, impotent, as Quinsana's olive green cross was pierced and shattered by a white flare from the meat ship. And he watched as Elena raked the meat with her lasers and cut it into quivering chunks, and the blast of engines destroying themselves sent the shards of ship arcing away from St Judy's Comet. And he could only watch, and not look away, as Elena turned too slow, too little, too late, as the burst seed-pod of the environment unit tore off her thruster legs and light sail and sent her spinning end over end, crippled, destroyed.

"Elena!" he screamed in both his voices. "Elena! Oh Jesus oh God!" But he had never believed in either of them, and so they let Elena Asado go tumbling endlessly toward the beautiful galaxy clusters of Virgo.

Earth's last rage against her children expired: twenty missiles dwindled to ten, to five, to one. To none. St Judy's Comet continued her slow climb out of the sun's gravity well, into the deep dark and the deeper cold. Its five hundred and twenty souls slept sound and ignorant as only the dead can in tombs of ice. Soon Solomon Gursky and the others would join them, and be dissolved into the receiving ice, and die for five hundred years while St Judy's Comet made the crossing to another star.

If it were sleep, then I might forget, Solomon Gursky thought. In sleep, things changed, memories became dreams, dreams memories. In sleep, there was time, and time was change, and perhaps a chance of forgetting the vision of her, spinning outward forever, rebuilt by the same forces that had already resurrected her once, living on sunlight, unable to die. But it was not sleep to which he was going. It was death, and that was nothing any more.

# Friday

Together they watched the city burn. It was one of the ornamental cities of the plain that the Long Scanning folk built and maintained for the quadrennial eisteddfods. There was something of the flower in the small, jewel-like city, and something of the spiral, and something of the sea-wave. It would have as been as accurate to call it a vast building as a miniature city. It burned most elegantly.

The fault line ran right through the middle of it. The fissure was clean and precise – no less to be expected of the Long Scanning folk – and bisected the curvilinear architecture from top to bottom. The land still quivered to aftershocks.

It could have repaired itself. It could have doused the flames – a short in the magma tap, the man reckoned – reshaped the melted ridges and roofs, erased the scorch marks, bridged the cracks and chasms. But its tector systems were directionless, its soul withdrawn to the Heaven Tree, to join the rest of the Long Scanning people on their exodus.

The woman watched the smoke rise into the darkening sky, obscuring the great opal of Urizen.

"It doesn't have to do this," she said. Her skin spoke of sorrow mingled with puzzlement.

"They've no use for it any more," the man said. "And there's a certain beauty in destruction."

"It scares me," the woman said, and her skin pattern agreed. "I've never seen anything *end* before."

*Lucky*, the man thought, in a language that had come from another world.

An eddy in his weathersight: big one coming. But they were all big ones since the orbital perturbations began. Big, getting bigger. At the end, the storms would tear the forests from their roots as the atmosphere shrieked into space.

That afternoon, on their journey to the man's memories, they had come across an empty marina; drained, sand clogged, pontoons torn and tossed by tsunamis. Its crew of boats they found scattered the length of a half-hour's walk. Empty shells stogged to the waist in dune faces, masts and sails hung from trees.

The weather had been the first thing to tear free from control. The man felt a sudden tautness in the woman's body. She was seeing it to, the mid-game of the end of the world.

By the time they reached the sheltered valley that the man's aura had picked as the safest location to spend the night, the wind had risen to draw soft moans and chords from the curves and crevasses of the dead city. As their cloaks of elementals joined and sank the roots of the night shell into rock, a flock of bubbles bowled past, trembling and iridescent in the gusts. The woman caught one on her hand; the tiny creature-machine clung for a moment, feeding from her biofield. Its transparent skin raced with oil-film colors, it quaked and burst, a melting bubble of tectoplasm. The woman watched it until the elementals had completed the shelter, but the thing stayed dead.

Their love-making was both urgent and chilled under the scalloped carapace the elementals had sculpted from rock silica. *Sex and death,* the man said in the part of his head where not even his sub-vocal withspeech could overhear and transmit. An alien thought.

She wanted to talk afterward. She liked talk after sex. Unusually, she did not ask him to tell her about how he and the other Five Hundred Fathers had built the world. Her idea of talking was him talking. Tonight she did not want to talk about the world's beginning. She wanted him to talk about its ending.

"Do you know what I hate about it? It's not that it's all going to end, all this. It's that a bubble burst in my hand, and I can't comprehend what *happened* to it. How much more our whole world?"

"There is a word for what you felt," the man interjected gently. The gyrestorm was at its height, raging over the dome of their shell. The thickness of a skin is all that is keeping the wind from stripping the flesh from my bones, he thought. But the tectors' grip on the bedrock was firm and sure. "The word is *die*."

The woman sat with her knees pulled up, arms folded around them. Naked: the gyrestorm was blowing through her soul.

"What I hate," she said after silence, "is that I have so little time to see and feel it all before it's taken away into the cold and the dark."

She was a Green, born in the second of the short year's fast seasons: a Green of the Hidden Design people; first of the Old Red Ridge pueblo people to come into the world in eighty years. And the last.

Eight years old.

"You won't die," the man said, skin patterning in whorls of

reassurance and paternal concern, like the swirling storms of great Urizen beyond the hurtling gyrestorm clouds. "You can't die. No one will die."

"I know that. No one will die, we will all be changed, or sleep with the world. But . . ."

"Is it frightening, to have to give up this body?"

She touched her forehead to her knees, shook her head.

"I don't want to lose it. I've only begun to understand what it is, this body, this world, and it's all going to be taken away from me, and all the powers that are my birthright are useless."

"There are forces beyond even nanotechnology," the man said. "It makes us masters of matter, but the fundamental dimensions – gravity, space, time – it cannot touch."

"Why?" the woman said, and to the man, who counted by older, longer years, she spoke in the voice of her terrestrial age.

"We will learn it, in time," the man said, which he knew was no answer. The woman knew it too, for she said, "While Orc is two hundred million years from the warmth of the next sun, and its atmosphere is a frozen glaze on these mountains and valleys." *Grief*, he skin said. *Rage. Loss.*

The two-thousand-year-old father touched the young woman's small, upturned breasts.

"We knew Urizen's orbit was unstable, but no one could have predicted the interaction with Ulro." Ironic: that this world named after Blake's fire daemon should be the one cast into darkness and ice, while Urizen and its surviving moons should bake two million kilometers above the surface of Los.

"Sol, you don't need to apologize to me for mistakes you made two thousand years ago," said the woman, whose name was Lenya.

"But I think I need to apologize to the world," said Sol Gursky.

Lenya's skin-speech now said *hope* shaded with *inevitability*. Her nipples were erect. Sol bent to them again as the wind from the end of the world scratched its claws over the skin of tecto-plastic.

In the morning, they continued the journey to Sol's memories. The gyrestorm had blown itself out in the Oothoon mountains. What remained of the ghost-net told Sol and Lenya that it was possible to fly that day. They suckled milch from the shell's tree of life processor, and they had sex again on the dusty earth while the elementals reconfigured the night pod into a general utility flier. For the rest of the morning, they passed over a plain across which grazebeasts and the tall, predatory angularities of the stalking Systems Maintenance people moved like ripples on a lake, drawn to the Heaven Tree planted in the navel of the world.

Both grazers and herders had been human once.

At noon, the man and the woman encountered a flyer of the Generous Sky people, flapping a silk-winged course along the thermal lines rising from the feet of the Big Chrysolite mountains. Sol with-hailed him, and they set down together in a clearing in the bitter-root forests that carpeted much of Coryphee Canton. The Generous Sky man's etiquette would normally have compelled him to disdain those ground bound who sullied the air with machines, but in these urgent times, the old ways were breaking.

*Whither bound?* Sol withspoke him. Static crackled in his skull. The lingering tail of the gyrestorm was throwing off electromagnetic disturbances.

*Why, the Heaven Tree of course,* the winged man said. He was a horrifying kite of translucent skin over stick bones and sinews. His breast was like the prow of a ship, his muscles twitched and realigned as he shifted from foot to foot, uncomfortable on the earth. A gentle breeze wafted from the nanofans grown out of the web of skin between wrists and ankles. The air smelled of strange sweat. *Whither yourselves?*

*The Heaven Tree also, in time,* Sol said. *But I must first recover my memories.*

*Ah, a father,* the Sky man said. *Whose are you?*

*Hidden Design,* Sol said. *I am father to this woman and her people.*

*You are Solomon Gursky,* the flying man withsaid. *My progenitor is Nikos Samitreides.*

*I remember her well, though I have not seen her in many years. She fought bravely at the battle of St Judy's Comet.*

*I am third of her lineage. Eighteen hundred years I have been on this world.*

*A question, if I may.* Lenya's withspeech was a sudden bright interruption in the dialogue of old men. Using an honorific by which a younger adult addresses an experienced senior, she asked, *When the time comes, how will you change?*

*An easy question,* the Generous Sky man said, *I shall undergo the reconfiguration for life on Urizen. To me, it is little difference whether I wear the outward semblance of a man, or a jetpowered aerial manta: it is flying, and such flying! Canyons of clouds hundreds of kilometers deep; five thousand kilometer per hour winds; thermals great as continents; mad storms as big as planets! And no land, no base; to be able to fly forever free from the tyranny of Earth. The song cycles we shall compose; eddas that will carry half way around the planet on the jet streams of Urizen!* The Generous Sky man's eyes had closed in rapture. They suddenly opened. His nostrils dilated, sensing an atmospheric change intangible to the others.

*Another storm is coming, bigger than the last. I advise you to take shelter within rock, for this will pluck the bitter-roots from the soil.*

He spread his wings. The membranes rippled. A tiny hop, and the wind caught him and in an instant carried him up into a thermal. Sol and Lenya watched him glide the tops of the lifting air currents until he was lost in the deep blue sky.

For exercise and the conversation of the way, they walked that afternoon. They followed the migration track of the Rough Trading people through the tieve forests of south Coryphee and Emberwilde Cantons. Toward evening, with the gathering wind stirring the needles of the tieves to gossip, they met a man of the Ash species sitting on a chair in a small clearing among the trees. He was long and coiling, and his skin said that he was much impoverished from lack of a host. Lenya offered her arm, and though the Ash man's compatibility was more with the Buried Communication people than the Hidden Design, he gracefully accepted her heat, her morphic energy, and a few drops of blood.

"Where is your host?" Lenya asked him. A parasite, he had the languages of most nations. Hosts were best seduced by words, like lovers.

"He has gone with the herds," the Ash man said. "To the Heaven Tree. It is ended."

"And what will you do when Orc is expelled?" The rasp marks on Lenya's forearm where the parasitic man had sipped her blood were already healing over.

"I cannot live alone," the Ash man said. "I shall ask the earth to open and swallow me and kill me. I shall sleep in the earth until the warmth of a new sun awakens me to life again."

"But that will be two hundred million years," Lenya said. The Ash man looked at her with the look that said, *one year, one million*

*years, one hundred million years, they are nothing to death.* Because
she knew that the man thought her a new-hatched fool, Lenya felt
compelled to look back at him as she and Sol walked away along
the tieve tracks. She saw the parasite pressed belly and balls to the
ground, as he would to a host. Dust spiraled up around him. He
slowly sank into the earth.

Sol and Lenya did not have sex that night in the pod for the
first time since Solomon the Traveler had come to the Old Red
Ridge pueblo and taken the eye and heart of the brown girl
dancing in the ring. That night there was the greatest earthquake
yet as Orc kicked in his orbit, and even a shell of tectodiamond
seemed inadequate protection against forces that would throw a
planet into interstellar space. They held each other, not speaking,
until the earth grew quiet and a wave of heat passed over the
carapace, which was the tieve forests of Emberwilde Canton
burning.

The next morning, they morphed the pod into an ash-runner
and drove through the cindered forest, until at noon they came to
the edge of the Inland Sea. The tectonic trauma had sent tidal
waves swamping the craggy islet on which Sol had left his
memories, but the self-repair systems had used the dregs of their
stored power to rebuild the damaged architecture.

As Sol was particular that they must approach his memories by
sea, they ordered the ash-runner to reconfigure into a skiff. While
the tectors moved molecules, a man of the Blue Mana pulled
himself out of the big surf on to the red shingle. He was long and
huge and sleek; his shorn turf of fur was beautifully marked. He
lay panting from the exertion of heaving himself from his customary element into an alien one. Lenya addressed him familiarly
– Hidden Design and the amphibious Blue Mana had been one
until a millennium ago – and asked him the same question she had
put to the others she had encountered on the journey.

"I am already reconfiguring my body fat into an aircraft to take
me to the Heaven Tree," the Blue Mana said. "Climatic shifts
permitting."

"Is it bad in the sea?" Sol Gursky asked.

"The seas feel the changes first," the amphiman said. "Bad.
Yes, most bad. I cannot bear the thought of Mother Ocean
freezing clear to her beds."

"Will you go to Urizen, then?" Lenya asked, thinking that
swimming must be much akin to flying.

"Why, bless you, no." The Blue Mana man's skin spelled puzzled surprise. "Why should I share any less fate than Mother Ocean? We shall both end in ice."

"The comet fleet," Sol Gursky said.

"If the Earth ship left any legacy, it is that there are many mansions in this universe where we may live. I have a fancy to visit those other settled systems that the ship told us of, experience those other ways of being human."

A hundred Orc-years had passed since the second comet-ship from Earth had entered the Los system to refuel from Urizen's rings, but the news it had carried of a home system transfigured by the nanotechnology of the ascendant dead, and of the other stars that had been reached by the newer, faster, more powerful descendants of St Judy's Comet had ended nineteen hundred years of solitude and brought the first, lost colony of Orc into the visionary community of the star-crossing Dead. *Long before your emergence*, Sol thought, looking at the crease of Lenya's groin as she squatted on the pebbles to converse with the Blue Mana man. Emergence. A deeper, older word shadowed that expression; a word obsolete in the universe of the dead. *Birth*. No one had ever been born on Orc. No one had ever known childhood, or grown up. No one aged, no one died. They *emerged*. They stepped from the labia of the gestatory, fully formed, like gods.

Sol knew the word *child*, but realized with a shock that he could not see it any more. It was blank, void. So many things decreated in this world he had engineered!

By sea and by air. A trading of elements. Sol Gursky's skiff was completed as the Blue Mana's tectors transformed his blubber into a flying machine. Sol watched it spin into the air and recede to the south as the boat dipped through the chop toward the island of memory.

We live forever, we transform ourselves, we transform worlds, solar systems, we ship across interstellar space, we defy time and deny death, but the one thing we cannot recreate is memory, he thought. Sea birds dipped in the skiff's wake, hungry, hoping. Things cast up by motion. We cannot rebuild our memories, so we must store them, when our lives grow so full that they slop over the sides and evaporate. We Five Hundred Fathers have deep and much-emptied memories.

Sol's island was a rock slab tilted out of the equatorial sea, a handful of hard hectares. Twisted repro olives and cypresses

screened a small Doric temple at the highest point. Good maintenance tectors had held it strong against the Earth storms. The
classical theming now embarrassed, Sol but enchanted Lenya.
She danced beneath the olive branches, under the porticoes,
across the lintels. Sol saw her again as he had that first night
in the Small-year-ending ring dance at Old Red Ridge. Old lust.
New hurt.

In the sunlit central chamber, Lenya touched the reliefs of the
life of Solomon Gursky. They would not yield their memories to
her fingers, but they communicated in less sophisticated ways.

"This woman." She had stopped in front of a pale stone
carving of Solomon Gursky and a tall, ascetic-faced woman with
close-cropped hair standing hand in hand before a tall, ghastly
tower.

"I loved her. She died in the battle of St Judy's Comet. Big
dead."

Lost.

"So is it only because I remind you of her?"

He touched the carving. Memory bright and sharp as pain
arced along his nerves; mnemotectors downloading into his aura.
*Elena*. And a memory of orbit; the Long March ended, the object
formerly known as St Judy's Comet spun out into a web of beams
and girders and habitation pods hurtling across the frosted red
dustscapes of Orc. A web ripe with hanging fruit; entry pods
ready to drop and spray the new world with life seed. Tectoforming. Among the fruit, seeds of the Five Hundred Fathers,
founders of all the races of Orc. Among them, the Hidden Design
and Solomon Gursky, four-armed, vacuum-proofed, avatar of
life and death, clinging to a beam with the storms of Urizen
behind him, touching his transforming *sur*-arms to the main
memory of the mother seed. Remember her. Remember Elena.
And sometime – soon, late – bring her back. Imprint her with an
affinity for his scent, so that wherever she is, whoever she is with,
she will come to me.

He saw himself scuttling like a guilty spider across the web as
the pods dropped Orc-ward.

He saw himself in this place with Urizen's moons at syzygy,
touching his hands to the carving, giving to it what it now
returned to him, because he knew that as long as it was Lenya
who reminded him of Elena, it could pretend to be honest. But
the knowledge killed it. Lenya was more than a reminder. Lenya

was Elena. Lenya was a simulacrum, empty, fake. Her life, her joy, her sorrow, her love – all deceit.

He had never expected that she would come back to him at the end of the world. They should have had thousands of years. The world gave them days.

He could not look at her as he moved from relief to relief, charging his aura with memory. He could not touch her as they waited on the shingle for the skiff to reconfigure into the flyer that would take them to the Heaven Tree. On the high point of the slab island, the Temple of Memory dissolved like rotting fungus. He did not attempt sex with her as the flyer passed over the shattered landscapes of Thel and the burned forests of Chrysoberyl as they would have, before. She did not understand. She imagined she had hurt him somehow. She had, but the blame was Sol's. He could not tell her why he had suddenly expelled himself from her warmth. He knew that he should, that he must, but he could not. He changed his skin-speech to passive, mute, and reflected that much cowardice could be learned in five hundred long-years.

They came with the evening to the Skyplain plateau from which the Heaven Tree rose, an adamantine black ray aimed at the eye of Urizen. As far as they could see, the plain twinkled with the lights and fires of vehicles and camps. Warmsight showed a million glowings: all the peoples of Orc, save those who had chosen to go into the earth, had gathered in this final redoubt. Seismic stabilizing tectors woven into the moho held steady the quakes that had shattered all other lands, but temblors of increasing violence warned that they could not endure much longer. At the end, Skyplain would crack like an egg, the Heaven Tree snap and recoil spaceward like a severed nerve.

Sol's Five Hundred Father ident pulled his flyer out of the wheel of aircraft, airships, and aerial humans circling the stalk of the Heaven Tree into a priority slot on an ascender. The flyer caught the shuttle at five kilometers: a sudden veer toward the slab sides of the space elevator, guidance matching velocities with the accelerating ascender; then the drop, heart-stopping even for immortals, and the lurch as the flyer seized the docking nipple with its claspers and clung like a tick. Then the long climb heavenward.

Emerging from high altitude cloud, Sol saw the hard white diamond of Ulro rise above the curve of the world. Too small yet to show a disc, but this barren rock searing under heavy $CO_2$ exerted forces powerful enough to kick a moon into interstellar space. Looking up through the transparent canopy, he saw the Heaven Tree spread its delicate, light-studded branches hundreds of kilometers across the face of Urizen.

Sol Gursky broke his silence.

"Do you know what you'll do yet?"

"Well, since I am here, I am not going into the ground. And the ice fleet scares me. I think of centuries dead, a tector frozen in ice. It seems like death."

"It *is* death," Sol said. "Then you'll go to Urizen."

"It's a change of outward form, that's all. Another way of being human. And there'll be continuity; that's important to me."

He imagined the arrival: the ever-strengthening tug of gravity spiraling the flocks of vacuum-hardened carapaces inward; the flickers of withspeech between them, anticipation, excitement, fear as they grazed the edge of the atmosphere and felt ion flames lick their diamond skins. Lenya, falling, burning with the fires of entry as she cut a glowing trail across half a planet. The heat-shell breaking away as she unfurled her wings in the eternal shriek of wind and the ram-jets in her sterile womb kindled and roared.

"And you?" she asked. Her skin said *gentle*. Confused as much by his breaking of it as by his silence, but *gentle*.

"I have something planned," was all he said, but because that plan meant they would never meet again, he told her then what he had learned in the Temple of Memory. He tried to be kind and understanding, but it was still a bastard thing to do, and she cried in the nest in the rear of the flyer all the way out of the atmosphere, half-way to heaven. It was a bastard thing and as he watched the stars brighten beyond the canopy, he could not say why he had done it, except that it was necessary to kill some things Big Dead so that they could never come back again. She cried now, and her skin was so dark it would not speak to him, but when she flew, it would be without any lingering love or regret for a man called Solomon Gursky.

*It is good to be hated,* he thought, as the Heaven Tree took him up into its star-lit branches.

The launch laser was off, the reaction mass tanks were dry. Solomon Gursky fell outward from the sun. Urizen and its children were far beneath him. His course lay out of the ecliptic, flying north. His aft eyes made out a new pale ring orbiting the gas world, glowing in the low warmsight: the millions of adapted waiting in orbit for their turns to make the searing descent into a new life.

She would be with them now. He had watched her go into the seed and be taken apart by her own elementals. He had watched the seed split and expel her into space, transformed, and burn her few kilos of reaction mass on the transfer orbit to Urizen.

Only then had he felt free to undergo his own transfiguration.

Life-swarm. Mighty. So nearly right, so utterly wrong. She had almost sung when she spoke of the freedom of endless flight in the clouds of Urizen, but she would never fly freer than she did now, naked to space, the galaxy before her. The freedom of Urizen was a lie, the price exacted by its gravity and pressure. She had trapped herself in atmosphere and gravity. Urizen was another world. The parasitic man of the Ash nation had buried himself in a world. The aquatic Blue Mana, after long sleep in ice, would only give rise to another copy of the standard model. Worlds upon worlds.

Infinite ways of being human, Solomon Gursky thought, outbound from the sun. He could feel the gentle stroke of the solar wind over the harsh dermal prickle of Urizen's magnetosphere. Sun arising. Almost time.

Many ways of being Solomon Gursky, he thought, contemplating his new body. His analogy was with a conifer. He was a redwood cone fallen from the Heaven Tree, ripe with seeds. Each seed a Solomon Gursky, a world in embryo.

The touch of the sun, that was what had opened those seed cones on that other world, long ago. Timing was too important to be left to higher cognitions. Subsystems had all the launch vectors programmed; he merely registered the growing strength of the wind from Los on his skin and felt himself begin to open. Solomon Gursky unfolded into a thousand scales. As the seeds exploded onto their preset courses, he burned to the highest orgasm of his memory before his persona downloaded into the final spore and ejected from the empty, dead carrier body.

At five hundred kilometers, the seeds unfurled their solar sails. The breaking wave of particles, with multiple gravity assists from Luvah and Enitharmon, would surf the bright flotilla up to interstellar velocities, as, at the end of the centuries – millennia

– long flights, the light-sails would brake the packages at their destinations.

He did not know what his many selves would find there. He had not picked targets for their resemblance to what he was leaving behind. That would be just another trap. He sensed his brothers shutting down their cognitive centers for the big sleep, like stars going out, one by one. A handful of seeds scattered, some to wither, some to grow. Who can say what he will find, except that it will be extraordinary. Surprise me! Solomon Gursky demanded of the universe, as he fell into the darkness between suns.

## Saturday

The object was one point three astronomical units on a side, and at its current 10 percent C would arrive in thirty-five hours. On his chaise lounge by the Neptune fountain, Solomon Gursky finally settled on a name for the thing. He had given much thought, over many high-hours and in many languages, most of them non-verbal, to what he should call the looming object. The name that pleased him most was in a language dead (he assumed) for thirty million years. Aea. Acronym: Alien Enigmatic Artifact. Enigmatic Alien Artifact would have been more correct but the long dead language did not handle diphthongs well.

Shadows fell over the gardens of Versailles, huge and soft as clouds. A forest was crossing the sun; a small one, little more than a copse, he thought, still finding delight in the notions that could be expressed in this dead language. He watched the spherical trees pass overhead, each a kilometer across (another archaism), enjoying the pleasurable play of shade and warmth on his skin. Sensual joys of incarnation.

As ever when the forests migrated along the Bauble's jet streams, a frenzy of siphons squabbled in their wake, voraciously feeding off the stew of bacteria and complex fullerenes.

Solomon Gursky darkened his eyes against the hard glare of the dwarf white sun. From Versailles' perspective in the equatorial plane, the Spirit Ring was a barely discernible filigree necklace draped around its primary. Perspective. Am I the emanation of it, or is it the emanation of me?

Perspective: you worry about such things with a skeletal tetrahedron one point three astronomical units on a side fast approaching?

Of course. I am some kind of human.

"Show me," Solomon Gursky said. Sensing his intent, for Versailles was part of his intent, as everything that lived and moved within the Bauble was his intent, the disc of tectofactured baroque France began to tilt away from the sun. The sol-lilies on which Versailles and its gardens rested generated their own gravity fields; Solomon Gursky saw the tiny, bright sun seem to curve down behind the Petit Trianon, and thought, *I have reinvented sunset*. And, as the dark vault above him lit with stars, *Night is looking out from the shadow of myself*.

The stars slowed and locked over the chimneys of Versailles. Sol had hoped to be able to see the object with the unaided eye, but in low-time he had forgotten the limitations of the primeval human form. A grimace of irritation, and it was the work of moments for the tectors to reconfigure his vision. Successive magnifications clicked up until ghostly, twinkling threads of light resolved out of the star field, like the drawings of gods and myths the ancients had laid on the comfortable heavens around the Alpha Point.

Another click and the thing materialized.

Solomon Gursky's breath caught.

Midway between the micro and the macro, it was humanity's natural condition that a man standing looking out into the dark should feel dwarfed. That need to assert one's individuality to the bigness underlies all humanity's outward endeavors. But the catch in the breath is more than doubled when a *star* seems dwarfed. Through the Spirit Ring, Sol had the dimensions, the masses, the vectors. The whole of the Bauble could be easily contained within Aea's vertices. A cabalistic sign. A cosmic eye in the pyramid.

A chill contraction in the man Solomon Gursky's loins. How many million years since he had last felt his balls tighten with fear?

One point three AU's on a side. Eight sextillion tons of matter. Point one C. The thing should have heralded itself over most of the cluster. Even in low-time, he should have had more time to prepare. But there had been no warning. At once, it *was*: a fading hexagram of gravitometric disturbances on his out-system sensors. Sol had reacted at once, but in those few seconds of stretched low time that it took to conceive and create this Louis Quattorze conceit, the object had covered two-thirds of the distance from its emergence point. The high-time of created things gave him perspective.

*Bear you grapes or poison?* Solomon Gursky asked the thing in the sky. It had not spoken, it had remained silent through all attempts to communicate with it, but it surely bore *some* gift. The manner of its arrival had only one explanation: the thing manipulated worm-holes. None of the civilization citizens of the Reach – most of the western hemisphere of the galaxy – had evolved a nanotechnology that could reconfigure the continuum itself.

None of the civilization/citizens of the Reach, and those federations of world-societies it fringed, had ever encountered a species that could not be sourced to the Alpha Point: that semi-legendary racial big bang from which PanHumanity had exploded into the universe.

Four hundred billion stars in this galaxy alone, Solomon Gursky thought. We have not seeded even half of them. The trick we play with time, slowing our perceptions until our light-speed communications seem instantaneous and the journeys of our C-fractional ships are no longer than the sea-voyages of this era I have reconstructed, seduce us into believing that the universe is as close and companionable as a lover's body, and as familiar. The five million years between the MonoHumanity of the Alpha Point and the PanHumanity of the Great Leap Outward, is a catch of breath, a contemplative pause in our conversation with ourselves. Thirty million years I have evolved the web of life in this unique system: there is abundant time and space for true aliens to have caught us up, to have already surpassed us.

Again, that tightening of the scrotum. Sol Gursky willed Versailles back toward the eye of the sun, but intellectual chill had invaded his soul. The orchestra of Lully made fete *galante* in the Hall of Mirrors for his pleasure, but the sound in his head of the destroying, rushing alien mass shrieked louder. As the solar parasol slipped between Versailles and the sun and he settled in twilight among the soft, powdered breasts of the ladies of the bed-chamber, he knew fear for the first time in thirty million years. And he dreamed. The dream took the shape of a memory, recontextualized, reconfigured, resurrected. He dreamed that he was a starship wakened from fifty thousand years of death by the warmth of a new sun on his solar sail. He dreamed that in the vast sleep the star toward which he had aimed himself spastically novaed. It kicked off its photosphere in a nebula of radiant gas but the explosion was underpowered; the carbon/hydrogen/nitrogen/oxygen plasma was drawn by gravity into a bubble of hydrocarbons around the star. An aura. A bright bauble. In Solomon Gursky's dream, an angel floated effortlessly on tectoplastic wings hundreds of kilometers wide, banking and soaring on the chemical thermals, sowing seeds from its long, trailing fingertips. For a hundred years, the angel swam around the sun, sowing, nurturing, tending the strange shoots that grew from its fingers; things half-living, half-machine.

Asleep among the powdered breasts of court women, Sol Gursky turned and murmured the word, "evolution."

Solomon Gursky would only be a God he could believe in: the philosophers' God, creator but not sustainer, ineffable; too street-smart to poke its omnipotence into the smelly stuff of living. He saw his free-fall trees of green, the vast red rafts of the wind-reefs rippling in the solar breezes. He saw the blimps and medusas, the unresting open maws of the air-plankton feeders, the needle-thin jet-powered darts of the harpoon hunters. He saw an ecology spin itself out of gas and energy in thirty million yearless years, he saw intelligence flourish and seed itself to the stars, and fade into senescence; all in the blink of a low-time eye.

"Evolution," he muttered again and the constructed women who did not understand sleep looked at each other.

In the unfolding dream, Sol Gursky saw the Spirit Ring and the ships that came and went between the nearer systems. He heard the subaural babble of interstellar chatter, like conspirators in another room. He beheld this blur of life, evolving, transmuting, and he knew that it was very good. He said to himself, *what a wonderful world*, and feared for it.

He awoke. It was morning, as it always was in Sol's Bauble. He worked off his testosterone high and tipped Versailles darkside to look at the shadow of his nightmares. Any afterglow of libido was immediately extinguished. At eighteen light-hours distance, the astronomical dimensions assumed emotional force. A ribbon of mottled blue-green ran down the inner surface of each of Aea's six legs. Amplified vision resolved forested continents and oceans beneath fractal cloud curls. Each ribbon-world was the width of two Alpha Points peeled and ironed, stretched one point three astronomical units long. Sol Gursky was glad that this incarnation could not instantly access how many million planets' surfaces that equaled; how many hundreds of thousands of years it would take to walk from one vertex to another, and then to find, dumbfounded like the ancient conquistadors beholding a new ocean, another millennia-deep world in front of him.

Solomon Gursky turned Versailles toward the sun. He squinted through the haze of the Bauble for the delicate strands of the Spirit Ring. A beat of his mind shifted his perceptions back into low-time, the only time frame in which he could withspeak to the Spirit Ring, his originating self. Self-reference, self-confession.

*No communication?*

*None,* spoke the Spirit Ring.

*Is it alien? Should I be afraid? Should I destroy the Bauble?*

In another time, such schizophrenia would have been disease.

*Can it annihilate you?*

In answer, Sol envisioned the great tetrahedron at the bracelet of information tectors orbiting the sun.

*Then that is nothing,* the Spirit Ring withsaid. *And nothing is nothing to fear. Can it cause you pain or humiliation, or anguish to body or soul?*

Again, Sol withspoke an image, of cloud-shaded lands raised over each other like the pillars of Yahweh, emotionally shaded to suggest amazement that such an investment of matter and thought should have been created purely to humiliate Solomon Gursky.

*Then that too is settled. And whether it is alien, can it be any more alien to you than you yourself are to what you once were? All PanHumanity is alien to itself; therefore, we have nothing to fear. We shall welcome our visitor, we have many questions for it.*

Not the least being, *why me?* Solomon Gursky thought privately, silently, in the dome of his own skull. He shifted out of the low-time of the Spirit Ring to find that in those few subjective moments of communication Aea had passed the threshold of the Bauble. The leading edge of the tetrahedron was three hours away. An hour and half beyond that was the hub of Aea.

"Since it seems that we can neither prevent nor hasten the object's arrival, nor guess its purposes until it deigns to com-

municate with us," Sol Gursky told his women of the bed-
chamber, "therefore let us party." Which they did, before the
Mirror Pond, as Lully's orchestra played and capons roasted over
charcoal pits, and torch-lit harlequins capered and fought out the
ancient loves and comedies, and women splashed naked in the
Triton Fountain, and fantastic lands one hundred million kilometers long slid past them. Aea advanced until Sol's star was at its
center, then stopped. Abruptly, instantly. A small gravitational
shiver troubled Versailles, the orchestra missed a note, a juggler
dropped a club, the water in the fountain wavered, women
shrieked, a capon fell from a spit into the fire. That was all.
The control of mass, momentum, and gravity was absolute.

The orchestra leader looked at Solomon Gursky, staff raised to
resume the beat. Sol Gursky did not raise the handkerchief. The
closest section of Aea was fifteen degrees east, two hundred
thousand kilometers out. To Sol Gursky, it was two fingers of
sun-lit land, tapering infinitesimally at either end to threads of
light. He looked up at the apex, two other brilliant threads spun
down beneath the horizon, one behind the Petit Trianon, the
other below the roof of the Chapel Royal.

The conductor was still waiting. Instruments pressed to faces,
the musicians watched for the cue.

Peacocks shrieked on the lawn. Sol Gursky remembered how
irritating the voices of peacocks were, and wished he had not
recreated them.

Sol Gursky waved the handkerchief.

A column of white light blazed out of the gravel walk at the top
of the steps. The air was a seethe of glowing motes.

*An attempt is being made to communicate with us*, the Spirit Ring
said in a flicker of low-time. Sol Gursky felt information from the
Ring crammed into his cerebral cortex: the beam originated from
a source of the rim section of the closest section of the artifact.
The tectors that created and sustained the Bauble were being
reprogrammed. At hyper-velocities, they were manufacturing a
construct out of the Earth of Versailles.

The pillar of light dissipated. A human figure stood at the top
of the steps: a white Alpha Point male, dressed in Louis XIV
style. The man descended the steps into the light of the flambeau
bearers. Sol Gursky looked on his face.

Sol Gursky burst into laughter.

"You are very welcome," he said to his doppelgänger. "Will

you join us? The capons will be ready shortly, we can bring you the finest wines available to humanity, and I'm sure the waters of the fountains would be most refreshing to one who has traveled so long and so far."

"Thank you," Solomon Gursky said in Solomon Gursky's voice. "It's good to find a hospitable reception after a strange journey."

Sol Gursky nodded to the conductor, who raised his staff, and the *petite bande* resumed their interrupted gavotte.

Later, on a stone bench by the lake, Sol Gursky said to his doppel, "Your politeness is appreciated, but it really wasn't necessary for you to don my shape. All this is as much a construction as you are."

"Why do you think it's a politeness?" the construct said.

"Why should you choose to wear the shape of Solomon Gursky?"

"Why should I not, if it is my *own* shape?"

Nereids splashed in the pool, breaking the long reflections of Aea.

"I often wonder how far I reach," Sol said.

"Further than you can imagine," Sol II answered. The playing Nereids dived; ripples spread across the pond. The visitor watched the wavelets lap against the stone rim and interfere with each other. "There are others out there, others we never imagined, moving through the dark, very slowly, very silently. I think they may be older than us. They are different from us, very different, and we have now come to the complex plane where our expansions meet."

"There was a strong probability that they – you – were an alien artifact."

"I am, and I'm not. I am fully Solomon Gursky, and fully Other. That's the purpose behind this artifact; that we have reached a point where we either compete, destructively, or join."

"Seemed a long way to come just for a family reunion," Solomon Gursky joked. He saw that the doppel laughed, and how it laughed, and why it laughed. He got up from the stone rim of the Nereid pool. "Come with me, talk to me, we have thirty million years of catching up."

His brother fell in at his side as they walked away from the still water toward the Aea-lit woods.

His story: he had fallen longer than any other seed cast off by the death of Orc. Eight hundred thousand years between wakings, and as he felt the warmth of a new sun seduce his tector systems to the work of transformation, his sensors reported that his was not the sole presence in the system. The brown dwarf toward which he decelerated was being dismantled and converted into an englobement of space habitats.

"Their technology is similar to ours – I think it must be a universal inevitability – but they broke the ties that still bind us to planets long ago," Sol II said. The woods of Versailles were momentarily darkened as a sky-reef eclipsed Aea. "This is why I think they are older than us: I have never seen their original form – they have no tie to it, we still do; I suspect they no longer remember it. It wasn't until we fully merged that I was certain that they were not another variant of humanity."

A hand-cranked wooden carousel stood in a small clearing. The faces of the painted horses were fierce and pathetic in the sky light. Wooden rings hung from iron gibbets around the rim of the carousel; the wooden lances with which the knights hooked down their favors had been gathered in and locked in a closet in the middle of the merry-go-round.

"We endure forever, we engender races, nations, whole ecologies, but we are sterile," the second Sol said. "We inbreed with ourselves. There is no union of disparities, no coming together, no hybrid energy. With the Others, it was sex. Intercourse. Out of the fusion of ideas and visions and capabilities, we birthed what you see."

The first Sol Gursky laid his hand on the neck of a painted horse. The carousel was well balanced, the slightest pressure set it turning.

"Why are you here, Sol?" he asked.

"We shared technologies, we learned how to engineer on the quantum level so that field effects can be applied on macroscopic scales. Manipulation of gravity and inertia; non-locality; we can engineer and control quantum worm-holes."

"Why have you come, Sol?"

"Engineering of alternative time streams; designing and colonizing multiple worlds, hyperspace and hyperdimensional processors. There are more universes than this one for us to explore."

The wooden horse stopped.

"What do you want, Sol?"

"Join us," said the other Solomon Gursky. "You always had the vision – *we* always had the vision, we Solomon Gurskys. Humanity expanding into every possible ecological niche."

"Absorption," Solomon Gursky said. "Assimilation."

"Unity," said his brother. "Marriage. *Love*. Nothing is lost, everything is gained. All you have created here will be stored; that is what I am, a machine for remembering. It's not annihilation, Sol, don't fear it; it's not your self-hood dissolving into some identityless collective. It *is* you, plus. It is life, cubed. And ultimately, we are one seed, you and I, unnaturally separated. We gain each other."

If nothing is lost, then you remember what I am remembering, Solomon Gursky I thought. I am remembering a face forgotten for over thirty million years: Rabbi Bertelsmann. A fat, fair, pleasant face. he is talking to his Bar Mitzvah class about God and masturbation. He is saying that God condemned Onan not for the pleasure of his vice, but because he spilled his seed on the ground. He was fruitless, sterile. He kept the gift of life to himself. And I am now God in my own world, and Rabbi B is smiling and saying, masturbation, Sol. It is all just one big jerk-off, seed spilled on the ground, engendering nothing. Pure recreation; recreating yourself endlessly into the future.

He looked at his twin.

"Rabbi Bertelsmann?" Sol Gursky II said.

"Yes," Sol Gursky I said; then, emphatically, certainly, "Yes!"

Solomon Gursky II's smile dissolved into motes of light.

All at once, the outer edges of the great tetrahedron kindled with ten million points of diamond light. Sol watched the white beams sweep through the Bauble and understood what it meant, that they could manipulate time and space. Even at light-speed, Aea was too huge for such simultaneity.

Air trees, sky reefs, harpooners, siphons, blimps, zeps, cloud sharks: everything touched by the moving beams was analyzed, comprehended, stored. Recording angels, Sol Gursky thought, as the silver knives dissected his world. He saw the Spirit Ring unravel like coils of DNA as a billion days of Solomon Gursky flooded up the ladder of light into Aea. The center no longer held; the gravitational forces the Spirit Ring had controlled, that had maintained the ecosphere of the Bauble, were failing. Sol's world was dying. He felt no pain, no sorrow, no regret, but rather a savage joy, an urgent desire to be up and on and out, to be free of this great weight of life and gravity. It is not dying, he thought. Nothing ever dies.

He looked up. An angel-beam scored a searing arc across the rooftops of Versailles. He opened his arms to it and was taken apart by the light. Everything is held and recreated in the mind of God. Unremembered by the mind of Solomon Gursky, Versailles disintegrated into swarms of free-flying tectors.

The end came quickly. The angels reached into the photo-sphere of the star and the complex quasi-information machines that worked there. The sun grew restless, woken from its long quietude. The Spirit Ring collapsed. Fragments spun end-over-end through the Bauble, tearing spectacularly through the dying sky-reefs, shattering cloud forests, blazing in brief glory in funeral orbits around the swelling sun.

For the sun was dying. Plagues of sunspots pocked its chromosphere; solar storms raced from pole to pole in mil-lion-kilometer tsunamis. Panicked hunter packs kindled and died in the solar protuberances hurled off as the photosphere prominenced to the very edge of the Bauble. The sun bulged and swelled like a painfully infected pregnancy: Aea was ma-nipulating fundamental forces, loosening the bonds of gravity that held the system together. At the end, it would require all the energies of star-death to power the quantum worm-hole processors.

The star was now a screaming saucer of gas. No living thing remained in the Bauble. All was held in the mind of Aea.

The star burst. The energies of the nova should have boiled Aea's oceans, seared its lands from their beds. It should have twisted and snapped the long, thin arms like yarrow stalks, sent the artifact tumbling like a smashed Fabergé egg through space. But Aea had woven its defenses strong: gravity fields warped the electromagnetic radiation around the fragile terrains; the quan-tum processors devoured the storm of charged particles, and reconfigured space, time, mass.

The four corners of Aea burned brighter than the dying sun for an instant. And it was gone; under space and time, to worlds and adventures and experiences beyond all saying.

# Sunday

Toward the end of the universe, Solomon Gursky's thoughts turned increasingly to lost loves.

Had it been entirely physical, Ua would have been the largest object in the universe. Only its fronds, the twenty-light-year-long stalactites that grew into the ylem, tapping the energies of decreation, had any material element. Most of Ua, ninety-nine followed by several volumes of decimal nines percent of its structure, was folded though eleven-space. It was the largest object in the universe in that its fifth and sixth dimensional forms contained the inchoate energy flux known as the universe. Its higher dimensions contained only itself, several times over. It was infundibular. It was vast, it contained multitudes.

PanLife, that amorphous, multi-faceted cosmic infection of human, transhuman, non-human, PanHuman sentiences, had filled the universe long before the continuum reached its elastic limit and began to contract under the weight of dark matter and heavy neutrinos. Femtotech, hand in hand with the worm-hole jump, spread PanLife across the galactic super-clusters in a blink of God's eye.

There was no humanity, no alien. No us, no other. There was only *life*. The dead had become life. Life had become Ua: Panspermia. Ua woke to consciousness, and like Alexander the Great, despaired when it had no new worlds to conquer. The universe had grown old in Ua's gestation; it had withered, it contracted, it drew in on itself. The red shift of galaxies had turned blue. And Ua, which owned the attributes, abilities, ambitions, everything except the name and pettinesses of a god, found itself, like an old, long-dead God from a world slagged by its expanding sun millions of years ago, in the business of resurrection.

The galaxies raced together, gravitational forces tearing them into loops and whorls of severed stars. The massive black holes at the galactic centers, fueled by billennia of star-death, coalesced and merged into monstrosities that swallowed globular clusters whole, that shredded galaxies and drew them spiraling inward until, at the edge of the Schwartzchild radii, they radiated super-hard gamma. Long since woven into higher dimensions, Ua fed from the colossal power of the accretion discs, recording in multi-dimensional matrices the lives of the trillions of sentient organisms fleeing up its fronds from the destruction. All things are held in the mind of God: at the end, when the universal background radiation rose asymptotically to the energy density of the first seconds of the Big Bang, it would deliver enough power for the femtoprocessors woven through the Eleven Heavens to rebuild the universe, entire. A new heaven, and a new Earth.

In the trans-temporal matrices of Ua, PanLife flowed across dimensions, dripping from the tips of the fronds into bodies sculpted to thrive in the plasma flux of ragnarok. Tourists to the end of the world: most wore the shapes of winged creatures of fire, thousands of kilometers across. Starbirds. Firebirds. But the being formerly known as Solomon Gursky had chosen a different form, an archaism from that long-vanished planet. It pleased him to be a thousand-kilometer, diamond-skinned Statue of Liberty, torch out-held, beaming a way through the torrents of star-stuff. Sol Gursky flashed between flocks of glowing soul-birds clustering in the information-rich environment around the frond-tips. He felt their curiosity, their appreciation, their consternation at his non-conformity; none got the joke.

Lost loves. So many lives, so many worlds, so many shapes and bodies, so many loves. They had been wrong, those ones back at the start, who had said that love did not survive death. He had been wrong. It was eternity that killed love. Love was a thing measured by human lifetimes. Immortality gave it time enough, and space, to change, to become things more than love, or dangerously other. None endured. None would endure. Immortality was endless change.

Toward the end of the universe, Solomon Gursky realized that what made love live forever was death.

All things were held in Ua, awaiting resurrection when time, space, and energy fused and ceased to be. Most painful among Sol's stored memories was the remembrance of a red-yellow tiger-striped angel fighter, half-crucified, crippled, tumbling toward the star clouds of Virgo. Sol had searched the trillions of souls roosting in Ua for Elena; failing, he hunted for any that might have touched her, hold some memory of her. He found none. As the universe contracted – as fast and inevitable as a long-forgotten season in the ultra-low time of Ua – Sol Gursky entertained hopes that the universal gathering would draw her in. Cruel truths pecked at his perceptions: calculations of molecular deliquescence, abrasion by interstellar dust clouds, probabilities of stellar impacts, the slow terminal whine of proton decay; any of which denied that Elena could still exist. Sol refused those truths. A thousand-kilometer Statue of Liberty searched the dwindling cosmos for one glimpse of red-yellow tiger-stripes embedded in a feather of fractal plasma flame.

And now a glow of recognition had impinged on his senses laced through the Eleven Heavens.

Her. It had to be her.

Sol Gursky flew to an eye of gravitational stability in the flux and activated the worm-hole nodes seeded throughout his diamond skin. Space opened and folded like an exercise in origami. Sol Gursky went elsewhere.

The starbird grazed the energy-dense borderlands of the central accretion disc. It was immense. Sol's Statue of Liberty was a frond of one of its thousand flight feathers, but it sensed him, welcomed him, folded its wings around him as it drew him to the shifting pattern of sun-spots that was the soul of its being.

He knew these patterns. He remembered these emotional flavors. He recalled this love. He tried to perceive if it were her, her journeys, her trials, her experiences, her agonies, her vastenings.

Would she forgive him?

The soul spots opened. Solomon Gursky was drawn inside. Clouds of tectors interpenetrated, exchanging, sharing, recording. Intellectual intercourse.

He entered her adventures among alien species five times older than Pan-Humanity, an alliance of wills and powers waking a galaxy to life. In an earlier incarnation, he walked the worlds she had become, passed through the dynasties and races and species she had propagated. He made with her the long crossings between stars and clusters, clusters and galaxies. Earlier still, and he swam with her through the cloud canyons of a gas giant world called Urizen, and when that world was hugged too warmly by its sun, changed mode with her, embarked with her on the search for new places to live.

In the nakedness of their communion, there was no hiding Sol Gursky's despair.

*I'm sorry Sol*, the starbird once known as Lenya communicated.

*You have nothing to sorry be for*, Solomon Gursky said.

*I'm sorry that I'm not her. I'm sorry I never was her.*

*I made you to be a lover*, Sol withspoke. *But you became some-thing older, something richer, something we have lost.*

*A daughter*, Lenya said.

Unmeasurable time passed in the blue shift at the end of the universe. Then Lenya asked, *Where will you go?*

*Finding her is the only unfinished business I have left*, Sol said.

*Yes*, the starbird communed. *But we will not meet again.*

*No, not in this universe.*

*Nor any other. And that is death, eternal separation.*

*My unending regret*, Sol Gursky withspoke as Lenya opened her heart and the clouds of tectors separated. *Good bye, daughter.*

The Statue of Liberty disengaged from the body of the star-bird. Lenya's quantum processors created a pool of gravitational calm in the maelstrom. Sol Gursky manipulated space and time and disappeared.

He re-entered the continuum as close as he dared to a frond. A pulse of his mind brought him within reach of its dendrites. As they drew him in, another throb of thought dissolved the Statue of Liberty joke into the plasma flux. Solomon Gursky howled up the dendrite, through the frond, into the soul matrix of Ua. There he carved a niche in the eleventh and highest heaven, and from deep under time, watched the universe end.

As he had expected, it ended in fire and light and glory. He saw space and time curve inward beyond the limit of the Planck dimensions; he felt the energy gradients climb toward infinity as the universe approached the zero-point from which it had spon-taneously emerged. He felt the universal processors sown through eleven dimensions seize that energy before it faded, and put it to work. It was a surge, a spurt of power and passion, like the memory of orgasm buried deep in the chain of memory that was the days of Solomon Gursky. Light to power, power to memory, memory to flesh. Ua's stored memories, the history of every particle in the former universe, were woven into being. Smart superstrings rolled balls of wrapped eleven-space like sacred scarabs wheeling dung. Space, time, mass, energy un-raveled; as the universe died in a quantum fluctuation, it was reborn in primal light.

To Solomon Gursky, waiting in low-time where aeons were breaths, it seemed like creation by *fiat*. A brief, bright light, and galaxies, clusters, stars, turned whole-formed and living within his contemplation. Already personas were swarming out of Ua's honeycomb cells into time and incarnation, but what had been reborn was not a universe, but universes. The re-resurrected were not condemned to blindly recapitulate their former lives. Each choice and action that diverged from the original pattern splintered off a separate universe. Sol and Lenya had spoken truly when they had said they would never meet again. Sol's point of entry into the new polyverse was a thousand years before Lenya's; the universe he intended to create would never intersect with hers.

The elder races had already fanned the polyverse into a *mille feuille* of alternatives: Sol carefully tracked his own timeline through the blur of possibilities as the first humans dropped back into their planet's past. Stars moving into remembered constellations warned Sol that his emergence was only a few hundreds of thousands of years off. He moved down through dimensional matrices, at each level drawing closer to the time flow of his particular universe.

Solomon Gursky hung over the spinning planet. Civilizations rose and decayed, empires conquered and crumbled. New technologies, new continents, new nations were discovered. All the time, alternative Earths fluttered away like torn-off calendar pages on the wind as the dead created new universes to colonize. Close now. Mere moments. Sol dropped into meat time, and Ua expelled him like a drop of milk from a swollen breast.

Solomon Gursky fell. Illusions and anticipations accompanied his return to flesh. Imaginings of light; a contrail angel scoring the nightward half of the planet on its flight across a dark ocean to a shore, to a mountain, to a valley, to a glow of campfire among night-blooming cacti. Longing. Desire. Fear. Gain, and loss. God's trade: to attain the heart's desire, you must give up everything you are. Even the memory.

In the quilted bag by the fire in the sheltered valley under the perfume of the cactus flowers, the man called Solomon Gursky woke with a sudden chill start. It was night. It was dark. Desert stars had half-completed their compass above him. The stone-circled fire had burned down to clinking red glow: the night perfume witched him. Moths padded softly through the air, seeking nectar.

Sol Gursky drank five senses full of his world.

I am alive, he thought. I am here. Again.

Ur-light burned in his hind-brain; memories of Ua, a power

like omnipotence. Memories of a life that out-lived its native universe. Worlds, suns, shapes. Flashes, moments. Too heavy, too rich for this small knot of brain to hold. Too bright: no one can live with the memory of having been a god. It would fade – it was fading already. All he need hold – all he must hold – was what he needed to prevent this universe from following its predestined course.

The realization that eyes were watching him was a shock. Elena sat on the edge of the fire shadow, knees folded to chin, arms folded over shins, looking at him. Sol had the feeling that she had been looking at him without him knowing for a long time, and the surprise, the uneasiness of knowing you are under the eyes of another, tempered both the still-new lust he felt for her, and his fading memories of aeons-old love.

Déjà vu. But this moment had never happened before. The divergence was beginning.

"Can't sleep?" she asked.

"I had the strangest dream."

"Tell me." The thing between them was at the stage where they searched each other's dreams for allusions to their love.

"I dreamed that the world ended," Sol Gursky said. "It ended in light, and the light was like the light in a movie projector, that carried the image of the world and everything in it, and so the world was created again, as it had been before."

As he spoke, the words became true. It was a dream now. This life, this body, these memories, were the solid and faithful.

"Like a Tipler machine," Elena said. "The idea that the energy released by the Big Crunch could power some kind of holographic recreation of the entire universe. I suppose with an advanced enough nanotechnology, you could rebuild the universe, an exact copy, atom for atom."

Chill dread struck in Sol's belly. She could not know, surely. She must not know.

"What would be the point of doing it exactly the same all over again?"

"Yeah." Elena rested her cheek on her knee. "But the question is, is *this* our first time in the world, or have we been here many times before, each a little bit different? Is this the first universe, or do we only *think* that it is?"

Sol Gursky looked into the embers, then to the stars.

"The Nez Perce Nation believes that the world ended on the

third day and that what we are living in are the dreams of the second night." Memories, fading like summer meteors high overhead, told Sol that he had said this once before, in their future, after his first death. He said it now in the hope that that future would not come to pass. Everything that was different, every tiny detail, pushed this universe away from the one in which he must lose her.

A vee of tiger-striped tectoplastic tumbled end over end forever toward Virgo.

He blinked the ghost away. It faded like all the others. They were going more quickly than he had thought. He would have to make sure of it now, before that memory too dissolved. He struggled out of the terrain bag, went over to the bike lying exhausted on the ground. By the light of a detached bicycle lamp, he checked the gear train.

"What are you doing?" Elena asked from the fireside. The thing between them was still new, but Sol remembered that tone in her voice, that soft inquiry, from another lifetime.

"Looking at the gears. Something didn't feel right about them today. They didn't feel solid."

"You didn't mention it earlier."

No, Sol thought. I didn't know about it. Not then. The gear teeth grinned flashlight back at him.

"We've been giving them a pretty hard riding. I read in one of the biking mags that you can get metal fatigue. Gear train shears right through, just like that."

"On brand-new, two thousand dollar bikes?"

"On brand-new two thousand dollar bikes."

"So what do you think you can *do* about it at one o'clock in the morning in the middle of the Sonora Desert?"

Again, that come-hither tone. Just a moment more, Elena. One last thing, and then it will be safe.

"It just didn't sit right. I don't want to take it up over any more mountains until I've had it checked out. You get a gear-shear up there . . ."

"So, what are you saying, irritating man?"

"I'm not happy about going over Blood of Christ Mountain tomorrow."

"Yeah. Sure. Fine."

"Maybe we should go out west, head for the coast. It's whale season, I always wanted to see whales. And there's real good seafood. There's this cantina where they have fifty ways of serving iguana."

"Whales. Iguanas. Fine. Whatever you want. Now, since you're so wideawake, you can just get your ass right *over* here, Sol Gursky!"

She was standing up, and Sol saw and felt what she had been concealing by the way she had sat. She wearing only a cut-off MTB shirt. Safe, he thought, as he seized her and took her down laughing and yelling onto the camping mat. Even as he thought it, he forgot it, and all those Elenas who would not now be: conspirator, crop-haired freedom fighter, four-armed space-angel. Gone.

The stars moved in their ordained arcs. The moths and cactus forest bats drifted through the soft dark air, and the eyes of the things that hunted them glittered in the firelight.

Sol and Elena were still sore and laughing when the cactus flowers closed with dawn. They ate their breakfast and packed their small camp, and were in the saddle and on the trail before the sun was full over the shoulder of Blood of Christ Mountain. They took the western trail, away from the hills, and the town called Redención hidden among them with its freight of resurrected grief. They rode the long trail that led down to the ocean, and it was bright, clear endless Monday morning.

# WANG'S CARPETS

## Greg Egan

*We are now heading into the world of ultra-extreme sf of which Greg Egan is arguably its most accomplished practitioner. Egan (b. 1961) is an Australian writer whose work builds on the current fascination for nanotechnology and virtual reality. This really took hold with his second novel,* Permutation City *(1995), wherein personalities become immortal by being copied into virtual reality.* Diaspora *(1997) brought together and further developed a sequence of stories that explore mankind's journey to the stars. The following story is part of that sequence.*

Waiting to be cloned one thousand times and scattered across ten million cubic light years, Paolo Venetti relaxed in his favourite ceremonial bathtub: a tiered hexagonal pool set in a courtyard of black marble flecked with gold. Paolo wore full traditional anatomy, uncomfortable garb at first, but the warm currents flowing across his back and shoulders slowly eased him into a pleasant torpor. He could have reached the same state in an instant, by decree – but the occasion seemed to demand the complete ritual of verisimilitude, the ornate curlicued longhand of imitation physical cause and effect.

As the moment of diaspora approached, a small grey lizard darted across the courtyard, claws scrabbling. It halted by the far edge of the pool, and Paolo marvelled at the delicate pulse of its breathing, and watched the lizard watching him, until it moved again, disappearing into the surrounding vineyards. The environment was full of birds and insects, rodents and small reptiles – decorative in appearance, but also satisfying a more abstract aesthetic: softening the harsh radial symmetry of the lone observer; anchoring the simulation by perceiving it from a multitude of viewpoints. Ontological guy lines. No one had asked the lizards if they wanted to be cloned, though. They were coming along for the ride, like it or not.

The sky above the courtyard was warm and blue, cloudless and sunless, isotropic. Paolo waited calmly, prepared for every one of half a dozen possible fates.

An invisible bell chimed softly, three times. Paolo laughed, delighted.

One chime would have meant that he was still on Earth: an anti-climax, certainly – but there would have been advantages to compensate for that. Everyone who really mattered to him lived in the Carter-Zimmerman polis, but not all of them had chosen to take part in the diaspora to the same degree; his Earth-self would have lost no one. Helping to ensure that the thousand ships were safely dispatched would have been satisfying, too. And remaining a member of the wider Earth-based community, plugged into the entire global culture in real-time, would have been an attraction in itself.

Two chimes would have meant that this clone of Carter-Zimmerman had reached a planetary system devoid of life. Paolo had run a sophisticated – but non-sapient – self-predictive model before deciding to wake under those conditions. Exploring a handful of alien worlds, however barren, had seemed likely to be an enriching experience for him – with the distinct advantage that the whole endeavour would be untrammelled by the kind of elaborate precautions necessary in the presence of alien life. C-Z's population would have fallen by more than half – and many of his closest friends would have been absent – but he would have forged new friendships, he was sure.

Four chimes would have signalled the discovery of intelligent aliens. Five, a technological civilization. Six, spacefarers.

Three chimes, though, meant that the scout probes had detected unambiguous signs of life – and that was reason enough for jubilation. Up until the moment of the pre-launch cloning – a subjective instant before the chimes had sounded – no reports of alien life had ever reached Earth. There'd been no guarantee that any part of the diaspora would find it.

Paolo willed the polis library to brief him; it promptly rewired the declarative memory of his simulated traditional brain with all the information he was likely to need to satisfy his immediate curiosity. This clone of C-Z had arrived at Vega, the second closest of the thousand target stars, twenty-seven light-years from Earth. Paolo closed his eyes and visualized a star map with a thousand lines radiating out from the sun, then zoomed in on the trajectory which described his own journey. It had taken three centuries to reach Vega – but the vast majority of the polis's twenty thousand inhabitants had programmed their exoselves to suspend them prior to the cloning, and to wake them only if and when they arrived at a suitable destination. Ninety-two citizens had chosen the alternative: experiencing every voyage of the diaspora from start to finish, risking disappointment, and even death. Paolo now knew that the ship aimed at Fomalhaut, the target nearest Earth, had been struck by debris and annihilated *en route*. He mourned the ninety-two, briefly. He hadn't been close to any of them, prior to the cloning, and the particular versions who'd wilfully perished two centuries ago in interstellar space seemed as remote as the victims of some ancient calamity from the era of flesh.

Paolo examined his new home star through the cameras of one of the scout probes – and the strange filters of the ancestral visual system. In traditional colours, Vega was a fierce blue-white disk, laced with prominences. Three times the mass of the sun, twice the size and twice as hot, sixty times as luminous. Burning hydrogen fast – and already halfway through its allotted five hundred million years on the main sequence.

Vega's sole planet, Orpheus, had been a featureless blip to the best lunar interferometers; now Paolo gazed down on its blue-green crescent, ten thousand kilometres below Carter-Zimmerman itself. Orpheus was terrestrial, a nickel-iron-silicate world; slightly larger than Earth, slightly warmer – a billion kilometres took the edge off Vega's heat – and almost drowning in liquid water. Impatient to see the whole surface firsthand, Paolo slowed his clock rate a thousandfold, allowing C-Z to circumnavigate the planet in twenty subjective seconds, daylight unshrouding a broad new swath with each pass. Two slender ochre-coloured continents with mountainous spines bracketed hemispheric oceans, and dazzling expanses of pack ice covered both poles – far more so in the north, where jagged white peninsulas radiated out from the midwinter arctic darkness.

The Orphean atmosphere was mostly nitrogen – six times as much as on Earth; probably split by UV from primordial ammonia – with traces of water vapour and carbon dioxide, but not enough of either for a runaway greenhouse effect. The high atmospheric pressure meant reduced evaporation – Paolo saw not a wisp of cloud – and the large, warm oceans in turn helped feed carbon dioxide back into the crust, locking it up in limestone sediments destined for subduction, as fast as vulcanism could disgorge it.

The whole system was young, by Earth standards, but Vega's greater mass, and a denser protostellar cloud, would have meant swifter passage through most of the traumas of birth: nuclear ignition and early luminosity fluctuations; planetary coalescence and the age of bombardments. The library estimated that Orpheus had enjoyed a relatively stable climate, and freedom from major impacts, for at least the past hundred million years.

Long enough for primitive life to appear—

A hand seized Paolo firmly by the ankle and tugged him beneath the water. He offered no resistance, and let the vision of the planet slip away. Only two other people in C-Z had free access to this environment – and his father didn't play games with his now-twelve-hundred-year-old son.

Elena dragged him all the way to the bottom of the pool, before releasing his foot and hovering above him, a triumphant silhouette against the bright surface. She was ancestor-shaped, but obviously cheating; she spoke with perfect clarity, and no air bubbles at all.

"Late sleeper! I've been waiting seven weeks for this!"

Paolo feigned indifference, but he was fast running out of breath. He had his exoself convert him into an amphibious human variant – biologically and historically authentic, if no longer the definitive ancestral phenotype. Water flooded into his modified lungs, and his modified brain welcomed it.

He said, "Why would I want to waste consciousness, sitting around waiting for the scout probes to refine their observations? I woke as soon as the data was unambiguous."

She pummelled his chest; he reached up and pulled her down,

instinctively reducing his buoyancy to compensate, and they rolled across the bottom of the pool, kissing.

Elena said, "You know we're the first C-Z to arrive, anywhere? The Fomalhaut ship was destroyed. So there's only one other pair of us. Back on Earth."

"So?" Then he remembered. Elena had chosen not to wake if any other version of her had already encountered life. Whatever fate befell each of the remaining ships, every other version of him would have to live without her.

He nodded soberly, and kissed her again. "What am I meant to say? You're a thousand times more precious to me, now?"

"Yes."

"Ah, but what about the you-and-I on Earth? Five hundred times would be closer to the truth."

"There's no poetry in five hundred."

"Don't be so defeatist. Rewire your language centres."

She ran her hands along the sides of his ribcage, down to his hips. They made love with their almost-traditional bodies – and brains; Paolo was amused to the point of distraction when his limbic system went into overdrive, but he remembered enough from the last occasion to bury his self-consciousness and surrender to the strange hijacker. It wasn't like making love in any civilized fashion – the rate of information exchange between them was minuscule, for a start – but it had the raw insistent quality of most ancestral pleasures.

Then they drifted up to the surface of the pool and lay beneath the radiant sunless sky.

Paolo thought: *I've crossed twenty-seven light-years in an instant. I'm orbiting the first planet ever found to hold alien life. And I've sacrificed nothing – left nothing I truly value behind. This is too good, too good.* He felt a pang of regret for his other selves – it was hard to imagine them faring as well, without Elena, without Orpheus – but there was nothing he could do about that, now. Although there'd be time to confer with Earth before any more ships reached their destinations, he'd decided – prior to the cloning – not to allow the unfolding of his manifold future to be swayed by any change of heart. Whether or not his Earth-self agreed, the two of them were powerless to alter the criteria for waking. The self with the right to choose for the thousand had passed away.

No matter, Paolo decided. The others would find – or construct – their own reasons for happiness. And there was still the chance that one of them would wake to the sound of *four chimes*.

Elena said, "If you'd slept much longer, you would have missed the vote."

*The vote?* The scouts in low orbit had gathered what data they could about Orphean biology. To proceed any further, it would be necessary to send microprobes into the ocean itself – an escalation of contact which required the approval of two thirds of the polis. There was no compelling reason to believe that the presence of a few million tiny robots could do any harm; all they'd leave behind in the water was a few kilojoules of waste heat. Nevertheless, a faction had arisen which advocated caution. The citizens of Carter-Zimmerman, they argued, could continue to observe from a distance for another decade, or another millennium, refining their observations and hypotheses before intruding . . . and those who disagreed could always sleep away the time, or find other interests to pursue.

Paolo delved into his library-fresh knowledge of the "carpets" – the single Orphean lifeform detected so far. They were free-floating creatures living in the equatorial ocean depths – apparently destroyed by UV if they drifted too close to the surface. They grew to a size of hundreds of metres, then fissioned into dozens of fragments, each of which continued to grow. It was tempting to assume that they were colonies of single-celled organisms, something like giant kelp – but there was no real evidence yet to back that up. It was difficult enough for the scout probes to discern the carpets' gross appearance and behaviour through a kilometre of water, even with Vega's copious neutrinos lighting the way; remote observations on a microscopic scale, let alone biochemical analyses, were out of the question. Spectroscopy revealed that the surface water was full of intriguing molecular debris – but guessing the relationship of any of it to the living carpets was like trying to reconstruct human biochemistry by studying human ashes.

Paolo turned to Elena. "What do you think?"

She moaned theatrically; the topic must have been argued to death while he slept. "The microprobes are harmless. They could tell us exactly what the carpets are made of, without removing a single molecule. What's the risk? *Culture shock?*"

Paolo flicked water onto her face, affectionately; the impulse seemed to come with the amphibian body. "You can't be sure that they're not intelligent."

"Do you know what was living on Earth, two hundred million years after it was formed?"

"Maybe cyanobacteria. Maybe nothing. This isn't Earth, though."

"True. But even in the unlikely event that the carpets are intelligent, do you think they'd notice the presence of robots a millionth their size? If they're unified organisms, they don't appear to react to anything in their environment – they have no predators, they don't pursue food, they just drift with the currents – so there's no reason for them to possess elaborate sense organs at all, let alone anything working on a sub-millimetre scale. And if they're colonies of single-celled creatures, one of which happens to collide with a microprobe and register its presence with surface receptors . . . what conceivable harm could that do?"

"I have no idea. But my ignorance is no guarantee of safety."

Elena splashed him back. "The only way to deal with your *ignorance* is to vote to send down the microprobes. We have to be cautious, I agree – but there's no point *being here* if we don't find out what's happening in the oceans, right now. I don't want to wait for this planet to evolve something smart enough to broadcast biochemistry lessons into space. If we're not willing to take a few infinitesimal risks, Vega will turn red giant before we learn anything."

It was a throwaway line – but Paolo tried to imagine witnessing the event. In a quarter of a billion years, would the citizens of Carter-Zimmerman be debating the ethics of intervening to rescue the Orpheans – or would they all have lost interest, and departed for other stars, or modified themselves into beings entirely devoid of nostalgic compassion for organic life?

*Grandiose visions for a twelve-hundred-year-old.* The Fomalhaut clone had been obliterated by one tiny piece of rock. There was far more junk in the Vegan system than in interstellar space; even ringed by defences, its data backed up to all the far-flung scout probes, this C-Z was not invulnerable just because it had arrived intact. Elena was right; they had to seize the moment – or they might as well retreat into their own hermetic worlds and forget that they'd ever made the journey.

Paolo recalled the honest puzzlement of a friend from Ashton-

Laval: *Why go looking for aliens? Our polis has a thousand ecologies, a trillion species of evolved life. What do you hope to find, out there, that you couldn't have grown at home?*

What had he hoped to find? Just the answers to a few simple questions. Did human consciousness bootstrap all of space-time into existence, in order to explain itself? Or had a neutral, pre-existing universe given birth to a billion varieties of conscious life, all capable of harbouring the same delusions of grandeur – until they collided with each other? Anthrocosmology was used to justify the inward-looking stance of most polises: if the physical universe was created by human thought, it had no special status which placed it above virtual reality. It might have come first – and every virtual reality might need to run on a physical computing device, subject to physical laws – but it occupied no privileged position in terms of "truth" versus "illusion." If the ACs were right, then it was no more *honest* to value the physical universe over more recent artificial realities than it was honest to remain flesh instead of software, or ape instead of human, or bacterium instead of ape.

Elena said, "We can't lie here forever; the gang's all waiting to see you."

"Where?" Paolo felt his first pang of homesickness; on Earth, his circle of friends had always met in a real-time image of the Mount Pinatubo crater, plucked straight from the observation satellites. A recording wouldn't be the same.

"I'll show you."

Paolo reached over and took her hand. The pool, the sky, the courtyard vanished – and he found himself gazing down on Orpheus again . . . nightside, but far from dark, with his full mental palette now encoding everything from the pale wash of ground-current long-wave radio, to the multi-coloured shimmer of isotopic gamma rays and back-scattered cosmic-ray *bremsstrahlung*. Half the abstract knowledge the library had fed him about the planet was obvious at a glance, now. The ocean's smoothly tapered thermal glow spelt *three-hundred Kelvin* instantly – as well as back-lighting the atmosphere's tell-tale infrared silhouette.

He was standing on a long, metallic-looking girder, one edge of a vast geodesic sphere, open to the blazing cathedral of space. He glanced up and saw the star-rich dust-clogged band of the Milky Way, encircling him from zenith to nadir; aware of the glow of every gas cloud, discerning each absorption and emission line, Paolo could almost feel the plane of the galactic disk transect him. Some constellations were distorted, but the view was more familiar than strange – and he recognized most of the old signposts by colour. He had his bearings, now. Twenty degrees away from Sirius – south, by parochial Earth reckoning – faint but unmistakable: the sun.

Elena was beside him – superficially unchanged, although they'd both shrugged off the constraints of biology. The conventions of this environment mimicked the physics of real macroscopic objects in free-fall and vacuum, but it wasn't set up to model any kind of chemistry, let alone that of flesh and blood. Their new bodies were human-shaped, but devoid of elaborate microstructure – and their minds weren't embedded in the physics at all, but were running directly on the processor web.

Paolo was relieved to be back to normal; ceremonial regression to the ancestral form was a venerable C-Z tradition – and being human was largely self-affirming, while it lasted – but every time he emerged from the experience, he felt like he'd broken free of billion-year-old shackles. There were polises on Earth where the citizens would have found his present structure almost as archaic: a consciousness dominated by sensory perception, an illusion of possessing solid form, a single time coordinate. The last flesh human had died long before Paolo was constructed, and apart from the communities of Gleisner robots, Carter-Zimmerman was about as conservative as a transhuman society could be. The balance seemed right to Paolo, though – acknowledging the flexibility of software, without abandoning interest in the physical world – and although the stubbornly corporeal Gleisners had been first to the stars, the C-Z diaspora would soon overtake them.

Their friends gathered round, showing off their effortless free-fall acrobatics, greeting Paolo and chiding him for not arranging to wake sooner; he was the last of the gang to emerge from hibernation.

"Do you like our humble new meeting place?" Hermann floated by Paolo's shoulder, a chimeric cluster of limbs and sense-organs, speaking through the vacuum in modulated infrared. "We call it Satellite Pinatubo. It's desolate up here, I know – but we were afraid it might violate the spirit of caution if we dared pretend to walk the Orphean surface."

Paolo glanced mentally at a scout probe's close-up of a typical stretch of dry land, an expanse of fissured red rock. "More desolate down there, I think." He was tempted to touch the ground – to let the private vision become tactile – but he resisted. Being elsewhere in the middle of a conversation was bad etiquette.

"Ignore Hermann. He wants to flood Orpheus with our alien machinery before we have any idea what the effects might be." Liesl was a green-and-turquoise butterfly, with a stylized human face stippled in gold on each wing.

Paolo was surprised; from the way Elena had spoken, he'd assumed that his friends must have come to a consensus in favour of the microprobes – and only a late sleeper, new to the issues, would bother to argue the point. "What effects? The carpets—"

"Forget the carpets! Even if the carpets are as simple as they look, we don't know what else is down there." As Liesl's wings fluttered, her mirror-image faces seemed to glance at each other for support. "With neutrino imaging, we barely achieve spatial resolution in metres, time resolution in seconds. We don't know anything about smaller lifeforms."

"And we never will, if you have your way." Karpal – an ex-Gleisner, human-shaped as ever – had been Liesl's lover, last time Paolo was awake.

"We've only been here for a fraction of an Orphean year! There's still a wealth of data we could gather non-intrusively, with a little patience. There might be rare beachings of ocean life—"

Elena said dryly, "Rare indeed. Orpheus has negligible tides, shallow waves, very few storms. And anything beached would be fried by UV before we glimpsed anything more instructive than we're already seeing in the surface water."

"Not necessarily. The carpets seem to be vulnerable – but other species might be better protected, if they live nearer to the surface. And Orpheus is seismically active; we should at least wait for a tsunami to dump a few cubic kilometres of ocean onto a shoreline, and see what it reveals."

Paolo smiled; he hadn't thought of that. A tsunami might be worth waiting for.

Liesl continued, "What is there to lose, by waiting a few hundred Orphean years? At the very least, we could gather baseline data on seasonal climate patterns – and we could watch for anomalies, storms and quakes, hoping for some revelatory glimpses."

A few hundred Orphean years? *A few terrestrial millennia?* Paolo's ambivalence waned. If he'd wanted to inhabit geological time, he would have migrated to the Lokhande polis, where the Order of Contemplative Observers watched Earth's mountains erode in subjective seconds. Orpheus hung in the sky beneath them, a beautiful puzzle waiting to be decoded, demanding to be understood.

He said, "But what if there *are no* 'revelatory glimpses?' How long do we wait? We don't know how rare life is – in time, or in space. If this planet is precious, *so is the epoch it's passing through.* We don't know how rapidly Orphean biology is evolving; species might appear and vanish while we agonize over the risks of gathering better data. The carpets – and whatever else – could die out before we'd learnt the first thing about them. What a waste that would be!"

Liesl stood her ground.

"And if we damage the Orphean ecology – or culture – by rushing in? That wouldn't be a waste. It would be a tragedy."

Paolo assimilated all the stored transmissions from his Earth-self – almost three hundred years' worth – before composing a reply. The early communications included detailed mind grafts – and it was good to share the excitement of the diaspora's launch; to watch – very nearly firsthand – the thousand ships, nanomachine-carved from asteroids, depart in a blaze of fusion fire from beyond the orbit of Mars. Then things settled down to the usual prosaic matters: Elena, the gang, shameless gossip, Carter-Zimmerman's ongoing research projects, the buzz of inter-polis cultural tensions, the not-quite-cyclic convulsions of the arts (the perceptual aesthetic overthrows the emotional, again . . . although Valladas in Konishi polis claims to have constructed a new synthesis of the two).

After the first fifty years, his Earth-self had begun to hold things back; by the time news reached Earth of the Fomalhaut clone's demise, the messages had become pure audiovisual linear monologues. Paolo understood. It was only right; they'd diverged, and you didn't send mind grafts to strangers.

Most of the transmissions had been broadcast to all of the ships, indiscriminately. Forty-three years ago, though, his Earth-self had sent a special message to the Vega-bound clone.

"The new lunar spectroscope we finished last year has just picked up clear signs of water on Orpheus. There should be large temperate oceans waiting for you, if the models are right. So . . . good luck." Vision showed the instrument's domes growing out of the rock of the lunar farside; plots of the Orphean spectral data; an ensemble of planetary models. "Maybe it seems strange to you – all the trouble we're taking to catch a glimpse of what you're going to see in close-up, so soon. It's hard to explain: I don't think it's jealousy, or even impatience. Just a need for independence.

"There's been a revival of the old debate: should we consider redesigning our minds to encompass interstellar distances? One self spanning thousands of stars, not via cloning, but through acceptance of the natural time scale of the light-speed lag. Millennia passing between mental events. Local contingencies dealt with by non-conscious systems." Essays, pro and con, were appended; Paolo ingested summaries. "I don't think the idea will gain much support, though – and the new astronomical projects are something of an antidote. We have to make peace with the fact that we've stayed behind . . . so we cling to the Earth – looking outwards, but remaining firmly anchored.

"I keep asking myself, though: where do we go from here? History can't guide us. Evolution can't guide us. The C-Z charter says *understand and respect the universe* . . . but in what form? On what scale? With what kind of senses, what kind of minds? We can become anything at all – and that space of possible futures dwarfs the galaxy. Can we explore it without losing our way? Flesh humans used to spin fantasies about aliens arriving to 'conquer' Earth, to steal their 'precious' physical resources, to wipe them out for fear of 'competition' . . . as if a species capable of making the journey wouldn't have had the power, or the wit, or the imagination, to rid itself of obsolete biological imperatives. *Conquering the galaxy* is what bacteria with spaceships would do – knowing no better, having no choice.

"Our condition is the opposite of that: we have no end of choices. That's why we need to find alien life – not just to break the spell of the anthrocosmologists. We need to find aliens who've faced the same decisions – and discovered how to live, what to become. We need to understand what it means to inhabit the universe."

*       *       *

Paolo watched the crude neutrino images of the carpets moving in staccato jerks around his dodecahedral room. Twenty-four ragged oblongs drifted above him, daughters of a larger ragged oblong which had just fissioned. Models suggested that shear forces from ocean currents could explain the whole process, triggered by nothing more than the parent reaching a critical size. The purely mechanical break-up of a colony – if that was what it was – might have little to do with the life cycle of the constituent organisms. It was frustrating. Paolo was accustomed to a torrent of data on anything which caught his interest; for the diaspora's great discovery to remain nothing more than a sequence of coarse monochrome snapshots was intolerable.

He glanced at a schematic of the scout probes' neutrino detectors, but there was no obvious scope for improvement. Nuclei in the detectors were excited into unstable high-energy states, then kept there by fine-tuned gamma-ray lasers picking off lower-energy eigenstates faster than they could creep into existence and attract a transition. Changes in neutrino flux of one part in ten-to-the-fifteenth could shift the energy levels far enough to disrupt the balancing act. The carpets cast a shadow so faint, though, that even this near-perfect vision could barely resolve it.

Orlando Venetti said, "You're awake."

Paolo turned. His father stood an arm's length away, presenting as an ornately clad human of indeterminate age. Definitely older than Paolo, though; Orlando never ceased to play up his seniority – even if the age difference was only twenty-five percent now, and falling.

Paolo banished the carpets from the room to the space behind one pentagonal window, and took his father's hand. The portions of Orlando's mind which meshed with his own expressed pleasure at Paolo's emergence from hibernation, fondly dwelt on past shared experiences, and entertained hopes of continued harmony between father and son. Paolo's greeting was similar, a carefully contrived "revelation" of his own emotional state. It was more of a ritual than an act of communication – but then, even with Elena, he set up barriers. No one was totally honest with another person – unless the two of them intended to permanently fuse.

Orlando nodded at the carpets. "I hope you appreciate how important they are."

"You know I do." He hadn't included that in his greeting,

though. "First alien life." *C-Z humiliates the Gleisner robots, at last* – that was probably how his father saw it. The robots had been first to Alpha Centauri, and first to an extrasolar planet – but first life was Apollo to their Sputniks, for anyone who chose to think in those terms.

Orlando said, "This is the hook we need, to catch the citizens of the marginal polises. The ones who haven't quite imploded into solipsism. This will shake them up – don't you think?"

Paolo shrugged. Earth's transhumans were free to implode into anything they liked; it didn't stop Carter-Zimmerman from exploring the physical universe. But thrashing the Gleisners wouldn't be enough for Orlando; he lived for the day when C-Z would become the cultural mainstream. Any polis could multiply its population a billionfold in a microsecond, if it wanted the vacuous honour of outnumbering the rest. Luring other citizens to migrate was harder – and persuading them to rewrite their own local charters was harder still. Orlando had a missionary streak: he wanted every other polis to see the error of its ways, and follow C-Z to the stars.

Paolo said, "Ashton-Laval has intelligent aliens. I wouldn't be so sure that news of giant seaweed is going to take Earth by storm."

Orlando was venomous. "Ashton-Laval intervened in its so-called 'evolutionary' simulations so many times that they might as well have built the end products in an act of creation lasting six days. They wanted talking reptiles, and – *mirabile dictu!* – they got talking reptiles. There are self-modified transhumans in *this polis* more alien than the aliens in Ashton-Laval."

Paolo smiled. "All right. Forget Ashton-Laval. But forget the marginal polises, too. We choose to value the physical world. That's what defines us – but it's as arbitrary as any other choice of values. Why can't you accept that? It's not the One True Path which the infidels have to be bludgeoned into following." He knew he was arguing half for the sake of it – he desperately wanted to refute the anthrocosmologists, himself – but Orlando always drove him into taking the opposite position. Out of fear of being nothing but his father's clone? Despite the total absence of inherited episodic memories, the stochastic input into his ontogenesis, the chaotically divergent nature of the iterative mind-building algorithms.

Orlando made a beckoning gesture, dragging the image of the

carpets half-way back into the room. "You'll vote for the micro-probes?"

"Of course."

"Everything depends on that, now. It's good to start with a tantalizing glimpse – but if we don't follow up with details soon, they'll lose interest back on Earth very rapidly."

"Lose interest? It'll be fifty-four years before we know if anyone paid the slightest attention in the first place."

Orlando eyed him with disappointment, and resignation. "If you don't care about the other polises, think about C-Z. This helps *us*, it strengthens *us*. We have to make the most of that."

Paolo was bemused. "The charter is the charter. What needs to be strengthened? You make it sound like there's something at risk."

"What do you think a thousand lifeless worlds would have done to us? Do you think the charter would have remained intact?"

Paolo had never considered the scenario. "Maybe not. But in every C-Z where the charter was rewritten, there would have been citizens who'd have gone off and founded new polises on the old lines. You and I, for a start. We could have called it Venetti–Venetti."

"While half your friends turned their backs on the physical world? While Carter-Zimmerman, after two thousand years, went solipsist? You'd be happy with that?"

Paolo laughed. "No – but it's not going to happen, is it? *We've found life.* All right, I agree with you: this strengthens C-Z. The diaspora might have 'failed' . . . but it didn't. We've been lucky. I'm glad, I'm grateful. Is that what you wanted to hear?"

Orlando said sourly, "You take too much for granted."

"And you care too much what I think! I'm not your . . . *heir*." Orlando was first-generation, scanned from flesh – and there were times when he seemed unable to accept that the whole concept of *generation* had lost its archaic significance. "You don't need me to safeguard the future of Carter-Zimmerman on your behalf. Or the future of transhumanity. You can do it in person."

Orlando looked wounded – a conscious choice, but it still encoded something. Paolo felt a pang of regret – but he'd said nothing he could honestly retract.

His father gathered up the sleeves of his gold and crimson robes – the only citizen of C-Z who could make Paolo uncomfortable to be naked – and repeated as he vanished from the room: "You take too much for granted."

The gang watched the launch of the microprobes together – even Liesl, though she came in mourning, as a giant dark bird. Karpal stroked her feathers nervously. Hermann appeared as a creature out of Escher, a segmented worm with six human-shaped feet – on legs with elbows – given to curling up into a disk and rolling along the girders of Satellite Pinatubo. Paolo and Elena kept saying the same thing simultaneously; they'd just made love.

Hermann had moved the satellite to a notional orbit just below one of the scout probes – and changed the environment's scale, so that the probe's lower surface, an intricate landscape of detector modules and attitude-control jets, blotted out half the sky. The atmospheric-entry capsules – ceramic teardrops three centimetres wide – burst from their launch tube and hurtled past like boulders, vanishing from sight before they'd fallen so much as ten metres closer to Orpheus. It was all scrupulously accurate, although it was part real-time imagery, part extrapolation, part *faux*. Paolo thought: *We might as well have run a pure simulation . . . and pretended to follow the capsules down.* Elena gave him a guilty/admonishing look. *Yeah – and then why bother actually launching them at all? Why not just simulate a plausible Orphean ocean full of plausible Orphean lifeforms? Why not simulate the whole diaspora?* There was no crime of heresy in C-Z; no one had ever been exiled for breaking the charter. At times it still felt like a tightrope walk, though, trying to classify every act of simulation into those which contributed to an understanding of the physical universe (good), those which were merely convenient, recreational, aesthetic (acceptable) . . . and those which constituted a denial of the primacy of real phenomena (time to think about emigration).

The vote on the microprobes had been close: seventy-two percent in favour, just over the required two-thirds majority, with five percent abstaining. (Citizens created since the arrival at Vega were excluded . . . not that anyone in Carter-Zimmerman would have dreamt of stacking the ballot, perish the thought.) Paolo had been surprised at the narrow margin; he'd yet to hear a single plausible scenario for the microprobes doing harm. He wondered if there was another, unspoken reason which had nothing to do with fears for the Orphean ecology, or hypothetical culture. *A wish to prolong the pleasure of unravelling the planet's mysteries?* Paolo had some sympathy with that impulse – but the launch of the microprobes would do nothing to undermine the greater long-term pleasure of watching, and understanding, as Orphean life evolved.

Liesl said forlornly, "Coastline erosion models show that the north-western shore of Lambda is inundated by tsunami every ninety Orphean years, on average." She offered the data to them; Paolo glanced at it, and it looked convincing – but the point was academic now. "We could have waited."

Hermann waved his eye-stalks at her. "Beaches covered in fossils, are they?"

"No, but the conditions hardly—"

"No excuses!" He wound his body around a girder, kicking his legs gleefully. Hermann was first-generation, even older than Orlando; he'd been scanned in the twenty-first century, before Carter-Zimmerman existed. Over the centuries, though, he'd wiped most of his episodic memories, and rewritten his personality a dozen times. He'd once told Paolo, "I think of myself as my own great-great-grandson. Death's not so bad, if you do it incrementally. Ditto for immortality."

Elena said, "I keep trying to imagine how it will feel if another C-Z clone stumbles on something infinitely better – like aliens with wormhole drives – while we're back here studying rafts of algae." The body she wore was more stylized than usual – still humanoid, but sexless, hairless and smooth, the face inexpressive and androgynous.

"If they have wormhole drives, they might visit us. Or share the technology, so we can link up the whole diaspora."

"If they have wormhole drives, where have they been for the last two thousand years?"

Paolo laughed. "Exactly. But I know what you mean: *first alien life* . . . and it's likely to be about as sophisticated as seaweed. It breaks the jinx, though. Seaweed every twenty-seven light-years. Nervous systems every fifty? Intelligence every hundred?" He fell silent, abruptly realizing what she was feeling: electing not to wake again after first life was beginning to seem like the wrong choice, a waste of the opportunities the diaspora had created. Paolo offered her a mind graft expressing empathy and support, but she declined.

She said, "I want sharp borders, right now. I want to deal with this myself."

"I understand." He let the partial model of her which he'd acquired as they'd made love fade from his mind. It was non-sapient, and no longer linked to her – but to retain it any longer when she felt this way would have seemed like a transgression. Paolo took the responsibilities of intimacy seriously. His lover before Elena had asked him to erase all his knowledge of her, and he'd more or less complied – the only thing he still knew about her was the fact that she'd made the request.

Hermann announced, "Planetfall!" Paolo glanced at a replay of a scout probe view which showed the first few entry capsules breaking up above the ocean and releasing their microprobes. Nanomachines transformed the ceramic shields (and then themselves) into carbon dioxide and a few simple minerals – nothing the micrometeorites constantly raining down onto Orpheus didn't contain – before the fragments could strike the water. The microprobes would broadcast nothing; when they'd finished gathering data, they'd float to the surface and modulate their UV reflectivity. It would be up to the scout probes to locate these specks, and read their messages, before they self-destructed as thoroughly as the entry capsules.

Hermann said, "This calls for a celebration. I'm heading for the Heart. Who'll join me?"

Paolo glanced at Elena. She shook her head. "You go."

"Are you sure?"

"Yes! Go on." Her skin had taken on a mirrored sheen; her expressionless face reflected the planet below. "I'm all right. I just want some time to think things through, on my own."

Hermann coiled around the satellite's frame, stretching his pale body as he went, gaining segments, gaining legs. "Come on, come on! Karpal? Liesl? Come and celebrate!"

Elena was gone. Liesl made a derisive sound and flapped off into the distance, mocking the environment's airlessness. Paolo and Karpal watched as Hermann grew longer and faster – and then in a blur of speed and change stretched out to wrap the entire geodesic frame. Paolo demagnetized his feet and moved away, laughing; Karpal did the same.

Then Hermann constricted like a boa, and snapped the whole satellite apart.

They floated for a while, two human-shaped machines and a

giant worm in a cloud of spinning metal fragments, an absurd collection of imaginary debris, glinting by the light of the true stars.

The Heart was always crowded, but it was larger than Paolo had seen it – even though Hermann had shrunk back to his original size, so as not to make a scene. The huge muscular chamber arched above them, pulsating wetly in time to the music, as they searched for the perfect location to soak up the atmosphere. Paolo had visited public environments in other polises, back on Earth; many were designed to be nothing more than a perceptual framework for group emotion-sharing. He'd never understood the attraction of becoming intimate with large numbers of strangers. Ancestral social hierarchies might have had their faults – and it was absurd to try to make a virtue of the limitations imposed by minds confined to wetware – but the whole idea of mass telepathy as an end in itself seemed bizarre to Paolo . . . and even old-fashioned, in a way. Humans, clearly, would have benefited from a good strong dose of each other's inner life, to keep them from slaughtering each other – but any civilized transhuman could respect and value other citizens without the need to have *been them*, firsthand.

They found a good spot and made some furniture, a table and two chairs – Hermann preferred to stand – and the floor expanded to make room. Paolo looked around, shouting greetings at the people he recognized by sight, but not bothering to check for identity broadcasts from the rest. Chances were he'd met everyone here, but he didn't want to spend the next hour exchanging pleasantries with casual acquaintances.

Hermann said, "I've been monitoring our modest stellar observatory's data stream – my antidote to Vegan parochialism. Odd things are going on around Sirius. We're seeing electron-positron annihilation gamma rays, gravity waves . . . and some unexplained hot spots on Sirius B." He turned to Karpal and asked innocently, "What do you think those robots are up to? There's a rumour that they're planning to drag the white dwarf out of orbit, and use it as part of a giant spaceship."

"I never listen to rumours." Karpal always presented as a faithful reproduction of his old human-shaped Gleisner body – and his mind, Paolo gathered, always took the form of a physiological model, even though he was five generations removed from flesh. Leaving his people and coming into C-Z must have taken considerable courage; they'd never welcome him back.

Paolo said, "Does it matter what they do? Where they go, how they get there? There's more than enough room for both of us. Even if they shadowed the diaspora – even if they came to Vega – we could study the Orpheans together, couldn't we?"

Hermann's cartoon insect face showed mock alarm, eyes growing wider, and wider apart. "Not if they dragged along a white dwarf! Next thing they'd want to start building a Dyson sphere." He turned back to Karpal. "You don't still suffer the urge, do you, for . . . *astrophysical engineering?*"

"Nothing C-Z's exploitation of a few megatonnes of Vegan asteroid material hasn't satisfied."

Paolo tried to change the subject. "Has anyone heard from Earth, lately? I'm beginning to feel unplugged." His own most recent message was a decade older than the time lag.

Karpal said, "You're not missing much; all they're talking about is Orpheus . . . ever since the new lunar observations, the signs of water. They seem more excited by the mere possibility of life than we are by the certainty. And they have very high hopes."

Paolo laughed. "They do. My Earth-self seems to be counting on the diaspora to find an advanced civilization with the answers to all of transhumanity's existential problems. I don't think he'll get much cosmic guidance from kelp."

"You know there was a big rise in emigration from C-Z after the launch? Emigration, and suicides." Hermann had stopped wriggling and gyrating, becoming almost still, a sign of rare seriousness. "I suspect that's what triggered the astronomy program in the first place. And it seems to have staunched the flow, at least in the short term. Earth C-Z detected water before any clone in the diaspora – and when they hear that we've found life, they'll feel more like collaborators in the discovery because of it."

Paolo felt a stirring of unease. *Emigration and suicides? Was that why Orlando had been so gloomy?* After three hundred years of waiting, how high had expectations become?

A buzz of excitement crossed the floor, a sudden shift in the tone of the conversation. Hermann whispered reverently, "First microprobe has surfaced. And the data is coming in now."

The non-sapient Heart was intelligent enough to guess its patrons' wishes. Although everyone could tap the library for results, privately, the music cut out and a giant public image of the summary data appeared, high in the chamber. Paolo had to crane his neck to view it, a novel experience.

The microprobe had mapped one of the carpets in high resolution. The image showed the expected rough oblong, some hundred metres wide – but the two-or-three-metre-thick slab of the neutrino tomographs was revealed now as a delicate, convoluted surface – fine as a single layer of skin, but folded into an elaborate space-filling curve. Paolo checked the full data: the topology was strictly planar, despite the pathological appearance. No holes, no joins – just a surface which meandered wildly enough to look ten thousand times thicker from a distance than it really was.

An inset showed the microstructure, at a point which started at the rim of the carpet and then – slowly – moved toward the centre. Paolo stared at the flowing molecular diagram for several seconds before he grasped what it meant.

The carpet was not a colony of single-celled creatures. Nor was it a multi-cellular organism. It was a *single molecule*, a two-dimensional polymer weighing twenty-five million kilograms. A giant sheet of folded polysaccharide, a complex mesh of interlinked pentose and hexose sugars hung with alkyl and amide side chains. A bit like a plant cell wall – except that this polymer was far stronger than cellulose, and the surface area was twenty orders of magnitude greater.

Karpal said, "I hope those entry capsules were perfectly sterile. Earth bacteria would gorge themselves on this. One big floating carbohydrate dinner, with no defences."

Hermann thought it over. "Maybe. If they had enzymes capable of breaking off a piece – which I doubt. No chance we'll find out, though: even if there'd been bacterial spores lingering in the asteroid belt from early human expeditions, every ship in the diaspora was double-checked for contamination *en route*. We haven't brought smallpox to the Americas."

Paolo was still dazed. "But how does it assemble? How does it . . . grow?" Hermann consulted the library and replied, before Paolo could do the same.

"The edge of the carpet catalyzes its own growth. The polymer is irregular, aperiodic – there's no single component which simply repeats. But there seem to be about twenty thousand basic structural units – twenty thousand different polysaccharide building blocks." Paolo saw them: long bundles of cross-linked chains running the whole two-hundred-micron thickness of the carpet, each with a roughly square cross-section, bonded at several thousand points to the four neighbouring units. "Even at this depth, the ocean's full of UV-generated radicals which filter down from the surface. Any structural unit exposed to the water converts those radicals into more polysaccharide – and builds another structural unit."

Paolo glanced at the library again, for a simulation of the process. Catalytic sites strewn along the sides of each unit trapped the radicals in place, long enough for new bonds to form between them. Some simple sugars were incorporated straight into the polymer as they were created; others were set free to drift in solution for a microsecond or two, until they were needed. At that level, there were only a few basic chemical tricks being used . . . but molecular evolution must have worked its way up from a few small autocatalytic fragments, first formed by chance, to this elaborate system of twenty thousand mutually self-replicating structures. If the "structural units" had floated free in the ocean as independent molecules, the "lifeform" they comprised would have been virtually invisible. By bonding together, though, they became twenty thousand colours in a giant mosaic.

It was astonishing. Paolo hoped Elena was tapping the library, wherever she was. A colony of algae would have been more "advanced" – but this incredible primordial creature revealed infinitely more about the possibilities for the genesis of life. Carbohydrate, here, played every biochemical role: information carrier, enzyme, energy source, structural material. Nothing like it could have survived on Earth, once there were organisms capable of feeding on it – and if there were ever intelligent Orpheans, they'd be unlikely to find any trace of this bizarre ancestor.

Karpal wore a secretive smile.

Paolo said, "What?"

"Wang tiles. The carpets are made out of Wang tiles."

Hermann beat him to the library, again.

"*Wang* as in twentieth-century flesh mathematician, Hao Wang. *Tiles* as in any set of shapes which can cover the plane. Wang tiles are squares with various shaped edges, which have to fit complementary shapes on adjacent squares. You can cover the plane with a set of Wang tiles, as long as you choose the right one every step of the way. Or in the case of the carpets, grow the right one."

Karpal said, "We should call them Wang's Carpets, in honour of Hao Wang. After twenty-three hundred years, his mathematics has come to life."

Paolo liked the idea, but he was doubtful. "We may have trouble getting a two-thirds majority on that. It's a bit obscure . . ."

Hermann laughed. "Who needs a two-thirds majority? If we want to call them Wang's Carpets, we can call them Wang's Carpets. There are ninety-seven languages in current use in C-Z – half of them invented since the polis was founded. I don't think we'll be exiled for coining one private name."

Paolo concurred, slightly embarrassed. The truth was, he'd completely forgotten that Hermann and Karpal weren't actually speaking Modern Roman.

The three of them instructed their exoselves to consider the name adopted: henceforth, they'd hear "carpet" as "Wang's Carpet" – but if they used the term with anyone else, the reverse translation would apply.

Paolo sat and drank in the image of the giant alien: the first lifeform encountered by human or transhuman which was not a biological cousin. The death, at last, of the possibility that Earth might be unique.

They hadn't refuted the anthrocosmologists yet, though. Not quite. If, as the ACs claimed, human consciousness was the seed around which all of space-time had crystallized – if the universe was nothing but the simplest orderly explanation for human thought – then there was, strictly speaking, no need for a single alien to exist, anywhere. But the physics which justified human existence couldn't help generating a billion other worlds where life could arise. The ACs would be unmoved by Wang's Carpets; they'd insist that these creatures were physical, if not biological, cousins – merely an unavoidable by-product of anthropogenic, life-enabling physical laws.

The real test wouldn't come until the diaspora – or the Gleisner robots – finally encountered conscious aliens: minds entirely unrelated to humanity, observing and explaining the universe which human thought had supposedly built. Most ACs had come right out and declared such a find impossible; it was the sole falsifiable prediction of their hypothesis. Alien consciousness, as opposed to mere alien life, would always build itself a separate universe – because the chance of two unrelated forms of self-awareness concocting exactly the same physics and the same cosmology was infinitesimal – and any alien biosphere which seemed capable of evolving consciousness would simply never do so.

Paolo glanced at the map of the diaspora, and took heart. *Alien life already* – and the search had barely started; there were nine hundred and ninety-eight target systems yet to be explored. And even if every one of them proved no more conclusive than Orpheus . . . he was prepared to send clones out further – and prepared to wait. Consciousness had taken far longer to appear on Earth than the quarter-of-a-billion years remaining before Vega left the main sequence – but the whole point of being here, after all, was that Orpheus wasn't Earth.

Orlando's celebration of the microprobe discoveries was a very first-generation affair. The environment was an endless sunlit garden strewn with tables covered in *food*, and the invitation had politely suggested attendance in fully human form. Paolo politely faked it – simulating most of the physiology, but running the body as a puppet, leaving his mind unshackled.

Orlando introduced his new lover, Catherine, who presented as a tall, dark-skinned woman. Paolo didn't recognize her on sight, but checked the identity code she broadcast. It was a small polis, he'd met her once before – as a man called Samuel, one of the physicists who'd worked on the main interstellar fusion drive employed by all the ships of the diaspora. Paolo was amused to think that many of the people here would be seeing his father as a woman. The majority of the citizens of C-Z still practised the conventions of relative gender which had come into fashion in the twenty-third century – and Orlando had wired them into his own son too deeply for Paolo to wish to abandon them – but whenever the paradoxes were revealed so starkly, he wondered how much longer the conventions would endure. Paolo was same-sex to Orlando, and hence saw his father's lover as a woman, the two close relationships taking precedence over his casual knowledge of Catherine as Samuel. Orlando perceived himself as being male and heterosexual, as his flesh original had been . . . while Samuel saw himself the same way . . . and each perceived the other to be a heterosexual woman. If certain third parties ended up with mixed signals, so be it. It was a typical C-Z compromise: nobody could bear to overturn the old order and do away with gender entirely (as most other polises had done) . . . but nobody could resist the flexibility which being software, not flesh, provided.

Paolo drifted from table to table, sampling the food to keep up appearances, wishing Elena had come. There was little conversation about the biology of Wang's Carpets; most of the people here were simply celebrating their win against the opponents of the microprobes – and the humiliation that faction would suffer, now that it was clearer than ever that the "invasive" observations could have done no harm. Liesl's fears had proved unfounded; there was no other life in the ocean, just Wang's Carpets of various sizes. Paolo, feeling perversely even-handed after the fact, kept wanting to remind these smug movers and shakers: *There might have been anything down there. Strange creatures, delicate and vulnerable in ways we could never have anticipated. We were lucky, that's all.*

He ended up alone with Orlando almost by chance; they were both fleeing different groups of appalling guests when their paths crossed on the lawn.

Paolo asked, "How do you think they'll take this, back home?"

"It's first life, isn't it? Primitive or not. It should at least maintain interest in the diaspora, until the next alien biosphere is discovered." Orlando seemed subdued; perhaps he was finally coming to terms with the gulf between their modest discovery, and Earth's longing for world-shaking results. "And at least the chemistry is novel. If it had turned out to be based on DNA and protein, I think half of Earth C-Z would have died of boredom on the spot. Let's face it, the possibilities of DNA have been simulated to death."

Paolo smiled at the heresy. "You think if nature hadn't managed a little originality, it would have dented people's faith in the charter? If the solipsist polises had begun to look more inventive than the universe itself . . ."

"Exactly."

They walked on in silence, then Orlando halted, and turned to face him.

He said, "There's something I've been wanting to tell you. My Earth-self is dead."

"*What?*"

"Please, don't make a fuss."

"But . . . why? Why would he –?" *Dead* meant suicide; there was no other cause – unless the sun had turned red giant and swallowed everything out to the orbit of Mars.

"I don't know why. Whether it was a vote of confidence in the diaspora" – Orlando had chosen to wake only in the presence of alien life – "or whether he despaired of us sending back good news, and couldn't face the waiting, and the risk of disappointment. He didn't give a reason. He just had his exoself send a message, stating what he'd done."

Paolo was shaken. If a clone of *Orlando* had succumbed to pessimism, he couldn't begin to imagine the state of mind of the rest of Earth C-Z.

"When did this happen?"

"About fifty years after the launch."

"My Earth-self said nothing."

"It was up to me to tell you, not him."

"I wouldn't have seen it that way."

"Apparently, you would have."

Paolo fell silent, confused. How was he supposed to mourn a distant version of Orlando, in the presence of the one he thought of as real? Death of one clone was a strange half-death, a hard thing to come to terms with. His Earth-self had lost a father; his father had lost an Earth-self. What exactly did that mean to *him*?

What Orlando cared most about was Earth C-Z. Paolo said carefully, "Hermann told me there'd been a rise in emigration and suicide – until the spectroscope picked up the Orphean water. Morale has improved a lot since then – and when they hear that it's more than just water . . ."

Orlando cut him off sharply. "You don't have to talk things up for me. I'm in no danger of repeating the act."

They stood on the lawn, facing each other. Paolo composed a dozen different combinations of mood to communicate, but none of them felt right. He could have granted his father perfect knowledge of everything he was feeling – but what exactly would that knowledge have conveyed? In the end, there was fusion, or separateness. There was nothing in between.

Orlando said, "Kill myself – and leave the fate of transhumanity in your hands? You must be out of your fucking mind."

They walked on together, laughing.

*    *    *

Karpal seemed barely able to gather his thoughts enough to speak. Paolo would have offered him a mind graft promoting tranquillity and concentration – distilled from his own most focused moments – but he was sure that Karpal would never have accepted it. He said, "Why don't you just start wherever you want to? I'll stop you if you're not making sense."

Karpal looked around the white dodecahedron with an expression of disbelief. "You live here?"

"Some of the time."

"But this is your base environment? No trees? No sky? No *furniture?*"

Paolo refrained from repeating any of Hermann's naive-robot jokes. "I add them when I want them. You know, like . . . music. Look, don't let my taste in decor distract you—"

Karpal made a chair and sat down heavily.

He said, "Hao Wang proved a powerful theorem, twenty-three hundred years ago. Think of a row of Wang Tiles as being like the data tape of a Turing Machine." Paolo had the library grant him knowledge of the term; it was the original conceptual form of a generalized computing device, an imaginary machine which moved back and forth along a limitless one-dimensional data tape, reading and writing symbols according to a given set of rules.

"With the right set of tiles, to force the right pattern, the next row of the tiling will look like the data tape after the Turing Machine has performed one step of its computation. And the row after that will be the data tape after two steps, and so on. For any given Turing Machine, there's a set of Wang Tiles which can imitate it."

Paolo nodded amiably. He hadn't heard of this particular quaint result, but it was hardly surprising. "The carpets must be carrying out billions of acts of computation every second . . . but then, so are the water molecules around them. There are no physical processes which don't perform arithmetic of some kind."

"True. But with the carpets, it's not quite the same as random molecular motion."

"Maybe not."

Karpal smiled, but said nothing.

"What? You've found a pattern? Don't tell me: our set of twenty thousand polysaccharide Wang Tiles just happens to form the Turing Machine for calculating pi."

"No. What they form is a universal Turing Machine. They can calculate anything at all – depending on the data they start with. Every daughter fragment is like a program being fed to a chemical computer. Growth executes the program."

"Ah." Paolo's curiosity was roused – but he was having some trouble picturing where the hypothetical Turing Machine put its read/write head. "Are you telling me only one tile changes between any two rows, where the 'machine' leaves its mark on the 'data tape' . . .?" The mosaics he'd seen were a riot of complexity, with no two rows remotely the same.

Karpal said, "No, no. Wang's original example worked exactly like a standard Turing Machine, to simplify the argument . . . but the carpets are more like an arbitrary number of different computers with overlapping data, all working in parallel. This is biology, not a designed machine – it's as messy and wild as, say . . . a mammalian genome. In fact, there are mathematical similarities with gene regulation: I've identified Kauffman networks at every level, from the tiling rules up; the whole system's poised on the hyperadaptive edge between frozen and chaotic behaviour."

Paolo absorbed that, with the library's help. Like Earth life, the carpets seemed to have evolved a combination of robustness and flexibility which would have maximized their power to take advantage of natural selection. Thousands of different autocatalytic chemical networks must have arisen soon after the formation of Orpheus – but as the ocean chemistry and the climate changed in the Vegan system's early traumatic millennia, the ability to respond to selection pressure had itself been selected for, and the carpets were the result. Their complexity seemed redundant, now, after a hundred million years of relative stability – and no predators or competition in sight – but the legacy remained.

"So if the carpets have ended up as universal computers . . . with no real need any more to respond to their surroundings . . . what are they *doing* with all that computing power?"

Karpal said solemnly, "I'll show you."

Paolo followed him into an environment where they drifted above a schematic of a carpet, an abstract landscape stretching far into the distance, elaborately wrinkled like the real thing, but otherwise heavily stylized, with each of the polysaccharide building blocks portrayed as a square tile with four different coloured edges. The adjoining edges of neighbouring tiles bore complementary colours – to represent the complementary, interlocking shapes of the borders of the building blocks.

"One group of microprobes finally managed to sequence an entire daughter fragment," Karpal explained, "although the exact edges it started life with are largely guesswork, since the thing was growing while they were trying to map it." He gestured impatiently, and all the wrinkles and folds were smoothed away, an irrelevant distraction. They moved to one border of the ragged-edged carpet, and Karpal started the simulation running.

Paolo watched the mosaic extending itself, following the tiling rules perfectly – an orderly mathematical process, here: no chance collisions of radicals with catalytic sites, no mismatched borders between two new-grown neighbouring "tiles" triggering the disintegration of both. Just the distillation of the higher-level consequences of all that random motion.

Karpal led Paolo up to a height where he could see subtle patterns being woven, overlapping multiplexed periodicities drifting across the growing edge, meeting and sometimes interacting, sometimes passing right through each other. Mobile pseudo-attractors, quasi-stable waveforms in a one-dimensional universe. The carpet's second dimension was more like time than space, a permanent record of the history of the edge.

Karpal seemed to read his mind. "One dimensional. Worse than flatland. No connectivity, no complexity. What can possibly happen in a system like that? Nothing of interest, right?"

He clapped his hands and the environment exploded around Paolo. Trails of colour streaked across his sensorium, entwining, then disintegrating into luminous smoke.

"Wrong. Everything goes on in a multidimensional frequency space. I've Fourier-transformed the edge into over a thousand components, and there's independent information in all of them. We're only in a narrow cross-section here, a sixteen-dimensional slice – but it's oriented to show the principal components, the maximum detail."

Paolo spun in a blur of meaningless colour, utterly lost, his surroundings beyond comprehension. "You're a *Gleisner robot*, Karpal! *Only* sixteen dimensions! How can you have done this?"

Karpal sounded hurt, wherever he was. "Why do you think I came to C-Z? I thought you people were flexible!"

"What you're doing is . . ." *What?* Heresy? There was no such thing. Officially. "Have you shown this to anyone else?"

"Of course not. Whom did you have in mind? Liesl? *Hermann?*"

"Good. I know how to keep my mouth shut." Paolo invoked his exoself and moved back into the dodecahedron. He addressed the empty room. "How can I put this? The physical universe has three spatial dimensions, plus time. Citizens of Carter-Zimmerman inhabit the physical universe. Higher dimensional mind games are for the solipsists." Even as he said it, he realized how pompous he sounded. It was an arbitrary doctrine, not some great moral principle.

But it was the doctrine he'd lived with for twelve hundred years.

Karpal replied, more bemused than offended, "It's the only way to see what's going on. The only sensible way to apprehend it. Don't you want to know what the carpets are *actually like?*"

Paolo felt himself being tempted. *Inhabit a sixteen-dimensional slice of a thousand-dimensional frequency space?* But it was in the service of understanding a real physical system – not a novel experience for its own sake.

And nobody had to find out.

He ran a quick – non-sapient – self-predictive model. There was a ninety-three percent chance that he'd give in, after fifteen subjective minutes of agonizing over the decision. It hardly seemed fair to keep Karpal waiting that long.

He said, "You'll have to loan me your mind-shaping algorithm. My exoself wouldn't know where to begin."

When it was done, he steeled himself, and moved back into Karpal's environment. For a moment, there was nothing but the same meaningless blur as before.

Then everything suddenly crystallized.

Creatures swam around them, elaborately branched tubes like mobile coral, vividly coloured in all the hues of Paolo's mental palette – Karpal's attempt to cram in some of the information that a mere sixteen dimensions couldn't show? Paolo glanced down at his own body – nothing was missing, but he could see *around it* in all the thirteen dimensions in which it was nothing but a pinprick; he quickly looked away. The "coral" seemed far more natural to his altered sensory map, occupying 16-space in all directions, and shaded with hints that it occupied much more. And Paolo had no doubt that it was "alive" – it looked more organic than the carpets themselves, by far.

Karpal said, "Every point in this space encodes some kind of quasi-periodic pattern in the tiles. Each dimension represents a different characteristic size – like a wavelength, although the analogy's not precise. The position in each dimension represents other attributes of the pattern, relating to the particular tiles it employs. So the localized systems you see around you are clusters of a few billion patterns, all with broadly similar attributes at similar wavelengths."

They moved away from the swimming coral, into a swarm of something like jellyfish: floppy hyperspheres waving wispy tendrils (each one of them more substantial than Paolo). Tiny jewel-like creatures darted among them. Paolo was just beginning to notice that nothing moved here like a solid object drifting through normal space; motion seemed to entail a shimmering deformation at the leading hypersurface, a visible process of disassembly and reconstruction.

Karpal led him on through the secret ocean. There were helical worms, coiled together in groups of indeterminate number – each single creature breaking up into a dozen or more wriggling slivers, and then recombining . . . although not always from the same parts. There were dazzling multicoloured stemless flowers, intricate hypercones of "gossamer-thin" fifteen-dimensional petals – each one a hypnotic fractal labyrinth of crevices and capillaries. There were clawed monstrosities, writhing knots of sharp insectile parts like an orgy of decapitated scorpions.

Paolo said, uncertainly, "You could give people a glimpse of this in just three dimensions. Enough to make it clear that there's . . . *life* in here. This is going to shake them up badly, though." Life – embedded in the accidental computations of Wang's Carpets, with no possibility of ever relating to the world outside. This was an affront to Carter-Zimmerman's whole philosophy: if nature had evolved "organisms" as divorced from reality as the inhabitants of the most inward-looking polis, where was the privileged status of the physical universe, the clear distinction between truth and illusion?

And after three hundred years of waiting for good news from the diaspora, how would they respond to this back on Earth?

Karpal said, "There's one more thing I have to show you."

He'd named the creatures squids, for obvious reasons. *Distant cousins of the jellyfish, perhaps?* They were prodding each other with their tentacles in a way which looked thoroughly carnal – but

Karpal explained, "There's no analog of light here. We're view-ing all this according to ad hoc rules which have nothing to do with the native physics. All the creatures here gather information about each other by contact alone – which is actually quite a rich means of exchanging data, with so many dimensions. What you're seeing is communication by touch."

"Communication about what?"

"Just gossip, I expect. Social relationships."

Paolo stared at the writhing mass of tentacles.

"You think they're *conscious*?"

Karpal, point-like, grinned broadly. "They have a central control structure with more connectivity than the human brain – and which correlates data gathered from the skin. I've mapped that organ, and I've started to analyse its function."

He led Paolo into another environment, a representation of the data structures in the "brain" of one of the squids. It was – mercifully – three-dimensional, and highly stylized, built of translucent coloured blocks marked with icons, representing mental symbols, linked by broad lines indicating the major connections between them. Paolo had seen similar diagrams of transhuman minds; this was far less elaborate, but eerily familiar nonetheless.

Karpal said, "Here's the sensory map of its surroundings. Full of other squids' bodies, and vague data on the last known positions of a few smaller creatures. But you'll see that the symbols activated by the physical presence of the other squids are linked to *these*" – he traced the connection with one finger – "representations. Which are crude miniatures of *this whole struc-ture* here."

"This whole structure" was an assembly labelled with icons for memory retrieval, simple tropisms, short-term goals. The general business of being and doing.

"The squid has maps, not just of other squids' bodies, but their minds as well. Right or wrong, it certainly tries to know what the others are thinking about. And" – he pointed out another set of links, leading to another, less crude, miniature squid mind – "it thinks about its own thoughts as well. I'd call that *consciousness*, wouldn't you?"

Paolo said weakly, "You've kept all this to yourself? You came this far, without saying a word –?"

Karpal was chastened. "I know it was selfish – but once I'd

decoded the interactions of the tile patterns, I couldn't tear myself away long enough to start explaining it to anyone else. And I came to you first because I wanted your advice on the best way to break the *news*."

Paolo laughed bitterly. "The best way to break the news that first alien consciousness is hidden deep inside a biological computer? That everything the diaspora was trying to prove has been turned on its head? The best way to explain to the citizens of Carter- Zimmerman that after a three-hundred-year journey, they might as well have stayed on Earth running simulations with as little resemblance to the physical universe as possible?"

Karpal took the outburst in good humour. "I was thinking more along the lines of the best way to point out that if we hadn't travelled to Orpheus and studied Wang's Carpets, we'd never have had the chance to tell the solipsists of Ashton-Laval that all their elaborate invented lifeforms and exotic imaginary universes pale into insignificance compared to what's really out here – and which only the Carter-Zimmerman diaspora could have found."

Paolo and Elena stood together on the edge of Satellite Pinatubo, watching one of the scout probes aim its maser at a distant point in space. Paolo thought he saw a faint scatter of microwaves from the beam as it collided with iron-rich meteor dust. *Elena's mind being diffracted all over the cosmos?* Best not think about that.

He said, "When you meet the other versions of me who haven't experienced Orpheus, I hope you'll offer them mind grafts so they won't be jealous."

She frowned. "Ah. Will I or won't I? I can't be bothered modelling it. I expect I will. You should have asked me before I cloned myself. No need for jealousy, though. There'll be worlds far stranger than Orpheus."

"I doubt it. You really think so?"

"I wouldn't be doing this if I didn't believe that." Elena had no power to change the fate of the frozen clones of her previous self – but everyone had the right to emigrate.

Paolo took her hand. The beam had been aimed almost at Regulus, UV-hot and bright, but as he looked away, the cool yellow light of the sun caught his eye.

Vega C-Z was taking the news of the squids surprisingly well, so far. Karpal's way of putting it had cushioned the blow: it was only by travelling all this distance across the real, physical universe that they could have made such a discovery – and it was amazing how pragmatic even the most doctrinaire citizens had turned out to be. Before the launch, "alien solipsists" would have been the most unpalatable idea imaginable, the most abhorrent thing the diaspora could have stumbled upon – but now that they were here, and stuck with the fact of it, people were finding ways to view it in a better light. Orlando had even proclaimed, "*This* will be the perfect hook for the marginal polises. 'Travel through real space to witness a truly alien virtual reality.' We can sell it as a synthesis of the two world views."

Paolo still feared for Earth, though – where his Earth-self and others were waiting in hope of alien guidance. Would they take the message of Wang's Carpets to heart, and retreat into their own hermetic worlds, oblivious to physical reality?

And he wondered if the anthrocosmologists had finally been refuted . . . or not. Karpal had discovered alien consciousness – but it was sealed inside a cosmos of its own, its perceptions of itself and its surroundings neither reinforcing nor conflicting with human and transhuman explanations of reality. It would be millennia before C-Z could untangle the ethical problems of daring to try to make contact . . . assuming that both Wang's Carpets, and the inherited data patterns of the squids, survived that long.

Paolo looked around at the wild splendour of the star-choked galaxy, felt the disk reach in and cut right through him. *Could all this strange haphazard beauty be nothing but an excuse for those who beheld it to exist? Nothing but the sum of all the answers to all the questions humans and transhumans had ever asked the universe – answers created in the asking?*

He couldn't believe that – but the question remained unanswered.

So far.

# UNDONE

## James Patrick Kelly

*I have always had a fascination for time-travel stories, but not simply with the hop from one year to another, but with the paradoxes and problems involved. There have been many excellent time paradox stories over the years, such as Robert A. Heinlein's "By His Bootstraps" and David Gerrold's* The Man Who Folded Himself. *The following story is not so much involved with paradoxes but how to cope with them.*

*James Patrick Kelly (b. 1951) has been a full-time writer since 1977, producing not just fiction but plays, poetry, planetarium shows and essays, plenty of them, including a regular magazine column about the internet. He received the Hugo Award for his short stories "Think Like a Dinosaur" (1995) and "$10^{16}$ to 1" (1999) and you'll find some of his best short fiction in the collections* Think Like a Dinosaur *(1997) and* Strange But not a Stranger *(2002).*

### panic attack

The ship screamed. Its screens showed Mada that she was surrounded in threespace. A swarm of Utopian asteroids was closing on her, brain clans and mining DIs living in hollowed-out chunks of carbonaceous chondrite, any one of which could have mustered enough votes to abolish Mada in all ten dimensions.

"I'm going to die," the ship cried, "I'm going to die, I'm going to . . ."

"I'm not." Mada waved the speaker off impatiently and scanned downwhen. She saw that the Utopians had planted an identity mine five minutes into the past that would boil her memory to vapor if she tried to go back in time to undo this trap. Upwhen, then. The future was clear, at least as far as she could see, which wasn't much beyond next week. Of course, that was the direction they wanted her to skip. They'd be happiest making her their great-great-great-grandchildren's problem.

The Utopians fired another spread of panic bolts. The ship tried to absorb them, but its buffers were already overflowing. Mada felt her throat tighten. Suddenly she couldn't remember how to spell *luck*, and she believed that she could feel her sanity oozing out of her ears.

"So let's skip upwhen," she said.

"You s-sure?" said the ship. "I don't know if . . . how far?"

"Far enough so that all of these drones will be fossils."

"I can't just . . . I need a number, Mada."

A needle of fear pricked Mada hard enough to make her reflexes kick. "Skip!" Her panic did not allow for the luxury of numbers. "Skip now!" Her voice was tight as a fist. "Do it!"

Time shivered as the ship surged into the empty dimensions. In threespace Mada went all wavy. Eons passed in a nanosecond, then she washed back into the strong dimensions and solidified.

She merged briefly with the ship to assess damage.

"What have you done?" The gain in entropy was an ache in her bones.

"I-I'm sorry, you said to skip so . . ." The ship was still jittery. Even though she wanted to kick its sensorium in, she bit down hard on her anger. They had both made enough mistakes that day. "That's all right," she said, "we can always go back. We just have to figure out when we are. Run the star charts."

## two-tenths of a spin

The ship took almost three minutes to get its charts to agree with its navigation screens – a bad sign. Reconciling the data showed that it had skipped forward in time about two-tenths of a galactic spin. Almost twenty million years had passed on Mada's home world of

Trueborn, time enough for its crust to fold and buckle into new mountain ranges, for the Green Sea to bloom, for the glaciers to march and melt. More than enough time for everything and everyone Mada had ever loved – or hated – to die, turn to dust and blow away.

Whiskers trembling, she checked downwhen. What she saw made her lose her perch and float aimlessly away from the command mod's screens. There had to be something wrong with the ship's air. It settled like dead, wet leaves in her lungs. She ordered the ship to check the mix.

The ship's deck flowed into an enormous plastic hand, warm as blood. It cupped Mada gently in its palm and raised her up so that she could see its screens straight on.

"Nominal, Mada. Everything is as it should be."

That couldn't be right. She could breathe ship-nominal atmosphere. "Check it again," she said.

"Mada, I'm sorry," said the ship.

The identity mine had skipped with them and was still dogging her, five infuriating minutes into the past. There was no getting around it, no way to undo their leap into the future. She was trapped two-tenths of a spin upwhen. The knowledge was like a sucking hole in her chest, much worse than any wound the Utopian psychological war machine could have inflicted on her.

"What do we do now?" asked the ship.

Mada wondered what she should say to it. Scan for hostiles? Open a pleasure sim? Cook a nice, hot stew? Orders twisted in her mind, bit their tails and swallowed themselves. She considered – briefly – telling it to open all the air locks to the vacuum. Would it obey this order? She thought it probably would, although she would as soon chew her own tongue off as utter such cowardly words. Had not she and her sibling batch voted to carry the revolution into all ten dimensions? Pledged themselves to fight for the Three Universal Rights, no matter what the cost the Utopian brain clans extracted from them in blood and anguish?

But that had been two-tenths of a spin ago.

## bean thoughts

"Where are you going?" said the ship.

Mada floated through the door bubble of the command mod. She wrapped her toes around the perch outside to steady herself.

"Mada, wait! I need a mission, a course, some line of inquiry." She launched down the companionway.

"I'm a Dependent Intelligence, Mada." Its speaker buzzed with self-righteousness. "I have the right to proper and timely guidance."

The ship flowed a veil across her trajectory; as she approached, it went taut. That was DI thinking: the ship was sure that it could just bounce her back into its world. Mada flicked her claws and slashed at it, shredding holes half a meter long.

"And I have the right to be an individual," she said. "Leave me alone."

She caught another perch and pivoted off it toward the greenhouse blister. She grabbed the perch by the door bubble and paused to flow new alveoli into her lungs to make up for the oxygen-depleted, carbon-dioxide-enriched air mix in the greenhouse. The bubble shivered as she popped through it and she breathed deeply. The smells of life helped ground her whenever operation of the ship overwhelmed her. It was always so needy and there was only one of her. It would have been different if they had been designed to go out in teams. She would have had her sibling Thiras at her side; together they might have been strong enough to withstand the Utopian's panic . . . *no!* Mada shook him out of her head. Thiras was gone; they were all gone. There was no sense in looking for comfort, downwhen or up. All she had was the moment, the tick of the relentless present, filled now with the moist, bittersweet breath of the dirt, the sticky savor of running sap, the bloom of perfume on the flowers. As she drifted through the greenhouse, leaves brushed her skin like caresses. She settled at the potting bench, opened a bin and picked out a single bean seed.

Mada cupped it between her two hands and blew on it, letting her body's warmth coax the seed out of dormancy. She tried to merge her mind with its blissful unconsciousness. Cotyledons stirred and began to absorb nutrients from the endosperm. A bean cared nothing about proclaiming the Three Universal Rights: the right of all independent sentients to remain individual, the right to manipulate their physical structures and the right to access the timelines. Mada slowed her metabolism to the steady and deliberate rhythm of the bean – what Utopian could do that? They held that individuality bred chaos, that function alone must determine form and that undoing the past was sacrilege. Being Utopians, they could hardly destroy Trueborn and its handful of colonies. Instead they had tried to put the Rights under quarantine.

Mada stimulated the sweat glands in the palms of her hands. The moisture wicking across her skin called to the embryonic root in the bean seed. The tip pushed against the seat coat. Mada's sibling batch on Trueborn had pushed hard against the Utopian blockade, to bring the Rights to the rest of the galaxy. Only a handful had made it to open space. The brain clans had hunted them down and brought most of them back in disgrace to Trueborn. But not Mada. No, not wily Mada, Mada the fearless, Mada whose heart now beat but once a minute.

The bean embryo swelled and its root cracked the seed coat. It curled into her hand, branching and rebranching like the time-lines. The roots tickled her. Mada manipulated the chemistry of her sweat by forcing her sweat ducts to reabsorb most of the sodium and chlorine. She parted her hands slightly and raised them up to the grow lights. The cotyledons emerged and chloroplasts oriented themselves to the light. Mada was thinking only bean thoughts as her cupped hands filled with roots and the first true leaves unfolded. More leaves budded from the nodes of her stem, her petioles arched and twisted to the light, *the light*. It was only the light – violet-blue and orange-red – that mattered, the incredible shower of photons that excited her chlorophyll, passing electrons down carrier molecules to form adenosine diphosphate and nicotinamide adenine dinucleo . . .

"Mada," said the ship. "The order to leave you alone is now superseded by primary programming."

"What?" The word caught in her throat like a bone.

"You entered the greenhouse forty days ago."

Without quite realizing what she was doing, Mada clenched her hands, crushing the young plant.

"I am directed to keep you from harm, Mada," said the ship. "It's time to eat."

She glanced down at the dead thing in her hands. "Yes, all right." She dropped it onto the potting bench. "I've got something to clean up first but I'll be there in a minute." She wiped the corner of her eye. "Meanwhile, calculate a course for home."

## natural background

Not until the ship scanned the quarantine zone at the edge of the Trueborn system did Mada begin to worry. In her time the zone had swarmed with the battle asteroids of the brain clans. Now the Utopians were gone. Of course, that was to be expected after all this time. But as the ship re-entered the home system, dumping excess velocity into the empty dimensions, Mada felt a chill that had nothing to do with the temperature in the command mod.

Trueborn orbited a spectral type G3V star, which had been known to the discoverers as HR3538. Scans showed that the Green Sea had become a climax forest of deciduous hardwood. There were indeed new mountains – knife edges slicing through ever-green sheets – that had upthrust some eighty kilometers off the Fire Coast, leaving Port Henoch landlocked. A rain forest choked the plain where the city of Blair's Landing had once sprawled.

The ship scanned life in abundance. The seas teemed and flocks of Trueborn's flyers darkened the skies like storm clouds: kippies and bluewings and warblers and migrating stilts. Animals had retaken all three continents, lowland and upland, marsh and tundra. Mada could see the dust kicked up by the herds of herbivorous aram from low orbit. The forest echoed with the clatter of shindies and the shriek of blowhards. Big hunters like kar and divil padded across the plains. There were new species as well, mostly invertebrates but also a number of lizards and some-thing like a great, mossy rat that built mounds five meters tall.

None of the introduced species had survived: dogs or turkeys or llamas. The ship could find no cities, towns, buildings – not even ruins. There were neither tubeways nor roads, only the occasional animal track. The ship looked across the entire elec-tromagnetic spectrum and saw nothing but the natural back-ground.

There was nobody home on Trueborn. And as far as they could tell, there never had been.

"Speculate," said Mada.

"I can't," said the ship. "There isn't enough data."

"There's your data." Mada could hear the anger in her voice. "Trueborn, as it would have been had we never even existed."

"Two-tenths of a spin is a long time, Mada."

She shook her head. "They ripped out the foundations, even picked up the dumps. There's nothing, *nothing* of us left." Mada was gripping the command perch so hard that the knuckles of her toes were white. "Hypothesis," she said, "the Utopians got tired of our troublemaking and wiped us out. Speculate."

"Possible, but that's contrary to their core beliefs." Most DIs had terrible imaginations. They couldn't tell jokes, but then they couldn't commit crimes, either.

"Hypothesis: they deported the entire population, scattered us to prison colonies. Speculate."

"Possible, but a logistical nightmare. The Utopians prize the elegant solution."

She swiped the image of her home planet off the screen, as if to erase its unnerving impossibility. "Hypothesis: there are no Utopians any more because the revolution succeeded. Speculate."

"Possible, but then where did everyone go? And why did they return the planet to its pristine state?"

She snorted in disgust. "What if," she tapped a finger to her forehead, "maybe we *don't* exist. What if we've skipped to another time line? One in which the discovery of Trueborn never happened? Maybe there has been no Utopian Empire in this timeline, no Great Expansion, no Space Age, maybe no human civilization at all."

"One does not just skip to another timeline at random." The ship sounded huffy at the suggestion. "I've monitored all our dimensional reinsertions quite carefully, and I can assure you that all these events occurred in the timeline we currently occupy."

"You're saying there's no chance?"

"If you want to write a story, why bother asking my opinion?"

Mada's laugh was brittle. "All right then. We need more data." For the first time since she had been stranded upwhen, she felt a tickle stir the dead weight she was carrying inside her. "Let's start with the nearest Utopian system."

## chasing shadows

The HR683 system was abandoned and all signs of human habitation had been obliterated. Mada could not be certain that everything had been restored to its pre-Expansion state because the ship's database on Utopian resources was spotty. HR4523 was similarly deserted. HR509, also known as Tau Ceti, was only 11.9 light years from earth and had been the first outpost of the Great Expansion. Its planetary system was also devoid of intelligent life and human artifacts – with one striking exception.

Nuevo LA was spread along the shores of the Sterling Sea like a half-eaten picnic lunch. Something had bitten the roofs off its buildings and chewed its walls. Metal skeletons rotted on its docks, transports were melting into brown and gold stains. Once-proud boulevards crumbled in the orange light; the only traffic was windblown litter chasing shadows.

Mada was happy to survey the ruin from low orbit. A closer inspection would have spooked her. "Was it war?"

"There may have been a war," said the ship, "but that's not what caused this. I think it's deliberate deconstruction." In extreme magnification, the screen showed a concrete wall pock-marked with tiny holes, from which dust puffed intermittently. "The composition of that dust is limestone, sand, and aluminum silicate. The buildings are crawling with nanobots and they're eating the concrete."

"How long has this been going on?"

"At a guess, a hundred years, but that could be off by an order of magnitude."

"Who did this?" said Mada. "Why? Speculate."

"If this is the outcome of a war, then it would seem that the victors wanted to obliterate all traces of the vanquished. But it doesn't seem to have been fought over resources. I suppose we could imagine some deep ideological antagonism between the two sides that led to this, but such an extreme of cultural psycho-pathology seems unlikely."

"I hope you're right." She shivered. "So they did it them-selves, then? Maybe they were done with this place and wanted to leave it as they found it?"

"Possible," said the ship.

Mada decided that she was done with Nuevo LA, too. She would have been perversely comforted to have found her enemies in power somewhere. It would have given her an easy way to calculate her duty. However, Mada was quite certain that what this mystery meant was that twenty thousand millennia had conquered both the revolution *and* the Utopians and that she and her sibling batch had been designed in vain.

Still, she had nothing better to do with eternity than to try to find out what had become of her species.

## a never-ending vacation

The Atlantic Ocean was now larger than the Pacific. The Med-iterranean Sea had been squeezed out of existence by the collision of Africa, Europe and Asia. North America floated free of South America and was nudging Siberia. Australia was drifting toward the equator.

The population of earth was about what it had been in the fifteenth century CE, according to the ship. Half a billion people lived on the home world and, as far as Mada could see, none of them had anything important to do. The means of production and distribution, of energy-generation and waste disposal were in the control of Dependent Intelligences like the ship. Despite repeated scans, the ship could detect no sign that any independent sentience was overseeing the system.

There were but a handful of cities, none larger than a quarter of a million inhabitants. All were scrubbed clean and kept scrupulously ordered by the DIs; they reminded Mada of databases populated with people instead of information. The majority of the population spent their bucolic lives in pretty hamlets and quaint towns overlooking lakes or oceans or mountains.

Humanity had booked a never-ending vacation.

"The brain clans could be controlling the DIs," said Mada. "That would make sense."

"Doubtful," said the ship. "Independent sentients create a signature disturbance in the sixth dimension."

"Could there be some secret dictator among the humans, a hidden oligarchy?"

"I see no evidence that anyone is in charge. Do you?"

She shook her head. "Did they choose to live in a museum," she said, "or were they condemned to it? It's obvious there's no First Right here; these people have only the *illusion* of individuality. And no Second Right either. Those bodies are as plain as uniforms – they're still slaves to their biology."

"There's no disease," said the ship. "They seem to be functionally immortal."

"That's not saying very much, is it?" Mada sniffed. "Maybe this is some scheme to start human civilization over again. Or maybe they're like seeds, stored here until someone comes along to plant them." She waved all the screens off. "I want to go down for a closer look. What do I need to pass?"

"Clothes, for one thing." The ship displayed a selection of current styles on its screen. They were extravagantly varied, from ballooning pastel tents to skin-tight sheaths of luminescent metal, to feathered camouflage to jumpsuits made of what looked like dried mud. "Fashion design is one of their principal pastimes," said the ship. "In addition, you'll probably want genitalia and the usual secondary sexual characteristics."

It took her the better part of a day to flow ovaries, fallopian tubes, a uterus, cervix, and vulva and to rearrange her vagina. All these unnecessary organs made her feel bloated. She saw breasts as a waste of tissue; she made hers as small as the ship thought acceptable. She argued with it about the several substantial patches of hair it claimed she needed. Clearly, grooming them would require constant attention. She didn't mind taming her claws into fingernails but she hated giving up her whiskers. Without them, the air was practically invisible. At first her new vulva tickled when she walked, but she got used to it.

The ship entered earth's atmosphere at night and landed in what had once been Saskatchewan, Canada. It dumped most of its mass into the empty dimensions and flowed itself into baggy black pants, a moss-colored boat neck top and a pair of brown, gripall loafers. It was able to conceal its complete sensorium in a canvas belt.

It was 9:14 in the morning on June 23, 19,834,004 CE when Mada strolled into the village of Harmonious Struggle.

## the devil's apple

Harmonious Struggle consisted of five clothing shops, six restaurants, three jewelers, eight art galleries, a musical instrument maker, a crafts workshop, a weaver, a potter, a woodworking shop, two candle stores, four theaters with capacities ranging from twenty to three hundred and an enormous sporting goods store attached to a miniature domed stadium. There looked to be apartments over most of these establishments; many had views of nearby Rabbit Lake.

Three of the restaurants – Hassam's Palace of Plenty, The Devil's Apple and Laurel's – were practically jostling each other for position on Sonnet Street, which ran down to the lake. Lounging just outside of each were waiters eyeing handheld screens. They sprang up as one when Mada happened around the corner.

"Good day, Madame. Have you eaten?"

"Well met, fair stranger. Come break bread with us."

"All natural foods, friend! Lightly cooked, humbly served."

Mada veered into the middle of the street to study the situation as the waiters called to her. ˜*So I can choose whichever I want?*˜ she subvocalized to the ship.

˜*In an attention-based economy*,˜ subbed the ship in reply, ˜*all they expect from you is an audience.*˜

Just beyond Hassam's, the skinny waiter from The Devil's Apple had a wry, crooked smile. Black hair fell to the padded shoulders of his shirt. He was wearing boots to the knee and loose rust-colored shorts, but it was the little red cape that decided her.

As she walked past her, the waitress from Hassam's was practically shouting. "Madame, *please*, their batter is dull!" She waved her handheld at Mada. "Read the *reviews*. Who puts shrimp in *muffins*?"

The waiter at the Devil's Apple was named Owen. He showed her to one of three tables in the tiny restaurant. At his suggestion, Mada ordered the poached peaches with white cheese mousse, an asparagus breakfast torte, baked orange walnut French toast and coddled eggs. Owen served the peaches, but it was the chef and owner, Edris, who emerged from the kitchen to clear the plate.

"The mousse, madame, you liked it?" she asked, beaming.

"It was good," said Mada.

Her smile shrank a size and a half. "Enough lemon rind, would you say that?"

"Yes. It was very nice."

Mada's reply seemed to dismay Edris even more. When she came out to clear the next course, she blanched at the corner of breakfast torte that Mada had left uneaten.

"I knew this." She snatched the plate away. "The pastry wasn't fluffy enough." She rolled the offending scrap between thumb and forefinger.

Mada raised her hands in protest. "No, no, it was delicious." She could see Owen shrinking into the far corner of the room.

"Maybe too much colby, not enough gruyere?" Edris snarled. "But you have no comment?"

"I wouldn't change a thing. It was perfect."

"Madame is kind," she said, her lips barely moving, and retreated.

A moment later Owen set the steaming plate of French toast before Mada.

"Excuse me." She tugged at his sleeve.

"Something's wrong?" He edged away from her. "You must speak to Edris."

"Everything is fine. I was just wondering if you could tell me how to get to the local library."

Edris burst out of the kitchen. "What are you doing, bean-headed boy? You are distracting my patron with absurd chit-terchat. Get out, get out of my restaurant now."

"No really, he . . ."

But Owen was already out the door and up the street, taking Mada's appetite with him.

~*You're doing something wrong,*~ the ship subbed.

Mada lowered her head. ~*I know that!*~

Mada pushed the sliver of French toast around the pool of maple syrup for several minutes but could not eat it. "Excuse me," she called, standing up abruptly. "Edris?"

Edris shouldered through the kitchen door, carrying a tray with a silver egg cup. She froze when she saw how it was with the French toast and her only patron.

"This was one of the most delicious meals I have ever eaten." Mada backed toward the door. She wanted nothing to do with eggs, coddled or otherwise.

Edris set the tray in front of Mada's empty chair. "Madame, the art of the kitchen requires the tongue of the patron," she said icily.

She fumbled for the latch. "Everything was very, very wonderful."

## no comment

Mada slunk down Lyric Alley, which ran behind the stadium, trying to understand how exactly she had offended. In this atten-tion-based economy, paying attention was obviously not enough. There had to be some other cultural protocol she and the ship were missing. What she probably ought to do was go back and explore the clothes shops, maybe pick up a pot or some candles and see what additional information she could blunder into. But making a fool of herself had never much appealed to Mada as a learning strategy. She wanted the map, a native guide – some edge, preferably secret.

~*Scanning,* ~ subbed the ship. ~*Somebody is following you. He just ducked behind the privet hedge twelve-point-three meters to the right. It's the waiter, Owen.*~

"Owen," called Mada, "is that you? I'm sorry I got you in trouble. You're an excellent waiter."

"I'm not really a waiter." Owen peeked over the top of the hedge. "I'm a poet."

She gave him her best smile. "You said you'd take me to the library." For some reason, the smile stayed on her face. "Can we do that now?"

"First listen to some of my poetry."

"No," she said firmly. "Owen, I don't think you've been paying attention. I said I would like to go to the library."

"All right then, but I'm not going to have sex with you."

Mada was taken aback. "Really? Why is that?"

"I'm not attracted to women with small breasts."

For the first time in her life, Mada felt the stab of outraged hormones. "Come out here and talk to me."

There was no immediate break in the hedge, so Owen had to squiggle through. "There's something about me that you don't like," he said as he struggled with the branches.

"Is there?" She considered. "I like your cape."

"That you *don't* like." He escaped the hedge's grasp and brushed leaves from his shorts.

"I guess I don't like your narrow-mindedness. It's not an attractive quality in a poet."

There was a gleam in Owen's eye as he went up on his tiptoes and began to declaim:

"That spring you left I thought I might expire
And lose the love you left for me to keep.
To hold you once again is my desire
Before I give myself to death's long sleep."

He illustrated his poetry with large, flailing gestures. At "death's long sleep" he brought his hands together as if to pray, laid the side of his head against them and closed his eyes. He held that pose in silence for an agonizingly long time.

"It's nice," Mada said at last. "I like the way it rhymes."

He sighed and went flat-footed. His arms drooped and he fixed her with an accusing stare. "You're not from here."

"No," she said. ˜Where am I from?˜ she subbed. ˜Someplace he'll have to look up.˜

˜Marble Bar. It's in Australia˜

"I'm from Marble Bar."

"No, I mean you're not one of us. You don't comment."

At that moment, Mada understood. ˜I want to skip downwhen four minutes. I need to undo this.˜

~.this undo to need I .minutes four downwhen
skip to want I¯ .understood Mada, moment
that At ".comment don't You .us of one not
you're mean I ,No" ".Bar Marble from I'm"
¯ *Australia in It's .Bar Marble*¯ ¯*up look to
have he'll Someplace*¯ .subbed she ¯?*from I
am Where*¯ .said she ",No" ".here from not
You're" .stare accusing an with her fixed he
and drooped arms His .flatfooted went and
sighed He ".rhymes it way the like I." .last at
said Mada ",nice It's" .time long agonizingly
an for silence in pose that held He .eyes his
closed and them against head his of side the
laid ,pray to if as together hands his brought
he "sleep long death's" At .gestures flailing
,large with poetry his illustrated He ".sleep
long death's to myself give I Before desire my
is again once you hold To keep to me for left
you love the lose And expire might I thought
I left you spring That" :declaim to began and
tiptoes his on up went he as eye Owen's in
gleam a was There ".poet a in quality attractive an not It's .narrow-mindedness your like
don't I guess I" .shorts his from leaves
brushed and grasp hedge's the escaped He
".like *don't* you That" ".cape your like I"
.considered She "?there Is" .branches the
with struggled he as said he ",like don't
you that me about something There's"
.through squiggle to had Owen so ,hedge
the in break immediate no was There ".me
to talk and here out Come" .hormones
wronged of stab the felt Mada ,life her in
time first the For ".breasts small with women
to attracted not I'm" "?that is Why ?Really"
aback taken was Mada. ".you with sex have
to going not I'm but ,then right All" ".library
the to go to like would I said I .attention
paying been you've think don't I ,Owen"
,firmly said she ",No" ".poetry my of some
to listen First"

As the ship surged through the empty dimensions, threespace became as liquid as a dream. Leaves smeared and buildings ran together. Owen's face swirled.

"They want criticism," said Mada. "They like to think of themselves as artists but they're insecure about what they've accomplished. They want their audience to engage with what they're doing, help them make it better – the comments they both seem to expect."

"I see it now," said the ship. "But is one person in a backwater worth an undo? Let's just start over somewhere else."

"No, I have an idea." She began flowing more fat cells to her breasts. For the first time since she had skipped upwhen, Mada had a glimpse of what her duty might now be. "I'm going to need a big special effect on short notice. Be ready to reclaim mass so you can resubstantiate the hull at my command."

"First listen to some of my poetry."

"Go ahead." Mada folded her arms across her chest. "Say it then."

Owen stood on tiptoes to declaim:

"That spring you left I thought I might expire
And lose the love you left for me to keep.
To hold you once again is my desire
Before I give myself to death's long sleep."

He illustrated his poetry with large, flailing gestures. At "death's long sleep" he brought his hands together as if to pray, moved them to the side of his head, rested against them and closed his eyes. He had held the pose for just a beat before Mada interrupted him.

"Owen," she said. "You look ridiculous."

He jerked as if he had been hit in the head by a shovel.

She pointed at the ground before her. "You'll want to take these comments sitting down."

He hesitated, then settled at her feet.

"You hold your meter well, but that's purely a mechanical skill." She circled behind him. "A smart oven could do as much. Stop fidgeting!"

She hadn't noticed the ant hills near the spot she had chosen for Owen. The first scouts were beginning to explore him. That suited her plan exactly.

"Your real problem," she continued, "is that you know nothing about death and probably very little about desire."

"I know about death." Owen drew his feet close to his body and grasped his knees. "Everyone does. Flowers die, squirrels die."

"Has anyone you've ever known died?"

He frowned. "I didn't know her personally, but there was the woman who fell off that cliff in Merrymeeting."

"Owen, did you have a mother?"

"Don't make fun of me. Everyone has a mother."

Mada didn't think it was time to tell him that she didn't; that she and her sibling batch of a thousand revolutionaries had been autoflowed. "Hold out your hand." Mada scooped up an ant. "That's your mother." She crunched it and dropped it onto Owen's palm.

Owen looked down at the dead ant and then up again at Mada. His eyes filled.

"I think I love you," he said. "What's your name?"

"Mada." She leaned over to straighten his cape. "But loving me would be a very bad idea."

## all that's left

Mada was surprised to find a few actual books in the library, printed on real plastic. A primitive DI had catalogued the rest of the collection, billions of gigabytes of print, graphics, audio, video and VR files. None of it told Mada what she wanted to know. The library had sims of Egypt's New Kingdom, Islam's Abbasid dynasty and the International Moonbase – but then came an astonishing void. Mada's searches on Trueborn, the Utopians, Tau Ceti, intelligence engineering and dimensional extensibility theory turned up no results. It was only in the very recent past that history resumed. The DI could reproduce the plans that the workbots had left when they built the library twenty-two years ago, and the menu The Devil's Apple had offered the previous summer, and the complete won-lost record of the Black Minks, the local scatterball club, which had gone 533–905 over the last century. It knew that the name of the woman who died in Merrymeeting was Agnes and that two years after her death, a replacement baby had been born to Chandra and Yuri. They named him Herrick.

Mada waved the screen blank and stretched. She could see Owen draped artfully over a nearby divan, as if posing for a portrait. He was engrossed by his handheld. She noticed that his lips moved as he read. She crossed the reading room and squeezed onto it next to him, nestling into crook in his legs. "What's that?" she asked.

He turned the handheld toward her. "Nadeem Jerad's *Burning the Snow*. Would you like to hear one of his poems?"

"Maybe later." She leaned into him. "I was just reading about Moonbase."

"Yes, ancient history. It's sort of interesting, don't you think? The Greeks and the Renaissance and all that."

"But then I can't find any record of what came after."

"Because of the nightmares." He nodded. "Terrible things happened, so we forgot them."

"What terrible things?"

He tapped the side of his head and grinned.

"Of course," she said, "nothing terrible happens anymore."

"No. Everyone's happy now." Owen reached out and pushed a strand of her hair off her forehead. "You have beautiful hair."

Mada couldn't even remember what color it was. "But if something terrible did happen, then you'd want to forget it."

"Obviously."

"The woman who died, Agnes. No doubt her friends were very sad."

"No doubt." Now he was playing with her hair.

~*Good question,*~ subbed the ship. ~*They must have some mechanism to wipe their memories.*~

"Is something wrong?" Owen's face was the size of the moon; Mada was afraid of what he might tell her next.

"Agnes probably had a mother," she said.

"A mom and a dad."

"It must have been terrible for them."

He shrugged. "Yes, I'm sure they forgot her."

Mada wanted to slap his hand away from her head. "But how could they?"

He gave her a puzzled look. "Where are you from, anyway?"

"Trueborn," she said without hesitation. "It's a long, long way from here."

"Don't you have libraries there?" He gestured at the screens that surrounded them. "This is where we keep what we don't want to remember."

~*Skip!*~ Mada could barely sub; if what she suspected were true . . . ~*Skip downwhen two minutes.*~

~.minutes two downwhen Skip~ . . . true were suspected she what if ;sub barely could Mada ~!Skip~ ".remember to want don't we what keep we where is This." .them surrounded that screens the at gestured He "?there libraries have you Don't" ".here from way long, long a It's" .hesitation without said she ",Trueborn" "?anyway, from you are Where" .look puzzled a her gave He "?they could how But" .head her from away hand his slap to wanted

She wrapped her arms around herself to keep the empty dimensions from reaching for the emptiness inside her. Was something wrong?

Of course there was, but she didn't expect

Mada ".her forgot they sure I'm, Yes"
.shrugged He ".them for terrible been have
must It" ".dad a and mom A" ".mother a
had probably Agnes" .next her tell might he
what of afraid was Mada .moon the of size the
was face Owen's "?wrong something Is"
~!Quiet~ ~. . . *memories their wipe to mechanism some have must They~* .ship the subbed
*~,question Good~* .hair her with playing was
he Now ".doubt No" ".sad very were friends
her doubt no ,Agnes ,died who woman The"
".Obviously" ".it forget to want you'd then
,happen did terrible something if But" .was it
color what remember even couldn't Mada

to say it out loud. "I've lost everything and all that's left is *this*." Owen shimmered next to her like the surface of Rabbit Lake.

"Mada, what?" said the ship.

"Forget it," she said. She thought she could hear something cracking when she laughed.

Mada couldn't even remember what color her hair was. "But if something terrible did happen, then you'd want to forget it."

"Obviously."

"Something terrible happened to me."

"I'm sorry." Owen squeezed her shoulder. "Do you want me to show you how to use the headbands?" He pointed at a rack of metal-mesh strips.

~*Scanning*,~ subbed the ship. "*Microcurrent taps capable of modulating post-synaptic outputs. I thought they were some kind of virtual reality I/O.*"

"No." Mada twisted away from him and shot off the divan. She was outraged that these people would deliberately burn memories. How many stubbed toes and unhappy love affairs had Owen forgotten? If she could have, she would have skipped the entire village of Harmonious Struggle downwhen into the identity mine. When he rose up after her, she grabbed his hand. "I have to get out of here *right now*." She dragged him out of the library into the innocent light of the sun.

"Wait a minute," he said. She continued to tow him up Ode Street and out of town. "Wait!" He planted his feet, tugged at her and she spun back to him. "Why are you so upset?"

"I'm not upset." Mada's blood was hammering in her temples and she could feel the prickle of sweat under her arms. ~*Now I need you*,~ she subbed. "All right then. It's time you knew." She took a deep breath. "We were just talking about ancient history,

Owen. Do you remember back then that the gods used to intervene in the affairs of humanity?"

Owen goggled at her as if she were growing beans out of her ears.

"I am a goddess, Owen, and I have come for you. I am calling you to your destiny. I intend to inspire you to great poetry."

His mouth opened and then closed again.

"My worshippers call me by many names." She raised a hand to the sky. ~*Help?*~

~*Try Athene? Here's a databurst.*~

"To the Greeks, I was Athene," Mada continued, "the goddess of cities, of technology and the arts, of wisdom and of war." She stretched a hand toward Owen's astonished face, forefinger aimed between his eyes. "Unlike you, I had no mother. I sprang full-grown from the forehead of my maker. I am Athene, the virgin goddess."

"How stupid do you think I am?" He shivered and glanced away from her fierce gaze. "I used to live in Maple City, Mada. I'm not some simple-minded country lump. You don't seriously expect me to believe this goddess nonsense?"

She slumped, confused. Of course she had expected him to believe her. "I meant no disrespect, Owen. It's just that the truth is . . ." This wasn't as easy as she had thought. "What I expect is that you believe in your own potential, Owen. What I expect is that you are brave enough to leave this place and come with me. To the stars, Owen, to the stars to start a new world." She crossed her arms in front of her chest, grasped the hem of her moss-colored top, pulled it over her head and tossed it behind her. Before it hit the ground the ship augmented it with enough reclaimed mass from the empty dimensions to resubstantiate the command and living mods.

Mada was quite pleased with the way Owen tried – and failed – not to stare at her breasts. She kicked the gripall loafers off and the deck rose up beneath them. She stepped out of the baggy, black pants; when she tossed them at Owen, he flinched. Seconds later, they were eyeing each other in metallic light of the ship's main companionway.

"Well?" said Mada.

## duty

Mada had difficulty accepting Trueborn as it now was. She could see the ghosts of great cities, hear the murmur of dead friends. She decided to live in the forest that had once been the Green Sea, where there were no landmarks to remind her of what she had lost. She ordered the ship to begin constructing an infrastructure similar to that they had found on earth, only capable of supporting a technologically advanced population. Borrowing orphan mass from the empty dimensions, it was soon consumed with this monumental task. She missed its company; only rarely did she use the link it had left her – a silver ring with a direct connection to its sensorium.

The ship's first effort was the farm that Owen called Athens. It consisted of their house, a flow works, a gravel pit and a barn. Dirt roads led to various mines and domed fields that the ship's bots tended. Mada had it build a separate library, a little way into the woods, where, she declared, information was to be acquired only, never destroyed. Owen spent many evenings there. He said he was trying to make himself worthy of her.

He had been deeply flattered when she told him that, as part of his training as a poet, he was to name the birds and beasts and flowers and trees of Trueborn.

"But they must already have names," he said, as they walked back to the house from the newly tilled soya field.

"The people who named them are gone," she said. "The names went with them."

"Your people." He waited for her to speak. The wind sighed through the forest. "What happened to them?"

"I don't know." At that moment, she regretted ever bringing him to Trueborn.

He sighed. "It must be hard."

"You left *your* people," she said. She spoke to wound him, since he was wounding her with these rude questions.

"For you, Mada." He let go of her. "I know you didn't leave them for *me*." He picked up a pebble and held it in front of his face. "You are now Mada-stone," he told it, "and whatever you hit . . ." – he threw it into the woods and it *thwocked* off a tree—

". . . is Mada-tree. We will plant fields of Mada-seed and press Mada-juice from the sweet Mada-fruit and dance for the rest of our days down Mada Street." He laughed and put his arm around her waist and swung her around in circles, kicking up dust from the road. She was so surprised that she laughed too.

Mada and Owen slept in separate bedrooms, so she was not exactly sure how she knew that he wanted to have sex with her. He had never spoken of it, other than on that first day when he had specifically said that he did not want her. Maybe it was the way he continually brushed up against her for no apparent reason. This could hardly be chance, considering that they were the only two people on Trueborn. For herself, Mada welcomed his hesitancy. Although she had been emotionally intimate with her batch siblings, none of them had ever inserted themselves into her body cavities.

But, for better or worse, she had chosen this man for this course of action. Even if the galaxy had forgotten Trueborn two-tenths of a spin ago, the revolution still called Mada to her duty.

"What's it like to kiss?" she asked that night, as they were finishing supper.

Owen laid his fork across a plate of cauliflower curry. "You've never kissed anyone before?"

"That's why I ask."

Owen leaned across the table and brushed his lips across hers. The brief contact made her cheeks flush, as if she had just jogged in from the gravel pit. "Like that," he said. "Only better."

"Do you still think my breasts are too small?"

"I never said that." Owen's face turned red.

"It was a comment you made – or at least thought about making."

"A comment?" The word *comment* seemed to stick in his throat; it made him cough. "Just because you make comment on some aspect doesn't mean you reject the work as a whole."

Mada glanced down the neck of her shift. She hadn't really increased her breast mass all that much, maybe ten or twelve grams, but now vasocongestion had begun to swell them even more. She could also feel blood flowing to her reproductive organs. It was a pleasurable weight that made her feel light as pollen. "Yes, but do you think they're too small?"

Owen got up from the table and came around behind her chair. He put his hands on her shoulders and she leaned her head back against him. There was something between her cheek and his stomach. She heard him say, "Yours are the most perfect breasts on this entire planet," as if from a great distance and then realized that the *something* must be his penis.

After that, neither of them made much comment.

## nine hours

Mada stared at the ceiling, her eyes wide but unseeing. Her concentration had turned inward. After she had rolled off him, Owen had flung his left arm across her belly and drawn her hip towards his and given her the night's last kiss. Now the muscles of his arm were slack, and she could hear his seashore breath as she released her ovum into the cloud of his sperm squiggling up her fallopian tubes. The most vigorous of the swimmers butted its head through the ovum's membrane and dissolved, releasing its genetic material. Mada immediately started raveling the strands of DNA before the fertilized egg could divide for the first time. Without the necessary diversity, they would never revive the revolution. Satisfied with her intervention, she flowed the blastocyst down her fallopian tubes where it locked onto the wall of her uterus. She prodded it and the ball of cells became a comma with a big head and a thin tail. An array of cells specialized and folded into a tube that ran the length of the embryo, weaving into nerve fibers. Dark pigment swept across two cups in the blocky head and then bulged into eyes. A mouth slowly opened; in it was a one-chambered, beating heart. The front end of the neural tube blossomed into the vesicles that would become the brain. Four buds swelled, two near the head, two at the tail. The uppermost pair sprouted into paddles, pierced by rays of cells that Mada immediately began to ossify into fingerbone. The lower buds stretched into delicate legs. At midnight, the embryo was as big as her fingernail; it began to move and so became a fetus. The eyes opened for a few minutes, but then the eyelids fused. Mada and Owen were going to have a son; his penis was now a nub of flesh. Bubbles of tissue blew inward from the head and became his ears. Mada listened to him listen to her heartbeat. He lost his tail and his intestines slithered down the umbilical cord into his abdomen. As his fingerprints looped and whorled, he stuck his thumb into his mouth. Mada was having trouble breathing because the fetus was floating so high in her uterus. She eased herself into a sitting position and Owen grumbled in his sleep. Suddenly the curry in the cauliflower was giving her heartburn. Then the muscles of her uterus tightened and pain sheeted across her swollen belly.

~Drink this.~ The ship flowed a tumbler of nutrient nano onto the bedside table. ˜*The fetus gains mass rapidly from now on.*˜ The stuff tasted like rusty nails. ˜*You're doing fine.*˜

When the fetus turned upside down, it felt like he was trying out a gymnastic routine. But then he snuggled headfirst into her pelvis, and calmed down, probably because there wasn't enough room left inside her for him to make large, flailing gestures like his father. Now she could feel electrical buzzes down her legs and inside her vagina as the baby bumped her nerves. He was big now, and growing by almost a kilogram an hour, laying down new muscle and brown fat. Mada was tired of it all. She dozed. At six-thirty-seven her waters broke, drenching the bed.

"Hmm." Owen rolled away from the warm, fragrant spill of amniotic fluid. "What did you say?"

The contractions started; she put her hand on his chest and pressed down. "Help," she whimpered.

"Wha . . .?" Owen propped himself up on elbows. "Hey, I'm wet. How did I get . . .?"

"*O-Owen!*" She could feel the baby's head stretching her vagina in a way mere flesh could not possibly stretch.

"Mada! What's wrong?" Suddenly his face was very close to hers. "Mada, what's happening?"

But then baby was slipping out of her, and it was *sooo* much better than the only sex she had ever had. She caught her breath and said, "I have begotten a son."

She reached between her legs and pulled the baby to her breasts. They were huge now, and very sore.

"We will call him Owen," she said.

# Begot

And Mada begot Enos and Felicia and Malaleel and Ralph and Jared and Elisa and Tharsis and Masahiko and Thema and Seema and Casper and Hevila and Djanka and Jennifer and Jojo and Regma and Elvis and Irina and Dean and Marget and Karoly and Sabatha and Ashley and Siobhan and Mei-Fung and Neil and Gupta and Hans and Sade and Moon and Randy and Genevieve and Bob and Nazia and Eiichi and Justine and Ozma and Khaled and Candy and Pavel and Isaac and Sandor and Veronica and Gao and Pat and Marcus and Zsa Zsa and Li and Rebecca.

Seven years after her return to Trueborn, Mada rested.

## ever after

Mada was convinced that she was not a particularly good mother, but then she had been designed for courage and quick-thinking, not nurturing and patience. It wasn't the crying or the dirty diapers or the spitting-up, it was the utter uselessness of the babies that the revolutionary in her could not abide. And her maternal instincts were often skewed. She would offer her children the wrong toy or cook the wrong dish, fall silent when they wanted her to play, prod them to talk when they needed to withdraw. Mada and the ship had calculated that fifty of her genetically manipulated offspring would provide the necessary diversity to repopulate Trueborn. After Rebecca was born, Mada was more than happy to stop having children.

Although the children seemed to love her despite her awkwardness, Mada wasn't sure she loved them back. She constantly teased at her feelings, peeling away what she considered pretense and sentimentality. She worried that the capacity to love might not have been part of her emotional design. Or perhaps begetting fifty children in seven years had left her numb.

Owen seemed to enjoy being a parent. He was the one whom the children called for when they wanted to play. They came to Mada for answers and decisions. Mada liked to watch them snuggle next to him when he spun his fantastic stories. Their father picked them up when they stumbled, and let them climb on his shoulders so they could see just what he saw. They told him secrets they would never tell her.

The children adored the ship, which substantiated a bot companion for each of them, in part for their protection. All had inherited their father's all-but-invulnerable immune systems; their chromosomes replicated well beyond the Hayflick limit with integrity and fidelity. But they lacked their mother's ability to flow tissue and were therefore at peril of drowning or breaking their necks. The bots also provided the intense individualized attention that their busy parents could not. Each child was convinced that his or her bot companion had a unique personality. Even the seven-year-olds were too young to realize that the bots were reflecting their ideal personality back at them. The bots were in general as intelligent as the ship, although it had programmed into their DIs a touch of naiveté and a tendency to literalness that allowed the children to play tricks on them.

Pranking a brother or sister's bot was a particularly delicious sport.

Athens had begun to sprawl after seven years. The library had tripled in size and grown a wing of classrooms and workshops. A new gym overlooked three playing fields. Owen had asked the ship to build a little theater where the children could put on shows for each other. The original house became a ring of houses, connected by corridors and facing a central courtyard. Each night Mada and Owen moved to their bedroom in a different house. Owen thought it important that the children see them sleeping in the same bed; Mada went along.

After she had begotten Rebecca, Mada needed something to do that didn't involve the children. She had the ship's farmbots plow up a field and for an hour each day she tended it. She resisted Owen's attempts to name this "Mom's Hobby." Mada grew vegetables; she had little use for flowers. Although she made a specialty of root crops, she was not a particularly accomplished gardener. She did, however, enjoy weeding.

It was at these quiet times, her hands flicking across the dark soil, that she considered her commitment to the Three Universal Rights. After two-tenths of a spin, she had clearly lost her zeal. Not for the first, that independent sentients had the right to remain individual. Mada was proud that her children were as individual as any intelligence, flesh or machine, could have made them. Of course, they had no pressing need to exercise the second right of manipulating their physical structures – she had taken care of that for them. When they were of age, if the ship wanted to introduce them to molecular engineering, that could certainly be done. No, the real problem was that downwhen was forever closed to them by the identity mine. How could she justify her new Trueborn society if it didn't enjoy the third right: free access to the timelines?

## undone

"Mada!" Owen waved at the edge of her garden. She blinked; he was wearing the same clothes he'd been wearing when she had first seen him on Sonnet Street in front of The Devil's Apple – down to the little red cape. He showed her a picnic basket. "The ship is watching the kids tonight," he called. "Come on, it's our anniversary. I did the calculations myself. We met eight earth years ago today."

He led her to a spot deep in the woods, where he spread a blanket.
They stretched out next to each other and sorted through the basket.
There was a curley salad with alperts and thumbnuts, brainboy and
chive sandwiches on cheese bread. He toasted her with mada-fruit
wine and told her that Siobhan had let go of the couch and taken her
first step and that Irina wanted everyone to learn to play an
instrument so that she could conduct the family orchestra and
the Malaleel had asked him just today if ship was a person.

"It's not a person," said Mada. "It's a DI."

"That's what I said." Owen peeled the crust off his cheese bread.
"And he said if it's not a person, how come it's telling jokes?"

"It told a joke?"

"It asked him, 'How come you can't have everything?' and
then it said, 'Where would you put it?'"

She nudged him in the ribs. "That sounds more like you than
the ship."

"I have a present for you," he said after they were stuffed. "I
wrote you a poem." He did not stand; there were no large, flailing
gestures. Instead he slid the picnic basket out of the way, leaned
close and whispered into her ear.

"Loving you is like catching rain on my tongue.
You bathe the leaves, soak indifferent ground;
Why then should I get so little of you?
Yet still, like a flower with a fool's face,
I open myself to the sky."

Mada was not quite sure what was happening to her; she had
never really cried before. "I like that it doesn't rhyme." She had
understood that tears flowed from a sadness. "I like that a lot."
She sniffed and smiled and daubed at edges of her eyes with a
napkin. "Never rhyme anything again."

"Done," he said.

Mada watched her hand reach for him, caress the side of his
neck, and then pull him down on top of her. Then she stopped
watching herself.

"No more children." His whisper seemed to fill her head.

"No," she said, "no more."

"I'm sharing you with too many already." He slid his hand
between her legs. She arched her back and guided him to her
pleasure.

When they had both finished, she ran her finger through the sweat cooling at the small of his back and then licked it. "Owen," she said, her voice a silken purr. "That was the one."

"Is that your comment?"

"No." She craned to see his eyes. "This is my comment," she said. "You're writing love poems to the wrong person."

"There is no one else," he said.

She squawked and pushed him off her. "That may be true," she said, laughing, "but it's not something you're supposed to say."

"No, what I meant was . . ."

"I know." She put a finger to his lips and giggled like one of her babies. Mada realized then how dangerously happy she was. She rolled away from Owen; all the lightness crushed out of her by the weight of guilt and shame. It wasn't her duty to be happy. She had been ready to betray the cause of those who had made her for what? For this man? "There's something I have to do." She fumbled for her shift. "I can't help myself, I'm sorry."

Owen watched her warily. "Why are you sorry?"

"Because after I do it, I'll be different."

"Different how?"

"The ship will explain." She tugged the shift on. "Take care of the children."

"What do you mean, take care of the children? What are you doing?" He lunged at her and she scrabbled away from him on all fours. "Tell me."

"The ship says my body should survive." She staggered to her feet. "That's all I can offer you, Owen." Mada ran.

She didn't expect Owen to come after her – or to run so fast. ˜*I need you.*˜ she subbed to the ship. "*Substantiate the command mod.*˜

He was right behind her. Saying something Was it to her? "No," he panted, "no, no, *no.*"

˜*Substantiate the com . . .*˜

Suddenly Owen was gone; Mada bit her lip as she crashed into the main screen, caromed off it and dropped like a dead woman. She lay there for a moment, the cold of the deck seeping into her cheek. "Goodbye," she whispered. She struggled to pull herself up and spat blood.

"Skip downwhen," she said, "six minutes."

".minutes six" ,said she ",downwhen Skip"
.blood spat and up herself pull to struggled She
.whispered she ",Goodbye" .cheek her into
seeping deck the of cold the ,moment a for
there lay She .woman dead a like dropped and it
off caromed ,screen main the into crashed she
as lip her bit Mada ;gone was Owen Suddenly
~ . . .com the Substantiate~ ".no ,no, no"
,panted he ",No" ?her to it Was .something
Saying. her behind right was He ~.mod command the Substantiate~ .ship the to subbed she
~.you need I~ .fast so run to or – her after come
to Owen expect didn't She .ran Mada ".Owen,
you offer can I all That's". feet her to staggered
She ".survive should body my says ship The"
".me Tell" .fours all on him from away scrabble she and her at lunged He "?doing you are
What ?children the of care take ,mean you do
What." ".children the of care Take" .on shift
the tugged She ".explain will ship The" "?how
Different" ".different be I'll ,it do I after
Because" "?sorry you are Why" .warily her
watched Owen. ".sorry I'm ,myself help can't
I" .shift her for fumbled She .her made had
who those of cause the betrayed have would she
easily How ".do to have I something There's"
.happy be to duty her wasn't It .shame and guilt
of weight the by her of out crushed lightness
the all ,Owen from away rolled She .was she
happy dangerously how then realized Mada
.babies her of one like giggled and lips his to
finger a put She ".know I" ". . . was meant I
what ,No" ".say to supposed you're something
not it's but" ,laughing, said she ",true be may
That" .her off him pushed and squawked She
.said he ",else one no is There" ".person wrong
the to poems love writing You're" .said she
",comment my is This" .eyes his see to craned
She ".No" "?comment your that Is" ".one the
was That" .purr silken a voice her ,said she
",Owen"

When threespace went blurry, it seemed that her duty did too. She waved her hand and watched it smear.

"You know what you're doing," said the ship.

"What I was designed to do. What all my batch siblings pledged to do." She waved her hand again; she could actually see through herself. "The only thing I can do."

"The mine will wipe your identity. There will be nothing of you left."

"And then it will be gone and the timelines will open. I believe that I've known this was what I had to do since we first skipped upwhen."

"The probability was always high," said the ship "But not certain."

"Bring me to him, afterwards. But don't tell him about the timelines. He might want to change them. The timelines are for the children, so that they can finish the revol . . ."

"Owen," she said, her voice a silken purr. Then she paused. The woman shook her head, trying to clear it. Lying on top of her was the handsomest man she had ever met. She felt warm and sexy and wonderful. What was this? "I . . . I'm . . ." she said. She reached up and touched the little red cloth hanging from his shoulders. "I like your cape."

"minutes six", said she ",downwhen Skip" .blood spat and up herself pull to struggled She .whispered she ",Goodbye" .cheek her into seeping deck the of cold the ,moment a for there lay She .woman dead a like dropped and it off caromed ,screen main the into crashed she as lip her bit Mada ;gone was Owen Suddenly ˜ . . . .*com the Substantiate*˜ ".no ,no, no" ,panted he ",No" ?her to it Was .something Saying. her behind right was He ˜.*mod command the Substantiate*˜ .ship the to subbed she ˜.*you need I*˜ .fast so run to or–her after come to Owen expect didn't She .ran Mada ".Owen, you offer can I all That's". feet her to staggered She ".survive should body my says ship The" ".me Tell" .fours all on him from away scrabble she and her at lunged He "?doing you are What ?children the of care take, mean you do What." ".children the of care Take" .on shift the tugged She ".explain will ship The" "?how Different" ".different be I'll ,it do I after Because" "?sorry you are Why" .warily her watched Owen. ".sorry I'm ,myself help can't I" .shift her for fumbled She .her made had who those of cause the betrayed have would she easily How ".do to have I something There's" .happy be to duty her wasn't It .shame and guilt of weight the by her of out crushed lightness the all ,Owen from away rolled She .was she happy dangerously how then realized Mada .babies her of one like giggled and lips his to finger a put She ".know I" ". . . . was meant I what ,No" ".say to supposed you're something not it's but" ,laugh

Mada waved her hand and watched it smear in threespace.

"What are you doing?" said the ship.

"What I was designed to do. ." She waved; she could actually see through herself. "The only thing I can do."

"The mine will wipe your identity. None of your memories will survive."

"I believe that I've known that's what would happen since we first skipped upwhen."

"It was probable." said the ship, "but not certain."

Trueborn scholars pinpoint what the ship did next as its first step toward independent sentience. In its memoirs, the ship credits the children with teaching it to misbehave.

It played a prank.

"Loving you," said the ship, "is like catching rain on my tongue.

ing, said she ",true be may That" .her off him
pushed and squawked She .said he ",else one
no is There" ".person wrong the to poems love
writing You're" .said she ",comment my is
This" .eyes his see to craned She ".No"
"?comment your that Is" ".one the was That"
.purr silken a voice her, said she ",Owen"

You bathe. . . ."

"Stop," Mada shouted. "Stop right now!"

"Got you!" The ship gloated. "Four minutes, fifty-one seconds."

"Owen,' she said, her voice a silken purr. "That was the one."

"Is that your comment?"

"No." Mada was astonished – and pleased – that she still existed. She knew that in most timelines her identity must have been obliterated by the mine. Thinking about those brave, lost selves made her more sad than proud. "This is my comment," she said. "I'm ready now."

Owen coughed uncertainly. "Umm, already?"

She squawked and pushed him off her. "Not for *that*." She sifted his hair through her hands. "To be with you forever."

# JUDGMENT ENGINE

## Greg Bear

*And so we reach the ultimate, at least so far as this
anthology is concerned. Here's what I consider one of the
most extreme sf stories currently around. It really does deal
with life, the universe and everything and, in a rather
curious way, brings us back to the earlier stories "Anomalies" and "The Creator".*

*Greg Bear (b.1951) is one of the most highly regarded
writers of high-tech hard science fiction, able to take it beyond
the bounds of nuts-and-bolts science into the mystical. This
became most evident with his 1983 award-winning story
"Blood Music", later adapted into the novel of the same name.
A scientist succeeds in merging his own DNA with the minutest
of nano machines, which immediately start to mutate and
replicate. Other novels dealing with nanotechnology were*
Queen of Angels *(1990) and* Slant *(1997). Other forms of
extreme sf will be found in* Eon *(1985) and* The Forge of God
*(1987). You'll find his shorter works in* The Collected
Stories of Greg Bear *(2002).*

## We

Seven tributaries disengage from their social = mind and Library
and travel by transponder to the School World. There they are

loaded into a temporary soma, an older physical model with eight long, flexible red legs. Here the seven become We.

We have received routine orders from the Teacher Annex. We are to investigate student labor on the Great Plain of History, the largest physical feature on the School World. The students have been set to searching all past historical records, donated by the nine remaining Libraries. Student social = minds are sad; they will not mature before Endtime. They are the last new generation and their behavior is often aberrant. There may be room for error.

The soma sits in an enclosure. We become active and advance from the enclosure's shadow into a light shower of data condensing from the absorbing clouds high above. We see radiation from the donating Libraries, still falling on School World from around the three remaining systems; We hear the lambda whine of storage in the many rows of black hemispheres perched on the plain; We feel a patter of drops on Our black carapace.

We stand at the edge of the plain, near a range of bare brown and black hills left over from planetary reformation. The air is thick and cold. It smells sharply of rich data moisture, wasted on Us; We do not have readers on Our surface. The moisture dews up on the dark, hard ground under Our feet, evaporates and is reclaimed by translucent soppers. The soppers flit through the air, a tenth Our size and delicate.

The hemispheres are maintained by single-tributary somas. They are tiny, marching along the rows by the hundreds of thousands.

The sun rises in the west, across the plain. It is brilliant violet surrounded by streamers of intense blue. The streamers curl like flowing hair. Sun and streamers cast multiple shadows from each black hemisphere. The sun attracts Our attention. It is beautiful, not part of a Library simscape; this scape is *real*. It reminds Us of approaching Endtime; the changes made to conserve and concentrate the last available energy have rendered the scape beautifully novel, unfamiliar to the natural birth algorithms of Our tributaries.

The three systems are unlike anything that has ever been. They contain all remaining order and available energy. Drawn close together, surrounded by the permutation of local space and time, the three systems deceive the dead outer universe, already well into the dull inaction of the long Between. We are proud of the three systems. They took a hundred million years to construct, and a tenth of all remaining available energy. They were a gamble. Nine of thirty-seven major Libraries agreed to the gamble. The others spread themselves into the greater magnitudes of the Between, and died.

The gamble worked.

Our soma is efficient and pleasant to work with. All of Our tributaries agree, older models of such equipment are better. We have an appointment with the representative of the School World students, student tributaries lodged in a newer model soma called a Berkus, after a social = mind on Second World, which designed it. A Berkus soma is not favored. It is noisy; perhaps more efficient, but brasher and less elegant. We agree it will be ugly.

Data clouds swirl and spread tendrils high over the plain. The single somas march between Our legs, cleaning unwanted debris from the black domes. Within the domes, all history. We could reach down and crush one with the claws on a single leg, but that would slow Endtime Work and waste available energy.

We are proud of Our stray thinking. It shows that We are still human, still linked directly to the past. We are proud that We can ignore improper impulses.

We are teachers. All teachers must be linked with the past, to understand and explain it. Teachers must understand error; the past is rich with pain and error.

We await the Berkus.

Too much time passes. The world turns away from the sun and night falls. Centuries of Library time pass, but We try to be patient and think in the flow of external time. Some of Our tributaries express a desire to taste the domes, but there is no real need, and this would also waste available energy.

With night, more data fills the skies from the other systems, condenses, and rains down, covering Us with a thick sheen. Soppers clean Our carapace again. All around, the domes grow richer, absorbing history. We see, in the distance, a night interpreter striding on giant disjointed legs between the domes. It eats the domes and returns white mounds of discard. All the domes must be interpreted to see if any of the history should be carried by the final Endtime self.

The final self will cross the Between, order held in perfect inaction, until the Between has experienced sufficient rest and boredom. It will cross that point when time and space become granular and nonlinear, when the unconserved energy of expan-

sion, absorbed at the minute level of the quantum foam, begins to
disturb the metric. The metric becomes noisy and irregular, and
all extension evaporates. The universe has no width, no time, and
all is back at the beginning.

The final self will survive, knitting itself into the smallest
interstices, armored against the fantastic pressures of a universe's
deathsound. The quantum foam will give up its noise and new
universes will bubble forth and evolve. One will transcend. The
transcendent reality will absorb the final self, which will seed it.
From the compression should arise new intelligent beings.

It is an important thing, and all teachers approve. The past
should cover the new, forever. It is Our way to immortality.

Our tributaries express some concern. We are to be sure not on
a vital mission, but the Berkus is very late.

Something has gone wrong. We investigate Our links and find
them cut. Transponders do not reply.

The ground beneath Our soma trembles. Hastily, the soma
retreats from the plain of history. It stands by a low hill, trying to
keep steady on its eight red legs. The clouds over the plain turn
green and ragged. The single somas scuttle between vibrating
hemispheres, confused.

We cannot communicate with Our social = mind or Library.
No other libraries respond. Alarmed, We appeal to the School
World Student Committee, then point Our thoughts up to the
Endtime Work Coordinator, but they do not answer, either.

The endless kilometers of low black hemispheres churn as if
stirred by a huge stick. Cracks appear, and from the cracks, thick
red drops; the drops crystallize in high, tall prisms. Many of the
prisms shatter and turn to dead white powder. We realize with
great concern that We are seeing the internal stored data of the
planet itself. This is a reserve record of all Library knowledge,
held condensed; the School World contains selected records from
the dead Libraries, more information than any single Library
could absorb in a billion years. The knowledge shoots through
the disrupted ground in crimson fountains, wasted. Our soma
retreats deeper into the hills.

Nobody answers Our emergency signal.

Nobody will speak to Us, anywhere.

More days pass. We are still cut off from the Library. Isolated,
We are limited only to what the soma can perceive, and that
makes no sense at all.

We have climbed a promontory overlooking what was once the Great Plain of History. Where once Our students worked to condense and select those parts of the past that would survive the Endtime, the hideous leaking of reserve knowledge has slowed and an equally hideous round of what seems to be amateurish student exercises work themselves in rapid time.

Madness covers the plain. The hemispheres have all disintegrated, and the single somas and interpreters have vanished.

Now, everywhere on the plain, green and red and purple forests grow and die in seconds; new trees push through the dead snags of the old. New kinds of tree invade from the west and push aside their predecessors. Climate itself accelerates: the skies grow heavy with cataracting clouds made of water and rain falls in sinuous sheets. Steam twists and pullulates; the ground becomes hot with change.

Trees themselves come to an end and crumble away; huge solid brown and red domes balloon on the plain, spread thick shell-leaves like opening cabbages, push long shoots through their crowns. The shoots tower above the domes and bloom with millions of tiny gray and pink flowers.

Watching all Our work and plans destroyed, the seven tributaries within Our soma offer dismayed hypotheses: this is a malfunction, the conservation and compression engines have failed and all knowledge is being acted out uselessly; no, it is some new gambit of the Endtime Work Coordinator, an emergency project; on the contrary, it is a political difficulty, lack of communication between the Coordinator and the Libraries, and it will all be over soon . . .

We watch shoots toppled with horrendous snaps and groans, domes collapsing with brown puffs of corruption.

The scape begins anew.

More hours pass, and still no communication with any other social = minds. We fear Our Library itself has been destroyed; what other explanation for Our abandonment? We huddle on Our promontory, seeing patterns but no sense. Each generation of creativity brings something different, something that eventually fails, or is rejected.

Today large-scale vegetation is the subject of interest; the next day, vegetation is ignored for a rush of tiny biologies, no change visible from where We stand, Our soma still and watchful on its eight sturdy legs.

We shuffle Our claws to avoid a carpet of reddish growth surmounting the rise. By nightfall, We see, the mad scape could claim this part of the hill and We will have to move.

The sun approaches zenith. All shadows vanish. Its violet magnificence humbles us, a feeling We are not used to. We are from the great social = minds of the Library; humility and awe come from Our isolation and concern. Not for a billion years have any of Our tributaries felt so removed from useful enterprise. If this is the Endtime overtaking Us, overcoming all Our efforts, so be it. We feel resolve, pride at what We have managed to accomplish.

Then, We receive a simple message. The meeting with the students will take place. The Berkus will find Us and explain. But We are not told when.

Something has gone very wrong, that students should dictate to their teachers, and should put so many tributaries through this kind of travail. The concept of *mutiny* is studied by all the tributaries within the soma. It does not explain much.

New hypotheses occupy Our thinking. Perhaps the new matter of which all things were now made has itself gone wrong, destabilizing Our worlds and interrupting the consolidation of knowledge; that would explain the scape's ferment and Our isolation. It might explain unstable and improper thought processes. Or, the students have allowed some activity on School World to run wild; error.

The scape pushes palace-like glaciers over its surface, gouging itself in painful ecstasy: change, change, birth and decay, all in a single day, but slower than the rush of forests and living things. We might be able to remain on the promontory. Why are We treated so?

We keep to the open, holding Our ground, clearly visible, concerned but unafraid. We are of older stuff. Teachers have always been of older stuff.

Could We have been party to some mis-instruction, to cause such a disaster? What have We taught that might push Our students into manic creation and destruction? We search all records, all memories, contained within the small soma. The full memories of Our seven tributaries have not of course been transferred into the extension; it was to be a temporary assignment, and besides, the records would not fit. The lack of capacity hinders Our thinking and We find no satisfying answers.

One of Our tributaries has brought along some personal records. It has a long shot hypothesis and suggests that an ancient prior self be activated to provide an objective judgment engine. There are two reasons: the stronger is that this ancient self once, long ago, had a connection with a tributary making up the Endtime Work Coordinator. If the problem is political, perhaps the self's memories can give Us deeper insight. The second and weaker reason: truly, despite Our complexity and advancement, perhaps We have missed something important. Perhaps this earlier, more primitive self will see what We have missed.

There is indeed so little time; isolated as We are from a greater river of being, a river that might no longer exist, We might be the last fragment of social = mind to have any chance of combating planet-wide madness.

There is barely enough room to bring the individual out of compression. It sits beside the tributaries in the thought plenum, in distress and not functional. What it perceives it does not understand. Our questions are met with protests and more questions.

## The Engine

*I* come awake, aware. *I* sense a later and very different awareness, part of a larger group. My thoughts spin with faces to which I try to apply names, but my memory falters. These fade and are replaced by gentle calls for attention, new and very strange sensations.

I label the sensations around me: other humans, but not in human bodies. They seem to act together while having separate voices. I call the larger group the We-ness, not me and yet in some way accessible, as if part of my mind and memory.

I do not think that I have died, that I am *dead*. But the quality of my thought has changed. I have no body, no sensations of liquid pumping and breath flowing in and out.

Isolated, confused, I squat behind the We-ness's center of observation, catching glimpses of a chaotic high-speed landscape. Are they watching some entertainment? I worry that I am in a hospital, in recovery, forced to consort with other patients who cannot or will not speak with me.

I try to collect my last meaningful memories. I remember a face again and give it a name and relation: Elisaveta, my wife, standing over me as I lie on a narrow bed. Machines bend over me. I remember nothing after that.

But I am not in a hospital, not now.

Voices speak to me and I begin to understand some of what they say. The voices of the We-ness are stronger, more complex and richer, than anything I have ever experienced. I do not hear them. I have no ears.

"You've been stored inactive for a very long time," the We-ness tells me. It is (or they are) a tight-packed galaxy of thoughts, few of them making any sense at all.

Then I know.

I have awakened in the future. Thinking has changed.

"I don't know where I am. I don't know who you are . . ."

"We are joined from seven tributaries, some of whom once had existence as individual biological beings. You are an ancient self of one of Us."

"Oh," I say. The word seems wrong without lips or throat. I will not use it again.

"We're facing great problems. You'll provide unique insights." The voice expresses overtones of fatherliness and concern; I do not believe it.

Blackness paints me. "I'm hungry and I can't feel my body. I'm afraid. Where am I? I miss . . . my family."

"There is no body, no need for hunger, no need for food. Your family – *Our* family – no longer lives, unless they have been stored elsewhere."

"How did I get here?"

"You were stored before a major medical reconstruction, to prevent total loss. Your stored self was kept as a kind of historical record and memento."

I don't remember any of that, but then, how could I? I remember signing contracts to allow such a thing. I remember thinking about the possibility I would awake in the future. But I did not die! "How long has it been?"

"Twelve billion two hundred and seventy-nine million years."

Had the We-ness said, *Ten thousand years*, or even *two hundred years*, I might feel some visceral reaction. All I know is that such an enormous length of time is geological, cosmological. I do not believe in it.

I glimpse the landscape again, glaciers slipping down mountain slopes, clouds pregnant with winter building gray and orange in the stinging glare of a huge setting sun. The sun is all wrong – too bright, violet, it resembles a dividing cell, all extrusions and blebs, with long ribbons and streaming hair. It looks like a Gorgon to me.

The faces of the glaciers break, sending showers and pillars of white ice over gray-shaded hills and valleys. I have awakened in the middle of an ice age. But it is too fast. Nothing makes sense.

"Am I all here?" I ask. Perhaps I am delusional.

"What is important from you is here. We would like to ask you questions now. Do you recognize any of the following faces/ voices/thought patterns/styles?"

Disturbing synesthesia – bright sounds, loud colors, dull electric smells – fill my senses and I close them out as best I can. "No! That isn't right. Please, no questions until I know what's happened. No! That hurts!"

The We-ness prepares to shut me down. I am told that I will become inactive again.

Just before I wink out, I feel a cold blast of air crest the promontory on which the We-ness, and I, sit. Glaciers now completely cover the hills and valleys. The We-ness flexes eight fluid red legs, pulling them from quick-freezing mud. The sun still has not set.

Thousands of years in a day.

I am given sleep as blank as death, but not so final.

We gather as one and consider the problem of the faulty interface. "This is too early a self. It doesn't understand Our way of thinking," one tributary says. "We must adapt to it."

The tributary whose prior self this was, volunteers to begin re-structuring.

"There is so little time," says another, who now expresses strong disagreement with the plan to resurrect. "Are We truly agreed this is best?"

We threaten to fragment as two of the seven tributaries vehe-mently object. But solidarity holds. All tributaries flow again to renewed agreement. We start the construction of an effective interface, which first requires deeper understanding of the nature of the ancient self. This takes some time.

We have plenty of time. Hours, days, with no communication. The glacial cold nearly kills Us where We stand. The soma

changes its fluid nature by linking liquid water with long-chain
and even more slippery molecules, highly resistant to freezing.

"Do the students know We're here, that We watch?" asks a
tributary.

"They must . . ." says another. "They express a willingness to
meet with Us."

"Perhaps they lie, and they mean to destroy this soma, and Us
with it. There will be no meeting."

Dull sadness.

We restructure the ancient self, wrap it in Our new interface,
build a new plenary face to hold Us all on equal ground, and call it
up again, saying,

*Vasily*

I know the name, recognize the fatherly voice, feel a new clarity. I
wish I could forget the first abortive attempt to live again, but my
memory is perfect from the point of first rebirth on. I will forget
nothing.

"Vasily, your descendant self does not remember you. It has
purged older memories many times since your existence, but We
recognize some similarities even so between your patterns. Birth
patterns are strong and seldom completely erased. Are you
comfortable now?"

I think of a simple place where I can sit. I want wood paneling
and furniture and a fireplace, but I am not skilled; all I can
manage is a small gray cubicle with a window on one side. In the
wall is a hole through which the voices come. I imagine I am
hearing them through flesh ears, and a kind of body forms within
the cubicle. This body is my security. "I'm still afraid. I know –
there's no danger."

"There *is* danger, but We do not yet know how significant the
danger is."

*Significant* carries an explosion of information. If their original
selves still exist elsewhere, in a social = mind adjunct to a Library,
then all that might be lost will be immediate memories. A *social =
mind*, I understand, is made up of fewer than ten thousand tributaries. A Library typically contains a trillion or more social minds.

"I've been dead for billions of years," I say, hoping to address
my future self. "But you've lived on – you're immortal."

"We do not measure life or time as you do. Continuity of
memory is fragmentary in Our lives, across eons. But continuity

of access to the Library – and access to records of past selves – does confer a kind of immortality. If that has ended, We are completely mortal."

"I must be so primitive," I say, my fear oddly fading now. This is a situation I can understand – life or death. I feel more solid within my cubicle. "How can I be of any use?"

"You are primitive in the sense of *firstness*. That is why you have been activated. Through your life experience, you may have a deeper understanding of what led to Our situation. Argument, rebellion, desperation . . . These things are difficult for Us to deal with."

Again, I don't believe them. From what I can tell, this group of minds has a depth and strength and complexity that makes me feel less than a child . . . perhaps less than a bacterium. What can I do except cooperate? I have nowhere else to go . . .

For billions of years . . . inactive. Not precisely death.

I remember that I was once a *teacher*.

Elisaveta had been my student before she became my wife.

The We-ness wants me to teach it something, to do something for it. But first, it has to teach me history.

"Tell me what's happened," I say.

## The Libraries

In the beginning, human intelligences arose, and all were alone. That lasted for tens of thousands of years. Soon after understanding the nature of thought and mind, intelligences came together to create group minds, all in one. Much of the human race linked in an intimacy deeper than sex. Or unlinked to pursue goals as quasi-individuals; the choices were many, the limitations few. (*This all began a few decades after your storage.*) Within a century, the human race abandoned biological limitations, in favor of the social = mind. Social = minds linked to form Libraries, at the top of the hierarchy.

The Libraries expanded, searching around star after star for other intelligent life. They found life – millions upon millions of worlds, each rare as a diamond among the trillions of barren star systems, but none with intelligent beings. Gradually, across millions of years, the Libraries realized that they were the All of intelligent thought.

We had simply exchanged one kind of loneliness for a greater and more final isolation. There were no companion intelligences, only those derived from humanity . . .

As the human Libraries spread and connections between them became more tenuous – some communications taking thousands of years to be completed – many social = minds re-individuated, assuming lesser degrees of togetherness and intimacy. Even in large Libraries, individuation became a crucial kind of relaxation and holiday. The old ways reasserted.

Being human, however, some clung to old ways, or attempted to enforce new ones, with greater or lesser tenacity. Some asserted moral imperative. Madness spread as large groups removed all the barriers of individuation, in reaction to what they perceived as a dangerous atavism – the "lure of the singular".

These "uncelled" or completely communal Libraries, with their slow, united consciousness, proved burdensome and soon vanished – within half a million years. They lacked the range and versatility of the "celled" Libraries.

But conflicts between differing philosophies of social = mind structure continued. There were wars.

Even in wars the passions were not sated; for something more frightening had been discovered than loneliness: the continuity of error and cruelty.

After tens of millions of years of steady growth and peace, the renewed paroxysms dismayed Us.

No matter how learned or advanced a social = mind became, it could, in desperation or in certain moments of development, perform acts analogous to the errors of ancient individuated societies. It could kill other social = minds, or sever the activities of many of its own tributaries. It could frustrate the fulfillment of other minds. It could experience something like *rage*, but removed from the passions of the body: rage cold and precise and long-lived, terrible in its persuasiveness, dreadful in its consequences. Even worse, it could experience *indifference*.

I tumble through these records, unable to comprehend the scale of what I see. Our galaxy was linked star to star with webworks of transferred energy and information; parts of the galaxy darkened with massive conflict, millions of stars shut off. This was war.

At human scale, planets seemed to have reverted to ancient Edens, devoid of artifice or instrumentality; but the trees and animals themselves carried myriads of tiny machines, and the ground beneath them was an immense thinking system, down to the core . . . Other worlds, and other structures between worlds, seemed as abstract and meaningless as the wanderings of a stray brush on canvas.

## The Proof

One great social = mind, retreating far from the ferment of the Libraries, formulated the rules of advanced meta-biology, and found them precisely analogous to those governing planet-bound ecosystems: competition, victory through survival, evolution and reproduction. It proved that error and pain and destruction are essential to any change – but more importantly, to any growth.

The great social = mind carried out complex experiments simulating millions of different ordering systems, and in every single case, the rise of complexity (and ultimately intelligence) led to the wanton destruction of prior forms. Using these experiments to define axioms, what began as a scientific proof ended as a rigorous mathematical proof: *there can be no ultimate ethical advancement in this universe, in systems governed by time and subject to change.* The indifference of the universe – reality's grim and mindless harshness – is multiplied by the necessity that old order, prior thoughts and lives, must be extinguished to make way for new.

After checking its work many times, the great social = mind wiped its stores and erased its infrastructure in, on and around seven worlds and the two stars, leaving behind only the formulation and the Proof.

For Libraries across the galaxy, absorption of the Proof led to mental disruption. From the nightmare of history there was to be no awakening.

Suicide was one way out. A number of prominent Libraries brought their own histories to a close.

Others recognized the validity of the Proof, but did not commit suicide. They lived with the possibility of error and destruction. And still, they grew wiser, greater in scale and accomplishment . . .

Crossing from galaxy to galaxy, still alone, the Libraries realized that human perception was the only perception. The

Proof would never be tested against the independent minds of
non-human intelligences. In this universe, the Proof must stand.

Billions of years passed, and the universe became a huge kind
of house, confining a practical infinity of mind, an incredible
ferment which "burned" the available energy with torchy brilliance, decreasing the total life span of reality.

Yet the Proof remained unassailed.

*Wait.* I don't see anything here. I don't *feel* anything. This isn't
history; it's . . . too large! I can't understand some of the things
you show me . . . But worse, pardon me, it's babbling among
minds who feel no passion. This We-ness . . . how do you *feel*
about this?

You are distracted by preconceptions. You long for an organic
body, and assume that lacking organic bodies, We experience no
emotions. We experience emotions. *Listen* to them > > > > >

I squirm in my cubicle and experience their emotions of first and
second loneliness, degrees of isolation from old memories, old
selves; longing for the first individuation, the Birth-time . . .
Hunger for understanding not just of the outer reality, beyond
the social = mind's vast internal universe of thought, but of the
ever-changing currents and orderliness arising between tributaries. Here is social and mental interaction as a great song, rich
and joyous, a love greater than anything I can remember experiencing as an embodied human. Greater emotions still, outside my
range again, of loyalty and love for a social = mind and something
like *respect* for the immense Libraries. (I am shown what the We-
ness says is an emotion experienced at the level of Libraries, but it
is so far beyond me that I seem to disintegrate, and have to be
coaxed back to wholeness.)

A tributary approaches across the mind space within the soma.
My cubicle grows dim. I feel a strange familiarity again; this will
be, *is*, my future self.

This tributary feels sadness and some grief, touching its
ancient self – me. It feels pain at my limitations, at my tight-
packed biological character. Things deliberately forgotten come
back to haunt it.

And they haunt *me*. My own inadequacies become abundantly
clear. I remember useless arguments with friends, making my

wife cry with frustration, getting angry at my children for no good reason. My childhood and adolescent indiscretions return like shadows on a scrim. And I remember my *drives*: rolling in useless lust, and later, Elisaveta! With her young and supple body; and others. Just as significant, but different in color, the cooler passions of discovery and knowledge, my growing self-awareness. I remember fear of inadequacy, fear of failure, of not being a useful member of society. I needed above all (more than I needed Elisaveta) to be important and to teach and be influential on young minds.

All of these emotions, the We-ness demonstrates, have analogous emotions at their level. For the We-ness, the most piercing unpleasantness of all – akin to physical pain – comes from recognition of their possible failure. The teachers may not have taught their students properly, and the students may be making mistakes.

"Let me get all this straight," I say. I grow used to my imagined state – to riding like a passenger within the cubicle, inside the eight-legged soma, to seeing as if through a small window the advancing and now receding of the glaciers. "You're teachers – as I was once a teacher – and you used to be connected to a larger social = mind, part of a Library." I mull over mind as society, society as mind. "But there may have been a revolution. After billions of years! Students . . . A *revolution!* Extraordinary!

"You've been cut off from the Library. You're alone, you might be killed . . . And you're telling *me* about ancient history?"

The We-ness falls silent.

"I must be important," I say with an unbreathed sigh, a kind of asterisk in the exchanged thoughts. "I can't imagine why. But maybe it doesn't matter – I have so many questions!" I hunger for knowledge of what has become of my children, of my wife. Of everything that came after me . . . All the changes!"

"We need information from you, and your interpretation of certain memories. Vasily was Our name once. Vasily Gerazimov. You were the husband of Elisaveta, father of Maxim and Giselle . . . We need to know more about Elisaveta."

"You don't remember her?"

"Twelve billion years have passed. Time and space have changed. This tributary alone has partnered and bonded and matched and socialized with perhaps fifty billion individuals and tributaries since. Our combined tributaries in the social = mind have had contacts with all intelligent beings, once or twice removed. Most have dumped or stored memories more than a billion years old. If We were still connected to the Library, I could learn more about my past. I have kept you as a kind of *memento*, a talisman, and nothing more."

I feel a freezing awe. Fifty billion mates . . . Or whatever they had been. I catch fleeting glimpses of liaisons in the social = mind, binary, trinary, as many as thousands at a time linked in the crumbling remnants of marriage and sexuality, and finally those liaisons passing completely out of favor, fashion, usefulness.

"Elisaveta and you," the tributary continues, "were divorced ten years after your storage. I remember nothing of the reasons why. We have no other clues to work with."

The "news" comes as a doubling of my pain, a renewed and expanded sense of isolation from a loved one. I reach up to touch my face, to see if I am crying. My hands pass through imagined flesh and bone. My body is long since dust; Elisaveta's body is dust. What went wrong between us? Did she find another lover? Did I? I am a ghost. I should not care. There were difficult times, but I never thought of our liaison – our *marriage*, I would defend that word even now – as temporary. Still, across *billions* of years! We have become *immortal* – her perhaps more than I, who remember nothing of the time between. "Why do you need me at all? Why do you need clues?"

But we are interrupted. An extraordinary thing happens to the retreating glaciers. From our promontory, the soma half-hidden behind an upthrust of frozen and deformed knowledge, we see the icy masses blister and bubble, as if made of some superheated glass or plastic. Steam bursts from the bubbles – at least, what I assume to be steam – and freezes in the air in shapes suggesting flowers. All around, the walls and sheets of ice succumb to this beautiful plague.

The We-ness understands it no more than I.

From the hill below come faint sounds and hints of radiation – gamma rays, beta particles, mesons, all clearly visible to the We-ness, and vaguely passed on to me as well.

"Something's coming," I say.

The Berkus advances in its unexpected cloud of production-destruction. There is something deeply wrong with it – it squanders too much available energy. Its very presence disrupts the new matter of which We are made.

Of the seven tributaries, four feel an emotion rooted in the deepest algorithms of their pasts: fear. Three have never known such bodily functions, have never known mortal and embodied individuation. They feel intellectual concern and a tinge of cosmic sadness, as if Our end might be equated with the past death of the natural stars and galaxies. We keep to Our purpose despite these ridiculous excursions, signs of Our disorder.

The Berkus advances up the hill.

I see through my window this monumental and absolutely horrifying creature, shining with a brightness comprised of the qualities of diamonds and polished silver, a scintillating insect pushing its sharply pointed feet into the thawing soil, steam rising all around. The legs hold together despite gaps where joints should be, gaps crossed only by something that produces hard radiation. Below the Berkus (so the We-ness calls it), the ground ripples as if School World has muscles and twitches, wanting to scratch.

The Berkus pauses and sizes up Our much less powerful, much smaller soma with blasts of neutrons, flicked as casually as a flashlight beam. The material of Our soma wilts and reforms beneath this withering barrage. The soma expresses distress – and inadvertently, the We-ness translates this distress to me as tremendous pain.

I explode within my confined mental space. Again comes the blackness.

The Berkus decides it is not necessary to come any closer. That is fortunate for Us, and for Our soma. Any lessening of the distance between Us would prove fatal.

The Berkus communicates with pulsed light. "Why are you here?"

"We have been sent here to observe and report. We are cut off from the Library—"

"Your Library has fled," the Berkus informs Us. "It disagreed with the Endtime Work Coordinator."

"We were told nothing of this."

"It was not our responsibility. We did not know you would be here."

The magnitude of this rudeness is difficult to envelope. We wonder how many tributaries the Berkus contains. We hypothesize that it might contain all of the students, the entire student social = mind, and this would explain its use of energy and change in design.

Our pitiful ancient individual flickers back into awareness and sits quietly, too stunned to protest.

"We do not understand the purpose of this creation and destruction," We say. Our strategy is to avoid the student tributaries altogether now. Still, they might tell Us more We need to know.

"It must be obvious to teachers," the Berkus says. "By order of the Coordinator, We are rehearsing all possibilities of order, usurping stored knowledge down to the planetary core and converting it. There must be an escape from the Proof."

"The Proof is an ancient discovery. It has never been shown to be wrong. What can it possibly mean to the Endtime Work?"

"It means a great deal," the Berkus says.

"How many are you?"

The Berkus does not answer. All this has taken place in less than a millionth of a second. The Berkus's incommunication lengthens into seconds, then minutes. Around Us, the glaciers crumple like mud caught in rushing water.

"Another closed path, of no value," the Berkus finally says.

"We wish to understand your motivations."

"We have no need of you now."

"Why this concern with the Proof? And what does it have to do with the change you provoke, the destruction of School World's knowledge?"

The Berkus rises on a tripod of three disjointed legs, waving its other legs in the air, a cartoon medallion so disturbing in design that We draw back a few meters.

"The Proof is a cultural aberration," it radiates fiercely, blasting Our surface and making the mud around us bubble. "It is not fit to pass on to those who seed the next reality. You failed us. You showed no way beyond the Proof. The Endtime Work has begun, the final self chosen to fit through the narrow gap—"

I see all this through the We-ness as if I have been there, have lived it, and suddenly I know why I have been recalled, why the We-ness has shown me faces and patterns.

The universe, across more than twelve billion years, grows
irretrievably old. From spanning the galaxies billions of years
before, all life and intelligence – all arising from the sole intelligence in all the universe, humanity – have shrunk to a few star
systems. These systems have been resuscitated and nurtured by
concentrating the remaining available energy of thousands of
dead galaxies. And they are no longer natural star systems with
planets – the bloated coma-wrapped violet star rising at zenith
over us is a congeries of plasma macromachines, controlling and
conserving every gram of the natural matter remaining, every erg
of available energy. These artificial suns pulse like massive living
cells, shaped to be ultimately efficient and to squeeze every
moment of active life over time remaining. The planets themselves have been condensed, recarved, rearranged, and they too
are composed of geological macromachines. With some dread, I
gather that the matter of which all these things are made is itself
artificial, with redesigned component particles.

The natural galaxies have died, reduced to a colorless murmur
of useless heat, and all the particles of all original creation –
besides what have been marshaled and remade in these three
close-packed systems – have dulled and slowed and unwound.
Gravity itself has lost its bearings and become a chancy phenomenon, supplemented by new forces generated within the macro-
machine planets and suns.

Nothing is what it seems, and nothing is what it had been when
I lived.

Available energy is strictly limited. The We-ness looks forward
to less than four times ten to the fiftieth units of Planck time –
roughly an old Earth year.

And in charge of it all, controlling the Endtime Work, a
supremely confident social = mind composed of many "tributaries," and among those gathered selves . . .

Someone very familiar to me indeed. My wife.

"Where is she? Can I speak to her? What happened to her – did
she die, was she stored, did she live?"

The We-ness seems to vibrate both from my reaction to this
information, and to the spite of the Berkus. I am assigned to a
quiet place, where I can watch and listen without bothering them.
I feel Our soma, Our insect-like body, dig into the loosening
substance of the promontory.

*     *     *

"You taught us the Proof was absolute," the Berkus says, "that throughout all time, in all circumstances, error and destruction and pain will accompany growth and creation, that the universe must remain indifferent and randomly hostile. We do not accept that."

"But why dissolve links with the Library?" We cry, shrinking beneath the Berkus's glare. The constantly reconstructed body of the Berkus channels and consumes energy with enormous waste, as if the students do not care, intent only on their frantic mission, whatever that might be . . . Reducing available active time by days for *all of us* –

*I know!* I shout in the quiet place, but I am not heard, or not paid attention to.

"Why condemn Us to a useless end in this chaos, this madness?" We ask.

"Because We must refute the Proof and there is so little useful time remaining. The final self must not be sent over carrying this burden of error."

"*Of sin!*" I shout, still not heard. Proof of the validity of primordial sin – that everything living must eat, must destroy, must climb up the ladder on the backs of miserable victims. That all true creation involves death and pain; the universe is a charnel house.

I am fed and study the Proof. Time runs in many tracks within the soma. I try to encompass the principles and expressions, no longer given as words, but as multi-sense abstractions. In the Proof, miniature universes of discourse are created, manipulated, reduced to an expression, and discarded: the Proof is more complex than any single human life, or even the life of a species, and its logic is not familiar. The Proof is rooted in areas of mental experience I am not equipped to understand, but I receive glosses.

**Law: Any dynamic system** (I understand this as *organism*) **has limited access to resources, and a limited time in which to achieve its goals.** A multitude of instances are drawn from history, as well as from an artificial miniature universe. Other laws follow regarding behavior of systems within a flow of energy, but they are completely beyond me.

**Observed Law: The goals of differing organisms, even of like variety, never completely coincide.** (History and the miniature universe teem with instances, and the Proof lifts these up for inspection at moments of divergence, demonstrating again and again this obvious point.)

Then comes a roll of beginning deductions, backed by examples too numerous for me to absorb:

*And so it follows that for any complex of organisms, competition must arise for limited resources.*

*From this: some will succeed, some will fail, to acquire resources sufficient to live. Those who succeed, express themselves in later generations.*

*From this: New dynamic systems will arise to compete more efficiently.*

*From this: Competition and selection will give rise to organisms that are \*streamlined,\* incapable of surviving even in the midst of plenty because not equipped with complete methods of absorbing resources. These will prey on complete organisms to acquire their resources. And in return, the prey will acquire a reliance on the predators.*

*From this: Other forms of \*streamlining\* will occur. Some of the resulting systems will depend entirely on others for reproduction and fulfillment of goals.*

*From this: Ecosystems will arise, interdependent, locked in predator-prey, disease-host relationships.*

I experience a multitude of rigorous experiments, unfolding like flowers.

*And so it follows that in the course of competition, some forms will be outmoded, and will pass away, and others will be preyed upon to extinction, without regard to their beauty, their adaptability to a wide range of possible conditions.* I sense here a kind of aesthetic judgment, above the fray: beautiful forms will die without being fully tested, their information lost, their opportunities limited.

*And so it follows . . .*

*And so it follows . . .*

The ecosystems increase in complexity, giving rise to organisms whose primary adaptation is perception and judgment, forming the abstract equivalents of societies, which interact through the exchange of resources and extensions of cultures and politics – models for more efficient organization. Still, change and evolution, failure and death, societies and cultures pass and are forgotten; whole classes of these larger systems suffer extinction, without being allowed fulfillment.

From history: Nations pray upon nations, and eat them alive, discarding them as burned husks.

*Law: The universe is neutral; it will not care, nor will any ultimate dynamic system interfere . . .*

In those days before I was born, as smoke rose from the ovens, God did not hear the cries of His people.

*And so it follows: that no system will achieve perfect efficiency and self-sufficiency. Within all changing systems, accumulated error must be purged. For the good of the dynamic whole, systems must die. But efficient and beautiful systems will die as well.*

I see the Proof's abstraction of evil: a shark-like thing, to me, but no more than a very complex expression. In this shark there is history, and dumb organic pressure, and the accumulations of the past: and the shark does not discriminate, knows nothing of judgment or justice, will eat the promising and the strong as well as birthing young. Waste, waste, an agony of waste, and over it all, not watching, the indifference of the real.

After what seems hours of study, of questions asked and answered, new ways of thinking acquired – re-education – I begin to feel the thoroughness of the Proof, and I feel a despair unlike anything in my embodied existence.

Where once there had been hope that intelligent organisms could see their way to just, beautiful and efficient systems, in practice, without exception, they revert to the old rules.

*Things have not and will never improve.*

Heaven itself would be touched with evil – or stand still. But there is no heaven run by a just God. Nor can there be a just God. Perfect justice and beauty and evolution and change are incompatible.

Not the birth of my son and daughter, not the day of my marriage, not all my moments of joy can erase the horror of history. And the stretch of future histories, after my storage, shows even more horror, until I seem to swim in carnivorous, *cybernivorous* cruelty.

## Connections

We survey the Berkus with growing concern. Here is not just frustration of Our attempts to return to the Library, not just destruction of knowledge, but a flagrant and purposeless waste of precious resources. Why is it allowed?

Obviously, the Coordinator of the Endtime Work has given license, handed over this world, with such haste that We did not have time to withdraw. The Library has been forced away (or worse), and all transponders destroyed, leaving Us alone on School World.

The ancient self, having touched on the Proof (absorbing no more than a fraction of its beauty) is wrapped in a dark shell of mood. This mood, basic and primal as it is, communicates to the tributaries. Again, after billions of years, We feel sadness at the inevitability of error and the impossibility of justice – and sadness at our Own error. The Proof has always stood as a monument of pure thought – and a curse, even to We who affirm it.

The Berkus expands like a balloon. "There is going to be major work done here. You will have to move."

"*No*," the combined tributaries cry. "This is enough confusion and enough being *shoved around*." Those words come from the ancient self.

The Berkus finds them amusing.

"Then you'll stay here," it says, "and be absorbed in the next round of experiment. You are teachers who have taught incorrectly. You deserve no better."

I break free of the *dark shell of mood*, as the tributaries describe it, and now I seem to kick and push my way to a peak of attention, all without arms or legs. "Where is the plan, the order? Where are your billions of years of superiority? How can this be happening?"

We pass on the cries of the ancient self. The Berkus hears the message.

"We are not familiar with this voice," the student social = mind says.

"I judge you from the past!" the ancient self says. "You are *all* found wanting!"

"This is not the voice of a tributary, but of an individual," the Berkus says. "The individual sounds uninformed."

"I demand to speak with my wife!" My demand gets no reaction for almost a second. Around me, the tributaries within the soma flow and rearrange, thinking in a way I cannot follow. They finally rise as a solid, seamless river of consent.

"*We charge you with error,*" they say to the Berkus. "*We charge you with confirming the Proof you wish to negate.*"

The Berkus considers, then backs away swiftly, beaming at us one final message: "There is an interesting rawness in your charge. You no longer think as outmoded teachers. A link with the Endtime Work Coordinator will be requested. Stand where you are. Our own work must continue."

I feel a sense of relief around me. This is a breakthrough. I have a purpose! The Berkus retreats, leaving us on the promontory to observe. Where once, hours before, glaciers melted, the ground begins to churn, grow viscous, divide into fenced enclaves. Within the enclaves, green and gray shapes arise, sending forth clouds of steam. These enclaves surround the range of hills, surmount all but our promontory, and move off to the horizon on all sides, perhaps covering the entire School World.

In the center of each fenced area, a sphere forms first as a white blister on the hardness, then a pearl resting on the surface. The pearl lifts, suspended in air. Each pearl begins to evolve in a different way, turning inward, doubling, tripling, flattening into disks, centers dividing to form toruses; a practical infinity of different forms.

The fecundity of idea startles me. Blastulas give rise to cell-like complexity, spikes twist into intricate knots, all the rules of ancient topological mathematics are demonstrated in seconds, and then violated as the spaces within the enclaves themselves change.

"What are they doing?" I ask, bewildered.

"A mad push of evolution, trying all combinations starting from a simple beginning form," my descendant self explains. "It was once a common exercise, but not on such a vast scale. Not since the formulation of the Proof."

"What do they want to learn?"

"If they can find one instance of evolution and change that involves only growth and development, not competition and destruction, then they will have falsified the Proof."

"But the Proof is perfect," I said. "It can't be falsified . . ."

"So We have judged. The students incorrectly believe We are wrong."

The field of creation becomes a vast fabric, each enclave contributing to a larger weave. What is being shown here could have occupied entire civilizations in my time: the dimensions of change, all possibilities of progressive growth. "It's beautiful," I say.

"It's futile," my descendant self says, its tone bitter. I feel the emotion in its message as an aberration, and it immediately broadcasts shame to all of its fellows, and to me.

"Are you afraid they'll show your teachings were wrong?" I asked.

"No," my tributary says. "I am sorry that they will fail. Such a message to pass on to a young universe . . . That whatever our nature and design, however we develop, we are doomed to make errors and cause pain. Still, that is the truth, and it has never been refuted."

"But even in my time, there was a solution," I say.

They show mild curiosity. What could come from so far in the past, that they hadn't advanced upon it, improved it, a billion times over, or discarded it? I wonder why I have been activated at all . . .

But I persist. "From God's perspective, destruction and pain and error may be part of the greater whole, a beauty from its point of view. We only perceive it as evil because of our limited point of view."

The tributaries allow a polite pause. My tributary explains, as gently as possible, "We have never encountered ultimate systems you call gods. Still, We are or have been very much like gods. As gods, all too often We have made horrible errors, and caused unending pain. Pain did not add to the beauty."

I want to scream at them for their hubris, but it soon becomes apparent to me, they are right. Their predecessors have reduced galaxies, scanned all histories, made the universe itself run faster with their productions and creations. They have advanced the Endtime by billions of years, and now prepare to seed a new universe across an inconceivable gap of darkness and immobility.

From my perspective, humans have certainly become god-like. But not just. And there are no others. Even in the diversity of the human diaspora across the galaxies, not once has the Proof been falsified. And that is all it would have taken: one instance.

"*Why did you bring me back, then?*" I ask my descendant self in private conference. It replies in kind:

*"Your thought processes are not Our own. You can be a judgment engine. You might give Us insight into the reasoning of the students, and help explain to Us their plunge into greater error. There must be some motive not immediately apparent, some fragment of personality and memory responsible for this. An ancient self of a tributary of the Endtime Work Coordinator and you were once intimately related, married as sexual partners. You did not stay married. That is division and dissent. And there is division and dissent between the Endtime Work Committee and the teachers. That much is apparent . . ."*

Again I feel like clutching my hands to my face and screaming in frustration. Elisaveta – it must mean Elisaveta. *But we were not divorced . . . not when I was stored!* I sit in my imagined gray cubicle, my imagined body uncertain in its outline, and wish for a moment of complete privacy. They give it to me.

## Tapering Time

The scape has progressed to a complexity beyond Our ability to process. We stand on Our promontory, surrounded by the field of enclaved experiments, each enclave containing a different evolved object, the objects still furiously convoluting and morphing. Some glow faintly as night sweeps across Our part of the School World. We are as useless and incompetent as the revived ancient self, now wrapped in its own shock and misery. Our tributaries have fallen silent. We wait for what will happen next, either in the scape, or in the promised contact with the Endtime Work Coordinator.

The ancient self rises from its misery and isolation. It joins Our watchful silence, expectant. It has not completely lost *hope*. We have never had need of *hope*. Connected to the Library, fear became a distant and unimportant thing; hope, its opposite, equally distant and not useful.

I have been musing over my last hazy memories of Elisaveta, of our children Maxim and Giselle – bits of conversation, physical features, smells . . . Reliving long stretches with the help of memory recovery . . . watching seconds pass into minutes as if months pass into years.

Outside, time seems to move much more swiftly. The divisions between enclaves fall, and the uncounted experiments stand on the field, still evolving, but now allowed to interact. Tentatively, their evolution takes in the new possibility of *motion*.

I feel for the students, wish to be part of them. However wrong, this experiment is vital, idealistic. It smells of youthful naiveté. Because of my own rugged youth, raised in a nation running frantically from one historical extreme to another, born to parents who jumped like puppets between extremes of hope and despair, I have always felt uneasy in the face of idealism and naiveté.

Elisaveta was a naive idealist when I first met her. I tried to teach her, pass on my sophistication, my sense of better judgment.

The brightly colored, luminous objects hover on the plain, discovering new relations: a separate identity, a larger sense of space. The objects have reached a high level of complexity and order, but within a limited environment. If any have developed mind, they can now reach out and explore new objects.

First, the experiments shift a few centimeters this way or that, visible across the plain as kind of restless, rolling motion. The plain becomes an ocean of gentle waves. Then, the experiments *bump* each other. Near Our hill, some of the experiments circle and surround their companions, or just bump with greater and greater urgency. Extensions reach out, and We can see – it must be obvious to all – that mind does exist, and new senses are being created and explored.

If Elisaveta, whatever she has become, is in charge of this sea of experiments, then perhaps she is merely following an inclination she had billions of years before: when in doubt, when all else fails, *punt*.

This is a cosmological kind of punt, burning up available energy at a distressing rate . . .

*Just like her*, I think, and feel a warmth of connection with that ancient woman. But the woman *divorced* me. She found me wanting, later than my memories reach . . . And after all, what she has become is as little like the Elisaveta I knew as my descendant tributary is like me.

The dance on the plain becomes a frenzied blur of color. Snakes flow, sprout legs, wings beat the air. Animal relations, plant relations, new ecosystems . . . But these creatures have evolved not from the simplest beginnings, but from already elaborate sources. Each isolated experiment, already having

achieved a focused complexity beyond anything I can understand, becomes a potential player in a new order of interaction.
What do the students – or Elisaveta – hope to accomplish in this
peculiar variation on the old scheme?

I am so focused on the spectacle surrounding us that it takes a
"nudge" from my descendant self to alert me to change in the
sky. A liquid silvery ribbon pours from above, spreading over our
heads into a flat upside-down ocean of reflective cloud. The
inverse ocean expands to the horizon, blocking all light from the
new day.

Our soma rises expectantly on its eight legs. I feel the tributaries' interest as a kind of heat through my cubicle, and I
abandon the imagined environment for the time being. Best to
receive this new phenomenon directly.

A fringed curtain, like the edge of a shawl woven from threads
of mercury, descends from the upside-down ocean, brushing over
the land. The fringe crosses the plain of experiments without
interfering, but surrounds Our hill, screening Our view. Light
pulses from selected threads in the liquid weave. The tributaries
translate instantly.

"What do you want?" asks a clear neutral voice. No character,
no tone, no emotion. This is the Endtime Work Coordinator, or
at least an extension of that powerful social = mind. It does not
sound anything like Elisaveta. My hopes have been terribly naive.

After all this time and misery, the teachers' reserve is admir-
able. I detect respect, but no awe; they are used to the nature of
the Endtime Work Coordinator, largest of the social = minds not
directly connected to a Library. "We have been cut off, and We
need to know why," the tributaries say.

"Your work reached a conclusion," the voice responds.

"Why were We not accorded the respect of being notified, or
allowed to return to Our Library?"

"Your Library has been terminated. We have concluded the
active existence of all entities no longer directly connected with
Endtime Work, to conserve available energy."

"But you have let Us live."

"It would involve more energy to terminate existing extensions
than to allow them to run down."

The sheer coldness and precision of the voice chill me. The end
of a Library is equivalent to the end of thousands of worlds full of
individual intelligences. *Genocide. Error and destruction.*

But my future self corrects me. "*This is expediency*," it says in a private sending. "*It is what We all expected would happen sooner or later. The manner seems irregular, but the latitude of the Endtime Work Coordinator is great.*"

Still, the tributaries request a complete accounting of the decision. The Coordinator obliges. A judgment arrives:

The Teachers are irrelevant. Teaching of the Proof has been deemed useless; the Coordinator has decided –

I hear a different sort of voice, barely recognizable to me – *Elisaveta*

"all affirmations of the Proof merely discourage our search for alternatives. The Proof has become a thought disease, a cultural tyranny. It blocks our discovery of another solution."

## A New Accounting

Our ancient self recognizes something in the message. What We have planned from near the beginning now bears fruit – the ancient self, functioning as an engine of judgment and recognition, has found a key player in the decision to isolate Us, and to terminate Our Library.

"We detect the voice of a particular tributary," We say to the Coordinator. "May We communicate with this tributary?"

"Do you have a valid reason?" the Coordinator asks.

"We must check for error."

"Your talents are not recognized."

"Still, the Coordinator might have erred, and as there is so little time, following the wrong course will be doubly tragic."

The Coordinator reaches a decision after sufficient time to show a complete polling of all tributaries within its social = mind.

"An energy budget is established. Communication is allowed."

We follow protocol billions of years old, but excise unnecessary ceremonial segments. We poll the student tributaries, searching for some flaw in reasoning, finding none.

Then We begin searching for Our own justification. If We are about to *die*, lost in the last-second noise and event-clutter of a universe finally running down, We need to know where *We* have failed. If there is no failure – and if all this experimentation is simply a futile act, We might die less ignominiously. We search for the tributary familiar to the ancient self, hoping to find the personal connection that will reduce all Our questions to one exchange.

Bright patches of light in the sky bloom, spread, and are quickly gathered and snuffed. The other suns and worlds are being converted and conserved. We have minutes, perhaps only seconds.

We find the voice, descendant tributary of Elisaveta.

There are immense deaths in the sky, and now all is going dark. There is only the one sun, turning in on itself, violet shading to deep orange, and the School World.

*Four seconds.* I have just four seconds . . . Endtime accelerates upon us. The student experiment has consumed so much energy. All other worlds have been terminated, all social = minds except the Endtime Coordinator's and the final self . . . The seed that will cross the actionless Between.

I feel the tributaries frantically create an interface, make distant requests, then demands. They meet strong resistance from a tributary within the Endtime Work Coordinator. This much they convey to me . . . I sense weeks, months, years of negotiation, all passing in a second of more and more disjointed and uncertain real time.

As the last energy of the universe is spent, as all potential and all kinesis bottom out at a useless average, the fractions of seconds become clipped, their qualities altered. Time advances with an irregular jerk, truly like an off-center wheel.

Agreement is reached. Law and persuasion even now have some force.

"Vasily. I haven't thought about you in ever so long."

"Elisaveta, is that you?" I cannot see her. I sense a total lack of emotion in her words. And why not?

"Not *your* Elisaveta, Vasily. But I hold her memories and some of her patterns."

"You've been alive for billions of years?"

I receive a condensed impression of a hundred million sisters, all related to Elisaveta, stored at different times like a huge library of past selves. The final tributary she has become, now an important part of the Coordinator, refers to her past selves much as a grown woman might open childhood diaries. The past selves are kept informed, to the extent that being informed does not alter their essential natures.

How differently my own descendant self behaves, sealing away a small part of the past as a reminder, but never consulting it. How perverse for a mind that reveres the past! Perhaps what it reveres is form, not actuality . . .

"Why do you want to speak with me?" Elisaveta asks. Which Elisaveta, from which time, I cannot tell right away.

"I think . . . *they* seem to think it's important. A disagreement, something that went wrong."

"They are seeking justification through you, a self stored billions of years ago. They want to be told that their final efforts have meaning. How like the Vasily I knew."

"It's not my doing! I've been inactive . . . Were we divorced?"

"Yes." Sudden realization changes the tone of this Elisaveta's voice. "You were stored before we divorced?"

"Yes! How long after . . . were you stored?"

"A century, maybe more," she answers. With some wonder, she says, "Who could have known we would live forever?"

"When I saw you last, we loved each other. We had children . . ."

"They died with the Libraries," she says.

I do not feel physical grief, the body's component of sadness and rage at loss, but the news rocks me, even so. I retreat to my gray cubicle. My children! They have survived all this time, and yet I have missed them. What happened to my children, in my time? What did they become to me, and I to them? Did they have children, grandchildren, and after our divorce, did they respect me enough to let me visit my grandchildren . . .? But it's all lost now, and if they kept records of their ancient selves – records of what had truly been my children – that is gone, too. They are *dead*.

Elisaveta regards my grief with some wonder, and finds it sympathetic. I feel her warm to me slightly. "They weren't really our children any longer, Vasily. They became something quite other, as have you and I. But *this* you – you've been kept like a butterfly in a collection. How sad."

She seeks me out and takes on a bodily form. It is not the shape of the Elisaveta I knew. She once built a biomechanical body to carry her thoughts. This is the self-image she carries now, of a mind within a primitive, woman-shaped soma.

"What happened to us?" I ask, my agony apparent to her, to all who listen.

"Is it that important to you?"

"Can you explain any of this?" I ask. I want to bury myself in her bosom, to hug her. I am so lost and afraid I feel like a child, and yet my pride keeps me together.

"I was your student, Vasily. Remember? You *browbeat* me into marrying you. You poured learning into my ear day and night, even when we made love. You were so full of knowledge. You spoke nine languages. You knew all there was to know about Schopenhauer and Hegel and Marx and Wittgenstein. You did not listen to what was important to me."

I want to draw back; it is impossible to cringe. This I recognize. This I remember. But the Elisaveta I knew had come to accept me, my faults and my learning, joyously, had encouraged me to open up with her. I had taught her a great deal.

"You gave me absolutely no room to grow, Vasily."

The enormous triviality of this conversation, at the end of time, strikes me and I want to laugh out loud. Not possible. I stare at this *monstrous* Elisaveta, so bitter and different . . . And now, to me, shaded by her indifference. "I feel like I've been half a dozen men, and we've all loved you badly," I say, hoping to sting her.

"No. Only one. You became angry when I disagreed with you. I asked for more freedom to explore . . . You said there was really little left to explore. Even in the last half of the twenty-first century, Vasily, you said we had found all there was to find, and everything thereafter would be mere details. When I had my second child, it began. I saw you through the eyes of my infant daughter, saw what you would do to her, and I began to grow apart from you. We separated, then divorced, and it was for the best. For me, at any rate; I can't say that you ever understood."

We seem to stand in that gray cubicle, that comfortable simplicity with which I surrounded myself when first awakened. Elisaveta, taller, stronger, face more seasoned, stares at me with infinitely more experience. I am outmatched.

Her expression softens. "But you didn't deserve *this*, Vasily. You mustn't blame me for what your tributary has done."

"I am not he . . . It. It is not me. And you are not the Elisaveta I know!"

"You wanted to keep me forever the student you first met in your classroom. Do you see how futile that is now?"

"Then what can we love? What is there left to attach to?"

She shrugs. "It doesn't much matter, does it? There's no more time left to love or not to love. And love has become a vastly different thing."

"We reach this *peak* . . . of intelligence, of accomplishment, immortality . . ."

"Wait." Elisaveta frowns and tilts her head, as if listening, lifts her finger in question, listens again, to voices I do not hear. "I begin to understand your confusion," she says.

"What?"

"This is not a peak, Vasily. This is a backwater. We are simply all that's left after a long, dreadful attenuation. The greater, more subtle galaxies of Libraries ended themselves a hundred million years ago."

"Suicide?"

"They saw the very end we contemplate now. They decided that if our kind of life had no hope of escaping the Proof – the Proof these teachers helped fix in all our thoughts – than it was best not to send a part of ourselves into the next universe. We are what's left of those who disagreed . . ."

"My tributary did not tell me this."

"Hiding the truth from yourself even now."

I hold my hands out to her, hoping for pity, but this Elisaveta has long since abandoned pity. I desperately need to activate some fragment of love within her. "I am so lost . . ."

"We are all lost, Vasily. There is only one hope."

She turns and opens a broad door on one side of my cubicle, where I originally placed the window to the outside. "If we succeed at this," she says, "then we are better than those great souls. If we fail, they were right . . . Better that nothing from our reality crosses the Between."

I admire her for her knowledge, then, for being kept so well informed. But I resent that she has advanced beyond me, has no need for me. The tributaries watch with interest, like voyeurs.

*("Perhaps there is a chance."* My descendant self speaks in a private sending.)

"I see why you divorced me," I say sullenly.

"You were a tyrant and a bully. When you were stored – before your heart replacement, I remember now . . . When you were stored, you and I simply had not grown far apart. We would. It was inevitable."

(I ask my descendant self whether what she says is true.

*"It is a way of seeing what happened,"* it says. *"The Proof has yet*

*to be disproved. We recommended no attempts be made to do so. We think such attempts are futile."*

*"You taught that?"*

*"We created patterns of thought and diffused them for use in creation of new tributaries. The last students. But perhaps there is a chance. Touch her. You know how to reach her.")*

"The Proof is very convincing," I tell Elisaveta. "Perhaps this *is* futile."

"You simply have no say, Vasily. The effort is being made." I have touched her, but it is not pity I arouse this time, and certainly not love – it is disgust.

Through the window, Elisaveta and I see a portion of the plain. On it, the experiments have congealed into a hundred, a thousand smooth, slowly pulsing shapes. Above them all looms the shadow of the Coordinator.

(I feel a bridge being made, links being established. I sense panic in my descendant self, who works without the knowledge of the other tributaries. Then I am asked: *"Will you become part of the experiment?"*

*"I don't understand."*

*"You are the judgment engine."*)

"Now I must go," Elisaveta says. "We will all die soon. Neither you nor I are in the final self. No part of the teachers, or the Coordinator, will cross the Between."

"All futile, then," I say.

"Why so, Vasily? When I was young, you told me that change was an evil force, and that you longed for an eternal college, where all learning could be examined at leisure, without pressure. You've found that. Your tributary self has had billions of years to study the unchanging truths. And to infuse them into new tributaries. You've had your heaven, and I've had mine. Away from you, among those who nurture and respect."

I am left with nothing to say. Then, unexpectedly, the figure of Elisaveta reaches out with a nonexistent hand and touches my unreal cheek. For a moment, between us, there is something like the contact of flesh to flesh. I feel her fingers. She feels my cheek. Despite her words, the love has not died completely.

She fades from the cubicle. I rush to the window, to see if I can make out the Coordinator, but the shadow, the mercury-liquid cloud, has already vanished.

"They will fail," the We-ness says. It surrounds me with its mind, its persuasion, greater in scale than a human of my time to an ant. "This shows the origin of their folly. We have justified Our existence."

*(You can still cross. There is still a connection between you. You can judge the experiment, go with the Endtime Work Coordinator.)*

I watch the plain, the joined shapes, extraordinarily beautiful, like condensed cities or civilizations or entire histories.

The sunlight dims, light rays jerk in Our sight, in Our fading scales of time.

*(Will you go?)*

"She doesn't need me . . ." I want to go with Elisaveta. I want to reach out to her and shout, "I see! I understand!" But there is still sadness and self-pity. I am, after all, too small for her.

*(You may go. Persuade. Carry Us with you.)*

And billions of years too late –

## Shards of Seconds

We know now that the error lies in the distant past, a tendency of the Coordinator, who has gathered tributaries of like character. As did the teachers. The past still dominates, and there is satisfaction in knowing We, at least, have not committed any errors, have not fallen into folly.

We observe the end with interest. Soon, there will be no change. In that, there is some cause for exultation. Truly, We are tired.

On the bubbling remains of the School World, the students in their Berkus continue to the last instant with the experiment, and We watch from the cracked and cooling hill.

Something huge and blue and with many strange calm aspects rises from the field of experiments. It does not remind Us of anything We have seen before.

It is new.

The Coordinator returns, embraces it, draws it away.

*("She does not tell the truth. Parts of the Endtime Coordinator must cross with the final self. This is your last chance. Go to her and reconcile. Carry Our thoughts with you.")*

I feel a love for her greater than anything I could have felt before. I hate my descendant self, I hate the teachers and their gray spirits, depth upon depth of ashes out of the past. They want to use me to perpetuate all that matters to them.

I ache to reclaim what has been lost, to try to make up for the past.

The Coordinator withdraws from School World, taking with it the results of the student experiment. Do they have what they want — something worthy of being passed on? It would be wonderful to know . . . I could die contented, knowing the Proof has been shattered. I could cross over, ask . . .

But I will not pollute her with me any more.

"No."

The last thousandths of the last second fall like broken crystals. *(The connection is broken. You have failed.)*

My tributary self, disappointed, quietly suggests I might be happier if I am deactivated.

Curiously, to the last, he clings to his imagined cubicle window. He cries his last words where there is no voice, no sound, no one to listen but Us:

*"Elisaveta! YES!"*

The last of the ancient self is packed, mercifully, into oblivion. We will not subject him to the Endtime. We have pity.

We are left to Our thoughts. The force that replaces gravity now spasms. The metric is very noisy. Length and duration become so grainy that thinking is difficult.

One tributary works to solve an ancient and obscure problem. Another studies the Proof one last time, savoring its formal beauty. Another considers ancient relations.

Our end, Our own oblivion, the Between, will not be so horrible. There are worse things. Much _____

# STUFFING

## Jerry Oltion

*We need to calm down a little after the last few stories and so, as a final* après-repas *– almost literally – here's a sly little piece by Jerry Oltion (b. 1957). We've already encountered Jerry in full hard-tech flow in collaboration with Stephen Gillett on "Waterworld", but here he's in a rather different mode.*

*Jerry claims he has been a gardener, stone mason, carpenter, oilfield worker, forester, land surveyor, rock 'n' roll deejay, printer, proofreader, editor, publisher, computer consultant, movie extra, corporate secretary, and garbage truck driver. He has also invented a new type of telescope mount that allows amateur astronomers to make homemade telescopes that track the stars while they're observing.*

*But he's also a prolific writer. He's written over a hundred short stories since his first sale to* Analog *back in 1982, plus fifteen novels. These include four* Star Trek *novels plus his most recent offerings* The Getaway Special *(2001) and its sequel* Anywhere But Here *(2005).*

When Dennis arrived in the park for their lunch date, he found Cheryl already basking in the sun. She was flat on her back in an open spot between two orange trees, arms and legs stretched wide to intercept the maximum amount of light, and wearing only a pair of dark sunglasses. Her skin was in maximum photosynthesis mode, and it intercepted so much light that she looked like a shadow on the ground, which gave Dennis an idea. He stepped softly around the other sunbathers until he stood at her feet, positioned his toes next to her heels, then leaned forward and stretched out his arms in the same posture as hers so his shadow fell over her in a nearly perfect outline.

"Hey, you're blocking my lunch," she said in a peevish tone, and then she must have opened her eyes. "Oh, it's you. Ha, ha. But you're still blocking my lunch."

"You look rather delectable there," he said. "Maybe I'll block it some more from a little closer in."

"You do that, and we'll get kicked out of the park. Scares the children, you know."

"Hmm. You're right." He stepped aside and stripped off his shorts, then sat down beside her while she scooted over to make room. He looked down the length of the colony, a mile-wide, ten-mile-long cylinder with three transparent windows running its entire length, trying to judge how much time they had before the afternoon rain reached them. The ring of misty fog that worked its way up the length of the cylinder each day looked at least an hour away; plenty of time for an unhurried meal, and maybe even time enough to use some of their recently acquired energy in a more private setting later.

He lay down on his back and took Cheryl's right hand in his left, careful to make sure hers was on top, although strictly speaking his higher body mass made maximum exposure more important for him than for her. "Ah, that feels good," he said as his skin pigment kicked into action and began flooding his system with sugar and oxygen.

"I love wintertime," Cheryl said. "I know we're only a couple million miles closer to the Sun than other times of year, but I swear I can feel it."

"It's possible." Dennis wiggled his butt to scratch an itch against the grass. "It's your source of sustenance; it wouldn't be surprising if you could sense the quality of it pretty accurately. Like the sense of taste, back when people still ate food."

She laughed. "Yeah, maybe our brains are starting to remap that whole cortical region. Instead of taste, now we're measuring voltage."

"Maybe."

They lay side by side for a while, just enjoying each other's company. They had started taking lunch together a few weeks ago after meeting by chance in line at a fast-flash booth and agreeing that neither of them liked the sudden shift in body chemistry they got from the high-intensity lamps. Cheryl had suggested a more leisurely, natural meal in the park, and they had had so much fun getting to know one another that they had made it a regular date.

"You know," Dennis said, "thinking about the solstice; there used to be a big traditional festival this time of year, back when the spacehabs were new. My great-grandmother told me about it. They called it 'Thanksmas.' People would buy each other gifts, and they would cook up a huge meal and stuff themselves silly, then exchange all their gifts, and—"

" 'Buy?' " Cheryl asked. "What's that?"

"Oh. It's a different kind of exchange that people did when they weren't giving things away. They kept track of who did useful work for other people, and they got some kind of points for it, and then when they wanted something that they couldn't make themselves they traded points with the guy who made it."

"Oh," said Cheryl. "That must have been before they had AIs to keep track of stuff like that."

"Yeah, I think so. And before they had nanofabs to do the producing. People actually had to do things they didn't like just to collect these points. But once a year they blew all their credit on this big feast and gift-giving thing, so life must not have been that bad or people wouldn't have given everything away like that."

"Or maybe they did it just to take their minds off of how awful it was the rest of the time," Cheryl said.

"Could be. The point is, people used to look forward to this time of year at least in part because of the big meal, so there's actually historical precedent for liking the solstice sunlight more than other times of the year."

"Ah, I see." She was quiet for a minute or so, but then she said, "So do you want to have a solstice meal? Get some big mirrors and intensify the sunlight in your back yard for an afternoon or something?"

Dennis considered that. The only real advantage to high-intensity sunlight was the speed at which you could recharge your body's energy, and that seemed kind of counter to the spirit of the occasion, at least what Dennis remembered from his great-grandmother's stories about it. "No," he said, "if we're going to observe Thanksmas, we ought to take our time and savor it the way they used to."

Cheryl rose up on one elbow to look at him. "What, you mean actually sticking food in our mouths? And swallowing it?"

"Huh? Eeew, no, I didn't mean that!" Then he realized the tone of voice she had used. "I mean . . . did you mean that?"

"No!" She lay back down, but a second later she was back up on her elbow again. "Okay, maybe I did. It . . . it sounds kind of sensual."

"Then by all means, let's do it!" He rose up for a kiss and ran his tongue along her lips, enjoying their delicious womanly flavor. Would food taste anything like that? He had no idea.

"We'll need to check with a doctor to make sure our bodies can still handle it," he said. "And we'll need to invite some friends. The whole point of Thanksmas was to share it with as many people as you could."

"Of course," she said. "What good's an intensely personal experience without friends there to watch you make a fool of yourself?"

"Exactly!" He lay back on the grass again. "So who should we invite?"

They settled on two friends each, for a total of six at the party. Since things could get kind of embarrassing while they re-learned how to do what people hadn't done for over a century, they decided to invite couples, who would at least presumably have developed some tolerance for each other's foibles. Dennis knew immediately who he would invite: his childhood friend Joachim and his wife, Teeliam. Joachim had always been an adventurous sort, climbing trees and running around the rain ring and hang-gliding from the zero-gravity middle of the colony down to the high-gee surface. He had even eaten a bug once on a dare, and claimed it hadn't been all that bad, so he already had some experience. Teeliam was a bit more conservative, but she had a good sense of humor about Joachim's peculiarities, so Dennis was willing to bet she would be okay at a food-feast. She accepted the invitation, at any rate, which was better than the first two sets of friends that Cheryl tried.

Cheryl eventually talked her sister, Frieda, and her sister's partner, Aylette, into joining them. Both women were skeptical, but Frieda wanted to meet this new man her sister had been spending time with, and Aylette decided she could use the experience for her Master's thesis on the evolution of fads in post-colonial societies.

"Oh, great," Dennis said when Cheryl told him about that. "Now it's going to be documented. No pressure."

Cheryl gave him a puzzled look. "What's to feel pressured about? We get some food; we eat it. How hard is that?"

Dennis laughed. "You haven't heard my great-grandmother's stories. Food doesn't come ready to eat; you have to cook it. People used to work for *days* preparing the Thanksmas meal. It had to be a work of art, and everything had to be ready at exactly the same time. Except for the pie, which you cooked while you were eating the other food."

"Why?"

"So it was still hot when you got to it. Pie came last."

"Why?" she asked again.

"How would I know?"

He vowed to learn by party time. He had two weeks, but the days evaporated surprisingly quickly once he had a deadline to meet. First off he had to find out if people could still eat an entire meal without damaging themselves, so he looked up a doctor and told him what he planned to do. When the doctor finished laughing he said, "Sure, it's still possible. We haven't had time to actually evolve away from our ancestral energy source. On the other hand, I'd advise you to reprogram your nanites to assist with the digestive process, just in case your endocrine glands are slow to respond after a lifetime of disuse. I can give you a program for that. You'll probably want to upload it a few hours before you eat so your body will already be prepared for the influx of food." Dennis felt a big weight slide off his shoulders until the doctor added, "Let me know how it works."

That wouldn't be possible without food, which wasn't something a person could just find in a storehouse somewhere. Dennis had to convince his apartment complex's nanofab AI that he had a legitimate need for the stuff, and once it agreed to make what he wanted, he had to decide what he did, in fact, want it to make.

There had to be a turkey, of course. He had a hard time convincing the AI that he wanted it already dead, and preferably without feathers or entrails, but from his research into cooking techniques he learned that very few people started with the whole turkey, and he saw no reason why he should either. Tradition was tradition, after all, and he wanted to do his Thanksmas dinner the same way his great-grandmother had done. That also meant potatoes, which he would boil and mash until they were smooth (never lumpy!), and gravy made with the molten fat from the turkey, and yams with both caramelized sugar and spun sugar melted over them – cooking seemed to involve a lot of melting – and deviled eggs, which involved yet another argument with the AI, who couldn't decide whether or not it needed to make a chicken first before it could make an egg.

And then there was the stuffing. Cheryl had gotten into the planning by this point, and she had uncovered perhaps the most controversial aspect of the whole holiday meal: what to put inside the turkey carcass while you cooked it. One source said it should be a mixture of spiced bread crumbs, and another source said it should be crackers and the cut-up "giblets" and more eggs (mixed in raw rather than deviled, thank goodness), and another source called for a different type of bread made from ground corn, while another swore that the best thing to put inside the turkey was a can of beer that would boil and steam the meat into perfect flavored tenderness from the inside out.

Of course all of the sources dismissed the other methods as hopelessly inferior, and Dennis couldn't remember which kind his great-grandmother had liked. "This must have been why the tradition died," he said to Cheryl when she showed him the results of her research. "Nobody could settle on what kind of stuffing to use."

She said, "I think we should just go with the easiest one. We're already making bread for the crescent rolls, so let's use bread crumbs and be done with it."

That made a great deal of sense, and the nanofab AI would undoubtedly like the idea, too, so that's what they decided to do. Then they complicated its job anyway by ordering olives and cranberry sauce and cheese spread and pickled cucumbers and half a dozen other condiments that the history texts swore were necessary for a traditional Thanksmas meal.

"Whoa, check this out," Cheryl said, pointing to a footnote at the end of the list. "It says here that fruit cake was mostly a 'Christmas' thing, and that Thanksgiving and Christmas were two separate holidays until the end of the twentieth century, when people realized that preparing for two big feasts in a row was driving them all crazy."

"No surprise there," Dennis said. Even with a nanofab to make the raw ingredients for him, this was turning into a major undertaking. The thought of doing it twice made him seriously doubt the sanity of his own sainted great-grandmother.

But as she had so often said to him before she left for a new life on Neptune's moon, Triton, "Nothing ventured, nothing gained." So Dennis persevered, and he and Cheryl finalized their menu and planned their strategy for preparing it all.

Then he had to figure out gifts for everyone. In a society where nanofabs could build anything a person wanted from its constituent atoms, it was hard to think of anything that his guests would want that they didn't already have, but Dennis delved into the history texts for that, too, coming up with a BB gun for Joachim, some frilly underwear for Teeliam, a bar of soap on a rope for Frieda, and a box of real paper stationery for Aylette. For Cheryl he directed the nanofabs to craft a pair of silver earrings with one-carat diamonds carved into the shape of little hearts. He nearly sent them back for recycling when the nanofab delivered two perfectly rendered human hearts, complete with aorta and pulmonary veins, but the reflections of light from them were so incredible that he decided to give them to her after all.

At last the day arrived. Dennis uploaded the modified metabolism program into his body's nanites and reminded his guests to do the same, then he and Cheryl swung into action, starting with the turkey, which they washed and stuffed and buttered and put in their specially created roaster in their specially created oven, covering it with a tent of aluminum foil despite several sources' admonition that that was cheating. That may have been true, but it was also true that the turkey's skin wouldn't dry out that way, and that's why practically everybody from the twentieth century all the way to the death of the whole concept of eating did it.

The smell of the raw bird and the dry bread inside it wasn't necessarily appealing, nor was its texture, but once it began to cook they were amazed at the aroma that wafted out of the oven. Dennis's abdomen gurgled loudly, and Cheryl laughingly accused him of doing it as a joke until her own did the same thing a few minutes later.

"It must be the nanites getting our bodies ready," she said.

They peeled the potatoes while the turkey cooked, arguing over whether to use a knife or the special slotted potato peeler that came with the kitchen utensil kit, and then they set the potatoes aside while they boiled the yams and the eggs in separate pots, then candied the yams and deviled the eggs.

Hour after hour they cooked the meal, and the smells permeating the apartment grew more and more complex all the while. Dennis's stomach was growling like a wild animal now, and there was a peculiar knotted sensation in it that became more and more insistent, until he could finally stand it no longer. When Cheryl poured a fan of olives out into a serving dish, he snatched one up, popped it into his mouth, bit down on it three or four times – sending a wild mix of salty, bitter, acidic and fruity flavors over his tongue with each bite – then swallowed the pieces. He felt them slide all the way down his throat, and when they hit bottom he knew he had done the right thing.

Cheryl stood there, her mouth wide open, waiting to see if he would fall over. He reached for another olive to feed his ravenous stomach, but at the last moment he popped it in Cheryl's mouth instead. He watched her roll it around with her tongue, then bite down on it, her eyes growing wider all the while; then she swallowed and he could actually see the lump pass down her throat.

"Oh my god," she whispered. "Why did they ever give this up?"

Dennis shook his head. "I have no idea."

They both looked at the dish of olives, then banged their knuckles together in their haste to grab another and another and another. Each one was as delightful as the first, assuaging one tiny step at a time the immense, burning, ravenous *hunger* in their stomachs.

"Stop," Cheryl said when the olives were half gone, pulling the dish away from Dennis's reach. "We've got to save some of these for our guests." She was breathing hard, her nostrils flaring wide with each inhalation, and at that moment Dennis would have devoured *her* if there hadn't been a whole room full of food waiting to be prepared and four friends coming over to share it.

He forced himself to calm down and roll out the dough for the rolls – which was probably why they were called "rolls", he supposed. His stomach growled again at the yeasty aroma of the raw bread, but he pushed his fist against his belly until it stopped.

"It's taking all my will power just to resist this stuff, and I'm a grown man who's never seen any of it before," he said. "How could children back then live with the anticipation?"

Cheryl was concentrating on the pie crust. A smear of white flour dusted the dark photosynthetic skin just above her navel, and Dennis couldn't resist the urge to lean down and lick it off.

"Hey!" she squealed, backing away and slapping him playfully on the head. "Don't you start that, or we'll never get this meal ready."

He took a deep breath. "Right. Wow. This is . . . when are those guys going to get here?"

"Soon. Why don't you start boiling the potatoes."

"Okay."

Each task required more and more focus, but he forced himself to follow the checklist until suddenly there came a banging at the front door.

"That's got to be Joachim and Teeliam," Dennis said, fleeing the makeshift kitchen to let his friends in.

It was indeed Joachim and Teeliam, panting heavily as if they had run the whole way from their apartment on the other side of the park. Joachim had leaves in his hair, and they both had orange stains around their mouths. Dennis had been prepared to apologize for his own appearance, but the moment he saw them he said, "What happened to you?"

"Our stomachs . . ." Joachim began, just as Teeliam said, "We've been getting these cravings. When we got to the park and smelled the fruit on the orange trees, we—"

"Oh no. You *ate* one?"

"More than one," Joachim said. "You wouldn't believe how good they are."

"Just the inside part," Teeliam added. Then she caught a whiff of the aroma coming from the apartment, and she pushed past Dennis. "Oh, wow. Wow, wow, wow. Excuse me, I'm just going to go check on this turkey of yours . . ."

"Oh yeah, let's see this thing," Joachim said, hot on her heels.

"Incoming!" Dennis called out to Cheryl. He would have followed to help her, but he saw Frieda and Aylette running out of the park, so he stayed to greet them at the door.

"You'll never believe what we just figured out!" Frieda said, shoving a soft white cylinder about an inch across into his mouth. "Can you believe it? It's a banana!"

The flavor was amazing. Smooth and sweet and exotic and oh, oh yeah.

Aylette said, "Who knew they were food? I always thought they were just genetically engineered sex toys."

"What have we been missing all our lives?" Frieda said. "And more to the point, *why?*"

"I've been asking that same question all afternoon," Dennis said. "Come on in and let's start eating!"

He didn't have to offer twice. With six people helping, the rest of the preparation went like a meteor strike, and within minutes the pies were in the oven and they were all sitting at the table, drooling at all the food while Dennis sliced slab after slab of flaky white meat from the turkey's breast. Only the presence of the knife kept everyone from snatching each piece as soon as it came free.

When he had carved six big slices, he held up the knife and said, "There's a traditional speech that the host makes before the meal," but he got no further before he was pelted with olives and pickles from all sides, so he lowered the knife and said:

"Dearlordwethankyouforthebountyplacedherebeforeusamen. Okay, let's eat!"

They didn't bother learning how to use forks and spoons, nor plates either for the first few minutes. They just grabbed what they could reach and stuffed it in their mouths. Nobody spoke; they just grunted and pointed and handed food back and forth until their stomachs stopped craving more.

Then they loaded up their plates and ate simply because it tasted so wonderful, and then they ate some more because they didn't want to stop. Finally, when the turkey was picked to the bone and every scrap of every other dish was gone as well, they pushed back from the table and staggered, groaning, into the living room where they could stretch out on the couches and let their meals digest.

"I expected more energy out of it," Joachim said, rubbing his distended belly.

"Me too," said Frieda. "But I feel like I just ran the length of the colony."

"I thought it was just me because I spent all day preparing it," Dennis said.

"It was all that eating," said Teeliam. "It really takes it out of you to shovel all that stuff into you."

"Mmm," said Cheryl. Her eyes were closed, and her breathing was slowing down.

Dennis wanted nothing more than to close his own eyes and drift off for a long afternoon nap, but the suddenness of their torpor alarmed him enough that he forced himself to stand up and go into his study, where he searched the historical archives for symptoms of overeating. He found several articles on weight gain and dieting, which he bookmarked just in case, but he found what he was looking for in an article on metabolism. Tryptophan, it said, was an essential amino acid formed from proteins during the digestive process, and it also had a pronounced soporific effect. Nothing to worry about, as long as you didn't try to operate heavy machinery after eating a big meal.

He went back into the living room to tell everyone, but they were already asleep, so he snuggled in next to Cheryl and did the same.

They awoke several hours later and exchanged their gifts, oohing and aahing over each of them, even the lame ones. Cheryl loved her earrings, and Joachim happily fired BBs at the turkey carcass until one of them bounced back and hit him in the eye. Cheryl gave Dennis a pair of warm socks, "Because I noticed that your feet sometimes get cold in the middle of the night."

Then it was time for pie. They weren't quite as excited about it as they were the rest of the meal, but the first bite changed that. They wound up dividing the whole thing into six pieces and cleaning the plate.

When they were done, they sat at the table and looked at the wreck of Dennis's apartment. The room they had cooked everything in was piled with dirty pots and pans, and the dining table was covered with dirty dishes and the platter with the turkey carcass on it, and the living room floor was scattered with the paper they had concealed the presents with until they had exchanged them, and even the guests were covered with smudges of grease and egg yolk and gravy.

"We are gloriously stuffed," Dennis said. "And I loved every minute of it. I still can't figure out why people gave this up."

Cheryl had an odd expression on her face. She looked down at her lap, then twisted around to look at her butt.

"What's the matter?" Dennis asked.

"Something feels funny down there," she said.

"Funny how?"

"Funny like really full. Like something wants to come out."

Now that she mentioned it, Dennis had been feeling the same thing for a while himself. He hadn't paid it much attention, since his stomach felt so much more distended, but the focus of pressure was definitely moving lower.

He felt a little bubble of gas escape, and the pressure eased a bit, but then the smell rose up to nose level and everyone scattered, gagging and waving their hands in front of their noses.

"I think we just figured out why people quit doing this," Cheryl said as she opened the window.

But it wasn't for another half hour, when they could no longer hold back the pressure, that they knew for sure.

# Other titles available from Robinson

### The Mammoth Encyclopedia of Science Fiction
Ed. George Mann

Compiled by expert science fiction editor and author George Mann, this is a concise, informative and entertaining reference guide to the world of SF. The reader is not only given a brief history of the birth and development of science fiction but also an A–Z guide to authors, illustrators, major SF magazines, movies and television on both sides of the Atlantic.

### The Mammoth Book of 20th Century Science Fiction Volumes I–II
Ed. David G. Hartwell

The definitive anthology that spans a hundred years of science fiction writing since its birth in the 1890s. It is guaranteed to change not only the way the science fiction field views itself but also the way the rest of literature views the field.

### The Mammoth Book of Science Fiction
Ed. Mike Ashley

In this anthology of stories containing some of the best science fiction produced over the last 50 years, 20 leading authors of the genre ask the question "What if . . ." and give their own fascinating versions of the changes that will happen in the future.

### The Mammoth Book of Best New SF 18
Ed. Gardner Dozois

The latest offering of the best new SF stories includes a host of masters as well as many bright young talents. Every aspect of the genre is embraced in this exciting volume, from cyberpunk and cyber noir to anthropological, military and adventure SF. The book also offers a thorough summation of the year and a recommended reading list.

*Robinson books are available from all good bookshops or can be ordered direct from the Publisher. Just tick the titles you want and fill in the form overleaf.*

| No. of copies | Title | Price | Total |
|---|---|---|---|
| | *The Mammoth Encyclopaedia of Science Fiction* Ed. George Mann | £9.99 | |
| | *The Mammoth Book of 20th Century Science Fiction Volumes I–II* Ed. David G. Hartwell | £7.99 | |
| | *The Mammoth Book of Science Fiction* Ed. Mike Ashley | £7.99 | |
| | *The Mammoth Book of Best New Science Fiction 18* Ed. Gardner Dozois | £7.99 | |
| | **Grand Total** | | £ |

Name: _____

Address: _____

_____ Postcode: _____

Daytime Tel. No. / Email: _____
(in case of query)

Three ways to pay:

1. **For express service telephone the TBS order line on 01206 255 800 and quote 'MAM'. Order lines are open Monday – Friday 8:30a.m. – 5:30p.m.**

2. I enclose a cheque made payable to **TBS** Ltd for £ _____

3. Please charge my ☐ Visa ☐ Mastercard ☐ Amex ☐ Switch (switch issue no. ___ ) £ _____

Card number: _____

Expiry date: _____ Signature: _____
(your signature is essential when paying by credit card)

**Please return forms (*no stamp required*) to, Constable & Robinson Ltd, FREEPOST NAT6619, 3 The Lanchesters, 162 Fulham Palace Road, London W6 9BR. All books subject to availability.**

**Enquiries to readers@constablerobinson.com.**
www.constablerobinson.com

Constable & Robinson (directly or via its agents) may mail or phone you about promotions or products. Tick box if you do not want these from us ☐ or our subsidiaries ☐.